Thanks! Enjoy! Love! Yvonne.

I Will Love You Forever

Part One

Yvonne Ray

Strategic Book Publishing and Rights Co.

Strategic Book Publishing and Rights Co., LLC
USA | Singapore

For information about special discounts for bulk purchases, please contact Strategic Book Publishing and Rights Co. Special Sales, at bookorder@sbpra.net.

ISBN: 978-1-62212-382-7

Book Design: Suzanne Kelly

Author's Note

First, I would like to thank everyone who encouraged me to publish this story. Those thanks include my friends from "Lit" and anyone who listened to me as I wrote this story. Special thanks go to three friends—Don, John, and Flora, who offered their opinions and suggestions even though I didn't always take them. Thank you.

I Will Love You Forever takes place during one of the most turbulent times in American history—pre-WWII and the war itself. Please be advised that racial epithets are used in this book and much of the subject matter is very adult in nature.

One last thing: All characters in this story, unless they are actual people in history, are purely fictional. Any resemblances to real people living or deceased are purely coincidental. The same applies to any events in the story.

I hope that you enjoy reading this as much as I have enjoyed writing it!

Yvonne Ray
Author

Chapter 1

LOS ANGELES, JUNE 1939

Twenty-year-old Kenjiro Takeda leaned over the rail of the ship, eager for his first sight of America. He had waited a very long time for this and could hardly believe it was actually happening. His parents, Hiroshi and Hana, had moved a few years before, set up the family nursery business in Los Angeles, and finally had enough money to send for him.

While he was in Japan and waiting for word that he should come, Kenji worked and saved every bit of money he could so that he could continue his education in his new country. His plan was to become a physician. He was an excellent student and graduated at the top of his class from the University of Nagasaki. His only concern was that his degree wouldn't mean much in the States and that he would have to start over. If he had to start over, then so be it; if not, then it was all to the good.

Kenji, as his parents called him, was tall for a Japanese man. He was just shy of six feet three inches with jet-black hair and expressive, soft brown eyes. Women found him attractive, although he didn't see why; as far as he was concerned, he was average looking. What he failed to understand was that it was the insecurity about his looks, along with his shy smile, that women found so attractive.

Even during the voyage, he found himself surrounded by single women who were with and without chaperones. A few of them had made offers that made his face burn, but aroused him at the same time. He always politely declined the offers. While he was no stranger to the charms of the opposite sex, he liked to be the aggressor, and to hear crude words coming from the mouth of a woman was embarrassing, especially since he didn't use crude words himself. The other issue was he had no idea where these women had been and had no desire to contract a sexually transmitted disease—or any other disease, for that matter.

The trip had been a long one with several people dying along the way, most of them elderly. Many people spent the voyage confined to their pallets, suffering from seasickness. He did what he could to alleviate their suffering, but he had a limited supply of the healing teas and herbs from home, and what he did have was gone in next to no time.

Before he knew it, he was being referred to as "the doctor," and he soon gave up trying to convince them otherwise. His calm, soothing manner was often enough to soothe frazzled nerves, and in turn, those who were calmed were able to calm others. He found that he really didn't mind going from person to person and talking with them, as it kept him busy and made the trip go faster.

By the time he reached the States, Kenji had delivered five babies; three of them were named in his honor, despite his protests. He had no real idea what he was doing but went by instinct and on memory, based on what he had read in medical journals. He also discovered that he loved the feeling of helping a new life into the world and decided he would go into obstetrics.

In his spare time, when he wasn't soothing shattered nerves or giving basic first aid, he practiced his English and taught those who wanted to learn to read and write in English so they wouldn't be totally at a disadvantage. In doing this, he discovered that he enjoyed teaching and saw it for what it was: another career opportunity.

Finally, he could see the shores of his new country. His heart pounded with an anxiety and happiness that almost overshadowed the thought of seeing his parents again. The letters they had sent him told him that things were going well, that they loved the United States and hoped he would as well. They told him about the people of many different races that lived in the States but also mentioned that they interacted with them rarely, and then it was only business-related and never on a personal basis.

Kenji was aware of other races, but had only interacted with the Europeans that his father had done business with and those who had attended university with him. The idea of interacting with so many different races of people thrilled him. He never really understood the concept of the separation of classes and felt there were things that could be learned from intermingling with other races. It wasn't an idea his parents or friends understood or agreed with. How he came to his beliefs he didn't know or understand any more than they did, but it was something that they agreed to disagree about, and it was never discussed.

It would be several hours before he could leave the ship, but he stood with his bags at his feet, transfixed as he watched the shores of his new home get closer. His excitement grew with each passing hour, and just when he thought that he could take it no longer, they docked. Kenji grabbed his bags and waited for what seemed hours before he and the others were allowed to disembark. When he was finally on land, he had to stop for a moment to get used to not moving.

"Kenjiro! Over here!" he heard a few minutes later.

Kenji turned to see his parents frantically waving at him. He grabbed his bags and hurried over to them, only to drop them so he could hug his parents. A few minutes later, they were on their way to the bus that would take them to his parents' home. During the walk, he saw his first live black person. He had seen pictures and thought the pictures didn't do them justice; they were a beautiful people.

He watched as the black man carried luggage for a white couple. He found himself wanting to touch the man's hair just to see what it felt like, and then he wondered if the man's dark skin was as smooth as it appeared to be. The second person he saw was a young black woman who he thought was quite attractive. It made him wonder why black people were referred to as apes.

His second thought was about the United States itself. As he watched the young black man struggle with the white couple's luggage, he wondered if it was all it was reputed to be. He had an inkling that it wasn't; he could already see the inequality. As they walked, he could see other indications that all was not as it was rumored to be. The occasional sign that said "For Whites Only" made him ask the question, "How is this equal?"

Patricia Ann Middleton waited at the station for Miss Abby's train to come in. She had no idea what time it was, but she didn't dare ask. The only thing she knew for sure was that she wasn't late. Her income helped supplement the money her father made from working at the train station and her mother made working as a housekeeper for a wealthy white family, and if she were late, her pay would be docked. She was also trying to save as much money as she could after helping with expenses, and so far she had ten dollars saved for what she called her "rainy-day fund."

To pass the time while she waited for Miss Abby, Patricia watched the newly arrived ship, fascinated by what appeared to be hundreds of Japanese getting off. In her mind, she wondered what it would be like to take a ship somewhere; the destination didn't matter, just so it was away from Los Angeles, where she had been born and raised.

At nineteen years old, she had never been outside of LA, let alone the state of California, but oh, how she wanted to go. Patricia was and always had been a dreamer, and it was something that her parents discouraged whenever she talked about going somewhere else.

"Stop that dreamin' and come back to earth!" her mother Hattie would say whenever she caught Patricia daydreaming. "It ain't no different no place else," she would add.

"But, Mama, how do you know that? We haven't been anywhere else," Patricia replied.

Hattie frowned; the way Patricia talked was too uppity and was the topic of gossip. Hattie knew where the uppity talk came from: that rich white woman Patricia worked for. She was the one who filled Patricia's head with crazy ideas about doing and going wherever she wanted, even going to college. The last conversation was over dinner the week before.

"Miss Abby thinks that I'm smart enough; she says that everyone is entitled to an education."

Her parents didn't respond. It would have been pointless, and it would have led to an argument. Patricia was as strong-willed as they came, and once her mind was made up, there was no changing it. In truth, Hattie wished Patricia could have the life she wanted, but she was afraid that Patricia would be disappointed when she found out things were the same everywhere.

The other thing Patricia didn't understand was this: The white woman was as trapped as they were; they just didn't realize it. They had the appearance of freedom only because they were white and could go almost anywhere they pleased, but they were still women in what was a man's world.

Patricia was a pretty girl with dark brown eyes that always had a mischievous sparkle in them; her skin was flawless, the color of chocolate caramel, and something that Miss Abby remarked on several times. She wasn't a thin girl by any stretch of the imagination, but she was comfortable with herself and had never put much stock in looks. She was of the opinion that it was what was on the inside that mattered.

She had her share of suitors, but none of them had what she looked for in a husband. She didn't know what she was looking for, only that none of the men trying to woo her were for her. Of all of them, she liked Vernon Monroe the least. He was probably the most handsome man she had ever seen, but she didn't like or trust him; he was ugly on the inside. He was at her door almost nightly, asking her to go for a walk with him, but she knew what he was really after and wanted no part of it.

That night was no different; she heard him knock on the front door of their tiny house, her father answering it, and the ensuing conversation.

"Evenin', sir, I was wonderin' if I could take Patricia on a walk."

He sounded so smug and polite, but Patricia knew better; she wasn't goin' on a walk or anywhere else with him.

"Evenin', Vernon," her father, John, replied. "I'll see if she wants to take that walk with you."

Patricia didn't give him the chance to ask. She went to the living room just as her father was coming to get her. When Vernon saw her, he gave her a predatory smile in anticipation that she might actually agree this time.

Patricia had tried to be nice when she told him countless times that she wasn't interested; now it was time to be blunt. When she got to the door, she pushed past him, not speaking until they were on the sidewalk in front of the house.

"Vernon Monroe," she said tersely, "let me see if I can make you understand something. I don't like you, and I'm not going to go on any walks or anywhere else with you, so stop wasting your time."

Vernon bristled; she was such an uppity bitch, thinking she was too good for him. One day soon, he was going to knock her off her high horse, but for now, he would play nice. "Why you want to be like that?" he asked. "All I want is a walk."

"Is that what you call it?" Patricia asked, laughing. "From what I hear, there's not too much walking involved. But whatever you're calling it, I want nothing to do with it."

"Who you savin' yourself for, girl?" Vernon asked, his tone snide. "You think somebody better than me gonna come along?"

That was exactly what she thought and was hoping for, but she wasn't going to tell him that, so she decided to end the discussion. "I'm going inside; good night, Vernon," she said and walked away before he could say anything.

Vernon watched her walk away with anger in his eyes. No bitch had ever told him no, and this bitch was no exception. Eventually she would give in; they all did.

Once in the house, Patricia peeked through the curtain and saw that Vernon was still outside, watching the house. She could tell by the way he held his body and the look on his face that he was angry. "Too bad," she muttered and closed the curtain.

Hattie had been peeking through the curtain and watching them talk. She worried for Patricia and feared for her future. If she wasn't careful, she would end up a lonely old woman with no one to care for her. However, she did agree with her on one thing: Vernon Monroe, no matter how handsome, was no good.

That had been a week ago, Patricia realized as she continued to wait for Miss Abby, and it didn't hurt her feelings that she hadn't seen Vernon since. She allowed her mind to continue its wanderings as she watched the Japanese people getting off the ship and greeting those there to pick them up. She didn't know a lot about Japan, but knew from the pictures she had seen that it was a beautiful country and a place she wanted to visit someday.

Her attention was drawn to a tall Japanese man as he rushed to meet his family, and for just a split second, their eyes met. His attention went back to his family, and hers was drawn by a shrill voice calling her name.

"Patricia!"

She turned to see Miss Abby standing behind her.

"I am so sorry, Miss Abby, I didn't know which way to look for you," she said.

"It's quite all right; no harm done, as I only just got here," Miss Abby replied as she looked around for someone to help with her luggage.

"I can help you, ma'am," said a voice that Patricia recognized.

"Why thank you!" Miss Abby said as she started to walk away.

Patricia ignored Vernon and followed Abby to where her luggage sat waiting for them.

Dinner at the Takeda home was a happy event; there was much news to give from home, some of it happy, some of it sad. Several births, deaths, and funerals had been missed, but Kenji had attended them in his parents' stead. Other than those things, nothing had changed.

As happy as Kenji's father, Hiroshi, was that Kenji was home, one thing marred it: something terrible was going to happen. He had known it since 1933 when Adolf Hitler became Chancellor of Germany. He remembered the sick feeling he got when he heard the news. His apprehension grew in 1936, when Hitler and Mussolini joined forces, and then again in 1938, when he heard about the destruction of Jewish property. He understood what no one else did: the world had a lunatic by the name of Adolf Hitler on its hands. The proof that they really didn't understand came when Hitler was named *Time* magazine's man of the year. The world was in for a very rude awakening.

Hiroshi had always been able to spot trouble; it was an ability he was proud of and, in 1933, he began to make plans to get his family out of Japan and to America. His gut told him that whatever Hitler was doing, somehow he was going to involve Japan. As he read the papers and letters from home, it seemed as though he had gotten Kenji out just in time.

As soon as he and Hana had arrived in Los Angeles, he bought a small nursery, and as soon as it became profitable, he began setting aside small amounts of cash. To date, he had eight hundred American dollars saved and hiding under the bed in a small box. If they didn't need it, then he would give it to Kenji for school expenses, but his instincts told him they were going to need it for survival. Hiroshi forced the negative thoughts out of his head and concentrated on the joy of being reunited with his only surviving child.

The next day, Kenji walked around Los Angeles, taking in the sights and trying to acclimate to his new surroundings. He was amazed at the variety of people he saw and understood why America was called the "melting pot." The blatant show of racism still surprised him, although he didn't know why. Japan was a racist society even among their own kind, the separation of the classes being a case in point, so racism wasn't a new concept for him.

He thought the surprise was because of what he had read about America and the letters his father had sent him. He had also read and memorized the Declaration of Independence and had taken it literally when it said, "All men are created equal." But even with the discrepancies in what he had been told and read, Kenji liked his new country. As he continued his walk, he thought about his education. In addition to school, he would have to find a job and help his parents at the nursery. He didn't know how he was going to manage it, but he would.

Patricia waited at the grocer's for Miss Abby's order, which included a small roast for dinner. The line was long, so she decided to wait outside, where it was relatively cooler. She leaned back against the building and allowed her mind to go wherever it wanted. She closed her eyes and traveled to France, Germany, and Japan, not paying attention to the fact that as she wandered in her daydreams, she was wandering out into the middle of the busy sidewalk.

"Get out of the way!" a male voice growled and roughly shoved her aside.

Before she knew what happened, Patricia found herself on the ground. She tried to move out of the way, and when she tried to get up, she found herself pushed down again. She was beginning to think she would never get up when she felt a hand on her arm.

Kenji had just rounded the corner when he saw Patricia standing by the wall of the grocer's and remembered her from the day before. He remembered that he had thought her very pretty and that she in no way resembled an ape. He watched as she absently wandered away from the wall and into the traffic of the sidewalk. It was obvious she wasn't aware of what she was doing as she wandered into the crowd. Helpless, he watched as someone pushed her down and kept going, without even looking back. He was further alarmed when no one stopped to help her up; instead, she was being kept down on the ground. Without thinking about it, he rushed over to her, touched her arm, and helped her up and back to the wall. Afterward, he wondered if he shouldn't have helped her, but then decided it was the right thing to do.

Patricia was grateful for the hand, no matter whom it belonged to, and didn't notice the color of it until she was standing. It was the tall Japanese man from the ship.

"Thank you," she said, not knowing if he could speak or understand English.

"You are welcome," Kenji replied. "Are you hurt?"

"No, I'm fine," she replied, looking up at him.

Kenji looked down at her, thought she was even prettier up close, and then walked away. As he turned the corner, he looked back, saw her watching him, and wished he had asked her name. After thinking about it, he realized it might have been improper for him to do so. He hadn't been too surprised to discover that her skin was as soft as it looked, and he hadn't missed the mischievous look in her eyes—even though she was on the ground and almost trampled.

Patricia watched Kenji walk away and wondered if he knew he could have gotten into trouble for helping her; but then again, maybe he wouldn't have. Neither of their races was welcome, so maybe no one paid attention. She heard her name being called, went into the store to pick up the order, and headed back to Miss Abby's house.

SEPTEMBER 1, 1939

Hiroshi listened along with the rest of the world as Hitler invaded Poland. What no one seemed to understand was that this was only the beginning; he wouldn't stop there. He glanced over at Hana and Kenji; he had come to the US with such high hopes for them, but it looked as though things were going to become more difficult. He thought about the money hidden under the bed that he had added another one hundred dollars to. The time was coming when they would have to sit down and plan, but there was still time for things to change. There was still time for someone to stop Hitler before he went much farther.

Patricia continued her studies under the guidance of Miss Abby, much to the dismay of her parents.

"Patricia, you gots to stop!" Hattie said one night. "People is talkin' 'bout you bein' uppity. It ain't that we don't want you to learn, but it ain't safe for you, and people are watching." When Patricia didn't respond, Hattie knew her words had been ignored.

"War's a comin'," John said as he walked into the room. "That Hitler ain't gonna stop with one tiny country," he said as he sat at the kitchen table. "I don't know what that gonna mean for us but—"

Vernon tapped on the door of the Middleton's home. He hadn't seen Patricia since he helped the woman that she worked for with her luggage. He hoped that maybe she had softened toward him and would take that walk with him.

Her father answered the door after peeking through the curtains to see who was there.

"Evenin', sir, is Patricia available for a visit?"

A few minutes later, Hattie was at the door.

"Evenin', ma'am," Vernon said, removing his hat.

"Evenin', Vernon," Hattie replied politely. "Patricia ain't acceptin' company tonight; she don't feel good."

Vernon swallowed his anger and forced himself to sound concerned. "Well, that's too bad; would you give her my regards?"

"I sure will," Hattie replied with a smile. "And thank you," she added.

Patricia listened from the other side of the door, wondering what she would have to do other than take the walk with him in order for him to leave her alone.

Hiroshi didn't rest well that night; he tossed and turned thinking about the money he had saved and what to do with it. It had to be easily accessible, which made a bank out of the question, and the money had to stay with them. He finally came to a decision: The money needed to be split between the three of them in case they were somehow separated. He would have Hana sew the money into the sides of each of their smallest bags and hope for the best. It was almost dawn before he closed his eyes and sleep took him.

Kenji couldn't sleep either. The possibility of war was a reason, but not the main one. He kept thinking about a certain young black woman he had helped a few weeks ago. He didn't know why he couldn't stop thinking about her or the mischievousness in her eyes that still made him smile whenever he thought about her. It had been a long time since a woman had made him smile like that.

He wondered how often she went to the grocer's and wondered if he would see her there again; if he did, he was going to ask her what her name was and hope he wasn't being improper.

SEPTEMBER 8, 1939

It was a Friday afternoon, and Patricia was at the grocer's for an unscheduled trip. She didn't mind; it gave her time to daydream without interruption. Ever since the incident weeks ago, she was much more careful not to go so far into her daydreams that she lost track of what she was doing. She had no desire to end up on the ground again. She found herself thinking about the Japanese man who had helped her. She had been surprised at how well he spoke English; even with his accent, she had no trouble understanding him. She handed the grocer the slip of paper containing the order for the day and went outside to wait.

"It'll be about an hour," the grocer called after her as she walked out of the door. "I hope Abby isn't in a hurry."

"No sir, she told me to wait for as long as it took," Patricia replied.

Kenji had started taking his walks about the same time of day when he had first met Patricia, and the route always took him past the grocer's. Today he was lucky; he saw Patricia standing in front of the store wearing a simple blue dress and sensible shoes, her hair pulled back into a tight ponytail that showed the roundness of her face. Like the last time he had seen her, she looked as if she was someplace far away, and he hoped she didn't end up on the ground again.

He crossed the busy street and walked up to her. "Hello."

Patricia snapped out of her reverie, surprised she had been spoken to. "Hello," she replied, smiling up at him.

Now that he had her attention, he didn't know what to say to her, but she spoke first. "Thank you again for helping me the other week."

"You are welcome," Kenji replied and walked away tongue-tied.

Patricia watched him walk away, giggled at his awkwardness, and wondered about it.

Kenji didn't leave; he just walked around the corner and peeked around it, watching Patricia. He didn't understand what had just happened; while shy, he had never been tongue-tied before. He wondered what it was about her that made him so nervous and almost attributed it to being in a foreign country and not knowing what was acceptable behavior and what wasn't. He realized that while that may have been a factor, it wasn't the main reason. He was nervous around her because she was a female and he found her attractive. Even as he thought it, he knew it could never be; his family would never accept her, and chances were her family would never accept him. He watched her for several more minutes and continued on his way, saddened that he wouldn't get to know her in the way he wanted to.

OCTOBER 8, 1939

For a month after he had first spoken to her, Kenji saw Patricia at least once a week—more often if he was lucky. Even though he swore he would ask her for her name, he never did because he was so nervous, so the routine was always the same. He saw her, walked up to her and said hello, and walked away. He looked forward to seeing her and was disappointed when he didn't. Other than Japanese people, hers was the only friendly face he knew. Today, he was going to ask her for her name.

Patricia saw him coming and smiled; she had come to enjoy seeing him, even though they never said more than "hello." Since it was another unscheduled trip to the grocer's, she would have at least an hour.

"Hello," Kenji said with a shy smile.

"Hello," Patricia said, returning the smile, and waited for him to walk away, surprised when he didn't.

"Please, may I ask your name?"

Patricia was surprised but pleased. "Patricia Middleton; what's yours?"

"I am Kenjiro Takeda; it is nice to meet you," he replied and walked away.

Patricia giggled and settled in to wait for her order.

"Patricia Middleton," Kenji murmured under his breath. He knew he should stop trying to see her; if he continued, it would only cause trouble for both of them, but he liked her. Seeing her had become the best part of his otherwise long week, and it gave him something pleasant to think about, other than what was happening in the world.

Like his father, he knew trouble was coming. Britain, France, Australia, and several other countries had already declared war on Germany, and it was only a matter of time before America got involved. He believed, as his father did, that at some point Japan would also become involved. The thought both frightened and saddened him. If Japan entered the war, what would happen to the Japanese in the United States? Would they all be sent back? It was a frightening thought and one that he pushed away by thinking about the girl with the mischievous brown eyes and infectious smile.

Vernon continued to pester Patricia for a "walk," and his annoyance grew with each increasingly rude rejection.

"Vernon, leave me be!" she told him the last time in a cold tone. "I don't like you, and I don't want to spend any amount of time with you!"

Vernon, forgetting where he was, lost his temper and raised his hand to hit her when he sensed someone staring at him—John Middleton.

"You touch her and I will kill your ass," he said softly, but the anger was evident in his voice. "Now, I've listened to her tell you every which way that she don't want your attention, but you keep comin' 'round. I likes and respects that you don't give up, but I sure as hell don't like or respect a man who raises his hand to a woman, 'specially if that woman be my girl. Now get goin' before I kill you, and stay away from my girl."

Vernon lowered his hand and tried to make light of what had just happened. "I didn't mean no harm; I was jus' playin'—"

"Damn straight you wasn't gonna do no harm!" John said, interrupting him. "Now scoot 'fore I change my mind about killin' you."

Vernon's smile froze as he backed away. John Middleton was a man of his word, and if he said he would kill him, then he would. He chanced a glance over at Patricia and decided the uppity bitch wasn't worth dying for, but one day he was going to have her, with or without her consent, and he was going to enjoy every fucking minute of it.

Patricia watched Vernon as he shrugged and then squared his shoulders. He smiled and then winked at her, letting her know he wasn't done with her. Patricia shuddered as she realized she had been right about him: he was ugly on the inside and she was going to have to watch herself. He was angry, and if he was going to hit her in front of her parents' home, what would he do if he caught her alone?

That night, as she got ready for bed, Patricia said Kenji's name several times. She liked it and wondered what it meant. She planned to ask him the next time she saw him—if he stayed long enough for her to get a word in. As she settled in for the night, she wished Kenji goodnight, wherever he was.

Kenji looked at the used medical journals he had found in the trash during his walks, but couldn't concentrate no matter how hard he tried. He was worried about the state of affairs in the United States: refugees from Germany and Poland were pouring in and reporting Hitler's discrimination of the Jews and other minority races. The stories sickened him; the world, it seemed, was going insane.

Like he had done so many times before, he pushed the ugly thoughts away and thought of Patricia. He hoped that she and her family were somewhere safe and that they hadn't run across the group known as the Klan. While he had no personal experience with them, he knew of those who did, and it had been far from pleasant. He finally closed the journal and gave up on reading. Instead, he got ready for bed and decided he would read in the morning.

It would be another week before Kenji and Patricia saw each other, but for him it seemed much longer than that. As he got ready for his walk, he tried to plan what he would say to her when he saw her. As he walked, his mind was on her and not on where he was going; he bumped into a man coming from the opposite direction.

"Watch where you're going!" the man snapped.

"My apologies," Kenji said with a bow.

The man seemed not to have heard the apology, as he continued to talk. "Think you own the damned sidewalk?" he asked. "If I had my way, every last fucking one of you would be crammed on the first boat out of here and be sunk at sea—and the niggers right along with you!"

The man didn't give Kenji a chance to reply before he stalked away. Kenji knew the Japanese weren't welcome, but still, the blatant anger surprised him. He watched the man walk away and wondered if he belonged to the group he had heard about. He continued his walk, but made sure he paid closer attention to where he was going. His heart stopped when he got to the grocer's; she wasn't there! Had she come early and he had missed her? He let out a sigh of relief when he saw her come out of the store; he realized she must have just arrived and placed her order.

Patricia saw Kenji before he saw her and wondered about the stricken expression on his face and then the look of relief that quickly replaced it. She was honest with herself: she was hoping to see him; he intrigued her. She heard the comments about the Japanese and wondered if any of them were true. The prevailing thought was that they were moving to the United States so they could take over. She didn't think it was true, so she asked her father about it.

"Could be," he replied. "There's so damned many of them!"

His answer didn't make sense, so she asked Miss Abby.

"Patricia, do you know what prejudice is?" Abby asked. "It's what you experience every day of your life. So do I, for that matter, but it's more subtle and only because I am an older white woman. You, on the other hand, have other things against you, things that cannot be hidden: your color and your sex. The Japanese have the same problem, but add to that the cultural and language differences.

"They are competing with native-born Americans for resources that are already tight and going to get even tighter, and that will make people less tolerant than they would ordinarily be. When people make comments such as those being made about the Japanese, it is out of fear and ignorance, and that is the definition of prejudice. Instead of trying to get to know them, assumptions are made. Do I think that they are here to take over? Of course not. I believe they are like people everywhere in that they want something better, and they came here to find it. I believe they chose this country because we're supposed to be the great melting pot and everyone is supposed to be treated as equals. I think we would agree that this isn't true—at least not yet. I want you to remember this, if you remember nothing else," Abby said. "There are good and bad people of every race, and that includes white people. Take each person as you meet them and decide from what you see or hear what kind of person they are. Never judge a person based on where he or she comes from or where they live."

It had been a very enlightening conversation, and as she now waited for Kenji to reach her, Patricia decided that she liked him and finally admitted that she missed him on the days she didn't see him.

"Hello, Patricia," Kenji said as he reached her.

"Hello, Kenjiro. What does your name mean?" she asked before he could walk away.

"It means 'second son who sees with insight,'" he replied. "What does Patricia mean?"

Patricia shrugged. "I don't know if it means anything; it's just a name," she replied. "So does your name mean that you have a brother?"

"I did, but he died before I was born," Kenji replied.

"I'm sorry," Patricia said, not knowing what else to say.

"Thank you, but it was many years ago."

"Where did you learn to speak English so well?" Patricia asked, changing the subject.

"At university, and I practiced on the trip here."

"You went to college?" Patricia asked. "I would love to do that!"

"Then why do you not go?" Kenji asked.

"Because it costs money, among other things—"

"Patricia! Stop yappin' with that Jap and come get your order!" the grocer called out.

"I have to go, but thanks for talking to me," Patricia said as she hurried into the store.

Kenji watched her hurry off and then continued his walk. He now had another problem that was going to complicate his life even more than the war he knew was coming: he was falling in love with Patricia Middleton, and he didn't know what to do about it.

Chapter 2

OCTOBER 8, 1939

"Nothing," Kenjiro muttered to himself. "Do nothing," he added. It was madness; they were in a world where neither of them was wanted, but their being together would be looked down on anyway. Once again he didn't understand. Two people should have the right to be together if they chose to be. He stopped himself; he had no idea what Patricia thought of him. He knew she liked him as a friend; he didn't think it went beyond that, but what if she by some chance felt as he did?

Patricia walked back to Miss Abby's carrying the heavy sacks of groceries; she was halfway there when she heard a voice behind her.

"Want some help with that?"

Patricia turned around to see none other than Vernon.

"No thanks, I'm almost there," she replied and turned around.

Vernon caught up to her. "Why don't you like me?" he asked.

"Because I don't," Patricia replied, "and besides, you showed your true colors when you were going to hit me."

"I was only havin' a little fun; I was just tryin' to scare you," Vernon said with what he thought was a friendly smile.

"Is that what that was?" Patricia asked. "My daddy didn't think you were having fun now, did he? And if I remember right, he told you to stay away from me, so what are you doing here?"

Vernon took a deep breath; he wanted to slap her senseless. *Why can't she be like all the rest of them?* he wondered. All the rest of them thought he was the best-looking Negro around, including some of the white women, but he wasn't so stupid as to mess with any of those. He liked his skin the way it was, and he definitely liked living, but here was this stupid bitch who was holding out on him.

Patricia stopped in front of Miss Abby's house. "Go home, Vernon, and stay away from me."

Vernon watched her walk away; his face was hot with anger. He knew who was giving her those uppity ideas, and he wished he could do something about her, but he would never get away with it.

Miss Abby watched the scene from her living room window, ready to intervene if needed. She could tell from Patricia's body language that she was uncomfortable, and she also noted the look of anger on the man's face. It took her a moment to realize who the man was: it was Vernon. He had helped her the last time she came in on the train. He was good-looking enough, but there was a mean streak a mile wide under that handsome exterior.

Miss Abby met Patricia by the door and took one of the sacks from her. "Patricia, was he bothering you?" she asked. Despite the differences in their skin color and age, Abby loved Patricia, which is why she took it upon herself to educate her as much as she could. The world wouldn't always be like this; there would be a time when Patricia would be able to go where she pleased and when she pleased. Abby realized it wouldn't happen in her lifetime, but it was going to happen.

"No ma'am, he wanted to help me with the groceries is all. The grocer told me to tell you that he'll be getting more of the fish you like on Friday and that he'll set some aside for you," Patricia said as she unpacked the groceries.

"Wonderful! Maybe I'll walk with you," Abby said.

"No! I mean, that's all right. I don't mind walking alone, and it is a long walk," Patricia replied. She didn't want anything to interfere with the possibility of seeing Kenjiro.

Abby looked at Patricia and wondered what was going on with her. For the past several weeks, she had all but begged to walk to the store. She wondered if a man was the reason, but didn't question her about it. But she felt obligated to warn Patricia about Vernon.

"Patricia, the young man that was outside with you; who is he?" she asked.

"That was Vernon Monroe; he's been after me to take walks with him, but I won't, and he keeps coming around. My daddy had to chase him off the other night," Patricia replied.

Abby hesitated and then spoke, "Patricia, be careful around him. I don't know him, but I get the feeling that he can be mean, and you didn't look like you enjoyed his attentions."

"I wasn't and you're right about him, Miss Abby. What do you know about Japan?" Patricia asked, changing the subject.

"Not a lot, I'm afraid, but I think it's a beautiful country—if the pictures I've seen are accurate. Why do you ask?"

"I guess I'm just curious about them," Patricia replied as she put the last item from the grocery store away. "I guess I'd better get going before it gets too much later," Patricia said.

"You be careful; I don't like you walking home by yourself," Abby said, her voice filled with concern.

"I'll be fine, Miss Abby, and I'll see you tomorrow morning," Patricia said as she gathered her things.

"Oh wait! I forgot that I have something for you," Abby said as she looked through the icebox. "Here it is!" she said, as she pulled out a plate of sliced roast beef. "I can't eat all of this, so take it home to your family. Just bring the plate back whenever you remember it," she said, handing the plate to a surprised Patricia.

"Miss Abby. . . . "

"Take it and hurry home before it gets too late," Abby said, urging Patricia toward the door.

Abby watched as Patricia headed down the sidewalk; she was frightened for Patricia, and Vernon wasn't the only reason. She sighed and closed the door, making sure to lock it. Afterward, she went to her massive library and started looking for any books that she might have on Japan.

Patricia allowed her mind to wander as she walked home: it started in France, then went to Italy, and finally to Japan, where it stayed for the rest of her walk home. She was so far into her thoughts that she didn't realize she was being followed by Vernon.

Her mother was waiting by the door, an anxious expression on her face.

"Mama? What's wrong?" Patricia asked.

"Your daddy ain't home yet; he should be here by now," Hattie said.

"Maybe he's just working late," Patricia said, not ready to worry just yet.

An hour later, there was still no sign of her father, and she was beginning to worry. "I'll go look for him," she said, standing up.

"You'll do no such thing! It's dark out there, and he wouldn't want you puttin' yourself in danger like that," Hattie said.

Another hour went by, and they were beginning to fear the worst when a frantic pounding on the front door made them both jump and scream.

"Hattie!" a male voice called. "Come quick!"

Hattie and Patricia ran to the front door and gasped. John was being supported by a man on each side. Blood ran from a cut on his head and from his mouth.

"Oh God! What happened?" Patricia asked as she helped the men bring her father in, mindless of the blood.

"He was helping a couple with their luggage and it was too much. He tried to tell them that he'd make a second trip, but they kept pilin' it on. When he tried to tell them again, they said he was bein' an uppity nigger and pushed him. When the luggage fell, they said he did it on purpose and they beat him and took his money, saying he had to pay for the damage to their things."

Patricia blinked back tears as she listened to the story; it had to be better than this somewhere. Her mother came back from the kitchen with a bowl of warm water and clean cloths. Patricia could see the tracks that tears had made down her plump cheeks.

"Thank you for bringing him home," she said.

"No problem, Miss Patricia; I just wish we could have helped him in some way," one of the men said.

"You helped him by bringing him home. You'd better get going; I don't want you to run into any trouble going home."

Between Patricia and her mother, they managed to get John into the bedroom and onto the bed, both of them crying as they took off his clothes and saw the bruises and cuts. They worked silently as they cleaned the cuts, each lost in her own thoughts. Hattie thought about how lucky they were that he hadn't been killed; Patricia thought that while she was thankful her father was alive, she had to get away from here. On the tail of that thought came another: Kenjiro.

Kenjiro reread the medical journals that he had found several times over; he had most of the articles committed to memory. Every time his mind wandered to Patricia, he forced it back to the task at hand. He looked over at his parents and as always marveled at the love they had for one another. He briefly wondered if he would feel a love like that, and Patricia came back to mind. He cursed under his breath and pushed Patricia from his mind. He wouldn't see her again; he would take another route for his walks and avoid the grocer's completely. It was for the best.

OCTOBER 15, 1939

It had been a week and Kenjiro hadn't been near the grocer's; when he caught himself heading in that direction, he went the opposite way. The problem was that instead of making him not think of her, it made him think about her even more. He wondered if she missed seeing him as much as he missed seeing her, but he steeled his resolve; he wasn't going to see her. He couldn't allow himself to feel more for her than he already did. "It's for the best," he murmured as he changed direction once again when he realized he was heading in the direction of the grocer's.

Patricia anxiously scanned the crowd for Kenjiro; he would be hard to miss with his height and skin color. She hadn't seen him in almost a week, and she wondered if he was all right. While she waited for the grocery order, she let her mind wander, but this time it went to Japan and stayed there. Miss Abby had gone through her library and found a few books on Japan, which she had happily lent to Patricia.

"Keep them for as long as you like; it's not likely that I'll be reading them," she said when she handed Patricia the books, wrapped in brown paper and tied with a bow. "As a matter of fact, why don't you keep them? Consider it a birthday present."

Patricia was excited and hugged Miss Abby so tight that she almost cut off her breath. "Thank you, Miss Abby! Thank you!" she said, over and over again.

Abby laughed at her enthusiasm; she loved it when someone was as excited about learning as Patricia was. The girl was a sponge, soaking up every bit of knowledge she could get her hands on.

Patricia snuck the books up into her room and began to read. Her plan was to surprise Kenjiro by telling him something she had learned about his country, and here it was a week later and she still hadn't seen him.

Unable to help himself, Kenjiro ended up across the street from the grocer's. He saw Patricia in her usual spot and tried to resist the urge to go to her, but he couldn't. "Just once more and I will not see her again," he told himself as he crossed the street.

Patricia stood straighter as she saw him cross the street and cringed as he was almost hit by a car in his haste. When he reached her, he looked at her as if he was committing her face to memory.

"*Ohayo*," she said softly.

Kenjiro's mouth dropped open; she had just said "hello" to him in Japanese. The pronunciation was a bit off, but he understood what she said. "*Ohayo*," he repeated back to her.

"Where have you been?" Patricia asked in her usual forthright way.

"I have been helping my parents," he replied, which wasn't a lie—just not the entire truth. "Have you been well?"

"I'm fine," she replied and then told him about the beating her father had received. She hadn't planned to tell him about it, but she felt like she could tell him anything.

Kenjiro listened intently and worried for her. "Your father, is he all right?"

"He's fine; he still has some bruises, but he'll live," she replied.

"I don't understand this land; your Declaration of Independence says that all men are created equal."

Patricia laughed. "It's equal if your skin is the right color," she said. "Kenjiro, you, me, and anybody else who isn't white isn't welcome here. I'm sure you've noticed the separate drinking fountains, and there are laws that keep us separate from the white man; they're called 'Jim Crow laws.'"

The longer Kenjiro was in America, the more he realized that, in many ways, America wasn't so different from Japan—only here he was among the discriminated against, whereas in Japan his family was in the upper class. Not nearly as wealthy as some, but they lived in comfort and wanted for nothing.

"What are these Jim Crow laws?" he asked.

"Well, basically they're laws to keep us separated from them; that's why you see the signs for separate entrances and at the drinking fountains."

"So you cannot sit in a public place with a white person?" he asked.

"Not unless I want to go to jail, and there's no white person worth that, with the exception of one," she replied. "There are some places that don't care—it's better here in California for black people than it is in other places, like the South."

Kenjiro gave some thought to what she said and wondered if those laws would apply to them. As it was now, people barely paid any attention to them as they talked. "Patricia, what of us?" he asked.

Patricia looked at him, confused by his question. "I don't understand what you mean," she replied.

"Would we be allowed to be seen together on a park bench?"

Patricia hesitated, not knowing how to answer him. She didn't know why he asked the question, but she didn't want to answer him.

"Patricia?"

"The truth of it is, even though no one wants either of our races around, there would still be problems. Would I mind sharing a park bench with you? I wouldn't mind at all," Patricia stopped when she realized she had said more than she meant to.

"Is it because of these laws that you can't go to college?" he asked.

Patricia breathed a sigh of relief when it seemed Kenjiro had missed what she said about sitting on the park bench with him.

"Partly—but it also costs money to go to school. But Miss Abby is teaching me. She's the one who gave me the books about Japan. Did I say it right?" she asked.

Kenjiro smiled down at her. "It was very close, but—"

"Patricia! Your order is up!"

She gave him an apologetic look. "I have to go, but I'm glad I got to see you."

Kenjiro gave her a slight bow, accompanied with a smile. "I am happy to see you too; when will you be back?"

"Patricia!" the grocer yelled at her. "Get your black ass in here and get this order!"

Kenjiro bristled at the way she had been spoken to, but bit his tongue. It would do no one any good if he ended up in jail or worse.

"I have to go, but I'm usually here on Fridays," she said as she walked into the grocer's.

He watched her walk into the store before he headed for home. He had been right in his assumption that although they were both unwelcome, there would be problems if they decided they wanted to be together. He smiled to himself as he remembered her admitting she would share a bench with him; it was another thought to cheer his days and nights.

When he got home, his father was hunched over the newspaper as usual, watching the progress of the war. He was still upset that the attempt on Hitler's life several weeks ago had failed; it would have stopped the war in its tracks, and now it looked like Russia was getting in on the act. Things were getting much worse; they all knew it but tried to act like it wasn't. As of yet, the United States hadn't entered the war, choosing neutrality, but that wouldn't last.

Hiroshi worked harder at trying to save more money, but no one was spending, and there were days he didn't have a single customer all day. And if he did, they didn't by anything. He was thinking of closing the nursery so he wouldn't have to pay the utilities to keep it open. There was no rent, as he bought the small greenhouse building as soon as he could, using almost all of the money that he came with, leaving just enough for him to buy food for him and Hana. They slept in the greenhouse for the first few months until they had saved enough for the small house that they still lived in.

Tonight they would make tentative plans in case something happened and they were separated. There was something else on his mind, too, and it concerned Kenjiro. A family acquaintance reported seeing him talking to one of the black women, not once but several times. It explained his walks at the same time each day and the smiles he thought no one noticed, but neither he nor Hana missed.

After their dinner of rice and fish, Hiroshi asked Hana and Kenjiro to remain sitting. "I think we all know that the United States is going to enter this war; it is just a matter of time. I think it is also safe to say that Japan is also going to enter the war, and it won't be on the side of the Americans. If our country joins Germany's side, then our life here as we know it will be over. We are already being treated with disdain, and that will only increase. I want us to try to stay together if at all possible, but if not, we have to have a place to meet. We still own the greenhouse, and if we are separated for any reason, we will meet there. There are bedrolls and some provisions there, enough for several days; just make sure no one sees you go there. I have been returning there every day, taking a few more supplies, but I am going to close it now. No one comes anymore, and those that do don't spend any money, so please be careful with the money that we have."

Hiroshi turned his attention to Kenjiro. "There is another thing that we must discuss," he said, "and it involves you, Kenji. It has gotten back to me that you have been visiting with one of the black women. That has to stop; she is not one of us, and it will only draw attention to us. And you have a betrothed in Japan, or have you forgotten that?"

In fact, he had forgotten. It wasn't that his future bride, Aki, wasn't beautiful—she was—but she didn't make him smile the way Patricia did. She didn't make him want to be with her the way Patricia did, and she didn't have an insatiable curiosity about the world like Patricia did. He was fully aware that, had he not seen Patricia that first time or any other time, he would be trying to find a way to get Aki here.

"I had forgotten that. But Father, I do not love her. She is beautiful but silly and petty," Kenjiro said softly.

"And she will grow up and make you a good wife and give you strong sons and beautiful daughters. It will do you well to remember your obligation to her. You are forbidden to see this black woman again; is that understood?"

Kenjiro almost said "yes" out of habit, but stopped himself. "No, Father, I don't understand. When you came here, you sent me letters telling me how wonderful this place was. While I waited for you to send for me, I read their Declaration of Independence. The part I loved the most was when it said that all men are created equal and that they are endowed by their creator with certain unalienable rights; among these are life, liberty, and the pursuit of happiness. I memorized the whole thing and

I clung to it because I sincerely believed life here would be different, that this truly was a place where these words would be true—but they're not. We have become among the discriminated against, and you continue to discriminate. Have you not looked around you? This country isn't what that paper says it is; that paper pertains only to certain people, the whites, while people like us and like Patricia are treated like scum. How is this so different from Japan, other than there we were the ones doing the discriminating?"

His parents stared at him; they had rarely seen his temper, and now he was riled.

"I will not stop seeing Patricia unless she wishes it, and I will not marry Aki," he added.

"Where have you learned this insolence?" Hiroshi asked angrily. "We have worked and sacrificed to bring you here, and this is how you show your gratitude? Is this . . . nigger more important to you than your family? Is she more important than your obligations? Would she forsake her family for you? What do you know of her? Can she read and write?"

Kenjiro took a deep breath; he had no right to speak to his parents as he did, but he wasn't going to give in. "I apologize for my tone and of course I am grateful that I am here, and I appreciate your sacrifices. But Father, was it not you who told me that I had to think on my own and that I had to decide for myself what is right and what is wrong? I have watched, and I have decided that the way we and the black people are being treated is wrong. The name you just called Patricia is wrong; for you to make me choose between you and her is not only wrong, but premature. I will not stop seeing her."

Patricia walked to Miss Abby's with her head in the clouds. She was happy that Kenjiro had reappeared after a week; she had missed him. When she got home, she would try to learn how to say "goodbye" in Japanese. She never heard Vernon come up behind her.

"Hello, Miss Uppity," he said snidely; he no longer even pretended to be nice.

Patricia kept walking and didn't respond.

"I bet if I made you drop those groceries, you wouldn't get paid. Miss Abby would take it out of your wages."

Patricia stopped and turned around to face him. "You wanted to know why I don't like you, well this is one reason right here. You're supposed to be a grown man, but you act no older than a ten-year-old. You stick your thing in anyone who'll let you, and you expect me to like you and then want to be with you in that way? Go find one of your friends that'll spread her legs for you, because I sure won't."

With that, she turned back around and started walking. Vernon saw red and picked up the first thing he saw and threw it at Patricia, just missing her head but grazing her cheek. She screamed in pain and dropped the sack of groceries. She looked up to see Vernon running down the street. She picked up the groceries and made it back to Miss Abby's, prepared to beg for her pay.

Abby saw her coming and frowned; Patricia was walking funny and looked like she had been crying. When she came into the house, Abby saw the blood running from her cheek.

"Dear Lord! Patricia!" she exclaimed as she took the bag from her.

"I'm sorry Miss Abby; I didn't mean to drop the groceries—"

"Shush about that and tell me what happened."

Patricia didn't want to be a tattletale, but she wasn't going to lie, either. "Vernon did it; he got mad and threw a rock at me. Miss Abby, please don't take my wages; I need them to help my family, since my daddy isn't back to work yet."

"Don't worry about that; this wasn't your fault," she replied absently. She thought about calling the police, but what would they do? Nothing, since Patricia was black.

She went to the kitchen and came back with a bowl filled with warm water and cleaned Patricia's face. The blood made it look much worse than it was, but it was deep enough that there would probably be a small scar, which was too bad because Patricia really did have lovely skin.

The bleeding finally stopped, but now it was dark—too dark for Patricia to walk home alone. Vernon might be waiting for her. Abby knew that Patricia's family didn't have a phone and that they would think the worst if she didn't go home. She thought of a taxi, but taxis wouldn't go to that area of town after dark. That left only one option: she would have to drive Patricia home herself. She hadn't driven the car in months; she wasn't even sure where the keys were.

After searching for a good twenty minutes, she located the keys and took a resisting Patricia to the car.

"Miss Abby, please, I can walk home."

"I'm not letting you walk home after what that man did to you! I would never forgive myself if anything happened to you. Now get into the car," Abby said, her tone brooking no nonsense.

Patricia climbed into the car and prayed for safety; she had ridden with Miss Abby before, and it was at best a harrowing experience. They made it to her house in no time and without mishap, but Patricia was worried about Miss Abby getting back in one piece.

When her father saw her face, he demanded to know what happened. Just as Patricia was about to say something, Abby spoke up. "It was that Vernon person; he's been following her to my house and harassing her. He threw a rock at her when he got angry."

Her father looked at Miss Abby. "Thank you for bringin' her home to us, but you'd better get going. Ain't safe for a woman to be out alone, even if she be white."

Abby nodded and went back to her car under the watchful eye of John Middleton. She returned home in one piece and was quite proud of herself. She didn't see Vernon watching her from across the street. The only thing that saved her life was the fact that she was a white woman and that Patricia would know that it was him. He slipped away before he was seen and headed toward home. He had to lie low for a while at least; John Middleton wasn't without friends, and they would be looking for him. He cursed himself for not having better control, but Patricia made him so mad.

It was a couple of days before Patricia went back to Abby's house. The cut on her cheek was healing, but as Abby had feared, there was going to be a scar—not a big one, but a scar nonetheless. Patricia looked at it in one of Abby's mirrors and felt her eyes burn with tears; what would Kenjiro think of her face now? She knew he thought she was pretty, but now. . . .

"Would you like me to walk to the store with you? Or we could drive," Abby suggested.

Patricia was almost tempted, but she declined. "I can't let him think that I'm scared of him," she replied. But there was another reason why she wanted to go alone: she wanted to see Kenjiro for the last time before he walked away from her. She didn't ask herself why it was so important what he thought of her; she only knew it mattered a great deal.

"Be careful, all right? Tell Joe to call me if you want me to come and get you."

"Yes ma'am."

Kenjiro waited across the street for Patricia to show up at the store; it was Friday and he arrived early. Finally he spotted her walking down the sidewalk, but she looked . . . different. He rushed across the street just after she had gone into the grocer's and was waiting for her when she came out. He noticed that she didn't look at him directly as she usually did; it was something that had taken him a while to get used to, but now that she wasn't doing it, he missed seeing the mischief in her eyes.

"*Ohayo*," he greeted.

"*Ohayo*," she repeated, but still didn't look at him.

"Patricia, what is wrong?" he asked.

She closed her eyes, took a deep breath, and looked up at him.

"Your face—who did this to you? Was it one of those Klan people?" he asked.

"No, it was . . . someone who was really angry at me. Miss Abby says I'll always have it."

"Where is this person?" Kenjiro asked.

Patricia realized he was angry and if she told him about Vernon, he would look for him. "No one that you know, but my daddy is looking for him."

Patricia looked away from Kenjiro, figuring that he had seen enough.

"Why do you look away from me?" he asked gently, and then he understood; she thought he would no longer find her pretty. "You are still very pretty," he told her in his softly accented English.

Patricia looked up at him; the mischievous sparkle in her eyes wasn't there—instead there was disbelief.

"I don't lie," he assured her. "You are more than pretty; you are *kirei*—beautiful," he added and watched her eyes light up and the mischievous glint return.

He asked her again about the person who had hurt her, but she wouldn't tell him anything. He would have to be content knowing that her father was looking for the man.

Vernon was tired of being indoors; he was horny and his hand just wasn't the same as being inside a responsive woman. It had been four days since he stupidly threw that rock at Patricia, and maybe her pops had cooled down enough that he wouldn't kill him. Vernon stuck his head out the door of his grandmother's house. She hadn't really wanted to let him in, because Vernon always equaled trouble, and the good Lord knew she had enough of that already.

Vernon kissed his grandmother goodbye before slinking out the door. He hadn't gone far when he saw the broad back of John Middleton. Just as Vernon turned around to go in the opposite direction, John called his name.

"Get your ass over here!" John shouted.

Vernon took off, only to run into a man every bit as big as John was.

"Goin' somewhere?" the man asked as he held onto Vernon.

John walked up to him and looked him up and down. "Now, I believes I told you to stay away from my girl and you didn't listen."

"I'm sorry! She just made me so mad with her uppity—"

"So nows you blamin' her?" John asked, his voice low with anger. "She ain't done nothin' to deserve what you done to her."

"No sir, you right; I shouldn't have done it," Vernon agreed in hope of getting off lightly.

"She got a scar on her face from here to here," John said as he traced an imaginary scar on Vernon's face. "Now I reckon that a good-lookin' fella like yourself wouldn't like a scar on your face."

Vernon tried to get away once he realized what was going to happen to him. When he couldn't get loose, he resorted to begging. "Please, Mr. John, I swear! I won't go near her again; I won't even speak to her iffin I see her."

"I know you won't because everyone I know is going to watch out for my girl, and if you look at her wrong, it will be the last thing you do. Do you understand me?"

"Yes sir; please don't do this!"

Vernon let out a shrill scream as John Middleton pulled out a knife and cut into his cheek. The cut was roughly the same length and deepness as the one that Patricia had, guaranteeing that he would have a scar. Vernon sobbed as he felt the warm blood run down his face. The man holding him gave him a rough shove, as if he were saying, "Just remember, nigger, you being watched."

Vernon sat on the ground sobbing for several minutes before he felt a hand on his shoulder.

"Come on, boy; let's get that cleaned up before infection sets in."

It was his grandmother. She loved him, but she knew it was only a matter of time before someone came after him. He was lucky he was still alive; John Middleton was not a man to be trifled with, and whatever Vernon had done, it had to have involved his daughter somehow.

"What you do to that girl?" she asked as she cleaned up Vernon's face.

"Nothin'!" he protested.

"Boy, I knows John Middleton, and he as peaceful as can be unless somebody he love been messed with, and I'm guessin' somethin' happened to his girl; now what did you do?"

Reluctantly, Vernon told his grandmother the whole story.

"Have you lost your mind? You lucky all he did was scar you! Stay away from that girl!"

DECEMBER 1939

The year was almost over, and the news grew even worse. There had been another attempt on Hitler's life, and once again it had failed. Another chance to kill the madman was gone, and Russia had attacked Finland and was now expelled from the League of Nations; this war was spreading, and soon every country would be involved. There was no such thing as a safe place, but here was better than anywhere else, Hiroshi decided as he rubbed his tired eyes.

The issue of Kenjiro and the black woman continued to plague him. In a way, this was his fault; he had taught Kenjiro to be a free thinker, and now when he needed his obedience, Kenjiro was exercising what he had been taught. Later, when Kenjiro had gone to his room, Hana talked to Hiroshi.

"If you continue to push him, he will do the opposite of what you wish. That is the way of children. Leave it alone and his fascination with this . . . woman will wear thin."

Hiroshi wasn't so sure; Hana didn't see Kenjiro's eyes when he talked about the black girl, nor did she see his eyes when he said he refused to stop seeing her, but there was nothing to be done. He could only hope that Hana was right and Kenjiro would see sense and realize that a pairing with this woman was impossible.

It was a pairing Kenjiro wanted, even if he himself hadn't realized it yet.

Patricia was no longer self-conscious about her scar; being upset about it wasn't going to make it go away, and Kenjiro wasn't bothered by it, which was all that mattered. She hadn't seen Vernon since that night, but had heard what her father had done to him. She wasn't sure how she felt about him having an almost identical scar; it almost made her feel like they were connected somehow, and she didn't like the feeling.

Kenjiro continued to meet her in front of the grocer's on Fridays, where she tried to surprise him by learning a new Japanese word every week. Sometimes it would take him several minutes to figure out what she was trying to say, and then he would gently correct her until she had it right.

"I have an idea," he told her one Friday. "Why don't I teach you a word a week?"

Patricia was thrilled and readily agreed. They began each meeting with a lesson, talked, and then reviewed the lesson. Patricia would practice the word all the way to Miss Abby's house and then on the walk home, which she no longer did alone. There was always someone nearby, whether she saw them or not, but even so, she remained alert.

Vernon watched from a distance. Why he couldn't leave her alone he didn't know, but she was like an itch he couldn't scratch, and he couldn't—or wouldn't—stop until it was satisfied. When he wasn't working at the train station, he spent his time in hiding watching her, which only made the itch worse.

JANUARY 1940

News from the war front hadn't changed, but the attitude toward the Japanese was growing worse. Hiroshi had closed the nursery just after Christmas, hoping for a few sales before then to add to their savings. It turned out to be a wise move, as he ended up selling the rest of his stock at a discounted rate.

It was then that he saw Patricia for the first time; she had come in to pick up a plant for her employer. He only knew it was her because of the way Kenjiro smiled when he saw her and rushed over to assist her. Hiroshi didn't understand it; if he had to want someone other than his betrothed, why couldn't she have been anything but what she was? Taking Hana's advice, he said nothing as he watched Kenjiro and the woman together.

Hiroshi pushed the issue of Kenjiro and the woman out of his mind; there were other pressing issues. He had just heard that America was requiring all "noncitizens" to register and be fingerprinted. He saw it for what it was: the Americans were preparing for war, and they wanted to know where their enemies, real or imagined, were. The Americans had also initiated the draft for the first time while they were at peace; war was at their back door.

There was no question as to whether they would go to register and be fingerprinted—of course they would go; it could only help. They would go to the nearest office on Monday to register. He knew that Kenjiro felt as though they were being treated as criminals, and he agreed with him, but if they had any hope of living a relatively normal life, they had to do what was asked of them.

Kenjiro lay on his bed thinking about Patricia; he wanted to know who had hurt her, but she still refused to say. The only thing she would tell him was that it was taken care of, and then she would beg him to tell her about Japan. He found himself wishing he could see her more often, but didn't know how to make that happen. He had already posted a letter to Aki and her family, breaking their engagement, but he hadn't received a response as of yet; maybe there wouldn't be one, or maybe she had already found another who would be able to deal with her childish ways. Kenjiro knew how he felt about Patricia, but he was unsure of her feelings toward him. One day he would ask her, but it couldn't be at the grocer's; the nursery was the only place that came to mind.

He forced Patricia from his mind and thought about what was happening; what was going to come after the fingerprinting and registration? He wondered. It wasn't going to stop there, and the government and Japanese knew it. Would they be sent back to Japan? It was a possibility, he supposed. It would be an expensive solution, but it could happen. He closed his eyes and wished Patricia a good night's sleep before falling asleep himself.

"They making them Japs register," Patricia's father said as they ate dinner.

Patricia's head snapped up; she hadn't heard about this. Miss Abby was away for the holidays and hadn't returned yet. "What do you mean, Daddy?" she asked.

"Word has it that the Japs have to go and register at the war office and get their fingerprints taken, and not only that—they's startin' to draft, the president is. If I was a younger man, I'd sign up myself and go kill a few Nazis."

"John Middleton, you stop that foolish talk!" Hattie said sharply.

Patricia wasn't paying attention; she wondered how she could go about getting a newspaper without buying one. If Miss Abby was home, she could say it was for her and no one would question it, but as it stood, she would have to wait until she saw Miss Abby at the train station in three days, unless she found another way.

The days passed slowly for both Patricia and Kenjiro as they waited for Friday to come.

Abby filled Patricia in on what was happening with the registration and the draft. "If you ask me, I think we're going to be in this war no matter what Roosevelt says about staying neutral. I don't know what to make of the Japanese registration unless—and this is just a guess—Roosevelt thinks Japan is up to something."

Patricia's heart dropped as she asked the next question. "Will they send them back to Japan?"

"I suppose it's possible, but I doubt it. War is an expensive proposition; if anything, they'll round them up and put them together so they can be watched."

"You mean like a camp of some kind?" Patricia asked, alarmed but trying not to show it.

"I think so, but of course I don't know for sure. Why the interest?" Abby asked.

"Just curious, ma'am; my daddy was talking about it but didn't know all of the facts."

JANUARY 7, 1940

By the time Kenjiro and his parents got to the registration office, the line was out the door and around the corner. They were in for a long wait. Kenjiro looked at the faces around him; some of them were impassive, some were angry, and some were confused. He himself felt anger and confusion. He still hadn't reconciled the words from the Declaration of Independence with what he had witnesses since he had arrived in this country a year ago. The anger was because they were being treated as though they were the enemy; as of yet, Japan had done nothing to antagonize America, and even if they had, he and these people were innocents. He looked down at his parents, curious as to what he'd see on their faces, and wasn't surprised to see acceptance. He accepted this because there was no other choice and because he had no desire to return to Nagasaki.

To pass the time, he thought about his last visit with Patricia or "*Kirei*," as he had started calling her, much to her delight. He could tell she was worried and had tried to ease her mind.

"It is just to register and be fingerprinted, so try not to worry," he told her, fighting the urge to touch her hand. *That, if anything, would cause a commotion*, he thought as he smiled at her.

The rest of the time was spent as it usually was, with him teaching her a new word and reviewing the past ones.

"You are a good student," he told her when she repeated all the words from their past lessons.

"You're a good teacher," she replied. She wanted to say more, but hesitated.

"Tell me," Kenjiro urged.

"I . . . I'm scared for you. What if they try to make you go back to Japan? Miss Abby thinks Japan is going to enter the war, and what will happen if they do?"

Kenjiro was touched by her concern, but had no answers for her questions. The only thing he was fairly certain of was that they wouldn't be sent back unless they were seen as a threat. He had heard rumors about a government man asking questions about some Japanese people, but they were no one he knew. He made a point of becoming close with as few other Japanese as possible; it was something he hated to do, but to him it was a necessary evil.

"I don't think they will send us back; there are too many of us, and there is no proof that Japan is going to enter the war," he told her.

Patricia wasn't convinced, but didn't say anything to contradict him. "Just be careful. I don't want anything to happen to you," she said.

"Patricia! Your order's up!"

Without thinking about it, Patricia reached out and touched Kenjiro's hand just for a second and then ran into the store.

Since that day, he had replayed that touch over and over in his mind.

"Kenjiro," his father called, "the line is moving."

He came out of his reverie to see that they had moved a few feet. The entrance to the building was still a long ways off, and he worried about his mother. She had never been the most energetic of people, and this standing was taking its toll on her. They should have brought a stool for her, but they thought they were leaving early enough that there wouldn't be a line; evidently everyone else had the same thought.

Kenjiro moved behind his mother and put his arms around her. "Lean against me; it will help."

When she began to argue, he teased her, "And you wonder where my stubborn gene comes from."

Hana chuckled as she leaned back and let Kenjiro support some of her weight. *He is a good son*, she thought as she sighed in relief.

Six hours later, they were finally in the door. They were tired, hungry, and in desperate need of a bathroom, and the process was slow.

"Do you swear your loyalty to the United States of America?" the man asked Kenjiro.

"Yes," he replied.

He heard the same question being asked of his parents and heard their answers. *Is this really happening?* he wondered, as he was fingerprinted as if he were a common criminal.

"Please, is there a bathroom nearby? My parents—"

The man interrupted him, "You can use the ones with the colored signs over them if they'll let ya—now move on."

Kenjiro waited for his parents, and then they made their way to the public bathroom.

His father balked. "We are not one of them! I will not use a toilet used by them."

Kenjiro, tired and hungry, snapped, "Get used to it, Father! As far as the white man is concerned, we might as well be one of them!"

He helped his mother into the bathroom and then stood guard at the door; to his surprise, they weren't harassed as they each took turns using the facilities and then getting a drink. They made their way back to the train station for the long ride home, buying food to eat on the train. Hana was asleep before she had eaten even half of her food. He gently took it from her hand and put it in his pocket for later; the day had been too much for her.

Hiroshi looked out of the window; to be thought of as being no better than those dark people angered him almost more than the fact that they had to register and be fingerprinted. He and Kenjiro didn't speak for the entire trip home, each of them lost in their own thoughts, although Hiroshi knew exactly where Kenjiro's thoughts were. Hana's advice wasn't working; if anything, he seemed even more taken by the girl. It was time for Hiroshi to do something to stop this madness.

Chapter 3

JANUARY 7, 1940

Hana slept for the entire train ride back to LA and then had to walk to their home. She was a tiny woman, and Kenjiro offered to carry her, but she adamantly refused.

Kenjiro and his father still hadn't spoken, and Kenjiro knew why: his father was angry that they had to use the same facilities as the blacks, and he was still angry over Kenjiro's refusal to stop seeing Patricia. The walk home was just as silent as the train ride back, and Hana worried about the discord between father and son. It was time for her to intervene and try to talk sense to Kenji; she had always managed to get him to see reason when his father couldn't. The one thing she wouldn't do was interfere with Kenjiro's walk. Hiroshi had tried that, and it didn't work; she would wait until afterward, when Hiroshi would be at a friend's house listening to the shortwave radio that he had managed to hide. If the man got caught, she could only hope Hiroshi wouldn't be there; if he was, he would be treated as a spy and there would be nothing they could do to help him.

When they got home, Kenjiro wished his parents good night and went to his room to reread the medical journals. He felt guilty about the divide between him and his father, but didn't know how to fix it unless he gave in and did as his parents wanted, and that wasn't going to happen. He would take his walk as scheduled and hoped to see Patricia to let her know he was all right. It gave him a warm feeling to know she worried for him, but at the same time, he didn't like that she worried over him; she had enough to worry about with her own family. When he finally fell asleep, it was with the memory of her brief touch on his hand.

Patricia couldn't concentrate on anything all day; she missed half of what Miss Abby said, requiring her to repeat it several times.

"Where is your mind today?" Miss Abby asked, looking at Patricia.

"I'm sorry, Miss Abby; I just didn't sleep well last night," Patricia replied.

"Is that man still bothering you? We'll tell your father if he is," Miss Abby said, peering at Patricia.

Patricia hadn't seen Vernon since her father gave him a scar that almost matched hers, although Vernon had been watching her.

"No ma'am, I haven't seen him since that night. Miss Abby? Can I ask you a question?"

"Of course you can," Abby replied.

"Is it wrong for people of different races to love each other?"

Whatever question she was expecting, this wasn't it. Abby took a few minutes to figure out how to answer her. "Well, society says it is, and some people and churches will even say that the Bible teaches against it. You know the verse, the one about not being unequally yoked? But is it wrong? I don't know, but what I do know is that life for the couple would be hell as well as for any children that they might have. Patricia, what's going on with you?"

"Nothing, Miss Abby, I was just curious," Patricia replied as she washed the dishes.

Abby didn't believe her, but didn't press—although she did decide to caution her. "Patricia, I don't know what's happening with you, but I hope you know you can come to me about anything. Having said that, I want you to be careful with whomever it is you're getting involved with—"

"There isn't anyone," Patricia interrupted. "I'm just asking."

Abby let the subject drop and helped Patricia with the dishes. She noticed that Patricia kept watching the clock and seemed to be moving her lips as if in silent prayer and wondered whom she was praying so hard for. That night, Abby drove Patricia home, as she had every night since the night Vernon threw the rock at her.

"Patricia. . . . "

"Goodnight, Miss Abby, drive safely," Patricia said as she got out of the car.

Abby waited until Patricia was indoors before pulling away. Vernon stood in the shadows fingering the scar he had received courtesy of John Middleton. He knew he should leave her alone; common sense told him that, but Vernon wasn't thinking. He wanted Patricia, and that was all there was to it. He just didn't know how to make it happen.

Patricia spoke to her parents and then excused herself to her room. Abby wasn't the only one who noticed that something was on Patricia's mind. Hattie tapped lightly on Patricia's door before going in.

"Patricia, what be bothering you? You been mopin' around for the last few days like you lost your best friend."

Maybe I have, Patricia thought to herself. "I'm fine, Mama; I guess it's all the talk about war that's got me so unsettled."

That wasn't a lie exactly; she was worried about a war, but not for all of the same reasons everyone else was. She was worried about Kenjiro and his family. It didn't occur to her that while he might care about her, his family wouldn't; to her, it was a given that when you cared for someone, their family was included in that care.

Hattie wasn't buying it any more than Abby, but let it go. The one thing she was sure of was that whatever ailed Patricia, a man was somehow involved. She could only hope it wasn't Vernon Monroe; she didn't care who it was, just so it wasn't him.

"Mama?" Patricia called as Hattie headed toward the door.

"Yes, baby?"

Patricia closed her eyes. Even at nineteen, she loved hearing her mother call her that; it gave her a sense of security, sort of like when Kenjiro called her "*Kirei*."

Hattie waited by the door for Patricia to say what was on her mind.

"Never mind, it isn't important. Goodnight," she said.

"Goodnight, baby," Hattie replied.

Patricia changed into her nightclothes and crawled into bed. She whispered a heartfelt prayer for Kenjiro and his family before saying a prayer for her own family. The final thing she prayed for was that Japan wouldn't enter the war.

JANUARY 8, 1940

Hiroshi read the newspapers with frustration. He still hadn't gotten over the treatment they had received the day before and that they had to use the bathrooms designated for the blacks. To add insult to injury, Kenji was in love with that black woman, even if he wasn't admitting it. He was awake all night trying to decide what he should do about it, and come morning, he still had no answers. He thought about writing to Aki's family and reneging on the broken engagement, but a letter would take too long; there was no guarantee they would even get it, and if they did, they wouldn't arrive in the States for weeks. He briefly thought about sending Kenjiro back, but that would take too much of their money, and if Japan entered the war, he would be expected to fight in the emperor's army.

He rubbed his tired eyes as he decided on what he should do, if anything. *Maybe the attraction will wear off*, he thought to himself and realized it was wishful thinking. Last night on the train, he had seen the smile on Kenjiro's faced and knew the reason for that smile. On the plus side, they were only talking, and as far as he knew hadn't spent any real time alone together. Maybe he should write that letter.

He jumped when Hana put a hand on his back and set a cup of tea in front of him.

"You worry about Kenji too much; he will make the right choice," she said.

Hiroshi wasn't so sure, but said nothing.

When Kenjiro came to the table, he bowed to his father. "I am sorry that we are in disagreement. Know that I am not deliberately trying to be disrespectful to you, but I cannot help what I feel and think," he said softly.

"And what of what we feel and think? Have you thought about that, or are you so wrapped up in this n—woman that you don't care about that? And what about her? Have you thought about what this will mean for her?" Hiroshi demanded.

The fact was that he had. He had come to the conclusion that he was being premature and that they would cross that bridge when and if they got to it; the other thing was it was for her to decide if she wanted a life with him. He took the time to remind his father of that fact. "Father, once again I must remind you that you are being premature . . . "

Hiroshi stood up, looked at Kenjiro, and walked out. Kenjiro knew better than to go after him; he was too angry and wouldn't listen to anything that he had to say anyway. He turned when he felt his mother touch his back.

"Sit down, Kenji; we must talk."

When they were sitting, Hana gave him a long, hard look, but her voice was soft when she spoke. "Your father means well; he only wants what's best for all of us, and this woman—"

"Her name is Patricia," Kenjiro interrupted.

"All right, this Patricia isn't what is best for this family," she continued.

Kenji thought about his question carefully before he asked it. "How do you know this? You haven't met her. You and father are making a judgment based on stereotype and prejudice."

Hana paused. "Tell me of her; tell me what makes her so special that you would break an engagement to a girl you have been planning to marry for years. Tell me what makes her so special that you would hurt us like this."

Kenjiro tried to sum Patricia up in a few words. "She makes me laugh and smile no matter how bad things seem, and she is *kirei* as well."

Kenjiro told Hana about how Patricia had surprised him by saying "hello" to him in Japanese and about her insatiable curiosity about the world outside of where she lived. It didn't take Hana long to realize Kenjiro was in love with this girl and nothing would sway him from pursuing this, except maybe guilt.

"I must admit that she sounds lovely, even though she is black, but Kenjiro, if you pursue this, how will you care for her? Not only that, but the sentiment against us grows, and who knows what will happen if Japan enters this war? If you won't think of us, think about her. Her life is already difficult because of her skin color, and yet you want to complicate it even more."

Kenjiro listened silently and waited for Hana to play her trump card.

"Your father worked hard to bring us here; surely you cannot choose this . . . Patricia over him? Over our family? She is and never will be one of us."

Kenji waited until she was finished before he spoke. "Mother, I was hoping you would understand, but I see that you don't. But once again, I remind you that this is a premature discussion. I don't know how Patricia feels about me. We haven't discussed it yet."

"Kenjiro, I am your mother and I know you are in love with this girl. Do you think I don't see the smiles you try to hide after one of your walks when you've seen her? Or how you become anxious if anything interferes with those walks? Even now, at the mention of her name, you smile, so don't do us a disservice by denying how you feel about her," his mother said sharply.

"I wasn't—"

"Yes, you were, and you are. If you cannot tell us how you feel about her, what are you going to do in the outside world?" Hana asked.

Kenjiro hadn't thought about it quite like that and realized his mother was right; by not saying anything, he was in effect saying he wanted his feelings to be kept secret.

"Very well, Mother, I am sorry you and Father believe I am being disrespectful to you when I am not. I am simply choosing whom I want to spend my life with, and it is not Aki. I love Patricia, and no, she isn't aware of it, but I do plan to tell her someday soon. I can only hope if you can't accept this that you do me the courtesy of not referring to her by the name Father calls her."

Hana was shocked; she had inadvertently forced his hand and he had chosen the woman over them. She wasn't even sure what she said that helped him decide the matter, but it wasn't important—they had lost their son to a black woman. But still she tried to get him to see reason. "Kenji, please think about what you are doing! You have said it yourself: we are no more welcome here than they are. What do you think will happen if you are together?" she asked frantically.

Kenji took his mother's hands in his and kissed them. "Mother, I love you and Father, but I won't be swayed by your arguments. I'm not saying they aren't worth considering, but I have to choose my own path. Both you and Father have taught me that. If Patricia doesn't feel as I do, then that is the end of it. It's time for my walk."

Kenjiro kissed her hands again and stood up to leave. Hana watched him with tears in her eyes; as much as she disagreed with him about the woman, she was proud of him. He showed strength and courage when he stood his ground with his father, and if he was determined to be with this Patricia, he would need it. She hoped the woman was half as strong as Kenji was.

Patricia got to the grocer's early, hoping to see Kenjiro. She regretted doing it; it only made the wait longer. Finally she saw him approaching from the distance and breathed a sigh of relief. She had slept poorly the night before, as she was too worried and frightened to sleep.

When he reached her, he bowed and said, "*Ohayo, Kirei*."

"*Ohayo*, are you all right? What happened?" she asked, not taking a moment to bask in his affectionate greeting.

Kenjiro was touched by her concern and tried to calm her. "We are fine; it was a very long day, but we are registered and fingerprinted. I thought of you," he added shyly.

"I thought about you, too. I was so afraid I wouldn't see you again," Patricia replied. "Was it horrible?"

"The wait was the worst of it, and the process was long. We arrived home rather late, but it is done. You haven't been sleeping well, have you?" he asked, seeing the dark circles under her eyes.

"Not really, but I'll sleep better now that I know you're all right."

"Patricia! Your order's up!" the grocer called out.

"I've got to go, but I'll see you on Friday," Patricia said as she walked away, relieved.

APRIL 1940

Patricia and Kenjiro continued to meet in front of the grocer's. Kenjiro continued her lessons and continued to be taken by her quest for knowledge not just about Japan, but of the world in general. What neither of them realized was that they were being watched by Vernon—and not just by him; Kenjiro's father had someone watching them as well.

Hiroshi still didn't know what to do about Kenjiro and the "nigger," as he had begun to call her whenever Kenjiro wasn't within earshot, but the war added to his upset. Denmark had surrendered to Germany after a five-year occupation, and as of yet, the Americans remained neutral, but the draft continued. Hiroshi felt deep in his gut that by this time next year, Japan would be in the war. He, Hana, and Kenjiro repeatedly talked about what they would do if that happened. The plan had never changed; they would stay together if they could, and if not, they would meet at the greenhouse.

Kenjiro half listened; he could recite the plan forward and backward in his sleep, but he had an additional worry: Patricia. He didn't want to leave her, and they had yet to talk about their feelings for each other. He was brought back to the present by his father telling him that he had received a letter from Japan.

Thinking it was from one of his friends, Kenjiro grabbed the envelope and ripped it open. When he saw the writing, his heart sank. It was from Aki.

Dear Kenjiro,

Of course I accept your apology for your previous letter! Your father has explained that you are simply nervous and has been generous enough to pay my passage to the United States. The boat leaves in two weeks, and I am very excited to be coming to you.

Until then,

Aki

Kenjiro stared at the letter in shock and then looked at the post date; it was over a month ago. Aki was on her way. He looked at the letter and then at his father, who met his stare with one of his own.

"I gave you every opportunity to end it with that . . . that woman, and yet you persisted in seeing her. Someone had to take control, so I wrote to Aki on your behalf; when she comes, you will marry her," Hiroshi said evenly.

Hana was shocked; she didn't know about the letter and would have tried to stop him if she had. The last time they had discussed it, Hiroshi had decided against it. She watched as father and son stared at each other with anger in their eyes. She looked at Hiroshi first and then Kenjiro; what she saw made her heart pound. She had never seen him this angry.

"I will not marry her even when she arrives. You have spent your money for nothing," he said softly, but with conviction.

"You will do as I say!" Hiroshi demanded.

"I will not obey you in this; even if Patricia were not a part of this, I would have refused to marry Aki. I do not love her and will not do her the disservice of pretending that I do, and I won't do Patricia the disservice of denying how I feel about her."

Hiroshi stammered in his anger, "You . . . you . . . fool! Aki's family is wealthy! They could pay for the education you need to be a doctor! Marry her and keep your little nigger girl on the side if you must have her, but—"

Kenjiro stood and left the table; there was nothing more to discuss. He wasn't going to be forced into a marriage just because of money and prestige. He went to his room and softly closed the door. He lay on his bed fully clothed and thought about Patricia; as always, his mood lightened.

"Hiroshi! What have you done?" Hana asked, appalled.

"What had to be done!" Hiroshi replied. "We tried it your way and it didn't work. He's more enamored with the girl than he was before.

"Because he loves her," Hana said quietly.

"He thinks he loves her!" Hiroshi stated coldly. "And I will rot before I allow him to disgrace this family!"

Hana didn't say anything for a long time; she rarely went against her husband, but she was in danger of losing her only living child.

"Hiroshi, you must listen to me; if you insist on Kenjiro marrying Aki, no more good will come of it than if he married Patricia. You must let him be, or else we will no longer have a son to give us grandchildren."

"No grandchildren would be better than the offspring he will produce with that black woman!" he retorted.

Hana looked at her husband as if seeing him for the first time. She knew he had racist views—so did she for that matter, but hers had tempered with time as she found that they were as discriminated against as much as the blacks, whereas Hiroshi's racist views seemed to grow. She understood that part of it was anger and maybe even some fear, but she had never heard such hatred in his voice, and it frightened her.

The next several days were awkward at best. Father and son barely spoke to each other, other than to talk about the progress of the war. Kenjiro continued with his walks and seeing Patricia when he could; he still hadn't decided when or how to tell her of his feelings for her. Most of his reluctance was due to fear that she wouldn't feel the same way, but even if she didn't, he was not going to marry Aki Kouki.

Friday finally came, and Patricia practically ran to the store. Kenjiro was waiting for her at the corner when she got there.

"*Ohayo, Kirei*," he greeted.

"*Ohayo*; you're early," she replied as they walked to the store.

"I was anxious to see you," he replied, smiling down at her.

"Really? How come?" she asked. "Hold on," she added as she went into the store. A few minutes later she came out. "We'll have some extra time today; Miss Abby forgot to call in her special order for her fish. It'll be an extra fifteen minutes," Patricia said as she took her place by the wall.

Vernon watched from across the street; he had followed her all the way from Miss Abby's. He watched as the Japanese man greeted her and noticed the smile he gave her and the way Patricia smiled at him in return. The beginnings of a plan began to form, but he had to wait and be patient. Patricia would do whatever he wanted her to do if he could just wait.

"Why did you want to see me so badly?" Patricia asked.

Now that the time was here, Kenjiro couldn't speak. This wasn't the place to tell someone that you loved them, so he changed his mind. "I just wanted to thank you for the concern you have shown to me and my family," he said.

He wasn't telling her the whole truth, and Patricia knew it, but then she was holding some things back herself. "You're welcome; I'm just glad that you're all right," she replied.

The rest of the visit passed quietly, with Patricia repeating the words Kenjiro had taught her over the months.

"Do you think you can teach me to speak in sentences?" Patricia asked.

"Of course, what would you like to learn to say?" Kenjiro replied.

"I don't know, maybe things like 'how are you today?' Or 'it's nice to meet you,'" she replied.

"We will start the next time we meet," Kenjiro said. "Patricia, I would like it if you were to call me Kenji. The only other people to call me Kenjiro are my parents."

Patricia didn't know what to say; for him to request that of her meant something. "Okay, if you want me to," she said softly.

"Thank you," Kenji said as he touched her hand so softly that she almost didn't feel it.

A small part of her wanted to stop what was happening between them; life was already hard enough without complicating it, but a bigger part of her wanted to keep going in spite of the odds. Patricia already knew how her parents would react and had a good idea of what his parents would say as well, but she found that she really didn't care so much. The optimist in her believed it would be all right; it had to be all right. She hadn't put a label on what she felt for Kenji; she wasn't quite ready for that just yet.

All too soon, her order was ready and they parted ways, but not before holding hands for a few brief seconds and squeezing lightly. Patricia told him all he needed to know in that brief squeeze—she cared for him, and he hoped she understood that he cared for her as well.

As he walked away, Kenji remembered Aki. She would arrive in a few weeks; he would face her as he should and apologize that she came so far only to be disappointed. He had no doubt that at that time his father would be angry enough to disown him, but so be it. His future lay with Patricia Middleton and no one else.

When Kenji arrived home, it was to a somber scene. His mother was crying as she held a letter in her hand.

"Mother? What is it?" Kenji asked as he rushed to her.

"Aki," was all she got out.

"What about her?" Kenji asked.

"She is not coming, they . . . she. . . . "

"She what?" Kenji asked, fearing the worst.

"She has married another; her family did not know this when they made her write the letter. They have returned the passage money your father sent," Hana replied.

Kenji breathed a sigh of relief; it seemed that Aki didn't want to marry him any more than he wanted to marry her.

"Does Father know?" he asked.

"No, and he will be so angry. Kenji, go to the greenhouse until he calms," Hana said. "He will say some very hurtful things to you about your Patricia."

"I will not leave you to face his anger alone; if I can't tolerate him saying things, then how will I tolerate anyone else? If she and I are to be together, it is something we will have to get used to."

"Kenjiro, please go. The tension between you is too much; one of you will say something you will regret," Hana begged.

Kenji dug his heels in. "I am not going to run and hide like a coward. I'm staying."

Hana nodded her head in acceptance and waited for the storm to begin.

Patricia practically skipped all the way back to Miss Abby's. Abby saw her coming and laughed at her; she remembered being so young and carefree, but she wondered about the cause of Patricia's good mood. She was still convinced it was a man, but she couldn't figure out who it might be. None of the men that came to mind were Patricia's type. *She would never be content to be a housewife, so who could it be?* she wondered.

Patricia greeted Abby with a warm smile and chattered like a magpie about everything and anything. Finally Abby could stand it no more. "Who is it that has you so happy?" she asked.

"Nobody," Patricia said as she put the groceries away. "I'm just happy."

"Patricia Middleton, no one makes you smile the way you're smiling, so who is it?" she pressed.

Patricia wanted to tell her, but she couldn't, at least not yet. She wanted this time to herself before she had to share it. "I promise to tell you, but not now," she finally said.

Abby looked at her suspiciously, but said no more.

Kenji and Hana waited for Hiroshi to come home, and when he did, he was in a foul mood. Kenji and Hana looked at each other and by mutual agreement decided to keep silent about the letter.

He barely acknowledged them as he stomped by them and into the bedroom. Hana finished dinner, hoping that whatever had Hiroshi so upset would have passed already, but it wasn't to be.

Dinner was tense as they ate in silence.

"Do you have no honor?" Hiroshi snarled finally. "You were seen with that nigger again! What of Aki? She is on her way here."

Hana and Kenji looked at each other, and Kenji spoke before she could. He would bear the brunt of his father's anger. "Father, Aki is not coming."

"Of course she is! I have the letter saying so," Hiroshi retorted.

"No, Father, another letter came today. Aki married another; she did it without the knowledge or consent of her family. She did not want to marry me. They sent the money back."

There was dead silence at the table as Hiroshi stood up and walked away. Hana and Kenji looked at each other, not speaking; Hiroshi's silence wasn't a good thing.

Kenji went to his room and tried to imagine what his father was up to; he had seen him like this before and knew there was more than anger involved. He was planning something. The most logical plan would be for his father to try to find another suitable bride for him, and it would have to be someone already here in the United States. He hadn't told Patricia too much about his country, but being an avid reader, she had read everything she could about Japan. He wondered if any of her reading mentioned anything about arranged marriages. The time was coming when they were going to have to talk; he just had to figure out when and where.

Patricia greeted her parents with hugs and kisses, startling the both of them; she only acted this way when she was happy about something. Like Abby, Hattie knew it had to involve a man, and like Abby, she couldn't imagine who it would be. But whoever he was, he must be someone special. Hattie went to Patricia's door and knocked before going in. She found Patricia lying on the bed fully dressed, eyes closed, and wearing the biggest smile she had ever seen on her face.

"Patricia, who is this man who got you so happy?" Hattie asked.

"I'll tell you soon, I promise," Patricia replied as she got up.

"Patricia. . . . "

"Soon, Mama, I promise," she repeated as she took her nightgown out of the drawer.

They were disturbed by John's big voice shouting, "Vernon Monroe, you a dead nigger!"

Patricia hadn't given Vernon any serious thought for weeks, but apparently he was still around and watching her. Patricia had a horrifying thought: what if he had seen her with Kenji? She relaxed. There was nothing to tell, and they were only talking, except for today when they held hands. *Did he see that?* she wondered and became anxious again.

Her father tapped on the open door and came into her room. "Patricia, that fool boy been following you all over the place. You be careful; he might hurt you worse than he did."

"Yes, Daddy," Patricia replied. He was worried and so was she, but for different reasons.

JULY 8, 1940

Hiroshi continued to keep a close eye on the war. The Prime Minister of Britain had resigned in the spring and there was a new prime minister: Winston Churchill. Germany invaded Denmark, Norway, Belgium, and the Netherlands and had accomplished this before the end of May, and to make matters worse, Italy jumped into the fray, declaring war on France and Great Britain. The only bright spots Hiroshi could see were that Japan was still out of the war, as was the United States—at least for the moment.

He closed the paper and pushed the war out of his mind. Kenji was still seeing the woman and had even managed to get Hana on his side.

"Hiroshi, leave him be. All you're doing is pushing him toward the forbidden fruit; he will still go to her even if he doesn't care for her just to prove to you that he is able to stand on his own."

"Are you agreeing with him? Are you saying I should encourage this?" he demanded angrily.

"No, of course not, but I am saying that you are pushing him into her arms by your actions. I am begging you to stop; I don't want to lose my son."

Hiroshi gave her words some thought but came to a decision. "Go to the store and buy enough to feed four; we are having company tonight," he said.

"Who's coming?" Hana asked.

"An acquaintance and his daughter, Dai," Hiroshi replied. "She is not as beautiful as Aki, but she will be a better match for Kenji."

Hana didn't argue. It would have been pointless; Hiroshi was going to do whatever he was going to do, with or without her help. She was tempted to warn Kenji but decided against it; Hiroshi had already accused her of siding with Kenji in his madness for the black girl.

Kenji overheard his parents talking in hushed tones as he headed out for his walk. It wasn't Friday, but he hoped to see Patricia anyway. It was rare for him to see her more than once a week, and when he did, there was little that could upset him. They had learned to stand close enough that they could actually touch without drawing attention to themselves; the brief hand-holding now occurred after every meeting.

Today he was leaving a little early. It was a special day; it was Patricia's twentieth birthday, and he hoped to buy her a small gift with the money he had saved before coming to America.

He was both excited and nervous because he had never bought a gift for a woman and had no idea of where to start. He headed out in the general direction of the grocer's, taking his time; if she was going to be there, it wouldn't be for another two hours or so. If he didn't see her, he would take his walk as usual and hope to see her. If that failed, it would have to wait until Friday.

As he walked, he allowed his mind to wander, but was careful to watch where he was going. He wondered if there was any place they could go where they could be together and not have problems. In his heart he knew no such place existed, but it didn't stop him from wishing there was. Kenji passed a jewelry store owned by a Japanese man who had been born in the United States. Kenji had passed the store before and the man had always acknowledged him, but this was the first time he ever stopped in. As far as Kenji could tell, the man fared no better than those who had immigrated; all the Americans saw was a Japanese man.

"What can I get for you?" the man asked politely.

"I am looking for a birthday gift for my mother," Kenji lied.

"I see," the man said. "What did you have in mind?"

"I . . . I don't know. Nothing big, but small; something that can be packed away without problems," Kenji replied.

The man showed Kenji what he had, which wasn't much, but Kenji's eye was drawn toward a simple gold necklace that was looped through a plain gold circle. It was small, but beautiful.

"How much for this?" he asked, hoping he had enough.

"That? Not so much. It has been there for a long time; three American dollars," the man said. "I am planning on closing the store soon. Things do not look good for our people," he added as he wrapped the necklace in a piece of brown paper. "I hope your mother likes it."

Kenji bowed to the man politely and continued on his way. His heart sank when he reached the grocer's and Patricia wasn't there. He waited for several minutes before giving up and going home.

"I don't mind going to the store for you," Patricia all but begged.

"It's your birthday and I'm not sending you to the store!" Abby protested as she set a wrapped gift in front of Patricia.

"Miss Abby!" Patricia gasped, the store temporarily forgotten.

"Happy birthday, Patricia! And I know I've never told you this, but if I were to have had a daughter, I would have wanted her to be like you—full of wonder and surprises. Open it!"

Patricia blinked back tears. She knew that Miss Abby cared about her, but she didn't realize just how much. Patricia carefully opened the gift, as she wanted to save the paper, which was a very pretty floral print. Inside was a beautiful red sweater; it was the one she always looked at in the Montgomery Ward catalog.

"Miss Abby, I can't take this! It's—"

"Perfect for you," Abby interrupted. "Try it on!"

Patricia put the sweater on and luxuriated in its softness; she had never felt anything as nice. Patricia took the sweater off and put it back in the box; she would only wear it for special occasions. Abby drove her home, sending along most of the birthday cake she had ordered for the occasion. The only thing that would have made her day perfect was if she had seen Kenji.

Patricia showed off her sweater to her parents before sharing the birthday cake with them.

"I'm sorry, baby, there ain't enough money to get you a nice gift like Miss Abby's, but we got you somethin'," her father said.

Hattie handed her a small package wrapped in old newspaper. Patricia's eyes filled with tears; they shouldn't have spent the money on a gift for her. Times were tight and were going to get tighter. Patricia took the package and carefully opened it. Inside was a book: *Around the World in Eighty Days*, by Jules Verne.

Patricia was speechless as she touched the book gently. Without a word, she hugged both of her parents; she would treasure that book for the rest of her life.

"I know it ain't much," her mother said.

"It's perfect. I love it, and I love you, too," Patricia said. "This has been a good birthday."

Patricia took her gifts and went to her room. She laid them on the bed and changed her clothes, her eyes never leaving the gifts. Finally she understood something, or rather admitted what she had known for some time: she loved Kenjiro and he loved her, but where they would go from here, she didn't know.

Chapter 4

JULY 8, 1940

Now that Patricia had admitted to herself that she was in love with Kenji, she was scared. She wanted to talk to her mother, but didn't think she would understand. She thought of Miss Abby, but she wouldn't understand either. It dawned on her that she and Kenji were on their own in this. She wondered if he had any idea what they should do. She changed into her night-clothes although it was early, knowing that her parents wouldn't bother her; they would assume she was reading the book she had just gotten for her birthday.

Patricia looked at the beautiful red sweater Miss Abby had given her and the book from her parents. She picked them up and put them in a small wooden box that she kept under her bed. She had had the box for years, and it had an odd assortment of things in it, including part of the money that she kept from her wages from Miss Abby. To date, she had fifteen dollars and some change. "For a rainy day," she would tell herself each time she put money in the chest, but so far the rainy day had never come. Patricia closed the box and put it back under the bed; she turned out the lamp and went to bed thinking of Kenji.

Kenji walked home fingering the small package in his pocket; he couldn't wait to see Patricia so he could give it to her. When he got home, he would make a small card and write "*Boku wa kimi wo it sumade aishuru tsumon da*—I will love you forever" on it and put the necklace with it.

He smelled food cooking even before he got into the house and wondered what was happening; he stopped short when he saw his father drinking saké with a man he didn't know. And then he saw the girl. He then knew what was happening. His father had already found a bride for him and was hoping he would just accept the decision.

Hana saw Kenji walk in and put two and two together and braced herself; Kenji was more like his father than he realized. She recognized the flash in his eyes, the stern set to his jaw that he had when his mind was made up, and he had already decided that he wasn't going to marry this girl.

Kenji bowed politely to the man and then to his father.

"Welcome home, Kenjiro; this is Joben Saito and his daughter, Dai."

Kenji politely acknowledged the girl with a polite smile and then turned to his father. He had to stop this before it went any further. "Father, please may I speak with you?"

Hiroshi excused himself and followed Kenji to the kitchen.

"She is pretty, isn't she?" Hiroshi asked.

"Yes, but I do not want her. I thought I was clear that I will marry whom I choose."

"And I thought I was clear in that you will do as I say," Hiroshi replied. "And besides, he has money to help you get started—"

"Father, I am not going to marry her. If you wish, I will tell them myself."

"And what reason will you give them?" Hiroshi shot back.

"The truth: that my heart belongs to another," Kenji replied.

Hiroshi was horrified; he couldn't believe Kenjiro would disgrace himself and his family like this. "You would do this thing? You would embarrass your mother like this? Once again, I will ask you: do you have no honor?"

Kenji didn't reply as he went back to the living room. Hiroshi watched, horrified, as Kenji informed the man and his daughter with deep apologies that he couldn't possibly marry Dai, as lovely as she was.

"My heart belongs to another; I am sorry," he added.

Joben looked at Hiroshi as if to say, "You cannot control your son?" Joben stood up and walked out, with Dai following closely on his heels.

Hiroshi turned to Kenji and walked away. He went into the bedroom and shut the door behind him. This wasn't the way it was supposed to be. By now, Kenji should be in medical school and anticipating his wedding to Aki; they shouldn't be arguing over a black girl who was more than likely an uneducated slut. They shouldn't be treated as if they were the enemy or as if they were one of the dark people. It was then that Hiroshi realized that he had lost control not only of his family but his life as a whole and it was time to take something back. It was time to deal with the issue of the black girl decisively.

Hiroshi stayed in the bedroom, not coming out until morning. He had a plan, but before it could be executed, he needed more information. Later that day, he walked to the grocer's where Kenji and Patricia met. He knew they met on Fridays and in the late afternoon; he would have someone watching to see what they did and if they went anywhere. He didn't think that they did, but he wanted to be sure. His plan also included the need for another male, preferably a black male; if Kenji saw the girl with another male, he would assume the worst and leave her alone. He would also ask his spy to look for any likely candidates.

Friday seemed to take a long time in coming. Patricia kept watching the clock, while at home Kenji paced. He really wished he could take Patricia somewhere nice to give her his birthday gift, but there was no help for it. Finally, it was time to go for his walk; he hoped nothing had happened to keep Patricia away. If it did, it could be another week before he saw her again. He touched the packet in his pocket that contained the note and the card. He carefully wrote the words in Japanese characters, the pronunciation, and the English meaning, one line on top of the other. What he really wanted was to say the words to her, but it wasn't possible. She would have to wait until she got home to open the gift. He hated this; he hated that he had to make do with seeing her once a week, and then only for an hour.

As he walked, he didn't notice that he was being followed; his mind was on other things, namely Patricia and how they could be together. The man following him was someone Kenji didn't really know, but who had his own agenda as far as Kenji's father was concerned.

Kenji crossed the street and waited for Patricia to come around the corner; as soon as he saw her, he couldn't help but smile.

"*Ohayo, Kirei*," he said with a smile and a little bow. "*Tanjoubi omedetou*—happy birthday."

Patricia smiled. "Thank you! Let me run this order in and I'll be right back."

A few minutes later, she was back. "Teach me how to say that," she said.

Kenji taught her how to say "happy birthday" in Japanese and told her he was sorry he had missed her birthday.

"It's all right; I did miss you, though. I tried to convince Miss Abby to let me come to the store because she was out of eggs, but she wouldn't let me because it was my birthday," Patricia said, talking fast.

Patricia was nervous; she only talked fast when she was nervous, and she knew that Kenji knew it by the way he smiled at her.

"I have something for you, but you cannot open it here. Wait until you are alone," Kenji told her. "Just know that I care for you," he added softly.

Patricia accepted the small package and slipped it into her pocket, not knowing that Vernon was watching her as well as the Japanese man, who had also noticed Vernon. Neither man left until Patricia and Kenji parted ways after their brief holding of hands.

"I'll be a son of a bitch!" Vernon murmured. "Little Miss Uppity is fuckin' a Jap." The thought angered him. *She'll spread her legs for a yellow son of a whore and not me?* he asked himself. If he had been thinking, he would have realized that once Patricia was in the house, she never left it, which left no opportunity for her to spread her legs for anyone.

The Japanese man watched Vernon carefully; he could tell that Vernon had some interest in the girl, but he needed to find out more before he took the information to Hiroshi or approached him.

Patricia toyed with the package in her pocket as she walked back from the store. As badly as she wanted to open it, she made herself wait. Time seemed to slow down once she got to Miss Abby's house. She found herself daydreaming about being somewhere else with Kenji and was unaware that she was being spoken to.

"Patricia!" Miss Abby shouted.

"Yes ma'am?" Patricia answered.

"You haven't heard a word I've said; where were you this time?" Abby asked.

Patricia smiled. "In Europe somewhere. France, I think," she replied.

"A lovely country; at least it was. So, Patricia, are you ready to tell me about this young man of yours?" Abby asked, changing the subject.

"Not yet. I want to keep it to myself for a while longer," Patricia replied truthfully.

"You are the strangest girl; when I was your age I couldn't wait to talk about my newest beau. I guess the times have changed."

Patricia didn't comment as she gathered her things to go home. Miss Abby was turning out to be quite a good driver, and Patricia no longer held onto the door handle and prayed so hard for safety. She jumped out of the car and spent several minutes with her parents before going to her room. As soon as she reached her room, she locked the door and took the small package out of her pocket. She looked at it for several minutes before carefully opening it.

She gasped when the necklace fell out attached to a small card. To her, it was the most beautiful thing that she had ever seen; it even surpassed the red sweater Miss Abby had given her. Patricia held the necklace in her hand as she read the card. She looked at the Japanese characters and then the pronunciation and said it slowly, not sure if she was pronouncing the words correctly. Finally, she read the meaning: "I will love you forever."

Hiroshi hadn't spoken to Kenji since the night he turned Dai Saito away; he could barely stand to look at him. The only reason he was still in the house was because of Hana; she would make his life miserable if he threw Kenji out, and no matter how angry he was, he couldn't do that to her. However, the problem would soon be solved. Of that he was certain.

Kenji sat in his room, wondering if Patricia had opened her gift and if she liked it. He murmured the words he had written on the card under his breath. They were in for a long hard ride. Like her, he realized they were going to be alone, but it didn't matter. They would survive.

SEPTEMBER 1940

Hiroshi's attention was divided between world events and events at home. He and Kenji hadn't really talked since July, becoming polite strangers. The Germans were bombing Britain during the day, making sure to bomb the airfields and factories as well; the British fought back by bombing Berlin just last month, but still no interference from Japan. That was until the twenty-seventh; Hiroshi's heart sank when he found out that Japan had become one of the Axis powers, along with Germany and Italy. He didn't see how the United States could remain neutral any longer, but they did, even though the draft conscription act had been passed.

Kenji continued to see Patricia, noting that she always wore the necklace on Fridays. He suppressed a smile as he remembered her attempts to repeat the words he had written on the card that he had given her for her birthday, but now she could say it almost flawlessly. After each meeting, they repeated the words to each other in Japanese and English, as well as briefly holding hands as they said them. Every time he saw Patricia wearing the necklace, he was pleased. He knew she didn't wear it all the time and wondered how she managed on Fridays.

"I put it in my pocket and as soon as I get to the corner, I put it on. When I get close to Miss Abby's, I take it off," she told him. "I wish I could wear it all the time," she said sadly.

"One day, you will; I promise," Kenji told her, certain he was telling her the truth.

As always, their time together flew, and each time it was a little more difficult to say goodbye. This last time, Kenji noticed a man watching them; he was sure he had seen the man before, not once but several times during his times with Patricia. The man was a friend of his father's, Joben Saito; he was the father of the girl, Dai. How long the man had been watching them he didn't know, but they had to be more careful. He didn't want to alarm Patricia, but she needed to know.

"Patricia, we are being watched by a friend of my father's. I believe it was he that initially told my father about us. We have to be careful; between now and Friday, let us see if we can come up with another place to meet. This is no longer a good place for us."

Patricia looked around until she spotted the nondescript Japanese man. "Why is he following us?" she asked nervously.

"My father is trying to keep us from being together; I don't know what he is planning, but Patricia, be careful. I know you have to go now; be safe and I will love you forever."

Patricia repeated the words and watched Kenji as he walked away. She looked around for the man, but he was gone. She walked home with a heavy heart; the reality of their situation was becoming even more concrete.

SEPTEMBER 30, 1940

Vernon was making his way home after a busy day at the train station. As he walked, he heard someone trying to get his attention; when he looked, it was a Japanese man. Vernon scowled and kept going; he had no use for the yellow people, except the one he wanted to kill: the one Patricia was obviously sweet on. He had given thought to going to her father, but John Middleton would just as soon kill him as look at him. But it was more than that; there had to be a way to get what he wanted from her without her blabbing to her father about it.

The Japanese man had started following Vernon as well as Kenji and Patricia, but stopped when he realized they had caught on. He knew where they met, so he concentrated on Vernon, watching him at work and on his days off. It didn't take him long to realize Vernon was obsessed with the girl; there was no love involved, but pure obsession. This man, Saito realized, was dangerous and capable of murder. If he killed the black whore, who was the only thing keeping his daughter from marrying into the Takeda family, then all would be well.

Joben knew that the Takeda family, while wealthy in Japan, was poor here, but that didn't matter. They were of a good name, and the son Kenjiro would be a wealthy doctor someday and add to the family honor. What the Takedas didn't know about Dai was that she was no longer pure; she had given herself to a man during the voyage to this country. There was no rape involved; she had admitted as much, and Kenjiro Takeda might be her last chance to marry into a decent family.

After following Vernon for about a week, Joben decided it was time to approach him. He waited until Vernon was walking alone before attracting his attention; up until this point, he had never spoken to one of the dark ones and prepared himself.

"Excuse me," he called.

Vernon kept walking, either not hearing or ignoring the man.

"Excuse me, please," Joben said louder.

Vernon finally stopped and turned around to see who was calling him. When he saw Joben, he frowned. "What the fuck you want, yellow man?" Vernon snarled.

Now that he was face to face with Vernon, Joben knew he was right in his assessment of him; he was dangerous.

"May we talk for a moment? I think we can help each other," Joben replied.

"You ain't got nothin' that can help me, so get the hell away from me," Vernon replied and started to walk away.

"Patricia," Joben said loudly enough that Vernon heard him.

Vernon stopped and turned around. What did this fool know about Patricia? "What about her?" Vernon asked.

"You want her; I can see it in the way you stare at her," Joben said. "But she does not want you; is that correct?"

Vernon was caught off guard. "How . . . ?"

"I've been following you, her, and the Japanese man she has been meeting, and as I said, I think we may be able to help each other," Joben said, plastering a fake smile on his pudgy face.

"Why would I want to help you?" Vernon asked. "What's in it for me?"

Vernon was hooked and Joben knew it; it was time to reel his fish in. "I will pay you fifteen American dollars and you can do what you wish with the girl," Joben said and then waited.

"What I have to do?" Vernon asked.

"The plans are being made; I will contact you when they're ready, but stay away from her until then," Joben replied as he walked away.

"Imbecile," Joben muttered under his breath. He was amazed that the man would actually take such a pittance to hurt one of his own kind. Joben wasn't fooling himself; he knew exactly what the black fool would do to the girl and hoped it would be enough to make Kenjiro turn from her—or that it would cause her death.

Vernon walked with a spring to his step; Patricia was going to be his and he could hardly wait. Plus he was going to be paid to do what he would have done for nothing; things were looking up. The thought of Patricia screaming beneath him excited Vernon; it had been a few days since he'd had any pussy and it was time.

Joben was quite pleased with himself as he tapped on the door to Hiroshi's home. Hana answered the door with a surprised look on her face.

"May I help you?" she asked.

"Please, is your husband home? I must speak to him," Joben said politely.

Hana nodded, bowed slightly, and let him in. "He is in the back," she said and led the way.

Hiroshi looked up when he heard Hana and Joben approach and frowned. Was the man stupid? He was not to come here until the issue of the black whore was settled. Hiroshi put on a friendly face and greeted Joben; Hana, however, wasn't fooled. Hiroshi's hatred of the black girl had gone beyond all reason. She understood that he felt the need to control something or someone, but this was going to end horribly. The longer this went on, the clearer it became that she was going to have to choose between her husband and her son. For the first time since this whole thing started, Hana understood how Kenji must feel; it was hard to love two people and then have to choose, especially when that choice shouldn't have to be made.

She still didn't like that this Patricia was black, but she also realized that had Patricia been white, Chinese, Spanish, or any other race, they would still be in this situation, and the same things would be happening. Kenji loved this girl, and she was reluctant to admit it, but the girl loved him, too. She didn't know how she knew this, but she did. The question was, what was she going to do? The time for hoping that Kenji and his father would reconcile their differences had long passed. Hana softly closed the back door and decided to try to talk sense into Kenji one more time in hopes that he would listen to her.

Kenji was reading some medical journals he had stumbled across during one of his walks. He was grateful for the finds, as he could finally throw some of the others away. From time to time, he would close his eyes, visualize Patricia, and hear her saying that she loved him, and then he would go back to his reading.

He was in the middle of an article on polio when his mother tapped on the door. She came in without giving him a chance to answer and sat on his small bed.

"Mother, what's the matter?" he asked, laying the journal down.

"Kenji, one of you must give in before something terrible happens! I know you love this girl, but it is tearing this family apart, and you must know that your father will never accept her or any children you have. I'm begging you to stop seeing her."

Kenji looked down at his hands and then back at his mother. "Mother, I love Patricia—"

"But does she love you?" Hana interrupted. "Is she willing to forsake all for you as you are for her?" she added, hoping the answer was no.

"Mother, Patricia and I have declared our love for each other, and one day—maybe not soon, but one day—she will be my wife. I know you and Father are disappointed in me and angry as well, but it is my hope that one day you will accept her as your daughter."

Hana started to rehash all the old arguments but stopped herself because it was pointless. Kenjiro's mind was made up, but was she willing to lose her only child because of whom he loved? The answer was no; she didn't agree with Kenji, but he was still her child. She would never accept the black girl as a daughter, but she would no longer stand between them. She had just chosen between her husband and her son.

Hana looked at Kenji with tear-filled eyes, stood, walked over to him, and hugged him. "I love you, Kenjiro. Perhaps you know something deep inside that we don't, but know that while I will not stand between you and this girl, I will never accept her as my daughter. If you marry her as you plan to, then I will not accept your children as my grandchildren, but you will always be my son." Hana kissed Kenji on his cheek and left the room.

Kenji sat, not moving for several minutes. He understood that his mother had in effect defied his father by not participating in whatever plans he was making. While she wasn't completely on his side, it was comforting to know that she hadn't disowned him. He could only hope that once she met Patricia, she would change her mind; realistically he didn't expect it to happen any time soon, if ever.

Hana went to her bedroom filled with mixed emotions, with the strongest one being pride. She was proud of Kenji and afraid for him, but he was facing his challenges as a man. She disagreed with Hiroshi on one thing: Kenjiro had honor. He may have disgraced them with his choice, but he had always acted with honor and integrity. About Hiroshi, she was beginning to wonder.

When they were alone, Joben quickly told Hiroshi of his observations and of his talk with Vernon.

"He is willing to hurt her for fifteen American dollars!" he exclaimed. "We could divide the cost in half," he added.

"I don't want her killed; I only want Kenjiro to see what she's really like—a slut. And it will be well worth the money if he walks away from her on his own."

Joben didn't agree; as long as the girl lived, she was a threat to Dai and himself. He saw how Kenji and the girl looked at each other. He didn't voice his thoughts, but nodded as if in agreement. He wouldn't tell the black oaf to kill the girl, but he hoped it would happen, even unintentionally.

By the time Joben left, a tentative plan had been made.

Patricia was restless; she tossed and turned so much that her bed looked like three people had fought in it. Unable to sleep, she got up and pulled the box from under her bed. She moved the sweater to the side and picked up the necklace and the note. She read the note several times before putting it and the necklace away again. She took the box back out, removed the necklace, and put it on, vowing never to remove it. The decision calmed her enough that she fell into an uneasy sleep, only to wake up an hour later.

She was well aware that Japan had joined the Axis powers, but didn't know what that meant for Kenji and his family; what she did know was that she was frightened for them. Her deepest fear was that one day he would simply be gone. She fell asleep praying for Kenji and the safety of his family.

By midweek, Patricia was exhausted, unable to sleep because of worry and anxiety. Miss Abby had finally had enough. Clearly, Patricia was worried and frightened by something, and she intended to find out what it was even if she had to play the "I'm your employer" trump card.

"Patricia, what's worrying you?" Abby asked, wanting to give her one more chance to volunteer the information.

"Nothing, Miss Abby," Patricia replied softly.

"Patricia Middleton, stop what you're doing and come with me," Abby said sternly.

Patricia's heart pounded; Miss Abby hadn't used that tone with her in over three years, and she wondered what triggered it now.

Abby sat on the sofa and patted the empty spot next to her. Patricia relaxed a little; apparently, she wasn't in any real trouble.

Abby was about to launch into her speech when she looked into Patricia's eyes and saw fear, anxiety, exhaustion, and worry; that she didn't see the usual sparkle and mischief in them worried her. She took Patricia's small dark hands into her small white ones and held them tight. "Patricia, I was going to make you tell me what was wrong, and before you tell me nothing, I know there is. You're not sleeping, your eyes lack that sparkle that always makes me want to smile, and what I see in them is fear and worry. I told you before that I think of you as a daughter and I love you as such, so please tell me what has you so frightened and let me help you."

Patricia stared at their hands clasped together and felt the first tears fall. "I . . . I can't," she whispered.

"Patricia, look at me," Abby said gently.

Patricia slowly raised her eyes to Abby's.

"Patricia, are you in trouble?" Miss Abby asked.

It took Patricia a few seconds to understand what Abby meant. "No! At least not that kind of trouble," she replied.

"All right, then why don't you tell me what kind of trouble that you're in," Abby said softly.

"It . . . it's not really trouble as far as we're concerned, but everyone else will think it is," Patricia replied.

Abby was confused; what had the girl gotten herself into? "Patricia, tell me what you're talking about. I promise I won't be angry, but you've got to tell me so I can help if I can," Abby insisted.

After a brief hesitation, the floodgates opened; Patricia told Abby everything.

"We love each other, Miss Abby; what if they take him away?" Patricia asked, crying.

Abby didn't say anything, but pulled Patricia into her arms and comforted her as she sobbed. It all made sense now: the sudden interest in Japan, the eagerness to walk to the store, and the smiles. Why she didn't put it together earlier, Abby didn't know, because all the clues were there.

When Patricia stopped crying, Abby gently pushed her away so she could look at her. "Has he told you that he loves you?" she asked.

"Yes ma'am, and he gave me this," Patricia said as she took the necklace from the inside of her dress.

"It's beautiful," Abby commented. "Who else knows about you two?"

Patricia told Abby about the Japanese man who had been following them.

Abby's mind was working; she loved star-crossed lovers, with Romeo and Juliet being her favorite couple. Every time she read the play, she would imagine all the ways she could have helped them be together, and now she could do it for real. She knew this was no game and that it could and would get ugly, but she was going to help in any way she could.

"Patricia, you need to be careful. I don't know a lot about Japanese culture, and I daresay that you know much more about it than I do, but I do know that you and your young man won't be accepted—not only by them, but by others as well. There is one thing that the white man and black man agree on, and that is that the Japanese are the enemy. The anti-Japanese sentiment has risen even more since Japan is in cahoots with Italy and Germany. Are you sure you can handle that?"

"Miss Abby, I love him," Patricia replied without hesitation.

"Have you told your mother?"

"No ma'am, I don't think she'd understand."

Abby smiled. "I would bet she already knows something. Maybe not the particulars, but she knows. I would also venture to say that your mother loves you and would try to help even if she doesn't agree with your choice. You need to tell her and then decide what to do about your father; he's the one who's going to have the problem."

Patricia nodded; she knew that Miss Abby was right.

"I know what we'll do; we'll have your mother over for tea and cake! We'll tell her together," Abby said.

"Miss Abby? Why are you helping me like this?" Patricia asked.

"Because I believe that people should be able to make their own choices without interference from others—and because I love a good love story," she replied. "And because I know what it's like to love someone and not be able to be with him or her," she added sadly.

"Miss Abby. . . . "

"Now, you cannot keep meeting in front of the grocer's; it's no longer safe there. I think I'll have my groceries delivered from now on," Abby said, grinning.

"But—"

"Let's get you home and we'll talk again tomorrow," Abby said, cutting Patricia off.

Patricia was amazed at how relieved she felt. She was still anxious and frightened for Kenji, but it felt good to let someone in on her secret. That Miss Abby would help her was an unexpected and welcome surprise; the next hurdle was her mother.

Abby went to the door with Patricia to talk with Hattie.

"Hello, Hattie," she said with a smile. "Patricia was telling me about the delicious pound cake you make, and I was wondering if I could persuade you to make one and bring it over tomorrow afternoon. I know this is short notice, but I took the liberty of bringing the ingredients along with me."

Hattie looked at Abby suspiciously; while she wasn't educated, she was far from stupid. This woman knew what was happening with her Patricia, and whatever it was, she wasn't going to like it.

"Yes ma'am; what time would you like that cake delivered?" Hattie asked.

"One would be perfect, and maybe you could help Patricia with cleaning the baseboards. I try to help her, but my back will no longer allow me to bend over for long. Of course you'll be compensated for your time," Abby said pleasantly.

Patricia was shocked; she had no idea that Abby had such a devious mind, but she was glad for it.

After Abby left, Hattie took Patricia by the hand and led her to the kitchen. "Patricia, what—"

"Please, Mama, not now, but I'll tell you tomorrow. I'll go get the cake ingredients and help you make the cake."

Hiroshi was actually having second thoughts about the plan. If anything happened to the girl, if she was hurt in any way, Kenji would never forgive him, and neither would Hana, for that matter. However, if things went as planned, all would be well. He swallowed his misgivings and decided to move forward with the plan.

The next morning, Patricia was up and dressed before her parents were. Her father would be leaving for work soon, trying to pick up every extra hour that he could. Her mother would be doing the wash for the Jenkins, the couple she sometimes worked for. She knew that her mother was worried about her and wondered about telling her about Kenji before she came over to Miss Abby's house. Patricia touched the necklace and decided to tell her.

She waited until she heard her father leave before going into the kitchen.

"Mama, I have to tell you something. Can we sit down for a minute?"

Hattie stopped what she was doing and sat down. The laundry could wait; she didn't have to deliver it for another couple of days. She noticed Patricia fiddling with a necklace and wondered where it came from.

"Where you get that?" she asked, looking at the necklace.

After saying a quick prayer, Patricia told her mother about Kenji. At first, Hattie didn't say anything; she hadn't expected this, but then she wondered if Miss Abby knew.

"That white woman know 'bout this?" she asked.

"I told her yesterday," Patricia replied and then realized that she had just hurt her mother.

"Why you tell her before me?" she asked quietly.

"Mama, it just came out and—"

"I been askin' you for months if there was a man and you flat out lied," Hattie said.

"I know, but Mama, I didn't know what to do. I didn't think you'd understand," Patricia said, crying.

"Why? Cos I don't use big fancy words? Cos I ain't white? Why you thought I wouldn't understand?"

"Mama, I'm sorry that I didn't tell you sooner but—"

"Patricia, you don't have to have no education to understand what it be like to love someone, whether it's right or wrong. That be something any woman would understand; all this time you been holdin' this in and then it's not me that you tell—it's that white woman who got your head filled with fancy ideas about doin' and goin' where you want. Since she be the one you trust so much, go to her."

Patricia watched as her mother stood up and walked away.

"Mama?" she called out, but Hattie didn't answer.

Patricia sat at the table, hoping that Hattie would come back and give her one of the big hugs that always seemed to make things better. When Hattie didn't come back after fifteen minutes, Patricia went to her room and packed a small bag. Once her mother told her father about Kenji, she wouldn't be allowed to stay. Crying softly, she pulled the wooden box from beneath her bed, took the sweater, the money, and the card from Kenji, and put them in her bag. At the last moment, she grabbed the book she had gotten for her birthday and the brown wrapper the necklace had come wrapped in and put those in her bag as well.

She stopped at the front door and whispered a soft "I'm sorry" into the air.

By the time she reached Abby's house, she could hardly see where she was going because she was crying so hard. The several nights of not sleeping, worrying about Kenji, and not seeing him had taken its toll. The final straw had been her mother's anger. Patricia tried to get herself under control but failed; when Abby opened the door, she fell into the older woman's arms and sobbed.

It took two cups of strong tea before Patricia calmed down enough to tell Abby what happened.

"Oh dear," Abby said, holding Patricia's hands. "She'll calm down, don't worry. She's just upset."

"But she wouldn't even look at me," Patricia said.

"I'm so sorry, but give her some time. She'll come around, and in the meantime, you'll stay with me," Abby said, patting Patricia's hands.

"Thank you, Miss Abby."

"You're welcome; now go wash your face and lie down in the spare bedroom," Abby said gently.

Abby watched Patricia walk away; she was exhausted, mentally and physically. She needed to see her young man.

Kenji was awake early; there was still one more day before he would see Patricia, and it seemed like an eternity. His father was already at the table when he went for breakfast; the two men looked at each other but didn't speak. There was nothing to say, and if either of them spoke, it would lead to an argument, and Kenji wasn't in the mood. He kissed his mother on the cheek, ate his breakfast, and went back to his room. It was too early to walk to the grocer's; Patricia wouldn't be there yet.

He sat at his desk, pulled out a medical journal, and began to read. It wasn't long before there was a tap on his door. Hiroshi stepped into the room; he was only here because Hana had begged him to reach some kind of compromise with Kenji.

Kenji put the journal down and looked at his father, but didn't speak.

"Kenjiro, please see reason; you cannot be with this girl. It isn't possible; we are now considered enemies of the government. If you love her as you say, you will not do his to her. Let her go to find one of her own kind to love her. If you agree to this, I will let you marry whomever you wish."

Kenji didn't respond for several minutes; he had to make his father understand that he couldn't and wouldn't be swayed. "Father, I appreciate your willingness to compromise, but I cannot and will not accept your terms. Patricia and I have declared our love for each other. My future, whatever it may be, is with her; the only thing that will change that is if she tells me that this is not what she wants. As long as we both breathe, we will be together. As I told Mother, nothing you can say or do will change that; Patricia will be my wife as soon as it is possible."

Hiroshi was so enraged that he couldn't speak—marriage? That wasn't going to happen; he wouldn't allow it to happen. Hiroshi stared at Kenji, who met his gaze without flinching. Hiroshi was the first to look away. It was decided. He was going to follow through with the plan; if the girl died, then so be it.

Hattie heard Patricia leave and didn't stop her. This was the fault of that white woman filling Patricia's head with ideas of fancy. Well, let her take care of her and her Japanese man!

After she calmed down, Hattie realized that Kenji or whatever his name was wasn't the issue; neither was the fact that he was Japanese, although it was a small part of it. It was the fact that Patricia hadn't trusted her enough to come to her; she had gone to Miss Abby, a white woman, for help. Hattie also realized something else: she was jealous of Miss Abby. She wanted to be the one to buy Patricia nice things instead of a ratty old book for her birthday.

Hattie sighed. She loved her baby girl, and all she ever really wanted was for her to be happy and to have opportunities that she never had and wanted, but wasn't that what Miss Abby was doing? As far as the Japanese man, she wished that he were anything but that, but Patricia loved him, and if he loved her as Patricia said he did, then so be it. But John was going to be another issue all together. She only hoped that Patricia understood what she was in for and that the Japanese man wouldn't run at the first sign of trouble. She stood up and sighed; she wouldn't be able to help much, but she would do what she could.

Patricia slept the morning away, only waking when Miss Abby told her it was time for lunch. Patricia wasn't hungry and toyed with her food.

"You have to eat, dear," Abby chided gently.

Patricia tried and got down a few bites before giving up.

"Patricia, what time does your young man get to the grocer's?" Abby asked.

"Around two or a little before; why?" Patricia asked.

"Just curious," Abby replied as she finished her sandwich. "We'll save yours for later," she added.

At one, the doorbell rang and Patricia answered it.

"Mama! I'm sorry!" she exclaimed, throwing her arms around Hattie, almost knocking the cake out of her hands.

"It's all right," Hattie crooned into Patricia's ear. "Shush now and let me in."

Abby watched the scene with relief; part of the problem was solved. Hattie wouldn't have come if she didn't want to help Patricia in some way.

"Hattie, I'm so glad that you came," Abby said, touching her arm.

"Well, this here is my baby, and I could never stay mad at her for long," Hattie replied.

Later, over tea and cake, the three women talked.

"Patricia, do you understand what the two of you are getting into? You'll have no real support other than each other and your mother and me. His family will more than likely disown him if they haven't already, and I think your father may disown you. Are you ready for that?" Abby asked.

"Mama, Miss Abby: This is the right thing for me. I know it'll be hard and I'm scared, but I don't want to be with anyone else."

"Patricia, honey, your father . . . you know you won't be able to stay at home, don't you? If it was up to me. . . . "

"I know, Mama. I understand. Miss Abby says I can stay here."

Hattie looked at Abby. "Why you doin' this? What you getting out of it?"

"Hattie, your Patricia is a beautiful, intelligent girl with a curiosity that I've never seen in all of my fifty years of life. I love her as if she were my own daughter, and like you, I want her to have every advantage that life has to offer. If I had the money, she would be in college somewhere learning to do whatever it is that she wants, but all I can do is teach her what I know. Times are going to change, and whether you believe it or not, there will be a time when we won't see those silly signs separating blacks from whites. Will it happen in our lifetime? Who knows, but I believe it will happen in Patricia's, and I want her to be ready. So what am I getting out of this? The knowledge that I helped somehow, if even a little, and I do so love a good love story."

Hattie nodded; her anger at Abby had been displaced. "I was plenty mad at you," Hattie said. "I thought that you was fillin' her head with things that wasn't goin' to ever happen, but maybe you're right, and I thank you for helping my baby. Patricia, I s'pose we better get it over with and tell your daddy; it ain't goin' to be any easier tomorrow."

Patricia took a deep breath and nodded; this probably scared her more than anything else did now.

Miss Abby insisted on driving them in case Patricia had anything she wanted to bring back.

John Middleton was sitting on the porch when they pulled up. He looked at the three of them with concern and then relaxed when Hattie and Patricia seemed fine.

"Thank you for drivin' them home, Miss Abby. I appreciate it."

"John," Hattie said softly. "We gots to talk; let's go inside."

John looked from woman to woman and knew he wasn't going to like what he was going to hear.

As Patricia talked, she could see the tenseness of his jaw line and the way his hands were clenched. He was going to explode.

For several seconds after she finished, there was a dead silence, and then he erupted. "A JAP? A FUCKING JAP? I'D RATHER SEE YOU WITH VERNON MONROE!" he screamed.

"Daddy—"

"Keep your mouth shut! I don't want to hear from you!"

John turned his attention to Miss Abby. "This is your doin'! She was fine before you came here telling her about this place and that! All she thinks about is goin' someplace that she can be whatever she want to be, but there ain't no such place! She walk around here talkin' like some white person, but she ain't white and she won't ever be white. Them things you tell her ain't true and ain't never goin' to happen, so now what? She in love with some dirty yellow bastard! How that happen? You let them meet up at your house when she supposed to be workin'?

"Patricia, go up to you room. You ain't leavin' this house unless someone with you!"

"Daddy—"

"Now!" John said.

"No," Patricia said softly.

"What you say to me, girl?" John asked.

"I said no. I'm not going to my room."

John was stunned; Patricia had never openly defied him. He moved to her grab her, but Hattie moved between them.

"John, leave her be; she's old enough to make her own choices."

John looked at Hattie in disbelief. "You accepting this?" he asked.

"I wish that it was different, but it ain't her fault that the one she chose is what he is."

John looked at a crying Patricia, who was once the little girl who could always make him laugh no matter how bad a day he was having, and saw a woman he didn't know and wondered when she had grown up. "Get out."

"Daddy—"

"You choose right now; if you stay here, you ain't gonna see that Jap."

Patricia stood up and tried to speak; she hugged her mother and walked out of the door without looking back, followed by Miss Abby.

In the car, she fell apart. This had hurt far more than she thought possible; her father had just disowned her, but even so, she still loved him and hoped he would love her again, too. She wanted to hear him call her his "little patty cakes" like he used to. For just a split second, she was ready to go back and agree just to make him happy, but then she felt the weight of the necklace around her neck and gripped it hard in her hand.

Kenji stayed in his room, skipping dinner; he didn't have the stomach for another go-round with his father, and he couldn't bear the look of pain in his mother's eyes. *This doesn't have to be difficult,* he thought to himself. *All they need to do is leave us be.* He closed his eyes and hoped that Patricia was all right; he hadn't seen her in a week and had no way of contacting her. Tomorrow was Friday and he could hardly wait.

OCTOBER 4, 1940

Patricia had finally fallen asleep sometime after three in the morning, with Abby sitting by the bed, holding her hand. Even though Abby had anticipated John Middleton's reaction, she was still unprepared for the intensity of it. She had never had children, but couldn't imagine turning her back on them if she did. She didn't care that John blamed her for Patricia falling in love with a Japanese man—it took some of the pressure off Patricia—but still, the intensity of his anger was frightening.

Patricia moaned softly, woke up disoriented, and looked around. Seeing Abby, she closed her eyes and went back to sleep. Abby sat with her until four o'clock in the morning, when she went to bed herself, leaving her door open in case Patricia called.

When Patricia woke up, the events of the week crashed down on her; she cried until her throat was raw and sore. Miss Abby came in with cool compresses and put them over her eyes without saying anything for several minutes.

"I'm going to go to the store; get dressed and I'll be back soon."

Patricia didn't even try to stop Miss Abby from driving to the store; she just didn't have the energy to argue with her. She lay in bed for another ten minutes before forcing herself to move. She washed her face and hands with cold water before fixing her hair into her characteristic ponytail and got dressed.

A glass of juice was waiting on the table, along with a sandwich and a note.

"Eat everything."

Patricia nibbled at the sandwich until it was gone and drank all the juice. She looked at the clock and realized with horror that Kenji had been at the grocer's and was already gone. Patricia sat on the sofa, hugged herself, and cried.

Kenji stood outside of the grocer's, patiently waiting; he was a good twenty minutes early, but he couldn't stand to be in the house any longer. As he waited, a car pulled up in front of him. An older woman looked at him for a few seconds before speaking.

"Are you Kenji?" she asked.

Kenji hesitated before answering. "I am he," he replied cautiously.

"Good, get in," Abby said.

"Excuse me, but who are you?" he asked.

"A friend; now get in if you want to see Patricia. She needs you."

That was all it took. Within seconds, Kenji was in the car. Unfortunately, Miss Abby had a very poor sense of direction and drove them around for almost an hour before finding her house.

Along the way, she questioned Kenji and was more than satisfied that he could and would take care of Patricia, but she warned him, "That girl is like a daughter to me, and she is risking everything to be with you. Be certain you want to do this before it goes any further."

Kenji looked over at Abby and assessed her before speaking. "I will tell you what I have told my parents: I love Patricia, and the only way that I'll walk away from her is if she wants me to or I have no more breath in me. I know it will be difficult—we both do—but we belong together no matter what anyone says."

Abby reached over and patted Kenji on his arm. "Good, now let me tell you about her week."

Kenji listened with sadness as Abby told him how Patricia's father had reacted; it was so much like his own father's reaction.

"But I think the worst of it was that she couldn't see you. She's exhausted physically and emotionally, and I think you can help with that."

Patricia was sitting on the end of the sofa when they came in; Kenji could tell by the way her body shook that she was crying. Abby gave him a gentle nudge toward Patricia and walked away.

"*Ohayo, Kirei*," he said softly as he sat on the sofa beside her.

Patricia didn't respond at first—he couldn't be here.

"Are you so angry with me that you will not greet me?" Kenji teased.

Patricia sat up and looked at him. "You're here?" she asked and threw herself into his arms, sobbing.

Kenji held her tight as she cried out the fears and frustrations of the past week. He spoke to her softly until she calmed down enough to talk.

"How?" Patricia asked.

"Your Miss Abby found me and brought me here. I wish I could have been with you when you talked to your father, but are you all right?" Kenji asked as he touched her face.

"I'm better now that I've seen you, but Kenji, what are we going to do?" Patricia asked.

"We start making plans to leave here," Kenji replied. "There has to be someplace we can go."

"But where? Your country is siding with Germany and Italy," Patricia replied. "And we have to have money in order to live; I've got fifteen dollars saved, but that won't get us far."

"I have ten dollars," Kenji replied. "That still isn't enough to get us far enough away from here, but it's a start. Patricia, I'm glad to be here with you, and I'm declaring my intent to marry you as soon as possible—that is, if you will accept."

Patricia didn't hesitate. "I accept."

Kenji cupped her face in his hands and slowly kissed her.

Patricia felt the room spin and then felt hot and dizzy. Kenji broke the kiss first and murmured against her lips, "I will love you forever; no matter what happens, always remember that."

Patricia nodded, not trusting herself to speak.

"All right, you two, we have some plans to make," Miss Abby said, interrupting them. "Kenji, I need a gardener; why don't you come by on Fridays? My landscaping could use some work."

Kenji looked at Patricia and then at Miss Abby, amazed that the woman was helping them. He would still see Patricia once a week, but it would be for longer than an hour. "I would be happy to help you with your landscaping," he replied, holding onto Patricia's hand.

"Good! How about I pick you up at the corner of the grocer's, say around ten o'clock? My yard needs a lot of work."

Abby excused herself to give Patricia and Kenji more time alone. Already the sparkle was back in Patricia's eyes, which was a good thing. Abby sat in the kitchen and began to draft a letter that she would drop off later.

An hour later, Patricia and Kenji were saying goodnight.

"Someday, I won't be leaving you alone at night, I promise," Kenji told Patricia as he kissed her one last time, before Miss Abby drove him back close to his home.

After they left, Patricia closed her eyes and prayed that what Kenji had promised would happen. She locked the doors and settled in to wait for Miss Abby to come back. She didn't see Vernon hiding behind a tree watching her with anger and lust on his face.

Chapter 5

Vernon watched the house with growing anger. The temptation to break in and take Patricia was almost too much to resist, but he managed. The Japanese man hadn't contacted him yet, and he didn't want to lose out on his fifteen dollars. He stood by and watched the house for a few more minutes before slinking off to find a willing woman to pass the time with.

Abby managed to find her way to where Kenji wanted to be dropped off without too much trouble. The one thing he wanted to know was why this woman wanted to help, and so he asked.

"Everyone keeps asking me that," she replied with a laugh. "One more time: I love that girl and I want her to be happy. Apparently, you're the one to help her do that; you could be orange for all I care as long as you love and care for her. I also love a good love story. Is that reason enough?"

"It is, and I thank you for both Patricia and I," Kenji said.

"You're welcome and be careful," Abby replied.

Hiroshi was waiting for Kenji when he came in. "Where have you been?" he demanded.

"I have a job; if I am going to have a wife, I will need to be able to support her," Kenji replied.

"What about your dream of being a doctor? You are even giving up on that for that—"

"If I am supposed to be a doctor, then it will happen," Kenji replied as he went to his room. He wanted to be alone so he could replay in his mind holding Patricia and kissing her for the first time.

Kenji went to his room, shut the door, and waited; one of his parents would be tapping on the door soon, and he didn't want to be disturbed while he thought about Patricia. A few minutes later, the anticipated knock came.

Hana stepped inside of the small, neat room and sat at Kenji's desk. "Your father is furious," she said softly.

"I know, but it cannot be helped," Kenji replied.

"Yes it can, but you choose not to. I know that I said I wouldn't interfere with you and this girl, but Kenji, I am begging you to stop this. Your father is becoming more unreasonable with each passing day. Between the anxieties of what will happen to us and your obsession with the black girl, he is at a breaking point."

Kenji closed his eyes and opened them again. "Mother, Father once told me that a man is responsible for his own actions and that a man cannot be made to do something he does not want to do. He is choosing to be angry and he is choosing to hate. Whether it is out of fear or misunderstanding, only he knows, but I have chosen my actions and will be responsible for them, as I have been from the beginning."

"But Kenjiro—"

"Mother, I have asked Patricia to marry me and she has agreed. We each have a little money and I have a job so I can add to our savings."

"Kenjiro, listen to me; you cannot do this! Your father . . . he will . . . don't do this!" Hana begged.

"Father will do what?" Kenji asked, suddenly alarmed.

"Nothing, he will do nothing," Hana said quietly as she got up and walked out of the bedroom, closing the door behind her.

Something was wrong; Kenji could feel it but couldn't think of what it could be. Patricia was safe at Miss Abby's house, so it wasn't that. He would have to watch his father carefully.

OCTOBER 10, 1940

It had been a week since Patricia moved in with Miss Abby and one day shy of the first time Kenji had held her and kissed her for the first time. Patricia still felt a little flushed when she remembered the kiss; she'd been kissed before, but she hadn't experience the same feelings she had with Kenji. For her, it was another confirmation that they were to be together.

Her father was still angry and wouldn't even consider the possibility of talking to her unless it was her saying she would give up seeing Kenji. Patricia went to see her mother whenever she knew that her father was at work, but as of yet hadn't told her that Kenji had asked her to marry him. Remembering the lesson from the week before, Patricia hadn't even told Miss Abby yet, and she wouldn't until she told her mother.

The question was if they could even get married to each other. Patricia knew that there were laws against whites marrying blacks and some of the other races, which included the Japanese, but she didn't know if it was illegal to for blacks and other races to marry. And if they married, where would they live?

She pushed the questions away. She had to get moving; Kenji was coming tomorrow to work on Miss Abby's yard, but not only that, it was his birthday. He would be twenty-one and she wanted it to be a special day.

Miss Abby loved birthdays almost as much as she loved love stories and wanted to help.

"Patricia, come to the library with me; I'm sure that there has to be a medical journal or two in there somewhere," she said.

After searching through the shelves for a good three hours, they found four books. One was on disease, one was on the heart, and two were reference manuals. Patricia dusted them off, wrapped them in newspaper, and attached a bow.

"Miss Abby, he's going to love these! Thank you!" Patricia said, hugging her.

"Somebody ought to get some use out of them," Abby replied as she returned the hug.

Patricia had her own gift for him; she made it because she didn't want to spend any of what little money they had. She had been working on the gift for weeks but had lost time during the events of the previous week. It was almost finished, needing only a few more stitches to complete it.

When it was done, she was pleased. She put it in a small box and wrapped it in newspaper before putting it under her bed.

Miss Abby had even made a birthday cake. Tomorrow couldn't come fast enough.

Vernon walked home; he was getting impatient. He hadn't heard from the Japanese man and was wondering what the holdup was. He was getting tired of waiting, and it was getting more difficult to stay away from Patricia, especially since he saw the Jap kiss her once. Vernon's mind ran wild with thoughts of what that Jap was doing to Patricia.

"By the time I'm done, he won't want your uppity ass," Vernon mumbled under his breath.

He hadn't quite gone a block or two when he heard a soft whistle. He turned around and saw the pudgy Japanese man motioning to him.

"Where the fuck you been, Jap?" Vernon asked.

"Making sure that all is ready," Joben replied, bristling; he hated these animals.

"Is it?" Vernon asked.

"Soon; meet me here tomorrow and I will tell you what to do," Joben said.

"Where my money?" Vernon asked.

"You will get it after you complete your end of the bargain. I know that you have been following the girl; stay away from her," Joben cautioned as he walked away.

Kenji no longer stayed at the house during the day, opting to spend his day walking or at the greenhouse reading until it was too dark to see. He was already counting down the hours until he would see Patricia and be able to hold and kiss her; it was the only birthday gift he wanted—that and to be able to marry her.

It was early yet, and he was already at the greenhouse. It was in need of dusting since it had been closed up for so long. To pass the time, Kenji began to clean and rearrange the greenhouse; he took stock of what supplies were there and reorganized them to his liking. By the time he was finished, the place was spotless and would be livable. As he cleaned, he had found coins here and there and put them in his pocket. He and Patricia would need every penny they could get their hands on. All told, he found twenty cents, which wasn't much, but it was something. Hoping that his father would be gone, Kenji headed for home.

Hana missed having Kenji around the house, but understood why he stayed away. As the days wore on, she became aware that Hiroshi was planning something; she even tried to find out what it was, but wasn't sure of what to do with the information even if he told her.

Hana heard the door open and then heard Kenji's soft footsteps; for as tall as he was, Kenji was graceful in his movements. Part of that was due to the martial arts training that Hiroshi had insisted he have. Kenji was an accomplished martial artist, and people who knew that about him often tried to get him to fight, but he hated violence of any kind. As a result, he kept that knowledge to himself. He still practiced in the privacy of his room, but over the past weeks began to take advantage of the space of the greenhouse. It not only kept him occupied, but the fluid movements calmed him.

Kenji greeted Hana with a kiss on the cheek and sat down at the table. "Where is Father?" he asked.

"Listening to the radio at Joben Saito's home," she replied as she fixed him a plate of food.

Hana debated if she should say anything about Hiroshi and decided against it after all. What could she say?

Kenji ate in silence, finished the food, and rinsed the dishes before heading to his room. He kissed Hana again before leaving the kitchen. *Eighteen more hours to go*, he thought as he took the washbasin and carried it to the bathroom to fill it with water. As the basin filled, he looked at himself in the mirror. His hair was longer than he usually liked, but it wasn't too bad, he thought. He carried the full basin to his room and washed himself from head to toe. When he got to his private area, he thought about making love to Patricia for the first time as her husband and hardened. He took a deep breath and pushed the thought away; there was no point in tormenting himself with thoughts like that. It could be months, if not years, before he could marry her.

Kenji finished his bath, redressed in clean clothes, left his room to empty the basin, and ran into his father.

Kenji bowed respectfully and continued on his way, ignoring the hard stare he felt boring into his back. When he came out of the bathroom and went back into his room, his father was sitting on his bed. Kenji took a breath and waited for the now familiar fight to begin.

"Tell me about her," Hiroshi said. "I want to understand what it is about her that will not allow you to see reason."

Kenji looked at his father with suspicion; it was much too late for this conversation. "Why are you asking me now?" Kenji asked as he set the basin down. "You have made it quite clear that you have no interest in knowing about her, so why now?"

"I think it is quite clear that we will never agree on this issue, and if you are determined to marry this girl, I want to know about her. Is that unreasonable?"

Alarm bells clanged in Kenji's head. He no longer trusted his father, which saddened him, but it was the truth. The feeling of wrongness hit him again, and he fought the urge to ask his father to leave; he didn't want him to know anything about Patricia.

Hiroshi waited; he could see the wheels turning in Kenji's head. Kenji had always been perceptive to the mood and feelings of others—that was part of what would make him an excellent physician if that nigger girl didn't hold him back. In a few days that would no longer be an issue. Hiroshi smiled at Kenji and indicated that he should sit down.

The alarms rang even louder in Kenji's mind, but he sat down.

"Tell me what's so special about . . . this Patricia," Hiroshi said as he smiled what he thought was a pleasant smile, but what Kenji saw was a smile of betrayal.

An hour later Hiroshi was gone and sitting outside. So the girl could read and write and could speak a little Japanese; that didn't change what she was. Kenji was not going to marry her; she would not be allowed to taint the Takeda bloodline.

Kenji spent the rest of the day in his room to avoid his father or the man who looked like his father. Kenji didn't know who the man in his room was, but it wasn't the Hiroshi Takeda who had encouraged him to think on his own and to face all challenges with honor, courage, and integrity. This man was filled with fear, anger, and prejudice, and his sense of honor was all but gone. It made Kenji wonder at the lengths his father would go to keep him from Patricia; would he kill him as he slept?

When it was quiet and he was sure his parents were sleeping, Kenji packed a small bag and left the house. He went to the only place that he could this late at night, the green house.

OCTOBER 11, 1939

Patricia was up early making the final preparations for Kenji's birthday; she could have sworn that Miss Abby was more excited about it than she was. Patricia laughed as Miss Abby fretted over the wrapping that covered the medical books she was giving Kenji.

"Miss Abby! He'll love it, I know he will," Patricia said, still laughing.

Miss Abby left a few minutes before ten to pick Kenji up; now that she knew where she was going, she didn't need to leave thirty minutes early. Patricia ran upstairs to change her clothes and fix her hair. She took the tie out and ran a brush through her hair. She was about to put it back into the ponytail and changed her mind. She stood at the mirror for several minutes, debating if she should go back to the ponytail and decided not. She had just managed to get dressed and put on the red sweater Miss Abby had gotten her for her birthday when she heard Miss Abby's voice.

Patricia smoothed down her hair and then her dress before going downstairs. Kenji had his back to the stairs, but Miss Abby saw her.

"Patricia! You look lovely!" she exclaimed.

Kenji turned around and stared at her. Patricia didn't look like a young girl but a woman, a woman he was going to marry, even if he did nothing else with his life.

"*Kirei*," he murmured.

Neither of them noticed that Abby had left the room, leaving them alone. Kenji walked to the stairs, his eyes on Patricia, and started toward her, only stopping when he reached the step that put him at eye level with her. His brown eyes glistened as he looked at her and then kissed her. Patricia's arms went around his neck as she returned the kiss, tentatively at first and then with more confidence. Kenji broke the kiss and looked at her; she had no idea of how beautiful he found her, even with the scar.

"Patricia. . . . "

"Happy birthday Kenji," she said, totally forgetting how to say it Japanese.

"It is a happy birthday; I am here with you," he replied and kissed her again.

Miss Abby made a sound to get their attention. "Breakfast is ready! Patricia made it for your birthday," Abby said.

Kenji realized there was so much they didn't know about each other beyond the fact that they loved each other; today they would have time to talk.

Patricia, he found, was a good cook; he enjoyed breakfast, especially since she had been the one to make it. After the dishes were cleared away, Miss Abby gave him his birthday gift. She sat perched on the edge of her chair, excited to see his reaction. For her, that was the highlight of giving gifts.

Kenji looked at the parcel in front of him and then at Miss Abby. "You have already done so much for us; I can't accept a gift from you," he said softly.

"Of course you can! And I think you'll be able to use those, so open it!" she urged.

Kenji's eyes widened when he saw the medical books. They looked as if they had never been opened. "Miss Abby. . . . "

"You're more than welcome; why don't you two go to the living room while I clean up here? I think Patricia has something for you."

Abby shooed them out of the kitchen, declining any offer of help with the dishes. "Go on, I haven't forgotten how to wash a dish!"

Patricia left Kenji sitting on the couch while she ran upstairs to get the gift. She took a deep breath and hoped he would like it.

Kenji watched her run up the stairs and wondered just how soon he could marry her. But then reality set in: between the two of them they had just over twenty-five dollars; it wasn't nearly enough money with which to start a life together.

Patricia came back downstairs with a small package and sat down next to Kenji. "It isn't much or anything as beautiful as the necklace you gave me, but I didn't want to spend any of the money we had, so I made it," she said and handed him the small box.

Kenji carefully removed the paper and opened the box. Inside was a man's handkerchief embroidered around the edges with small blue flowers. In one corner, Patricia had embroidered the words "I will love you forever" in Japanese and the same words in English in another corner.

Patricia watched anxiously as Kenji looked at the handkerchief in silence. Her heart sank when he didn't say anything.

"I can make another one—"

She didn't get to finish her sentence because Kenji was hugging her tightly against him and speaking in Japanese. When he finally released her, he took her hands in his and kissed them. "Patricia, this is . . . beautiful and I will always keep it with me."

Patricia laughed. "If you use it, it has to be washed."

"I will never use it," Kenji replied. "But it will never leave my person."

Miss Abby watched from the kitchen with tears in her eyes and walked away. The two of them needed to be together without her present; she trusted that they wouldn't do anything inappropriate.

Vernon waited for the Japanese to show up; the man hadn't given a time, so he was there early. The man showed up two hours later, walking as if he had all the time in the world. Vernon fought the urge to punch him in his pudgy face and then walk away, but there was Patricia.

Joben knew that Vernon would be angry and he simply didn't care; he would have let the oaf wait longer except he was already in the area and didn't want to come back. He hoped the fool was intelligent enough to follow simple instructions.

"Listen to me carefully," Joben said slowly, as if he were talking to a child. "Monday morning the girl will get a message to meet Kenji at the greenhouse on Tuesday morning; do you know where it is?"

"Just tell me and I'll find it," Vernon said gruffly.

"Very good. No one will be there; you are to do whatever it is you people do to your females. You are to make it appear as though she invited you there; do you understand?" Joben asked.

Vernon was angry. "I ain't stupid!" he snarled.

"Of course not," Joben said, not telling Vernon that in all likelihood the girl would be the last female he would ever be with. Kenji would still kill the man even if it appeared that the girl invited him there—at least that is what Joben hoped would happen.

The last thing to do was find someone to give the girl the message, but it had to be someone she knew and trusted. He headed back after going over the directions with Vernon; how to get a message to the girl? She no longer walked to the store, so that wasn't an option. Kenji had a job somewhere, but his parents didn't know where. It was only Friday; he had a few days to figure it out.

Joben stopped and turned around; on a hunch he walked back to where Vernon still stood. "Do you know where the girl works?" he asked.

"Yeah I know; she work for some white woman," Vernon replied.

"I have another job for you," Joben said.

Kenji spent the day with Patricia; he thought it was the best day of his life, and he wanted more days like this. He appreciated how Miss Abby gave them as much privacy as she could, allowing them to kiss and hold each other as much as they wanted to. They would never be able to repay her for her kindness to them.

Miss Abby drove Kenji home just before dark, leaving Patricia alone in the house. Patricia walked around the house, straightening things up, imagining that it was her and Kenji's house. She knew it would be many years before they would be able to buy a house, but it helped to pretend. As wonderful as today was, she knew that bad times were coming, and they needed every good memory they would experience together.

Kenji spent the night at the greenhouse. He didn't want to spoil the day by fighting with his father. Once settled, he took out the handkerchief Patricia had embroidered and wondered how many times she poked herself as she put in the small stitches and how long it had taken her to complete it. He carefully folded it and put it in his bag until he could find a wallet or something to carry it in. He closed his eyes to the memory of kissing her on the stairs and holding her. It would be another week before he saw her again, a lifetime.

OCTOBER 13, 1940

Vernon touched the note in his pocket as he waited for a chance to leave the note for Patricia. So far, the white woman hadn't left the house, but Patricia's mother came and had been there for an hour already. Vernon didn't know if there was a backup plan or not, but if there wasn't, he was still going to take Patricia somewhere and do as he pleased with her.

Finally, Abby came out of the house, followed by Patricia's mother. Vernon watched as they got into the car and drove off. He waited for a few minutes just in case they came back. When he was sure they were gone, he ran across the street, stuck the note in the door, and knocked hard.

He just made it across the street in time to see Patricia disappear with the note in her hand. *Soon, bitch*, he thought as he walked away.

Patricia was in the kitchen when she heard the knock on the door; her first thought was that Miss Abby had forgotten something, but when she got to the door, no one was there. She looked around and then saw the note. After looking around again, she took the note and went indoors. She turned it over several times before opening it.

Patricia,

I cannot wait until Friday to see you; meet me tomorrow at ten at my father's greenhouse.

I will see you then.

Kenjiro

The note struck her as odd. It was too formal, but she dismissed it, excited about having another day with Kenji before the week was up. She ran up the stairs, taking the note with her. She laid the note on the dresser and began to gather the laundry. If she was going to be gone for part of the day tomorrow, she'd better get some work done today. Patricia hummed as she washed the clothes and hung them out to dry. She did not think to mention where she was going to Miss Abby when she got back from taking her mother home because she could go wherever she wanted without permission. The only thing she told Miss Abby was that she was going to the grocer's in hopes of seeing Kenji.

"Patricia, be careful. If you don't see him, come back," Miss Abby advised.

Kenji was sitting at the kitchen table when his father came in.

"Father," Kenji said politely.

"Kenjiro," his father replied. "Are you well?"

"I am," Kenji replied and said no more.

"You have been rising early; where do you go?" Hiroshi asked.

Kenji hesitated. "I was looking for a place for Patricia and me to live," he replied.

Hiroshi's jaw clenched, but he said nothing, which surprised Kenji. Hana stood by watching and was as surprised as Kenji that Hiroshi didn't comment.

"You still mean to marry her?" Hana asked.

"Yes," Kenji replied. "If you would like for me to leave, I will."

"You have a place?" Hiroshi asked.

"Yes," Kenji replied.

It wasn't much, but it was a small room in a house owned by an old man. In exchange for rent, Kenji would do odd jobs around the house. The tricky part had come when Kenji told the man about Patricia.

"Ain't no never mind; I always liked a bit of dark meat myself," the man replied.

Kenji was offended but said nothing; the fact was they couldn't live together at Miss Abby's if they were unmarried, and not even if they were. He had already started working on the man's house and getting the room ready. He hadn't told Patricia yet, not sure of how she would feel about them living together without being married. The other option was for him to live in the room and Patricia to stay with Miss Abby; at least that way he could see her more often. Somehow, he knew Patricia would choose the second option.

OCTOBER 14, 1940

The Greenhouse

Patricia looked at the note again and thought it odd; it just didn't sound like Kenji, but then she had only ever gotten one note from him. She shook off her misgivings and headed toward the greenhouse, happy to be seeing him again.

She reached the greenhouse right at ten and looked around; she didn't remember Kenji telling her it was closed, but she may have just forgotten. She almost didn't go in, but she did not see Vernon hiding in a corner.

"Kenji?" she called as she walked through the greenhouse.

"Kenjiro," Hiroshi said. "I was wondering if you would go to the greenhouse and take a few supplies with you."

"Of course, Father, I'll leave in a few minutes," Kenji replied.

"Kenji? Where are you?" Patricia called, suddenly nervous.

"Hello, Miss Uppity," a voice behind her said.

Patricia turned around to see the leering face of Vernon Monroe. The note hadn't been from Kenji, she realized, but it wasn't from Vernon either; he could barely write his name, so who . . .

Kenji picked up the bag of canned goods and headed out; his father was looking at him with anticipation, although Kenji couldn't think of what he could be anticipating. He took his time walking to the greenhouse; he had nowhere to be until the afternoon, when he would go to the old man's house and work on the room.

"Look at you, all prettied up for that Jap," Vernon said as he walked toward her.

"What are you doing here?" Patricia asked as she backed away.

"You know you the only one I ain't been with?" Vernon asked, ignoring her question. "And the way I sees it, you owe me for this scar your daddy gave me."

"Vernon, go away and I won't tell anybody," Patricia said as she looked around for anything she could defend herself with.

"Who you goin' to tell? Your daddy? I heard he's plenty mad at you for takin' up with that yellow man. We could come to an agreement 'tween us; let me have what I wants and I'll leave you and your Jap alone," Vernon said as he took another step toward her.

"Who told you that I'd be here?" Patricia asked, trying to keep him talking.

"Don't knows his name and it don't matter. When we done, I get paid for doing what I would have done for nothin'."

"Someone paid you to do this? Vernon, for once in your life, use your head and walk away."

"I can't do that; I got a job to do," Vernon replied.

Patricia was backed against a table; she felt around, hoping for anything that could help. Her hand bumped against a handle and grabbed it.

Kenji was less than halfway to the greenhouse, his head in the clouds as he thought about Patricia living with him as his wife. He decided not to ask her to live with him out of wedlock. The first time that he made love to her, he wanted to be married to her. He just hoped it wouldn't be years before that happened.

Vernon took another step toward Patricia. "Come on, this don't have to be ugly," he said, attempting to calm her.

"Stay away from me, Vernon," Patricia said, holding the handle of the unknown tool tighter in her fist.

Suddenly, Vernon lunged at her, his hands on her shoulders. Patricia screamed and swung at him with the tool in her hand. Vernon stopped, grabbed his neck, and looked at Patricia in surprise before removing his hand and looking at it.

Kenji was almost to the greenhouse when he heard Patricia scream. He dropped the bag of food and took off running. He heard her crying as he ran through the building looking for her. He panicked when he saw blood on the floor and followed the trail. Kenji found her a few seconds later crouched in a corner holding a garden tool in a death grip.

"Patricia, *Kirei*," he called softly as he walked toward her, trying to see if she was hurt. As far as he could tell, the blood wasn't hers. She was very frightened but unhurt.

"Patricia," he called again. "It is me, Kenji."

Patricia slowly opened her eyes, fully expecting to see a body on the floor. There was blood but no body. She stood up on shaky legs and almost fell down. Kenji caught her and sat on the floor, taking her with him.

"Who did this?" he asked when she had stopped crying.

"V-Vernon, he said that somebody paid him. I got a note yesterday. I thought it was from you; I didn't think it sounded like you, but I wanted to see you so I came. Vernon was already here," Patricia said and started to cry again. "I thought I killed him; there's so much blood."

Kenji held her and looked around. The greenhouse had been locked; he had locked it himself. He also realized he had the answer to the question he had asked himself several nights before. He now knew how far his father would go to gain his obedience.

He helped Patricia to her feet and led her out of the greenhouse, only stopping to pick up his small overnight bag. She needed a place to sit and calm down, but the closest place was his parents' home; from there he would take her back to Miss Abby's house.

The bag of food he had dropped when he heard Patricia scream was gone; he ignored the stares as he walked with his arm around Patricia to his parents' house.

He heard his parents talking in the kitchen as he led Patricia to a chair and gently set her down.

"Wait here," he said as he kissed her forehead.

When he turned around, both his parents were staring at him, shocked, especially his father.

Kenji didn't speak for several seconds as he stared at his parents. When he spoke, it was to his mother first. "Mother, this is Patricia. Someone gave her a note telling her to come to the greenhouse to meet me. When she got there, a man was waiting inside for her and was going to rape her and possibly kill her. I brought her here because this was the only place I could think of where she could rest. After she is rested, I will take her from here, never to come back. I love you, but I cannot remain your son if you cannot accept Patricia as your daughter."

Hana let out a sob and turned to Hiroshi. "What have you done?" she asked. "I warned you! I told you to leave them be."

She turned back to Kenji. "I am so sorry, but I didn't think he would try to harm her. I would have told you if I had known."

Kenji looked at his father. "You asked me on more than one occasion if I had any honor. My question to you is what happened to yours? In your quest to control, you lost your honor and your integrity. It pains me to say this, but you are not my father. The man who was my father would never have participated in a plan to hurt someone; the man who was my father would have attempted to understand even if he didn't agree with me. You didn't try to understand; you allowed hatred and fear to guide you. After this moment, you will not see me again. I will also give you a warning: tell Joben Saito to stay out of my path. If I see him, I will kill him."

Patricia's heart hurt as she listened to Kenji break ties with his family; it hurt her to hear him threaten to kill because it was against everything he believed, but she knew if he saw the man, he would kill him. She noticed that of his parents, only his mother visibly reacted to what happened, and she felt for her; she was trapped between the two people she loved the most and had lost one of them.

Kenji held his hand out to her and led her out of the house. It took them some time to get back to Miss Abby's house. She opened the door as soon as she heard them on the porch.

"Patricia! What happened?" she asked as she let them in. "Are you hurt?"

"No ma'am, I'm fine," Patricia said tiredly.

Abby got her a glass of water and a wet washcloth with which to wipe her face. "Are you sure you're not hurt?" she asked.

Patricia assured Abby that she was fine and then told her the whole story.

"Vernon Monroe did this?" she asked.

"Yes ma'am," Patricia replied quietly.

Abby was quiet for several minutes, obviously in deep thought. "Kenji, stay here with her and don't leave; I'll be back."

"Where are you going?" Patricia asked.

"To see your father; he may be still angry with you, but you are still his daughter, and I doubt that he would let this pass, no matter how angry he is. Now stay put and rest."

John was sitting out front when Abby pulled up. He didn't stand or acknowledge her when she came to the porch.

"I'm here about Patricia," Abby said.

"I don't know no Patricia," John said, looking away from her.

"Fine, then you don't want to hear about how she was almost raped and murdered this afternoon. I'm sorry to have wasted your time."

John's head snapped back to Abby. "She all right?" he asked.

"She's frightened, but she's fine."

"She say who done it?"

"Vernon Monroe," Abby replied, fully aware that she had just signed the man's death warrant.

"Thank you for comin' by," John said as he stood up.

"Is Hattie here? I think Patricia needs her mother."

A few minutes later, Hattie and Abby were headed back to the house.

While Abby was gone, Kenji held Patricia as she dozed off. He had been so close to losing her, and for what? Simply because his father didn't like the color of her skin. As far as he was concerned, Patricia was his family.

He hadn't quite believed his mother when she said she didn't know what was happening. He believed she may not have known the details, but she knew his father was up to something and chose not to warn him. He tried to understand her position, and to some degree he did. Every day he was in the house, she was in a position where she had to choose between husband and son. That was no longer an issue; he meant it when he said he wasn't going back.

Patricia stirred at the sound of voices, jumping up when she recognized her mother's voice.

Hattie hugged Patricia tight and kissed her cheek. "You all right, baby?" Hattie asked, not noticing Kenji at first.

"I'm all right, Mama," Patricia replied.

Hattie noticed Kenji and gave him a level stare. "You him?" she asked.

"I am Kenjiro Takeda; it is an honor to meet you," Kenji said with a bow.

"Yeah, well, we'll see 'bout that," Hattie replied as she hugged Patricia again.

Vernon made his way to his grandmother's house; no one would help him when they saw the blood, and word that John Middleton was looking for him didn't help. He banged on his grandmother's door until she turned on the lights. When she saw him, she shook her head but let him in.

"Boy, what you do this time?" she asked as she cleaned the wound on his neck. It was deep, but he would live.

"Nothin'! He still mad 'bout the other time," Vernon said.

"Uh huh, what I hear is that you try to force yourself on that girl and she cut you. That true?"

Vernon could never lie to his grandmother; even as a child, he could never lie to her. Finally, he told her the truth. She sighed; she heard the stories about the girl and the Jap but she wasn't sure they were true, but here was Vernon confirming it. That John Middleton had disowned the girl wouldn't matter to him; Patricia was still his girl and there was nothing that would change the fact that her grandson would be dead within twenty-four hours.

"Why couldn't you leave that girl alone?" she asked. "You didn't love her."

Vernon didn't answer; it didn't matter anyway. He could only hope that his death would be quick. Vernon kissed his grandmother goodbye for the last time and walked out. He didn't try to hide and didn't run or fight when two of John's friends found him. An hour later, Vernon Monroe was dead at the hands of John Middleton.

Chapter 6

OCTOBER 14, 1940

"What is this place?" Abby said, peering into the growing darkness, looking at the large unkempt house.

"It isn't much, but I have found a place for Patricia and me to live after we marry. An old man owns it, and in exchange for rent, I am taking care of the property. We will have one room, maybe two, and share the rest of the house with him," Kenji replied.

"Is he aware that Patricia is black?" Abby asked as she continued to take in the disrepair of the house and ill-kept yard.

"He knows and he says it doesn't matter. I wish I could do better for her; she deserves so much more than this, and one day I'll be able to give her what she deserves, but I must ask a favor of you. Don't tell her about it unless she asks. I know that I don't have the right—"

"You have my word," Abby interrupted. "I'll come back for you at eleven; you two have a lot to talk about as far as what you're going to do."

Abby made it back home to find Patricia sound asleep on the couch. She checked the doors and windows before rousing Patricia and sending her to bed, but once in bed, Patricia couldn't sleep, and as a result, neither could Abby.

Hana wondered where Kenji had gone. He wasn't at the greenhouse; she walked there to look for him. Hiroshi tried to stop her and then tried to go with her, but she refused; she was much too angry and hurt to want to talk to him.

When she got to the greenhouse, she used a candle to give her some light. In the dim light she saw the drops of blood on the floor and followed them to where they ended. She saw the garden tool lying on the floor and started to cry. Her husband was going to let that girl die. Kenji was right; he had lost all honor and integrity. He was not the man she'd married and had two children with, one now deceased years ago, leaving only Kenji, whom she had just lost.

Hana corrected herself. She'd lost Kenji the moment they had refused to make any attempt to see his point of view about the girl. They had forced his hand, but she did try to warn Hiroshi and Kenji both. The question that she asked herself was: Would it have turned out differently if they had at least listened to him? After all, he had been right when he told them he was only doing what they had taught him, and that was to think for himself. He'd been right to say they'd tried to force him to see things their way.

There was one thing that she was sure of: If she had said something, even though she didn't know the specifics, today more than likely wouldn't have happened. In her silence, she had helped her husband not only in his plan to keep Kenji from the girl, but to cause her physical harm. Despite what she'd said, did she really agree with her husband? She wondered.

Hana walked around the greenhouse not bothering to call for Kenji; she knew as soon as she walked in that he wasn't there. As she walked out, she realized that while she didn't want Kenji to marry the girl, she didn't want anything to happen to her, either. The realization did little to assuage her guilt and sense of loss. In one day she had figuratively lost both her husband and son, but not to death—death would have been easier to handle.

Hiroshi watched Hana walk out of the house, his heart heavy. Hana, he knew, would never forgive him for what he had done. She would remain his wife and as dutiful as ever, but things between them would never be the same, and for him that was the only unacceptable loss. Kenji and the nigger girl could both burn in hell as far as he was concerned.

The money. Kenji had a little over three hundred dollars in American money sewed into the lining of his small overnight bag. Apparently Kenji had forgotten about it, just as he and Hana had. The question was: How was he going to get it back? He didn't know where Kenji went after he took the girl to wherever she lived, or even where to begin looking for him.

Joben Saito sat sipping tea with his daughter attending him; he hadn't heard anything, so he was under the assumption that all had gone well. Hiroshi would have been at his house if it hadn't.

"Remember, Dai, you must be the perfect wife to Kenjiro Takeda. Do not ruin this chance," he told her as she poured him another cup of tea.

"Yes, Father," she replied as she bowed and left the room. Tears burned her eyes. She didn't want to marry anyone, especially someone who was in love with another, but she would do as she was told. It was the least that she could do since she had brought dishonor to her family by giving herself to the man on the ship. Fortunately, a pregnancy hadn't resulted from the tryst, and for that she was grateful.

Hana didn't acknowledge Hiroshi when she returned from the greenhouse, going straight to their room and softly closing the door behind her instead of leaving it open as she usually did.

Hiroshi looked at the closed door with anger; she was still his wife, and he was not going to allow her to ban him from their marital bed. He got up and walked to the door and was surprised to find it locked; he banged on the door in anger and frustration and then dug the key out of his pocket.

Hana was sitting on the bed when he walked in, her expression unreadable as he looked at her. He could have punished her for her insolence but didn't; she had always been the perfect wife to him, and he did love her. He also realized that she was reacting out of anger and pain. In the morning she would feel better and they could discuss how to get the money back from Kenji.

Kenji looked around the small room. Patricia did deserve so much better than this, and one day she would have it. He had already taken out the trash that covered the small bed and cluttered the room. It was actually bigger than he thought it was. He drug the mattress out of the room and out the back door, then propped it up against the side of the house to air out; he would beat it with a broom later.

The old man was in the kitchen when he came back into the house.

"That girl of yours, she cook?" he asked.

"Yes," Kenji replied, "why do you ask?"

"I need a cook and housemaid," the man replied. "I'm prepared to barter for her services; after all, this ain't no slave state."

"What are you offering?" Kenji asked.

"What is it you want?" the man countered.

Kenji thought. He still had to tell Patricia about the house, and he wasn't sure how she would feel about him volunteering her services. But if he could get them more space than that one room. . . .

"We would like more than one room to call our personal space," Kenji replied.

"Is that all?" the man asked. "Well, hell, you can have half the house for all I care. As you can see, there's more than enough space for all of us."

Taking advantage of the man's willingness to compromise, Kenji made another demand. "There is more: we would like Sundays and Mondays as our personal time."

The man considered the request. "I don't got no issue with that; do we have a deal?" he asked.

"I haven't spoken to her about this place yet; I wanted to get it ready before I brought her here. If you will allow it, I would like to get the rest of it ready for her and we will discuss it together," Kenji replied.

The man laughed. "You're one smart cookie, ain't ya? Do what you need to do," the man said and walked away.

Kenji stood staring at the man's back. He was already honoring his promise to give Patricia better. At the thought of her, he felt a pang in his heart and hoped she was all right. He couldn't stay with her as long as he wanted to; Abby was already helping them enough, and they couldn't and wouldn't cause trouble by drawing more attention to her.

Kenji walked through the house, looking at the rooms that would be theirs, choosing the biggest room that was farthest from the old man's rooms as their bedroom. He decided the room next to it could be the library or sitting room, whatever she wanted. Kenji stopped; there was still the issue of a marriage. He had to find out whether they could marry. As soon as he could, he would go to the library to do some research, but in the meantime, he had a house to get ready.

Hana looked at Hiroshi but didn't speak; she had nothing to say to him.

"Hana, I know you are angry and upset, and that you are not in the mood to discuss this, so I am going out for a short time. I will return, and this door had better not be locked," Hiroshi said, looking at her, his expression grim.

Hana didn't reply, the expression on her face passive as Hiroshi turned away from her and left the room. After he left, Hana let the tears of grief flow and wondered if there wasn't some way for her to get her son back.

Joben was settling in for the evening when Hiroshi knocked on his door. He sent Dai to answer the door while he got out his best saké. Hiroshi was coming for a celebration drink, he thought. Joben walked into the living room with a smile that froze when he saw the expression on Hiroshi's face.

"We have failed. The girl still lives and the man that we hired is, no doubt, dead. Probably at the hands of Kenjiro; he knows of your involvement and has vowed to kill you if you should cross his path," Hiroshi said.

Joben was stunned; how could it have failed?

"The girl stabbed the man we hired before Kenjiro saw them together. The man was already gone by the time Kenjiro got to the greenhouse. Whether Kenjiro saw him or not, I don't know, but if he did, the man is dead," Hiroshi said. "Afterward, he brought her to my home where, in front of her, he disowned us and vowed to kill you. I am here to warn you to stay out of his path."

Joben was initially frightened and then relaxed. Kenji wanted to be a doctor; it wouldn't be in him to kill or hurt anyone intentionally. The threat was just him talking out of anger and nothing more.

Hiroshi saw that while Joben was initially frightened, he wasn't any longer. "Did you not hear me? He will kill you if he sees you anywhere near that girl, or even if you cross his path," Hiroshi said.

"Hiroshi, I wasn't aware that you were so melodramatic! The boy only spoke out of anger; he isn't capable of deliberately hurting anyone. He's a healer," Joben said calmly.

"Joben, listen to me: I know my son, and he meant it. You didn't see the look in his eyes when he said it or the look in his eyes when he disowned me as his father. It's true that Kenji is a healer, but he is also of the Takeda line. We are fiercely loyal and protective to the ones we love, and he loves this girl. I'm warning you to stay away from him; there is no longer any chance that he will marry your daughter. You will have to set your eyes on another groom for her."

After Hiroshi left, Joben gave serious thought to what he had been told and resigned himself to finding another groom for his daughter. The Takedas were by far the best choice; he would now have to settle for a family with a lesser name.

As Abby watched Patricia rest, she let her mind wander back to 1914. It was June and the Great War had just started. She was a young twenty-five-year-old single woman at the time. Her family had been pushing her to marry her then-suitor, Monty, but she wanted nothing to do with it or him. Eventually he got tired of waiting for her and married someone else. She had just heard that he was the father of a brand-new baby boy.

"Good for him," she'd murmured, meaning it.

The problem was that she wasn't interested in men, period. She didn't find them attractive in any way, but was more drawn toward women. It was an urge she had managed to suppress until she met Lorena Butler.

Lorena was a beautiful, petite, mulatto girl who had a perpetual smile on her face and an infectious giggle. She had been one of the new maids hired by the head housekeeper. Abby was immediately drawn to the girl who was just shy of twenty when she started working for the family.

It wasn't long before they became friends, much to the displeasure of her parents.

"She's a servant and not your equal; it would do you well to remember that," her mother had told her repeatedly.

Over the course of a year, their friendship had progressed to the point where they had no secrets from each other, often seeking each other out during the day. Abby couldn't remember what it was that led them to that first stolen kiss, but she knew that from that moment on, her life would never be the same. She had found a woman who felt as she did about men. Neither of them hated men, but the thought of being touched by a man sexually was repulsive.

After that first kiss, they stole away together as much as possible. Abby remembered with a longing that never diminished—even after twenty-five years—the first time she and Lorena had made love. She also remembered, with great pain, the last time they made love. It was when they were caught.

Abby had started sneaking Lorena to her room at the end of Lorena's workday. Lorena lived with her family but told them she was staying at the house to help with some extra cleaning and that she would stay overnight. They never questioned her about it.

One night, after they thought that everyone was in bed, Abby and Lorena began to make love. Abby's father had still been up and heard giggling coming from Abby's room as he passed by.

Curious, he'd stopped outside of the door; he hadn't been aware that Abby had an overnight guest, and he wondered when the friend had arrived because the guest hadn't been present at dinner.

Without knocking, he opened the door to see Abby with her head between Lorena's legs. That was the last time Abby had ever seen Lorena.

Tears burned Abby's eyes at the memory; she still missed Lorena and her giggles, she missed the warmth of her body as they made love. Three months after they were caught, Abby's father had made her marry Lionel Devault. He was a handsome man and, on the surface, very polite and kind, but the reality was that he was a brute.

By the time he died, they had been married for fifteen years, with the first five years being nothing short of hell for Abby. Finally, in desperation, she gave him permission to seek his pleasure elsewhere, just as long as he was discrete and left her alone. Recognizing the deal of a lifetime, Lionel had agreed. The beatings stopped, and life got better. They made the social appearances together, but at home, they never spoke and slept in separate bedrooms. Her parents died thinking they had fixed her "problem," although they never understood why there had never been any children.

"I really do understand," Abby murmured to a now-sleeping Patricia.

Hattie paced the small living room, waiting for John to come back. He was out with some of his friends, looking for Vernon. She knew he was still angry at Patricia, and would be for a long time, but Vernon had taken his own life into his hands when he touched Patricia. John would kill for her, no matter how angry he was at her. Hattie only hoped he wouldn't get caught.

Vernon's body was found behind some crates, just after midnight, by two drunks looking for a place to sleep. After they checked his pockets for money and took his coat, they left him where he was. He wouldn't be discovered again until early in the morning.

OCTOBER 15, 1940

Patricia was still asleep when Abby heard a knock on the door. She approached cautiously and was surprised to see John Middleton standing there holding a wooden box.

"This belongs to her, and tell her that Vernon won't be botherin' her no more." He set the box on the porch swing and turned to leave.

"Daddy?" Patricia called.

John turned and looked at her briefly before turning from her and walking away.

Abby put her arm around Patricia and hugged her. There was nothing she could say that would make things any better. Only time and Kenji could do that. She led a crying Patricia to the kitchen and made her a cup of strong tea, sweetened with honey. She wasn't going to insist that Patricia eat; it would have been pointless.

Hiroshi sat at the breakfast table while Hana silently served him; she hadn't spoken to him since the day before, but cried quietly. It was time to bring up the issue of the money; even if she was upset, it had to be talked about.

"Hana, we have to find out where Kenjiro is staying. His bag contains over three hundred dollars. He is not entitled to that money; he has dishonored us and has chosen that ni—"

"Stop it!" Hana exclaimed. "You've done enough damage already, and I won't help you do more. I knew you were planning something, and I kept silent. I should have said something to Kenji but I didn't, and that girl was almost raped. Last night I lay awake all night wondering if there was a way to save my family. I wondered if there was a way to get my son back, and there is. With or without your consent, I'm going to find Kenji and beg his forgiveness, and I'm going to try to accept the one he has chosen to love, even if I don't agree with his choice. I love my son enough to do that. What of you? Do you love your son enough to try to accept this girl?"

Hiroshi couldn't believe his ears. Hana was siding with Kenjiro? "I forbid you to do this," he said sternly.

Hana gave him a sad smile. "You have just answered my question. As far as the money goes, it's his. He and Patricia will need it. There's something else: Throughout this entire ordeal, you've questioned Kenji's honor and his integrity, but it's your own you should be questioning. Kenji never lied to us about his feelings for this girl once he knew what they were. He has always acted with honor, integrity, and courage, the three things you taught him. He made every effort to talk with us about it and her, and we wouldn't allow it; we tried to sway him our way by appealing to his sense of guilt.

"Hiroshi, you didn't have to choose the path that you chose; we could have just let them be, or we could have at least met her. I allowed you to put me in a position where I had to choose between my child and my husband, and almost every time I have chosen you. Now I'm choosing my child. If I have to consider this girl as my daughter to get my son back, then so be it."

"Hana, you must listen to me! We cannot allow this to . . . "

Hana walked away, leaving Hiroshi talking to air.

Kenji woke up after just sleeping a few hours; he couldn't rest for thinking about Patricia and how she was. He was going to see her tomorrow, but he couldn't wait; he had to be sure that she was all right. He decided to stop at the library on his way there; maybe he could find out about the possibility of them being married.

Having made his decision, he did a few repairs around the house and took a bath. By ten o'clock, he was on his way to the library. He made it to the library for the most part without incident; he was accosted a couple of times, but he ignored the men and kept going. He was more bothered by the attitude of the children than he was by the adults; they were already being taught hatred and no tolerance for those different from themselves.

The library was large and airy, and he wondered why he hadn't thought to come here before. Maybe he and Patricia could spend some time here together; he would bring it up to her.

"Help you?" a terse voice asked.

"Yes, please," Kenji replied politely. "I am looking for the section on your laws."

The librarian, a younger woman, eyed him suspiciously. "What laws are you looking for?" she asked.

Kenji didn't want to give specifics, so he said, "Laws in general, and also I am interested in your medical journals."

Reluctantly, the librarian pointed him to the law section and then told him where the medical journals were. "You're not planning on making some poison to kill us, are you?" she asked as he walked away.

Kenji stopped and turned around. "Excuse me?" he asked, thinking he had to have misheard her.

"Are you deaf? I asked if you were planning to make some kind of poison to kill us," she replied, her voice tight with the irritation of having to repeat herself.

Kenji couldn't believe she would ask him that and then expect that he would tell her. "No, I hope to become a physician someday, and I like to read the journals," he replied.

The librarian gave him a dubious look and then turned away. Kenji glanced at the clock; he would spend a couple of hours here and hope he would have some good news for Patricia—they both needed it. He kept an eye on the clock as he read through a law book that looked the most promising. Seeing nothing that would prohibit them from marrying, he chose another book with the same results.

He glanced at the clock; he had been at the library for almost ninety minutes. He looked through one more book and once again found nothing. As far as he could tell, there was nothing to keep them from legally getting married. That it wouldn't be a Japanese wedding was of very little concern to him; that his parents wouldn't attend saddened him, but that couldn't be helped. He was more concerned for Patricia. He had met her mother briefly and they hadn't really talked, the both of them focusing on Patricia. He hoped, if only for Patricia's sake, that her mother would attend. A woman should have her mother at her wedding.

Kenji ignored the stares and comments as he walked to Abby's house. It took a while, but it gave him time to figure out how to tell Patricia about the house and the old man's offer. As he walked, a car sped by, and the occupant threw something out of the window, called him a name, and kept going. Things were escalating, and he wondered about his mother. This whole thing had been hard on her, but he still couldn't shake the feeling that she knew something was happening and chose not to tell him. It didn't matter anymore, but what did matter was that she was safe. As much as he wanted to go check on her, he wasn't going to. When they had rejected Patricia, they had rejected him.

Patricia and Abby were polishing the silver when Kenji knocked on the door.

"I'll get it, Miss Abby," Patricia said quietly as she lay down the fork she was polishing.

Abby's heart broke for Patricia and Kenji both; she wished she could do more to help them. She jumped up and ran to the living room when she heard Patricia cry out, only to find her in Kenji's arms and crying.

Kenji looked up to see Abby looking at them and apologized. "I am sorry to come uninvited, but I had to make sure Patricia was all right. I won't stay long."

"Of course you'll stay as long as you need and want to!" Abby exclaimed. "You're always welcome here, and besides, you're just what the doctor ordered. Sit down and I'll bring you something cold to drink; that's quite a walk you just took."

As soon as Abby was gone, Kenji kissed Patricia gently and led her to the couch. "Patricia, are you all right?" he asked, missing the sparkle in her eyes.

"Daddy came by this morning; he said that Vernon won't be bothering me anymore and . . . then he left. He wouldn't talk to me," Patricia said, crying. "I don't understand! Who are we hurting?"

"*Kirei*, we are hurting no one, and those that say that we are, are wrong. My parents and your father are choosing to be hurt, and they are living according to what they have been taught and have no interest in learning anything different. In the end, the only thing that matters is what we feel for each other. What the world thinks doesn't matter," Kenji told her as he pulled her close.

"But your family! At least I have my mom. . . . "

"Patricia, you are my family now. Who knows, maybe my parents will change their minds, but even if they do, you will always come first."

Abby listened at the door. She was convinced that whatever happened, as long as they held on to each other, they would survive. She made a little noise so they knew she was coming back into the room. She handed Kenji a cold glass of iced tea and then handed one to Patricia before taking one for herself.

They sat quietly, sipping their tea. Kenji broke the silence first. "I spent some time at the library on my way here. I was trying to find out if it was illegal for us to marry."

Patricia sat up. "And?" she prompted.

"I found nothing that says we can't, and I looked through several books. They are very specific in stating that whites cannot marry blacks and other minorities, but it said nothing about the minority races marrying. Then again, it didn't say we could, either. I plan to do further research, but if I find that we can marry, I would like to do so as soon as possible," Kenji said.

Abby said nothing as Kenji told her what he had found out. *Even if they could marry, who would do it?* she wondered.

"I have more to tell you," Kenji said. "I found a place for us to live."

Patricia listened as Kenji explained the living situation and what the man wanted in exchange for rent.

"That's all he wants?" she asked.

"Yes, and I believe him to be a man of his word. I think he is lonely; he has no family, and that is why he's willing to compromise. I've been working on his house for the past few days, and it was this morning that he approached me with this offer. I didn't want to accept before speaking with you, Patricia. I know it's not much, and I know you deserve so much better than this, and one day you'll have it, but for now will you—"

"Yes, I don't care if I have to scrub the baseboards with a toothbrush, so tell him we accept," Patricia said and then stopped, an expression of sadness crossing her face. She had always dreamed of the white gown and of her father proudly giving her away. Unless he changed his mind, that wasn't going to happen. In the scheme of things, she didn't even care about the dress and everything else that symbolized what a wedding was; she only wanted her daddy to be there with her when she got married. She pushed the thought away; she had to concentrate on what was happening and not on what she wished for.

"So when can I see the house?" she asked.

"It isn't ready yet; I'm still cleaning it and getting it ready," Kenji replied.

"I can help you clean; it'll go faster that way," Patricia said, happy to do something that would keep her busy and allow her to spend more time with Kenji.

An hour later they were piled into Miss Abby's car to go see the house. When they arrived, Patricia looked at the old house and saw possibilities. Kenji led her and Abby into the house and introduced them to Ralph, as he wanted to be called.

"So you're the one he's sweet on; I can see why," Ralph said as he looked Patricia up and down.

Feeling uncomfortable, Patricia moved closer to Kenji, who put an arm protectively around her waist. Ralph lost interest in Patricia when he saw Abby. Abby noticed his interest but didn't react, hoping he would take the hint. He followed Abby around like a puppy as they went from room to room in the part of the house where Kenji and Patricia would be staying.

Like Patricia, Abby saw the possibilities. *But, first of all, that hideous green paint has to go*, she thought. White paint would open the rooms up nicely, and she had some in the shed.

"Not bad at all," she said. "The color is awful, but that can be fixed with a couple of coats of paint, and I'm sure I have some drapes packed away that we could alter to fit the windows. We'll have to tell your mother; I'm sure she'll want to help," Abby gushed.

Patricia watched as Abby walked around the room and wondered why she was really helping them. She knew what she had told them, but sensed there was more to it. They left Kenji at the house, promising to come the next morning with more cleaning supplies.

On the way back, Abby suggested they see if Hattie was able to help.

"I don't know, Miss Abby, my daddy might be home," Patricia replied.

"True, but Patricia, he needs to see that you're the same sweet girl he's always loved, except you've grown up. You don't even have to speak to him; just let him see you. He'll eventually come around," she said.

John wasn't home when they got there; Hattie was making dinner. They could smell the scent of beans and potatoes from the front door.

"Mama?" Patricia called.

Hattie came to the door, wiping the flour from her hands. "Patricia! You all right?" she asked, concerned.

"I'm fine, Mama, we just . . . Kenji found a place for us and we . . . I was wondering if you wanted to help us fix it up," Patricia asked nervously.

Hattie looked at Patricia for several long seconds before she spoke. "You ain't just gonna move in there with him, are you?"

"No, Mama," Patricia replied. "He's looking into seeing if we can get married."

"What you doing here?" John's voice boomed from behind them, making them all jump.

"John—" Hattie began.

"You ain't welcome here, so scoot!" John said, ignoring Hattie.

Tears blurred Patricia's eyes; her father really hated her.

Hattie stepped out onto the porch and hugged Patricia tight and whispered in her ear, "Give him some time; he'll come round."

Patricia hugged her mother back and hoped she was right.

"So, Hattie, is nine o'clock all right to come get you?" Abby asked.

"Nine be fine," Hattie replied.

By the end of October, Germany had invaded Romania, and Italy attempted to invade Greece but failed. Hiroshi watched the progress of the war even more nervously, but was relieved to see that Japan hadn't made any moves on the United States, though that could change at any time.

"Hana, our plan still stands even without him," he said. Hiroshi couldn't bring himself to say Kenji's name without becoming enraged.

Hana made a point of saying it every chance she got, such as now. "Do you mean Kenji, our son?" she asked.

"I have no son," Hiroshi said sternly.

Hana sighed; she had made little progress locating Kenji, but she hadn't given up. She talked with whomever she saw, asking if they had seen him. Most people politely said no, but those who knew of his "dishonor" wouldn't speak to her.

Hiroshi found himself glad for each failed attempt to find Kenji; he never thought he would see the day when he would say he hated his son, but he did. Kenji was to be their future heir; he was to add honor to the family name, but he made a selfish decision, totally disregarding the obligations to his family.

Kenji was no closer to figuring out if he and Patricia could marry than he was before. What he needed was to find a lawyer who could answer his questions, but lawyers weren't free, and he didn't want to use their meager savings to talk to one. So every chance he got, he went to the library and kept coming to the same conclusion—but he had to be sure.

The house was coming along nicely; even Ralph was amazed at the difference and asked if they could do his side of the house as well. It turned out that Ralph just loved women, no matter the color, size, or shape. He sidled up to Hattie after taking in her large breasts and behind. As with Abby, he followed her around the house, his eyes glued to her ass.

Other than their initial meeting, Kenji and Hattie had never talked, but she watched him whether he was aware of it or not. One afternoon, Abby and Patricia went to the store, leaving the two of them alone. It was only a matter of time until it happened, and Kenji was glad for it; they needed to talk.

"Why her?" Hattie asked suddenly. "Of all the girls in this place, why my Patricia?"

Kenji stopped what he was doing and turned around to face Hattie. "Please, sit," he said, indicating the only chair in the room. When she sat down, he sat on the floor in front of her.

He began with the very first time he saw Patricia. "I had just gotten off the ship and was meeting my parents. The very first black person I had ever seen in my life was a male, and I remember thinking that he no more resembled an ape than I did. Patricia was the second black person I had ever seen in my life, and I thought her quite pretty. Later I would change that to *Kirei*—beautiful."

"That's what you be calling her?" Hattie asked.

"Yes. After that man cut her face with the rock, she was concerned that I would no longer think her pretty because of the scar. I have called her *Kirei* ever since," Kenji told her.

He went through their meetings and how he fell in love with her. "She makes me smile even when there isn't much to smile about," he said. "She even learned to say some words in Japanese," he added, smiling as he could faintly hear her voice speaking his native language.

Hattie smiled at Kenji for the first time, revealing the beautiful young woman she had been at one time. Kenji still thought her beautiful and knew what Patricia would look like when she was older.

"Her daddy used to say the same thing; she do have a way of making things seem better. I need you to understand somethin'; that girl is my baby, and that's the main reason why I'm here. You love her—I can sees that—and she loves you, but I wish it wasn't so. Life is already hard, and you two done made it harder."

"I understand, and I regret that things are as they are, but I will give you my word that I will die to keep her safe," Kenji replied, meeting Hattie's gaze.

Hattie believed him and, in spite of her misgivings, liked him; anyone who loved her baby the way he did couldn't be all bad, and he was a definite improvement over Vernon Monroe.

"I wants to say one thing: if she ever needs me, you find a way to let me know," Hattie said.

"Agreed, and I would like to say that it is an honor to marry your daughter. I promise to love and care for her," Kenji pledged.

That was all it took; Hattie could see why Patricia had fallen for the tall, soft-spoken Japanese man. She still wished it was different, but she understood.

Patricia and Abby came back just after Kenji and Hattie finished their talk. Hattie watched as Kenji looked after Patricia's comfort. Japanese or not, he was a good man; Patricia could have done much, much worse.

By the end of 1940, Roosevelt was nominated for another term, and Hungary and Romania had become part of the Axis powers.

Kenji watched the war with as much interest as his father. He had a feeling of intense foreboding and questioned whether he and Patricia should wait until after the war to get married. When he mentioned it to Patricia, she balked.

"What if it never ends or lasts for ten years? What are we supposed to do?" she asked.

Kenji was glad she didn't interpret his question as him changing his mind; nothing was further from the truth, but he was thinking of her. What he thought would happen, he didn't know, and he worried for her. They still had most of their savings from before they met, and each of them set aside as much as they could from their wages earned from Miss Abby. Both he and Patricia tried to refuse the money, although they needed it.

"You have helped us in so many ways; it isn't right that we take your money," Kenji told Abby one afternoon.

Abby sighed. "I help you because I want to, and I've come to care for you as much as I do Patricia. And besides, you're going to need it."

Kenji had to admit that she was right; they couldn't afford not to take it. Over the last several months, their meager savings grew from twenty-five dollars to sixty dollars. It still wasn't much, but if they had to leave, it would help.

They still hadn't figured out whether or not they could get married. Abby had written a letter to a friend who was an attorney and hadn't heard back from him. In the meantime, they tentatively planned a wedding. The only one among them that knew a minister personally was Patricia, and she wasn't sure he would agree to do the ceremony.

"I can have my mama ask him," she said, although she was almost certain the man would say no.

"Let's see what my friend says," Abby suggested. "It's going to be a moot point if it won't be legal."

The only thing they could do was wait, but it was becoming more difficult for the both of them. Kenji was more than ready to make love to Patricia, but was holding onto the promise he had made to himself to wait until their wedding night. Patricia, for her part, was becoming more anxious as well. The light petting sessions weren't enough for either of them, leaving them wanting more.

One day, Abby dropped Patricia off at Kenji's house while she ran some errands. As soon as she was in the door, Kenji held her close and kissed her. Patricia playfully bit his lower lip, earning a moan, thinking she had hurt him. She pulled back to apologize, but Kenji wouldn't let her go. Instead he pulled her even tighter against him, letting her feel his hardness against her stomach. Patricia had seen him erect before but had never felt it; he always excused himself and came back a few minutes later, under control. But today, it was different. She jumped when he slipped his tongue into her mouth and touched hers; as many times as they had kissed, he'd never done that, and she found that she liked it.

Kenji felt his control slipping and pulled away. "Patricia—*Kirei*, we have to stop," he told her, his breathing ragged.

"But I—"

"Not like this; I want us to be married when we make love," he told her as he stepped back.

"When will that happen?" Patricia asked. "How long do we have to wait?"

"It's hard, but *Kirei*, it will be so worth the wait," Kenji soothed.

"What if it isn't legal, then what?" Patricia asked as tears of frustration ran down her cheeks.

Kenji tried hard not to think about that, but she had a valid point, and if that was the case, they had a decision to make. Nevertheless, at the moment both of them needed release from their physical needs. He tried to remember what time it was that Abby had left and what she'd said she had to do. By his calculations, she had only been gone for fifteen minutes or so; she was also going to an unfamiliar place and would probably get lost. He decided to take a chance.

"Patricia, in addition to wanting us to be married before we make love, there is another reason—I don't want to take the chance of you getting pregnant before we are married. It's not that I don't want children with you, I do, but I want us to have time to ourselves, and we can't afford a child right now. Can you understand that?" he asked as he stroked her face.

She did, and she even agreed to a point, but the question remained: what if they couldn't get married? She knew her mother would be disappointed if she gave herself before she was married, but she already belonged to and with Kenji.

"Patricia, there are ways to make love without the fear of pregnancy. I can show you, but we have to hurry; I don't want Miss Abby walking in on us."

It didn't take Patricia long to decide. "Yes," she said, "show me."

Kenji led her to the bedroom, sat her on the neatly made bed, and sat beside her. Now that they were actually going to do something, Patricia was nervous. Kenji pulled her close for a kiss, repeating the kiss from earlier, only this time he didn't stop. Patricia pressed closer, wrapping her arms around his neck. Kenji tightened his arms around her and lay back on the bed, holding her close. He moved from her lips to her neck and kissed it lightly before licking it with the tip of his tongue.

Patricia gasped and then moaned as Kenji sucked on her neck. She wasn't prepared for the feelings of pleasure that tightened her nipples and traveled down to between her legs. Kenji's hand traveled from her back to her front and squeezed her breasts; he had touched them before, but this was different. Instead of slow light caresses, he pinched her nipples lightly, making them harden as he kneaded her large breasts in his hands.

Not knowing what to do with her hands, Patricia let them wander. She started with his face and made her way to his chest. She could feel his heart racing beneath her hands and held them there for just a few seconds. Kenji took her hand and slowly eased it down over his stomach and rested it on his erection. He moaned softly at the contact and began to rub her hand up and down his shaft until she caught on.

Kenji let his hand drift over her hips, stopping to caress her behind before continuing to move downward until he reached the hem of her skirt and slowly lifted it up. When it was over her hips, he slipped his hand underneath and touched her most private of places for the first time through her underwear. He felt her moisture and wished for the thousandth time that they were married.

Patricia kept rubbing Kenji through his pants and wondered what he would feel like in her hand. Tentatively, she touched the zipper of his slacks, paused, and then took hold of it.

Kenji made no move to stop her as he moved her underwear to one side and touched her. He was somewhat surprised to find that her pubic hair was coarse, but it wasn't an unpleasant surprise. He spent several minutes stroking her mons, and it wasn't long before she was moving her hips forward, searching for more contact.

He jumped and then moaned as she shyly reached inside his slacks and found his shaft. Patricia was surprised at how soft it felt, but hard at the same time. He left her neck and went back to her lips, saying her name just before he kissed her. Kenji slipped a finger between her inner lips and began to tease her throbbing center until she was moaning into his mouth. Patricia quickened her strokes on his erection, jumping when she felt him release into her hand with a moan, and then she cried out as the first orgasm of her life washed over her.

Kenji took a handkerchief from his pocket and cleaned Patricia's hand before pulling her back into his arms. They lay quietly in each other's arms until they heard Abby pull up in front and beep her horn. They kissed one last time before going to help Abby with whatever purchases she made on her travels.

As soon as Abby saw them, she knew something had happened. Both of them seemed more settled, and she could only hope that whatever they did didn't result in a pregnancy. Things were complicated enough without that. She greeted them as though she didn't notice anything different about them. Patricia and Abby left a couple of hours later. For both Kenji and Patricia, this was by far the hardest goodnight they had ever experienced.

Abby knew that the waiting was wearing on them, and she hoped the letter from her friend came soon.

As soon they were in the privacy of the car, Abby spoke frankly with Patricia. "Patricia, I know this has been a long, drawn-out ordeal for the two of you, but please be careful. What we don't need is a pregnancy to further complicate things."

Patricia didn't reply but looked out of the window for several minutes, trying to gather her thoughts. "Miss Abby, what are we going to do if we can't get married?" she asked quietly.

Abby reached over and patted Patricia's arm; she had no answers. She whispered a silent prayer that a letter would be waiting for them when they got home.

Kenji lay on the bed he and Patricia had just made love on and wanted her back in bed with him. He knew that Abby knew something had happened, even though she acted like she didn't notice. The question that Patricia asked rang in his mind: What if they couldn't legally marry? As far as he was concerned, if that was the case, they would live together as man and wife, and if interracial marriage ever became legal, they would get married then. He suspected that Patricia would feel the same way. The next time they saw each other, they would have to talk about it.

Abby and Patricia eagerly looked through the mail only to be disappointed once again. Abby hugged Patricia and whispered in her ear, "Maybe tomorrow."

Patricia nodded, unable to speak because her throat was so tight. She went to her room, threw herself on her bed, and cried herself to sleep.

Abby heard her crying and started crying herself as she thought about Lorena.

Chapter 7

JANUARY 1, 1941

Kenji and Patricia celebrated Christmas and New Years at the house with Ralph and Abby. As of yet, there had been no word from Abby's lawyer cousin. Between the two of them, Kenji and Patricia decided if they hadn't received word by the end of January, they would get married and hope they weren't breaking any laws, although Kenji's research indicated they wouldn't be.

Patricia was a little sad; this was the first Christmas she wasn't with her parents. She had given thought to going to their house, but decided she didn't want to see the disgust in her father's face when he saw her. Hattie had already seen both her and Kenji, giving them a box that contained several candles.

"You never know when you might need them," she said as she hugged Patricia and smiled at Kenji.

Abby gave them a new comforter for the bed they had yet to sleep in together, although they made some form of love on it frequently. As of yet, Patricia hadn't told her mother or Abby about their plans to marry by the end of January if they hadn't heard from Abby's cousin.

Kenji stood by the window, looking out in the direction where his parents lived, and hoped they were well. Patricia had tried on a number of occasions to get him to at least visit his mother.

"No, *Kirei*, if they cannot accept you, then they cannot accept me," he told her.

Patricia kept trying because she knew he missed his mother just as much as she missed hers, the difference being that she had some contact with hers.

Patricia looked over at Abby and saw her sad expression; she was missing someone, too, she thought—maybe her husband, but Patricia didn't think so. Abby almost never talked about him, and when she did, it was very briefly. Patricia wondered who it was that she missed so much.

Christmas at the Takeda household was quiet. Hana no longer talked to Hiroshi unless it was absolutely necessary, and Hiroshi didn't seem to care. All his attention was focused on the progress of the war. He still wished he had the money from Kenjiro, but that was a lost cause. Hana was Kenji's champion; if Hiroshi even brought him up in a negative way, Hana walked away, indicating that she wasn't interested in anything Hiroshi had to say unless it was to talk about reconciliation.

Hana continued to walk around their neighborhood, hoping to find someone that had either seen Kenji or knew where he had gone. As the news of his dishonor to his family spread, fewer and fewer people spoke to her. Hana was frustrated, but determined to find Kenji and hoped that he would at least talk to her.

Before Patricia and Abby left for the night, Kenji pulled Patricia aside for a goodnight kiss.

"I wish you weren't leaving," he told her. "The bed is very lonely without you in it."

Patricia understood what he meant; she didn't want to leave, but Abby wouldn't allow her to stay, saying that until they were married, it wouldn't be proper. Patricia leaned into Kenji, wrapping both arms around his waist. It had been a long, hard year and a half, and she was ready for it to be over. She gave him a final squeeze before pulling away.

"We'll see you tomorrow; sleep well."

Kenji watched her leave with a lump in his throat. This shouldn't be so difficult; they were two consenting adults. That they were of different races and nationalities should make no difference, but the reality of it was it did. He glanced at the clock and thought about going for a walk but changed his mind; it was no longer safe for anyone of Japanese descent to be out after dark. He went to what he and Patricia decided would be the study and took down one of the medical journals Abby had given him for his birthday and began to read.

The ride to Abby's was quiet until Abby broke the silence. "You're planning to marry even if we don't hear from my cousin." It wasn't a question but a statement of fact and acceptance. Abby was actually surprised they had waited this long; she knew she couldn't have waited.

"Yes ma'am," Patricia replied. "We both feel like we've waited long enough. We've been waiting for months to hear from your cousin, but we'll give it to the end of this month."

That surprised Abby, as well as the fact that they had been able to refrain from sexual intercourse—again something she doubted she would be able to do, if she liked men.

"When are you going to tell your mother?" Abby asked.

"The next time I see her; maybe she can talk to her minister about marrying us," Patricia replied.

"Patricia, what if he refuses? What will you do?"

She and Kenji had already talked about that, too, and decided they would just have to live together out of wedlock. What difference could it possibly make? Almost everyone was against them, and they needed and wanted to be together.

"Patricia?" Abby called.

"If that happens, we'll live together as if we were married," Patricia said quietly and then waited for the fallout.

Abby was silent for several minutes before she spoke again. "I understand and expected as much, but your parents won't. I would suggest that you tell your mother sooner rather than later to give her some time to get used to the idea. Where would you like to have the wedding?"

They had talked about that, too, and decided to have it at their house. Kenji would talk to Ralph about having a couple of extra days off after the wedding for their "honeymoon."

"As soon as we are able, I will take you on a proper honeymoon," he had said, hugging her.

Patricia couldn't have cared less about a honeymoon; she was eager to begin her life as Kenji's wife, and the rest of the world could take a flying leap.

Hattie came over to see Patricia a week later.

"How's Daddy, Mama?" Patricia asked, trying to gauge whether her father was any closer to forgiving her.

"If you askin' if he still mad, the answer is yes. Baby, you has to understand he was taught that the races just don't mix for anything other than business; we was all taught that," Hattie replied.

"He's never going to forgive me, is he?" Patricia asked sadly.

"I don't know 'bout that," Hattie replied. "I wish I could say different, but I do knows he don't hate you. You are still his baby girl."

"Then why doesn't he try to understand?" Patricia asked. "Why won't he at least talk to me about it?"

"Baby, your daddy is as stubborn as his own daddy and his daddy before him. He got a long memory, and his feelins run deep. You just gonna have to try to be patient and hope he come around, but even if he do, he ain't gonna want to see your man," Hattie said.

Patricia was now at the same place Kenji had been; he wouldn't acknowledge his mother until she acknowledged her.

"All right, Mama, let me know if he changes his mind about Kenji, but would you tell him that I love him?" Patricia replied.

"I'll tell him. What else on your mind?" Hattie asked.

Patricia took a deep breath and told Hattie about her and Kenji's plan to marry by the end of the month, even if they hadn't heard from Abby's cousin.

"What if it ain't legal?" Hattie asked. "Then you and him be livin' in sin!"

"Mama, we've been waiting for this letter for months. For all we know, Miss Abby's cousin is sick or dead! We don't want to wait any longer."

"Why can't you wait until after the war? Your daddy say it won't be too long a war once we jump in," Hattie argued.

"He can't know that," Patricia replied, "and that's what they said about the Civil War. Mama, even if we wait, it doesn't change the question about whether it will be legal or not."

Abby sat quietly, listening to mother and daughter talk. Hattie was weakening; she could see it.

"You goin' to do this with or without me, ain't you?" Hattie asked, resigned to the fact that Patricia was going to marry Kenji.

"Yes, Mama, I am," Patricia replied, taking Hattie's hand in hers. "I want you to know that I love you and I don't mean any disrespect, but Mama, I love him, and my place is with him."

Hattie nodded but felt led to make Patricia aware of one more reality. "Patricia, you do this and he might not ever forgive you. You knows that, don't you?"

Tears ran down Patricia's face; it was something she had already thought about and knew it was true, but it was a chance she was prepared to take. "I know," she said softly.

Abby was crying, too; she was remembering the night she and Lorena had been found in bed together. After Lorena was taken to who knew where, her parents stood in front of her with looks of disgust and anger on their faces. They were so angry that they couldn't speak, and it wasn't until she married Lionel that they began speaking to her again.

"Abigail," her mother said the night before the forced wedding, "your father and I want you to know that all is forgiven. It was the black girl's fault that you were doing such a disgusting thing—"

"No it wasn't," Abby interrupted. "I wanted to do it and I loved doing it! I hate the touch of men," she blurted out.

Her mother was horrified; from that moment on, she and her parents were at odds, and they never really forgave her, although they said they did. After she had been married to Lionel for almost six months, Abby had managed to believe they really had forgiven her, but it was all a façade.

Even now the memory stung, but at least Patricia had her mother to stand with her, even though she didn't agree with her.

"Miss Abby? Are you all right?" Hattie asked.

"I'm fine; I just love weddings," Abby replied, forcing a cheerful smile on her face. "Hattie, Patricia says maybe your minister would perform the ceremony; do you think he will?"

Hattie frowned. "I don't think so; it seems that God has taken a dislike to the Japs—Japanese. That's what he's preachin', anyway. He already come to me askin' if we need to lay hands and anoint Patricia for what he call her 'unnatural affliction.'"

So much for that, Patricia thought as Hattie talked. They would have to do their own ceremony and face whatever consequences arose from it.

Kenji was working on the windows when Ralph called to him.

"Come on over here; I want to show you somethin'," he said as he walked away. Ralph looked much better than he did several months ago, having gained fifteen of the thirty-five pounds he had lost, a fact he attributed to Patricia's cooking.

Kenji climbed down from the stepstool and followed Ralph into what he called the "general area."

When they were sitting, Ralph began to talk. "I like you and your girl; you been more like family to me than my own family—when I had one—and she's one hell of a cook, too!" he said as he settled back in his chair. "I know you planning to marry her, so I want to give you a gift. It ain't much, but I ain't got no use for them anymore. I dug 'em up the other day after we talked and cleaned 'em up a little."

Ralph handed Kenji a small box. "Go on, open it," he urged.

Kenji looked at the box and then at Ralph, and he opened the box. "Ralph . . . we . . . I cannot take these. . . . " Kenji stammered.

"'Course you can! You can't get married without the rings, can ya?"

Kenji stared at the plain gold bands and couldn't see how he could take them without paying for them. He did a quick calculation in his head; they had close to eighty dollars. Maybe he could pay Ralph ten for the rings and they would just absorb the cost.

"Please allow me to pay you something for these; I cannot just take them," Kenji replied.

Ralph grinned; he had already anticipated this and had an amount in mind. "A dollar."

"What?" Kenji asked. "That isn't near what these are worth."

"A dollar, that's all I'm askin' for them," Ralph insisted.

Kenji smiled in gratitude; he understood what Ralph had done. He had given him something, but not really because Kenji had to pay for it.

Ralph watched as Kenji excused himself and went to get the dollar. Whether Kenji knew it or not, Ralph already considered himself paid in full for the rings; he hadn't felt so good or happy in years, and it was due to Kenji and his woman, who never failed to make him smile. He felt badly for them, though; bad times were coming, and he hoped they were strong enough to weather the storm.

Hana continued her walks, actually becoming a little stronger physically because of them. More and more people refused to talk to her, so she decided to branch out in the hopes that the people outside her immediate area didn't know about Kenji and his woman. A few did but still talked with her; it wasn't until a week later that she got lucky.

JANUARY 14, 1941

Hana decided to try to simulate Kenji's route, although she didn't know what it was exactly. She headed out in the direction he always did and started walking. Eventually, she ended up near the grocer's, where Kenji and Patricia had always met. She thought about going inside to ask questions but decided against it, not wanting to draw attention to herself. As it was, people—black and white alike—were already staring at her.

Abby was in the store at the time, picking up her order.

"Where's your girl been?" Joe asked as he packed the sack.

"Under the weather, I'm afraid," Abby replied as she paid for her purchases.

"Get another one then," Joe replied as he handed her the sack.

"I'll take that under advisement," Abby replied a bit tersely.

Just as she turned around, she saw a petite Japanese woman looking into the store; the woman looked familiar somehow. Who did she remind her of? Abby racked her brain—Kenji! Abby hurried out of the store and followed the woman down the sidewalk, finally catching up to her at the corner.

"Excuse me?" Abby called to the woman.

Hana stopped and turned around, fully prepared for the usual offer of work. "No, miss, I do not do laundry," Hana said before Abby could speak.

Abby was confused and then realized what was happening. "No, please, could I speak with you for just a moment?"

Hana gave Abby a wary look, but nodded her consent. The two women moved away from the corner and headed back toward the store.

"Who are you?" Hana asked abruptly.

"Are you Kenji's mother?" Abby asked, ignoring Hana's question.

Hana froze; what did this woman know about Kenji? "I am his mother; do you know where he is? Is he safe?"

"He's fine, but he misses you," Abby said, carefully watching the woman's expression. The bag of groceries was getting heavy. Abby looked around to see how far away her car was; maybe she could put the bag in the car, at least.

"Can you wait here?" Abby asked. "I have to take my groceries to the store."

Hana nodded and watched as Abby walked back to the grocer's. A few minutes later she was back. "They'll deliver them tomorrow," Abby said, answering Hana's unspoken question.

The next obstacle was finding a place where they could talk privately; the only place immediately available was Abby's car. There was a small flower garden not far from where they were; maybe they could talk there.

"Follow me," Abby said and led the way.

Several minutes later, they were sitting in the garden, as far away from other people as they could get.

"Tell me of Kenji," Hana said as soon as they were sitting.

"As I said, he's fine. You've raised a good man," Abby said.

"Thank you; where does he live?" Hana asked. "I want to see him and apologize."

Abby hesitated, not knowing what she should do—meeting Kenji's mother was so unexpected. "I won't tell you that, at least not now," Abby said. "I want to talk to him first, and if he agrees, we'll go from there."

Hana understood. This woman, a white woman at that, was protecting a child that wasn't hers.

"Please, the girl, Patricia, is she well?" Hana asked.

"She's fine no thanks to . . . she's fine," Abby replied.

"Are Kenjiro and her . . . still together?" Hana asked reluctantly.

"They are," Abby replied and offered no further information. For all she knew, Kenji's mother was just gathering information to take back to his father.

The two women parted after agreeing to meet in the garden in two days' time. Abby watched Hana walk away; she had sensed genuine concern for Kenji and, surprisingly, for Patricia. Abby walked toward her car to drive home; she didn't notice the well-dressed white man watching her from across the street.

JANUARY 15, 1941

Kenji touched the rings and imagined placing the smallest one on Patricia's finger. Wedding rings weren't part of the Japanese wedding, and he had never worn jewelry of any kind, but was looking forward to wearing this particular piece of jewelry. He and Patricia had talked and decided to include something from a Japanese wedding ceremony into their own. Neither of them saw it as a problem, since the likelihood of finding a minister to marry them was low.

Kenji hadn't told her about the rings yet because he wanted to clean them up just a bit more. Ralph had done a good job, but with his poor eyesight had missed several places. The rings now shone as if they were brand new; he would show them to her the next time he saw her, which would be later today.

Hiroshi watched Hana; something had changed. The worried look that had become part of her since the day Kenji left was gone. She had to have found him or at least she knew where he was; maybe he could still recover the money.

Hana knew that Hiroshi was watching her and even knew what he was thinking and decided to meet him head on. "I know you are wondering about my sense of relief," she said quietly. "I have been told that our son is alive and well. I don't know where he is, but he is safe."

Hiroshi didn't speak for several seconds, his mind working. Maybe he could feign regret and find out where Kenji was and maybe, just maybe, he had let the nigger girl go and things could go back to the way they were before.

"I have been thinking these past few days," Hiroshi said softly. "I miss our son, too. I admit that in the past I acted without honor and integrity and would like to seek the forgiveness of Kenjiro."

Hana's eyes widened and then narrowed. "Does this mean you will accept the girl as well?"

Hiroshi hesitated for just a second too long, telling Hana what she needed to know.

"You still act with hatred and dishonor," she said softly. "You do not miss him, and you will never accept the girl for what and who she is—the woman our son loves and has chosen to be his wife."

Hiroshi stood up, once again enraged. "You accept her now?" he asked. "You will accept this tainting of our bloodline? I would rather see him marry a Japanese whore!"

"Hiroshi, the world as we knew it has changed and will continue to change. We can either change with it or do as you are doing and hold on to old prejudices. I'm honest enough to admit that I wish Kenji were not in love with this girl, but he is; he has chosen her over us. It is unfortunate that he even had to make that choice, but the fact remains that he is still our son. I have decided to accept this girl, maybe not as a daughter but as his wife, and if you want Kenji back in our lives, you must do the same."

Hiroshi looked at Hana as if he had never seen her before; surely she couldn't believe what she had just said. But she did, Hiroshi could see it in her eyes. She had become the enemy. He hated this country that at one time he considered to be the greatest place on earth. He came here filled with hope and dreams for his family and it took them away; he had nothing. If someone would have offered him free passage back to Japan, he would have taken it and left Kenji with his nigger and Hana there with them. He no longer cared whether Japan entered the war or not, but if it did, he would help as much as he could from here.

Hiroshi gave Hana a sad look and walked away; there was nothing left to say. They had each chosen their paths.

Hana let the tears fall as she watched Hiroshi walk away; she knew she had just lost him forever. If Kenji didn't forgive her, then she was all alone.

Patricia cried when she saw the rings; she hugged Ralph so tightly that he patted her back to let her know he needed air.

"You're welcome," he said after Patricia thanked him for the fifth time. "They was just collectin' dust."

Abby let them have their time alone before bringing up the subject of Kenji's mother. She smiled at Patricia's excited giggles and Kenji's soft voice that was filled with amusement when he replied to her. *They are definitely good for each other*, she thought as she waited for them to come out. Their children would be beautiful, and she hoped they would make major contributions to the world.

Kenji and Patricia came from the kitchen, holding hands; inside this house they could be what they were: a young couple in love looking forward to a life together.

Abby smiled at them and asked them to sit down. "Kenji, I was at the grocer's today, and I saw a woman who looked familiar." Abby told them the story and waited for a response.

"You spoke with my mother? Is she well?" Kenji asked, still holding on to Patricia's hand.

"She seems well, but Kenji, she misses you. She would like to talk to you; she said she wanted to apologize," Abby said.

Kenji looked at Patricia and then back at Abby. "What of my father?"

"She didn't mention him, and I didn't ask. Kenji, she did ask about Patricia; she wanted to know if she was all right. I really think she wants her son back and is willing to accept Patricia in order to do that. I'm meeting her tomorrow; what would you like me to tell her?"

"Kenji," Patricia said softly, "you have to go see her regardless of how she feels about me. If you don't and something happens, you'll feel guilty for the rest of your life."

Kenji was quiet for several minutes. "Then you go with me," he said.

"Kenji, I—"

"No, that is how it will be; you will come with me when I meet with my mother," he insisted.

Reluctantly, Patricia agreed.

"Good!" Abby replied. "Patricia and I will pick you up at eleven; I told your mother that I would meet her at eleven-thirty. Now, let's talk about this wedding. Patricia, your mother was right in thinking her pastor wouldn't marry you, so it looks like you do your own wedding, even though it won't be considered legal. We still have two weeks to hear from my cousin, but I really don't expect it to happen, so let's proceed."

"Miss Abby? Could we wait until my mama's here?" Patricia asked.

Abby smiled. "Of course, my apologies! I'm just so caught up in making plans, which reminds me, we have to get you a new dress—"

"Miss Abby, I have something I could wear," Patricia interrupted.

"Patricia, I've told you many times that I think of you as a daughter, and if I had one, I would want her to be just like you. If this were her wedding, this is exactly what I would be doing, so please allow me this honor of providing for your wedding."

Kenji watched and listened to the exchange between the women; he wished there were more people like Abby in the world. They owed her so much, and there was no way they could ever repay her for her kindness toward them, but at the same time, he was grateful they had her on their side.

The afternoon and evening passed quietly, with Abby excusing herself several times to go chat with Ralph. She really did like the old coot, even though he still mentally undressed her.

"Why don't we make dinner tonight?" she asked. "That way the lovebirds can have some time alone."

Ralph gave it some thought. "Sure, why the hell not?" he replied with a grin.

Abby went back to their part of the house and found them where she'd left them. "You two have the evening off. Ralph and I are cooking dinner, and no arguments," she said when Patricia started to object. "We should be ready by five; we'll call you," she added as she left the room.

Patricia and Kenji looked at each other, not quite believing their good fortune. Kenji stood up and held out his hand to Patricia. When she took it, he pulled her to her feet and into his arms; he held her for just a moment before kissing her.

"Two weeks more and you won't have to leave here at night, and I can make love to you as a husband makes love to his wife."

Patricia felt herself moisten at his words; her nipples hardened as she imagined what it would be like to be with him like that, to not have to worry if Miss Abby would be back before they finished kissing and touching each other to orgasm. Two more weeks.

Kenji led Patricia to their bedroom and closed the door behind them before taking her into his arms again. "I love you, Patricia," he said, his voice choked with emotion.

Patricia hugged him tightly and rested her head on his chest. She listened to his heart as it beat fast, but then so was hers; they were really going to be together.

Kenji gently guided her to the bed and sat her down on it before sitting next to her. Looking into her eyes, he began to slowly unbutton her top. He had never seen her breasts before, and now that he had the time, he wanted to explore. When the blouse was undone and her breasts were before him clothed in a white bra, Kenji's breath caught. He took a finger and traced a path along the material of the bra that touched Patricia's skin.

Patricia's eyes never wavered from Kenji's as he unbuttoned her blouse; it didn't occur to her to be shy or embarrassed; this was Kenji and he loved her. As his fingertips skimmed her chest, Patricia began to unbutton Kenji's shirt, not stopping until she was touching his bare chest. She had felt him before when, while kissing, she would put her hands under his shirt, something that he really seemed to like, especially when her hands brushed across his nipples. Now, she tweaked a nipple and was rewarded with a gasp and a moan.

Kenji took her hands in his and held them for several minutes as he looked at her before kissing her, gently at first and then with more intensity. He left her lips and kissed a trail to her shoulder, releasing one of her hands so he could move a bra strap from her shoulder, baring the skin beneath it.

Patricia ran a hand through his hair; it was longer than what was usually worn, but she liked the silky feel of it as it slipped through her fingers. Kenji had released her other hand and was sliding the other bra strap down her shoulder, kissing it as he had the other.

"*Kirei*," he murmured against her shoulder as he pulled the bra down, revealing her large, dark breasts. Kenji sat back to look at her face and then let his gaze drift downward. Slowly he reached out, took a breast in his hand, and ran a thumb over the erect nipple.

Patricia bit back a moan as Kenji ran his thumb over and over the nipple before taking the neglected breast into his free hand and doing the same thing. She reached over and kissed his lips, his neck, and finally a nipple. She heard him murmur something in Japanese, but the only word she understood was "*Kirei*."

Kenji eased her back onto the bed and took a nipple into his mouth after giving it a gentle kiss and a lick. Patricia moaned as she arched her back, trying to push more of herself into his mouth. Kenji sucked hard and then soft, adding gentle nips while he rolled and pinched the other nipple. Patricia reached down between them and began to stroke him through his pants as Kenji sucked and nipped each nipple until they were swollen and sensitive to even the lightest of touches from his tongue.

Patricia was close, but so was he. Patricia unzipped his slacks, reached in, took him into her hand, and began to stroke him slowly. She cried out as she felt a hand between her legs, the stroke matching hers; she didn't know which of them changed the pace first, but it wasn't long before they climaxed together.

Kenji held Patricia close as she recovered from the orgasm; as far as he could tell, they had another hour, give or take a few minutes, and he was going to take full advantage of it. He turned on his side and had Patricia face him. Her skirt was bunched around her hips and had to be uncomfortable. A few minutes later, the skirt and blouse were draped across a chair, along with his slacks. Kenji pulled Patricia tight against him and began a slow but steady grind against her. Patricia could only close her eyes and go along for the ride; several minutes later, her face was buried in his chest as she climaxed for the second time that day. Kenji pulled away just before his own climax; he didn't want to risk a pregnancy. Understanding, Patricia wrapped her hands around his erection and stroked him to completion.

They were dressed and sitting in the living room when Abby came to get them for dinner; she took in their relaxed appearance and knew that they had made love. She no longer worried about a possible pregnancy. If it was going to happen, it would have happened by now.

Dinner passed by in a blur, and before they knew it, Kenji and Patricia were saying goodnight.

"Soon, *Kirei*," he told her as he held her close.

Hiroshi watched Hana with growing interest; he had decided to start following her in the hope that she would lead him to Kenji and the rest of the money. He didn't say anything as Hana went to her room, the room that had been Kenji's, for the night and shut the door.

JANUARY 16, 1941

Hana was up early, nervous about seeing Kenji; she prayed that he would forgive her and look at her as his mother again. She practiced the apology in her mind and then added one for Patricia; she was sure he would bring her if he agreed to meet with her.

She made her way to the kitchen and made breakfast for her and Hiroshi without speaking to him; he had made his position quite clear. The one thing she wanted to remind Kenji of was the money; knowing him as she did, she was almost positive he had forgotten about it. After breakfast, Hana cleaned the kitchen and left the house without speaking to Hiroshi, unaware that he was planning to follow her.

Patricia slept fairly well, a fact she attributed to making love with Kenji just before dinner—that and the delicious dinner Abby and Ralph had put together. Ralph had been holding out on them; he was quite the cook.

"I used to own a restaurant, but it went belly up, along with everything else," he said when everyone complimented him on his cooking.

"Well," Abby said, "maybe when this war is over, you should reconsider reopening."

Ralph smiled. "Maybe I should."

Patricia crawled out of bed and headed to the bathroom; Abby was still asleep and would be for another hour. Patricia looked at herself in the mirror; she touched the scar that marred her otherwise perfect complexion. It wasn't a big scar, but still she wished it wasn't there. She washed her face and hands before going down the stairs to put the tea kettle on. As she got the tea ready, she wondered about Kenji's mother and what she was like. The one time she had seen her, they didn't speak, and she wondered if they would speak this time.

Kenji was awake early as well; he was nervous about the meeting with his mother. What would she say when he told her that he and Patricia were going to be married in two weeks? He hoped Abby was right in her assessment of his mother. He really did miss her.

Hiroshi followed Hana as she walked to the greenhouse. *What could she want here?* he wondered as he watched her unlock the front door and go in. He slipped in behind her and watched as she walked from one end of the building to the other. He watched as she looked at what appeared to be bloodspots on the floor; she felt guilty, he realized.

Hana spent an hour at the greenhouse before she left and headed toward the garden to meet the white woman and, hopefully, Kenji. As she walked, she practiced her apology to Kenji and Patricia; if asked, she would be honest: she didn't want Kenji to marry this girl.

Hana got to the garden early. The morning was cool, so she found a sunny spot to sit in while she waited for the woman to come. Hiroshi waited across the street to see what was going to happen. He was just about to give up when he saw a car pull up and Kenjiro climb out. He helped the older white woman out and then her . . . the nigger that made Kenji act with dishonor. Even from where he stood, Hiroshi could see how Kenji and the woman looked at each other. They loved each other, that was clear, but it still shouldn't have happened. Kenji should have been the dutiful son and done as he was told. He should have married Dai Saito; he should have. . . . Hiroshi stopped himself. The bottom line was that Kenji did none of the things he was supposed to, in effect ruining the Takeda name.

Hana stood up when she saw the white woman's car. Her heart pounded as she watched Kenji help the woman from the car and then help Patricia. He looked well and happier than she had ever seen him, and it was all because of the girl.

Kenji approached his mother with Patricia at his side; no one spoke for several minutes.

"Mother, are you well?" Kenji asked.

"I am well, and I can see that you are, too. Kenji—"

"Sit, there is no need for formalities," Kenji said, indicating the bench. He offered Patricia the seat at the end of the bench and he sat between them.

"Mother, before you say whatever it is you want to say, I would like for you to meet Patricia Middleton, soon to be Patricia Takeda. We are going to be married in two weeks' time. Patricia, this is my mother, Hana Takeda."

The two women looked at each other until Patricia broke the silence. "*Konnichiwa, hajimemashite.*" Hello, it is very nice to meet you.

Hana was stunned; Patricia's pronunciation was a little off but was almost perfect. She looked at her and saw the same mischievousness that everyone who knew her saw. She didn't reply for several minutes, as she continued to assess Patricia.

"*Konnichiwa, hajimemashite*," Hana replied softly. "Kenji, I came here to ask your forgiveness for whatever role I played in the attempt to harm Patricia. I ask the same forgiveness of Patricia. I knew your father was planning something, but I didn't think it involved causing Patricia physical harm. I ask that you acknowledge me as your mother and I, in exchange, will acknowledge Patricia as your chosen. I cannot accept her as a daughter, but who knows? That may come later."

Kenji looked at his mother as if trying to decide if she were trying to trap them. "What of Father?" he asked.

"I am sorry, but his views have not changed, and I don't think they will anytime soon, if at all. He is very angry and disillusioned; he is not the same man who came here in 1933," Hana replied quietly.

"Why have you changed your mind?" Kenji asked. "The last time we spoke, you were quite clear on your position."

Hana hesitated, trying to think of the best way to answer his question. "Throughout this entire thing, I have been caught between your father and you. I held out hope that you would see reason and understand that even though you love th—Patricia that it could not and should not be, but that didn't happen.

"I knew he was up to something, as I said, but I swear to you, had I known that he meant to harm her, I would have said something. As much as I didn't want you to be with her, I never wanted her hurt, especially in the way she was going to be hurt. Patricia, please understand that I never meant you any ill will; I just didn't—"

"You didn't want our line tainted," Kenji finished for her. "But what about now? At some point, there will be children. Would you deny them the privilege of knowing you?"

Hana bit her lip as she thought about the question. "Kenji, I am here because I love you enough to accept Patricia as your chosen; if there are children, I will recognize them as my grandchildren."

"What of Father? What will you tell him?" Kenji asked, for the first time fully understanding Hana's position.

"Your father and I are . . . estranged. He no longer cares about anything other than what he considers to be your betrayal and the war. He has been seen visiting with people who are very pro-Japan. I am worried about him, but we no longer talk."

Kenji felt a sense of sadness and some guilt; had he done this? Was falling in love with Patricia the cause of the destruction of his family? No, he decided. The problems were already there; falling in love with Patricia had brought them to the fore. There wasn't anything he would have changed about falling in love with her, and he wouldn't have done anything differently.

"Kenjiro, I humbly ask for the forgiveness of you and Patricia," Hana said and bowed her head.

Kenji took Patricia's hand in one hand and Hana's in the other. "Mother, I accept your apology. It is for Patricia to decide whether she accepts or not."

Up until this point, Patricia had been silent. She could see that Hana meant what she said and also realized what it must have taken for her to ask forgiveness not only from Kenji but her. "I accept," Patricia said softly, giving Kenji's hand a gentle squeeze.

Abby could see the relief in Hana's face and in Kenji's as well. It struck her that it was the mothers that rallied around their children while the men still acted like stupid jackasses. She wondered, not for the first time, if the world wouldn't be a better place if women ran it.

Hiroshi watched, enraged, as Kenji hugged Hana; her betrayal was now complete. He no longer cared about the money; Kenji and his whore could choke on it as far as he was concerned. As for Hana, he still loved her, but she was no longer his wife. They would still live together to keep up appearances, which was a good thing for him, given what he was contemplating. Hiroshi gave Hana, Kenji, and Patricia one last look before he walked away, followed by the man that had followed Abby the day before.

"Kenjiro, there is one last thing: do you still have your small overnight bag?" Hana asked.

"Yes, why do you ask?" Kenji replied.

"Do you remember what's inside of it?" she asked, not wanting to say too much.

Kenji frowned and then remembered; there was more than three hundred American dollars sewn into the lining of the bag. Once Hana had sewn it in, he had forgotten about it, concentrating on the issues with Patricia.

"I remember now. It is at our home if you want to come and get it," Kenji replied.

"No, I want you to have it. You will need it more than I will. I just wanted to remind you that it is there."

"Mother—"

"No, I insist, and I have something else for you, but do not open it until you are home," Hana said, pressing a small package into his hands.

"Would you like to come see our home?" Kenji asked.

Hana hesitated and declined. "I have to go now, but I would like to see your home."

"Our wedding will be in two weeks; will you attend?" Kenji asked, knowing that she would probably say no, and he wasn't disappointed.

"No, Kenji; your father already feels betrayed by me, and I will not cause him any more distress even if we are . . . not together."

Hana refused the offer of a ride home, preferring to walk instead. As she walked home, she reconsidered whether she should go to the wedding or not. There was still time to change her mind, she realized, as she continued on her way home.

Abby dropped Kenji and Patricia off, saying she had errands to run and would be back in an hour or so. Kenji wasted no time in taking Patricia to their bedroom where they made love, forgetting about the package Hana had given them.

Afterward, as Kenji held her, Patricia asked about the package. "What do you think it is?" she asked.

Kenji got up, retrieved the package, and brought it back to the bed. "You open it," he told her as he handed her the package.

"But it's for you," Patricia replied, handing him the package back.

"It belongs to the both of us, whatever it is, so open it," Kenji urged.

Patricia took the package and opened it; there was a small figurine of a Japanese man. "Who is it?" she asked as she turned the figurine over in her hands.

"This is Fukurokujo; he is the god of happiness, wealth, and longevity. Mother is wishing us to have a good life together," Kenji explained as he took the figurine from Patricia. "We have to pick a good place for him to sit," he added as he pulled her back into his arms. Abby had been gone for about forty-five minutes and would be back any time now.

Kenji was right on the money; he was getting good at timing Abby's returns. They had just redressed when she beeped her horn, signaling her return.

"Patricia! Where are you? I brought your mother back with me!" Abby called.

Hattie hugged Patricia but nodded at Kenji; they understood each other, and that was all she wanted.

"The place looks real nice," Hattie said as she looked around.

"Well, you helped make it this way," Patricia replied. "I'm glad you're here; I was hoping you would help me plan our wedding."

"You hear from Miss Abby's cousin?" Hattie asked.

"No, Mama, we haven't, and we've been waiting for a long time. We're going to get married anyway; Kenji has looked into it a lot over the past few months, and we don't think it's illegal," Patricia replied.

"You don't think?" Hattie asked. "And what if it is? Then what?"

"Mama, we're getting married in less than two weeks—"

"You got a minister who'll do it? Because Pastor Griffin say he not going to do it," Hattie interrupted.

"No, Mama, we're going to marry ourselves," Patricia said quietly.

"That ain't legal, and you be livin' in sin!" Hattie protested.

Patricia knew this was how Hattie would react, but she stuck to her guns. "Mama, please understand. We've been waiting for months now, and it's time to move on."

Hattie turned to Abby. "You agree with this?"

"I wish I could say no, but Hattie, you have to admit that they've done everything they possibly could to legally get married. We are all aware that Patricia won't be recognized as Kenji's legal wife, but what matters is that they will believe themselves to be married, and in the eyes of God, they will be."

There were several minutes of silence before Hattie spoke. "Your daddy can't find out about this."

Everyone let out a sigh of relief, but Patricia was saddened by the thought that her father wouldn't be at the wedding and that he wouldn't know about it. Kenji, sensing her mood, pulled her aside and hugged her; he knew how close Patricia had been to her father. There was really nothing he could say to make her feel any better.

By the end of the evening, the wedding was planned; it wasn't too different from the original plan—it wasn't hard to plan a wedding where there would be a total of five people in attendance. Abby planned to take Patricia and Hattie shopping in the morning and was going to order a nice roast for the wedding dinner. Hattie volunteered to make the cake, and Ralph offered to prepare the rest of the dinner.

JANUARY 30, 1941

Patricia was so excited that she didn't sleep the whole night. She packed her few belongings and got ready to move into the house with Kenji and Ralph. On more than one occasion, she thought that theirs was a strange household: an older white man, a black woman, and a Japanese all under one roof. Patricia touched the necklace that she hadn't removed since the day she told her mother about Kenji. In just four hours, she would be married. It still hurt her that her father wouldn't be there, but nothing could be done about it; she was just happy that her mother was coming.

Kenji was up early; he and Ralph had been up late talking about whatever came to mind.

"You're a brave man, you know it?" Ralph had asked

"No, I'm just a man who knows what he wants," Kenji replied. "And I am a man in love."

Ralph laughed. "I been there a time or two, but I never loved anyone the way you love Patty."

The wedding was just a little over four hours away. Kenji took a bath and washed his hair. He was going to ask Ralph to cut it, but he liked the feeling of Patricia's hands running through it when they made love. After the wedding, he would get Patricia to cut it for him. His clothes were washed, pressed, and hanging in the closet; the rings sat on the table beside the bed. Kenji sat on the bed he would soon be sharing with Patricia and closed his eyes. Two years it had taken them to get to this point, and it was finally here.

Hana sat in her room, trying to decide what she was going to do. Part of her wanted to go to the wedding, but part of her. . . . She had seen Kenji three times since the initial meeting; each time he asked her to reconsider, and each time she told him no. Before they parted ways the last time, he told her to be at the garden by one if she was going to come; Abby would be there waiting for her.

Hana stood up and went to her closet. She was going. If she was going to accept Patricia as Kenji's wife, then she needed to go to the wedding. She hadn't told Hiroshi about the wedding; it would only anger him, and he would start repeating the litany of offenses leveled at him by the United States, Kenji, and herself.

When she left the house, Hiroshi wasn't home, for which she was grateful; she didn't want to have to explain where she was going and the small envelope containing one hundred dollars that she was going to give as a gift to Kenji and Patricia.

She arrived at the garden early; Hana had always enjoyed the quiet of the mornings and usually took the time to think. This morning her thoughts were not so much on Kenji, but Hiroshi. His disillusionment was leading him to make unwise decisions. She had overheard him talking to Joben Saito a few nights before, and whatever they were planning sounded both illegal and dangerous. She wished she could talk to Kenji, but she wasn't going to ruin his wedding day with this. Maybe once they were settled. . . .

"Where you goin' so early?" John Middleton asked as Hattie dressed in her best dress.

"I goin' to Miss Abby's; she havin' a party that she need help with an—"

"Woman, stop lyin'," John said. "You never could lie. Where you goin'?" he asked again.

"Miss Abby's," Hattie replied and said no more.

John didn't say anything for several minutes, but when he did, his voice was filled with a quiet resignation. "She marryin' that Jap, ain't she?"

"John—"

"Don't ever mention her name; I don't have a daughter," John said and walked away.

At this, Hattie grew angry. "John Middleton! Don't you turn your back to me!"

John turned around and looked at her.

"That girl is your daughter no matter what she done! And really? What she do wrong exceptin' falling in love with someone we don't care for, and that be only because he not from here. I wish to God that he wasn't a Jap, but he is and she loves him. You should see the way he look at her; it be the same way you look at me when you thinks I ain't watchin'—except he makes sure she knows he's looking at her. Now the way I sees it, you have two choices: you keep sayin' you don't know her or you accept her as the woman she is."

John didn't respond but turned away and walked into the kitchen. Hattie sighed and finished getting ready for the wedding.

Abby was at the garden right at one, after taking Patricia to Kenji's house.

"Now you promised to stay out of sight; he's not supposed to see you before the wedding!" Abby had told her as she got out of the car.

"Not even for a second?" Patricia had asked.

"Not even for a second. Your dress is in Ralph's extra bedroom, and to make sure you and Kenji don't see each other, your mama is already there."

Hana got into the car, looked out the window, and then looked at Abby. "You have been good to my son; thank you."

Abby smiled and patted Hana's hand. "I love weddings!" she said in response.

Hattie helped Patricia fix her hair; as she did, she had to ask once more. "Baby, is you sure about this? It ain't too late to change your mind."

Part of the reason for Patricia's sleeplessness the night before was because she asked herself the same question: Did she really want to do this? No matter how she sliced it, the answer was always yes. She wanted to marry Kenji.

"I asked myself the same thing last night, and Mama? I love him, and I want to do this," Patricia replied with conviction.

Hattie nodded and helped Patricia into the cream-colored dress with matching shoes. Hattie reached into her bag and brought out a pearl necklace. "This belonged to my mama; she wore it on her weddin' day, and I wore it on mine. You get to wear it today, and if you have a daughter, she'll wear it at hers."

Patricia touched the necklace and then hugged Hattie. “Thank you, Mama!” she cried.

Hattie put the necklace around Patricia’s neck, on top of the one Kenji had given her for her birthday.

“You sure is a pretty bride!”

Chapter 8

Abby didn't respond at first. *How does Nick know about Hiroshi Takeda?* she wondered, but then remembered that he worked for the government

"I know who he is, and that's all; why do you ask?"

"What about his son Kenjiro? What do you know about him?" Nick asked.

"I know he's a good man. Nick, why are you asking about the Takedas?" Abby asked.

Nick ignored her question and asked one of his own. "Do you think Kenjiro Takeda could be a spy for Japan?"

Abby almost choked on the sip of tea she had just taken. "Are you crazy? Of course he isn't! He just got married today to a very lovely girl—"

"Yes, I know, Patricia Middleton," Nick interrupted.

"Then you know that he can't possibly be a spy," Abby replied sharply.

Nick was silent for several minutes. "I'm inclined to agree with you. We've been watching him, and he has no close ties to the Japanese community, although he's Japanese. That could be his cover, but as I said, I don't believe him to be a spy; he wouldn't jeopardize the girl like that. His father, on the other hand, is another story. His mother, we're not sure about yet."

"We? Who is this *we*?" Abby asked.

Nick gave Abby a long, hard look, as if trying to decide if he could trust her or not and then decided he could. "Abby, I didn't answer your letter because I couldn't; I was out of the country. I was in Europe."

"Europe? What were you doing there?" Abby asked, surprised.

"I can't tell you much, but we think Japan is planning something big, and we know they have spies planted here. Abby, I work for the United States government. I assess possible threats to our security."

"And you think Hiroshi Takeda is a threat to our security," Abby stated.

"He's been seen with another Japanese immigrant who has been trying to round up support for Japan," Nick said.

"And that makes him suspect? Maybe they're just friends and Hiroshi has nothing to do with whatever this other man has planned, if anything," Abby replied.

"That's always a possibility, but it doesn't look that way," Nick replied. "I need you to do something for me."

Abby gave Nick a wary look and waited for him to continue.

"I want you to find out what you can about Hiroshi Takeda and report back to me."

Abby stared at him. "Nick, how am I supposed to do that? I don't know the man."

"No, but you know his wife; I saw her today in the garden waiting for you to pick her up," Nick said.

"You can't be serious!" Abby said.

"I am very serious," Nick said. "Oh, and to answer the question in your letter, as far as I know, there is nothing that prevents people of two different nationalities and races to marry as long as one of the races isn't white. So will you help me out? It's a matter of national security."

"Can I think about it?" Abby asked.

"Yes, but not for long. I'll be back tomorrow evening."

After Nick left, Abby went to bed but couldn't sleep. Nick had just put her in a very awkward position

Hiroshi was sitting at the kitchen table when Hana returned. He was poring over the papers, reading about the war. Japan still hadn't made any moves on the United States, and Hiroshi wondered why; they had already invaded China, Manchuria, and Korea all before 1940, so why the hesitation to declare war on America?

He was disturbed by Hana coming in. He noticed she was dressed in her best kimono and wondered where she had been. He decided to ask and then wished he hadn't.

"Where have you been? I came home to no dinner," he said dryly.

Hana had debated on what to tell Hiroshi in case he asked and decided on the truth. Hiroshi would find out at some point anyway, and she wanted it over with. "I have been to the home of our son; he married the girl today," Hana said.

"So he has tainted our family name," Hiroshi said quietly.

Hana waited for the outburst that never came and was actually more nervous than she would have been if it had. She said nothing and waited. Instead of saying anything more, Hiroshi returned to reading the paper; he truly no longer cared. As far as he was concerned, Kenjiro and Hana were as dead to him as the son they had buried years ago.

Hana went to her room and shut the door. She would no longer cook or clean for Hiroshi; he no longer considered her his wife. She had known that for quite some time, but it didn't hit home until today—ironically, the day Kenji married the girl.

Hana chided herself; she had to stop thinking of Patricia as "the girl." She was Kenji's wife, and she had agreed to accept her as such. She had also made an unspoken agreement with Patricia's mother; they had to get along to help their children, and she wondered what that would entail.

Hana couldn't deny that while she still disagreed with Kenji's decision, she was proud of him. He had acted with the courage and integrity of men many years his senior; he had also acted with honor in that he was true to himself and Patricia.

Her mind went back to Hiroshi; what was he doing with Joben Saito? Hana had never liked the man and liked him even less when she found out he was trying to pass his daughter off as a virgin. She heard the whole sordid story from someone who had come on the same boat. She never told Hiroshi what she knew, as it would just make him angry, and he was angry enough as it was. She heard the front door open and then close. She knew where he was going: Joben Saito's house.

Joben waited patiently for Hiroshi to arrive. It had taken some time, but between the disillusionment due to the United State's treatment of the Japanese and the dishonor brought to his family by his son Kenjiro, it didn't take much to convince Hiroshi that he should help Japan. Hana's refusal to disown Kenji and her acceptance of the black girl had sealed the deal. Joben really did want Dai to marry into the family, but it was for more than one reason, and as it turned out, he really didn't need for Dai to marry Kenji in order to get part of what he wanted: the strength of the Takeda name behind his efforts.

"What is it, my friend?" Joben asked as he took in Hiroshi's sad expression.

"It is done; I now have no one. Kenjiro married the nigger today, and Hana is in support of him. Both he and Hana are dead to me," Hiroshi said.

Joben secretly rejoiced, although he outwardly commiserated with Hiroshi. "I am sorry, my friend. Come, sit, and I will pour you some tea."

Hiroshi followed Joben into his office and sat down. He looked at the flag of Japan hanging from the wall and wished he had never left.

Patricia woke up several times, almost expecting to hear Abby's voice warning them of her arrival. Kenji woke up every time she did, but for different reasons; he wanted to reassure himself that Patricia was here with him and that she wasn't just the dream he had been having every night for months. They made love several times that night, always drifting off to sleep for a short while afterward.

"Kenji?" Patricia called softly during one of the times they were awake.

"Yes, *Kirei*?"

"What do you think is going to happen? With the war, I mean," she clarified.

"I don't know," he replied, giving her a little squeeze. "But after we have our time alone, we need to sit down and plan what we're going to do."

Deep down, they both knew it was only a matter of time before the United States entered the war, whether Japan provoked them or not. By unspoken agreement, they spoke no more of the war until after their "honeymoon."

Abby lay awake, trying to decide what she should do about Nick's request. There were two good things that came out of Nick's visit: one, she now knew that Kenji and Patricia could legally marry if they could find someone to do it, and two, she now knew the government didn't think Kenji was a spy—at least not yet.

The issue was what to do about his father; if she told Kenji, he would go to his father and put himself back under suspicion, so no, she wouldn't tell him—but what about Hana? Abby didn't think she was a spy any more than she thought Kenji was—but Hiroshi? She didn't know about him. Given the way he had reacted to Patricia and Kenji's relationship, she wouldn't put it past him, but then, John Middleton had reacted almost as badly. Did that make him a spy?

It all came down to whom she owed her loyalty to, she decided. Kenji and Patricia absolutely, Hana not so much, but then she did come to support Kenji, and it was obvious that she loved her son. Hiroshi was another matter; she owed him nothing except for a good swift kick in the balls for what he tried to have done to Patricia. If she did what Nick wanted, it would put Hana in the middle, and Hana would probably go to Kenji for help. He would go to his father, in effect putting himself back under more suspicion. She had to talk to Hana before Hana talked to Kenji. The decision made, Abby finally went to sleep.

JANUARY 31, 1941

Patricia woke up first and was going to get up to make breakfast; Kenji opened his eyes and held her in place.

"Where are you going?" he asked.

"It's after eight; I was going to make breakfast," she replied.

"Stay in bed with me; we've waited for this for so long, and I'm not yet ready for it to end," Kenji said as he pulled her tightly against him.

"Aren't you hungry?" she asked.

"Yes, but I would much rather lay here with you in my arms than eat," Kenji replied with a kiss that went from her lips to her neck.

Patricia moaned and pressed against him, his erection trapped between them. Kenji's kisses moved from her neck to her shoulder and kept moving downward until he was at her breast. Patricia murmured his name as he kissed a nipple before taking it into his mouth to gently suckle on it before releasing it to tend to the other.

Kenji left her breasts and moved to her soft stomach, kissing it with kisses that to Patricia felt like the touches of a butterfly. When he got to her mound, she froze. *What is he doing?* she wondered.

Kenji felt her tense and stopped, remembering this was all new to her. "It's all right; just relax," he told her softly as he kissed her thigh.

Patricia took a deep breath and moaned when she felt a kiss on the inside of her thigh. Kenji was now kneeling between her legs, gently holding her outer lips apart. He took a moment to look at what belonged to him and no one else before taking her into his mouth and having his first taste of her This was something he had only done once before and had decided afterward that this pleasure should be reserved for one's wife.

Patricia cried out when she felt his tongue flick across her throbbing nub; she grabbed his pillow and covered her face to muffle the screams as she came for the first time in Kenji's mouth. As her orgasm waned, Kenji slid into her and thrust until he felt his orgasm approaching. Regretting that he had to do it, he pulled out and felt her waiting hands wrap around him, stroking him to completion.

Afterward, Patricia relaxed against him and closed her eyes. They had really done it! She repeated her name in her head several times. Patricia Ann Takeda—she liked the sound of it, she decided as she dozed off again.

Kenji listened to the sound of Patricia's even breathing for several minutes before closing his eyes again; for the moment all was well.

Abby got up after sleeping for only a few hours. She had made her decision, but she was still concerned about Kenji finding out about his father. She wondered if Nick could protect him in any way, although she suspected not, which meant it was up to her to keep Kenji out of the loop, and that meant she had to convince Hana not to go to him about Hiroshi. She wondered what Nick and the government were up to and how Hiroshi Takeda figured in to it.

She sat at the table thrumming her fingers, deep in thought as she waited for the water for her tea to boil. "This is going to get ugly," she murmured to herself as she stood to take the tea kettle from the stove. As the tea bag steeped, Abby decided to call her attorney to be sure that he had the letter she had given him almost a year ago. If anything happened to her for any reason, she had written a list of instructions that were to be followed to the letter. Another copy of the letter was in her jewelry box just in case, and another copy was at the bank; her attorney was aware of the locations of the additional letters.

Satisfied that all would be taken care of, Abby drank her tea. When she was finished, she decided to visit Hana Takeda and hope that her husband wasn't home. The thing was, she had to phrase things in such a way that Hana wouldn't be aware that her husband was being watched by the United States, and she had no idea how to do that. Today would be the best day to make her visit, because she was sure Kenji and Patricia wouldn't venture out for another couple of days at least, and definitely not today.

Hana didn't sleep well; even though she and Hiroshi were no longer together, she was frightened for him. He hadn't come home last night, and she knew he was still with Joben Saito. She couldn't say anything to him because he wouldn't listen and because he no longer considered her his wife, but still, maybe she should try. If she didn't, she would be making the same mistake she had made with Kenji, which had almost ended horribly for Patricia. She got out of bed, dressed for the day, and prepared to wait for Hiroshi to come home.

Hiroshi walked in an hour later, looked at Hana, and went to the bedroom. Hana steeled her nerves and followed him.

"Hiroshi, please listen to me," Hana said.

Hiroshi acted as if she hadn't spoken and began to undress.

"I don't know what it is that you and Joben are planning, but I know it's something illegal and dangerous. Please sever your ties with this man before it's too late."

Hiroshi continued to ignore her as she talked.

"I know he's partly responsible for the incident at the greenhouse; does that not tell you what kind of man he is? It's true that you have acted in hatred and dishonorably, but you can stop this and regain the respect of our son. Hiroshi, please!" Hana begged.

Hiroshi stopped what he was doing and looked at her. "There's no reason for me to listen to you. You and Kenjiro are dead to me; both of you have dishonored me and the Takeda name. You, along with Kenji, chose a nigger over this family, and don't deny it. When you chose Kenji, you left me. You chose to accept her as Kenji's wife instead of disowning him as you should have and siding with me, your husband.

"As to what kind of man Joben Saito is, he's a man who knows where the future lies, and it is with Japan. I curse the day I stepped foot in this country, and if I could leave it, I would. And I would leave you, Kenji, and his nigger here."

Hana was shocked by the vehemence in his voice, but she had to try once more. "Hiroshi, do you know why Joben was so anxious for his daughter to marry Kenji? It's because on the voyage here, she gave herself to a sailor on the ship. Did he tell you this? If he didn't, then that's proof he cannot be trusted. . . . "

"Even if what you say was true, I would still have chosen Dai Saito, spoiled or not, over the whore Kenji has dishonored himself and our family with," Hiroshi replied harshly.

"Hiroshi, you must see reason! We agreed to be loyal to this country! And what you're saying about Japan is treason; they will hang you, Joben, and anyone else who agrees with you." she said.

Her words fell on deaf ears as Hiroshi pushed her out of the room and closed the door in her face. *This time, if anything happens, I'll have a clear conscience*, Hana thought as she walked away.

Hana walked to the garden, wanting to be out of the house if Hiroshi came out of his room. She found a quiet corner and reflected on her life. Her marriage to Hiroshi had been an arranged one, but they had fallen in love and assumed the same would happen for Kenji and Aki. For the most part, their life was good: they were of the right social class and Kenji was a healthy boy who had an innate respect for others, no matter their station in life. Their youngest son was already dead by the time Kenji was two, and they had been unable to have another child.

Kenji was always curious, and they encouraged that desire to learn as well as encouraging him to think for himself. If they had wanted him to be the type of son who would blindly obey, then that is where they made their mistake. Never in a thousand years did she imagine she would be considered dead by her husband

and almost disowned by her son and that her son would marry a black girl. *Life is funny*, she thought as she enjoyed the warmth of the sun on her face.

Abby drove to the garden first, hoping to see Hana; she really didn't want to go to her house and run into her husband. Abby parked the car and walked around the garden. She found Hana sitting in her favorite spot.

"Good morning, Hana," Abby said.

"Good morning; please join me," Hana invited.

Abby sat down but didn't speak for several minutes, trying to decide how to begin. "It was a lovely wedding, wasn't it?" she asked.

"Yes, it was . . . different," Hana said with a small smile.

"I'm sure it was different from the weddings in your country," Abby agreed. "Hana, would you agree that we have to do everything possible to keep Kenji safe?"

Hana turned to look at Abby. "Is he in trouble because he married that . . . Patricia?" she asked anxiously.

"No, they're fine, and it turns out they can legally marry, but that's not the problem. Hana, Kenji was being watched and probably still is."

Hana frowned. "Watched? By whom?"

"Hana, I don't know how to go about saying this except to just say it: If there are any problems with your husband, don't tell Kenji. If you do, he'll go to him and come under suspicion again, and this time they may arrest him. They only let him go this time because he didn't interact with other Japanese, instead keeping to himself. Whether that was by choice or not, I don't know, but it took him off the list of people suspected of being spies."

"By people suspected of being spies, you mean Japanese, do you not?" Hana asked. "My . . . husband, is he on this list?"

Abby hesitated, not sure of how to answer the question without giving anything away. "I can't really say, but I think we should err on the side of caution and not tell Kenji if his father is into anything that could be construed as treason," she said, fully aware that she had just tipped Hana off.

"How do you know this?" Hana asked.

"I can't tell you that, but please keep Kenji out of whatever your husband is into, if anything, and please don't tell your husband where Kenji lives. Can you promise me that?" Abby asked.

After a brief hesitation, Hana nodded her agreement.

Nick watched the two women from across the street; he was certain Abby was telling the woman not to tell her son about his father, but he was relatively sure Abby was going to help him. If she refused, he would threaten to arrest Kenjiro Takeda under the suspicion of being a spy to gain her cooperation, and if that didn't work, he'd arrest the girl as well.

He would feel guilty if it came to that, but this was war, and there was no room for sentiment. Nick also knew Abby would never forgive him if he followed through on his threat, but once again, he reminded himself, this was war.

John refused to speak to Hattie, even when she spoke to him. He couldn't believe that Patricia had really married the Jap and that Hattie had gone to the wedding. He loved Patricia—that would never change—but she had done something that shouldn't be done even in the best of times. He didn't care about how the Jap looked at her or how much they loved each other; what mattered is what people were saying. Even his friends were whispering behind his back about his girl and the Jap, and it wasn't complimentary. He didn't defend her because he agreed with them. Did he miss her? He did, but that didn't change anything.

"You gonna disown me, too?" Hattie asked as she put a plate of eggs in front of him.

"You shouldna went," he said quietly. "You shoulda stopped her; she listens to you."

Hattie sat down. "John, we talkin' about the same girl? When she ever listened to me? And jus' so you know, I tried to talk her out of it, but her mind was made up. Now I'm sorry you mad, but it's done, and ain't nothin' to be done 'bout it," she said.

"You ain't there when theys be talking about it behind my back, and what can I say? Nothin'! Cos they right; she ain't had no business marryin' that Jap, and you had no business bein' there," John said, pushing the plate of eggs away angrily.

"That what this about? What they say?" Hattie asked. "I never thought I see the day when John Middleton be concerned 'bout what other peoples think. But you know what? I'm proud of her; she stood tall and did what she thought to be right, no matter what anyone else says, jus' like we taught her. I only sorry you didn't see how beautiful and happy she looked."

Hattie got up from the table, leaving John with his now-cold eggs and angry thoughts. No matter what Hattie said, Patricia shouldn't have married the Jap, and he had no plans of talking to her unless it was her telling him that she had left him.

Hattie peeked at John and recognized the set to his face, and knew that nothing she said had made a difference.

Patricia had finally persuaded Kenji to let her out of bed; she was hungry, and she needed the bathroom. While she was in the bathroom, Kenji made the bed and waited for her to come out. He twirled the ring on his finger, still not quite believing that he and Patricia had married. He wondered what his father said when his mother told him, but then decided maybe he didn't want to know.

A tap on the bedroom door pulled his mind from his thoughts; he opened the door to a tray with plates of food from their wedding dinner, including slices of cake and glasses of iced tea. Kenji stuck his head out of the door to thank Ralph, but he was already gone.

"Was that Ralph?" Patricia asked as she came out of the bathroom.

"Yes, he brought us food," Kenji said, setting the food on the table.

He kissed Patricia as he passed her on his way to the bathroom. When he came out, Patricia had the food set out and was waiting for him. Together they had their first meal alone as man and wife; afterward, they took the dishes to the kitchen and looked for Ralph to thank him. They found him in the front, sitting on the steps and daydreaming.

"Thank you for fixing us a tray; that was very nice of you," Patricia said, touching Ralph's arm.

"Come up for air, did ya?" Ralph teased.

Patricia blushed and wondered just how much Ralph had heard throughout the night. Kenji gave Ralph a slight smile but didn't respond. The three of them sat on the steps watching the traffic go by; Kenji put his arm around Patricia and wondered if he would be able to walk down the street with his arm around her, unmolested. If it happened, it wasn't going to be anytime soon, he thought as he pulled her tighter against him.

It didn't occur to any of them that they were doing anything out of the norm until a car drove by and the driver yelled out at them while throwing trash into Ralph's yard.

No one said anything as the car zoomed off. Kenji got up, stared at the car as it turned a corner, and picked up the trash before returning to the steps.

"Don't worry about it," Ralph said. "There's always going to be ignorant people." Ralph stood up and patted Patricia on the shoulder before going into the house, leaving the door open.

Kenji sat down next to Patricia and put his arm around her; they needed to talk about her safety. "Come, *Kirei*, we have things to discuss," Kenji said, standing up and holding out his hand.

Not yet! Patricia thought. She wanted more time before the real world intruded even more than it had just done, but she also knew Kenji was right. They had things to discuss, and procrastinating wasn't going to make it go away. She took Kenji's hand and followed him into the house and to their living room, where they sat on the couch.

"Patricia, I don't want you to go out alone. By now, the news of our marriage has probably spread, and it isn't safe for you to be out alone."

"But what about you?" she asked. "It's not safe for you either."

"No, but I can protect myself," Kenji replied. "Promise me you won't leave the house alone; either I or Ralph has to be with you."

Patricia balked, but in the end agreed.

"I just want to say that I don't like this and that I'm only agreeing because you won't stop until I do."

Kenji laughed. "You learn quickly, but there's more." He had really wanted to wait to talk about the next topic, but like his father, he had a sense of knowing when trouble was coming, and it was headed their way.

"*Kirei*, if anything happens to me—"

"Stop!" Patricia said. She didn't want to hear it. She didn't want to think about the possibility that something could happen.

Kenji put his arms around her and waited till she settled to continue. "If anything happens to me, go to Miss Abby's and stay there. Be sure to take the small bag that has the money in it and the money in the box under the bed."

"Nothing's going to happen; it can't!" Patricia exclaimed anxiously.

"I wish I could promise you that it won't, but I cannot make that promise. *Kirei*, these are only plans in case something happens. I need to know you'll be safe," Kenji said, kissing her.

Abby waited for Nick to come to the house; she would do as he asked now that she had talked to Hana. She knew she had given Hana a not-so-subtle warning about her husband, but it couldn't be helped. If Nick was angry about it, then so be it.

She thought about how her life had changed over the past year; it had gone from quiet and boring to being involved in the romance of Patricia and Kenji to being involved in the government.

As she waited, she put on the kettle for tea. Tomorrow she would go see Kenji and Patricia and tell them they could legally marry; she couldn't wait to see the look of excitement on their faces.

Nick arrived a short while later and declined the offer of tea.

"What have you decided?" he asked, getting straight to the point.

"I've decided to help you—as much as I can, at any rate," Abby replied as she sipped at her tea.

"Good; I knew I could count on you," Nick replied. "So tell me, what did you and Hana Takeda talk about this morning?" he asked.

Abby stared at him. He had followed her? The very idea of it made her angry, but she answered the question. "We talked about the wedding and Kenji," Abby said. "And before you ask, I told her that Kenji was being watched by the government and for the moment he is safe. I also told her not to tell Kenji anything about what his father might be into because he might go to him and go back on your list of suspected spies. Did I tip her off about her husband? Probably, and if you're angry about it, too bad!"

Nick didn't say anything for several minutes, giving Abby a chance to cool down. "I expected as much," he said. "I would have been surprised had you done differently."

"What?" Abby asked, surprised.

"Abby, you forget how well I know you. You always were for the underdog, and in this case, the underdogs are Kenjiro Takeda and Patricia Middleton, whom you should know that I was very willing to use to gain your compliance if you refused to help me," Nick replied with a small smile.

Abby was flabbergasted; this wasn't the Nick she knew and had been friends with for more than fifteen years. This Nick was cold and calculating, and he was willing to put their friendship on the line, which told her something: all hell was going to break loose, and soon. She found herself hoping that Kenji and Patricia had made plans just in case; knowing Kenji, she was sure they had.

"Just what were you going to do to ensure my cooperation?" Abby asked.

"Does it matter?" Nick asked.

"It does; what were you going to do?" Abby repeated.

"I was prepared to have Kenjiro Takeda arrested under the suspicion of being a spy for Japan," Nick replied, not seeing the point in telling her he would have used Patricia as well if he had to.

"Even though you knew it wasn't true?" Abby asked, appalled.

"Yes," Nick replied. "I told you it was a matter of national security, but seeing as you have agreed to help me voluntarily, Kenjiro Takeda is safe for now—unless he does something to arouse our suspicions.

"What did Hana Takeda have to say?"

"Not much, only that she agreed that we need to keep Kenji out of this," Abby replied softly.

"How did she react to the suspicions about her husband?" Nick asked.

"You were there! What do you think?" Abby snapped angrily.

Nick didn't respond to her anger; it was justified, and he had put her in a very difficult position.

It was a stroke of luck that she had written to him. At the time, he didn't know why she was asking the question about interracial marriage, but it got him thinking. He had sent someone to watch her and could hardly believe it when he got the reports about her involvement with Kenjiro Takeda and the girl, whom he found out that Abby was quite fond of.

And then there was Joben Saito's involvement with Hiroshi Takeda on the attempt to harm the girl. Abby was the perfect way to get information on Hiroshi Takeda. Nick believed that initially Hiroshi Takeda wasn't aware of Joben Saito's loyalties, but even after he found out, he was constantly seen with the man and others with the same sentiment.

They knew Joben Saito was specifically sent here to spy and gather support for Japan wherever he could. There was also the issue of Saito's daughter and her involvement, but to date, she was rarely seen outside of the house, so there was no easy way of getting to her. So how much she knew or how actively involved she was, they didn't know.

"Abby, I'm sorry. I didn't want to involve you, but I had no choice."

"Get out, Nick," Abby said softly and walked away.

Nick sat for another moment before standing to leave. He had just lost his dearest friend, but it couldn't be helped. The security of the country was more important than one friendship.

"Wait," Abby said as Nick walked away. "I want something from you," she said coldly.

Nick waited for her demands.

"I want your word that you will do everything possible to keep Kenjiro and Patricia Takeda safe and out of this. If anything is going to happen to the Japanese here, I want to know before it happens."

Nick nodded. It was the least he could do.

Hana sat on her bed, wondering what to do. Abby, in so many words, had warned her that Hiroshi was being watched, and if he was being watched, so was Joben. Should she try talking to Hiroshi again? Maybe if he stopped now, he wouldn't be arrested.

Hiroshi wasn't home when she got there, and she assumed that he was with Joben, where he had been spending more and more time—even sleeping there.

Hana decided she would try to talk to Hiroshi one last time; after that, there was nothing more she could do. It wasn't that she didn't love her husband, but she couldn't support him in the things that mattered to him, namely the hatred he now carried for the United States and his role in whatever he and Joben were planning.

Not knowing what else to do, Hana settled down to wait for Hiroshi to come home.

Joben poured Hiroshi another glass of saké, encouraging him to drink it. They had just finished the preliminary plans for reaching out to other Japanese who felt as they did. They already had a sizable group of fifteen, and from what they could tell, there were many more, but until Japan made a decisive move against the United States, they remained hidden, keeping their views to themselves.

As much as he hated to admit it, Hiroshi missed Hana and even Kenji to some degree, but that meant nothing in the whole scheme of things. Just as they wouldn't change their views, he wasn't going to change his, and even if he wanted to change, he suspected it was much too late for that. Of everything that had happened, the thing Hiroshi regretted the most was the loss of Hana. Even now, if she were to come to him and beg his forgiveness, he would grant it to her on the condition that she no longer see Kenji and that she renounce the nigger he had married. For Kenjiro, there would never be forgiveness, even if he crawled on his belly, kissed his boots, and committed *hari kari*. Hiroshi was somewhat surprised at what little emotion he felt at the thought of Kenji's death.

Hiroshi walked home only slightly inebriated to find Hana sitting in the living room.

"Hiroshi, we must talk," Hana said as he walked past her, barely looking at her.

He stopped to look at her, saw her as the young, shy bride of so many years ago, and wished they could go back to that time. "Unless it is to ask my forgiveness and to renounce him and that nigger, we have nothing to discuss," he said.

Hana ignored the comments and continued speaking. "Hiroshi, you and Joben are being watched by the United States government. You must stop seeing him!"

"How do you know this? Are you working with them?" he asked accusingly.

"Of course not, but—" Hana stopped herself; it was no use. Hiroshi had chosen, and she could only hope his choices didn't harm Kenji or her.

FEBRUARY 10, 1941

Abby checked the roast and potatoes in the oven. Patricia, Kenji, and Ralph were coming over for dinner. She had invited Hattie, who couldn't get away. Patricia's father had become more unreasonable instead of better in accepting Patricia's marriage to Kenji. Hattie saw Patricia every week, but only when John was at work, and only for an hour or so. Abby would pick her up, and they would spend an hour or so visiting before Abby took her back home. She had invited Hana, too, but she had declined, not wanting to feed into Hiroshi's accusations that she was working for the government.

Abby glanced at the television, which had just been delivered that morning. She had actually seen one demonstrated at the 1939 World Fair but opted not to buy one, figuring it was another fad, but time had proved her wrong. The deliveryman turned it on just to make sure it worked and then turned it off. The television was in a large case with a ten-inch screen and had cost her almost four hundred dollars, but she justified it by saying that she really was frugal with her money and that it was an investment.

She couldn't wait to see the look on their faces when they saw the television; she didn't know what channels or programs were available, but they'd find out.

Nick was waiting by her car when she went out; she hadn't been able to find out much from Hana—only that Hiroshi still met with Joben Saito, but never at the house. Hana didn't know where they met, but would have been surprised if it was at Joben's home, although Hiroshi spent a lot of time there.

"What do you want, Nick?" Abby asked.

"Just checking in to see if you heard anything new," he said, leaning against her car.

"No, I haven't heard anything; now move," Abby said as she climbed into the car.

Nick watched her as she backed away and drove off. He really hated his job and couldn't wait to go back to being a lawyer.

Kenji, Patricia, and Ralph were waiting when she arrived. Patricia was holding a warm apple pie she and Ralph had made together, combining their two recipes. Apparently, Abby and Kenji were supposed to be the guinea pigs for this culinary experiment.

Nick was gone by the time Abby got back with her dinner guests, much to her relief. She made them wait in the kitchen, as she made sure the television was completely covered before calling them into the living room.

"All right, sit down and close your eyes!" Abby said excitedly. When she was sure their eyes were closed, she took the sheet off the television. "You can open them now!" she said.

All three of them were speechless, but it was Ralph who recovered first. "Abby, is that a television?" he asked.

"It is, and it just came today. What do you think?" she asked.

"It's beautiful!" Patricia said, awed. Her parents would never be able to afford anything like that. For that matter, neither would she and Kenji.

"I thought I would invest in one so when and if they start broadcasting the war, we could watch," Abby said.

Dinner was delicious, and the pie was a definite success, although Kenji wasn't exactly impartial; he loved Patricia's cooking, and he was gaining an appreciation for American food. He found that his slacks were getting a little snug around his waist, and he set up a small area in the back to begin his workouts again. It wasn't long before his slacks weren't tight around his waist and his stomach was hard and flat. Patricia often sat outside and read while he worked out, and Kenji taught her a few basic defensive moves. He made it seem like a game, but he really wanted her to be able to defend herself, at least enough to get away from an assailant.

After dinner, they sat around the television set as Abby switched it on and turned the channel knob. All of them jumped when they heard just a few words and then nothing but static.

Kenji was awed by the advances in technology and wondered what advances had been made in the field of medicine. He still thought about medical school, but the money just wasn't there, and he wasn't about to touch the money they had saved, especially since Patricia would need it if anything happened. He consoled himself with the fact that he had the one thing that he needed sitting next to him and that he was still young at twenty-two.

Patricia looked over at Kenji and wondered what he was thinking about; he caught her looking at him and smiled. He wouldn't trade his life with her for anything, even if he was offered a full scholarship at the most prestigious medical school in the country. He put his arm around her and gave her a squeeze. It was going to work out; he just had to have faith.

Hattie sat staring at John; she was getting to the end of her rope. She missed Patricia and had wanted to go to Abby's for dinner, but John wouldn't allow her to go. For the most part, she did as he said, but that was coming to an end, as far as her seeing Patricia was concerned.

"John, you wrong to keep a mama from her child," she said.

"We ain't got no child," he replied, not looking at her.

"Maybe you don't, but I does, and her name is Patricia Ann Takeda—"

"Hattie—" John said, his voice filled with warning, which Hattie ignored.

"Patricia Ann Takeda is our girl, and I won't let you stop me from seeing her anymore. You cans huffs and puffs all you want, but I am goin' to see our daughter. You can come with me if you want; she'll be glad to see you," Hattie added.

"Go see her if you has to, but don't tell me nothin' about it," John said and walked out, slamming the door behind him.

"Why you gots to be so stubborn?" Hattie murmured under her breath and then decided that she wouldn't bring up the subject of Patricia again unless he did. The important thing at the moment was that he would no longer stop her from seeing Patricia.

The rest of February passed quietly, with Kenji and Patricia celebrating Valentine's Day in bed. Kenji still had to constantly remind himself not to get too carried away when they made love. There had been two or three times when he didn't pull out in time and they worried about a possible pregnancy and breathed a sigh of relief when Patricia's period came. He looked forward to the time when he could release inside of her without the worry of whether she would get pregnant or not. The times that he had released inside of her were extremely pleasurable, but the anxiety of a possible pregnancy overrode that pleasure. He wondered if there was some kind of birth control available; something natural would even be better. They would still have to be careful, but maybe if they used something, the accidental releases wouldn't be as stressful. He would ask his mother the next time he saw her, and he would do some research on his own.

The end of February came and went with Kenji wondering what was happening with Japan. He wasn't the only one.

Hiroshi scanned the papers and listened to the radio non-stop; he no longer acknowledged Hana when he saw her, instead turning away to discourage any conversation. It was the end of February, and Japan, as far as he was concerned, was just sitting on its ass. *What is the holdup?* he wondered as he tossed the paper across the table. Germany and Italy had attacked Yugoslavia, Greece, and the Island of Crete, so where was Japan in all of this?

Joben urged patience. "What is it that the Americans say? 'Good things come to those who wait.' Patience, Hiroshi; the emperor knows what he is doing."

Hiroshi picked up the paper and reread it; there were stories of supposed concentration camps where people of Jewish origin were sent to be used as slave labor or killed. He didn't believe it; it was just propaganda meant to elicit sympathy since some countries, the United States included, were severely limiting the immigration of Jews. Hiroshi laughed; so much for welcoming everyone with open arms. Just another lie as far as he was concerned, but to be honest, he hoped the stories *were* true. He wished the blacks could be included or at the very least sent back to where they came from. If not that, they needed to be made into what they had once been: slaves.

Hiroshi had developed a hatred for all things American, only dressing as an American so he wasn't conspicuous; he only used his native tongue when he was with like-minded people, and only in private. He no longer spoke Japanese with Hana, if he even spoke to her at all; he no longer trusted her.

Tonight he was meeting with Joben, who had managed to secure a shortwave radio, and they were going to talk to a contact in Japan. When Hiroshi asked Joben where the radio had come from, Joben became secretive, bringing back Hana's words about his honesty. Still, Hiroshi went, excited to hear from his homeland, and disregarded any misgivings he had about Joben.

Joben greeted Hiroshi at the door and led him to his office, where four other men waited. Joben quickly made introductions and sat at his desk. Several minutes later, a voice in their native tongue filled the room. Hiroshi blinked back tears at the sound of it and once again questioned why he had ever left. He had come to the conclusion that his way of thinking really wasn't that different than that of the man he had once called a lunatic.

The voice on the radio didn't say much but said enough that Hiroshi knew soon Japan would make a move on the United States. He listened as Joben gave the information they had managed to gather about any military bases and locations. Joben also informed the voice that the Japanese, both American-born and immigrants, were being watched. After urging caution, the voice was gone.

Two things occurred to Hiroshi: one, he was now officially a traitor to the country he had sworn allegiance to, and two, if they were caught, they were dead. There was a third thing, he realized: He was now trapped. Even if he wanted out, he wouldn't be able to leave. Joben would kill him first. *It's a good thing he don't want to leave*, he thought to himself.

JUNE 1941

The world watched, shocked, as Germany invaded Russia, one of its Allies. The Russians were taken by surprise, as they had signed a treaty with Germany in 1939, but apparently that agreement meant nothing to Hitler. Three million soldiers and 3,500 tanks were sent into Russia, prompting Stalin to sign a mutual assistance treaty with Britain. The United States offered the same lend-lease agreement to Russia that it did to Britain; the Americans were slowly being pulled into the war.

Hiroshi watched the events unfold with interest. Japan was already at war with China and had been since 1937. *When and where will they attack the Americans?* Hiroshi wondered as he poured over the newspaper and listened to the radio with growing excitement. Japan's time to take its place in the world was coming, and he was a part of it.

Hana watched Hiroshi with tears in her eyes; the man that she knew would never have delighted in war or the prospect of it. She slipped out of the house and headed toward the garden, where she would sit for several hours and think. She had come to trust and like Abby and considered her to be the only true friend she had. Like Kenji, she stayed away from other Japanese to protect herself and him as well, but it was a lonely existence. To some degree, she knew Abby was using her to obtain information about Hiroshi, but there really was no information to give.

Hiroshi had become even more secretive about his comings and goings, and Hana didn't dare ask him about it. She had the sense that Hiroshi was capable of murder if he felt threatened, and she had no wish to die at his hands.

She thought about walking to Kenji's home but decided against it; it would be dark before she made it back to her own home, and she didn't want to be caught out after dark. Other than the usual racial epithets and stereotypical comments, she was left alone, but why chance it?

As she sat in the garden, she thought about Patricia. She was a strong woman, and in spite of the fact that Patricia was black, Hana could no longer deny that Kenji had chosen well. That Patricia loved Kenji was obvious, and in spite of herself, Hana liked her and her mother, even though the only thing they had in common was that they loved their children. Mothers, Hana realized, were the same. No matter what part of the world they lived in or their social status, their children came before anything else. She wished fathers felt the same way.

Patricia wanted to bake a cake, but realized they were almost out of eggs. Kenji was in the back with Ralph, working on the steps, and she hated to disturb them just for eggs. The store wasn't far, just a few blocks, and she thought she could be there and back before they missed her. Her gut told her not to go, but her stubborn streak took over.

She peeked out of the window and saw that both men were engrossed in what they were doing. She took another minute to look at Kenji working with his shirt off. *He's handsome even though he's covered in sweat,* she thought as she left the window. Patricia went to the money jar, took out some money, and slipped out the front door.

The trip to the store was for the most part uneventful; she purchased the eggs and decided to buy a loaf of bread and headed home. She was three blocks away from home when the trouble started.

"Hey, Mikey!" a voice called out. "Ain't that the nigger that lives with that Jap?"

There was a moment of silence as Mikey looked at her. "Kinda looks like her, don't it? But then, they all kinda look alike," he replied.

Patricia kept walking, pretending not to hear what was being said. Soon there was a young man about her age on either side of her.

"It *is* her!" Mikey said, looking at her.

"You like Jap cock?" the other boy, named Adam, asked her.

"She must; she married to one, ain't she?" Mikey asked.

"I'll bet she likes white cock, too; my dad says they all do," Adam said as he felt Patricia's behind.

Patricia bit her lip and kept walking. The one named Mikey stopped her by standing in front of her.

"We was talking to you, nigger; do you like white cock?" he asked.

Adam stood behind her, reached around, and knocked the sack containing the eggs and bread out of her hands while Mikey reached for her breasts. Patricia kicked behind her and connected with Adam's shin, making him release her. She tried to push Mikey out of the way. When he held her against him, she kneed him and took off running, tears blinding her. She wasn't watching where she was going and fell down. When she got up, she took a quick look behind her and saw that the men were gaining on her. She began to run and ran straight into Kenji, who was being followed by Ralph, who was carrying a baseball bat.

The men stopped their pursuit when they saw Kenji and Ralph, instead calling insults from where they were before walking away.

Mindless of who was watching, Kenji held Patricia until she caught her breath and then led her home while Ralph walked behind them, keeping watch.

Patricia knew that Kenji was angry with her, but knew that he would care for her before letting her know just how angry he was. She would hear from Ralph later, and he wouldn't be as gentle with her as Kenji was going to be.

Kenji took her to the bedroom, sat her on the bed, and took off her shoes without saying a word. When her shoes were off, he eased her back onto the bed and looked at the abrasions on her knees. He didn't speak as he went into the bathroom and came back with cool washcloths and washed her knees; it stung, but Patricia didn't say anything. After he finished, Kenji got into bed with her and held her tightly against him.

Patricia started to shake when she realized just how lucky she had been. People had watched as the two men assaulted her and had done nothing. They were going to let those men rape her, she realized.

Kenji held her as she cried. He wouldn't have to say anything to her; she now understood the danger. That she had experienced it angered him; that she couldn't walk to the store unmolested angered him. He took a deep breath to calm himself and rubbed Patricia's back until she calmed.

"I'm sorry; I wanted to make a cake, and we were almost out of eggs. I shouldn't have gone," she said softly when she could talk.

"No, you shouldn't have, but you shouldn't have been treated like that either," Kenji said and then fell silent.

As she suspected, Ralph wasn't gentle with her at all.

"Patty, what in the hell were you thinking?" he asked.

When she told him about the cake, he exploded.

"A damned cake? You put yourself in danger for a god-damned cake? Patty Takeda, if you were my woman, I'd whip your ass till you couldn't sit!"

"Ralph," Kenji said softly but with authority after they got back to the house, "she understands."

"Just don't do it again; my heart can't take so much excitement," Ralph said and walked away muttering about "that damned cake."

Patricia stood looking after him with tears in her eyes; in her stubbornness, she had jeopardized all of them.

"*Kirei*, come here," Kenji said gently.

When Patricia reached him, he hugged her tightly and kissed her head.

"We were both very frightened for you. That's why he's so angry. He cares for you as though you were a daughter, but he is right. Please don't do that again."

After that day, she never went out alone; either Kenji or Ralph went with her. Even though they were called names, no one touched them.

Abby watched for the mail with excitement; she was expecting two packages. One was for Patricia's birthday, and the other was for Kenji's birthday, although it wasn't until the fall. She decided to order his early just in case something happened that disrupted the mail.

For Patricia, she had ordered a reproduction of the classics, and for Kenji, she had ordered the latest editions of the medical journals she had given him for his last birthday, as well as some others she thought he would like.

Her good mood was spoiled by Nick's arrival. He had been showing up at her house unannounced several times a week, asking the same question: "Have you learned anything?"

"No, I told you Hana hardly ever sees her husband, and he doesn't talk to her if she does," Abby said hotly.

"Does she at least know where he goes?" Nick asked.

"She thinks he spends most of his time at Joben Saito's house, and that's all she knows. Jesus, Nick! Can you not show up so often?" Abby asked.

"All right, Abby, but I need more information than you're giving me."

"Here's a question for you," Abby said. "If you're so damned sure Hiroshi Takeda and Joben Saito are spies, why don't you just arrest them?"

Nick ignored the question and walked away, passing the mailman on the way to his car. There had to be a way to get more information that wouldn't endanger Abby or Hana, although Hana wasn't his main priority. He had someone watching Joben

Saito's home; that was how he knew that Abby's information was accurate.

The key, he believed, was Dai Saito, but her father watched her like a hawk. Intel from Europe supported the thought that Japan was going to declare war on the United States, but the actual plans were still unclear. Whether Joben Saito knew anything also wasn't clear, but it was doubtful; he was too low on the totem pole. But he had to be reporting to someone, and that's whom they wanted. The thought was that Dai Saito might be able to help.

JULY 8, 1941

Abby had another surprise for Kenji and Patricia. She had found a minister who would marry them if they got a license, and she was working on that—or rather, Nick was. He was due any moment with the license, and the minister was coming for dinner.

Abby hummed as she put the finishing touches on the cake while Hattie set the table. Hattie had been beside herself with happiness that Patricia and Kenji would no longer be "living in sin." The only other person who knew was Ralph, and Abby knew he could keep his mouth shut. Abby invited Hana and was going to pick her up at the garden at three; she hadn't talked with her to let her know about the impromptu wedding.

Nick tapped on the door around one, holding the marriage license. Abby didn't know how he pulled it off, nor did she care, but she gratefully accepted the envelope.

"Will Hana Takeda be here?" he asked as she took the envelope.

Abby now understood why he had so easily agreed to help her. Quid pro quo.

"Yes, she'll be here," she said.

"I've always enjoyed weddings," Nick said with a smile that didn't quite reach his eyes.

Abby sighed before speaking. “Be sure to bring a gift for the newlyweds; money is always nice.”

Nick smiled again; this time the smile reached his eyes.

“Hey, Patty, why don’t you wear that dress you wore the day you and Kenji got married?” Ralph said, hoping he wasn’t overdoing it.

He bugged her so much about it that Patricia finally gave in but wondered what the big deal was. Ralph had never cared about what she wore before. When she asked him about it, he mumbled something about a woman looking nice for her birthday and walked away.

Kenji also wondered about Ralph’s behavior because he had pressed Kenji’s shirt and slacks so well that they looked professionally done. When Kenji asked him about it, he made a comment similar to the one he made to Patricia. “A man should look nice for his woman’s birthday.”

Ralph himself was dressed in his best clothes, which surprised Kenji and Patricia even more because he hated dressing up.

Kenji took Patricia aside to give her the gift from his mother. It wasn’t much, but he knew she would like it. He had to ask his mother about it, but she found it, and he was pleasantly surprised when she agreed to give it. It was a tea set from Japan; it was the set his grandmother had given to his mother when she married his father, and it was to be passed on to the woman he married. He hoped Patricia wouldn’t mind that it was supposed to go to Aki and hoped she understood that his mother giving it to her meant something: she had accepted her.

He sat her on the couch and had her close her eyes as he went to get the box he had hidden on the top shelf of their closet. He hoped this gift would mean as much to Patricia as it did to him. She sat on the couch with her eyes closed, trying not to peek.

“You can open your eyes now,” he said as he sat the box on the couch next to her.

Patricia opened her eyes and looked at the box. "Is that for me?"

"It's a gift from my mother; my grandmother gave it to her when she married my father, and now she is giving it to you," Kenji said softly.

Patricia opened the box and looked inside. Tears sprang to her eyes when she saw the tea set; she understood what it meant. Kenji's mother had finally accepted her as Kenji's wife and her daughter; she didn't know why the change, and it didn't matter.

"It's beautiful! How do I thank her?" Patricia asked.

"When she comes to our home, serve her tea in it; she will understand," Kenji said, wiping away a tear from Patricia's face.

Patricia kissed him and wished they weren't going out so they could spend her birthday in bed, but they would have tonight. "I love you," Patricia murmured against his lips.

"Hey, you two! Abby's here!" Ralph called.

"I love you, too, *Kirei*," Kenji replied as he took her hand and led her to the door.

Hana was already in the car and said happy birthday to Patricia in Japanese. "*Tanjoubi omedetou, Patricia*."

"Thank you, and thank you for the beautiful tea set," Patricia replied.

Hana, smiled, nodded, and said no more.

Hattie was finishing making dinner while Nick and the minister talked. Abby beeped her horn, signaling her arrival as she pulled into the garage. The smell of roasting chicken wafted outside, making Patricia's stomach rumble.

She and Kenji were both surprised by the extra guests, but said nothing. Abby made the introductions and then handed Patricia the envelope containing the marriage license.

"Happy birthday!" she exclaimed as Patricia read the license.

"Is this real?" she asked, as she handed the paper to Kenji with shaking hands.

"It's for real," Abby said happily. "We have my friend Nick to thank for it; he cut through a lot of red tape for us, and there's more. We have a minister here to marry you!"

Both Patricia and Kenji were speechless; while they considered themselves married, legally they weren't recognized as such. Patricia could now legally change her last name.

She looked over at Ralph, who gave her a grin. "You knew," she said.

"Yep," he said and then added, "What are we waitin' for?"

Patricia hugged her mother, then Abby, and finally Hana, who was at first startled and then returned the hug. She walked over to Nick, looked up at him, and whispered a soft, heartfelt thank you to which he whispered, "You're welcome."

Everyone stood while, for the second time that year, Kenji and Patricia exchanged vows. Then they signed the marriage certificate. Afterward, they all sat down for the combination wedding and birthday dinner. What surprised Abby was that Nick didn't approach Hana, and she wondered why. Instead, he just watched her without speaking to her; what was he up to?

Hiroshi, Joben, and three other men huddled around the shortwave radio listening to news from Japan. The feeling of excitement filled the small office as they listened to the progress of the war. All of them ignored Dai as she dutifully served them tea. Dai was very good at appearing to be aloof, but she heard every word and stored it away for possible future use.

She was her father's daughter and had learned from him that everything was important and never to forget anything. She knew what would happen if her father was caught, and she simply didn't care. He didn't care about her, and she had no desire to be sent back to Japan and would do whatever was necessary to keep that from happening. Her only problem was getting away from her father long enough to figure out to whom she should take her information. She was playing a dangerous game, and if caught, her father would kill her without remorse. She had to bide her time and hope she wouldn't be too late.

The rest of the summer and fall passed quietly for Kenji and Patricia, with Kenji's twenty-third birthday celebrated at Abby's house in October. Hattie and Hana were both there, surprising everyone by talking together quietly and occasionally laughing. Hattie surprised everyone once again when she hugged Kenji and gave him a kiss on the cheek as she wished him a blessed birthday.

Nick was there as well, but while he chatted with Kenji, he didn't approach Hana other than to say hello. Abby wondered if he had decided that Hana wasn't a spy, but it still didn't make sense that he didn't talk to her more than he did.

Thanksgiving was held at Kenji and Patricia's house, with Ralph insisting that he prepare the meal. Hana had arrived early, walking from her house to Kenji's. There were very few people out since it was a holiday, so she was left in peace as she walked. Hiroshi wasn't home when she left, for which she was glad; she had no desire to see him or to feel his angry glare as she left.

Both Patricia and Kenji were surprised to see her at their door so early, but welcomed her in. While Kenji visited with his mother, Patricia took out the tea set she had yet to use and made tea. She had no idea if there was some protocol or ritual she was supposed to follow but decided it wouldn't matter if there was.

She took a deep breath and carried the tray with the tea set on it to the living room.

"I made tea," she said softly when Kenji and Hana looked up at her.

She saw Kenji's smile of approval and then Hana's.

She set the tray on the coffee table, poured a cup of tea, and handed it to Hana.

"You honor me, Patricia," Hana said and bowed her head.

Hana's acceptance of her was complete.

Kenji watched as Patricia served their mother with pride; she had not just honored Hana; she had honored him as well.

Thanksgiving dinner was one of the happiest days of Kenji's life; he had his mother and his Patricia in his life. He gave no more thought to his father and hadn't in some time. For that day, there was no talk of war or anything morbid or sad. It was a day of happiness and peace.

DECEMBER 6, 1941

Once again, Hiroshi wondered about Hitler's sanity. The man wasn't listening to his generals, stories of concentration camps ran rampant, and part of the German forces still had Leningrad under siege and had its sight on Moscow—that was in October. Now it was December, and the Russians were having the coldest winter on record, with the temperatures dropping to twelve degrees Celsius. "What madness!" Hiroshi muttered. "Why doesn't he leave Russia while he still can?" He had already called off the attack on Moscow, so why stay?

On the positive side, the Japanese were occupying Saigon, Vietnam, but what were they going to do about the Americans? Their contact in Japan assured them that soon, the United States would be on its knees, but when? They had been hearing that for months, and still nothing!

He went to bed that night not speaking to Hana. As a matter of fact, he didn't even know if she was in the house or at the greenhouse, and he didn't care.

Joben Saito eyed his daughter with growing suspicion. She was acting differently but trying not to show it. He also noticed her hovering longer than she needed to when he sent and received broadcasts from Japan. The only thing that saved her life was that she hadn't been out of the sight of someone at all times. He wondered what it was she thought she knew and whom she was going to take it to. He had actually considered letting her "sneak out" to see where she went but decided it was much too risky; she might actually know something. He was now convinced that she did; he could tell by the way she paced restlessly, and her frequent offers of saké validated what he knew. She was trying to get out, but the question remained: where was she going to go?

Much to Dai's frustration, Joben drank only tea. She knew it was over by the way he looked at her; he knew what she was up to. She finally gave up and went to her room and closed the door; whatever happened now, she was going to be tied to her father. That she tried to help wouldn't matter; where was the proof? She only had her word, and they wouldn't believe her—except that she did have information. It would help, she hoped.

Abby had done all she could do and hoped she never saw Nick again and made a point of telling him so.

"You have used me as your information gatherer for the last time; don't come back."

"Abby, listen to me. I didn't want to use you, but I had to. We think Japan is going to attack us. We needed every bit of information we could get."

Abby stared at him, incredulous. "You can't be serious!" she said.

"I'm serious," Nick said. "The problem is that we don't know when or where."

"And you think Hiroshi Takeda is apart of that?"

"Maybe not directly, but we do know he has been spying here and reporting to Joben Saito."

"What about Hana? Do you believe she's involved?" Abby asked anxiously.

"Personally, no, but if they arrest Hiroshi and she's there, she'll be arrested, too, and there won't be anything I can do to help her. The same goes for her son and his wife. Abby, I'm sorry."

Abby wasn't listening; she glanced at the clock. It was early yet, barely eight. Hana wouldn't be at the garden; it was too late for that. She would be at home. She had to be warned; she was owed that much. And then there was Patricia and Kenji.

"Nick, I forgive you, but I have to go," Abby said, standing up and looking for her purse.

"Where are you going?" Nick asked.

"I have to warn Hana not to be at home for the next several days," she replied as she headed toward the door, leading Nick by the hand.

Nick followed her out and tried to talk sense to her. "You don't know when or—"

"Nick, my gut is telling me I have to warn her; now get out of my way!" she said as she rushed past him.

Hana lay on her bed wondering what was going to become of her, Kenji, and now Patricia. She had a sick feeling in her stomach; it was a feeling she hadn't had since before their youngest child died. Something horrible was going to happen, but she didn't know what. She could only hope that it didn't involve Kenji and Patricia; that it would involve Hiroshi, she was sure.

"Hiroshi, what have you done?" she whispered into the darkness.

She had just closed her eyes when there was a banging on the door. Startled, she got up and put on a house robe before going to the door.

Hiroshi came out of his room at the same time, but didn't speak as he walked with Hana to the door. *Some habits die hard*, he realized as they reached the door.

As soon as Hana opened the door, several men pushed their way in.

"Hiroshi Takeda, Hana Takeda, you are both under arrest for treason against the Unites States of America."

Hana was stunned. Treason? She had done nothing! She looked at Hiroshi, who gave her a blank stare back. She then realized she was going to be thought of as guilty just because she was married to Hiroshi.

Abby got to Hana's house just as they put Hana and Hiroshi in a car. Tears ran down her face as she realized she was too late.

Joben Saito sat with his feet propped up and sipped the saké Dai had offered him several times. He was proud that he had been able to help Japan, if only a little, and looked forward to helping even more. The pounding on the door startled him. Thinking that it was Hiroshi, he jumped up and opened the door to several men.

"Joben Saito, you are under arrest for the act of treason against the United States of America," a man said in a loud, booming voice.

Joben was stunned; he had been so careful. How had they caught on? His first thought was that Hiroshi had turned on them, but he didn't think so. Then he thought of Dai, but she was always watched, so who had betrayed them? He looked up to see Dai looking at him with tears in her eyes.

"Th . . . there's a radio in the office," she said softly. "It's under the floorboard of his desk."

Joben stared at her, disbelieving that she would betray him to his face.

As several men went into the office, the man addressed Dai, reading off the same charge of treason as he did for her father, and then led them to a car.

Kenji and Patricia had just finished making love for the second time that evening. Both of them felt inexplicably nervous, although they didn't know why. They were almost asleep when they heard Abby frantically beeping the horn of her car and then banging on the door.

They heard Ralph's voice and Abby's frantic one, and then Ralph yelling at them to get up and get dressed. They looked at each other and had just finished dressing by the time Abby made it to their part of the house.

"Miss Abby? What's wrong?" Patricia asked as she took in Abby's appearance.

"You have to come with me now!" she said, grabbing Patricia's hand.

As he had practiced so many times in his mind, Kenji grabbed the box from underneath the bed and the small overnight bag from the closet, and at the last moment he grabbed the tea set and the figurine of the Japanese god his mother had given them. Patricia was already in the car with Abby and Ralph when he ran out of the house, not bothering to lock it behind him. He suspected they wouldn't be coming back to it anytime soon, if ever. He jumped into the car, took a very frightened Patricia into his arms, and hugged her.

They arrived at Abby's house in record time, which was a minor miracle; Abby had horrible night vision. As she drove, Abby tried to decide how to tell Kenji about his parents and decided on the truth.

When they were all sitting, Abby told them everything. Kenji held Patricia's hand so tightly that she gave his a squeeze to let him know he was hurting her.

"I have to go to them," he said, standing.

"Kenji, you can't," Abby said. "If you go, they'll arrest you, too, and you have Patricia to think about. Your mother knew that, and that's why she never told you about your father's activities."

"What am I supposed to do?" Kenji asked. "Let them suffer in jail?"

"There's nothing we can do tonight," Abby said. "First thing in the morning, I'll call Nick. Maybe he can do something for your mother, but Kenji, your father committed treason," Abby said kindly.

"But—"

"I think you and Patricia need some time to talk; you can use her old room," Abby said.

When they were gone, Ralph swore, "Oh fuck!"

"My sentiments exactly," Abby said.

For the first time since they had met, Kenji was the one who needed comforting. Patricia led him to the bed and sat down, pulling him with her. She didn't say anything as she wrapped her arms around him and held him as he tried not to cry.

"Kenji, it's all right to cry," she said softly and kissed his head. She felt his arms go around her waist and the first sob as it shook his body. Patricia cried with him; as much as his father had hated her, she still felt for him and especially for Hana. She said a prayer that they would be treated well and that Hana would be released. Eventually, Kenji fell into a restless sleep with his head resting on Patricia's breasts and her arms around him.

DECEMBER 7, 1941

Abby was up early, unable to rest any longer. She made her way to the kitchen, jumping when she heard Ralph say, "Mornin', Abby."

"Oh, good morning. I was just going to make some tea; would you care for some?"

"I'm not a tea drinker, but what the hell! Sure," Ralph said as he sat down.

Kenji and Patricia came into the kitchen a few minutes later, holding hands; Kenji looked like hell, his eyes red and swollen from crying. Abby offered them tea, which they gratefully accepted. To all of them, the previous night had a surreal feel, but they knew it had happened.

The morning passed quietly as each of them tried to process the events of the previous night. At some point, Ralph turned on the television, hoping for some news. Kenji and Patricia were sitting on the couch with their arms around each other, and Abby had just come in from the back yard and sat down when the announcement came on.

Japan had just that morning attacked the naval base at Pearl Harbor. Kenji, Patricia, Abby, and Ralph all stared at the television, horrified.

Chapter 9

Abby, Ralph, Kenji, and Patricia watched the news in shock. All of them had known that Japan would attack the United States, but none of them had ever imagined it would be on American soil. Hana and Hiroshi were temporarily forgotten as they stared at the television.

Jim Daly of CBS was talking about the attack. "We interrupt this program to bring you a special news bulletin. The Japanese have attacked Pearl Harbor, Hawaii, by air."

Abby sat down heavily, unable to speak. Ralph cursed softly, while Kenji held Patricia even tighter against him, not knowing what to say. His first thought after recovering from shock was for Patricia; would Ralph and Abby penalize her for what his country had just done?

Patricia looked at Kenji and saw the worry on his face; she already knew what he was thinking, but her concern was for him. What was going to happen to him? Would they arrest him as a spy, like his parents? She said a silent prayer that he wouldn't be taken away from her. If they decided to send him away, she was going with him, no matter what he said.

They sat in silence for almost an hour before Kenji gently pushed Patricia away and stood up. "I have to leave; I cannot and will not endanger you by staying here. I only ask that you take care of Patricia."

Abby snapped out of her fog. "What? What are you talking about?" she asked.

"I'm leaving before anything happens to any of you," Kenji said quietly.

"Boy, sit your ass down! You're not going anywhere," Ralph said angrily. "You didn't fly the plane that dropped those bombs."

"But—"

"Kenji, please," Patricia said. "He's right; you didn't do anything wrong."

"I know that, as do you, but the people outside of this house don't. They will only see that I'm Japanese, and that alone makes me guilty. We have been seen as the enemy for a long time now, and the attack has just confirmed what many already believed to be true. If I stay here, then everyone in this house will be seen as being traitors, not necessarily by the government but by other Americans."

Abby spoke next. "You should know by now that I don't give a flying leap what everyone else says or thinks. This is my house, and you're staying! If I get arrested, then so be it, so stop the silly talk about leaving."

"Kenji," Ralph said. "We are your friends no matter what happens, I think you know that. Now, you could leave and you'd have our word that we would take care of Patty, but what would it change? Nothing at all. I say that you stay here with us, and we'll deal with things as they come up. So here's my suggestion: You stay here with Patty while me and Abby go back to the house and pack up whatever food is there and our clothes. Just make sure to stay inside. What do you think?"

Much to Patricia's relief, Kenji agreed, albeit reluctantly. Abby went to get dressed while the rest of them watched the news, still not quite believing what they were seeing. Kenji knew his mother wouldn't be released now; his father he no longer cared about. That Hana had been arrested was his father's fault, and for all of his talk about honor and integrity, Hiroshi Takeda had made choices that endangered his family. For that, Kenji would never forgive him.

Hana heard about the attack and began to cry. There was no doubt in her mind that she would either hang or be sent to prison along with Hiroshi and everyone else that was arrested last night. Her one consolation was that Kenji was still safe and that he had friends and Patricia. She was glad she had met Patricia and that Kenji had her; he was going to need her.

Hana jumped when a man came into the small room where she was being held. Her eyes widened as she recognized him. Nick.

Hiroshi's reaction to the bombing was different than Hana's; he shed no tears over the attack but rejoiced. Unbeknownst to him, the day before, President Roosevelt had pled with Emperor Hirohito to use his influence to avoid war. Had he known that, he would have been angry at the audacity of the American president, given the way he had allowed the Japanese in his country to be treated.

Now, as he sat in the tiny interrogation room, he was pleased with the small part he had played in the success of the Japanese attack on America. That he might die was of no concern; that Hana could die saddened him, but war had casualties. That Hana was one of them was unfortunate. That Kenji was still free angered him, but there was nothing that could be done about that. He briefly thought about implicating him, but disregarded it after remembering that Kenji had been watched and determined not to be a spy. He only knew that because Hana had told him during the ride here.

There was something else Hiroshi wasn't aware of: the man he thought of as a friend and ally was painting a very interesting picture of him to the government.

Joben Saito was excited about the attack as Hiroshi. He was still disappointed in Dai's betrayal, but he would have done the same thing, and he wasn't ashamed to admit that to himself. What she told them didn't matter anymore; it was too late for the information to be acted on, and not only that, she was implicated because she knew so much.

When an agent came into the room, Joben lost some of his bravado. As happy as he was about the attack, he had no desire to die. Before the man even asked the first question, Joben started talking. By the time he was finished, he had the man believing that Hiroshi Takeda was the leader of the spy ring.

Dai Saito sat quietly, wondering what was going to happen to her. She knew that the information she had was now useless. As far as the United States was concerned, she was a spy, and no amount of denial on her part was going to change that.

A tear ran down her face as she realized she could very well be sent back to Japan or be hanged.

John and Hattie Middleton were shocked by the news. Hattie's first thought was of Patricia and her safety; John's first thought was that Patricia had married the enemy. He had a mind to make Hattie show him where Patricia lived so he could drag her home kicking and screaming, but he didn't. For one, he knew Hattie would never tell him, and for two, Hattie would never forgive him if he did.

"Damn it, girl!" he muttered under his breath as his friends talked about the attack. None of them were stupid enough to make a comment about Patricia in front of him; they would talk behind his back later.

Hattie could only hope that Patricia and Kenji were safe; as the day wore on, people were getting angrier, and the talk about "killing some Japs" only got worse. Against John's wishes, Hattie started to walk toward Abby's house.

Abby and Ralph hadn't been gone long when the phone rang.

Patricia answered the phone with shaking hands. “Hello?”

“Abby?” a male voice asked.

“No sir, she isn’t home right now; can I take a message?” Patricia asked.

“Patricia? This is Nick, Abby’s friend. Where is she?”

“She went to our house a little while ago.”

“Is your husband there with you?”

Patricia hesitated; what if he was coming to arrest him?

Nick, understanding her hesitation, assured her that he wasn’t going to arrest Kenji. “I just want to be sure you’re both safe,” he said.

“He’s here,” Patricia confirmed.

“Good. Both of you stay indoors and tell Abby that I called.”

“Mr. Nick? Is Kenji’s mother all right?” Patricia asked.

“She’s fine. I have her in a room by herself, and I’ll do what I can, but Patricia, it doesn’t look good. I’ll call back later.”

Patricia hung up the phone and went back to Kenji, whose eyes were glued to the television set.

“That was Mr. Nick, Miss Abby’s friend,” Patricia said softly.

Kenji’s attention shifted from the television to her. “What did he say?” he asked anxiously.

“He said your mother is all right and that he’ll try to help her but that it doesn’t look good. He also said that we need to stay indoors.”

Kenji didn’t say anything as he took Patricia into his arms; he didn’t say anything, but he had the feeling that his days of holding her were numbered. Kenji released her, stood up, and held his hand out to her. When she took it, he led her up the stairs and into her room. He needed and wanted to make love to her; those times were numbered as well.

Patricia had become more sensitive to his moods the longer they had been together. She needed to love him as much as he needed to love her. Patricia followed him into the room and undressed; there was none of the playfulness that had become a major part of their lovemaking. It was as gentle as always, but with an edge of desperation and fear. Kenji remembered to pull out at the last minute; a pregnancy right now was more out of the question than ever.

Patricia cried into his chest as the orgasm washed over her, clinging to him, not allowing him to move when it was over.

"*Kirei*," Kenji said softly. "Promise me something," he said when she finally let him move.

"No."

"You don't know what I'm requesting," he said softly as he touched her tear-streaked face.

"Yes I do," Patricia replied, "and the answer is no. I will not promise to love somebody else or to let someone else love me if anything happens to you, and do you know why? Because nothing is going to happen to you, because I refuse to believe that we won't get through this, and because I promised to love you forever and. . . . "

Kenji held her as she sobbed; he wouldn't try to make her promise. He recognized the stubborn tone in her voice and knew it would have been pointless. He would just have to try to have as much faith as she did. He looked at the clock and mentally calculated how much time they had before Abby and Ralph got back. Not long, he realized, as he snuggled Patricia closer to him.

"I need for you to promise me something," Patricia said, holding him tighter to her.

"If it's what I was going to get you to promise me, then my answer is also no," Kenji said, ignoring the beeping horn of Abby's car.

"I want you to promise me that you'll try to come back to me if they take you away," Patricia said, crying again.

"You have my word," Kenji replied, kissing her.

Several minutes later they were downstairs, helping to unpack the food.

"We got there in good time," Ralph said. "There were groups of people out looking for any unsuspecting Japanese on the street, and they were headed toward our house when we left."

"I grabbed as many of your personal items as I could, concentrating on clothes; we figured we'd go back in a few days," Abby said.

"Thank you both," Patricia said, hugging Abby.

"Yes, thank you," Kenji agreed as he picked up a suitcase to carry upstairs.

"Miss Abby, your friend Nick called. He said he would call you later," Patricia said.

"Did he say anything about Hana?" Abby asked.

Patricia told Abby what Nick had told her. Abby felt a sense of guilt; if only she had left earlier, Hana would be here with them.

The knock on the door startled them; Ralph made the women stay in the kitchen while he answered the door.

"Hattie! What are you thinking, being out and about?" Ralph asked as he pulled her into the house.

"For once, I'm not the one in danger," she replied. "Is Patricia here?" she asked, looking around.

"Mama!" Patricia exclaimed, throwing herself into Hattie's arms.

"You all right? Where's your man?" Hattie asked.

"Upstairs; Miss Abby came to get us last night. Hana is in jail for being a spy and—"

"Hana, a spy?" Hattie interrupted. "I's don't believe it."

"Neither do we," Abby interjected. "Nick is trying to help, but he says it doesn't look good. Sit down and let me get you something to drink," Abby said as she headed toward the kitchen.

The television was still on, and Jim Daly was still talking about the attack. Kenji came down the stairs and looked at Hattie warily, not knowing what to expect. It wouldn't have surprised him if she came to try to talk Patricia into leaving him.

Instead, Hattie stood up and hugged him. "I sorry 'bout your mama; I jus' whispered a little prayer for her."

He was touched by the simple sincerity of Hattie's words and hugged her tightly before kissing her on the cheek. "Thank you; that means much to me," he said, his throat tight.

They sat down and watched the news together. Abby looked at Kenji and Patricia and prayed they would be strong enough to endure what was coming.

Nick called back later in the evening with bad news. "I tried to get Hana Takeda released, but they still think she's a part of the spy ring. I'm sorry; I'll keep trying, but. . . . "

"Thank you for trying," Abby said. "Where will they take her?"

"I don't know yet. I'll let you know, but you won't be able to see her no matter where she ends up," Nick cautioned.

"Do you think Kenji can speak to her on the phone?" Abby asked.

"That isn't advisable, even if I were to listen in. We don't want to give them any reason to suspect him of spying. Just keep him in the house until things calm down. I'll be around later tonight."

Abby hung up, heartsick. Things weren't going to die down any time soon; Patricia and Kenji had some decisions to make.

DECEMBER 8, 1941

Everyone was glued to the television; the United States and Britain declared war on Japan one hour after President Roosevelt delivered a speech to the Joint Session of Congress. The Americans were now officially at war, and the Japanese living in America were now officially the enemy. Many Japanese business owners were shocked to find all of their assets and businesses seized by the Department of the Treasury. Kenji was thankful they didn't have a bank account or a business. By the end of the day, the Netherlands and New Zealand had declared war on Japan, and more would follow. The Second World War had begun in earnest.

Patricia and Kenji sat up late, weighing their options. They talked about relocating, but to where? They had over five hundred dollars, but that wouldn't last long, even if they were very careful. The sentiment toward the Japanese wouldn't be any different than where they were, and not only that—what would they do for work? Patricia might be able to find something, but not him, and Kenji refused to have Patricia support him. They talked for hours before deciding to stay where they were. Their friends, family, and support were here; if they moved, they would lose that. The one thing Kenji didn't say was that Patricia would be taken care of if something happened.

DECEMBER 9, 1941

The madness continued. Every man of legal age, white and black, wanted to go kill some "Japs and Nazis"; Japanese language schools were closed; China and Australia officially declared war on Japan.

Patricia could no longer watch the news; it frightened her too much. Each passing day was another day in fear; she woke up at night afraid that someone would come banging on the door and drag Kenji away, accusing him of being a spy. Kenji tried to reassure her, but what could he say? The thing she feared could very well happen.

Instead of watching the news for hours, he began watching it in the morning, noon, and at night for just long enough to find out what was happening. The rest of the time he spent with Patricia. Sometimes they read together; sometimes they talked and made plans for when the madness was over.

Kenji would go to med school, they decided, and Patricia would go to college, too. She didn't know for what yet, but she had time to figure it out. They would have three children, with at least one of them being a girl, and they would travel wherever they wanted. The dreaming helped both of them; it gave them something to look forward to.

"Where would you like to go to first?" Kenji asked.

"I don't know, maybe Paris," she replied. "What about you?" Patricia asked as she drew abstract designs on his stomach with her fingertips.

"My dream is to take you to Japan," Kenji said, catching her hand in his and bringing it to his lips. "There are so many places I would like to show you."

When they were alone and just talking as they were, it was almost easy to forget that there was a war going on and that their future was uncertain, but each day brought the reality back to them.

By the end of December, Germany and Italy had declared war on the United States; the United States, along with the United Kingdom, had declared war on Germany and Italy, as well as on Romania and Bulgaria. India had declared war on Japan, thousands were starving in Leningrad, and Hitler had become Commander-in-Chief of the German army.

Kenji watched and listened with sadness. So much death already, and there was more to come. He spoke with Nick frequently, looking for information about his mother.

"I wasn't able to help her. I'm sorry," Nick said during the last phone call.

"What will happen to her?" Kenji asked.

"Prison for now, but I don't know where. Is there any message for her?"

"Tell her we love her and that we are well," Kenji replied.

*

Hiroshi was still in shock; where did the Americans get the idea that he was the leader of the so-called spy ring? Who would have told them such a thing? Not Hana; he was sure of that. Was it one of the other men? His mind rejected what he finally admitted to himself later that night: Joben Saito.

Hiroshi replayed Hana's warning in his head; she had been right. Joben was not to be trusted, and it was now too late to change anything. They had been at the same location for almost a month; he hadn't seen or spoken to anyone other than the agent, who questioned him on a daily basis.

"Who did you report to? What else is Japan planning?"

Hiroshi gave up trying to convince the man that he probably knew more than he Hiroshi did. He asked about Hana, but the question was always ignored.

It was now the end of December, and he still had no idea what was going to happen to him. With nothing more to do than think, Hiroshi thought about the past two years and wondered if he would have changed anything if given the chance, and there was—there was one thing he would have changed. He would have left Kenji in Japan, even if it meant he would have to fight in the emperor's army. That would have been better than him making the choices that he did.

Hana lay on her cot and tried to sleep; she had no idea what was happening in the outside world other than what Nick told her. Her only real concern was Kenji and his safety; she no longer thought about or cared about Hiroshi. It was because of him that she was here; it was because of him that she had almost lost her son. She no longer owed him her loyalty.

JANUARY 1, 1942

Things at Abby's house had settled into a quiet routine. Ralph and Abby made another trip to the house, only to find it ransacked. They walked through the rooms in disbelief, taking whatever wasn't destroyed.

"Bastards," Ralph hissed as he took in the damage.

"Let's go," Abby said as she looked around. "There's not much here," she said sadly.

Ralph cursed again and followed Abby out of the house.

Kenji and Patricia lay on the bed holding hands; they had just made love, and Kenji hadn't pulled out in time.

"*Kirei*, we have to make plans in case there is a child and I am—"

Patricia stopped him as she always did whenever he started to talk about something happening to him. "Please don't," she said softly.

This time, Kenji insisted. "I know this frightens you, but we have to talk about it, as we should have long before this. If there is a child and I'm not here for whatever reason, I want you to stay with Abby and Ralph. If you meet someone who will care for you—"

"*No!* Stop it!" Patricia screamed at him, flew off the bed, and huddled in a corner on the floor.

Kenji got up, walked over to her, sat on the floor, and put his arms around her. "Patricia—"

"No, I don't want to talk about this," she said, sobbing.

Kenji held her tighter and talked even as Patricia tried to stop him. "If you meet someone who will love you and our child, let him care for you."

"No."

Kenji kept talking, determined to have his say. "I won't be angry with you if you find that you love this person in return; I just want you to be safe and happy."

"No."

"*Kirei*—"

"No! Stop talking like I'm going to lose you!" Patricia said, crying. "I refuse to believe that we're not going to raise our baby, if there's one, together. I refuse to believe or accept that we won't do all the things we've talked about together, and you need to stop thinking you're going to leave me."

Kenji said no more and hoped she was right; his gut told him they would be separated for a while at least. He hoped a pregnancy hadn't resulted from his failure to pull out from her, but if it did, they would deal with it.

They stayed sitting on the floor long after they heard Ralph and Abby come in. Kenji convinced Patricia to move to the bed, where they stayed for the rest of the night, missing dinner.

They missed the announcement that prohibited travel by "all suspected enemy aliens" and the order to surrender all weapons. It wouldn't have mattered anyway; Kenji had no weapons and had no place he wanted or needed to go to.

Ralph was going to call them for dinner, but Abby stopped him.

"Leave them be; they'll eat when they're ready."

"Abby, what's going to happen to them?" Ralph asked.

"Nothing, I hope," she replied.

JANUARY 2, 1942

Kenji and Patricia didn't appear until lunchtime. It was obvious that Patricia had been crying, but no one acknowledged it, with the exception of Kenji. Abby noted how he always touched her or hugged her as if he was storing the feel of her for a rainy day. Patricia, she noticed, was doing the same. Abby also noticed that the sparkle in her eyes was gone and replaced by a fear she hadn't seen since Patricia first told her about Kenji—but it was worse.

Patricia picked at her food until Kenji pulled her aside. "*Kirei*, you have to eat. What if there is a baby growing?" he asked, touching her stomach. "You must take care of yourself so that we will have a healthy baby."

Patricia nodded and made more of an attempt to eat.

Lunch was just about over when there was a banging on the door. Patricia and Abby both screamed, and both men jumped to their feet.

"Kenji, stay here with the women," Ralph said as he walked to the living room.

John made Hattie tell him where Patricia was. He had had it with all of the snide comments about Patricia and the Jap cock that she was sucking; he was tired of the comments about her being a traitor not only to the United States, but to her race as well. He walked to Abby's house, ignoring Hattie's pleas for him to stop; she tried to keep up with his long strides but soon gave up, arriving at Abby's house several minutes after he did.

John banged on the door, not caring who saw or heard him; he was taking Patricia home even if he had to kill the Jap to do it.

"Who in the hell are you?" Ralph asked, glaring at John.

"Where's Patricia?" John demanded, ignoring Ralph's question.

"Who's asking?" Ralph asked, knowing full well who John was.

"Daddy?" Patricia cried when she heard John's voice. She ran from the kitchen into the living room, thinking that he had come to talk to her.

When John saw her, he fought the urge to tell her that he had never stopped loving her. The urge disappeared when he saw Kenji for the first time.

"Get your things; you comin' home," John said, his voice harsh.

"What? No, I—"

"I said, *get your things*! You ain't staying with that!" John said, pointing at Kenji.

Hattie finally caught up with him and tried to talk to him. "John, let's go home. We can talk to her later, when you ain't so mad."

John turned to Hattie. "You jus' as much at fault as that white woman. You let her do what she want, and look it; she married to . . . that yellow bastard!"

Patricia gasped; she had never heard her father's voice filled with so much hatred and anger, and she also heard the underlying hurt.

John pushed past Ralph in an attempt to reach Patricia; he was about to grab her when Kenji moved in front of her, blocking John's path.

"Move!" John bellowed.

Kenji remained where he was, calmly staring back at John.

"That's my girl people are talkin' about! They callin' her traitor and everything else, and it's because of you!" John screamed into Kenji's face.

"Patricia is my wife. The only way that she leaves here is if she chooses to do so," Kenji replied, not flinching or moving.

John raised a fist and got ready to swing when Abby spoke, "John Middleton, back away or I swear to God I will shoot you."

John looked at Abby with a mixture of surprise, hate, and anger before speaking to Patricia. "You got one more chance to come home."

Patricia stepped from behind Kenji and took his hand. "I am so sorry that you're angry and hurt, but Daddy, Kenji is my husband. I know it's not easy for you to understand, but I love him, and I'm not coming home," Patricia said, her voice shaking. "I just wish you would try to understand."

"Understand what? That my girl turned her back on her family? That she marry to a man that attacked this country? What I'm s'posed to understand?" John asked.

"Nothing except that I love you and I love him," Patricia said as she reached for her father.

For just a second, she thought he was going to reach for her, too, but at the last second, John backed away. He turned his back on Patricia and walked out of the house. Patricia knew she would never see her father again. He would never forgive her, she knew that with certainty.

Hattie watched the exchange between father and daughter with tears running down her face. She wasn't even going to try to talk sense to him; he had already decided that he would never forgive Patricia. She ran up the steps, into the house, and hugged Patricia. Hattie didn't say anything; what was there to say?

She did speak to Kenji. "She just lost her daddy; make sure that she don't lose you, too."

Hattie kissed Patricia and left without speaking to Ralph or Abby. Patricia stood, staring at the door; she no longer had a father. She tried to fight back the tears, but failed miserably. Kenji took her upstairs, undressed her and then himself, and got into bed with her. Patricia let out a low moan and then a sob as she began to grieve for a father she had lost, not because of death but because of hatred.

JANUARY 19, 1942

"I want to come with you," Patricia said as Kenji got ready to go to be reregistered.

"No, *Kirei*. There will be a long wait, and it will be late when I come back."

Patricia didn't give up; she remembered the last time he had gone to register. It had been the longest day of her life. "Kenji—"

"No, *Kirei.* Stay here with Abby and be sure to eat," he admonished.

They still didn't know if Patricia was pregnant or not, and Kenji was working under the assumption that she was until they knew differently.

Abby watched Patricia as she struggled not to cry and panic. She remembered that day, too, and made a decision.

"You know, it's been a while since I've been anywhere; why don't we all take the train? While Kenji takes care of business, Patricia and I could shop."

"That sounds like a plan to me," Ralph said. "But I have a better idea; why don't we drive?" he asked. "Me and Kenji can take turns."

It didn't take Kenji long to figure out what was happening; they were thinking of Patricia. She would be upset from the moment he left until he was back.

They all waited for his vote, even though he was outnumbered.

"Only if you promise not to ask to wait in line with me," he told Patricia.

Patricia hugged him and went to get dressed. While Abby dressed, Ralph made sandwiches and Kenji waited.

He hadn't heard any news of his mother, other than she was still being detained. He worried for her health, although the last time he had seen her, she looked better than ever. He had Nick's assurances that she was well and wasn't being mistreated.

As he waited, Kenji decided it was just as well that Patricia was coming with him; it had been a hard two weeks for her. She hadn't seen her mother since the day John showed up to try to take her home by force. For two days afterward, Patricia barely ate anything. The sparkle he loved so much was back in her eyes, but when the president announced that all "suspected enemy aliens" in the west had to reregister, Kenji had watched the sparkle dim.

He smiled when he heard her excited giggles as she talked with Abby about what she should wear. He hoped she wore the red sweater; red looked good on her. And he hoped that she decided to wear her hair down, although he would be surprised if she did. She only wore her hair down for special occasions, and he wasn't counting today as one of those.

Their first anniversary was in less than two weeks; although they were legally married on Patricia's birthday in July, January 30 was the one they chose to celebrate. He did a mental calculation of their funds and decided he would have Abby buy Patricia a small gift, maybe some perfume. When he heard Patricia in the bathroom, he ran up the stairs and grabbed some money from the box hidden under the bed.

He made it back downstairs just as Patricia came out of the bathroom.

"Ralph, a favor if you please," Kenji said and told Ralph what he wanted.

"Sure we can; is there a scent that you like?" Ralph asked.

Kenji hadn't really thought about it. "I will trust your judgment," he replied as he handed Ralph the money.

The drive there was uneventful. Ralph drove while Abby sat in the front with him, proving herself to be quite the backseat driver.

"Damn it, woman!" Ralph exclaimed. "Will you let a man drive?"

Kenji and Patricia blocked out the bickering coming from the front seat and talked quietly between them. Patricia was a few days past her time, but Kenji wasn't ready to say she was pregnant just yet. He found himself having very mixed emotions about a possible pregnancy. Part of him wished and hoped for it, but the practical part of him wished and hoped that she wasn't; things were too uncertain.

As they agreed, Kenji got out at the registration office; the line was already long and growing longer by the minute. Kenji took Patricia's hand and kissed it before closing the car door and walking away. Patricia watched Kenji walk toward the back of the line, scanning the faces of those closest to her. *So many people*, she thought as they drove away. *Surely the government can't think all of them are enemies, can they?* she wondered.

"It's frightening, isn't it?" Abby asked as she looked at the long line of Japanese people, not missing the looks of fear, anger, and apprehension she saw on their faces.

"Frightening" wasn't the word Patricia had in mind; "horrifying" was more like it.

Kenji stood in line and settled in for the long wait; he toyed with his wedding band as he remembered the last time he was here. So much had happened since then. He scanned the faces around him and saw what he had seen the last time—with one exception. This time, there was fear; the feeling that things were going to take a turn for the worse struck him.

Ironically, the same man who had fingerprinted and registered him the last time reregistered him this time, but gave no sign that he recognized Kenji. The process was as slow, if not slower, than the last time, even though they had the names in front of them.

"Do you swear loyalty to the United States of America?" the man asked, clearly bored.

"Yes," Kenji replied.

He answered the several questions after that one as quickly as he could and then left. He spotted the same restrooms he and his parents had used before and headed toward them. Just as he was reaching for the handle, someone spoke.

"Whatcha think you doin', Jap? That says it for coloreds, and you ain't colored."

Kenji turned to look at the speaker. "I would like to use the restroom and then be on my way," he replied politely.

The man looked Kenji up and down before speaking again. "Scoot! You ain't usin' this toilet; go find an alley or someplace."

Kenji was going to press the issue but didn't. The last thing he needed was to draw attention to himself. He looked around to see if Abby and Ralph were back yet. Not seeing them, he walked back over to the spot where they were going to pick him up.

By the time they got there, he thought he was going to burst. Ralph stopped by the side of the road as soon as he could so Kenji could relieve himself.

He poured a capful of water so he could wash his hands before touching Patricia and got back into the car. As he reflected on the day, especially the incident with the restroom, he wondered if they really wanted to bring a child into a world so filled with hate and intolerance.

JANUARY 30, 1942

It was their anniversary, and Patricia wasn't pregnant. Kenji waited for Patricia to come out of the bathroom; he held her anniversary gift in his hands and hoped she would like it. Abby had managed to sneak the purchase past Patricia by saying it was for herself.

Kenji smelled it just before wrapping it in some pretty paper Abby had tucked away. It smelled like spring flowers, and he thought it perfect for Patricia. He could smell their anniversary dinner cooking and wished they were celebrating alone. But, he reminded himself, they wouldn't be celebrating at all if it weren't for the people preparing the meal, so it was fitting that they be there.

Hattie was coming, too; they had only seen her once since the first of January. Patricia's father never came up; the fact that it was their fathers who disowned them wasn't lost on Kenji. In that moment, he made a conscious decision: He would never turn his back on his children no matter what they had done. They would always have the love of him and Patricia.

Patricia finally came out of the bathroom wearing her best dress and the red sweater; she had decided to wear her hair down just because he liked it that way.

"Come sit by me," Kenji said, patting the empty spot next to him.

Patricia blushed at the smile he gave her, surprised that he still affected her that way. When she was sitting, Kenji kissed her.

"*Kekkonkinen bi omedeto, Kirei* (Happy Anniversary, Beautiful)," Kenji said and handed her the gift.

Patricia looked at the gift and tried to repeat what Kenji had said in Japanese but couldn't quite do it. "Happy anniversary," she said instead. "When did you buy this?" she asked as she opened the package.

"I had Miss Abby buy if for me the day I had to register," Kenji replied.

"You sneak!" Patricia exclaimed when she saw the bottle of perfume.

Abby had even had her smell it under the guise of asking for her opinion.

"Thank you!" Patricia said as she threw her arms around his neck. She opened the bottle and put a little behind her ears. "Do you like it?"

"I like it," Kenji replied and once again wished they were alone.

Hiroshi sat in his cell, fully aware of what the date was; it was the day Kenji and Hana had completed their betrayal of him and dishonored the Takeda name. He had no idea what was happening as far as the war went; his captors made a point of not informing him unless it was something negative about Japan, and he hadn't seen a newspaper or listened to a radio since his arrest.

He did know that Joben, Dai, and Hana, as well as some others, were somewhere in the same building, but he had never seen them. He did ask to speak to Hana once and was denied; he doubted she would have spoken to him anyway.

Hiroshi also wondered what Joben got out of the information he had given the Americans; did they promise to release him if he helped them? He was a fool, he realized. He should have listened to Hana when she had warned him about Joben; he would have been more careful.

Hana knew no more than Hiroshi did about the war. Her only thoughts were on her only child and his wife. Today was their first anniversary, and she hoped it was a good one.

Nick still came to see her once a week and gave her updates on Kenji and Patricia. The fact that the Japanese had to reregister didn't bode well for Kenji—or anyone else, for that matter. When Nick came to see her next, she had a favor to ask of him. If she was correct, that should be today.

Nick showed up two hours later. "How are you holding up?" he asked as he sat down at the small table.

"I could be better, but then I could be worse," Hana replied with a small smile that didn't quite reach her eyes. "What news of my son and his wife?"

"They're fine. They're still living at Abby's, along with that old guy Ralph. Hana, I'm still trying to get you out of here, but they're still convinced that you know something. Is there anything you can think of that would help?" Nick asked for what had to be the hundredth time.

"There is nothing; I only know what I've told you. I don't know whom Joben reported to, and I made a point of never asking Hiroshi what they talked about."

"Hana, Joben says he reported to Hiroshi," Nick said.

Hana frowned. "No, that isn't right. Joben Saito is a liar if he told you that. He's the one who persuaded Hiroshi to become a traitor to this country. Would he have done it anyway? Probably, but Joben is the one who organized the meetings and fed into Hiroshi's feelings of disillusionment and anger.

"Have you spoken to Joben's daughter, Dai? If anyone would know what happened in that house, it would be her. Joben made her a virtual prisoner in his home after Kenji refused to marry her."

Nick had never talked to the girl, but he had heard that she did have some information that would have been valuable if they could have gotten it in time. The agent in charge of her was convinced of her guilt and did little to find out exactly what the girl knew. What if she did know who the leader was and whom they reported to? She would also be able to verify whether Hana knew any more than what she was telling. He had to talk to that girl or get the agent responsible for her to talk to her.

"Hana, I've got to go; do you need anything?" Nick asked.

"Yes, I have a favor to ask," Hana said.

Nick sat across the table from Dai Saito and looked at her for several minutes before speaking to her. "Why should I believe you aren't a spy?" he asked.

"Why would you believe I am?" she shot back. "Because I'm Japanese? Because my pig of a father is a spy?" she asked bitterly. "Believe it or not, there are many of us who are loyal to this country, in spite of the way we have been treated."

Nick ignored her outburst. "So who was the ringleader? Hiroshi Takeda?" he asked.

Dai looked at Nick and laughed. "You cannot be serious! Hiroshi Takeda is not a leader but a follower, and he is led by emotion. My father is the only reason that he is this deeply involved," Dai said and then she paused. "My father, is he the one who told you that Hiroshi Takeda was the leader?"

Nick's silence was all she needed to know it was true.

"My father is the consummate liar. The only reason he even approached the Takedas was because he wanted the power of their name to lure people to him. As a matter of fact, the two of them tried to get Kenjiro to marry me, but he refused, saying his heart belonged to another. Is it true that he married a black woman?"

"It's true, but back to your father: do you know who his contact in Japan was?" Nick asked.

"What will I gain by giving you this information?" Dai asked.

"I'm not in the position to offer you anything; that has to come from your agent."

"Him?" Dai asked. "He has no interest in what I have to say. He looks at me and only sees that I'm Japanese, but you—you're different. Why is that?"

Nick honestly didn't know and said so. "Miss Saito, all I can do is promise you that I will speak to your agent. It will go a long way if you tell me what you know; if it checks out, maybe we can work something out."

"Will you let me out of this place?" Dai asked.

"I can't promise you that," Nick replied.

"You're honest; you could have lied."

"I could have, but then you wouldn't trust me to keep my word, would you?" Nick asked.

Thirty minutes later, Nick was on his way to Hiroshi's home. Once there, he found the overnight bags with no difficulty and then headed over to Abby's.

He tapped on the door and waited for someone to answer. Ralph peeked through the window before opening the door.

"Nick! What are you doing here so late?" Ralph asked.

"I know it's late, but I need to talk to Kenji and Patricia; are they still up?"

"In the dining room with Abby and Hattie," Ralph said, stepping aside to let him in.

Nick went to the dining room, carrying the two small bags. All conversation stopped when they noticed him.

"Nick? What's happened?" Abby asked anxiously.

"Those bags belong to my parents; is my mother all right?" Kenji asked.

"She's fine," Nick replied. "She wanted me to bring these to you and told me to tell you 'happy anniversary.'"

Kenji made no move to take the bags; instead, he looked at Nick. "You are sure she's all right?"

"I just left her a couple of hours ago and she was fine," Nick said, holding the bags out to Kenji.

Kenji took the bags and put them on the table without speaking. He knew why his mother had sent Nick with the bags, but he was reluctant to take the money. If she was released, she would need both her share and his father's share.

"Will she be released?" Patricia asked.

Nick blew out a breath, trying to decide what to tell them. "I don't know yet."

"That's not a 'no,'" Abby said.

"But it's not a 'yes' either," Nick said. "New information has surfaced and needs to be verified before anything else can happen, but don't get your hopes up. Kenji, as far as your father goes, his fate is pretty much sealed. What's going to happen to him, I don't know."

"The only one I'm concerned about it my mother," Kenji replied.

"All right then; I have to get back. I'll keep you posted," Nick said as he left the dining room.

"Do you think they'll let Hana go?" Abby asked.

"Don't know," Ralph said. "But I agree with Nick; let's not get our hopes up.

FEBRUARY 6, 1942

Nick sat across from Hana and asked her all the same questions, which Hana answered in the same way. Even though he knew the answers, Nick asked anyway, as a matter of protocol. Today, however, there was a difference; this was the last time he would ask her those questions. Hana was being released. Dai Saito was a goldmine of information, most of which exonerated Hana and completely implicated her father. Hana would always fall under suspicion because of her nationality, but for the moment, she was no longer considered a spy.

"Hana, we're letting you go," Nick said and watched her reaction.

Hana looked at Nick in disbelief. Surely he wouldn't joke about such a thing?

"I'll take you to your house to gather a few things, and then I'll take you over to Abby's. She's made room for you there," Nick said.

"Why can't I stay at my home?" she asked, recovering from her surprise.

This was one of the things Nick hadn't told her. "The Department of the Treasury seized control of all Japanese property, businesses, and bank accounts. You no longer have a home. I'm sorry."

"Everything is gone?" Hana asked quietly.

"I'm sorry," Nick repeated.

Hana was released an hour later. Nothing felt real to her as she watched the scenery pass as Nick drove her to what used to be her home. When they arrived, Nick followed her from room to room as she packed the things most important to her. Hana slowly walked by the room that had been Hiroshi's; she contemplated whether there was anything in there she wanted and decided not.

She went to her room, packed her clothing, and walked out without another glance. What would be the point? Her life in this house was over. There was a measure of sadness at the thought. There had been so many happy times here, but of late, the memories had been sad and painful.

Nick waited patiently as Hana went to the kitchen and packed her tea set, just in case something had happened to Patricia's. The last thing she did before leaving the house forever was to pack any nonperishable foods to take to Abby's home.

Hana stopped at the front door, took one last look around, and walked out.

Abby's house was abuzz with excitement as they prepared for Hana's arrival. Kenji and Patricia gave up their room for Hana and moved down to the basement, which as far as they were concerned was perfect. It gave them the illusion that they were living in their own apartment. That they had to go up two sets of stairs to use the bathroom was of no consequence. The only major issue was a bed. Once they heard about Hana's pending release, Ralph and Abby went back to Ralph's house to see if any of the beds were salvageable. If they were, they'd bring one back and put the mattress in the back yard to air out.

As it turned out, the only bed that was in good shape was Kenji and Patricia's. While they were there, they packed up any extra linens they could find and extra kitchen utensils. After they were finished, they left the house for the last time.

Kenji and Patricia worked on the basement, moving boxes to one corner to make room for their bed and a dresser.

"It's almost like having our own place, isn't it?" Patricia asked.

"It is," Kenji agreed. "But this isn't what I want for you."

"I know it isn't, but I don't mind, and who knows? Maybe we'll have our own little house someday," Patricia replied cheerfully.

"Maybe," Kenji replied, smiling at her.

He had given up on trying to get her to face the possibility that something could happen to him; it caused her too much pain. Kenji realized her optimism was what kept her grounded and made her who she was, and who was he to take that from her? His one consolation was knowing that if something did happen to him, Patricia would be cared for. He had already spoken to Ralph and Abby, who had both promised him that Patricia and their child, if there was one, would be cared for. It was a conversation Patricia knew nothing about, and he wanted it to stay that way.

Nick beeped the car horn as he pulled into Abby's garage. They had decided it was best this way because while the neighbors hadn't complained too much about one Japanese, they would about two.

Hana was greeted with tearful kisses and hugs.

"Mother, are you well?" Kenji asked as he looked her up and down before hugging her again.

"I am fine. Nick has been very kind to me," Hana replied.

Patricia hugged Hana next. "I'm so glad you're here."

Hana hugged Patricia the hardest of all. Here was a woman who had been discriminated against by others, including her, but yet had found it within herself to forgive. Hana fully understood why and how Kenji fell in love with Patricia. When they had a moment alone, she would tell him that.

Dinner was a very noisy and happy affair. Even Nick seemed to be relaxed and carefree as he told jokes and laughed with the rest of them. For a few hours, no one thought about what was happening around the world and in Washington, DC.

Hiroshi heard about Hana's release from the agent in charge of his case.

"Yep, she got lucky, and if you ask me, I think her agent is sweet on her."

Hiroshi's eyes flashed. Impossible! Hana would never betray him like that! And then he remembered what he had told her: "You and Kenjiro are dead to me."

But still, she wouldn't . . . would she?

FEBRUARY 24, 1942

Ralph was reading the morning paper, looking for any postings on new laws regarding the Japanese. So far, a curfew was initiated, but that was old news, and there were more and more stories about the extermination of the Jews in Germany and Poland in concentration camps. Ralph wasn't sure if he believed the stories. War was one thing; it was expected that people would die, unfortunately, many of them innocent, but to deliberately try to kill off a whole race of people? That was just craziness, but then again, it wouldn't be the first time. And if it were true, it wouldn't be the last time, either.

"Crazy-assed bastards," Ralph swore under his breath as he continued to read. He stopped reading when he saw the heading: "Executive Order 9066."

"What in the fuck is that?" he wondered as he continued reading. "Oh, fuck me," he swore softly as he began to understand what was happening. The United States was planning to inter the Japanese.

"Oh fuck," Ralph swore again and set the paper down.

Chapter 10

Ralph reread the article and cursed again. His first thought was how he was going to tell everyone what he had just found out; his second thought was how they would react when they heard the news.

"Shit!" he swore softly.

It was early yet and no one else was up, something for which he was glad. Abby would be up next; he would talk to her and see if she had any ideas on how to break the news to Kenji, Patricia, and Hana. Maybe her friend Nick knew something or might be able to help in some way. He certainly hoped so; the one thing Kenji had been afraid of might really be happening.

Abby came down the stairs an hour later and said good morning to Ralph, and it took her a moment to realize that he didn't respond.

"Ralph?" she asked. "What's the matter?"

"We got a big problem," Ralph replied and showed Abby the article.

"Oh my God!" Abby said, sitting down, still holding the paper.

"What are we going to tell them?" Ralph asked.

"Nothing until I talk to Nick."

"How are you going to keep it from them? Kenji watches the news three times a day without fail," Ralph reminded her.

Abby looked at the clock and decided to call Nick.

"What do you know about this Executive Order 9066?" she asked, not giving him a chance to say hello.

"It's because of Pearl Harbor," Nick replied. "The fear is that the Japanese here will side with Japan and perform acts of sabotage internally. Of course, there's no proof that will happen, but people are afraid."

"Where are they going to send them?" Abby asked.

"That's information I'm not privy to; I only know what I do because a friend of mine works at the White House and was there when Roosevelt signed the order. I wish I had more information, but I'll keep you posted if I hear anything else," Nick said. "Abby, the interment is for the West Coast; now might be a good time for Kenji, Patricia, and Hana to think about moving out to the East Coast."

"They've talked about moving and have decided not to; their concern is how they would live. They have some money, but it wouldn't last long. Kenji's concern is how he would support them when the money ran out, and he refuses to have Patricia support them," Abby replied. "The other thing is this: Here they have friends and support. If they move, they'll have no one, and if anything happens to Kenji, Hana and Patricia will be alone."

"Abby, I understand, but if they want to stay together, they may have to move," Nick said.

"You're right," Abby conceded sadly.

"Stay close to the phone; I'll keep you posted," Nick said and hung up.

"Well?" Ralph asked anxiously.

"He's not high enough up on the totem pole to be privy to any information, but he'll keep us posted on anything he finds out. He also suggested that Kenji, Patricia, and Hana move to the East Coast."

"They won't go," Ralph said with certainty.

"I know, but it's like Nick said; it may be their only chance to stay together. But here's something else: Even if they could stay together wherever they sent Kenji and Hana, Kenji wouldn't allow Patricia to go. It would be too dangerous for her; she won't take it well."

"Fuck, Abby! Those two can't catch a break, can they?" Ralph said.

Patricia snuggled closer to Kenji and held him tight; she had awoken with a feeling of dread.

"What's wrong, *Kirei*?" Kenji asked as he turned on his side so he could look at her.

"Nothing," Patricia replied.

"You don't cling to me so tightly for nothing," Kenji said, kissing her. "Tell me what you're thinking about," he urged.

Patricia hesitated, trying to put her feelings into words. "Did you ever have the feeling that something was going to happen and there was nothing you could do about it?"

"Yes," Kenji replied. "What is it you think is going to happen?"

"I don't know, but do you think we can stay in bed for a little while longer?" Patricia asked.

"We can stay here all day if you wish," Kenji replied. Like Patricia, he sensed that something major was coming.

Hiroshi heard about Executive Order 9066 and grunted with disgust. In his mind, it only confirmed what he had come to believe, that the United State's profession of being a land that treated all equally was a lie. That the Japanese people were going to be locked up simply because they were Japanese was ludicrous and proved his point. He didn't see or want to see that he was just as guilty in that he put all blacks together and thought them an ignorant race of people. He had no proof of this; they were black, and that was all that mattered. He failed to see that this was the exact same thinking as the United Sates regarding the Japanese—not about the intelligence, but about them being spies and traitors just because Japan attacked on American soil.

He hadn't heard any news of Hana since her release, but one thing weighed on his mind. Was Hana with the American agent? His own agent seemed to enjoy tormenting him with the possibility. Hiroshi had been the only man Hana had ever been with; he was the one who deflowered her on their wedding night, and the thought of her with another man angered him; that the man was one of the enemy infuriated him. Not once during his imprisonment did Hiroshi admit that he was where he was because of his own decisions; not once did it occur to him that he had placed his family in danger by the decisions he made. He did wonder where they would end up, if they would end up at the same place, and what would happen if they did. Would they acknowledge each other? Probably not, and to be honest, it wouldn't hurt his feelings if they didn't.

Hiroshi wondered about Joben Saito and his daughter, Dai. Were they still here? What other lies had Joben told about him? Hiroshi's agent stopped questioning him about whom he reported to about the same time they released Hana. What had she told them? Nothing, because she knew nothing; she had made a point of knowing nothing, so how had she been released? Had she prostituted herself? She wouldn't have done that, would she? But then again, she did side with Kenji and accept the nigger girl as a daughter, so it was very possible that she gave herself to her agent in exchange for her freedom. So now she was a slut, he mused.

Because he wasn't allowed to have a newspaper, Hiroshi didn't know about the battle for Bataan, which had begun January 7, 1942, and was still raging, or that Singapore had surrendered to his native country. Whenever he asked for news of the war, he was only told about Japanese losses. Hiroshi knew what the agent was trying to do and refused to be baited; he wouldn't allow himself to become despondent. The emperor would prevail, and who knew? Maybe there would be a place for him in the emperor's government.

Joben Saito was a different story; for all of his talk about faith in the emperor, he had tried to denounce Japan. He had volunteered every piece of information he knew in the hopes that he would be released, as Hana Takeda had been. Joben conveniently forgot that Hana wasn't a spy but he was. There was also another thing he failed to realize: Dai had given the same information to the agent that had gotten Hana released.

Unlike Hiroshi, Joben no longer wanted to know about the progress of the war. His main objective was how he was going to obtain his freedom.

The morning he found out that he and the Japanese on the West Coast were going to be interred, he went into shock.

"But I have told you everything! I have cooperated with you!" he screamed at his agent.

"You didn't tell us anything we didn't already know," his agent replied dryly.

"Hana Takeda, how did she obtain her freedom?" Joben asked.

The agent wasn't going to respond but then changed his mind. "We received information that exonerated her."

Dai. She knew much more than he realized; was she free as well?

"My daughter, is she still here?" Joben asked.

The agent hesitated again. "No, she has been moved to another facility," he replied. As much as he despised the man sitting across from him, the agent couldn't bring himself to tell Joben that Dai had been released the week before. That would be the last act of kindness Joben Saito would ever receive.

Nick called his friend who worked at the White House in hopes of getting more information on EO 9066.

"Mitch? Nick here. Did you find out anything else about this order?"

"Yes, but why are you so interested in this?" Mitch asked.

"Just curious is all," Nick replied, knowing that his friend wouldn't buy the excuse.

"Uh huh, well anyway, the order also includes Germans and Italians, but mostly the ones located on the East Coast," Mitch replied.

"Any ideas of where they're going to take the Japanese?" Nick asked. He was pushing his luck, and he knew it.

Mitch hesitated before replying. "Nick, I don't know what you're into and I don't want to know, but be careful. The word got around about how you got those two Japanese women released, and people are beginning to talk. But to answer your question, they're looking at a variety of places. I don't know where exactly, but I do know that General Dewitt is planning on making the western half of the three West Coast states and the southern third part of Arizona military zones."

"What does that mean exactly?" Nick asked.

"It means that anyone who is of Japanese descent is going to have to move at some point. When? Who knows?" Mitch replied. "By the way, you didn't hear any of this from me," Mitch added before hanging up.

"Damn it!" Nick swore.

Kenji and Patricia didn't come up from the basement until late afternoon after spending the morning making love and talking about their plans. The feeling of impending doom that Patricia had experienced earlier was considerably lessened but not gone.

"Good, you're up. We need to talk," Abby said.

A feeling of foreboding hit Patricia hard, and she grabbed Kenji's hand. He gave it a reassuring squeeze and led her to the living room, where Ralph and Hana were already seated. Abby sat down and waited until Kenji and Patricia were situated.

"Miss Abby, what's wrong?" Patricia asked.

Abby didn't want to tell them, but what choice did she have? Maybe they would reconsider and move, although she doubted it. "Kenji, the president has signed an executive order called 9066."

"What is that?" Patricia asked, already fearing the worst.

Patricia, Kenji, and Hana listened in shock as Abby told them what she knew.

"Kenji, maybe you should reconsider your decision about staying here and going to the East. You can always come back after the war is over," Abby said. "I know you're concerned about how you'll support Hana and Patricia after you get there, but—"

"This is where our friends and family are," Kenji said, interrupting Abby. "If we move east, I won't be able to find a job there any more than I am able to find one here, and then what will happen to Patricia and my mother? If it were just me, I would take that chance, but that is not the case. At least here, if something happens, I know Patricia will be cared for."

Patricia couldn't speak. *This can't be happening!* she thought to herself. They weren't going to lock up a group of people because of their ethnicity, were they? But then she remembered the stories of the concentration camps in Germany and Poland; those people were being killed just because they were Jewish and gypsies or because they didn't fit the mold of a "perfect" German. This was 1942, for God's sake! She began to tremble as the realization of what could happen hit her: they would make Kenji go away, and he would make her stay with Miss Abby and Ralph.

"We don't know anything for certain yet," Abby said. "Nick is trying to find out and will let us know what's happening."

"They . . . they can't do this, can they?" Patricia asked.

"Patty, this is war," Ralph said kindly. "They'll do whatever they think is necessary, even if it's wrong."

"But . . . they didn't do anything!" she objected.

"No, *Kirei*, we didn't except that we are Japanese, but before we panic, why don't we wait to see what Nick tells us?" Kenji asked calmly. He had known that something like this was going to happen; he had known it since the first time they had gone to register. He and Patricia needed to have that conversation whether she wanted to or not; they had to think about every eventuality, with the ultimate goal that they wouldn't be separated, if at all possible. They would talk later when she calmed down and when they had more information from Nick.

The only one who hadn't spoken was Hana. Her heart broke as she watched Kenji soothe Patricia. *When will they have peace?* she wondered as she felt a stab of guilt at the part she had played in their past sufferings. She whispered a prayer to every god she could think of, including the Christian one, that they would come out of this intact and together.

For several minutes, no one spoke; what was there to say?

Nick sat at his kitchen table trying to determine the best way to break the news. There was no good way, he realized as he stood up to go to Abby's. He understood what the government was doing, but he didn't agree with it; they had the people that they knew to be spies in custody, so why do this? The part that sickened him was the majority of the Japanese that would be interred were American citizens. They had pledged their allegiance to this country just as he had, yet that didn't count for anything.

Just as he was about to leave, his phone rang. Mitch.

"Heads up, they're planning to ask the Japanese to move out of the proposed military zones, so if you know of anyone you want out of there, let them know. I heard that one of the places they're looking at for a camp is somewhere in the central part of the state—Manzanar, I think it's called."

"Manzanar? That's over two hundred miles from here," Nick said.

"You know the place?" Mitch asked.

"I know of it," Nick said. "I know that American Indians lived in the area for a long time, but the town itself was established by ranchers and miners somewhere around 1910. It was abandoned in 1929 or 1930, when LA bought out pretty much all of the water rights. Jesus, Mitch! They're thinking of putting people there?"

"I didn't know you were such a history buff, but yeah, that's what I'm hearing. I also heard that they're looking at some of the Southern and Eastern states, too," Mitch said.

"Thanks for the info; I owe you." Nick said and hung up.

He sighed and headed over to Abby's house.

Kenji and Patricia were in the basement trying to process what was possibly going to happen. *No*, Kenji thought, *it isn't a possibility—it is going to happen, and soon.* Patricia's head was resting on his chest, her favorite place, especially when she was frightened, as she was now. The big battle would be convincing her to stay with Abby and Ralph, where he knew she would be safe. He found himself wishing he had forced this talk sooner, but there was no getting around it now.

"Patricia . . . *Kirei*—"

"I know what you're going to say, and the answer is still no," Patricia interrupted.

"I wasn't going to ask that you find someone to care for you if something should happen to me. I think we are in agreement that there will be no one else for either of us, but we have other things to discuss," Kenji said.

"If it's about you leaving, I don't want to talk about it—"

"*Kirei*, we have to talk about it. We no longer have the luxury of putting it off," Kenji replied.

Patricia was already shaking, but her voice was firm when she spoke. "Fine," she said. "If they take you, then I'm going, too, and you can't stop me."

"*Kirei*—"

"No! I am your wife, and where you go, I go, and I don't care where it is!" she exclaimed.

Kenji closed his eyes and braced himself. He had never spoken to Patricia in the way he was about to. "Patricia," he said firmly enough that it got her attention. "This isn't up for discussion. You will not go with me, no matter where they send me. I need to know that you are safe and cared for; I have already discussed this with Ralph and Miss Abby, and they have agreed to care for you until I return, and I promise you that I *will* return."

"Kenji—"

"No, *Kirei,* my mind is made up. I don't know what kind of place they're planning to send us to, and I will not have you suffer needlessly," Kenji said.

"Don't you understand?" Patricia asked. "I'll suffer here, too! I'll worry and be scared that something's going to happen to you. I would rather suffer physical hardship with you than the mental hardship of not knowing if you're alive or dead or if you're being mistreated."

Kenji saw her point, but he didn't bend; she was staying here. Patricia saw the set to his jaw and knew she had just lost the battle.

Please, God, she prayed silently. *Let this be a big mistake.*

Kenji blinked back tears; he never wanted to speak to her like that again. It wasn't abusive by any stretch of the imagination, but their marriage had always been a partnership. They always made decisions together, but he had just taken that right from her. That it was for her good and safety didn't matter; he didn't like doing it. He was going to apologize but thought better of it; if he did, she would try to sway him, and he couldn't allow that—he might actually give in. He held her so tightly against him that she couldn't move, but she didn't object; she was holding him just as tightly.

Nick knocked on the door and waited for someone to answer. Over the months, Nick had come to like Kenji and Patricia and thought of them as friends. Both of them were intelligent people who needed a break, and it just wasn't happening. He was also realizing that he liked Hana, too, and not in what he considered to be a good way. The fact that people were already questioning his motives for getting her and Dai Saito released didn't bother him as much as why they thought he did it. He would have to start being more careful; for all he knew, he was being followed, although he didn't think so—and if he was? There'd be nothing to report. Everyone knew about Abby and her houseguests, and the house was being watched, even though Abby wasn't aware of it; he saw no point in telling her.

Hana opened the door after checking to see who it was.

"Hello, Hana," Nick said with a slight bow.

"Hello, would you like to come in?" Hana asked softly. She stepped back to let Nick in and offered him tea.

"No thanks; where is everyone?" he asked.

"Kenji and Patricia are in their room; Abby and Ralph are in the back yard. Would you like me to get them?" Hana replied.

"Please," Nick replied.

A few minutes later, they were all assembled in the living room. Nick took a deep breath and told them what he knew.

"Kenji, I understand why you don't want to leave here, but this thing is going to happen. I think you need to reconsider your decision. I don't know if Patricia can go with you when you're sent away, and not only that, you could end up on the East Coast anyway, and she'll be here. If you go voluntarily, at least you'll be together."

In fact, Kenji had been rethinking his position ever since he and Patricia had talked earlier. While she slept, he did a mental count of their available funds. Counting the money that Hana had, they would have close to a thousand American dollars, but they would have to pay for a place to live out of that, and food. The fact remained that he wouldn't be able to get a job, and he didn't want Patricia to have to support him and Hana, and besides, there was no guarantee that she would find a job.

"Kenji, maybe he's right," Patricia said. "I don't mind working. I'll scrub toilets if I have to, if it means that you won't have to go to one of those places."

Kenji wavered, but it was the thought of Patricia scrubbing anyone's toilet that stopped him from changing his mind. "No, we stay," he said firmly.

"Kenji," Ralph said. "Use your head! We'll help you with the money part if that's what the problem is. I own some land up in the Carolinas. There's a cabin up there; it ain't much, but it's solid. You, Patty, and Hana could go there."

"Kenji, please, let's go!" Patricia begged.

"There is another option," Nick said.

Everyone looked at him expectantly.

"Hawaii. The Japanese there aren't subject to be interred simply because the island is already under martial law. The question is whether they will let more Japanese in. Patricia wouldn't be a problem—or not much of one, anyway—but Kenji and Hana would be."

"Where would we live?" Patricia asked.

"I have a small house there you could use," Nick said, not quite believing that he was trying so hard to help them.

They were disturbed by a banging on the door. Nick made them all stay put while he answered it.

Hattie waited anxiously for the door to open. As soon as it did, she rushed in, looking for Patricia. "Thank the Lord!" she said, hugging her.

"Mama? Is Daddy all right?" Patricia asked.

"He's fine, but I had to come to check on you; we heard 'bout what theys wantin' to do. Your man, he all right? And his mama?" Hattie asked.

"We are fine," Hana said, hugging Hattie. It didn't escape her that a year ago she never would have done such a thing, but times had changed.

"Mama, we're thinking about moving east, or maybe to Hawaii," Patricia said.

Hattie sat down while Abby went to get her a drink. "It won't be easy no matter where you goes; you know that," she said. "But you'd be together."

They talked about the pros and cons of each location until late evening.

"I think Patricia and I need time to talk more about this," Kenji said finally.

"I understand," Nick said. "In the meantime, I'll see what I can find out about Hawaii."

MARCH 1942

Ralph read the papers and watched the news, along with Kenji.

"Fools!" Ralph exclaimed when he read about the siege of Leningrad. "Why doesn't the stupid son of a bitch realize it's over?" Ralph asked, talking about Hitler. "His men are dying of cold and starvation, and the fool tells them to stay put! That's the kind of leader somebody needs to shoot dead!"

Kenji didn't respond; for one thing, Ralph didn't expect him to, and secondly, he and Patricia were still trying to decide where they should go. He knew time was running out, but he had to make the best decision for everyone involved. They were leaning toward Hawaii, mostly because of the weather. Kenji didn't think his mother could take the sometimes-harsh Eastern winters.

He was also disturbed to hear that construction of a camp called Manzanar had begun; he was further disturbed to hear that several hundred Japanese-Americans had volunteered to build the camp. He understood the rationale; they could take their families with them and eliminate the chance for separation, but to build the place that would ultimately become a prison for you and your family? Kenji didn't see it, but supposed if he were in that position, he might have made the same decision.

By the end of March, the first groups of Japanese had begun to move to the camp. Others were moved to a detention center near Seattle, Washington. Other temporary sites were set up in Merced, Tulare, Marysville, and Fresno, California. It was really happening, and it was time for him, Patricia, and his mother to leave. Hawaii, Kenji decided.

Just as he was going to call Nick with his decision, the phone rang.

"Kenji, it's too late," Nick said.

"Too late for what?" Kenji asked, his heart already sinking.

"Effective today, no one of Japanese descent can leave the West Coast. I'm sorry."

Kenji couldn't speak. This was his fault; he had taken too long to decide, and now it was too late.

"Kenji? Are you there?" Nick asked.

"I'm here."

"I'm going to try to get you to Hawaii. Be ready to go because if it happens, it's going to happen fast. I've got to go."

Kenji stood with the phone receiver pressed to his ear. He was still standing there when Patricia found him.

"Kenji? What's wrong?" she asked worriedly.

"Come, *Kirei*, we must talk," he said, hanging up the phone and taking her hand.

Kenji led her to the basement, closing the door behind them so they wouldn't be disturbed. "*Kirei*, I waited too long deciding where we should go."

"What do you mean?" Patricia asked.

"As of today, no one of Japanese descent can leave the West Coast."

It took several minutes before Patricia understood what he was trying to tell her. "We can't leave? They're going to make you go to one of those places?" she whispered.

"Nick is going to try to get us to Hawaii, so we must be ready to go at a moment's notice. *Kirei*, I am so sorry that I waited so long."

Patricia's initial reaction was anger. Not just at Kenji, but at the world as a whole; this just shouldn't be happening! She swallowed her anger and put her arms around him. This wasn't the time for blame; it wouldn't have changed anything, and she didn't want to spend what could be their last times together being angry with him. She'd save that for when they got through this mess.

"*Kirei—*"

Patricia silenced him with a kiss.

"We'd better tell the others and your mother," she said gently.

Kenji had been waiting for her to yell and scream at him for letting the chance for them to leave pass them by and was surprised when it didn't happen. Instead, she accepted what was happening, but he had no doubt that when this was over, if it was ever over, she would let him know just how angry she'd been, and he would listen to her without complaint.

Kenji and Patricia came up from the basement, holding hands. Ralph, Abby, and Hana were sitting in the living room watching the news.

"Ralph, Miss Abby, Mother, we have some disturbing news," Kenji said.

They all looked at him and saw the expression on his face.

Kenji, with Patricia holding his hand, broke the news to them. "Mother, be ready to go and pack lightly. I'm sorry that I took so long to decide. . . . "

"Kenjiro, it will be all right," Hana said as she stood. She walked over to him and hugged him. "We will be fine; we are of the Takeda line, one of the strongest. We will get through this."

Patricia and Kenji went back to the basement to pack. Kenji looked over at Patricia as she went through her things; she had been through so much just because she loved him, and because of his indecision, she would suffer more.

Patricia felt his eyes on her and turned around to see his tear-streaked face.

"*Kirei*, I am so sorry that my indecision causes you more pain."

Without speaking, Patricia slipped out of her dress and walked over to him. When she was standing in front of him, she looked up at him and began to unbutton his shirt.

"Patricia—"

"Shhh. . . . Don't talk," Patricia said as she slid the shirt off his shoulders and kissed his chest. Kenji's arms went around her as she unbuckled his belt and undid the button at the top of his slacks. With her eyes glued to his, she unzipped his slacks and reached inside to take his erection into her hands.

The slacks slid to the floor and Kenji stepped out of them, standing in front of the bed totally nude. Patricia, in a rare show of aggression, pushed him back until his the back of his knees were against the bed, pushed until he was sitting down, and then pushed his chest until he was lying down with his legs hanging over the side of the bed.

As many times as they had made love, there was one thing Patricia had never done. And Kenji had never asked her to do. She had never taken him into her mouth; Kenji assumed that when she was ready, she would do it without him saying anything. He watched as Patricia tried to decide where to start, but he remained silent in anticipation of the pleasure he would feel when she finally took him into her mouth.

Patricia took a tentative swipe at the head of Kenji's penis, jumping when he jumped. She peeked up at him to see him watching her, his brown eyes filled with a look that she knew all too well and loved. Gaining a little confidence, she licked again and then took the head into her mouth and sucked on it like a lollipop while rubbing the underside of his erection with her hand.

Kenji began saying words in Japanese that she didn't understand, but got the gist of; he liked what she was doing. Patricia wrapped her hand around him as far as it would go and sped up her strokes as she increased the intensity and speed of her sucking on the head of his cock.

She was completely caught off guard when Kenji screamed as he released into her mouth for the first time. She was also surprised that she liked the slightly sweet and salty taste of him. Patricia released his softening member from her mouth and lay beside him, her head on his chest.

After he recovered, Kenji pushed Patricia onto her back and pulled the bra straps over her shoulders. He loved her breasts, especially her nipples; he loved the feel of them in his mouth as he licked and suckled on them and this time was no different. Before he took the first nipple into his mouth, he looked at her.

"Boku wa kimi wo it sumade aishurutsu mon da" (I will love you forever).

Reluctantly, he left her now-swollen and slightly sore nipples and made his way down the soft, rounded belly that she complained so much about, but that he loved; he loved her exactly as she was. *She's beautiful now, but when she is with child, she will be radiant*, Kenji thought as he kissed her stomach. All of these thoughts gave him even more determination to come back to her, no matter what it took.

Kenji continued his journey down Patricia's body, bypassing her mound and kissing her all the way down to her feet. She was very ticklish, and he did it because he loved the sound of her giggles when she was aroused; it was the combination of a giggle and a moan. It was a giggle he never heard unless she was aroused, as she was now. Kenji played for a few minutes before going back to where he really wanted to be—with his face buried between her legs.

Patricia opened for him as wide as she could, crying out when she felt his warm tongue caress her nub. Patricia was always surprised at the strength of the emotions she felt for Kenji, especially when they made love; it always brought her to the brink of tears, but this time she cried. For all she knew, this could be the last time they made love; she prayed it wasn't so, and the innate optimist in her had the same hope.

When she came, it was with his name on her lips.

Kenji moved up her body and slid into her, almost not caring whether he released inside of her or not. The only thing that stopped him was the thought that this time she would get pregnant, and he had no wish for her to go through a pregnancy alone. He wanted to go through every single step with her, including the delivery; he wanted to be the first to greet their child when he or she came into the world.

When he was close, he pulled out and collapsed on top of her, emptying on her stomach. He stayed where he was, as Patricia liked for him to do; this time she wanted him to stay put longer than usual, hugging him to her. Reluctantly, she let him go so they could clean up and finish packing.

Afterward, they stayed in the basement, skipping dinner. They talked about their plans, but this time, it didn't help. Both of them were frightened, but more for each other than for themselves.

Nick pulled every string he had and called in every favor he was owed, and it was all for nothing. All he could do now was keep his ear to the ground and find out where Kenji and Hana would be taken when the time came. He hoped it wasn't Manzanar; the weather there could be brutal, with temperatures reaching over one hundred in the summer and below freezing in the winter, as well as windstorms in the summers. Kenji would be able to tolerate it—he was young—but Hana was a different story. She wasn't old—she was his age, mid-forties—but she was petite. The cold would go right through her. Nick wondered why he was so concerned about her welfare; he told himself it was because he liked her as he would a friend and that was all.

He was now faced with having to tell them that he wasn't able to help. He was going to take the coward's way out and do it by phone, but decided to do it in person; he owed them that much. He had spoken with his friend Mitch several times and had been given the names of several other camps.

"We've got over a hundred thousand Japanese here on the West Coast, and that's including those who were born here," he reminded Nick. "Between me, you, and the gatepost, this is wrong! I can understand containing those who are immigrants and aren't US citizens, but all of them?"

Nick changed the subject; he didn't know who was listening, if anyone. He didn't believe that Mitch was reporting on him, but he wasn't taking any chances.

"Thanks for the updates! We'll need to get together soon," Nick said before hanging up.

Abby answered the door this time. She had a hopeful expression on her face that died when she saw his face.

"I tried everything I could think of to help," Nick said dejectedly. "I'm sorry."

Abby hugged him. "You tried, and you've helped us in so many other ways. I'll go get them."

Patricia started crying when Nick told them the news. Kenji put his arms around her and fought back tears of his own.

"I am so sorry," Nick said for the third time.

"How much time do they have?" Ralph asked.

"I don't know yet. They've already moved some people to the camp in Manzanar. Hiroshi Takeda, Joben Saito, and the others arrested on December 6 are being taken to other camps, but I don't know where. If I hear anything, I'll let you know."

Kenji and Patricia went back down to the basement. Kenji wasn't going to unpack, but Patricia made him.

"I don't want to be reminded that you're going to leave me behind," she said quietly.

Instead of reminding her that he would only have to pack again, Kenji unpacked. Neither of them spoke as they lay on the bed with their arms around each other.

"There has to be something we can do to help them!" Ralph insisted.

"I'm all ears," Abby replied.

"We could drive them to my place in the Carolinas," Ralph said.

"We'd never make it; we'd get stopped," Abby replied.

"What about a closer state, like Arizona?" Ralph asked. "We could take them to the northern part of the state and—"

"Ralph, how would we get them across the border? They're probably going to have checkpoints or something," Abby said.

"This isn't right."

"No, it's not," Abby agreed.

APRIL 1942

The entire household was on pins and needles. No one knew when or if Kenji and Hana would have to report to the Civil Control Station. Kenji and Patricia took each day as a gift and spent most of each day alone. Kenji no longer watched the news or read the paper, trusting Ralph to keep him up to date. There were things he would rather have not known about, such as the twenty-four thousand sick and starving troops, both American and Filipino, trapped on Bataan; the eventual fall of Bataan to the Japanese; and the subsequent death march. That humans could be so cruel to each other never failed to surprise and disturb him. Eventually, he asked Ralph not to tell him any more about the war; he only wanted to concentrate on his time with Patricia.

Hana and Hattie had become more than two mothers who got along because they loved their children; they became friends in spite of John's protests.

"You as bad as she is! Socializin' with the enemy," he said when Hattie got ready to go to Abby's house.

"John, our baby is goin' through a hard time, and she need her daddy. Can't you forget for one minute how mad you is at her and go to her just this once?" Hattie asked.

"She ain't my baby!" John spat out.

"You knows what? I think you and Kenji's daddy are jus' alike. Both of ya thinking 'bout yourselves instead of you children. Well, look where it got him; he in jail somewhere, and if you ain't careful, you be in jail, too—but only a different kind. Your girl, your Patty Cakes, is hurtin'; her man is gonna be taken away from her to who knows where, and she's scared. Are you tellin' me that you don't care 'bout that? I ain't askin' you to care 'bout him, but I am asking you to care 'bout your girl."

For just a second, Hattie thought she had gotten through, but then she saw John square his shoulders and clench his jaw. "John Elias Middleton, You has gots to be one of the most stubborn and stupidest men I knows! I only hope you get right with Patricia before you can't."

Hattie left John standing in the kitchen and headed out of the front door, where Abby was waiting for her.

"How are they?" Hattie asked when she was settled in the front seat.

"Scared, but for each other more than for themselves," Abby replied. "Hattie, she's going to need you when the time comes. We'll work it out so you can be at the house daily, even if I have to pay you to make up for any lost income."

"Abby, that girl means more to me than any amount of money; she needs me, then I'll be there," Hattie replied.

Neither woman could say when Hattie had become comfortable enough to stop using "Miss" or when she stopped calling

Ralph "Mr. Ralph," and it didn't matter. They were all friends and a family in a strange kind of way.

Hattie hugged Patricia, then Kenji, and finally Hana. "It will be all right," she assured them. "I been praying every day, and I believes that it will turn out right."

All of them hoped so and whispered silent prayers. Even Ralph, who claimed not to believe in the existence of God or any other higher power, began to pray only for Patricia, Kenji, and Hana, but never for himself.

As the month of April passed by, everyone became cautiously hopeful. Everyone was just beginning to relax a little when Ralph came home one day with a flyer.

MAY 3, 1942

Ralph was out for a walk when he noticed a flyer being handed out to any Japanese person passing by. He politely asked for one and was given one after being scrutinized. He found a place to sit and read the flyer:

> *WESTERN DEFENSE COMMAND*
> *Wartime civil control administration*
> *Presidio of San Francisco, California*
> *May 3, 1942*
> *INSTRUCTIONS*
> *TO ALL PERSONS OF*
> *JAPANESE ANCESTRY*
> *LIVING IN THE FOLLOWING AREAS*

Ralph read the flyer with a sinking heart. Kenji, Hana, and all the Japanese were going to be evacuated by twelve noon on Saturday, May 9, 1942. He finished reading the flyer with eyes blurred with tears; in his mind, his family was being ripped away from him. Kenji had become like a son to him and Patricia like a daughter. His heart hurt for them as most parents' would.

Unable to go home, Ralph walked around until he absolutely had to go home. He couldn't put off telling them; it was already the third, but when he walked in and heard Patricia's happy giggle, he couldn't make himself tell them. He would let them have tonight before he lowered the boom. Tomorrow would be soon enough.

Chapter 11

Ralph went to his room, bypassing the kitchen, and looked at the flyer again. He cursed when he realized he had missed a vital piece of information. As head of the family, Kenji had to report to the Civil Control Station either tomorrow or the following day for instructions. Ralph heard Patricia giggle again; it was a giggle he hadn't heard for a while now, and here he was about to take away their moment of happiness.

He had to tell them now so Kenji could decide which day he wanted to go, but they deserved another night of being happy, didn't they? Ralph agonized for almost an hour before he decided he had to tell them tonight; he could see no way around it.

Patricia, he knew, would be devastated; maybe he should tell Kenji first and let him decide the best way and time to tell her. That, he decided, was the best option. The next thing was to get Kenji alone for a few minutes. He heard someone coming up the stairs and recognized the footsteps as Abby's; he got off the bed and tapped on her door.

Abby was just about to change her clothes when Ralph tapped on the door. She opened the door to greet him when she saw the tears in his eyes.

"Ralph?"

Unable to speak, Ralph thrust the paper into Abby's hand and waited for her to read it. Abby looked at Ralph and then quickly scanned the paper. She felt the color drain from her face, and she felt faint. "What are we going to do?" she whispered.

"Nothin' we can do," Ralph replied gruffly. "I figured we should tell Kenji first and then let him tell Patty."

Both of them closed their eyes when they heard Patricia, Kenji, and Hana laughing. Abby held Ralph's hand and let the tears fall; she agreed with Ralph that the best thing to do was to let Kenji tell Patricia.

The opportunity to talk to Kenji alone didn't come until later. The women were in the kitchen doing dishes, and Kenji was in the library reading. Ralph lightly knocked on the door to get Kenji's attention and sat in the empty chair next to him. Instead of speaking, he handed Kenji the paper, much in the same way he had handed it to Abby earlier in the evening.

Kenji paled as he read the paper. He paled even more when he saw the dates he needed to go to the office.

"I am so sorry," Ralph whispered. "If there was anything I could do to help you, I would."

Kenji couldn't speak; he was going to have to tell Patricia that he and Hana had to leave her. He would tell her tonight and spend all day tomorrow doing whatever he could to reassure her. But reassure her of what? He didn't even know where they would be going. What if it was the East Coast? He forced himself to slow down and deal with one thing at a time.

"The only thing I will need from you is to know that you and Abby will keep your word and care for Patricia," Kenji said, once he found his voice.

"You have my word," Ralph said. "And I know you have Abby's word, too."

Kenji nodded and looked toward the door; he had to tell her, and the sooner the better. He thanked Ralph, stood, and folded the paper.

Patricia was in the kitchen with Hana and Abby, looking so happy that he thought about putting it off until tomorrow, but changed his mind; her reaction would be the same no matter when he told her. He had to tell his mother, too, but Patricia was his priority. He decided to hand the paper to Hana and let her read it for herself and leave it to Abby and Ralph to comfort her.

"*Kirei*, come with me," Kenji said, holding out his hand.

Right before his eyes, Kenji saw the sparkle in Patricia's eyes dim and then disappear. Patricia took his hand, not looking at anyone else, and followed him to their room.

Abby, Ralph, and Hana knew the exact moment Kenji told Patricia he had to leave because they heard her gut-wrenching sob and his tear-filled voice trying to comfort her.

No one slept that night, as Ralph and Abby sat with Hana while Kenji and Patricia stayed in the basement. Abby called Nick to see if there was anything he could do from his end, already knowing the answer.

"There's nothing I can do to stop it, but I'll try to find out where they're going," he said. "How's Hana?"

"Better than Patricia is right now," Abby replied. "Isn't there something we can do?"

"I wish there was, but there isn't. But that doesn't mean I won't keep trying. Just tell them I'm sorry," Nick said before hanging up.

Patricia was numb; she couldn't cry anymore, and there was nothing to talk about. They were going to make Kenji and Hana go to one of those places, and Kenji's resolve that she wasn't going with them remained strong. She had just spent the last two hours begging him to let her go, him holding her as she begged.

"I'll . . . I'll sneak on the bus," she threatened, knowing it was an idle threat; she'd stick out like a sore thumb. She went so far as to say that she's steal Abby's car, leading Kenji to make a mental note to tell Ralph and Abby to make sure they kept the car keys hidden. Patricia would kill herself trying to reach him; she couldn't drive.

Four hours after receiving the news, Patricia had finally calmed down. They had decided that he would go to the office in the morning and get it over with so they could have the rest of their days uninterrupted.

Kenji began to sing to her softly in Japanese until she drifted off to sleep; when she woke up, she wanted to know what the song meant.

"It's a song about a soldier who had to leave his beloved because of a war. They loved each other very much, just as we love each other. The night before he had to leave, he made a promise to her that he would return to her, never to leave her again."

"Did he keep his promise?" Patricia asked.

"He did, although it took him many months after the war to find her, but he never gave up. She never gave up on him coming home; she turned down many offers of marriage to wait for him. When they finally found each other, he kept his word, and he never left her again."

"That's a beautiful story," Patricia said.

"*Kirei*, I am like that soldier in the song. I have to go, but I swear to come back to you even if it takes me years, and once we are together again, I will never leave your side. One of the things that I loved and love about you is your optimism. Even when things were at their worst, you believed they would get better. I need you to believe that we will be together again and that we will have many beautiful children and grandchildren together. We each have to believe that; can you do that?"

Patricia couldn't speak; she was crying again, but she nodded her head yes. She clung to Kenji and fell into a fitful sleep. Kenji stayed awake long past midnight, hoping he would be able to keep his word and return to her. He wanted to go check on Hana, but whenever he moved, Patricia whimpered and moved closer to him. Finally he gave up and fell asleep, holding her tightly against him.

Everyone was in the kitchen when they came up from the basement. Hana looked exhausted but not frightened; Abby and Ralph just looked sad. Patricia grabbed her sweater when Kenji grabbed his coat to go to the Civil Control Station, which was located at the Japanese Union Church on San Pedro Street in LA; Ralph was in the car waiting for him.

"*Kirei*, where are you going?" Kenji asked.

"With you," Patricia said as she put her sweater on.

"No, *Kirei*, stay here with Abby and my mother; we shouldn't be too long. When I come back, we'll spend the day in bed."

"No."

Kenji raised his eyebrows. "No?"

"No, I'm coming with you even if I have to walk," Patricia said stubbornly.

"That's my girl," Abby murmured, glad to see some of Patricia's spunk.

After arguing with Patricia for more than fifteen minutes, Kenji gave in, but with a stipulation. "You must stay in the car with Ralph."

Reluctantly, Patricia agreed. The church wasn't too far away from Abby's house, but the line was around the corner, down the street, and extended for several blocks. Before Kenji could remind her of her promise to stay in the car, Patricia was out and walking toward the end of the line.

Kenji caught up with her and grabbed her arm. "What are you doing? You agreed to stay in the car with Ralph."

"I know, but I want to wait with you," Patricia said softly. "Please?"

Kenji ignored the dirty looks and derogatory comments spoken in Japanese and hugged Patricia to him and then headed toward the back of the line. It took hours before they reached the front of the line. After a while, people were so tired that they no longer paid any attention to Patricia, but when someone walked down the line offering water, they were ignored. Ralph came to the rescue several times by bringing them something to eat and drink while they waited, earning angry glares from the others in line.

Finally at the front of the line, Kenji received his instructions, which were exactly like the ones on the flyer at home. The only thing that was new was he found out where he and Hana would be going.

"She going with you?" the man asked.

"No," Kenji said before Patricia had a chance to speak.

"Probably for the best," the man said and waved them on.

"That was it?" Patricia asked as she walked to the car on very sore and tired feet.

Abby and Hana were anxiously waiting when they got back. Kenji sat Patricia down, took off her shoes, and examined her swollen ankles and feet.

"I wish you had stayed here, where you would have been comfortable," Kenji said as he began to massage her feet.

Patricia didn't reply because she had fallen asleep in the chair. Abby got a blanket and covered her as Kenji continued to rub her feet.

MAY 8, 1942

The week flew by so fast that no one could believe that the next day Kenji and Hana had to report to the Civil Control Center to be transported to the camp. Both Hana and Kenji were packed and ready to go. Fortunately, because Nick knew what the area was like, they were ready with mittens, extra socks, and blankets. Kenji left most of the money with Patricia, with him and Hana each taking a hundred dollars just in case. He stowed his luggage in Hana's room so Patricia wouldn't see it; he didn't want any reminders that he was leaving to distract from their last evening together.

They ate breakfast with Abby and Ralph before going back to their room, where they talked, cried, and made love. They only left the basement for meals and to use the bathroom and periodically to check for news from Nick. The later it got, the more the hope that Nick would be able to do something diminished. By midnight, all hope was gone; Kenji and Hana would be leaving in the morning.

"When this is over," Kenji said, "we will travel wherever you want to go."

It was a very familiar conversation meant to give hope and to soothe, but it didn't work. Patricia fought back tears, trying to be brave, but failing.

At one point, she sat up and took off the necklace Kenji had given her for her birthday. Tearfully, she put it around his neck. "Give it back to me when we're together again," she said as she kissed him.

Kenji pulled her back toward him when she went to move away. He buried his face in her neck and kissed it slowly, savoring the feel of her against his lips. In a few hours, all he would have would be memories to live on. He took his time exploring her with his lips, his eyes closed, trying to commit her to memory; no one knew how long he would be gone.

He could tell Patricia was crying again by the way her body shook; he didn't tell her not to cry because he was crying himself. He made love to her breasts, paying special attention to her nipples as his hands touched her everywhere he could reach. He stopped long enough to tell her that he loved her and to repeat his promise to come back to her. He did all of the things that made her giggle in the way he loved to hear when they made love, but this time there were sobs mixed with the giggles.

Kenji took his time in tasting her, drawing her pleasure out for as long as he could before she came, throbbing on his tongue. Without stopping, Kenji kissed a wet trail back up to her nipples, taking one and then the other into his mouth as he slid into her and stilled.

They lay that way for several minutes—their mouths pressed together, taking in each other's breaths. Kenji moved first, slowly pulling back and then sliding back in again. Patricia reached for his hands, and their fingers intertwined as Kenji thrust into her faster and harder. Patricia freed her hands, opened her legs wider, and wrapped her arms around his waist. She could tell that he was close, but she held on, not wanting him to pull out. In her mind, she hadn't gotten pregnant in all of this time—it wasn't going to happen now.

"*Kirei*!" Kenji moaned as he came deep inside of Patricia's womb. Patricia came shortly afterward, still holding on to him and sobbing. Neither of them spoke as Kenji pulled out of her, lay beside her, and pulled her tight against him.

MAY 9, 1942

Patricia and Kenji cleaned up and dressed in silence, too afraid to speak because they'd both start crying again. No one ate breakfast, but Abby made sandwiches for Hana and Kenji to eat on the bus.

Nick came just as they were getting into the car to go to the center. Abby took one look at him and could tell he hadn't gotten any more sleep than they had.

He went to Kenji and shook his hand. "I . . . I don't know what to say except that I wish this wasn't happening. There's a man there by the name of Mitch Dalton; he's a friend of mine. If you need anything, tell him, and he'll reach me. I'll help Patricia as much as I can, so try not to worry about her too much. I'll try to come up as often as I can, and I'll bring any letters or messages from here and vice versa. Just watch your back up there."

"Thank you for your friendship and kindness," Kenji said, accepting Nick's extended hand.

Nick went to Hana next. "Take care of yourself, and the same goes for you as far as Mitch is concerned; let him know if you need anything, and I'll try to get it for you."

Abby looked at Nick closely; he was in love with Hana Takeda, even if he hadn't admitted it to himself. If he hadn't, it was because one, she was still a married woman, and two, she was Japanese. Abby also knew that even if Hana hadn't been married, Nick still wouldn't have admitted how he felt about her; Hana's race would have stopped him, something that she found quite sad. Nick followed them to the center, transporting Patricia and Kenji; he didn't talk, allowing them the time to talk between themselves.

Nick watched them through the rearview mirror as Kenji wiped Patricia's tears away with a handkerchief that was beautifully embroidered and wondered if Patricia had been the one to do it. Nick parked the car and carried Kenji's luggage so he could hold Patricia for as long as possible before having to leave.

Patricia was literally shaking as they approached the bus that would take Kenji away. Boarding the bus took some time, as people had to find places for their luggage. Kenji took the opportunity to hold Patricia and reassure her that he and Hana would be all right. She tried one more time to get him to change his mind about her going with him.

"No, *Kirei*," he said gently. "I want you to stay where you will be safe."

Kenji was the last to board the bus; Hana had already said her goodbyes and boarded, reserving a seat for Kenji.

Patricia fought the urge to hold on to him when he kissed her and pulled away; she blinked back her tears so she would appear strong for him in front of everyone watching. "Be careful!" she admonished after kissing him again.

"Let's go!" someone yelled from the bus.

Kenji looked at the speaker and then back at Patricia. "*Boku wa kimi wo it sumade aishurutsu mon da* (I will love you forever)," he whispered in her ear as he hugged her

Patricia's throat tightened. "*Boku wa kimi . . . wo . . .* " She hesitated and then continued, "*It sumade aishurutsu mon da.* (Please be careful and come home)."

Kenji gave Patricia one last hug and kiss before he walked toward the bus.

Abby, Ralph, Nick, and now Hattie, who had just arrived, surrounded her as Kenji walked away. Tears ran down Patricia's face as she struggled not to run after him. They watched as Kenji got on the bus, sat down, and strained to see Patricia. As soon as the bus pulled away, Patricia fell apart; she no longer cared who was watching as she dropped to the ground, hugged herself, and sobbed.

"Come on, baby girl; let's get you home," a voice she hadn't heard in over a year said as arms went around her.

"Daddy?"

"Come on, get up and you can rest at Miss Abby's," John said, helping her up.

John had followed Hattie to the church to see the Japanese being taken away. He had been unprepared to see the strength and pain Patricia showed as she said goodbye to Kenji. Even so, he wasn't going to approach her; he was just going to walk away until he saw her fall to her knees in sadness and pain. For those few minutes, he forgot he was angry with her. She was his Patty Cakes, and she needed her daddy.

Patricia stood up, threw herself into John's arms, and sobbed.

"It'll be all right, baby; he look like he a strong man," John soothed.

Hattie and Abby watched in relief as father comforted daughter. John walked with his arm around Patricia's waist, almost supporting her. Hattie sat on one side of her in Nick's car while John sat on the other side; both of them had an arm around her.

No one spoke on the drive back to Abby's house, not knowing what to say. John helped Patricia into the house and sat her on the couch.

"We needs to talk, but not now," John said. "If it all right with Miss Abby, I'll come tomorrow or the next day."

Patricia nodded and lay down on the couch. She had never felt so helpless, frightened, and alone. She hadn't been this frightened even when Vernon was going to rape and kill her in the greenhouse. She didn't respond when she felt a warm blanket cover her as she cried herself to sleep.

MANZANAR, CALIFORNIA

Kenji choked back a sob as the bus pulled away, taking him away from Patricia. Hana reached over and took his hand in hers and gave it a reassuring squeeze. The only consolation he had was that Patricia was going to be safe, even if he wasn't sure of his own safety. He toyed with the necklace around his neck and thought about Patricia; they should have left when they had the chance. They would have managed somehow. He recalled his words to Patricia about having faith that he would return. He meant it and resolved that whatever he had to do to get back to her, he would do it. He was going to be that soldier in the song and return to his beloved, even if it took him years.

Hana stroked Kenji's knuckles like she used to do when he was young and needed comfort; the reality of it was that it was just as comforting for her as it was for him. She wondered what had become of Hiroshi; was he still in prison, or was he being moved to one of the camps? Her curiosity wasn't because she cared for him—she didn't—she just wanted to know. It didn't occur to her to ask Nick when she had seen him that morning, but then there were other things taking precedence over one man who didn't care about his family.

Hana felt a fierce pride for Patricia; she saw how she had struggled to let Kenji go and how she tried to control her fear, pain, and grief. Hana had also seen the one thing Kenji hadn't; if he had, he would have jumped off the bus to go to her. Hana saw Patricia fall to her knees and hold herself when she thought the bus was far enough away that no one would see. Patricia, she decided, was a much stronger woman than she was. Hana recalled the first time Hiroshi went away for a business trip. How she had cried and begged for him not to go, and here was Patricia, who didn't know when or if she would see Kenji again, showing a strength and courage that put her to shame. Kenji had chosen well.

Hana glanced over at Kenji to see how he was doing, but his eyes were closed and his cheeks wet with tears, a small smile that contained sadness on his lips. He was thinking about Patricia and missing her, as she was no doubt missing him.

They arrived at the camp later that afternoon. Hana and Kenji were shocked at how barren the land was, but were awed by the beauty of the mountains that surrounded the camp. Later, Kenji would learn the names of the mountains were Mount Whitney and that the camp was nestled between the Sierra Nevada Mountains and the White-Inyo Range.

Once Kenji finished looking at the mountains, he looked around the camp. His eyes widened when he saw the barbed-wire fence and the eight watchtowers spread along the fence. They widened even more when he saw what they would be living in: the barracks were made of pine covered with tar paper. *This is where we're expected to live?* he wondered as he and Hana went to their assigned area. The floors were bare and would be freezing in the winter, but he counted them as lucky; some families weren't placed together.

He left Hana to organize their space as he walked around the camp. He counted thirty-six residential blocks, two staff housing blocks, two warehouse blocks, a garage block, a hospital, and a military police compound. Kenji continued his walk until he ended back at the barracks where he and Hana were staying. He located the mess hall, the two communal bathhouses, and noted the lack of privacy. *This*, he thought as he continued his walk, *is unbelievable—that people could be herded together and forced to live in housing that's inadequate and lacking privacy.* He was glad he hadn't given in and let Patricia come with them.

Kenji realized he had to keep busy in order not to despair and miss Patricia so much. Later, after he and Hana were settled, he would go to the hospital and volunteer there and anyplace else that needed help. Patricia had insisted that he pack his medical journals, and now he was glad she had; when he wasn't doing anything, he would continue to read them.

Several children ran by Kenji, and he wondered whom they belonged to; he stopped an older woman who seemed to be the caretaker and asked her about them in Japanese.

"Those children are all from orphanages and foster homes. The government said they had to come here as well, even though they're hardly old enough to be enemies of the government," she said.

"Who cares for them?" Kenji asked, grateful that he and Patricia didn't have children. The child would have had to come here as well as Patricia; there was no way she would have agreed to be separated from him and their child.

"There is an orphanage here," the woman replied. "We could always use teachers, if you're interested."

"Couldn't the orphanages where they came from keep them?" Kenji asked.

"I believe they tried," the woman said. "There are three orphanages I know of that fought for the children: the Mary Knoll Home for Japanese Children; the Shonien, which is located in Los Angeles; and the Salvation Army's Japanese Children's Home in San Francisco. And these are the largest ones, but no one listened. So we have these children, who are total innocents, paying for something they had no hand in," the woman added sadly.

"Are you a teacher?" Kenji asked in Japanese.

"I was, but I must warn you, be careful with whom you speak our native tongue; we're not to speak it, although I'm not sure how they expect those of us who don't speak English to communicate."

"I would like to help," Kenji said in English. "I can teach those who wish to learn how to read and write in English, and I'm sure that my mother would like to help in the orphanage."

"Any and all help would be appreciated," the woman replied. "What's your name?"

"I am Kenjiro Takeda, and my mother is Hana Takeda. It is an honor to meet you."

"I am called Shinju Yamada. I'm in charge of the orphanage; I thank you and your mother in advance for any help you may offer us."

They talked for a few more minutes, with Kenji promising to bring Hana by the orphanage the next day. Kenji hadn't thought to ask how many children there were, but it really didn't matter. One child having to live here was one child too many.

Hiroshi looked at the barracks with disgust. He bit back the urge to complain, as he was in enough trouble as it was. His agent had made it clear to him that he was lucky he wasn't dead when Hiroshi complained about going to a camp.

"Look, you ungrateful son of a bitch!" he had said. "If I had my way, you'd be hanging instead of living off the money of this country."

Now, looking around, Hiroshi thought he would have just as soon died. *The niggers live better than this*, he thought as he sat on his cot. Hiroshi had arrived two weeks before and for the most part kept to himself; every once in a while he would see someone he knew, but turned around before they saw him. The one person he didn't want to know that he had been seen was standing now not more than fifteen feet in front of him. Joben Saito.

Hiroshi spent his days wandering around the camp and wondering if there was a way to escape. It was much too soon to start asking questions about the surrounding area, and there were other problems: he had no money and he didn't know anyone. The way he saw it, he had two choices: he could try to fit in and stay out of trouble or bide his time. He opted for the latter choice.

It didn't take long for Hiroshi to figure out that there was some dissension between two groups of internees, the Japanese American Citizens League and several of the first-generation Japanese. Instead of joining either group, Hiroshi sat back and watched. He wanted to see who would come out on top. Discretely, he tried to find out what the point of contention was between the groups, and as far as he could tell, it was a matter of respect. The JACL acted as representatives to the administration, but the elders didn't share their views, making for very lively meetings where nothing was accomplished.

In a way, Hiroshi was disgusted. Japanese fighting against Japanese when they needed to band together? He had learned his lesson well; he kept his mouth shut, keeping his opinions to himself. His sixth sense about trouble had kicked in, and he didn't want to be involved unless it was to his benefit.

Joben Saito had arrived at the camp the week before Hiroshi. His reaction to the camp was the same as Hiroshi's and Kenji's had been. He found it hard to believe that he had nothing and that for the basics of life, he was dependent on the very people he had conspired against. His goal wasn't escape but survival, and he would kiss as many white asses he needed to in order to reach that goal.

He still didn't know where his daughter, Dai, was or even if she was still alive. The father in him was concerned because he did love her, but the spy for the emperor in him was furious with her; she had used information he had painstakingly gathered for her own gain. He had conveniently forgotten that he was going to use the same information for himself to the same end.

Unlike Hiroshi and Kenji, Joben stayed in the quarters he shared with a family of six, only leaving for meals and to use the communal bathrooms and showers. Joben counted himself fortunate that the children were all older, with the youngest being twelve and the oldest seventeen. They spent much of the day out and about, exploring and helping with the construction of whatever buildings were going up.

The real reason that Joben stayed hidden was because he had seen Hiroshi Takeda arrive at the camp. Joben knew that Hiroshi knew it was he who made the agents at the prison believe Hiroshi was the leader of the spy ring. He was also positive that Hiroshi hadn't taken it well and wouldn't pass on an opportunity to exact revenge; the trick was going to be staying out of his way until they were released. Then he could disappear, maybe move to the East or the South.

Joben was also aware of the tensions between the two groups of Japanese and, like Hiroshi, decided to stay out of it until the dust settled and then decide what he was going to do, if anything. For the moment, his main goal was survival, and if joining one of the groups ensured that, then he would do it.

There was one thing Joben wasn't aware of: Hiroshi had already seen him.

Kenji and Hana ate a quiet dinner in the mess hall. From time to time, they would see someone who had come on the bus with them who would make a comment about Patricia. Kenji tensed but pretended not to hear; he was bound and determined that he was going home to her, and getting into a fight wasn't the way to do it. He was already dreading the night, when he knew he would miss her the most. He lay down his fork and stopped eating.

"Kenjiro, you have to eat," Hana said softly.

Kenji didn't respond, but picked up the fork and forced himself to finish his meal. Hana was right; he had to eat and do the things he did at home, including his training. He would fill his days with so much activity that when night came, he would be too exhausted to miss Patricia. As he sat at the table, the thought that he shouldn't have married Patricia crossed his mind and then was gone. He knew that if she was given the choice, she would do all of it again, and so would he.

Patricia roused from her sleep and started to ask Kenji why he had let her fall asleep on the couch, when she remembered that he wasn't there to ask.

"Patricia?" Hattie asked as she moved to the couch.

"Mama?" Patricia said and laid her head on Hattie's lap like she had done when she was a child. "What if something happens to him and I don't know it?"

Hattie rubbed Patricia's arm. "Patricia, honey, I know that it's hard and that you scared, but have a little faith. I don' believe God put you through this for nothin'."

Patricia didn't reply for several minutes, and then she told Hattie the story that Kenji told her about the soldier and his beloved.

"It sound like he planning on comin' back, and what that means is that you have to take care of yourself. Abby left you some soup on the stove, and I want you to eat it," Hattie said firmly.

Patricia really had no appetite, but she forced the soup down before going down to the basement to her and Kenji's room.

"You don't hafta sleep down there; you can use Hana's room if you want," Hattie said.

"No, you sleep there; I'll sleep in our bed downstairs," Patricia replied.

The basement door had barely closed behind her when the tears came. She cried as she changed for bed, and by the time she was in bed, she was sobbing.

Kenji lay on his cot and had never felt so lonely. Patricia was only a little over two hundred miles away, but she might as well have been on the moon. He touched the necklace around his neck and then touched his wedding band. *This place is wrong on so many levels*, he thought as he closed his eyes.

"Kenji," his mother called to him.

"Are you all right?" Kenji asked, concerned.

"Don't worry so much about me," Hana said. "I am stronger than I look. I just wanted to tell you something. Patricia is a strong woman, and she will survive this, just as you will. I also wanted to tell you that I am proud of you and that I am proud to call Patricia my daughter."

Kenji swallowed hard before he responded. "Thank you, Mother; that means a lot to me. There's an orphanage here," he said, changing the subject.

"Here?" Hana asked, surprised.

Kenji told her about the conversation he had with the woman who was in charge of the orphanage.

"I told her that you would help with the children," he said.

"I would like that; it will give me something to do," Hana replied.

MAY 10, 1942

Kenji was awake early; he missed Patricia so badly that his chest hurt. He fought the urge to stay in bed, knowing that it would only make things worse. Hana was already up, her cot neatly made and a broom next to it. It didn't take long for Kenji to understand the reason for the broom; his blankets were covered in dust from the night before. Dust flew from his hair as he ran a hand through it. He would have to come up with a way to minimize the amount of dirt and dust that came into their quarters; if he didn't, they were both looking at respiratory problems.

Kenji got up, dressed, and made his bed after using the broom to beat the dust from the blankets. What he really wanted was a bath, but he knew that the lines for the showers would be long and decided to try to take his showers as early in the morning as he could.

Hana was already in the dining room eating breakfast when Kenji got there.

"Good morning, Mother," he said as he sat down with his breakfast.

"Good morning," Hana replied with a small smile. "I thought we could walk to the orphanage after breakfast."

Kenji nodded his agreement. "I also want to stop at the hospital to see if I can volunteer there," he said as he took a sip of tea. He thought about Patricia and wondered how she was. "I love you, *Kirei*," he whispered as he took the last sip of his tea.

Kenji took Hana around the camp, showing her where things were before taking her to the orphanage. They found Shinju helping one of the younger children get dressed for the day.

"Shinju, this is my mother, Hana," Kenji said. "I told her about the orphanage, and she would like to help."

"Thank you; we will need all the help we can get," Shinju replied.

"How many children are here?" Hana asked.

"Right now, almost one hundred," Shinju replied.

"One hundred? All of them without parents?" Hana asked.

"Yes, some of them were in foster homes but were taken away and brought here," Kenji said, repeating the information Shinju had given him.

Hana looked at the children; the older ones were helping the younger ones get ready for breakfast. "Kenji, I'm going to stay and help Shinju. Why don't you go to the hospital?"

"I'll come back for you later," Kenji said as he kissed Hana on the cheek.

As Kenji walked to the hospital, he looked at the faces of the people passing him. The expressions on their faces were almost identical to the expressions he had seen while they were waiting to be registered: anger, fear, and resignation.

He found the hospital to be larger than he had originally thought it to be. For the first time since his arrival, Kenji felt a sense of peace. Nothing would make him stop missing Patricia, but this would help him cope and give him some purpose. Kenji walked around until he found someone he thought could help him.

"I am Kenjiro Takeda," he said, introducing himself to the man looking at a chart.

"Yes, what of it?" the man asked, not looking up from the chart.

"I would like to volunteer to help," Kenji said.

The man looked up from his chart and gave Kenji an appraising look. "What is it you want to do?" he asked.

Misunderstanding the question, Kenji replied, "I would like to be a physician when this is over."

"That's not what I asked, but it will do. Be here at six tonight," the man said tersely.

"Please, may I ask your name?" Kenji asked.

"Dr. Mynt," the man responded and then walked away.

Hiroshi was out and about when he first saw Kenji and Hana. He was so shocked that he almost ran into the person walking in front of him. *How long have they been here?* he wondered and decided not very long; they still had that slightly shocked expression on their faces. He also wondered what barracks they were in and if he should make himself known to them. *What would be the point?* he asked himself as he walked away and headed toward the dining hall.

Joben Saito was another matter altogether; Hiroshi planned to have a talk with Joben sometime soon. Hiroshi had already been quietly spreading rumors about Joben's betrayal to the others in his group, taking care not to reveal that he was one of the betrayed. He started with the family Joben was sharing space with and then picked out random people he saw Joben talking to. Hiroshi wanted him completely isolated before he spoke with him and decided what he wanted to do with him.

Joben was now the enemy.

Joben couldn't understand the attitude change of the family he shared space with. While they had never been overly friendly, now they refused to look at or even speak to him. Even the people he usually greeted when he was on his way to the shower or dining room no longer spoke to him. When he tried to ask what was happening, no one replied except to call him "*uragirimono*"—"backstabber" in Japanese.

The only thing he could figure out was that someone was talking. He didn't think of Hiroshi because, as far as he knew, Hiroshi didn't know he was here. But who else could it be?

Patricia woke up bleary-eyed and exhausted; she slept for a few minutes at a time, always waking to find Kenji gone. She spent the day down in the basement, not even bothering to get dressed; she only left the basement to use the bathroom and immediately returned, not speaking to anyone.

Abby, Ralph, and her mother left her alone for the first day, figuring that she needed the time to adjust, but when day three passed without her eating or drinking anything, they decided to take action.

Every hour, one of them went down to the basement, if only to talk to her. The designated person took either a glass of water or a glass of juice with them. Sometimes the water or juice would be gone and sometimes not; they all agreed not to push the food just yet. As long as she was drinking, she would be all right for a few days without food.

On the fifth day, Patricia got an unexpected visitor.

"Baby girl, you has to eat somethin'," John Middleton said gently as he came down the stairs carrying a tray with a sandwich and juice on it.

"I'm not hungry," Patricia replied, not reacting to the fact that it was her father bringing her the food.

"Eat anyways; Miss Abby made this for ya," he said and sat the tray on the small table by the bed.

Patricia looked at the food and then looked away. "Why are you here, Daddy?" she asked tiredly. "Is it to tell me that you're glad Kenji's gone? Because if you are, I get it—I'm not your daughter anymore."

John rubbed his face, trying to think of a way to let Patricia know that he still loved her even though he wasn't happy with the choice she had made. "Patty Cakes, I ain't here to tell you that I'm glad your man is gone. I ain't never made no secret about how I felt about you and him, and I ain't changed my mind on that.

"Now, your mama been tellin' me for a long time now that you is still my girl, and she right 'bout that. Baby, I am sorry he got taken away, but only because you hurtin' because of it. I watched you the day they took him, and girl, you a Middleton through and through. What you needs to do right now is remember that and pull yourself together. You has to be ready for whatever come your way. You can't be sick if he come home, can ya?"

Patricia could hardly believe what she was hearing; she had her father back. While he would probably never accept Kenji, he accepted her back as his daughter, which begged a question.

"Daddy, I am so glad that you're here, but I have to ask you something," Patricia said. "I know that you don't like Kenji or rather what he is, but he is and will always be my husband. Will you be able to respect him as my husband? Because if you can't. . . . "

"Patricia, I can't tell you that I understand why you married a Jap because I don't, but I does understand love. If he come home, he will have my respect as another human bein' and because he your man. That be all that I can give ya," John said.

"It's enough," Patricia cried and threw herself into her father's arms and cried.

Patricia came up from the basement in time for dinner. John and Hattie had already gone home.

Ralph stopped what he was doing and gave her a hug and whispered assurances in her ear. "He's going to be fine, Patty, I know he is," he said as he hugged her again.

"Thank you," Patricia said, blinking back tears. Kenji had been gone for almost a week, and it was time to start getting used to life without him, no matter how temporary it might be.

Abby hugged her next and kissed her cheek. "We're going to get through this," she promised.

Patricia forced down the light supper that Abby had prepared and insisted on cleaning up.

"Go relax; you've been taking care of me for the past week," she said when Ralph and Abby started to clear the table. Abby stayed in the kitchen and kept her company while Ralph watched the news; she no longer cared to hear about the dead and dying. The battle of the Coral Sea was over and done after lasting for four days; on the fifteenth, the bill creating the Women's Auxiliary Army Corp (WAAC) became law. Under normal circumstances, Abby would have been thrilled, but the concern about Patricia and Kenji overrode any elation she may have felt.

"What is that, exactly?" Patricia asked, wanting to talk about anything so she wouldn't think about Kenji.

"According to the news and the papers, they're the first women to serve in the military in roles other than nurses. They go through basic training and wear uniforms, too. The men aren't taking too kindly to it, but that doesn't surprise me," Abby said. "And my personal opinion is that the bill only passed because there's a shortage of men. What the women will be doing, I'm not sure, but it's about damned time."

"Are they going to let colored women in?" Patricia asked.

"The paper says they'll start training in Des Moines, Iowa, in July and that there are going to be one hundred twenty-five enlisted and over four hundred who are candidates for officer training, and forty of those are black," Abby replied. "See, Patricia? Things are changing already."

"Maybe, but I'll bet you they'll still be segregated," Patricia replied.

"I'm sure they will be, but it's a step in the right direction."

"Miss Abby? Do you think Kenji and Hana are all right?" Patricia asked.

Abby hesitated, not wanting to give Patricia pat answers. "I think that if they weren't, Nick would have told us. Remember, he has that friend working up there," Abby replied.

Patricia swallowed hard and nodded. "Do you think they'd let me in to see him?"

"I don't know, Patricia. That would be a question for Nick, and there is the issue of gas, but I suppose if we saved our coupons, we could manage. But Patricia, don't get your hopes up," Abby cautioned.

Patricia made herself calm down; Abby was right. They wouldn't know if they could visit until they talked to Nick, and it would be a long drive.

The first week at the camp passed slowly in some ways and quickly in others. The slow times were when Kenji had nothing to do but read his medical journals and think about Patricia. His plan to run himself ragged so far hadn't worked; he was always exhausted when he went to bed, but sleep still didn't come easily. Part of it was because of the windstorms that sometimes came at night, and the other part of it was because he was so worried about Patricia. It wouldn't be until the second week that he would fall into a deep, exhausted sleep.

Hana, for the most part, seemed to adjust to camp life and loved working with the children. She was right, Kenji realized; she was stronger than she looked. Kenji taught English to those who wanted to learn, which was difficult because the use of Japanese was prohibited, but he managed. He also found that he really enjoyed his shifts at the hospital, often staying way past the time when he should have gone home. Dr. Mynt was a good if not gruff teacher and recognized that Kenji had the makings of an excellent physician, but hadn't told him that.

Hiroshi watched Joben, Kenji, and Hana from a distance. Hana, he thought, looked as beautiful as ever, and he felt a small twinge of guilt as he thought about his role in her being here. He still had ill feelings toward Kenji, but Hana didn't deserve what had happened to her. She never should have been arrested that night, he realized, but then, they would have ended up here anyway.

He did have to wonder about Kenji's whore, if she had given him any whelps yet. If she had, then the Takeda line was forever ruined and would never be restored to purity.

"Hiroshi? Is that you?" Hana asked from behind him.

Hiroshi stiffened and then relaxed; it was only a matter of time before either Kenji or Hana spotted him. "Hello, Hana," Hiroshi said, greeting her as if she was an acquaintance instead of his wife.

"Hello, Hiroshi; are you well?" Hana asked, searching his face.

"I am well," Hiroshi replied and decided to cut the conversation short. "I must go now," he said and walked away.

Later, over dinner, she told Kenji that his father was at the camp.

"Mother, stay away from him. No good can or will come from associating with him," Kenji advised.

Sadly, Hana had to agree.

Before they knew it, a month had gone by. Kenji received a letter from Patricia that was delivered by Nick.

"Is she well?" Kenji asked as he anxiously took the letter.

"She's better. The first week was rough for her, but she's all right, other than she misses you," Nick replied. "How is your mother?"

"She is well, but the dust here makes it difficult to sleep well," Kenji replied.

Nick waited while Kenji wrote a quick letter to Patricia assuring her that both he and Hana were well and reminding her to take care of herself and that they had plans to finalize. He ended the letter by telling her that he loved her and she was never far from his thoughts.

After Nick left, he decided he would buy a notebook from the commissary and start writing in it. When Nick came, he would have him give the notebook to Patricia. That way Patricia could be a part of his life without actually being there, and it would offer her some reassurances.

JUNE 1942

Patricia was finally sleeping at night; the fact that both Kenji and Hana were both doing well went a long way toward helping her rest. Her father came with Hattie at least once a week to visit, and by unspoken mutual agreement, they didn't talk about Kenji.

One morning, Patricia woke up feeling slightly sick to her stomach. Her period was late, but she attributed it to the stress of the past month and didn't worry about it. She lay in bed and reread the letter from Kenji several times over; as sweet as it was to hear from him, it only made her miss him more. She missed him during the day, but as always it was worse at night and they still hadn't found out whether it would be possible for them to visit Kenji and Hana, although she suspected it wasn't going to happen anytime soon, if at all.

The papers were filled with stories about people of Jewish descent being killed in gas chambers and being sent to "the east"; Mexico declared war on Germany, Italy, and Japan; and the United States declared war on Bulgaria, Hungary, and Romania. The Battle of Midway was over; the USS *Yorktown* sank, along with four Japanese carriers and a cruiser.

"So much destruction," Ralph murmured every time he read the paper. He had stopped telling Abby what was happening in the war arena; it upset her too much, and Patricia had more than enough to handle without hearing about it. The only time he got to talk about the war was with Nick and the other old men in the park.

"What do you think, Nick?" Ralph asked. "Is this going to be a quick war?"

"I wouldn't bet on it," Nick replied. "If anything, it's spreading, and it's going to get worse, if you ask me."

"What about Kenji and Hana? Any talk of letting the Japanese go?" Ralph asked.

"I wish to God that I could say yes, but it looks like they're going to keep the Japanese interred until the end of the war."

"The same for the Italians and Germans out east?" Ralph asked.

"From what I hear, no one's going anywhere until the war is over," Nick said.

"Damn," Ralph said softly. "It just isn't right."

By the end of the month, Patricia knew she was pregnant; she didn't know what to do or how to tell anyone, so she didn't say anything.

It was her mother who noticed something was amiss and cornered her. "Patricia, what's wrong, and don't say nothin'," Hattie said.

"Mama. . . . " was all she got out before she burst into tears.

"Baby, what is it?" Hattie asked, almost fearing the worst.

Patricia took a deep breath to calm herself; this was the one thing Kenji didn't want, at least now—a baby.

"Mama, I'm pregnant," Patricia blurted out and started crying again.

"That all?" Hattie asked, hugging her. "You ain't the first or the last woman to get pregnant."

"I know, but Mama, we . . . he . . . what am I going to do?" Patricia asked.

"What do you mean what are you going to do?" Hattie asked. "You're gonna have a baby, and we're gonna help you."

"Do I tell Kenji?" Patricia asked.

"What you think you should do?" Hattie asked.

"No, I won't tell him," Patricia said firmly. "If I do, he'll try to come back, and I want him back in one piece."

Hattie didn't argue with her because she saw Patricia's point and agreed with her. Abby and Ralph, however, didn't.

"Patty, he needs to know!" Ralph exclaimed.

"I agree," Abby said.

"But he'll try to leave to come here, and then what?" Patricia asked. "They could kill him or throw him in jail or something. I'm not telling him, and I don't want Nick to tell him either."

Later that night, as Patricia lay in bed, she hugged herself and wondered about her decision not to get word to Kenji about the baby. If she knew for sure that he wouldn't try to leave the camp, she would tell him, but knowing him as she did. . . . No, she couldn't risk it. She would rather have him angry at her than dead or in prison because he tried to get to her, but what if he died there? He could die there not knowing that he had a son or daughter. Patricia closed her eyes and said a prayer that Kenji and Hana would return safely and that Kenji wouldn't be too angry with her.

JULY 1942

Hiroshi still hadn't approached Joben Saito, but knew that his life was miserable. He continued to watch Hana and Kenji from a distance, careful to stay out of sight.

He heard bits and pieces about the war from the guards and whoever happened to be talking about it.

"The Japs have control of Guadalcanal," he heard one of the guards say.

Hiroshi stopped and then moved on when the men stopped talking. *So Japan hasn't been defeated*, he thought to himself as he tried to find a place where he could listen for further information. By the time he found a place to listen, the conversation had shifted from Japan to Stalingrad, of which Hiroshi had no interest.

Further down the road he heard another interesting tidbit: The Germans were systematically deporting the Jews from the so-called "Warsaw Ghetto" to someplace called Treblinka and were meeting resistance. None of the news bothered Hiroshi; he had become purely pro-Japan and if offered a chance to return, he would do it, even if he had to become a foot solder in the emperor's army.

Life at the camp for Hana and Kenji settled into an uncomfortable routine, with the discomfort coming from the windstorms, waking up covered in dust as a result, and the hot temperatures during the day. Kenji took some of his clothes and cut them into strips in an attempt to block off some of the holes allowing the dust in. Hana took one of her kimonos and fashioned scarves to cover their heads and mouths at night so they could breathe better and to minimize the dust in their hair when they woke up; their efforts helped some, but didn't eliminate the problem.

It had been almost three months since they arrived, and being released was no longer discussed. Many of the internees were concerned about money; they had lost everything before being interred and were under the understanding that they would be paid army wages for working in the factories in the camp. The fact that they hadn't been paid was further cause for the trouble that Hiroshi, Kenji, and Joben saw coming. Of the three, Kenji was the only one who had decided he wasn't going to get involved; his only goals were to learn as much as he could from Dr. Mynt and to get home to Patricia.

Nick made another visit and delivered a letter from Patricia; as always, Kenji asked about Patricia's wellbeing.

"She's good," Nick replied. There was something about Nick's response that hit Kenji the wrong way, but he let it pass for the moment.

"Your mother is still all right?" Nick asked.

"She is as well as can be expected," Kenji replied. "What of Miss Abby, Ralph, and Hattie?"

"They're good; Patricia's father has started talking to her again, so that's a good thing," Nick said.

"Good, I know she missed him," Kenji said as he ran a finger over the letter Patricia had sent. "What are you keeping from me?" Kenji asked pointedly.

"What do you mean?" Nick asked.

"I mean that you are keeping something about Patricia from me; what is it? Is she ill?"

"Not really; she's fine," Nick said.

"What do you mean by not really? Is she ill or not?" Kenji asked, growing more alarmed by the second.

"She's not sick; calm down," Nick said.

"Then what is it?" Kenji asked.

"Kenji, she's fine," Nick said. "Let's leave it at that."

"Nick, if you don't tell me what is happening with Patricia, I'll leave here—I'll walk if I have to. Now tell me what's wrong with Patricia."

Nick sighed; there was no way he could get around telling Kenji that he was going to be a father. "All right, but you've got to promise me that you won't do anything stupid, like try to leave," Nick said.

Kenji hesitated, but then agreed.

"I mean it; you cannot try to leave here. Do you understand that?" Nick asked.

"I understand, now tell me," Kenji said impatiently.

"Kenji, she's pregnant."

"Wh . . . what?" Kenji asked. "I have to go to her, I—"

"You have to stay put," Nick interrupted. "This is why she didn't want you to know."

"Is she really all right?" Kenji asked as he tried to take in the fact that he was going to be a father.

"She's really fine," Nick said.

Kenji handed the notebook to Nick. "Give this to her," he said softly.

After Nick left, Kenji went to his and Hana's space, sat down on his cot, and cried. Patricia was going to have their baby without him. He fought with great difficulty the urge to leave from where he sat, but he agreed with Nick—it would be a stupid thing to do.

He was still lying on the cot when Hana came in.

"Kenji?" she called, concerned.

Kenji didn't respond at first; Hana called his name again and sat on her cot.

"Patricia, she is going to have our baby," Kenji said quietly.

Hana didn't know what to say; she could only imagine how Kenji felt. Patricia would have the baby without him there, and who knew when they would be released. The child could grow up not knowing his father, and Patricia had to be frightened.

Hana moved closer to Kenji and took his hand. "She will be a good mother, just as you will be a good father. I know that you will miss the birth of your child, and that is and will be painful, but use it as inspiration to get through this."

Kenji squeezed his eyes shut to stop the tears. He had to see Patricia; he had to see for himself that she was all right. If he could do that, he would be all right, but how was he going to make that happen?

Chapter 12

Kenji didn't sleep at all that night. His mind was on Patricia and their coming child. Would they make her bring the baby here or send them somewhere else? And Patricia, was she really all right or was Nick telling him what he wanted to hear? The only thing he knew for sure was that he needed to see her, to touch her and the belly that held his son or daughter. He made another promise to himself: he would never miss the birth of another one of their children. No matter where he was or what was happening, he would be there. In making that promise, Kenji realized that he really believed he and Patricia would be reunited, and that meant that he couldn't do anything rash.

He took the handkerchief that Patricia had given him for a birthday gift from his pocket and held it tightly in his hand as he touched the necklace around his neck. He missed her and, try as he might to keep busy, he still missed her. He put the handkerchief back in his pocket, closed his eyes, and tried to sleep. The winds howling outside didn't help much, but eventually sleep did come.

He woke as he did almost every morning, his blankets covered with dust. His hair was mostly dust free because of the scarves that Hana had fashioned from one of her kimonos. Hana, he noticed, hadn't slept in her cot but sometimes she didn't, preferring to sleep at the "children's orphanage" where there wasn't as much dust, and they had toilets and showers for the children that she sometimes used.

Kenji got up and dusted off both his and Hana's cots before getting dressed and going to breakfast, where he planned to find a quiet corner and reread the letters from Patricia that Nick brought with him each time he visited.

He took a cup of tea and a plate of food and went to a corner to read, starting with the most recent letter first.

Dear Kenji,

I hope that you're doing all right. I can't tell you how much I miss you and how many times during the day I think about you and pray for the safety of you and your mother. I reread your letters so many times that I think I have them memorized—actually, I know I do. Nick keeps us informed of any changes, but so far there is no news on how soon you and Hana can come home. To keep busy, Ralph has been trying to teach me how to play chess, but to be honest with you, I don't understand the game. I keep trying because I know that he's trying to help me not to be so scared and to keep me busy. I don't know about you, but the nights are the worst part of the day for me. Even after all of these weeks, I wake up and expect to find you next to me and when you're not . . .

Miss Abby is doing well and has taken up knitting. I think she's making something for you and your mother for Christmas and, at the rate she's going, she'll be done long before then. We saved all of our coupons and bought enough sugar and butter so that we had cake for my birthday. I know how you like sweets, so I ate an extra piece for you, and when you come home, we'll bake the biggest cake that we can fit into the oven.

Are you still reading your medical journals? I'm still planning on you going to medical school and me going to college to be a teacher. Do you think I'd be good at that? Or should I think about studying something else? I guess I have time to figure it out, it's not like I'm old or anything.

Nick gave me the notebook and it helps me so much. I'm still scared, but not as bad as I was before the notebook. I read it every night before I go to sleep. I started one too and will send it with Nick the next time he drives up there. I hope to be able to come with him sometime, but he doesn't know yet if we'll be allowed to see each other. I'm getting long winded, so I guess I'll close. Just be careful and know that I love you.

Patricia

July 10, 1942

Kenji folded the letter and whispered a prayer that Nick could bring Patricia to see him, but with the pregnancy, he wasn't sure that it would be a good idea. He was glad that he thought of writing in a notebook and sending it with Nick, especially since it brought Patricia some comfort, but it helped him too. The second notebook was already over half full and probably would be full by the time Nick came back again.

He finished his now-cold meal and stood to leave when he saw his father. Hiroshi looked at him and turned away, telling Kenji all that he needed to know—his father had not forgiven him nor would he ever forgive him. It was probably just as well, because it meant that there would be little to no contact between them.

Patricia knelt on the bathroom floor in front of the toilet, throwing up. She hadn't been able to keep anything down, other than sips of water, for the past week. Finally, Abby had had enough and called the doctor to the house. She also made Patricia move up from the basement and into her old room.

"You need to be where we can hear you if you need help," Abby said, with the full support of Ralph and Hattie.

Patricia really didn't want to move, but eventually stopped arguing with them and agreed to move back upstairs. When the doctor first came to the house, he was all sweetness and light, congratulating Abby on her marriage to Ralph. Later, Ralph would tell Patricia that it was all that he and Abby could do not to burst into laughter.

The doctor's attitude changed when he realized that Patricia was the patient.

"I don't treat coloreds," he said and started to leave.

"Hold on a damned minute!" Ralph said blocking the door. "That girl is pregnant and she's sick. You're not leaving here until you've seen her and done something for her."

When the doctor started to protest, Abby spoke up.

"How would you feel if that was your wife or child and no one would help them simply because they were the wrong color?" she asked. "But it's not even that, it's about helping another human being regardless of their race and station in life," she added.

Feeling shamed, the doctor went to see Patricia, with Abby in attendance. He asked Patricia a few questions and then handed Abby a packet containing a powder that he said would settle Patricia's stomach.

"Will it hurt the baby?" Patricia asked.

"No!" the doctor snapped, earning him a glare from both Patricia and Abby.

"If you don't want that, try some mint tea. It can help soothe the stomach as well," he said as he snapped his bag shut.

"How much for the visit?" Abby asked.

The doctor mumbled something and rushed out of the room without looking back.

Patricia was too afraid to take the powder, because she didn't know what it was. She sipped on mint tea for the next couple of days and, after two or three days, the nausea began to subside and she was able to hold down broth. By the end of the week, she was able to eat small portions of her meals and was beginning to feel better. She passed the time by learning to play chess with Ralph, reading the notebook from Kenji, and writing in a notebook that Nick would take to Kenji on his next trip. Hattie and John came to visit at least once a week and usually stayed for dinner. John knew about Patricia's pregnancy, but so far hadn't commented on it, and Patricia didn't push.

After the last trip to Manzanar, Nick confessed to telling Kenji about the baby.

"Nick you promised!" Patricia said.

"I know, but Patricia, I swear that he knew something was up," Nick replied.

"What did he say?" Patricia asked.

"He was going to do what you thought he might. He was going to try to come to you, but I talked him out of it," Nick said.

"Nick, I have to see him. If I don't, he'll leave and get himself killed," Patricia said.

Nick blew out a breath; he just didn't see how he could make it legally happen.

"Give me some time to see what I can do, but Patricia, don't get your hopes up," he cautioned.

Patricia sat on the bed writing in the notebook that was more than a quarter full. She tried to write in it every day, but ended up writing for hours about anything and everything that came to mind.

> *Nick told me that you know about the baby and that you wanted to come home. As much as I want you here, I don't want you to get hurt doing it, so please stay there. Ralph, Abby, and my parents have been taking good care of me and making sure that I'm eating and getting plenty of rest. The doctor was here because I couldn't keep any food down, but I'm fine now and haven't thrown up in a few days. I was thinking about names for the baby and realized that other than the names of your family I don't know any Japanese names. What do you think about giving the baby a Japanese and an American name? Maybe when you send your next notebook you can let me know what you think about that and come up with some suggestions.*

Patricia kept writing, telling Kenji that she was talking to the baby and telling it all about him. The more she thought about it, the more she began to believe that Nick telling Kenji about the baby was a good thing; it would give him something else to focus on, as long as he stayed put. From that point on, whenever she wrote in the notebook, she talked about the baby and made sure to ask his opinion on things that she knew he would find important.

AUGUST 1942

Ralph slammed the paper down in disgust. It was the end of the month, and the Germans were still advancing on Stalingrad and actually were quite close. Brazil declared war on the Axis powers, the Guadalcanal campaign had begun, Churchill met with Stalin in Moscow, and supposedly there was going to be a second front sometime in 1942, but there was no word on what was going to happen to the Japanese in the internment camps or when they would be released.

It went without saying that if the Japanese weren't freed by the time Patricia had the baby, she would have to keep it under wraps, as it would be considered Japanese as opposed to black. The Civilian Exclusion Order No. 34 stated that people with as little as one-sixteenth of Japanese blood were eligible for internment, and because Korea was being occupied by Japan, Korean-Americans were also included. Ralph was surprised that the Chinese weren't included as well and wouldn't be surprised if they were included at some point.

His mind went back to Patricia and the baby. She wouldn't survive if they took it from her. She would try to go to the camp with it, and there was no guarantee that she would end up at the same place as Kenji. Tonight he and Abby would talk to her and make sure that she understood that she couldn't allow the baby to be seen.

The next thing he thought about was getting Patricia up to Manzanar at least once before the winter and before she had the baby. It would go a long way toward helping Kenji and her—at least emotionally. He knew that Nick was working on something, but so far he hadn't said anything about what he was planning.

Abby and Hattie put their heads together and started accumulating baby supplies for Patricia. She wanted to go shopping with them, but too many people knew she was married to a Japanese. Now that her pregnancy was beginning to show, Abby didn't think it was a good idea that she be seen. Patricia wasn't happy, but accepted it and spent the afternoon writing in a notebook, *talking* to Kenji.

> *My tummy that I used to complain so much about is bigger now, but I'm not complaining. I'm not sick at all anymore, and I'm able to eat everything on my plate. I don't know who will deliver the baby when it's time, since the doctor that was here made it clear that he doesn't treat colored people and he only helped that one time because Ralph wouldn't let him leave until he did. But we have some time to figure it out. Have you given any thought to the names? I still like the idea of a Japanese and an American name together.*
>
> *It feels like years since you've been gone, but it's only been four months. Nick has been keeping his ear to the ground, hoping to hear some news of the release of the Japanese, but so far nothing. Kenji, I won't lie to you and tell you that I'm not scared or that I haven't entertained the thought of taking the car and trying to come to you, although I won't. I won't because I would probably kill myself and the baby trying to get to you or get lost in the process of getting there. I want you to promise me that you won't try anything rash to see me. I would rather have you alive and able to see our baby than to have you dead and just be a memory. I know that I mention this every time, but I feel like I have to,*

especially when I miss you as much as I know that you miss me.

Nick is still working on a way that we can see each other at least once before the baby is born and the winter sets in up there. As near as we can tell, the baby will be born in January or February, and Nick has promised that he will get a camera and take a picture of the baby so that you can see it. I know that it won't be as good as the real thing, but at least you'll be able to see what she looks like.

Kenji, I love you. Please be safe, and I hope to see you soon. Please tell your mom that my mother, Ralph, and Abby think of her often, and that all of us are praying for your release.

Patricia

August 20, 1942

Nick had a plan. It took some doing and calling in some favors, but it would work. He hadn't said anything to Patricia yet, waiting until he had everything set up. During one of his visits to the camp, he had driven around its perimeter. The camp itself covered 540 acres, but there were spots along the perimeter that weren't always well guarded. One section of the perimeter, behind the camp hospital where Kenji spent much of his time, was in a blind spot. Through his friend Mitch, Nick had met Dr. Mynt who, in spite of being gruff, actually liked Kenji. Nick tucked the information away for future use as he was given a tour of the hospital by Dr. Mynt.

"What's this space used for?" Nick asked when they were walking through a part of the hospital that apparently wasn't being used.

"Overflow and storage," Dr. Mynt replied, giving Nick a curious look.

Nick thanked the doctor for the tour and left the hospital in search of Hana and Kenji. He was shocked when he ran into

Hiroshi. The two men stared at each other for several seconds before Nick spoke.

"Stay away from Hana," Nick said without preamble.

Hiroshi didn't reply, but tried to walk around Nick, who stopped him.

"Do you understand what I said?" he asked.

"I understand," Hiroshi said. "I understand that you lust after a married woman, but you can have her. She and Kenjiro are both dead to me. Now, please let me pass."

Nick let Hiroshi by and wondered if anyone else had noticed that he was attracted to Hana Takeda. It wouldn't be a good thing for either of them if the wrong people noticed. He had to be more careful so, instead of looking for Hana, he looked for Kenji. He had two notebooks from Patricia, as well as a box of cookies and a new medical journal from Abby.

He found Kenji sitting in the mess hall, reading an old letter from Patricia.

"I've got some new reading material for you," Nick said as he sat down.

"Patricia—"

"Is fine. She sent some things for you," Nick said, setting the parcel on the table.

Kenji didn't touch the package, but looked at Nick as if trying to decide if he were lying.

"I swear to you she's fine, and I have a little gift from me to you," Nick said as he reached into his jacket pocket and pulled out an envelope.

Kenji took the offered envelope and opened it, expecting something official. His breath caught when a black and white photo fell onto the table. It was a picture of Patricia holding up a sign that said I LOVE YOU. His hands shook as he picked up the picture and looked at her smiling face.

"*Kirei*," he murmured as tears ran down his face. "Thank you," Kenji said to Nick as he stared at the picture of Patricia. He was relieved to see that she looked well, but was saddened that he couldn't quite make out the swell of her belly.

Nick swallowed a lump as he watched Kenji look at the picture of Patricia and touch it lovingly. He cleared his throat and suggested that Kenji open the parcel. Reluctantly, Kenji lay the picture down and pulled the parcel closer to him. The box of cookies was on top of the notebooks and the medical journals and, although the intent was to comfort, in that moment all Kenji could think of was how much he missed Patricia.

"Nick, I miss her so much," Kenji whispered.

"I know you do and she misses you. The notebooks? They help, that's why she sent some to you," Nick replied.

"If they find out about the baby and make her go to a camp, please make it here. Don't let them send her anywhere else," Kenji begged, crying again.

Nick wiped at his eyes, which had become wet with his own tears. *This is so fucking wrong*, he thought to himself as he nodded his promise to Kenji, although he had no idea of how he could keep it.

Nick spoke when he thought he could trust his voice again.

"We've talked, and Patricia knows that she can't take the baby outside of the house other than in the back yard. Even now, we're keeping her indoors, since she's beginning to show," Nick said.

"Is . . . is she beautiful?" Kenji asked, his voice choked with emotion.

"Look at the picture," Nick said. "I took it just a couple of days ago, but yes, Kenji, she is beautiful and she's healthy."

Kenji dried his eyes, only to have them fill with tears again when he looked at the picture of Patricia. This war couldn't be over soon enough to suit him. As he took out the handkerchief that Patricia had embroidered for him, Kenji wished that he had a wallet or something more secure to carry the picture in, but this would have to do. He did a quick pat of the pockets of his slacks to make sure that the money was still there. He hated to carry around so much money, but it was the only secure place he could think of. Leaving the money in their quarters was out of the question.

Seeing his predicament, Nick pulled out his own wallet, emptied it, and handed it to Kenji. "I have others that I like better," he said.

Kenji, however, refused to accept the wallet without paying something for it. After looking around to be sure that he wasn't being watched, he pulled out a dollar bill and handed it to Nick. "I insist on paying for it," Kenji said, his tone firm.

Kenji carefully folded the picture so that it fit into the wallet and then added the letters from Patricia. The two men talked for several minutes while Kenji added a note to the last entry of his notebook, before parting ways. Kenji went to the hospital where he could begin to read the notebooks from Patricia before his shift started. Her notebooks had become his lifeline as his had become hers.

"You're early," Dr. Mynt said when Kenji passed him in the hallway.

"Yes, I have some reading that I would like to do," Kenji replied.

"The storage room is empty," Dr. Mynt muttered and walked away.

Kenji liked the doctor in spite of his gruffness. He also liked the fact that Dr. Mynt was giving him more responsibility: letting him perform simple procedures, such as stitches, letting him assist with the more complicated procedures and surgeries, and teaching him as they went along.

Dr. Mynt glanced back just as Kenji walked to the back hall heading toward the storage room. "That boy is going to be one hell of a doctor," he muttered as he continued on his way.

Kenji went into the storage room, shut the door, and locked it behind him. He sat on one of the bare mattresses, pulled out the wallet he had just bought from Nick, and took out the picture of Patricia. She was even more beautiful than he remembered, "I love you too, *Kirei*," he said as he put the picture away.

He opened the box of cookies and took one out after counting how many there were. Twenty-four, now twenty-three he counted. If he ate only one a day, they would last just over three weeks. He closed his eyes and took the first bite of the cookie, chewing slowly and savoring the sweetness and the subtle lemon flavor. He took his time finishing the cookie before opening the first notebook from Patricia.

Hiroshi watched as Kenji and Nick talked and wondered if Kenji was spying for the United States. He discounted the idea when he saw Kenji crying as he looked at what appeared to be a picture. Hiroshi then realized that whatever they were talking about, it had to have something to do with the black girl Kenji had married. If Kenji had been working for the government, they wouldn't be talking in the open like this. Hiroshi walked away in search of the other object of his attentions, Joben Saito.

Joben Saito saw Hiroshi before Hiroshi saw him. It had taken him some time, but Joben finally figured out that it was Hiroshi who was the cause of the cold reception he had been receiving. Joben stepped back just as Hiroshi turned his way; he wasn't ready to deal with him just yet.

Hana loved her work at the orphanage so much that she spent most of her time there. She met with Kenji for meals and sometimes slept in their assigned area, but the laughter of children soothed her as nothing else could. She felt for Kenji. Finding out that Patricia was pregnant had been hard on him, and it had taken a lot of talking on her part to keep him at the camp. After a few days, he seemed to calm down, although he was hurting inside. She hadn't seen Hiroshi since that last time, and she had made no efforts to find him. She had nothing to say to him. She thought she had seen Joben Saito once, but she wasn't sure. She had only seen the man for a few seconds. As she brushed the hair of a little girl, Hana wondered what Patricia would give Kenji—a boy or a girl.

SEPTEMBER 1942

Patricia had already read through Kenji's notebooks twice; she was still worried, but now it was more a matter of missing him than of being scared for him. She cried when Nick told her that Kenji cried when he saw the picture of her.

"His exact word was *Kirei*," Nick told her. "Patricia, he's doing as well as can be expected; he's keeping busy and so is Hana, for that matter."

Nick's words comforted Patricia some, but the real comfort came from Kenji's notebooks.

Kirei, I cannot tell you how much I miss you! I am glad that you are better, but if the nausea returns try the mint tea again. I don't know what it was that the doctor gave you but I'm glad that you didn't need it. It is only late August but already the nights grow cool; it won't be much longer before we will be needing the gloves and warm clothing that we have packed away. As always we wake up covered in dust whenever we sleep in our quarters so whenever possible, I sleep at the hospital and mother sleeps at the orphanage.

I have one small piece of unpleasantness that I want to address, actually two. The first thing is this: I have made Nick promise me that if by some chance it is found out that you are pregnant with my child that you are to be brought here. It is not the best place for you or our child, but at least we would be together. Kirei, I know how strong-willed you can be but please, do as Nick and the others tell you and stay out of sight.

The next piece of news is this: my father is here, as is Joben Saito. I have seen my father and he would not acknowledge me, but he has spoken to Mother. I have encouraged her to avoid him, as he could get her into trouble again. As I did before, I stay to myself, not interacting with anyone other than my mother on a personal level. I am still teaching English to those who wish to learn it and I spend much of my time at the hospital.

There is a doctor there who is quite gruff in his mannerisms; he reminds me a little of Ralph, but at any rate, he has been teaching me as we go along. I am able to do simple procedures and I sometimes assist him in surgery. I am grateful that you insisted that I bring my medical journals and yes I read them often but only after I read the letters from you, even though I have them memorized.

I know that it seems as though I am rambling, but this keeps me sane; if I concentrate enough as I write, I can almost convince myself that I am talking to you, but what stops the illusion is when I reach out to touch you and you aren't here. I cannot even begin to imagine how beautiful you must be with our child growing within you. If I could be granted just one wish, it would be to see you, hold and kiss you, and touch your stomach.

Patricia bit her lip to keep from crying as she closed the notebook to pick up another one; this one had the hastily written letter on the last page.

Kirei, you are even more beautiful than I could even imagine! Please take care of yourself so that we have a healthy baby. Whenever you become frightened, remember the song about the soldier who had to leave his beloved. I am coming back to you and our baby, no matter what I have to do to get to you. I will love you forever, Kenji.

The tears escaped, although she tried to stop them. Patricia rubbed her stomach and began to sing softly until she drifted off to sleep. She didn't hear Nick, Ralph, and Abby talking quietly downstairs, making plans.

"We'll have to leave early," Nick said. "So be ready."

"Next Sunday?" Abby asked.

"Yes, but don't say anything to Patricia, just in case something happens," Nick advised.

Abby nodded in agreement. If they told Patricia and it didn't happen, she would be heartbroken, and she had had more than her fair share of pain.

"So let me get this straight," Ralph said. "We drive up there and go to the post behind the hospital and some doctor is going to let Patty in? How do you know that you can trust him or the guard at the watchtower?"

"The guard is a friend of Mitch's and is being given a weekend night off in exchange for his help. The doctor likes Kenji and yes, he is aware of the situation," Nick replied.

"And where is this reunion going to take place?" Abby asked.

"The hospital," Nick replied. "There's a storage area that is sometimes used for patient overflow, but it's usually empty. No one goes back there much and the doc says that he could block off one of the rooms for them to use."

"Just how much time will they have?" Abby asked.

"Kenji's entire shift, which is about ten to twelve hours, sometimes longer because he doesn't leave when he's supposed to," Nick replied. "The doctor is going to ask him to start earlier so that they can have more time together," Nick added.

"And what will we be doing all of that time?" Ralph asked.

"We could visit with Hana for a while and there is a town not far from there," Nick said. "What do you think? Will Patricia be all right to travel?"

"I think that you wouldn't be able to keep her here," Abby replied. "Nick, we don't know how to thank you," she added.

"Don't thank me yet," Nick replied. "Things could change."

Abby smiled at Nick. "You've done a wonderful thing for them, so why don't you do something wonderful for yourself?" she asked.

"Like what?" Nick asked.

"Like admitting that you're in love with Hana Takeda, and don't bother denying it," Abby said.

"Abby, even if I were in love with her, she's still married...."

"To a man that considers both her and Kenji dead," Abby interrupted. "There has to be a way for them to be legally divorced and . . . "

"Abby, stop," Nick said. "Even of that were the case, I wouldn't act on it."

"Why ever not? Just because she's Japanese?" Abby asked.

"Isn't that reason enough?" Nick countered.

"No, it isn't! Look at Kenji and Patricia," Abby replied.

"Exactly, look at them," Nick said. "Both of them are miserable because they can't be together and even if they could be, their lives would be hell. The only reason that they're even married is because of you, and Abby, not everyone is like you and Ralph."

"I don't disagree with that, but Nick, people have got to stop being afraid and start standing up for what they believe. Patricia and Kenji have faced and are facing what appear to be insurmountable odds, yet they're making it and they still love each other. I can't tell you what to do, but I can tell you that real love only comes once if you're lucky and if you pass it up, not only are you a fool but you're a coward as well," Abby said as she stood up and walked away.

SUNDAY, OCTOBER 11, 1942

Patricia was already awake when Abby tapped on her door. Abby had finally told her last night that she would get to see Kenji, after almost six months. The best part was that he didn't know that she was coming and his birthday would be in a few days. She, Abby, and Ralph stayed up and baked cookies from what little supplies that they had left. Hattie also baked cookies, adding to the dozen that they had come up, with making the grand total three dozen cookies. Patricia dressed with care, pulling her hair into a ponytail with plans of letting it loose just before she saw Kenji, that's if she remembered. The last thing she did was to spray on some of the perfume Kenji had given her for her birthday.

Nick was already downstairs waiting and had the car loaded with bags that contained the knitted hats and mittens that Abby had made over the summer, along with extra socks and thermal underwear that Patricia had ordered from the mail-order catalog. Patricia gave herself one last critical look before rubbing her ever-growing stomach.

"We're going to see your daddy today," she said softly. "You would make him really happy if you moved so that he could feel you."

Patricia smiled as the baby kicked, as if it understood what she was saying. On her way out of the room, she grabbed the red sweater from the back of the chair and went downstairs. A few minutes later, they were on their way.

To Patricia, who had never been outside of LA, it seemed like a different world and the trip seemed to take forever, but the closer they got, the more excited she grew. She could hardly wait to feel Kenji in her arms and to see his face when he touched her stomach.

"We're about thirty minutes away," Nick said as he looked into the rearview mirror.

Abby held onto Patricia's hands as they shook with nerves and excitement and a bit of sadness. Leaving him here would be hard, Patricia realized, and then pushed the thought away, choosing to think about the hours that they would be able to spend together.

Kenji was up and dressed, already on his way to the hospital. Dr. Mynt asked him if he wouldn't mind coming in and helping with some general cleaning and other things before the start of his shift. The ironic thing was that, for once he had slept fairly well; he had actually started sleeping better after he got the notebooks and picture of Patricia. They seemed to confirm her existence and gave him the determination to survive this place to be with her. The morning was cold but not unbearably so, and for once there was no wind. The sun was just beginning to rise over the mountains, making the scenery look like something out of a book or a painting. It was a view that he would have loved to share with Patricia, and someday he would.

Dr. Mynt was in his office when Kenji got there and didn't even look up when Kenji tapped on his door.

"Start in that storage room all the way to the back and take your time," Dr. Mynt said.

Kenji frowned; usually Dr. Mynt was in a hurry and wanted things done as soon as possible, but he didn't argue with him as he headed down the hallway to the back storage room.

Patricia looked around the small room and sat on a chair to wait for Kenji, taking note of the mattress lying in the corner, already made up. She jumped with every sound and her heart pounded. A few minutes later, the knob of the door began to turn.

Patricia stood up shaking as the door slowly opened.

Kenji walked in and didn't notice her at first because he was finagling with the doorknob.

"*Ohayo*, Kenji," Patricia said softly.

Kenji froze and shook his head.

"Are you so angry with me that you won't greet me?" she asked using the same line that he had used with her from what seemed like an eternity ago.

Kenji looked up and stared at her in disbelief.

"*Kirei*? You are really here?" he asked, still making no move toward her.

"I'm really here," Patricia replied.

Before she knew what was happening, Kenji had practically run across the room and was hugging her. Both of them were crying and trying to talk at once. After the initial shock had worn off, Kenji kissed Patricia's face all over before kissing her lips. Neither of them noticed that someone had quietly closed the door, giving them privacy.

They kissed for several minutes until Kenji pulled away and ran his hands down Patricia's body beginning with her face, moving to her shoulders, and down her arms, not stopping until they rested on her stomach. Patricia laid her hands on top of his and prayed that the baby would move. For several seconds nothing happened and then the baby moved beneath Kenji's hands, which had begun to shake.

"Our child is strong," Kenji said as he rubbed her stomach, pausing when the baby moved again. They stood close together for several minutes before Kenji made her sit down.

"I'm fine," Patricia protested.

"You have had a long trip, rest for a while. . . ."

"Kenji, are you really all right?" Patricia asked as she touched his face and brushed his hair back out of his eyes as he knelt in front of her.

"Other than missing you I'm fine," Kenji replied. "The picture and the notebooks help but you being here. . . . We owe Nick and the others so much," he added.

A tap on the door startled them; both of them had the same thought that she had just gotten there and that it couldn't be time to leave yet.

"Wait here," Kenji said as he kissed her.

He carefully opened the door and saw no one but a cart with two covered trays that had been left by the door. Kenji quickly pulled the cart inside and rolled it over to Patricia.

"You must eat," he said gently as he uncovered the food.

Food was the furthest thing from Patricia's mind, but she didn't say anything, she knew that Kenji would have insisted and she wasn't about to take away his chance to be the doting husband and father-to-be, for today she would let him take care of her.

Patricia ate everything on her plate even though she was full; she was worried that if she didn't Kenji would think that something was wrong, but when he tried to get her to eat some of his, she put her foot down.

"Kenji, I'm full and you've lost weight, so you eat," she insisted

"I want to be sure that you and the baby have enough."

"Kenji, look at me," Patricia said. "I've gained more than twenty pounds! I'm fine, now please eat."

While Kenji ate, Patricia wondered where the nearest bathroom was, but waited until he was finished to ask.

"It is too big of a risk to take you there; wait here," Kenji said as he pushed the cart to the corner of the room.

He slipped out of the room and was gone for so long that Patricia began to worry that something had happened.

Kenji came back with blankets, two buckets, washcloths, towels, and a bucket of water on a utility cart. He quickly hung the blankets and set the two buckets behind them, creating a make-shift bathroom. While Patricia used the "bathroom," he cleared the cart of its trays and set the bucket of water, towels, and washcloths on the cart. Out of his pocket, he pulled a bar of soap and set it next to the washcloths, his only wish being that the water was warm.

"Kenji," Patricia said softly, attracting his attention.

Kenji turned to see Patricia standing behind him completely nude and holding her hand out to him. Instead of rushing over to her, Kenji took a moment to really look at her. He knew that this was the last time he was going to see her before she had the baby. In a few months, she would be even bigger and more beautiful and he would miss it, he would miss the birth of their first child.

"Kenji, come here," Patricia said, still holding her hand out.

Kenji slowly walked over to her, his eyes never leaving hers. Patricia took his hands and placed them on her bare stomach and held them there.

"I talk to her," Patricia said as she stroked Kenji's hands. "I tell her about you and how much you love us. I don't know if she can hear me, but I tell her the story about the soldier so that she'll know that you're coming home to us and you are coming home," she added, her voice filled with the conviction of her belief.

Kenji didn't respond, but kissed her as she began to unbutton his shirt. When she reached the last button, she began to undo the belt to his slacks. Kenji caught her hands in his and placed them on his chest over his pounding heart and held them there for several seconds before releasing them to pull Patricia tight against him. His hands ran over her bare back down to her behind and squeezed her buttocks gently.

Patricia relaxed and enjoyed the feeling of him getting reacquainted with her body, but she needed to touch him too. Patricia wrapped her arms around Kenji's waist and pressed her larger-than-usual breasts and her pregnant stomach into him, prompting Kenji to hold her tighter.

Kenji wanted nothing more than to bury himself deep inside of her, but forced himself to wait. To him, holding her was every bit as important as the rest of it. As he held her, he caught the scent of the perfume that he had given her for her birthday and the tears started; it brought back the memory of a happier time.

Kenji pulled away, took Patricia's hand and led her to the mattress in the corner, kissing her before he helped her down. Patricia scooted over to make room for him while he took off his shirt and removed his pants. Her nipples were already tingling in the anticipation of his touch and she was wet between her legs. It was a reminder of how much she had missed this part of their relationship; it had been the part of their life that she tried not to think about and for the most part she was successful.

Patricia opened her arms to him, crying when she finally felt the full length of his naked body pressing into hers.

"I need you," she whispered as she kissed his chest, took a nipple into her mouth and sucked one and then the other as she took his erection into her hand and squeezed.

Kenji placed his hand on top of hers and held it still; he didn't want his first release in months to be like this.

"*Kirei*, don't, not like this," he murmured as he kissed her lips and trailed kisses down her neck, just as he had during their last night together. He stopped at Patricia's breast, taking one hard nipple into his mouth and flicking his tongue over the tip as he rolled the other nipple between his fingers.

The sensation traveled straight from Patricia's nipples to between her legs, where she was throbbing. Kenji could hear the sobs in her voice and was tempted to give her what they both needed, but he wanted and needed to hear that giggle that she only had when she was aroused. He reluctantly left her nipples and kissed his way to her stomach and stopped.

"Take care of each other," he murmured with his lips pressed against Patricia's stomach. The baby moved, the feeling light against his lips as if in acknowledgement of his request. Kenji made his way to Patricia's feet and kissed them, chuckling when he heard that giggle.

He made his way back up her body until he was at her crotch; he nuzzled his cheek against the coarse hair of her mound and his mouth watered at the thought of tasting her again. Patricia moved restlessly against him, telling him in a nonverbal way to get on with it. He slipped his tongue between her outer and inner lips and stilled, taking the time to savor what he considered to be the sweet taste of her fluids.

Patricia gasped and then cried out when Kenji's tongue finally touched her throbbing nub. When he finally took her into his mouth and sucked, she covered her mouth with a pillow and screamed into it as she came for the first time in months. Her screams turned into sobs as Kenji planted a soft kiss on her nub before moving so that he was positioned between her legs.

"Patricia, *Kirei*, please look at me," Kenji said as he touched her vaginal opening with the tip of his erection.

Patricia opened her eyes and looked up at him, crying out as he slowly but gently slid into her until he was in as far as he could go. He began to thrust slowly, careful not to put too much weight on her stomach, and moments later he moaned his release. Moving carefully, Kenji pulled out, wishing he could stay inside of her like he had in the past, and lay behind her with both arms around her.

Neither of them spoke for several minutes as they caught their breath; for just a little while they had managed to forget where they were and what was happening around them.

*

Hana hugged both Abby and Ralph, but smiled shyly at Nick.

"Patricia is here, too?" she asked.

"She's with Kenji," Abby said. "How are you? Is there anything that we can get for you?"

"No, I am fine and you have done more than enough by coming here to see us," Hana replied.

Ralph's eyes were filled with anger as he looked around the camp and took in the inadequate housing. The inhabitants had done a great deal to make the place homelike he noticed, as he took in the gardens and the fruit trees that were from the original farmers before the town had been abandoned. He was actually surprised that they bore fruit; it was a testament to the skill of some of the detainees. He was also surprised at the number of businesses that flourished; there was a dress shop, a furniture shop, as well as some factories and schools. If it hadn't been for the housing, the fence surrounding the camp, and the watchtowers, he wouldn't have known that he was in a camp.

What really amazed him was that some of the detainees were actually performing experiments for the California Institute of Technology. They were experimenting on extracting rubber from a small woody plant called a guayule, in an attempt to help with the war effort. "That's more than I would have done," he muttered under his breath. He was further angered to find out that the detainees had yet to be paid for their services and were being asked to "volunteer" their services to keep the operations that were needed running.

"What the fuck is this?" Ralph asked, disgusted. "Just how long do they think that these people are going to stand for not being paid? They already have nothing and you mark my words, trouble is coming, and I only hope that Kenji and Hana don't get caught up in it," he added as he stomped off.

They watched him walk off and let him have his time alone. Abby handed the bags containing the gifts to Hana, who took them gratefully.

"There are mittens and hats in there, as well as thermal underwear that Patricia ordered for you and Kenji. I think that she has a few letters in there for him and I believe that there's one in there for you, as well as a small gift," Abby said.

"Patricia has written me?" Hana asked, surprised but pleased.

"Yes and there's a letter from Hattie, too. Hana, we all miss you and Kenji; when this is over don't worry about a place to stay, your room is waiting for you," Abby said, patting Hana's arm.

Hana placed her hand on top of Abby's.

"Thank you for all that you have done, but mostly thank you for all that you have done for Kenji. Today will go far in easing his mind about Patricia and the baby; he is . . . distraught that he won't be able to be with her when the time comes."

"Why can't we sneak them out of here?" Ralph asked from behind them.

"Ralph. . . ."

"No, let's think about this," he insisted. "Do they do roll call?" he asked Nick.

"No but . . ."

"Other than the hospital and the orphanage, where else do they have to be?" he pressed.

"Ralph. . . ."

"Hana, are either of you close with anyone who would miss you?" he asked, ignoring Nick.

"Just the woman at the orphanage and Kenji has become friendly with the doctor that he works with," Hana replied, not fully grasping what Ralph was suggesting.

"Where do you spend most of your time?" Ralph asked.

"I am usually at the orphanage and Kenji is either there or at the hospital; why are you asking?" Hana replied.

"If you didn't show up, would the woman at the orphanage report you missing?"

"I . . . I don't know," Hana replied slowly.

"The doctor at the hospital, would he report Kenji as missing?" Ralph asked.

"I don't know. I have never met him," Hana said, suddenly understanding.

Ralph turned to Nick. "Tell me why we can't get them out of here," he challenged.

"All right, how about this? If we get caught, all of us will go to prison. You, me, and Abby will be tried as traitors and Hana and Kenji could be given a sentence that could exceed the time that they would be here," Nick replied.

"But we don't know how long that would be," Abby said softly. "It could be years," she added.

"Patricia would go to prison, too; her baby would be born in prison and who knows where it would end up," Nick said. "I think that it's too much of a risk and I don't think that Kenji will agree for the reasons that I just stated."

"Nick is right," Hana said softly. Kenji wouldn't want to risk your lives or freedom and neither would I. You have all risked enough for us."

Ralph wasn't ready to concede. "I think we should let Kenji decide for himself."

As Patricia dozed in his arms, Kenji watched her sleep. In one of her letters she had mentioned that the nights were the worst time of the day for her. He hadn't told her that it didn't matter what time of day it was, he missed her equally. Their day together was coming to an end; the note on the lunch tray told him that they had four hours left and that had been two hours ago. Kenji kissed Patricia's shoulder to wake her; he wanted to make love to her once more before she had to leave.

Patricia opened her eyes and turned to face him.

"It's almost time, isn't it?" she asked.

"Yes, *Kirei*, it is," Kenji replied.

"I don't want to leave you here," Patricia said as a tear slipped down her face. "I wish that there was a way to take you with us."

Kenji didn't respond. What could he say, other than to repeat his promise to come to her as soon as he could. A tap on the door told him that their dinner had arrived. Reluctantly, he got up to get the cart. As with the other two meals, there was no one in sight as he pulled the cart into the room. Patricia was up and using the 'bathroom" when Kenji turned around; she was out and washing her hands by the time he had the food uncovered.

She sat staring at the food, her appetite completely gone. Kenji didn't encourage her to eat because he couldn't eat himself and it would have been pointless. He stood up, walked around the small cart, stood behind Patricia, and put his arms around her.

"Come back to bed with me," he whispered to her.

An hour later they lay wrapped in each other's arms. Patricia was trying hard not to cry again; she had cried the entire time they made love for what would be the last time for a long time. After a few more moments of hugs and kisses, they got up to clean up and get dressed. To both of them it was too much of a reminder of the day that Kenji left for the camp, but in some ways this parting was more painful.

They were barely dressed when there was a tap on the door.

"Kenji! It's me, Ralph, open up!"

Kenji and Patricia looked at each other and opened the door together. Ralph ducked in, gave Kenji a hug and began to explain why he was there.

Kenji listened silently while he watched Patricia's face. He saw the hope in her eyes as she listened to the plan. His first reaction was to grab Patricia's hand and run to the car, but the practical part of him came forward. When Ralph finished, Kenji stood mute.

"Kenji?" Patricia said.

He wanted to say yes, but he couldn't.

Patricia watched his face and knew that he was going to say no.

"Kenji, please!" she said softly.

"*Kirei*, I want to. I want to leave this place and sleep tonight holding you and our baby, but I can't."

"Why not? Why can't you come with us?" Patricia asked, trying not to cry.

"Because I cannot and will not ask our friends to put themselves at risk anymore than they have," Kenji replied.

"I think that's for us to decide," Ralph interjected, although he had promised to remain quiet after he presented the plan.

"You are right, but there's more. Patricia, if we were to be caught, all of you could go to prison as traitors. Our baby could be born in prison and then taken away from us. He could end up in a place like this, with neither of us to keep him safe. I would rather be here than to have that happen," Kenji said.

"Don't do this to us again. Don't make me leave you again!" Patricia begged.

Kenji wavered, the memory of the last wrong decision came forward, but he was right this time, he knew he was and he steeled his resolve.

"*Kirei*, I won't take that risk."

Patricia stopped crying, anger and confusion shone in her dark eyes.

"You don't love me," she said quietly.

Kenji looked as if he'd been slapped.

"*Kirei* . . ."

"If you loved me and this baby you'd come with us, you wouldn't make me leave you again! Please come with us, please?"

Kenji took Patricia in his arms and kissed her.

"I am choosing to stay because I love you and our child. Patricia, if we all end up in prison, who will protect you and the baby? Where will our baby end up?" Kenji asked.

"Then I'm staying here," Patricia said.

"Patty. . . ." Ralph said softly.

"If you won't come with us, then I'm staying here," Patricia said stubbornly.

"*Kirei*, that isn't possible. The winter is coming and the dust. . . ."

"I don't care! I said that I would be with you no matter what. I'm not going!"

"Ralph, could I please be alone with Patricia?" Kenji asked.

As soon as Ralph was gone, Kenji sat on the chair and pulled Patricia into his lap, holding her as she sobbed. When she quieted, he spoke to her softly.

"Patricia, believe me when I say that I want to come with you, but I can't and won't jeopardize the lives of those who have cared for and helped us and if you think about it, you know that what I say is true. I want you to go back and take care of yourself and our baby. . . ."

"Kenji, we have to go," Ralph said through the door.

"Patricia, it's time," Kenji said, kissing her.

"No . . . "

"I promise we'll be together again soon," he said, hugging her tightly.

"Kenji!" Ralph called again.

Patricia stood on shaky legs and walked with Kenji to the door. They kissed one last time before Kenji opened the door and gently pushed Patricia into Ralph's arms. He watched Ralph lead Patricia away and questioned his choice, but then stuck by it.

He closed the door, sat on the mattress that he had spent most of the day on with Patricia, and cried. Dr. Mynt slipped into the room, sat on the mattress beside him and put a hand on Kenji's shoulder.

"That was a hard choice to make," he said, the gruffness that Kenji had become accustomed to gone. "But son, you did the right thing by her and that baby you've got coming."

Dr. Mynt sat with Kenji until he drifted off to sleep. Before leaving, he covered Kenji with the blanket that lay on the floor at the foot of the mattress, closing the door behind him when he left.

The ride home was quiet, with the exception of Patricia's sobs, which finally quieted when she fell asleep with her head in Abby's lap. Hana had also chosen to remain behind for many of the same reasons that Kenji did and she didn't want to leave him.

"He will need me," she said when Nick tried to convince her to come with them. "And the end result will be the same if we are caught. I will come with you only if Kenji does."

Neither Nick nor Ralph spoke, each lost in his own thoughts. Nick was thinking about what Abby said to him about Hana. She was right about one thing, he was a coward; today Kenji and Patricia had shown him that. When he got home, he would see if he could find some way for Hana to divorce her husband and he would see if there was some legal loophole with which he could get both her and Kenji free.

Ralph just didn't understand it; Kenji and Hana could have been their way home with them right now. The chance wouldn't present itself again until spring, and that was only if they had the same amount of cooperation that they did this time. He understood Kenji's point of view to a certain degree, especially in regard to Patricia and the baby, but maybe he and Nick could make a return trip without the women. It would take them out of the mix; he would talk to Nick about it the next time they were alone.

Kenji woke up stiff and grainy eyed; Hana was sitting on the chair waiting for him to wake up and smiled at him weakly. He sat up, rubbed his reddened and swollen eyes, and looked at her.

"Mother, did I make the right decision?" he asked.

"I think for now, yes," Hana replied as she moved to sit next to him on the mattress.

"Her face when I said that I wasn't going with them, she was so hurt. She questioned whether I loved her," Kenji said, laying his head on Hana's shoulder like he did when he was a child and needed comforting.

"Kenjiro, she knows that you love her. When she spoke it was out of anger, fear, and pain. This is the second time that she had to leave you, when she thought that there might be a chance for you to be together."

Kenji closed his eyes and made a decision: if the opportunity ever arose again, he would take it. He wouldn't and couldn't do this to her again.

When they arrived at Abby's house, Patricia went to the basement instead of upstairs to Hana's room. She changed her clothes, climbed into bed, and curled into as tight a ball as her stomach would allow, and cried herself back to sleep.

Chapter 13

Patricia woke up sad and stiff from lying in the same position for too long. The visit with Kenji had been bittersweet; she was happy to have had the time with him, but she was so . . . angry—that was it, she was angry that she had to leave him there, but even angrier when he didn't come with them when he had the chance. She also felt guilty; for her to accuse him of not loving them was wrong and unfair. It had just been too much when he made her leave without him.

"I am so sorry that I said that," she said into the air and then hoped that he knew she didn't mean it. She made her way upstairs to the bathroom, reluctantly; she admitted to herself that she needed to move back into her old room where the bathroom would be close. When she was finished in the bathroom, she changed her clothes, sat on the bed, and began to write in the half-filled notebook:

> *October 12, 1942*
>
> *I am so sorry for what I said to you before we left. I know that you love us and that you were thinking of us, but Kenji, it was so hard leaving you again. Yesterday was wonderful and sad at the same time, but if given a chance to come again, I would take it even if it hurt like it did yesterday. I'm glad you got to feel the baby move; he's active, isn't he? Please stay safe and be sure to use the thermal underwear I sent for you and your mother.*
>
> *I love you,*
> *Patricia*

Patricia tore the note from the notebook and put it in the front so Kenji would see it first. As an afterthought, she sprayed the note with some of the perfume Kenji had given her for her birthday and closed the notebook. It would be at least two weeks before Nick went up to see Kenji and Hana again, but until then, she would keep writing.

Kenji moved as though he were in a dream; he alternately understood and stood by his decision to stay and wished that he had gone with Patricia and the others. Deep down, he knew he had made the right decision, but he kept seeing the pain on Patricia's face when he told her she had to leave without him. For her to doubt even for one second that he didn't love her felt like a knife twisting in his heart, even though he understood why she had lashed out at him. If the opportunity came again, he wasn't going to say no; if another opportunity came, then it was meant to be.

He kept himself busy, working at the hospital all day and then going to the orphanage in the evening. By the time he got back to his and Hana's quarters, he was exhausted. Hana had given him the package from Patricia unopened, hoping it might cheer him up some. The wind howled outside, blowing the dust in through the cracks. Their cots were already covered with dust, which meant that Kenji had to clean them off before he could go to bed. He almost didn't do Hana's since it would be covered again by morning, but did it anyway. When he was finished, he looked at the package from Patricia, sat down, and opened it. There were sugar cookies, thermal underwear, hats, and mittens. There was also a letter from Patricia and Hattie for Hana, as well as a notebook from Patricia.

Kenji reached into his pocket and pulled out the wallet that held his one and only picture of Patricia. He carefully took the photo out, laid back on the bed, and looked at it.

"I am so sorry, *Kirei*," he whispered as he kissed the picture and put it back in the wallet. He opened a package of thermal underwear, stripped, and put them on, as well as the hat and the mittens; it was going to be cold tonight. He settled down in the cold cot and began to read the notebook from Patricia.

By the end of October 1942, the German advance into Stalingrad had come to a halt; the age for conscription was lowered to eighteen; and Admiral William Halsey was given command over the Naval forces in the South Pacific. In the UK, clergymen and various political leaders were meeting to protest Germany's treatment and persecution of the Jews, and the Japanese continued to send reinforcements to Guadalcanal.

"Stubborn bastards," Ralph mumbled as he read the paper. Another article caught his attention: the 100th Infantry Battalion had become active.

"What the fuck?" Ralph muttered as he read the article. The force consisted of 1,400 Nisei—second-generation Japanese. Ralph continued to read with amazement, finding it hard to believe that these people would fight for a country that considered them the enemy. On one hand, he understood: they wanted to prove their loyalty, and maybe in their position, he would have done the same thing. As much as he hated the idea of Kenji being in the camp, he was glad that he wasn't second-generation Japanese; he would have enlisted, as much as he hated violence and loss of life. He would have done it for Patricia and the baby, and if he had died . . . Ralph pushed the thought away; it was still possible that Kenji could die in the camp from sickness or something else.

He had yet to talk with Nick about getting Kenji and Hana out of Manzanar, and he wanted to do it soon. The problem was that either Abby or Patricia was always around, and he wanted to talk in private. Ralph was worried about Patricia; she seemed to have gotten over the disappointment of Kenji's decision, but he knew how badly it had hurt her.

Ralph went back to the newspaper article about the Nisei; he found it interesting that while the Nisei were allowed to volunteer, they generally weren't allowed to fight in the Pacific

Theater, whereas no limitations were placed on Americans of German or Italian descent who fought against the Axis powers in Europe. It was a matter of numbers, Ralph realized; there were many more people of German and Italian descent than there were of Japanese descent.

"Humph!" Ralph snorted. "That's like telling a woman that she's good enough to fuck but not good enough to be your wife," he muttered as he continued reading. His mind went back to Kenji and Hana; he knew from Nick that the internees still hadn't been paid.

"Nick, that's a recipe for disaster," he said when Nick told him.

"I know, I know," Nick said worriedly. "The good thing is that Kenji and Hana have some money and are able to survive, but if that place erupts into a riot, they won't be safe."

Ralph looked at Nick for several minutes before speaking. "You're sweet on her, aren't you?"

Nick was going to deny it, but instead told the truth. "I guess I am."

"Well, it's about damned time you admitted it," Ralph said and then went back to the previous topic. "It's not a question of *if* but *when* things are going to get out of control."

NOVEMBER 1, 1942

Patricia folded and refolded the diapers and clothes that Abby and her mother had bought for the baby. They bought colors that could be worn no matter the sex of the baby—a boy, Patricia thought. She would love for their first baby to be a boy; Kenji would be thrilled no matter what sex the baby was, but she wanted a boy for him. Every day, she talked to the baby about everything and anything, often reading out loud with one hand on her stomach, slowly rubbing it. When she wrote in the notebook, she read out loud what she was writing; it helped her to not miss Kenji so much.

It had been almost two weeks since she saw Kenji, and she was finally over the fact that he hadn't come back with them when he had the chance. It was as he said, when she had a chance to think about it, she would realize he was right. But it still hurt. She still felt guilty over her accusation that he didn't love her, and she swore to never say anything like that again. It had to have hurt him to hear her say that, especially after he had chosen her over his family.

Patricia's father, John, had finally acknowledged her pregnancy. It was hard not to say anything when she was so big, but when he said something, it wasn't what she expected.

"It be nice to have a grandson to play ball with," was all he said.

Patricia was stunned; so was everyone else, for that matter. "Daddy, I—"

"Don't go getting no ideas 'bout me and your man being friends," John interrupted. "But a man shouldn't blame the children for his parents' mistakes."

He had just let her know that he still wasn't happy with them, but she didn't care. The fact that he would accept their child and treat him or her as a grandchild was more than enough.

Kenji began to hear more and more rumblings around the camp about the lack of money. It occurred to him that it was becoming increasingly dangerous to have so much money on him. Of the two hundred dollars he and Hana had between them, they had one hundred and seventy left. They spent money only when absolutely necessary, and Kenji considered the notebooks and pens necessary. He had started writing two lines in one space in order to get the maximum use from each notebook; it made the writing slower, but it helped to fill his time.

Hana spent all of her time at the orphanage now that the weather had turned cold, leaving Kenji alone in their quarters. The camp was bursting at the seams as more and more people came, making the opportunity for disease to spread rise even more. Already, he could hear the coughs and the complaints of fever from those around him, and the hospital was becoming very busy. He had no doubt that the room where he and Patricia spent the day would soon be used as an isolation room. His goal was to remain healthy; he had begun to eat all of his meals and kept up his training to keep his body and mind strong. He was not going to die here; he had other plans for his death, which included Patricia when they were old and had done everything they had talked about doing together.

Hiroshi continued to watch the two groups that were at odds with each other. The meetings between the Japanese American Citizens League and some of the first-generation Japanese continued to be nothing more than shouting matches and fights. The death threats and beatings against those of the pro-administration group continued as well. Things were coming to a boiling point, and it was just a matter of time before the pot boiled over.

Joben Saito fell on the side of the pro-administration side; that in and of itself was no big surprise to Hiroshi. Joben was a coward as far as he was concerned, and his time was coming.

As far as Hana and Kenji were concerned, Hiroshi could honestly say that he cared nothing about them. That agent threatening him about Hana had taken care of the last positive feelings he had for her. The agent obviously had feelings of some kind for her in order for him to seek him out as he did. Kenji, he simply hated. He was a traitor of the worst kind; he not only betrayed his country, he betrayed his family and his race—and for what? A black woman who was probably screwing someone else this very moment?

Hiroshi pulled his coat tighter around him; it wasn't nearly warm enough for this kind of weather. In all of his planning, he never thought he would end up a captive, totally dependent on someone else for the basic things one needed to live.

Joben Saito sat quietly in his space; he was also aware that things between the two groups of Japanese were escalating, with each side participating in gang activity. He distanced himself from that part of the conflict, as it would do the opposite of what he wished; he wanted to appear compliant in the hopes that the right people would notice.

For the most part, he stayed to himself, and not by choice; the only people who spoke to him were the members of the JACL, and that was only because they thought he agreed with them. Did he? On some level he supposed he did, but then he would have agreed with the other side if it suited his purpose. No one in the JACL seemed to mind that he was first-generation Japanese—only that he agreed with them.

As far as Hiroshi Takeda was concerned, Joben stayed as far away from him as he could. He wanted to survive this place and find his daughter, Dai; lately he had been thinking of her more and more as a father who was worried about his child. He had wronged her and he knew it; he should have let her go wherever it was she wanted to run to, and he never should have involved her in his plans. His hope was that she escaped to the east and was safe somewhere, so that when this was over he would have a place to go.

He also thought about his part in the planning to hurt the black girl; what had he been thinking? Joben realized with a start that he was having regrets, and in his experience, that only happened when a person knew they were going to die. He had no plans of dying, but still the idea that he was having regrets frightened him.

There was another meeting tonight between the two groups; something told him he should stay away, and he decided to obey that voice. He didn't even go out for meals.

Kenji now spent most of his time at the hospital, eating and sleeping when he could. As he had suspected, the hospital was busy and all available spaces were in use, making him grateful that Patricia had come when she did.

He found himself thinking about her much more than usual as the time for the baby's birth drew near. He hoped she was well and taking care of herself; he would give anything to talk to her just once.

Abby poured Ralph a cup of coffee and then one for herself before she sat down.

"What are you thinking about, old man? And before you say 'nothing,' I know better," she said.

"Where's Patty?" Ralph asked.

"Upstairs sleeping; why?" Abby replied. "Ralph, what—"

"Listen, me and Nick are going to try to get Kenji and Hana out of there," he said urgently.

"What? Kenji won't come, you know that," Abby said.

"I think he will," Ralph said. "You didn't see his face when he pushed Patty out of the door. He almost changed his mind, but we can't tell Patty. If he does refuse to come, I don't think I can stand seeing her hurt like that again."

"When were you thinking of doing this?" Abby asked.

"I don't know yet; Nick is checking a few things out. But Abby, you do realize what could happen if Kenji and Hana are found here, don't you?" Ralph asked.

"I know the risks, and I simply don't care," Abby replied. "What I do care about is Patricia and that baby; we have to have another place for them to go to if things go badly."

"What about her folks?" Ralph asked.

Abby hesitated; they would take Patricia and the baby, but she didn't know about Kenji, and that still left the issue of Hana. "Patricia and the baby they would take, but not Kenji if John has anything to say about it, and that still leaves Hana."

"There's my house," Ralph said. "I could move back in and they could all stay with me."

Abby hesitated; she had grown used to having people around, but Ralph did present a viable option. They would have to go see what condition the house was in; they hadn't been there in months.

Nick sat at his desk, absently tapping his fingers as he thought about the plan to get Kenji and Hana out of Manzanar. He knew they were both safe from the reports he got from his friend Mitch. The hospital was filled to capacity and then some, which meant they couldn't use the storage area, but they could use the back door. While it was cold and it had snowed once, the roads to the camp were still open, and there was no indication that any storms were on the way. This week would be the best time, but everything wasn't ready; Ralph was going to talk to Abby tonight, and it was agreed to keep Patricia out of the loop.

The plan was to have Hana and Kenji stay with Abby, but there had to be a backup plan. Nick knew that Abby's house was no longer being watched since Kenji and Hana were gone, but his was. Ralph's old house wasn't being watched, which made it another possibility. Realistically, they wouldn't be able to try to get Kenji and Hana out until December at the earliest, the spring at the latest. Nick made plans to drive up to the camp in the next day or two.

By the end of November 1942, the Naval Battle of Guadalcanal had ended. The United States had heavy losses, but managed to maintain control of the sea. During the battle, the USS *Juneau* was sunk; included in its casualties were the five Sullivan brothers.

The 6th German Army at Stalingrad was surrounded, and Hitler continued to order that there was to be no surrender, but there was no word on the release of the thousands of Japanese still in interment camps.

Nick found Hana at the orphanage looking none the worse for wear. If anything, she seemed to be thriving under the less-than-ideal conditions; she seemed stronger than before and not as fragile as Nick remembered.

"Hello, Hana," Nick said.

"Nick, is everything all right? Patricia and the baby?" Hana asked anxiously.

"Everything is fine, including Patricia and the baby. Could we talk for a moment?" Nick asked.

"Of course," Hana replied. She spoke to the little girl she had been reading to and followed Nick to a quiet corner.

"You look well," Nick said.

"I am all right; the warm things Patricia and Abby sent have been very helpful," Hana replied.

"Good," Nick said and then hesitated. "Hana, I don't quite know how to go about this, so bear with me. I know that you and Kenji's father are no longer together, even though you're still married, and I know—at least I hope you know that I . . . I've come to care for you in a way that I didn't want to because you're married and—"

"I am Japanese," Hana finished for him.

"Yes," Nick agreed. "But the Japanese part has become less and less important to me; actually, it no longer matters. I look at Kenji and Patricia, and I see how hard they struggle to be together no matter what the odds are, and well, I can help you legally divorce Hiroshi so you can be with whoever you want."

Hana didn't know what to say. She suspected that Nick had feelings for her, but never thought he would act on them because of the reasons he just stated. As for herself, she was attracted to Nick, but hadn't allowed herself to think that there could be anything between them mainly because she was married, but also because of her race.

Did she want to be free of Hiroshi? Yes, she did; should she admit to Nick that she had been harboring feelings for him? Yes, she decided. If he could admit how he felt about her, then she needed to be honest with him and do the same.

"I would like to be free of Hiroshi; it has been a long time since he considered me his wife, and I no longer care for him as a wife should care for her husband," Hana replied.

"Hana, do you feel anything for me at all?" Nick asked.

"Yes," Hana admitted. "But Nick, you could be treated as a traitor and lose your job if we were found out."

"I'm not worried about that," Nick replied. "My concern is for you and Kenji; is he all right?"

"He's better, but he misses Patricia so much, and the closer the time of the baby's birth comes, the more restless he is," Hana replied.

"Hana, if we came again, do you think you could convince Kenji to leave with us?" Nick asked.

Hana thought a minute before replying, "I think I could."

"You need to come with him; he won't come unless you do," Nick said.

Hana already knew that and didn't disagree; the question was when this would happen.

Nick answered her question before she had a chance to ask it. "Ralph and I are hoping to do this before the baby is born, but at the latest it will be in the spring. I plan to make a trip up here by the first of the year, weather permitting, but be ready in case it's before that. The only thing I can tell you is that we'll be leaving from behind the hospital and that you won't be able to bring too much with you other than what you'll be wearing, which reminds me—make sure the both of you are wearing your thermal undergarments," Nick said as he stood. He glanced around and then touched Hana's hand. "Be safe," he murmured before he took off in search of Hiroshi.

He found him in his barracks reading a newspaper that had been thoughtlessly tossed in the trash. Nick didn't say anything about the paper as he sat down uninvited on the cot opposite of Hiroshi.

"What do you want?" Hiroshi asked.

"Nothing much," Nick said as he reached into his pocket and pulled out the divorce papers. "I only need for you to sign the papers agreeing to give Hana a divorce."

That got Hiroshi's attention. "Why should I sign anything?" he asked as he wondered what he could possibly get out of signing the papers.

"You obviously don't care for or love either her or your son," Nick replied. "I believe that your words were 'they are dead to me,' so why would you want to be married to a dead woman?"

"True, but why does this matter to you?" Hiroshi asked, already knowing the answer.

"That," Nick said, "is none of your concern, but I am willing to do something for you in exchange for your signature."

"What is it that you could possibly do for me?" Hiroshi asked. "Can you arrange my release from this place? Can you get me my business and home back?"

"No, and I won't lie to you and tell you that I can, but I can get money to you. I know you haven't been paid and that the money you have must be getting low," Nick replied.

"I have money enough," Hiroshi replied, but what he would need was money for whenever he was released from here. Whenever that happened, he was going back to Japan, never to return to the United States. He would find another wife, preferably one young enough to give him more children, and he wouldn't repeat the mistake he made with Kenji; he would start a new Takeda line.

Nick waited; he was in no hurry, as he had made arrangements to spend the night at Mitch's place, and he knew where Kenji was.

"I will sign if you will agree to pay my way back to Japan when this is over," Hiroshi said, "and I want it in writing."

Nick had come prepared; he knew Hiroshi wouldn't just sign the divorce papers out of the goodness of his heart. "Agreed," Nick said and handed the divorce papers over to Hiroshi.

Hiroshi looked over the papers and grunted. The American, he noticed, had left nothing to chance; part of the agreement was that he was to have no contact with Hana or Kenji for the rest of their interment and afterwards. If it was found out that he had initiated contact with either of them, then any financial agreement between he and Nick would be null and void, but the divorce would remain final. Without speaking, Hiroshi signed the papers and handed them back to Nick, who took them, tucked them into his pocket, and left Hiroshi to read his paper.

Nick found Kenji where he thought he would find him: at the hospital. Dr. Mynt offered him the use of his office for privacy.

"Patricia?" was the first thing that came out of Kenji's mouth when he saw Nick.

"She's fine, and she sent this," Nick said, handing Kenji the notebook.

Kenji looked at the latest date and relaxed.

"Kenji, I need to talk to you about a few things, the first thing being about your mother," Nick said.

"What about her?" Kenji asked.

"I don't know whether you've noticed or not—everyone else has, but . . . I have feelings for her, and I have for quite some time. I haven't acted on them because for one, she was married, and two, because she's Japanese. The latter reason has become irrelevant, and today, I told her how I felt about her, and she has feelings for me, too."

Kenji was surprised that he hadn't noticed, but then again, he was focused on him and Patricia.

"Anyway," Nick continued, "I just talked with your father, and he agreed to grant your mother a divorce."

"What did he want in return?" Kenji asked.

"Why do you think he would want anything?" Nick asked.

"Because I know my father; what did he demand from you?" Kenji asked again.

"That when this was over, I fund his return trip back to Japan, but there are stipulations that he has to follow in order for that to happen, the main one being that he has to stay away from you and your mother. He cannot initiate any contact with either of you; if he does, my end of the bargain is null and void, while he has to keep his end of the deal," Nick explained.

"And he agreed to this?"

"Yes," Nick replied. "But I have a question for you: how do you feel about your mother and me?"

"I have to admit to being surprised, but it isn't an unpleasant one," Kenji replied. "I only want for her to be happy and cared for no matter who it is that can do that for her, but I am pleased it is you."

Nick let out a breath that he hadn't been aware he was holding. Now for the rest of it. "Kenji, if we, meaning Ralph and I, came back for you and your mother, would you leave?"

Here it was, Kenji realized. This was his second chance to leave this place and to be with Patricia and their baby. What should he do? He knew what he had promised himself, but the issues were the same as before; if they got caught. . . . The memory of Patricia's face the last time he said "no" came to mind.

"Does Patricia know of this?" Kenji asked.

"No, and we're not going to tell her," Nick said.

"What of my mother? Have you spoken to her about this?"

"Yes, and she will only leave if you do," Nick replied.

Kenji was silent for so long that Nick didn't think he was going to answer. *Shit*, he thought, *he's going to say "no."*

"I will agree under two conditions," Kenji said.

"All right, I'm listening," Nick replied.

"The first one is this: if something happens, you let me turn myself in before your involvement becomes known."

"All right; what's the other condition?"

"That you swear to me that if I go to prison or if I am killed, you will care for my mother, Patricia, and my child," Kenji replied.

"I agree," Nick said, without hesitation and with relief.

"When are we leaving?" Kenji asked.

"We're planning by the New Year," Nick replied. "We have a few more things to work out, but as I told your mother, be ready at a moment's notice. Wear your thermal underthings at all times, and pack lightly—bring only the things that are the most important to you."

"Where will we live?" Kenji asked.

"Abby's, since her house is no longer being watched," Nick replied. "What we're working on is a second place in case something happens. Ralph is thinking his house, but my house isn't out of the realm of possibilities either, although it's being watched. Don't worry about that; we want you home in time to see that baby born."

Kenji was moved to tears that these people would put themselves at risk for him, Patricia, and his mother. That Nick cared for Hana sweetened things a bit; he wouldn't have to worry so much about her.

"I have to get back to work," Kenji said, extending his hand toward Nick. "Thank you many times over," he said, clasping Nick's hand in his.

"You're welcome, and Kenji? Stay here at the hospital as much as you can. Maybe Dr. Mynt will let you keep your things here. I don't know for sure, but I think trouble is coming, and tell your mother to stay at the orphanage or here with you."

Kenji nodded in agreement. Nick was right; trouble was coming.

DECEMBER 1, 1942

"Damn it!" Ralph swore as he watched the news.

"Now what?" Patricia asked, as she tried to get into a more comfortable position.

"Gas rationing!" Ralph exclaimed. They knew it was coming, but it still was a shock.

The war was affecting everyone in some way, but Patricia was more concerned about something else—they still hadn't found anyone to deliver the baby. The closer the time came, the more she missed Kenji and the more frequently she found herself in tears. She was, in a word, petrified.

Hattie tried to calm her by telling her that millions of women had babies without doctors or their husbands being present, but it didn't help. She wanted and needed Kenji to be with her. "It's not going to happen," she murmured to herself and told herself that she had to be strong for her and the baby.

DECEMBER 5, 1942

The trouble that Kenji, Ralph, and Nick thought was coming began. The leader of the JACL, Fred Tayama, was attacked by six masked men while he slept. Harry Ueno, the leader of the Kitchen Workers Union, was arrested for the beating, although there was no real proof that he was involved. Ueno was taken to Independence, California, the nearest town, and kept there in the local jail.

Kenji happened to be at the hospital when they brought Tayama in.

"What in the hell did they think would happen?" Dr. Mynt asked as he examined Tayama. "You got people living in close quarters; it was bound to happen."

Kenji excused himself and went in search of Hana; the warning bells in his head were ringing loud and clear. He found her in their quarters going through their things.

"Mother, come with me," Kenji said. "Tonight is just the beginning."

He helped her go through their things, leaving most of it behind. The only things he took for himself were the notebooks and letters from Patricia and a change of clothing. Hana took the letters from Patricia, Abby, and Hattie, and two changes of clothes. Kenji hurried her to the hospital and went to find Dr. Mynt.

"Please, may she stay here? She will help in anyway that she can," Kenji said.

"There are some babies that need to be fed," Dr. Mynt said and walked away.

DECEMBER 6, 1942

Approximately two thousand internees joined together in support of Ueno. Out of the two thousand, five were chosen to negotiate his release. When the crowd became agitated, the director of the camp agreed to bring Ueno back from Independence to the camp's prison in the hopes of appeasing the crowd. Even so, thousands of internees had gathered to demand Ueno's release and to voice other grievances. Things escalated when the crowd began to arm themselves with anything that could be used as weapons, prompting the director to call for the military police.

Kenji was assisting Dr. Mynt with another patient when he heard the ruckus down the hall. Both he and Dr. Mynt looked at the door and headed toward it. They watched as a small group of people started looking in rooms in search of Tayama.

"Where is he?" someone yelled.

Kenji stepped out in front of the group when they came down the hall. "This is a place of healing and not of violence; please leave," he said calmly.

"Tell us where Tayama is and we'll leave!" another voice said.

"Whatever your problems are with this man, they will not be settled here," Kenji said.

Dr. Mynt stepped forward. "I've called for the military police, so unless you want to join your friend Ueno in jail, I would suggest that you leave."

Reluctantly, the group left, peering into any rooms they passed on the way out.

Outside, things were escalating: a group of five hundred internees had surrounded the police station and were demanding the unconditional release of Ueno, even as the selected five were negotiating with the police chief, and the crowd continued to grow in size.

By evening, the soldiers assigned to the front of the building had drawn a line in the sand. The internees ignored the line and continued to move forward. To break up the crowd, tear gas was released, and then there was a shot—then another as soldiers began firing into the crowd, although the order to shoot hadn't been issued.

Kenji heard the shots and his heart sank as he wondered how many had died.

Hiroshi saw his opportunity and took it. He slipped in behind Joben Saito, who was so engrossed in what was happening that he wasn't paying attention to what was happening around him. Joben felt a pressure and then a pain in the kidney area of his back and fell to the ground.

Hiroshi had just added the term murderer to the list of names used to describe him, but to him, it wasn't murder—it was justified. Joben Saito was partially responsible for his being here; he had taken advantage of his disillusionment instead of approaching him as a man and presenting his options to him. Hiroshi slipped away, unseen in all of the chaos, and went back to his quarters.

The casualties included a seventeen-year-old who was killed and eleven others who were wounded. The protesters that were considered problems were removed from the camp and taken to local jails; others were taken to a WRA isolation center in Moab, and those who were non-US citizens were sent to Department of Justice camps.

Kenji was the one who identified Joben Saito's body and noted that his was the only body that didn't have a bullet wound; his gut told him his father had something to do with the death of the man, but he had no proof.

At the sight of the body of the seventeen-year-old, Kenji wept. This child would never get to make his mark upon the world; the world would be denied his knowledge and whatever skills he possessed. Suddenly, he couldn't wait to leave this place; he had had enough.

Nick received word of the Manzanar "incident" from his friend Mitch the next day.

"It was a hell of a thing, and to be honest with you, I'm surprised there weren't more casualties," Mitch said.

"The Takedas—are they all right?" Nick asked.

"As far as I know," Mitch replied. "But you remember Joben Saito?"

"Yeah, what about him?" Nick asked.

"He's dead, and it wasn't from a gunshot. What do you think about that?"

"Interesting," Nick replied; he had his suspicions just as Kenji had, and like Kenji, he couldn't prove anything. "Are you certain the Takedas are safe?"

"Like I said, as far as I know," Mitch replied.

"All right, thanks," Nick said and hung up before Mitch could ask any questions.

They would have to wait until things settled down up there before they could even think about getting Kenji and Hana out; he, however, would make another trip up there just on the off chance that there would be an opportunity. He looked at the calendar; it was December 7, one year since the attack on Pearl Harbor.

By the end of December 1942, gas rationing had been in effect for a month, Rommel was trapped in Tunisia, the Germans were trapped at Stalingrad, the Japanese seemed to be ready to abandon Guadalcanal, and it had been eight months since Kenji and Hana went to Manzanar and three months since Kenji and Patricia had last been together.

But to the both of them, it felt like years.

JANUARY 1943

Things at the camp had finally calmed down; all of the camp's operations were resumed, and the schools reopened. Kenji and Hana were on pins and needles, not knowing when Nick and Ralph would appear. Kenji was even more worried about Patricia; the baby could be born any time between now and February. He just wanted to hear her voice to know she was all right.

Taking a chance, he approached Dr. Mynt. "I know it is against the rules for me to make a phone call, but could you please call my wife and ask if she is well?"

Dr. Mynt looked at Kenji for several minutes and then told him to sit down. "Son, you're going to be a hell of a doctor someday, and I don't say that often. I'll make that call for you under one condition."

Kenji waited for him to finish.

"When this damned mess is over, I want you to call me," Dr. Mynt said and wrote his number down on a card and handed it to Kenji. "Do I have your word?"

Kenji would have promised the man the sun, moon, and stars if that was what it took to talk to Patricia. "You have my word," Kenji replied as he pulled out his wallet and slipped the card inside.

"Good, now what's the number?"

Abby was in the process of making Patricia a cup of mint tea when the phone rang. She glanced at the clock and wondered who could be calling so late; Nick had left a few minutes before, so it couldn't have been him.

"Hello? Yes, this is she. May I ask who's calling? Just a minute!" Abby said excitedly.

"Patricia! There's a phone call for you!" Abby called, "Ralph, help me get her up!"

"Who is it?" Patricia asked, not really wanting to move now that she was comfortable.

"You'll see, now come on!" Abby insisted.

A few minutes later, Patricia was holding the receiver to her ear. "Hello?"

"*Kirei*?"

"Kenji? Is that you?" Patricia asked, not trusting her ears.

"Yes. *Kirei*, are you all right?"

"I . . . we're fine; I just miss you. Are you all right?" Patricia asked through her tears.

"I miss you, too, and yes, Mother and I are both fine," Kenji replied.

"Your father, is he all right too?" Patricia asked.

The question, though a simple one, threw Kenji; that she would ask after a man who had planned to have her raped and killed surprised him, but then he remembered that her forgiving nature was one of the many reasons he loved her.

"Yes, *Kirei*, he is well," Kenji replied. "I had to hear your voice; I will rest better knowing that you and the baby are well. I have to go now, but *Kirei*, believe me when I tell you that I am coming home to you and our child. I love you," he said and then hung up.

Patricia stood holding the receiver to her ear, the tears streaming down her face, but she felt better. Kenji and his family were all right.

By end of January 1943, Iraq had declared war on the Axis powers, the RAF began a two-night bombing in Berlin, the Allies captured Tripoli, and Germany initiated a new conscription law—men between the ages of sixteen and thirty-five and women between the ages of seventeen and forty-five were open to be drafted.

The German forces in Stalingrad were near collapse, the last of the Japanese in Guadalcanal had been evacuated undetected by the Americans, and a large part of the German 6th Army at Stalingrad surrendered, in spite of Hitler's orders to stand firm.

And there was still no word about the release of the interred Japanese.

Ralph watched Patricia closely; she was scared and rightfully so. It looked as if her mother and Abby would have to deliver the baby without the help of a doctor. He prayed that nothing would go wrong and that the baby would be born healthy and strong. *He'll need to be strong in order to survive in this crazy world he's being brought into*, Ralph thought. He had hoped to hear from Nick by now and was getting impatient. He was about to go up to Manzanar alone, except he didn't have the connections Nick did.

Hattie had moved in temporarily, since they didn't know exactly when the baby was due, and it was a comfort to Patricia to have her mother close by.

Ralph and John had become friends of sorts, especially when John asked him to teach him how to play chess, a game Patricia had never gotten the hang of. John, however, took to it like a fish to water.

"You sure you haven't played this before?" Ralph asked when John beat him in yet another game.

"No sir," John replied. "It ain't that hard once you understand who you protectin'."

"You would have made one hell of a strategist," Ralph said, meaning the compliment.

"I don't know exactly what that is, but I thank you for the compliment," John said as he set the board up again.

They were partly through the next game when the phone rang. Hattie and Abby were upstairs with Patricia, making sure they had everything they needed for the baby, so Ralph answered the phone.

"Yep. All right," was all he said, and then he hung up.

John left for home after spending a few minutes with Patricia and Hattie, leaving Ralph alone with his thoughts. Tonight, if all went well, Kenji and Hana would be home and safe; he hadn't said anything to Hattie yet, but he would leave that to Abby. He wrote a quick note and slid it under Abby's door; it was short and to the point.

Abby,
I'm going to run an errand with Nick; be back as soon as we can. Have hot tea and some soup ready; we're going to need it.
Ralph

Ralph slipped on his heavy coat, put on his hat and gloves, and walked out to the corner, where Nick waited.

FEBRUARY 1, 1943

Kenji was doing some extra cleaning for Dr. Mynt, and so was Hana. Whenever they were going to leave, Dr. Mynt found something else for them to do. Something was happening, and Kenji suspected what it was: Nick and Ralph were coming tonight or sometime soon. When he had a moment, he pulled Hana aside.

"Mother, do you have what you want from our quarters?"

"I have everything I need, and yes, I am wearing the underthings that Patricia sent us. Do you need to go back there?" she asked, concerned.

"No, but I have a question: what about the orphanage? How did you explain your absence?" he asked.

"I told her there were children here at the hospital that needed a mother's touch," Hana replied with a smile.

Kenji relaxed; it wouldn't do to have the woman question Hana's whereabouts, but to their advantage, the camp had grown in size; there were thousands of Japanese here, and they wouldn't be missed for quite some time, if at all.

Nick and Ralph drove out of town and stopped along the road. Nick had already padded the trunk of his car with blankets, but it would still be cold. After doing a quick check that there was water and sandwiches in the trunk, they took off again in the direction of the camp. Neither man spoke during the entire drive to the camp; when they neared the road taking them to the back of the hospital, Nick turned off the lights. The howling wind covered the sounds of the car's engine as they approached the back of the hospital.

Ralph saw the light first. "What is that?" he asked.

"Sentry," Nick replied. "Don't say anything; let me do the talking," he added as he rolled to a stop.

"What you doing out here?" the sentry asked, shining his light into the car.

"We're friends of Doctor Mynt, visiting from Independence," Nick replied.

"Havin' another one of his poker games, is he?" the sentry asked with a chuckle.

"That he is," Nick agreed, not quite believing their luck.

"Been to a few of 'em. Gotta watch him though; I swear that the man cheats! Well, go on, then, and try to keep hold of some of your money," the sentry said and waved them on.

To Nick, it was luck; to Ralph, it was confirmation that they were doing the right thing.

Nick pulled as close to the back of the hospital as he could, got out, and opened the trunk. It would be a tight fit, especially for Kenji with his height, but it couldn't be helped.

Ralph ran up the back steps and banged on the door four times and stepped back. The door was opened by none other than Dr. Mynt. Ralph stepped inside and waited while Dr. Mynt went to get Hana and Kenji.

"Kenji and Hana, there's some trash that needs to be taken out. Take everything with you; I don't want to draw any unwelcome visitors," he said gruffly.

Kenji understood. Ralph and Nick were here. He looked At Dr. Mynt and nodded; he could have sworn that he saw tears in the doctor's eyes. Dr. Mynt nodded back and walked away toward the front of the hospital. Kenji and Hana went to where they had their few belongings hidden and went out into the cold night air, where Nick and Ralph waited. Nick gave Hana a brief hug and kiss on the cheek as Kenji climbed into the trunk of the car; when he was settled, he helped Hana in and then covered them with the thick blankets, putting the food and water where they could reach them.

When they were on their way, both he and Ralph remembered the sentry; they hadn't been there long enough to play cards. They could only hope they didn't see him, and if they did, Nick had a story ready about there being some kind of emergency that cancelled the card game. Fortunately, the sentry was nowhere to be seen—probably huddled in a corner somewhere trying to stay warm.

It had started to snow, so Nick slowed down until they were out of the mountains. He wanted to stop and check on his passengers, but he didn't dare take the chance.

Kenji hugged Hana close to him; she was freezing in spite of the blankets and thermal underwear.

"Soon, Mother," he murmured into her hair. To distract her from thinking about how cold she was, he asked her about Nick. "So how long have you had feelings for Nick?"

Hana knew what he was up to and played along, finding that it actually helped. After a while, they noticed they weren't quite so cold, indicating that they were out of the mountains. It was only then Kenji allowed himself to believe that soon he would be holding Patricia and her pregnant belly against him.

Hattie and Abby watched the clock, which seemed like it hadn't moved. Soup was simmering on the stove in anticipation of four cold and hungry people. Patricia was sound asleep upstairs after crying for several minutes on Hattie's shoulder. As much as Hattie wanted to tell her what she knew, she didn't dare. Abby had told her about their visit to Manzanar and how Patricia had reacted when Kenji wouldn't come back with them, and she wouldn't put her through that again.

Several hours later, both women jumped at the sound of Nick's car horn. Abby went through the kitchen and opened the garage door. She had moved her car as far over as she could to give Nick room to squeeze his car in. They had decided it would look suspicious if her car was parked on the street as opposed to the garage.

Nick got out, opened the trunk, and helped Hana out. She was immediately greeted with hugs and kisses by both Hattie and Abby.

Kenji needed a little help out, as he was stiff from being in the same position for so long. "Where's Patricia?" he asked as soon as he could stand.

"Upstairs, but. . . . "

Kenji never heard the rest of the sentence; he was already in the house and up the stairs. He stopped in front of the door to the room where Patricia lay sleeping. He looked at the bathroom and decided to go there first; once he was in bed with her, he wasn't getting out unless he absolutely had to.

He rushed into the bathroom, used the toilet, stripped, and quickly washed off. He put only his shirt and trousers back on and carried the rest of the clothing to the bedroom, dropping them on the floor as soon as he stepped inside. Patricia was on the side closest to the wall, he noticed—the place where he usually slept whenever they used this room.

Quietly, Kenji closed the door and stripped. He stood by the bed for several minutes just looking at her before he eased in beside her. She didn't wake up at first but snuggled into him as she always did when they slept together; he felt a warm tear hit his skin, and he realized that she thought she was dreaming.

"*Kirei*," he said softly.

Patricia moaned and began to cry in her sleep.

"*Kirei*, wake up; I'm here like I promised," Kenji said as he kissed her.

Patricia's eyes were closed as her arm went around his waist and she pulled him closer. Suddenly, her eyes snapped open and she was face to face with Kenji. "This isn't real; I'm dreaming," she murmured.

"No, *Kirei*, this is no dream," Kenji assured her. "I'm really here."

Patricia threw her arms around Kenji's neck and cried in relief and joy as Kenji held her.

Neither of them spoke for almost an hour. Patricia kept touching Kenji's face and hair, still not believing that he wasn't a figment of her imagination, so vivid only because she wanted him to be with her so badly. Kenji let her touch as much as she wanted while he kept his hands on her stomach, crying when he felt the baby move beneath his hands.

"How long do we have?" Patricia asked, already preparing herself.

"I'm not going back; Mother is here, too," Kenji said.

"They let you go?" Patricia asked.

"No, *Kirei*, Nick and Ralph came for us. We will have to stay hidden until the war is over, but I will be here when our baby comes. Sleep now; I'll be here when you wake up," Kenji promised.

Patricia resisted; she was too afraid that when she woke up Kenji wouldn't be in bed with her. Kenji turned so that as much of him as possible was touching her and began to stroke her back while he sang another song about a soldier that had come home to his true love. Finally, unable to keep her eyes open, Patricia fell back to sleep.

Chapter 14

At first, Patricia thought she was dreaming—until she felt a warm muscular body cradling hers. Kenji was still asleep and snoring softly in her ear, but she didn't mind; she would never complain about his snoring for as long as she lived. She lay one of her hands on top of Kenji's, which was resting on her stomach. He was really here. She didn't care if they had to stay in the basement for years; if that was what it took to keep him with her, then she would do it. The immediate problem was that she had to go to the bathroom, but she didn't want to wake Kenji. She waited for as long as she could before she absolutely could not wait any longer.

It took Kenji a minute to reorient himself, but when he woke up, he did quickly. He followed Patricia to the bathroom and waited outside of the door for her to come out before going in himself. He hoped she wasn't ready to get up yet; he wanted to spend more time in bed just holding and talking with her. At some point, they would need to talk about what she needed to do if he was caught, but not today or tomorrow, either; he wanted her to be happy for just a little while longer.

Patricia waited for Kenji while he used the bathroom and then followed him back to the bedroom. Patricia got into bed first and was followed by Kenji; for long minutes neither of them spoke, and when they did, it was Patricia who broke the silence.

"Kenji, I'm so sorry for what I said to you that night. I know you love us, but it was so hard leaving you again, and I wanted you to come home with us so badly."

"*Kirei*, I know it was out of fear and pain that you spoke," Kenji said. "So no apologies are needed. That was the hardest thing I have ever had to do, and I hope I will never have to leave you again. But enough sadness; we have had more than our share. It's time to start getting ready for our baby, and sadness has no place in that," Kenji said as he held her tighter against him.

Hana woke up with a start and then remembered where she was; at first she thought it was Hiroshi lying in bed with her and then remembered it was Nick. He was going to leave, but she had asked him to stay; there had been no lovemaking, but Nick slept with his arms around her—something Hiroshi had never done.

She could smell food cooking and her stomach rumbled. Nick, feeling her stir, woke up; the smell of the cooking food made his stomach growl as well. Out of respect for Hana, Nick got out of bed and went upstairs, leaving her alone to get dressed.

"Morning," he greeted Ralph and Abby when he reached the kitchen.

"Morning; there's some coffee if you want some, and I think the bathroom's free," Abby said.

"Have Kenji and Patricia surfaced yet?" Nick asked as he poured himself a cup of coffee.

"No, and I don't expect that they will for a while yet," Abby replied. "How's Hana?"

"All right, I think. She's still adjusting to the fact that she's a free woman," Nick replied as he took a sip of the coffee and then set it down to head for the stairs. "I think I'll use the bathroom," he said as he took the stairs two at a time.

By the time he made it back downstairs, Hana was dressed and waiting her turn for the bathroom. One thing became clear to Ralph: there were too many people living in Abby's house, and someone was bound to notice. A few options ran through his mind. He could move back to his house; Nick had his own place, and since he and Hana seemed to be an item, maybe he could sneak her into his house, leaving Patricia and Kenji to stay with Abby. It would be safer for all of them that way, and it would also provide other places for them to go to if the need arose.

He and Abby had gone back to his house to see what needed to be done, and all it needed was a good cleaning and straightening up. That was something he, Abby, and Hattie could do, and it wouldn't take too long, especially if Patricia helped—she wouldn't feel right about them doing all of the work and would go with them. He would give it a couple of days before he brought it up, but for now, what he considered his family was together.

It occurred to Ralph that had this happened twenty years ago, he wouldn't have lifted a finger to help them. It wouldn't have been because he didn't want to; he would have been too afraid to. He recalled the one incident that made him swear to himself that he would never let fear rule him again.

He was living in his cabin in South Carolina at the time; his wife Ada had just passed on, and he was at odds with their children, who blamed him for her death. In a way, he supposed it had been his fault. She was sick, and he hadn't wanted to spend the money for a doctor; it was too hard to come by. The great flu epidemic of 1918 was over, and they had come through it unscathed, although an estimated fifty million people had died. But whatever was wrong with Ada, it wouldn't pass. By the time Ralph called the doctor, it was too late, and Ada died.

The children—two boys, eleven and thirteen at the time—had gone to live with Ada's folks in the city, leaving him alone, and that was the last time he ever saw them. One morning not too long after Ada died and the boys left, Ralph was out checking his traps when he heard voices and then a howl of pain. He followed the voices until he came to a clearing, where a group of men had a black man tied with his chest to a tree. He himself didn't have any bad feelings toward anyone no matter their skin color, but he was in the minority, and he wondered what the black man had done to make the white men so angry.

He watched as the men began to take turns whipping the man. Ralph was sickened; he knew that the intent was to kill the man as painfully as possible, and he wanted to help the man. He wanted to stop the whipping, but he was afraid—after all, he was just one man, and they would kill him for interfering.

After watching for a few more minutes, he slunk away and went back to his cabin. He didn't go back until evening, when he was sure the group of white men would be gone. What he saw made him vomit. What was still tied to the tree in no way resembled a human being; it was a bloody mass of flesh.

Crying, he went back to his cabin, got a shovel and a tarp, and headed back to the clearing. He cried as he dug the grave for the black man, not even knowing his supposed crime or his name. It didn't matter, Ralph decided. No human being deserved to die like that. He dug the grave deep enough that the animals wouldn't be able to dig it up; he cut the man's body down and wrapped him in the tarp.

"I'm sorry that I didn't help you," he murmured as he dragged the tarp-wrapped body to the grave and rolled it in. By the time he was done, Ralph was covered in sweat, dirt, and the blood of the dead man.

He left South Carolina shortly after that, not bothering to contact his children to tell them where he had gone. That had been twenty-five years ago, and for all he knew, his boys could be in Europe serving their country—or they could be dead. Suddenly it was important that he find out. What he would do with the information once he had it, he didn't know, but he had to know where they were.

"Ralph?" Abby called, concerned.

Ralph swiped at his face, noticing that his hand was wet. "What?" he asked gruffly, wiping his face with his hand again.

"Nothing," Abby replied, giving him a curious look.

The four of them ate breakfast in silence, making sure to leave enough for Patricia and Kenji. Nick decided it was time for him to go home, but wanted a few minutes alone with Hana.

"Ralph and I will clean up this mess," Abby said, standing up.

"I'll help you," Hana said, standing as well.

"No, dear, why don't you walk Nick to the car?" Abby said.

"But. . . . "

"Hana, come with me," Nick said, taking her hand and leading her to the garage.

Once in the garage, Nick pulled Hana into his arms. They had to talk about what they wanted, but for now, this would do until they had the time to talk.

"I'll be back later; stay in the house and don't answer the phone or door," Nick said as he pulled away. "We'll talk later," he added as he bent down and kissed Hana for the first time on her lips.

Hana's breath caught; Hiroshi's kisses had always been perfunctory, and there was no real emotion to them, although he loved her—or he had at one point. But this kiss was different; she liked it, but didn't know how to convey the sentiment. Nick seemed to understand and kissed her again before leaving. Hana watched him get into his car and thought of how strange and unpredictable life was.

Hiroshi had several very anxious days. He knew that the way Joben had died was under suspicion; there was talk of it around the camp, especially by those who knew him. On one hand, Hiroshi knew he was safe; anyone could have killed Joben, and there was so much going on that night that no one saw him do it. On the other hand, if anyone suspected him, it would be Kenji, Hana, or the American agent, but they would be unable to prove anything.

It was hard to believe that he had actually killed someone, but he had, and he had gotten away with it. The only thing left to do now was to wait for release and dream of his return to Japan. There were times when he wondered about Hana and Kenji, but all he had to do to kill the curiosity was remember the agreement between him and the American. Hiroshi knew that Nick would keep his word as long as he kept his, and if all went well, he would be back in Nagasaki within the year and would have a new wife soon after. She would be young enough to give him sons to restart the Takeda line, and he would not make the same mistakes that he had with Kenji.

His main point of contention now regarded the Japanese units that were going to fight for the United States. He just didn't understand it, because many of the men volunteering were internees, as were their families. The 100th Infantry Battalion had done so well in training that the United States reversed its decision regarding Japanese-Americans serving in the armed forces.

"Traitors and fools," he mumbled to himself.

A few days later, Hiroshi and other internees were expected to answer a loyalty questionnaire. He found out later that the questionnaire was used to register the Nisei—the second-generation Japanese—for the draft. Question number 27 of the form asked, "Are you willing to serve in the armed forces of the United States Army on combat duty wherever asked?" Hiroshi wondered how Kenji would have answered that one if he had been born Nisei. Question number 28 asked, "Will you swear unqualified allegiance to the United States of America and faithfully defend the United States from any and all attack by domestic and foreign forces and forswear any form of allegiance or obedience to the Japanese Emperor, or any other foreign government, power or organization?"

Hiroshi again wondered how Kenji would have answered and knew the answer. He had already turned his back on Japan, as had Hana; her answer would have been the same—they would have said yes. What he wanted to know were the results of the questions asked. What he found out later was that more than seventy-five percent said they would be willing to enlist and serve in the United States armed forces; all of these Hiroshi considered traitors. Hiroshi was further angered when he learned that eighty-six percent of those who answered the loyalty questionnaire had answered positively. Many of those who were young or fluent in English were permitted to leave for schools or jobs in the Midwest and the East.

"I am surrounded by traitors," Hiroshi mumbled as he headed back to his quarters.

FEBRUARY 1943

"It's about fucking time!" Ralph exclaimed to himself. He was the only one really following the war news anymore, as everyone was focusing on Patricia and when the baby would come. As he watched her, he was glad they had gone back for Kenji and Hana; just seeing her smile had been worth it, and it had given him a measure of peace that he had done something right.

The Battle of Stalingrad was finally over, and the entire German 6th Army had surrendered; Guadalcanal was finally secured; Nuremberg, Germany, had been bombed; and shoes were being rationed in the States. Ralph chuckled at the shoe rationing. Abby had thrown a fit; shoes were her one true vice.

Kenji and Patricia had moved back down to the basement, their rationale was that they liked the feeling that they had their own space, even though it was just an illusion. Kenji solved the bathroom problem by emptying out the closet and running a rope from one end of the basement to the other to hang their clothes up on and turning the closet into a small but private bathroom, which meant that he was on latrine duty, but he didn't mind. He made sure there was always a supply of water, soap, and towels handy for use afterwards.

One corner of the basement became the "nursery," and Ralph helped with that. He and Kenji built several shelves to store the baby's things and then carried the things down for Patricia to arrange however she wanted.

For his part, Kenji couldn't stop touching Patricia or her stomach; he was going to witness the birth of their first child, and not only that, he was going to deliver the baby himself. They had it all worked out; it would be just the two of them until it was time for the baby's actual birth. Then Hattie and Hana would come and hold Patricia's hands while he delivered the baby. Abby would be there for moral support and a pair of extra hands. Several times a day, Kenji read the medical books until he was certain he would be able to handle any minor issues. They all prayed that the birth would go smoothly and without complications. Kenji also checked his supplies several times a day, arranging and rearranging things until he was satisfied that they were in the order he wanted.

Patricia was at the point where she wasn't comfortable no matter what position she was in, and if she was comfortable, it didn't last for long. It had become too much of an ordeal for her to climb the stairs up to the second floor to take a shower; getting upstairs to the kitchen was as far as she could go, so Kenji patiently and lovingly bathed her daily, leaving no place unwashed. Each day found Patricia more nervous, to the point where she couldn't eat. Kenji didn't force it, but made sure she took in as much fluid as she could handle.

One night, feeling particularly guilty, Patricia tried to get Kenji to go rest on the couch upstairs. "I'm keeping you up and you're exhausted," she said.

"Think of it as practice for medical school," Kenji replied as he kissed her. "And I promised you I would never leave your side, so I stay," he added, kissing her cheek and then her stomach.

Ralph was on retrieval duty; once Patricia went into labor, he was supposed to go get Hattie and John, and it was a duty he took seriously. He frequently checked to be sure that the car's tires were intact and that there was gas in the tank, even if he had just checked the day before and the car hadn't moved from its spot. He also started the car up at least once a day.

Hana and Abby boiled white towels and washcloths and sealed them in plastic after they were dry, as per Kenji's instructions. They also boiled Abby's sewing scissors and thread and sealed them in canning jars—something Kenji thought up—and stored everything in the basement, where the baby would be born. Kenji checked the seal on the jars several times a day; the last thing he wanted was for Patricia or the baby to get ill because of infection. There were two never-used wash basins that had been sterilized with boiling water and then placed in plastic for Kenji to wash his hands. When Patricia went into active labor, it was Ralph's job to start heating water and to keep it ready.

Hattie was working frantically to finish a baby quilt that she had started when she found out Patricia was pregnant, and since she had delivered a few babies herself was going to be Kenji's "second."

They kept the names they had chosen for the baby to themselves, even though they were pestered incessantly for hints. Finally, they were as ready as they were going to be. Kenji talked with Patricia about what to expect in the hopes of taking away some of her apprehension and taught her breathing exercises meant to calm and relax.

FEBRUARY 16, 1943

Patricia had finally drifted off into an uncomfortable sleep with Kenji's arm around her and a hand on her stomach. As tired as he was, Kenji couldn't sleep. He loved the feel of the baby moving under his hand and wondered if it was a boy or a girl; he would be happy with either and only wanted him or her to be healthy and for Patricia to be safe. When the baby finally settled down, Kenji closed his eyes and was soon snoring softly into Patricia's ear.

She wasn't sure what woke her, the feeling that the bed was wet or the pain, but she woke Kenji, not sure of what else to do. "Kenji, wake up," she whispered.

"*Kirei*? What's wrong?" he asked.

"I think . . . I don't know if anything is; I just had a cramp and I need the bathroom," she replied.

Kenji helped her up to their bathroom and went to change the sheets. He looked at the wet spot and then back toward the bathroom; he suspected that she might be in labor but didn't say anything, in case it was a false alarm. When he changed the bed, he added towels to absorb the fluid and blood that would occur when the baby was born.

"Ouch," Patricia said about twenty minutes later and then again after about another twenty minutes.

"*Kirei*, I think you're in labor," Kenji said calmly.

"The baby is coming?" Patricia asked nervously.

"I believe so, but we have time," Kenji assured her with a kiss. "I'll wake Ralph so he can go get your parents."

Several minutes later, Kenji was back downstairs and in bed with her. "Sleep while you can," he advised as he pulled her tight against him.

"I'm scared," Patricia admitted softly.

"I know you are, but we'll be fine; now rest."

To Patricia that was like telling the mountain to move into the sea; she couldn't sleep, but she tried to rest. She heard her parents talking in the kitchen with Abby several minutes later; she found the sound of their voices comforting and fell asleep, only waking when the contractions came.

Labor began in earnest sometime around one o'clock in the morning. Patricia grabbed Kenji's hand and squeezed hard enough to wake him.

"All right, *Kirei*, let's get you into a more comfortable position," he said as he stood and slid in behind her, so her back rested against his chest and she was sitting between his legs.

"That's better," Patricia agreed.

"Good, now let's rest, and when the next contraction comes, we breathe together," Kenji told her.

Patricia closed her eyes and tried to relax; just as she fell asleep, another contraction came. She bit her lip so she wouldn't cry out and wake Kenji.

"*Kirei*, I'm awake. Breathe with me," he whispered in her ear.

Several hours later, the contractions were coming more frequently and with increasing intensity. Patricia had never felt such pain and hoped never to feel it again anytime soon.

"What time is it?" she asked.

"Eight," Kenji replied and wiped her face with a cool cloth and moistened her dry lips with a clean cloth dipped in water. "Soon our baby will be here," he soothed as he rubbed her lower back. She was now lying on her side; the sitting position was no longer comfortable. Several times she walked around the basement with Kenji's arm around her, and sometimes they just stood with their arms around each other, breathing together. When the contractions were too severe for Patricia to safely be out of bed, Kenji put her to bed and lay with her.

By ten o'clock, Hana, Hattie, and Abby were surrounding the bed. Hana and Hattie were on each side holding a hand, and Abby was at the head, wiping Patricia's face with cold, wet cloths. Neither woman holding her hands complained as Patricia squeezed their hands and cried out. All of the women whispered words of encouragement to her as the labor progressed.

"*Kirei*, it's time; push as hard you can," Kenji said.

Patricia pushed for what felt to her to be hours, and still there was no baby. She was in tears; she was exhausted and frustrated.

"Hattie, Mother, please come here," Kenji said.

When they reached him, he gave them instructions. "I need to talk with Patricia for a few moments; if you see the baby's head, call to me."

Hattie, who had delivered several babies, nodded in understanding while Hana looked pale and uncertain.

Kenji went to the head of the bed and kissed Patricia's hot, sweaty face before wiping it with a cool cloth that Abby handed him. "*Kirei*, close your eyes for just a few minutes and listen to my voice."

Patricia hesitated and then closed her eyes. Kenji pressed his lips against her ear and spoke. "We are almost done; our baby will soon be here, and if it is a girl, she will be as beautiful and as strong as her mother, and she will be a Takeda; if it is a boy, he will be beautiful, strong, and he will be a Takeda as well. I will love you and our child forever; now release our child into my hands." Kenji kissed a crying Patricia on her lips and murmured, "I love you."

Patricia took a deep breath and waited for Kenji to take his place at the foot of the bed. Hana and her mother returned to her side, and each took a hand and gave it a squeeze.

Kenji touched Patricia's knee to get her attention. "*Kirei*, look at me," he said softly and waited for her to comply. "When the next contraction comes, push as hard as you can."

When the next contraction came, Patricia pushed as hard as she could.

"Good, *Kirei*," Kenji encouraged.

Three pushes later, Kenji smiled at her. "Her head is coming; she's almost here!" he exclaimed, having no idea of the sex of the baby.

Ten minutes later, a tiny cry filled the basement.

"A boy! It's a boy!" Kenji exclaimed as he checked the baby's nose and mouth before wrapping him in a warm towel. "*Kirei*, we have a beautiful baby boy!" he said as he cried.

Everyone was crying as Kenji lay the baby on Patricia's stomach and clamped the umbilical cord off before cutting it.

Patricia sobbed as Hana picked the baby up and placed him in her arms. She counted his fingers and toes to make sure all of him was there. *Kenji was right; he is beautiful*, she thought as she kissed their baby for the first time. She could hear the shouts coming from upstairs as the men heard the news of the baby's arrival. She was so tired, but she felt so good, especially since she had gotten her wish that their first baby be a son.

Kenji left the foot of the bed long enough to kiss Patricia and his son before going back to watch her. He wanted to be sure she had delivered the entire placenta and wasn't bleeding excessively. He checked her stomach just as Dr. Mynt had taught him and was satisfied that Patricia was all right. Patricia let each grandmother and Abby hold the baby while Kenji cleaned her and then changed the bed. Only when that was done were the men allowed to come downstairs to see the baby.

Ralph was out-and-out crying; John was trying not to cry, and Nick's eyes were wet. John gave up trying not to cry the moment he held the baby in his arms. In that moment, he forgot that his grandson was half-Japanese; all he saw was his grandson, and without thinking about it, he held out his hand to Kenji, who after a hesitation born of surprise took John's hand in his and shook it. Ralph held the baby next, and then Nick, who of the three was the least comfortable holding a baby.

"Hey, does this kid have a name?" Nick asked as he held the baby.

"He does," Kenji said. "Our plan was to give our child an American and Japanese name, and that is what we have done. His name is Nikorasu Ralph. Nikorasu is Japanese for Nicolas. I wouldn't be here if not for the two of you coming back for Mother and me. I would have missed the birth of my son. We're honored to name our son after the two men that made this possible: you, Nick, and Ralph."

Neither man knew what to say; Nick spoke first. "Don't you want a Kenji Junior or something?" he asked, but he was obviously surprised and pleased.

"Yeah, and Ralph's no name for a kid," Ralph added, just as pleased.

"Nikorasu Ralph will be his name," Kenji said as he took the baby from Nick and kissed his tiny, dark head.

Several minutes later, the basement was quiet with the exception of the quiet murmurings of Kenji and Patricia talking between themselves.

"He is so beautiful," Patricia said as she stroked the baby's face.

"And so are you," Kenji said as he sat behind her with his arms around her, looking over her shoulder at the baby. "You did well," he added, kissing her shoulder.

"So did you," Patricia replied. "As soon as this is over, we have to find a way to get you into medical school," she added sleepily.

She nursed Niko one more time before falling asleep. Kenji sat in the rocking chair by the bed and watched her sleep while he rocked the baby; for the second time since their meeting, everything was perfect. The first time being the day they married.

By the end of February 1943, Joseph Goebbels, the German propaganda minister, announced a "total war" against the Allies; General Dwight D. Eisenhower was selected to command the Allied armies in Europe; members of the White Rose movement—an anti-Nazi youth group—were arrested, and two of the members—brother and sister Hans and Sophie Scholl—were executed for high treason.

At Featherstone POW camp in New Zealand, 240 Japanese prisoners refused to work. A Lt. Adachi was shot by the camp adjutant, which led to the prisoners either charging or appearing to do so. The end result was thirty-one dead and seventy-four wounded, with some of the wounded dying later on the Japanese side, and one dead and six wounded on the New Zealand side. Later New Zealand would be exonerated, but it was discovered that cultural differences played a major role in the event and that the prisoners were not aware that under the Geneva Convention, compulsory work was allowed.

Baby Niko brought a sense of normalcy to the house; it was hard not to smile when he was in the room and easy to forget that in the outside world there was a war going on and that there was the danger that Kenji and Hana could be caught. After much discussion, it was agreed that Hana would go with Nick and that Ralph would stay with Abby, Kenji, Patricia, and the baby, but his house would be made ready just in case it was needed.

There was an uneasy peace between John and Kenji, but John was trying, and to Patricia it was more than she could have hoped for.

Ralph continued to read up on the war news, informing them of what he considered pertinent. "They got Ike Eisenhower now; he'll kick some ass!" he said.

Kenji rarely responded to the war news anymore, but when he heard about the execution of the Scholls, he mourned just as he had mourned upon hearing about the event at Featherstone and the deaths at Manzanar. He could barely stand to hear about the concentration camps, but he forced himself to listen; he never wanted to forget the damage this war had done. Like Ralph, he searched the newspapers for news of the release of those still in the interment camps, but saw nothing, and Nick had nothing to report either.

Hana was upstairs packing her things when Patricia came to see her.

"Are you all right with going with Nick?" she asked.

"I . . . this is new to me, but as I learned to adapt to life at the camp and to accept you as a daughter, I will learn to adapt to this," Hana replied.

"Do you miss him? Kenji's father, I mean?" Patricia asked.

"No, and I haven't for a very long time," Hana replied. "I think we were comfortable with each other, but we never really loved each other. We were told to marry, and we did it without question; it wasn't until you and Kenji happened that the cracks in our marriage came forth. I don't hate him, and I wish him no ill will, but he is no longer of any concern to me."

Patricia stopped Hana from packing so she had her full attention. "Hana, we never intended for you and Hiroshi to separate. All we wanted was to be together and—"

"Patricia, none of what happened is your fault," Hana said. "You and Kenji were just the motivating factor and nothing more; what matters is that Kenji is happy, and that is because of you and now the baby. I'm on my way to being happy, and that is also because of you and your courage. I'm honored and proud to call you daughter," Hana said and hugged Patricia. "Be happy and take good care of my son and my grandson."

Patricia promised and ran down the stairs. She took out the blue tea set Hana had given her for her birthday and quickly made tea. When she heard Hana come down the stairs, she walked to her and bowed. "Will you join me for tea before you go?"

Kenji watched as Hana graciously accepted Patricia's offer of tea; the only thing missing was his father. As angry as he was at him, Kenji missed him. He missed the man that had taught him so much, and wished things had been different.

While Kenji reacted to the news of Featherstone with mourning, Hiroshi reacted with anger. It only proved that the Allies were barbarians, but he had little knowledge of the conditions of the prisoners held in Japanese POW camps. What little he heard, he didn't believe; it was nothing more than propaganda, just as the extermination of the Jews was propaganda, whose only goal was to make the Americans and others opposed to the Axis powers hate them enough to be willing to fight against them.

Here it was the end of February, and he had long stopped listening to the rumors about being released. If release were imminent, he would have heard from the American who was in love with Hana.

Not long after Hana and Kenji escaped, it occurred to Hiroshi that he could take comfort in the flesh without guilt, as he was no longer married. With so many women around, he had no problem finding willing partners. The truth was that when he, Hana, and Kenji were still living in Japan, he took advantage of the whores. The only time he had sex with Hana was when he wanted her pregnant. After Kenji was born, he tried for months to impregnate Hana; when it didn't happen, he gave up, deciding it was her fault and not his. After that, he didn't touch her again and took his pleasure with the *shoufu*—whores. Hiroshi was sure Hana knew or at the very least suspected, but being the dutiful wife, she never questioned him.

It wasn't too long before he found a steady bed companion at the camp to keep him warm at night, and it wasn't too much longer after that before he forgot about Hana completely, unless it was in relation to the deal he had made with Nick.

Cabin fever. As glad as he was to be with Patricia and Niko, Kenji wanted to be outside; he wanted to feel the March breeze and the sun on his face for just a few minutes. He hadn't seen the outdoors since February, when Nick and Ralph came for him and Hana. He needed just a few minutes; he could almost hear the outdoors call to him.

He went to the library, which now doubled as his workout room, and shut the door to begin his meditation and workout.

As always, it helped but not for long; the temptation to peek his head out of the back door became almost too much for him. He had to get out; he missed the long walks he took before the camp and in the camp when he wasn't working.

Ralph watched Kenji and knew what he was thinking, and if he didn't do something soon, Kenji would do something stupid. The neighbors had long become used to seeing Ralph around and thought he was Abby's husband, so there was no problem with him going out.

Ralph went to the back yard and into the shed. He saw several old trellises he could use as. . . . An idea began to form. Ralph dragged the trellis out of the shed and propped it against the house and then went back into the house for the car keys; before he left, he cornered Kenji.

"I know you want to go outside; it's been weeks, but don't you dare put Patty and that baby in harm's way for a bit of fresh air. You hear me?" he asked.

The mention of Patricia and the baby being in danger had the desired effect. Kenji nodded and headed up to the shower. There was another issue, and Kenji didn't know how to address it. He needed his wife. He wanted and needed to make love with Patricia, and not just the heavy petting they had been doing for the past few weeks. By his calculations, it was safe for them to make love, with the only issues being another pregnancy and having the time alone without interruption.

Abby watched Kenji run up the stairs and smiled. Patricia had already talked with her about needing some time alone with Kenji, and Abby had happily agreed to help by keeping Niko upstairs with her for the night. The diapers and all that she would need were already in her room, as well as a makeshift crib made out of one of her dresser drawers. Patricia had been pumping her breasts and saving the milk for the past day or so, and several bottles were in the freezer as well as several in the bottom part of the refrigerator. The plan was that Patricia would hand the baby to Abby and tell Kenji that she needed to talk with him privately in their room and then tell him that Abby was going to babysit for the night.

Abby knew Ralph had something up his sleeve, but she didn't ask what it was; she had an idea of what he was up to, but decided to wait and see if she was right.

Patricia was in the kitchen giving the baby a bath when Kenji came up behind her.

"I miss you," he murmured against her neck.

"I miss you, too," she replied as she washed Niko's dark, curly hair. "He looks like you," Patricia commented as she examined the baby's skin, which was dark but not as dark as hers.

"He looks like both of us," Kenji replied as he wrapped his arms around her waist.

"I guess he does," Patricia agreed. "But I hope he'll be tall like you."

"Why is that?" Kenji asked, curious as to what her answer would be.

"I don't know; I guess when you stand over me like you are now, I feel safe, and if he has a sister, I want her to feel safe. I know it's silly. . . . "

"It's not silly," Kenji said, kissing her head. "I'm glad you feel safe with me, and who knows? Maybe he'll be taller than I am. Let me finish Niko's bath while you go sit with Abby."

Patricia didn't argue. The one thing her mother kept commenting on was how Kenji helped in the care of the baby.

"When you was a baby, as soon as you spit a little or messed you pants, you daddy handed you off. It's good that he helps you."

John had other opinions. "What you doin', man? You makin' it hard for the rest of us! That be the job of the mama," he said when he saw Kenji changing Niko's diaper.

"But I helped make him, did I not?" Kenji asked, not seeing the issue.

"Yeah, but you did your part," John said.

"I don't understand," Kenji said. "He is my baby, too, so why shouldn't I help in his care?"

The women laughed as John threw up his hands and walked away.

Abby was looking at a magazine when Patricia came in.

"Thank you so much for watching the baby tonight," Patricia said.

"I'm happy to do it; so is everything ready?"

"I think so; there's milk is in the freezer, but there are four bottles in the bottom, so you should have more than enough," Patricia replied.

Kenji came in carrying a squeaky clean baby and sat down next to Patricia. "He should sleep well tonight; I gave him a massage as I finished his bath."

"He looks comfortable, but let Auntie Abby hold him for awhile," Abby said, holding out her arms.

Kenji got up, took the baby over to Abby, and settled him in her arms. Just as Kenji was about to sit down, Patricia stopped him.

"Could we go downstairs for a minute? I want to show you something."

Kenji looked at Abby, who said, "Go on; me and Niko are just fine."

Kenji followed Patricia downstairs to the basement, wondering what she wanted to show him.

"Close the door behind you," she called back.

Kenji ran back up the stairs to close the basement door and ran back down. When he reached the bedroom, he stopped short. Patricia was lying on the bed completely nude with her arms outstretched toward him. Kenji couldn't move. He felt exactly as he had the very first time he had seen her unclothed—awed. The fact that she hadn't lost the weight she had gained from the pregnancy meant nothing to him; to him she was as beautiful as ever. She was his *Kirei* and the mother of his child.

"The baby—"

"Will be fine; Abby is going to watch him tonight," Patricia said as she waited for Kenji to grasp what was happening.

"Do you have any idea of how much I missed you when I was in that place?" he asked, still not moving but watching her.

"I think I do, because I missed you too, and I was scared so much of the time," Patricia said.

This was the first time since Kenji was home that they talked about the camp. It was something they needed to talk about, but other things had taken precedence. But now they had a chance to breathe and to talk. Kenji looked down at Patricia; the time for talk would be later.

Patricia watched as Kenji stripped and walked toward her, stopping at the side of the bed to look at her. She felt herself grow warm, even though the basement air was cool. She moved over when Kenji decided to get into bed with her and moved closer when he was in beside her.

Kenji kissed her lightly at first, as if he were taste-testing something sweet; then he kissed her harder, as if he had decided that what he had tasted was much to his liking. He nudged Patricia's lips open with his tongue and slipped it in, touching hers with his. As he kissed her, he reached behind her head and pulled the tie loose, freeing the ponytail she still wore, and ran his hands through her hair.

Patricia moaned into his mouth, wrapped her arms around his neck, and pressed against him as tears ran down her face. Kenji was crying, too, his tears mixing with hers as they kissed; they each had so many pent-up emotions: fear, anxiety, and pain, but predominately love that they hadn't been able to express for months.

Kenji wanted nothing more than to slide into Patricia and just stay there, not moving, but he wanted to taste her, too; it had been far too long since he had felt her hard nipples in his mouth or felt her throbbing against his tongue as she came. He wanted to hear that giggle mixed with a moan as he kissed her feet and knees; he just . . . wanted.

He pulled back from her and kissed her eyes, her nose, her cheeks, and her lips again before he closed his eyes to see how many of her pleasure spots he could find just by touch. He knew she had many, and he planned to take his time and find all of them, but first he had to hear that giggle. He kept his eyes closed as he kissed her neck, sliding his lips along her skin, never losing contact. He smiled when she gasped and then moaned when he found a spot. Sometime he stayed for a minute or two and teased the spot until she was whimpering, and then he moved on to the next spot and repeated the teasing.

Kenji's cock throbbed just thinking about how ready Patricia was for him; he felt the moisture at the tip of his erection and ignored it. Her words that he didn't love her went through his mind. By the time he was done, she would never think that again, no matter what was happening. It was then that he realized those words had hurt more than he thought or cared to admit. But it wasn't the actual words themselves; it was the emotion behind them and because at the time she said them, she had really believed it, and that was unacceptable.

He forced himself to go even slower in searching for her pleasure spots; when he finally reached her feet and kissed them, he heard that giggle, and he wanted to hear it again. He kissed the other foot, keeping his eyes closed as he listened to her giggle and moan several more times. He loved that sound and wished he could somehow record it and listen to it whenever he wished.

Slowly he kissed and licked his way back up to her mound and stopped. He nuzzled against it and moaned when he felt her hands in his hair, twisting it between her fingers and pulling it lightly. Unable to resist any longer, Kenji slipped his tongue between her vaginal lips and took his first taste of her in weeks; he felt his balls tighten and pull up tight against him and stopped tasting her long enough to take several deep breaths to regain control of himself. He could hear Patricia saying his name as he flicked his tongue over her nub; it wouldn't be long before she would be climaxing over his tongue and screaming into a pillow. *Someday*, he thought to himself, *she won't have to do that.* They would have their own house, their own bedroom, and the only thing they would have to worry about would be the children hearing them, and when the children were gone. . . .

So close, Patricia thought as Kenji made love to her. Each time she thought she would explode, he moved to another part of her body until finally he was between her legs, his tongue teasing her to the point of climax and then retreating. Just when she thought she couldn't possibly take anymore, Kenji latched onto her nub and suckled it until she was screaming into the pillow she had covered her face with.

Kenji kissed his way back up her body, only stopping when the head of his throbbing erection was at her opening, and then he slammed into her hard enough that it took her breath away. Then he stopped. He wanted to savor the feel of her surrounding him. He put as much of his weight on her as possible without hurting her and began to move. "*Kirei*," he moaned when he felt her hands on his butt cheeks.

Patricia squeezed each cheek in her hands and bucked up against him; he was close, and she could tell he was getting ready to pull out. As much as she didn't want him to, she knew he had to; it was much too soon for another pregnancy, even though she was fairly certain she wouldn't get pregnant because she was still breastfeeding.

Kenji said something in Japanese, pulled out, and ground himself into Patricia's soft belly and came. He was going to roll off her, but she stopped him; she liked the feel of his weight on top of her. Finally he moved, even though she protested.

"I'm going to crush you or smother you if I don't move," Kenji teased and kissed her.

He lay with her in his arms for several minutes before getting up and gathering some wet cloths to clean her and then himself. After they were clean, Kenji held her close and started to talk about the camp.

"I wouldn't have wanted you there; it was hot in the summer and cold during the winter, especially at night. The housing was barely adequate; we woke up covered in dust every morning that we slept in our space, and some nights it was hard to sleep because of the wind howling. Add that to the fact that I missed you. . . .

"There was an orphanage there; all of these children were taken from their foster homes and orphanages because they are Japanese or part Japanese; what did the government think they could do? They are just children. Mother worked there and started sleeping there because there was less dust, and she enjoyed the children while I worked at the hospital and taught English to those who wanted to learn.

"*Kirei* . . . I wish I had gone with you that first time, but I couldn't. Do you understand? I couldn't leave, and it had nothing to do with not loving you, but everything to do with the fact that I do."

Kenji told her about the incident where the seventeen-year-old died because the soldiers fired into the crowd and what he considered to be the murder of Joben Saito. "It was then that I decided if another chance to come home to you happened, then it was meant to be and I would take it. I want you to understand something: no matter what happens, even if I am arrested and put in prison, I will always love you, and I don't ever want you to question that again."

Patricia realized how much she had hurt him. That day could have been the last time they were together, and she left him hurting because of something she had said out of fear.

"Kenji, I'm sorry. After I got home and thought about it, I understood. I just—"

Kenji shushed her with a kiss. "It's over now, and I don't need an apology. I just needed for you to understand."

"I understand," Patricia said as she sucked a nipple between her lips as she reached down and took his cock into her hand and began to stroke it until it was hard. Kenji moaned in anticipation of being inside of Patricia's mouth; it had been several days since it had last happened, and it was something he never requested from her. The fact that she did it without his asking made it all the sweeter.

Patricia teased him much as he had teased her, but instead of going all the way to his feet, she stopped at his cock. Kenji cried out as Patricia took as much of him as she could into her mouth without gagging; she swirled her tongue around the head and then flicked it across the underside, where the head met the shaft. Taking her mouth from the head, she gently took one ball into her mouth and sucked on it gently, making Kenji almost buck her off the bed. Releasing one ball, she took the other into her mouth and gave it the same treatment as she rapidly stroked the shaft and head of his erection. When she felt him grow in her hand, Patricia took the head back into her mouth and sucked hard, and swallowed as Kenji released into her mouth, crying out her name.

Afterward, Patricia dozed while Kenji lay awake thinking about where they would go after the war was over—if it was ever over.

Nick had managed to get Hana from Abby's house to his without incident. He refused to have her hide in the trunk again, although she assured him she would be fine.

"No, we're not doing that again," Nick said. "Just lay down in the back seat and keep covered, and we'll be home in ten minutes."

True to his word, ten minutes later Nick was pulling into his garage. He hadn't noticed anyone watching, but that didn't mean they weren't. After he checked the house, he took Hana inside and showed her where she would be sleeping.

"This is your room," he told her. "The bathroom is down the hall to the right; everything you need should be in there. You have the run of the house, but don't go outside and stay away from the windows. If I'm not home, don't answer the phone or the door; the same applies if I'm home. From time to time people will come to drop something off; if that should happen, stay in your room with the door closed and be quiet. Any questions?"

Hana looked around the room and shook her head no. It didn't escape her that the house was very masculine, with not one feminine touch present; Nick, she figured out, had never been married, and she wondered why.

"Have you never married?" she asked.

"Almost, but no," Nick replied as he turned her bed back for her.

"Why almost?" Hana asked.

"It's a long story, but just suffice it to say that I wasn't rich enough and I didn't come from the right family. Are you hungry or thirsty?" Nick asked, changing the subject.

"No, I am fine," Hana replied.

"Okay then; I'm going to turn in. I'll see you in the morning," Nick said and left the room, closing the door behind him.

That had been over a month ago, and he and Hana still slept in separate rooms, but it wasn't because he wanted it that way. He was waiting for Hana to adjust to her new life as a single woman, and he finally admitted to himself that he was nervous. To date, they hadn't even talked about their relationship or how they felt about each other; he was coming to realize that she was waiting for him.

Nick always made dinner, even though Hana offered. He knew she was getting bored, but he wanted her to understand that she was there because he wanted her to be and that she wasn't his servant—she didn't need to wait on him hand and foot.

The problem was, Nick didn't know how to approach her. Finally he decided to just say what he felt and what he wanted. Their dinner conversation was always the same: the war, the baby, and the interment camps, after which they cleaned the kitchen and each retreated to their rooms.

This night, Nick stopped Hana before she left the table. "Hana, we need to talk," Nick said as she stood up.

Hana sat down, looked at Nick, and then looked down at her hands.

"Could you please look at me?" Nick asked and then waited until Hana was looking at him.

"Hana, I took you from that camp because I wanted to. You're here because I want you to be here, but I don't want you to think that you owe me anything. I also don't want you to think that I brought you here to be my servant. The last time I was at the camp I asked you if you had feelings for me; is that still true, or has that changed?"

Hana was stymied; she had never discussed her feelings with Hiroshi. It was just assumed that she was happy, and she supposed that in some ways she had been. It was assumed that they would grow to care for each other, and if not, then so be it, but here was Nick asking her what her feelings were.

"I still have feelings for you," Hana replied, looking down.

"Hana, I'm not going to lie to you," Nick said. "I didn't want this, and we've talked about why, but now I do. I have to admit I'm ashamed I let something as trivial as your race keep me from admitting my feelings for you, but you were still married. Over the past three years, I've watched Patricia and Kenji overcome incredible odds because they love and believe in each other, and to be honest, it made me feel like a coward.

"I know this is hard for you, being here with me, and we're not married, but Hana, would you at least sleep with me? If you don't want to make love yet, that's fine, but I want to feel you next to me," Nick said and then waited for Hana's response.

As nervous as Hana was, she was relieved. She thought Nick's feelings for her had changed, but she had been too afraid to ask. She had liked the feel of his arms around her as she slept that night at Abby's and had wondered ever since the night he brought her home why he took her to a separate bedroom. Now she understood his concerns and his reasons.

Was she prepared to sleep with a man she wasn't married to? She knew that, unlike Kenji and Patricia, she and Nick couldn't marry, and if she had sex with him, what would that make her? A *shoufu*—a whore? She knew what Hiroshi would say, but he wasn't a part of this; he was no longer her husband. *What would Kenji think?* she wondered. He would be happy for her, she thought; he wouldn't think of her as a whore or a slut, and he had already given Nick his approval.

Nick watched as Hana struggled to make a decision, but remained silent; he couldn't help her with this. They sat at the table for another thirty minutes before Hana finally said something. "I did not think you wanted me any longer."

Nick didn't ask her why she would think something like that; he already knew the answer. It was because he, in his efforts to let her get acclimated to being around him, hadn't made any moves toward her.

"Hana, that isn't true," Nick said. "I just wanted to give you time to adjust to being here, and I didn't want you to think you had to sleep with me. I want you to sleep with me because you want to and not because you think you owe me something, so the question is this: do you want to sleep with me?"

It took Hana another several minutes to reply. "It isn't a question of want," she replied. "It is a question of why and what I will be if I do. Will you come to see me as a *shoufu*—a whore who is paying her way with her body?"

While he wasn't surprised Hana would think that he didn't want her, the fact that she could think he might see her as a whore did. He reminded himself that he had to remember where she came from, and it just wasn't her culture that would think that—if she had been an American woman, people would have thought the same thing. The problem was that he didn't know what to say to her to make her understand that he never could or would think that of her.

"The why," she continued, "has to do with the reason that you stated about me thinking that I owe you something. I must ask your indulgence for a while longer as I examine my motives for sleeping with you. It's not because I don't care for you that I hesitate; it's because I need more time to reconcile what I want and need with what I was taught and know."

What could he say? If he had talked with her sooner, they would be past this point, but he hadn't, and here they were. He could only hope she didn't take too long to "reconcile" herself.

They cleaned up the supper dishes and went to their separate rooms.

Somewhere around eleven, Nick woke to the sound of his door opening and then closing. Hana stood just inside his bedroom, saying nothing and not moving.

"Hana? Are you all right?" Nick asked, sitting up.

At the sight of his bare chest, Hana almost left. Hiroshi was the only man she had ever seen naked, and never in bed—he had always worn a covering of some sort, even when they made love. The night at Abby's, Nick had slept with his clothes on, and she hadn't thought about how he slept here at home—obviously shirtless, but what about the rest of him?

Now that she was here in his room, Nick didn't want her to leave. He could see that she was uncomfortable, and he thought he knew why. "Hana, sweetheart, I won't hurt you. Come to bed."

When Hana didn't move, Nick tried again, "Is it because I don't have a shirt on?"

Hana found her voice. "I . . . yes."

"Thank God I have pajama bottoms on," Nick mumbled as he reached for the top to the pajamas. He usually slept nude, but since Hana moved in, he slept in pajama bottoms. It had been quite the adjustment for him, but he hoped to someday go back to sleeping nude.

"Better?" he asked after the top was on and buttoned up.

"Thank you," Hana said softy.

"It's all right; will you come to bed now?" Nick asked.

Hana slowly made her way to the bed, wearing one of Nick's pajama tops as a nightgown. The sleeves were rolled up, but the hem to the top fell an inch or two past her knees. Hana had braided her waist-length hair into a single braid that was draped over her left shoulder. She had no idea of how beautiful she truly was, Nick realized; she also had no idea what she was doing to him dressed as she was.

Nick shifted in bed, trying to find a comfortable position for his cock; it wasn't going to go down, so there was no point in even trying to hide it.

Hana climbed into the bed, turned on her side so that her back was to his chest, and waited. Nick moved closer and put an arm around her, resisting the urge to pull her as tight against him as possible. Nick lay awake long after Hana had fallen asleep.

By the end of March 1943, Niko was six weeks old and what Hattie considered a "good baby," meaning that he rarely cried and when he did, it was because he was in need of something. John, to the surprise of everyone, warmed up to Kenji even more. No one commented, not wanting to halt any progress he was making toward total acceptance.

Ralph continued to be the source of war information if anyone really wanted to know anything, but the big question was: when were the interred Japanese going to be freed? Many of the men were serving in the armed forces, and the general consensus was that it should count for something, but as it was, it didn't.

On the war front, the Battle of the Bismarck Sea was over. Over the course of three days, the combined forces of the United States and Australian forces sank eight Japanese troop transports near New Guinea. Rommel was forced to retreat in Tunisia; the Battle of Medenine would be his last battle there.

The German liquidated the Jewish ghetto in Krakow, the second largest and one of the oldest cities in Poland. The Jewish population of the city was moved to the walled-in section of Krakow that would become known as the "Krakow ghetto." From there they were sent to extermination camps, such as Auschwitz and the concentration camp at Plaszow.

Reports of the execution of twenty-two thousand POWs and Polish nationals in the Katyn Forest massacre began to seep into the West. The massacre was carried out by the Soviet Secret Police, who would later blame the massacre on the Germans.

General Patton led his tanks into Tunisia, and seventy-six Allied prisoners of war escaped from Stalag Luft III in Sagan, a small town in Western Poland. Of the seventy-six that escaped, seventy-three were recaptured. Fifty of the seventy-three were executed; twenty-three were sent back to the prison camps, and the remaining three made it to freedom.

The Japanese failed in their attempt to reinforce a garrison at Kiska, which was a part of the Aleutian Islands of Alaska. Due to poor leadership, there were heavy losses on both sides.

Hiroshi fumed; would he ever leave this accursed place? News of the war continued to seep in, and he was growing more and more restless. What was the emperor waiting for? Why was he not yet victorious? He asked his bed partner this question several times. She never responded because she wasn't expected to; her only goal was to be warm at night and to bide her time until she was free.

Stories of the Japanese treatment of the POWs in their camps continued to seep in.

"I heard that they give those people hardly anything to eat and then force them to work," Hiroshi heard a soldier say.

"I heard that, too," the other man replied. "And I heard they're torturing them, too. Maybe we ought to do that here; tit for tat, right?"

For the first time, Hiroshi began to wonder if the stories about the Japanese POW camps were true. Both of the men talking seemed to be genuinely angry and were very serious about doing the same thing here. He was then forced to wonder about the stories of the Jews in the concentration camps: were those true? While he felt that the Japanese race was the superior race, that didn't mean he thought people should be tortured or starved and certainly not exterminated. They would have their place in the world; just as the blacks had once been slaves, these other races could be servants as well.

Hiroshi had to ask himself another question: if the stories were true, then what would he do? "I have no choice but to continue to follow the emperor," he said quietly. Leaving Japan is what had gotten him here in the first place, and learning what he did in no way changed his plans to go back home.

Kenji and Patricia were often wakened early by Ralph's working at the back of the house.

"What is he doing?" Kenji asked one morning when it seemed that the racket started earlier than usual.

Although Patricia could go outside, she didn't, even though Kenji encouraged her to.

"If you can't go out, then I won't either," she replied, and it was for that reason she didn't know what Ralph was doing.

The project wasn't finished until the end of March. Ralph waited impatiently for Kenji and Patricia to surface with the baby. When they did, he didn't give them a chance to sit down to breakfast. He took the baby and handed him to Abby.

"Come on, I've got something to show you," Ralph said, grabbing Kenji's arm.

"Ralph . . ." Kenji said when he saw he was being led to the back door.

"Just come on!" Ralph insisted. "You too, Patty."

Patricia warily followed Ralph to the back door, where she and Kenji both jumped back when he flung the door open. Ralph had taken the trellises and made a small room off the back door; the lattice work made it virtually impossible to see who was sitting inside. The front of the small room faced the back of Abby's yard, where there was a vacant house. The yard of the vacant house was taken care of once a week, so Kenji couldn't go out during that day, but the evening would be safe. Both Kenji and Patricia looked at the room, speechless, and then they both started talking at the same time.

"Ralph, this is. . . . I don't know what to say," Kenji said

"It's beautiful!" Patricia chimed in.

"I know it's not the same as the walks Kenji here likes, but at least you can get some fresh air," Ralph said.

Patricia gave Ralph a hug and kissed him on the cheek. "Thank you! Thank you!" she said several times.

"Yes, Ralph, thank you," Kenji added and shook Ralph's hand.

A few minutes later, Kenji, Patricia, and the baby were sitting in the small room enjoying the fresh air. Kenji closed his eyes and smiled as the March breeze caressed his face and ruffled his hair. He put an arm around Patricia and pulled her close to his side. *Someday*, he thought, *someday we will be able to be seen together out in the world.*

Abby gave Ralph his second kiss of the day. "That was a nice thing you did for them," she said.

Ralph blushed and then grinned. "They sure look happy, don't they?" he asked and then thought to himself that it was about time.

Nick and Hana slept together every night Nick wasn't away. That first week had been the hardest one for them, but for different reasons. For Hana it was because she had never been with another man and because they weren't married; for Nick it was because he wanted to make love with her. He was confused as to what he should do. He thought about forcing the subject, but then again, he had promised her that he wouldn't push. But a month had passed since they had begun sleeping together, and as far as he could tell, they were no closer to making love than they had been then.

Hana sensed Nick's frustration and knew she couldn't sleep in the same bed with him forever and not expect him to want more. It wasn't even a question of whether she wanted him or not; she couldn't get past the fact that they weren't married. There was nothing that could be done about that; legally marriage was impossible. But what if they did what Kenji and Patricia had done? They still wouldn't be legally married, but in her mind they would be. The issue was how to bring it up to Nick. She didn't believe that he would be angry; he had told her a number of times that he loved her, to which she responded in kind, which only served to confuse Nick even more.

She made dinner that night and waited for Nick to come home. She hoped he had some word on when the internees would be released. She had just gone upstairs when she heard the front door open; she almost went down the stairs when she heard a voice respond to Nick's.

Nick was speaking loudly to the other person, a woman. Hana's first reaction was anger and then jealousy, even though it was obvious by the way Nick talked to the woman that their relationship was nothing more than professional.

"Did you finally hire someone to cook for you?" the woman asked.

"Yes, she leaves it in the oven for me; we must have just missed her," Nick lied smoothly.

"Smells good," the woman said, clearly hoping for a dinner invitation.

"It does," Nick agreed, "but she's really good at cooking just enough for me, so I'll see you tomorrow."

Hana heard the door close and then waited a few minutes before going downstairs, just in case the woman came back.

Nick turned to look at her as she walked down the stairs. That had been too close for comfort. He needed to devise some way of letting Hana know when he was bringing someone home with him. He could tell just by looking at her that she had something she wanted to say and that she would wait for him to ask her what it was.

Dinner was quiet, with the conversation being about the release of the interred and the fairness of including the Nisei in the draft.

"If they're serving this country, then why are they and their families not freed?" Hana asked.

It was a good question and one that Nick didn't have the answer to, but he knew she was stalling. He was tired and wasn't in the mood to dance around whatever Hana's issue was. "Hana, if you have something to say, please just say it."

"I . . . I think I know what's wrong, why I cannot be with you as you wish," Hana said.

"Are you saying you don't want to be with me in the same way?" Nick asked.

"No, I'm not saying that, I . . . this is difficult for me, so please be patient as I try to explain myself."

"I'm sorry I was so short," Nick said. "Take your time."

Haltingly, Hana told him what she thought she needed and then waited for his response.

“Hana, if there was any way I could legally marry you, I’d do it,” Nick said. “But there isn’t—at least not now—but if having a wedding between the two of us will ease your mind, then I’m all for it.”

Hana looked down at her hands; Nick was going to give her what she wanted and needed. There was nothing to stop her from being with him as she wanted to be.

“When would you like to get married?” Nick asked, hoping she would say tonight.

“A bride must have time to prepare for her husband,” Hana said softly. “Tomorrow night.”

Nick started to suggest tonight, but kept his mouth shut. He had waited this long; what was one more night?

MARCH 31, 1943

As soon as Nick left for work, Hana began her preparations. She began by undoing and washing her hair and then taking a long bath. She spent the day cleaning the one kimono she had that was in fairly decent shape, and by the end of the day, it was presentable. It wasn’t perfect, but it would do. There was only one thing left that Hana wanted and needed: Kenji’s blessing.

Nick left work thirty minutes early and went to a jeweler’s located several blocks from his office. Unfortunately, he wouldn’t be able to wear a wedding band, but Hana could. He chose two bands: one for him and one for her, since they came in a set. As he drove home, Nick made a decision. He would wear the band when at home and take it off when he left for the office.

Nick chuckled at his predicament. Here he was, an agent for the United States government, and he was going to “marry” a woman who was considered an enemy of said government. Not only that, he had engaged in several activities that would be considered treason, and if caught, prison was the least of the punishments he could receive. “I’ll have to make sure I’m not caught,” he said to himself.

While he was in the restroom at work, he heard a piece of information he decided to keep to himself. It involved the release of the Japanese in the interment camps. There were two reasons why he kept the information to himself: one was that he didn't want to get anyone's hopes up, and secondly, the office was filled with so many rumors that he had no real way of verifying it unless he called Mitch, and even then the information might not be accurate. It was better not to say anything, he decided.

At the end of the day, Hana stayed upstairs just in case Nick had someone with him. When she heard him call her name, she went down the stairs and was greeted with a kiss.

"Are we ready to do this?" Nick asked, looking down at her.

"Almost," Hana replied. "There is one more thing I must have."

Nick tensed. "What do you need?"

"I want and need the blessing of my son," Hana said.

Nick relaxed, walked over to the phone, picked it up, and called Abby's house. "Abby? Nick here; is Kenji nearby? Can I talk to him?"

Hana waited nervously for Nick to talk to Kenji. She was planning to do it herself, but it was better for Nick to do it.

"Kenji? Nick here. . . . Yes, she's fine; it's her I wanted to talk to you about. You already know how I feel about her, and I would like to marry her. . . . Yes, I know it's not legal, but it would be like your and Patricia's first wedding. Tonight. . . . Yes, I wish there was a way to get you all here or for us to come to you, but it's too dangerous. . . . I agree, but Kenji, let me ask you this: do we have your blessing?"

Hana held her breath and released it with a gush when Nick smiled and then nodded at her.

"He would like to speak with you," Nick said, holding the phone toward her.

They talked for a minute or two before hanging up. There was nothing to stop her from being with Nick now; Kenji was in agreement with their marriage and voiced the same sentiment he had with Patricia.

"Maybe someday you'll be able to marry Nick publicly, as I'll be able to marry Patricia. I am glad you're happy, and I'll tell Patricia as soon as I hang up."

Hana turned to Nick and smiled shyly. "We have his blessing."

An hour later, Nick and Hana stood face to face in the bedroom. Hana was dressed in her kimono, and Nick was still in his suit and tie. They each said a few words that to them meant they were married, and then Nick brought out the rings.

"I know from talking to Kenji that rings aren't usually a part of your ceremony, but I would like it if you wore one. I can't wear one to work, but I can wear it here at home when we're together. Will you wear a wedding band?" Nick asked.

Hana held out her hand in acceptance of the ring. Tears ran down her face as Nick slid it onto her finger. She realized that while she loved Kenji and the child that had died, she had never really loved Hiroshi. She had accepted him because she had to; there was no choice. Her father chose Hiroshi for her because he was smart, ambitious, and came from a good family with money. Hana had considered herself lucky in that Hiroshi had never mistreated her, and because of that, she thought she loved him, and he her.

She loved Nick as a woman was supposed to love her husband, and for once, in spite of the situation that they were in, she was happy. And she understood why Kenji wouldn't give Patricia up.

When the ring was on her finger, she took the other ring and slid it onto Nick's hand. As far as they were concerned, they were married.

Nick pulled Hana into his arms and kissed her. He held her tight against him, wanting her to feel his hardness. Hana tried to pull back, but Nick wouldn't let her. He loosened his hold only when he felt her relax in his arms. This was something she was just going to have to get used to, he decided. He wondered what Hana and Hiroshi's sex life had been like. Did Hiroshi take care of himself only, or did he see to Hana's pleasure as well? His hunch was the former, and that was about to change.

"You are so very beautiful," Nick said as he stroked Hana's cheek.

Hana blushed and looked away. Hiroshi had always told her she was beautiful, but there was never any real emotion behind the sentiment—not like there was when Nick said it.

"Hana, look at me," Nick said, tipping her face up to his. "Thank you for this."

"It is I who should be thanking you for all you've done for me and my family and for . . . this," Hana replied as she stood on her tiptoes and kissed Nick's chin. It was the first time she had initiated physical contact of any kind with him; she was nervous, but it felt good. She never would have done such a thing with Hiroshi; he would have considered it too forward and chastised her for it.

Nick pulled her closer against him, reached behind her, and undid the simple bun she had put her hair up in. He loved the feel and smell of her hair, especially just after it was washed. Nick pulled back and began to untie the belts that held the kimono together. The kimono fell open, revealing the slip underneath. For several seconds, Nick didn't move; he almost expected Hana to bolt, but was relieved when she didn't.

Hana's heart was racing by the time Nick slid the kimono off her shoulders and let it slide to the floor; she resisted the urge to pick it up. Hiroshi would never have allowed her to leave her clothing on the floor, no matter the reason. Even on their wedding night, he took care to make sure they hung everything up before going to the marriage bed that first time. She remembered being nervous, but not excited as she was now; she watched Nick as he stood in front of her and undressed. When she tried to look away, Nick stopped her.

"Hana, there's nothing to be embarrassed about. It's normal for a married couple to see each other naked," he said.

Hana swallowed hard and nodded. She wished she was as at ease about these things, as Patricia and Kenji seemed to be, but she supposed it would come in time.

In no time, Nick was down to his boxers and leading Hana by the hand toward the bed. Nick stopped by the side of the bed;

he seemed to be considering something. He understood she was nervous, but she was more nervous than she should be for an experienced woman. Given what he knew about Hiroshi Takeda, he had to wonder if Hana had been cared for in bed.

"Hana, other than to get you pregnant, did you and Hiroshi make love?" he asked.

Hana blushed, which told him either she was embarrassed because sex wasn't discussed in their home or because of the answer. "Hiroshi believed the only purpose for sex with one's wife was for procreation and nothing more."

"Wait, what are you saying?" Nick asked.

"I . . . I'm saying that after Kenji was born, we tried to have more children. When I didn't conceive, Hiroshi no longer found me attractive. He . . . he went elsewhere."

Nick was shocked; whatever he had been expecting, it wasn't that. "Are you saying he was unfaithful to you?" he asked.

Hana didn't reply; that she had not been able to give Hiroshi what he wanted most—more sons—was her secret shame. It never occurred to her that she wasn't at fault, but Hiroshi was.

Nick did the math in his head; Hana hadn't been touched in more than twenty years. He now fully understood her nervousness and why she thought he didn't want her. "Hiroshi was and is a fool in more ways than one," Nick said as he hugged Hana to him.

Nick eased her onto the bed and sat next to her for a few minutes with his arms around her. As far as he was concerned, Hana was a virgin who needed to be treated gently.

"Lie down," Nick said and then lay next to her when she was in bed. He wanted her naked, but he had to take one step at a time, his hope being that she would remember any passion she felt from lovemaking in the past—if there was any passion.

Nick took the time to remind Hana of how beautiful he thought she was and that he loved her. For several minutes, they talked until he felt her gradually relax, and then he began to slowly make love to her, starting with soft kisses on her face and neck as his hand slid under the slip, touching the soft skin of her stomach and then down over her hips. As of yet, Hana had yet to touch him, and he wondered if he needed to give her permission.

"Hana, it's all right to touch me."

Hesitantly, Hana placed a hand on Nick's arm and then moved it to his shoulder and left it there. Nick moved his shoulder to encourage her to keep touching but soon gave up when it became obvious she wasn't taking the hint. Hana's slip was now up over her hips, and he was stroking the exposed skin, making his way to her mound, where he stopped and waited for a few seconds before slipping a finger between her folds.

Hana gasped and clutched Nick's arm. Nick's lips hovered above her slip-clad breasts and then took a nipple into his mouth and sucked it through the thin material of the slip. Hana cried out as Nick sucked her nipple and fingered her now-wet and throbbing nub until she climaxed. That had never happened with Hiroshi, although she knew he climaxed. She was caught completely by surprise by the orgasm, not sure of how she was supposed to respond. She bit her lip in an attempt not to cry out.

Nick lay on his back and pulled Hana on top of him; her slip had ridden up to her waist. Nick reached up and pushed Hana's hair behind her ear and pulled her closer for a kiss; there was less reticence and more active involvement on Hana's part. She now understood and knew what she had been missing during her time with Hiroshi: passion, love, and genuine caring. It struck her as ironic that she would find those things with a man whom Hiroshi thought to be an enemy.

Nick reached down and tried to slide his shorts down. He pulled Hana forward until she was sitting on his stomach and then managed to get the shorts down. He gently pushed Hana back so she was sitting on his cock and ground against her before lifting her up enough so he could slide into her.

"Nick?" Hana called, her voice filled with uncertainty.

"Sweetheart, it's all right," Nick soothed as he rocked his hips back and forth. He stopped long enough to remove Hana's slip. He took a breast in each hand and ran a thumb over each nipple until they were hard points against his thumbs. He began to move his hips again, adding a swivel when he was as far inside of Hana as he could go. Hana gave up on trying to keep silent and cried out with Nick as another orgasm approached. Nick's orgasm came just as Hana's was ending.

Afterward, Hana had the first real restful sleep she had had in months. Nick lay awake for a short time afterward, holding Hana as she slept. A few minutes later, he was asleep, too.

By the end of May 1943, racial tensions between American Marines and New Zealand troops of the Maori origin—indigenous Polynesians—resulted in the Battle of Manners Street, a small-scale riot in which there were no casualties. Bolivia declared war on Germany, Italy, and Japan; the last units of the Afrika Korps in the northern corner of Tunisia surrendered; the Wehrmacht—the armed forces of Nazi Germany—announced the discovery of the mass graves of the Poles allegedly killed by the Soviets in the Katyn massacre.

The chief architect of Japanese naval strategy, Admiral Yamamoto, was killed when his plane was shot down by American P38s while he was on an inspection tour. The Warsaw Ghetto massacre continued, but would be over by the end of May, when the ghetto was destroyed.

German and Italian armed forces in Tunisia surrendered to Britain; over thirty thousand Chinese civilians were killed by the Japanese over a four-day period during the Changjiao massacre. The German Afrika Korps and the Italians surrendered to Allied forces in North Africa; there were more than 250,000 prisoners taken.

Josef Mengele became the Chief Medical Officer of Auschwitz. Mengele would become known as the "angel of death." He was one of the SS physicians responsible for determining who would die and who would be forced into labor. He would be more widely known for the experiments he performed on the prisoners of the camp, including women and children, many of whom died.

The French resistance was formed.

MAY 1943

Ralph's makeshift anteroom went a long way toward helping Kenji cope with being cooped up indoors. He, Patricia, and Niko spent as much time in the room as possible. Abby took the baby one night a week to give Kenji and Patricia alone time, and John and Kenji finally talked.

Kenji was in the library reading when John found him. Patricia and the other women were in the kitchen, and Ralph was working on the car.

John stood in the doorway of the library, watching Kenji as he went through his workout. He couldn't help but be impressed with the way Kenji moved so effortlessly. He waited until Kenji was finished before going into the library.

"I wants to talk to ya, if you has a minute," John said.

"Of course; would you like to sit down?" Kenji replied.

John sat down and gave Kenji a long hard look, the intent being to make Kenji flinch or look away. When it didn't happen, John gave a nod of approval. "I ain't gonna lie to ya, I wasn't happy 'bout you and my girl," John said.

"I am aware of that," Kenji said. "It was a very difficult time for Patricia."

"Yeah, well, I wasn't havin' no picnic myself," John replied. "What I wants to tell you is this: I still don't understand it, but I ain't mad 'bout it no more either. I see how you cares for her and that baby, and she's happy, like Hattie says she is. I'm only going to say this one time: take care of my baby and my grandson. You don't and your ass is mine."

John stood up and walked out of the library. He had gone as far as he could go in his acceptance of Kenji, and that had taken some time.

Patricia saw her father as he left the library and wondered what had happened between him and Kenji. "Kenji? Is everything all right? I just saw my father leave."

"It's fine; we just had a talk, and I think we understand each other," Kenji replied as he took the offered glass of water. "Where's the baby?"

"My mother has him in the little room," Patricia replied. "Do you think this will ever end?"

"I don't know, *Kirei*," Kenji replied. He felt and understood her frustration; he knew that things weren't going well for the Axis powers, but they still fought in spite of the surrenders in Africa and the Soviet Union. Japan was having its problems, too. As the stories about the treatment of the POWs leaked out, Kenji was sickened and worried. What if the Americans began to mistreat those in the internment camps?

Kenji had another concern: Ralph. He didn't like the way Ralph was looking; his color was off and he seemed to have trouble breathing when he walked. When Kenji asked about his health, Ralph denied being sick.

"I'm fine; you just concern yourself with Patty and the baby."

"Ralph—"

"Kenji, I'm fine! Now stop hovering over me like an old woman."

As of yet, Kenji hadn't said anything to anyone about his concerns; all he had was a feeling and not much else, other than Ralph's appearance. He decided to watch Ralph for a little while longer before he raised the alarm.

Ralph still followed the war news; with Nick's help he found out that one of his sons, the oldest, had died in 1941 at Pearl Harbor, and the other son was back in South Carolina after losing an arm in a battle with the Nazis. Nick had even found a phone number. Ralph carried the number around in his pocket, not sure of what to do with it. Several times, he picked the phone up only to hang it up. What would he say to him? "I'm sorry about your mother? I'm sorry about Luke, and I'm so damned sorry that you lost your arm?"

Ralph browsed through the paper and came across an article about the Tuskegee Airmen.

"Well, I'll be damned," he muttered.

He was amazed that the two races that were discriminated against were willing to die for the country that discriminated against them.

"They're better people than I am," he muttered as he read.

He read the article with growing interest; the military was as segregated as anything else, he noted. That struck him as odd; he felt that if a man or woman was willing to serve and die, the least that could happen is they would be treated as equals. He was further surprised when he read that the group had been formed in 1940 and was a part of the 332nd Fighter Group.

"Well hell!" he swore. "We got these pilots and we're not using them?"

The article also included some background on the airmen. It wasn't until First Lady Eleanor Roosevelt inspected the program in 1941 and was taken on a thirty-minute flight by African-American Chief Civilian Instructor C. Alfred Anderson that the program got a much-needed publicity boost. The program officially began in June of 1941 and consisted of forty-seven officers and 429 enlisted men, with the officers being predominately white.

It occurred to Ralph that maybe things would change as Abby said they would; however, he knew he wouldn't live to see it to its conclusion. He also knew he wouldn't live to see the end of the war.

Ralph touched his wallet, which contained his youngest son's phone number; his mouth was dry as he imagined how the phone call would probably go.

"Hello, son; this is your father."

Ralph could almost feel the chill that would come from the other end of line. The phone call would end not long after that, with Lawrence not saying a word. But still, he had to try to talk to his son one last time. If nothing came of it, then that was the way it was.

Ralph looked around; the house was quiet. Abby and Hattie had gone to the store; Kenji, Patricia, and the baby were down in the basement. If he was going to do this, now was the time.

Ralph stood up slowly and made his way to the phone, taking out his wallet as he walked. He looked at the phone as if it were a snake that was going to bite him at any second. Ralph took a deep breath, and with a shaking hand picked up the receiver and almost put it down. Steeling his nerve, Ralph called his son. The phone rang four times before someone picked it up, a boy who sounded like he was around fourteen or fifteen.

"Hello?"

Ralph froze; did he have a grandchild?

"Hello? Anybody there?"

"Ah yes, could I please speak to your father?" Ralph asked and held his breath.

The boy had been well trained; without hesitating, he asked Ralph to identify himself.

"I . . . I'm someone that hasn't seen your father for a very long time," Ralph replied, his throat now tight.

He could hear someone in the background asking who was on the phone.

"Don't know—some man asking for you. Didn't say who he was," the boy said, not bothering to cover the mouthpiece.

"All right, you go on and do your chores."

Ralph heard the sounds of the phone changing hands; he wanted to hang up, but forced himself to stay on the line. He might not have a second chance.

"Who is this?" the voice at the other end demanded.

"L-Lawrence?" Ralph stammered.

"Yes, who is this and what is it you want?"

"Lawrence, this is your father," Ralph blurted out.

There was several seconds of icy silence.

"What?" Lawrence asked, surprise and wariness in his voice.

Ralph swallowed hard. "This is your father," he repeated.

He could hear a woman in the background asking who was on the phone. His eyes burned when he heard the response.

"Nobody." And the line went dead.

Ralph stood holding the receiver in his hand. This was his fault, he thought as he hung up the phone. The thought that he should have contacted his boys long ago ripped through him. He let the tears fall and hurried to his room when he heard Abby and Hattie return with their purchases; he couldn't face anyone. With all they had been through together, Ralph had never told them about his boys or what had happened to make him leave South

Carolina, and he was certain he never would. Abby and the rest of them, including Hattie and John, were now his only family.

Tomorrow, he planned to go to the bank; there was something there that he needed to get before it was too late.

MAY 29, 1943

Life at Nick's had settled into a comfortable, but quiet existence. Hana was always up before Nick, although he insisted she stay in bed with him for "just ten more minutes."

"Those ten minutes will turn into twenty minutes, and you'll be late for work," Hana said.

Nick sighed; she was right. He was never late for work, and that couldn't change. As it was, people were questioning why he left right after work instead of sitting around for a few minutes afterward and chatting. He would have to start doing that again.

Reluctantly, he let Hana out of bed. She was a different woman, freer and lighter of heart, and she had gotten over Nick's sleeping in the nude, although she preferred to wear something.

Hana hurried down the stairs to start breakfast while Nick got ready for work. She was just pouring the coffee when he sat at the table, looked at the paper, and put it down, choosing to watch Hana instead.

Feeling his gaze on her, Hana turned around and smiled at him. "Yes?" she asked.

"Nothing, I just like looking at you," Nick replied.

Hana blushed; she never knew how to respond to things like that, so she said nothing and carried the cups of coffee to the table.

"I'm going to be a few minutes late tonight," Nick said and then explained why.

"I understand," Hana replied.

"I won't be too late, but things have to go back to being like they were before so I don't arouse any more suspicions," Nick explained, even though he knew she understood.

Nick had been gone for about an hour by the time Hana went upstairs to make the bed and clean the bathroom. She walked past the dresser and then doubled back; Nick's wedding ring wasn't there. He always left it on the dresser as he walked out of the bedroom to go to downstairs for breakfast. Hana pulled out the top drawer, thinking it might have fallen in, and then looked under the dresser. Frantically she searched the bathroom before accepting the fact that Nick had gone to work wearing his wedding band. She could only hope he realized it before he got to work and took it off; he would have a very difficult time explaining how he got married without anyone's knowledge.

Nick pulled out of the garage wishing he had called in sick. It was hard being away from Hana, especially since he knew he was being watched at the office and had no way of knowing if someone was watching the house during the day. Every morning before he left for work, he admonished Hana to stay indoors and not to answer the phone under any circumstances. He knew she did as he asked, but he still worried for her.

He parked in his usual spot, grabbed his briefcase, and went into the building, speaking and nodding to people as he went. He made his way to his office and saw his friend and partner waiting outside of his door.

"Morning, Nick," Howard said as Nick unlocked the office door.

"Morning," Nick replied as he sat his briefcase on his desk. It was then that he realized he was still wearing his wedding band. All hope that Howard hadn't noticed vanished when Nick realized Howard was staring at his hand.

Howard walked back to the door, shut it, and sat down in the chair across from Nick's desk. "Nick, we're partners and friends, right?"

"Yes," Nick replied.

"We've been through some things together, haven't we? I mean, we saved each others' asses a few times," Howard said, looking at Nick.

"Yes, we have," Nick agreed.

"Then tell me, what the fuck is going on with you? And before you say 'nothing,' let me run through the list of odd behaviors that have been noticed, and not just by me. It all started with that Japanese woman, Hana Takeda, and then you helped another one bargain her way to freedom. You seemed to be yourself again, and then you started doing weird shit like the drives up to Manzanar. Granted it was on your own time, and I know Mitch is up there, but Nick, it was more than that, and we all know it. So I looked to see who else was up there, and imagine my lack of surprise when I saw Hana and Kenji Takeda's names on the list.

"And there's more: You used to be the last one out of here, and now you're out of here like a bat out of hell. When people ask what you did on your days off, you're vague; you find reasons not to show up at social events when you were always the first to ask where and when; and now you show up wearing a fucking wedding band. I'm only going to ask you one more time: what in the fuck are you doing?"

Nick was shocked; his partner, who had always appeared aloof and uninterested in things, had been watching him like a hawk. The question was, had he gone to anyone with his observations, and what were they going to do about it? He wasn't worried about losing his job—he never wanted it to begin with, but because of his experience with international law and affairs, he had been given no choice.

Instinctively he lied, but mixed the truth in with it. He didn't trust Howard; Hana's safety depended on his caution. "About the women, I guess I was just a soft touch and I believed them when they said that they weren't a part of the spy ring. And as it turned out, they weren't. I know we're at war, but to put innocent women in prison? I couldn't do it. Regarding my trips up to Manzanar, you're right: it's none of your damned business what I do on my time off, and I resent the fact that you felt the need to examine my motives for going up there. Last, but not least, I got married; is that a crime?"

Howard was quiet for several minutes. "Why haven't we met her? When did you get married and where?" he finally asked.

Something snapped and Nick had had enough. "None of your motherfucking business! I'm done here; I never wanted this job to begin with."

Howard realized he had pushed too hard; he had to find out what Nick was into. "Nick, calm down," Howard said, with his hands held out in surrender. "I'm sorry, but I had to ask."

"Had to?" Nick asked. "Who sent you in here?"

"Nick—"

"Who in the hell sent you here to interrogate me like I'm a damned spy?" Nick asked, cutting Howard off.

"All right," Howard said. "Those words were yours, not mine."

Understanding dawned on Nick. That's exactly what they thought: they thought he was a spy. "You can't be serious!" Nick exclaimed.

"Nick, all the things I mentioned in and of themselves aren't wrong, but when you put all of the pieces together, they paint an entirely different picture. As to who sent me here, no one did, but you are being watched, both here and at home."

Nick sat down in his chair; what were his options? Telling Howard about Hana was out of the question; he just didn't quite trust him now. He couldn't quit—it would only draw more suspicion. He again decided to go with a version of the truth.

"All right, I was attracted to Hana Takeda. I checked up on her when I went up to Manzanar, took her and her son extra blankets and things like that. I know I haven't been myself, but I'm tired of this war. The only thing I want to do is go back to practicing law and leave this intrigue shit to those who want to do it."

"I can understand that," Howard said. "But that doesn't explain why you didn't tell anyone that you got married and why we haven't met her."

"Howard, I hate this job. When I leave here, I go home to my wife and try to forget about this place and this damned war. I do that by keeping my home life completely separate from this place. Surely you can understand that," Nick said, hoping Howard would buy it.

"I guess I do," Howard replied. "Can you at least tell me her name, or does that violate the keeping-home-from-work-separated rule?"

Not seeing that he had too much of a choice, Nick told Howard Hana's name.

"Good, old-fashioned name," he replied. "I hope to meet her when this is over," he said as he stood up. "And Nick? Watch yourself."

Nick sagged with relief when Howard left his office. Hana had to be frantic by now; she always put his wedding band on the kitchen counter so he could slip it on as soon as he got home. He thought about calling, but she wouldn't answer the phone. He couldn't leave early, as it would arouse suspicions—or would it? By lunchtime, everyone would know he was married, and it wouldn't be the first time a newly married man left an hour or so early on a Friday.

"So you got hitched?" one of the secretaries asked.

"Yes, a couple of months ago," Nick replied.

The secretary didn't say anything, but looked at Nick, her eyes filled with disappointment—and she wasn't the only one.

"Was there something else?" Nick asked.

"No; she must be something to be able to get a ring on your finger," she replied and walked away.

Hana didn't know what to do; she had Nick's work number, but was too afraid to call it; what if he didn't answer the phone?

She thought about calling Patricia, but then what? Patricia could call her back, but she wouldn't be able to answer the phone, and she would be exactly where she was now: anxious and frightened.

Hana looked at the phone again. She could call, and if someone other than Nick answered, she would hang up. She reached for the phone and then stopped; she would wait.

By three o'clock, Nick couldn't stand it anymore. He had to get home to Hana and let her know everything was all right, at least for now. He had actually entertained the idea of moving Hana to Ralph's house, but disregarded the idea; chances were that he would be followed, and the one place he knew wasn't being watched would be compromised.

He packed up his briefcase and headed toward the door, waving and smiling at the catcalls about going home to fuck his new wife. In the end, the accidental wearing of the wedding band had turned out to be a blessing in disguise that he hadn't anticipated.

Hana was waiting by the front door when he walked in. Nick saw the lines of fear and worry on her face and hugged her.

"It's all right," he said, kissing her.

"I didn't know what to do! I was so worried about you," Hana said, hugging Nick back.

"I know, and that's why I'm home early," Nick replied and told her about the conversation he had with Howard.

They were headed toward the kitchen when someone banged on the door. Hana froze; she recognized an angry sound when she heard it.

"Sweetheart, go upstairs and don't come out no matter what," Nick said and gave her a quick kiss.

Hana started to object, but was pushed toward the stairs. "Go!" Nick said as he headed toward the front door.

Hana ran upstairs to their bedroom and hid in the back of the closet, making sure she was well concealed.

Satisfied that Hana was hiding, Nick opened the door to see his partner Howard with two other men.

"Where is she, Nick?" Howard asked.

Chapter 15

"Where is who?" Nick asked calmly.

"Hana Takeda; she's been reported missing," Howard replied, trying to look around Nick.

"And you think she's here?" Nick asked, incredulous. "Are you out of your mind?"

"Where is she?" Howard asked again.

"How would I know? And how do you know she's missing? There are several thousand Japanese in that camp," Nick said, as he tried to think of a way to keep Hana from being found.

"The woman at the orphanage where Takeda worked got worried when she didn't see her for several weeks and—"

"Hold it, Hana Takeda hasn't been seen in weeks and this woman is just now reporting it?" Nick interrupted. "And then you barge in on me and ask me where she is?"

"Nick, we all knew you were sweet on her, and it's like I said: you haven't been yourself."

"I see, so that makes me guilty of what?" Nick asked angrily. "Who authorized this?"

"Where's your wife? I'd like to meet her," Howard said, avoiding Nick's question.

"I don't think so," Nick replied coldly. "I plan on introducing her to my friends, and you are not my friend. Now get the hell out of my house."

"Be advised that you are on suspension until Hana Takeda is found. And if we find out that you knew where she is or assisted her in any way—"

"Get the fuck out of my house," Nick said. "I'm not going to tell you again."

"Come on, Howard," one of the other agents said.

"Nick, I'm sorry," the other agent said before he walked away.

Nick waited a few minutes, locked the door, and ran up the stairs to check on Hana. "Hana, you can come out; it's all right now."

Hana came out of the closet, visibly shaken. Nick held her until she stopped shaking. He had made the same error Kenji had; he should have gotten her out of the house sooner. That way he could have let Howard search the house. Getting her out now was going to be impossible; his every move was going to be followed. But there was another issue: Kenji, Patricia, and the baby.

"Sweetheart, are you all right?" Nick asked.

"I . . . I think so," Hana replied. "Maybe I should go back."

"You're not doing that, and besides, it's not possible. But right now, I need to call Abby and warn them. I have a feeling Howard is going to pay them a visit."

Patricia had just finished giving the baby a bath when the phone rang. She wrapped Niko in a towel and carried him with her to answer the phone.

"Hello?"

"I need to speak to Kenji immediately," the male voice on the other end of the phone said.

"Who is this?" she asked.

"A friend; now get him on the phone!"

Patricia hesitated; this could be a trap.

"Damn it! Get him on the phone now!" the voice roared, making Patricia jump.

Ralph walked into the kitchen and saw the look on Patricia's face. "Patty? What's wrong?" he asked.

"A man on the phone wants to talk to Kenji, but he won't say who he is," she replied.

Ralph took the phone from Patricia and barked into it, "Who is this?" After a few seconds, he relaxed. "Why in the hell didn't you just say who you were?" And then to Patricia he said, "It's all right; go get him."

Kenji was in the library reading when Patricia tapped on the door. He reached for the baby as soon as he saw them.

"There's a man in the phone who wants to talk to you; Ralph is talking to him now. He says it's all right for you to talk whoever it is."

Kenji frowned; the only person other than Nick that would call him would be Dr. Mynt.

"Thank you, *Kirei*," he said and handed the baby back to her. "Don't worry," he added and kissed her cheek.

Ralph handed the phone to Kenji and went to find Patricia.

"Patty, we have to move Kenji and the baby," he said.

"Why? What's happened?" she asked, alarmed.

"Hana has been reported missing; they're searching for her now. We have to get Kenji and the baby out of here before it's too late. Now go make sure you have everything you need in your emergency bag and meet me by the car in twenty minutes. Make sure the baby is padded good; he's going to have to ride in the trunk with Kenji."

"The trunk?" Patricia asked, horrified.

"Yes, Patty, the trunk; if we get stopped and they ask to see Niko. . . . Just go get ready. I'll get Abby from the back yard."

Patricia's throat was tight as she hurried to the basement stairs. She could hear Kenji talking on the phone in soft, hushed tones. He was trying not to scare her, but it was way too late for that. She laid Niko on the bed and pulled out the suitcase that was already packed with two changes of clothes for her and Kenji, and baby supplies for Niko. The first tears had just fallen when Kenji came down the basement stairs. He hugged her tight and kissed her in an attempt to reassure her. This war had scarred her; she would always be afraid of not seeing him again.

"*Kirei*, it's only my mother they're looking for. Dr. Mynt has them convinced that I live at the hospital, and so far they haven't asked to see me. We'll go to Ralph's house and stay there until this is over."

"But what about your mother and Nick?" she asked.

"I don't know, *Kirei*, but for now we must go. Do we have everything we need for Niko?"

"Yes, and there are some things over at Ralph's house," Patricia replied.

Abby was anxious in the kitchen when they came up from the basement. "There's food and anything else we might need over there. Ralph and I are going with you; people will just assume we went on a trip or something," she said.

"But my parents—"

"They already know if they come and no one is here that we had to leave," Abby assured her.

"I can't believe this is happening," Patricia whispered.

"Patricia, it's going to be all right; now go to the car and I'll be right out."

Kenji was already in the trunk waiting for Patricia to come out with Niko. By the time Patricia was satisfied that both Kenji and Niko were as comfortable as possible, Abby came out of the house, carrying a small bag. The suitcase was tied to the top of the car, giving the appearance that Ralph, Abby, and Patricia would be gone for several days.

Patricia could hear Niko crying and Kenji's soft voice soothing him, and she started to cry herself. She prayed silently that everything would be all right, just as Abby and Kenji believed it would be, and then she prayed for the safety of Nick and Hana. She would feel so much better if they were all together, but it wasn't possible.

The drive to Ralph's house seemed to last for hours before they pulled into the back yard. Ralph got out first, looked around, and unlocked the door to the house. Next he unlocked the trunk, took the baby from Kenji, and hurried into the house. He was nervous because it was daylight, but they had no real choice; someone could be at Abby's even now. Kenji climbed out of the trunk once Ralph gave him the all-clear sign; he found Patricia in the living room hugging Niko and crying.

"Patricia, *Kirei*, we are safe now."

"But Nick and your mother may not be, and what if they find you? And—"

Kenji wrapped his arms around Patricia. "It will be all right. I won't believe that we have been through so much only to be pulled apart again. Mother and Nick will be fine."

Patricia nodded her head in understanding. Kenji was right; surely God wouldn't be so cruel as to pull them apart, would he? He wouldn't, Patricia decided; he couldn't. It wouldn't be fair, but then the world wasn't fair, so why should it be any different for them?

"Patricia," Abby said softly, "give Niko to me; you and Kenji need some time together."

When Patricia started to argue, Abby silenced her with a look Patricia hadn't seen in a long time and held out her arms for the baby. Patricia handed Niko over to Abby, albeit reluctantly.

"Abby—" she started to say, but Abby had already started to walk away.

"*Kirei*, come with me," Kenji said, taking her hand.

He led her to the rooms where they had lived for the first several months of their marriage. Patricia looked around the living room and couldn't help but smile; in spite of everything, this was one of the places where she had been the happiest. Kenji led her to the couch where they had made so many plans for their lives together and sat down, pulling her down with him. He pulled her close to his side and put an arm around her.

For several minutes, neither of them spoke; when Kenji felt Patricia was calmer, he spoke. "*Kirei*, someday this war will be over and we'll be able to live in peace with Niko and our family, but until then, we do what we can to keep the war outside."

"How can we do that?" Patricia asked. "We have to hide, and we jump every time someone comes to the door or the phone rings, and if they find us here, then what? They'll make you go back to the camp or send you to prison and I—we—"

"Patricia, listen to me. I know you're frightened, but try not to be."

"Aren't you scared?" Patricia asked.

Kenji hesitated before answering. "Yes, *Kirei*, I am, but I refuse to let that fear rule me. Instead, I take joy in every moment I have with you, Niko, and our family. I have faith that we will do all of the things we planned when we sat here on this couch."

Patricia laid her head on Kenji's shoulder; she wanted to believe him, and deep down she did. She was just tired of the hiding, and the stress was getting to her. She fell asleep listening to Kenji repeat the list of things they were going to do together and with their children.

Nick looked out the window and saw a black car parked on the corner; he was being watched. Any ideas of trying to get Hana out were shot to hell. As long as she stayed out of sight, they were fine, but they never knew when Howard would come pounding on the door demanding to search the house. Hana stayed upstairs just in case that happened, and all she would have to do is get back into the closet and be quiet. She had suggested again that she give herself up, but that wouldn't help anything—Nick would still go to prison and she would go back to the camp.

"No, Hana, and don't suggest it again," Nick said firmly. "I've thought about this, and our best option is to stay put and keep you out of sight."

Nick beat himself up over the ring. "If only I had remembered to take it off," he muttered to himself. But then he realized something: this still would have happened even if he hadn't worn the ring. Hana being reported missing was the thing that initiated Howard's barging in on him.

Nick moved away from the window and went upstairs, where Hana was waiting in their bedroom. She was worried about Kenji, Patricia, and the baby. Nick didn't blame her; he was worried, too. He tried to call Abby's house and became alarmed when no one answered. It meant one of two things: that they had been warned somehow or that they had been arrested, with the latter being the most likely. He felt sick to his stomach as he imagined what they had to be going through, especially if that ass Howard was in charge of the questioning.

Nick sat on the bed next to Hana and hugged her; he felt her shaking against him as she imagined all of the worst-case scenarios.

"Hana, maybe they got out."

"But maybe they didn't," Hana replied. "What will become of Niko?" she asked as tears ran down her face. "He's just a baby."

Nick didn't reply; he knew the answer as well as she did. Niko would be placed in an orphanage in one of the camps. He whispered a prayer for all of them; it couldn't hurt.

Hiroshi was out and about enjoying the warmth of the day; it wasn't hot yet, but pleasant. The rumors about Joben Saito's death had stopped long ago; people simply lost interest. Things at the camp had settled down, until yesterday. From what he understood, Hana had been reported missing over a week ago. The woman at the orphanage where Hana worked had been the one to report it.

As soon as he got wind of the disappearance, Hiroshi, who now had contacts everywhere in the camp, looked into it. No one could really remember seeing Hana since February, but no one thought much of it since they knew she usually stayed at the orphanage. Why no one had noticed that their quarters were covered in weeks' worth of dust, Hiroshi didn't understand, but there was something else that didn't make sense: Kenji wasn't reported as missing. There was no way Hana would have left without Kenji, so where were they?

After what the military police did what they called a thorough search, Hana was proclaimed missing. There was much speculation about what happened to her, ranging from a rumor that she killed herself to one that someone got her out of the camp. Hiroshi believed the latter, and he even knew who would do it: the American agent. But that didn't explain why Kenji would still be here, unless he really wasn't and no one had reported him missing yet. Like Hana, Kenji spent very little time in the barracks; it was common knowledge that he spent almost all his time at the hospital and orphanage, where he taught English to those who wanted to learn. So no one would think about him not being in the barracks, either.

By May 22, it was clear that Hana was gone. Hiroshi thought about telling the military police what he knew, but if he did that, he wouldn't be able to get back to Japan, as Nick wouldn't keep his end of the bargain. If Hana was caught and put back in the camp and Nick imprisoned, the same would happen. It was in Hiroshi's best interest that Hana be "found."

The first thing he did was visit the orphanage. He found the woman who reported Hana missing and introduced himself. "I am Hiroshi Takeda, the husband of Hana."

"Where is she? Is she all right?" the woman asked.

Hiroshi weighed his options and went with intimidation. "You will go to the police and tell them you were mistaken. Hana is here in the camp, but has not been here because she is ill. Do you understand?" Hiroshi asked coldly.

"No, but—"

"You will go to the police immediately and tell them you were wrong and that I came to you and reported Hana ill. If you don't do this. . . . " Hiroshi left the unspoken threat hang in the air, staring at the woman until she nodded her head in compliance.

"Good, and if I hear that you have done other than what I have instructed . . . the camp is a large place," Hiroshi said with a smile before walking away.

The next evening, the military police found Hiroshi in his assigned space in the barracks. "We hear your wife isn't missing; where is she?"

Hiroshi's bedmate stepped forward. "I am Hana Takeda; I am sorry for the trouble, but I have been ill and did not want to make the children ill as well."

The police left shortly afterward, apparently satisfied that they had spoken to Hana Takeda. Hiroshi looked at the woman who had posed as Hana; it was too bad that he couldn't take her back to Japan with him. Nick wouldn't pay for her, and besides, she didn't want to go back.

Hiroshi nodded at the woman and walked out, confident that he was still going back to Nagasaki. What he would do once he got there, he didn't know, but there had to be a place somewhere for one of the emperor's most loyal subjects.

It had been almost a week since Howard had come banging on Nick's door. Nick never left the house, unless it was to go get the paper. There was always a car parked on the street watching him and the house. Nick recognized some of the car's occupants: they were people he had talked with and had even been to their homes for social gatherings. He wasn't nearly as angry with them as he was with Howard, whom he had really considered a friend.

Nick had a lot time to think since he was on suspension; if by some miracle he was able to go back to work, he would tell them to shove the job right up their asses, and he would reopen his law practice. Later he changed his mind; he would go back because he would be able to keep his ear to the ground and get a heads-up about any information that came up about Hana and Kenji. The one thing he wouldn't do was accept that asshole Howard back as his partner. Nick understood on one hand that Howard had a job to do, but this went beyond that. Howard wanted to move up the ladder and was willing to use his partner to do it; he was a self-serving bastard.

MAY 30, 1943

Nick was in the kitchen making tea for him and Hana when there was a tap on the door. Nick quickly looked to be sure that Hana wasn't in sight and went to answer the door.

"What do you want, Howard?" Nick asked.

Howard shuffled nervously on his feet and didn't say anything for several seconds. One of the agents standing behind him made a coughing sound in his throat.

"Nick, it seems that I owe you an apology."

Nick narrowed his eyes and looked at Howard; he didn't trust him, but he didn't say anything.

"It seems that Hana Takeda isn't missing; she's at the camp. The woman who reported her missing said she made a mistake and that the husband showed up and assured her that Hana was not missing, but ill."

"What you're saying to me is that you didn't do a full investigation before you came to my home and accused me of aiding and abetting an enemy of this country," Nick said dryly. "And let's not forget that you also implied I was a spy for Japan."

"Nick, you have to admit—"

"I don't have to admit a damned thing," Nick hissed.

Howard swallowed hard; he had just fucked up royally, and not just his friendship with Nick. The promotion he was working so hard to get was gone.

"I am also here to tell you that you are officially off of suspension; you will be compensated for the days you missed because of—"

"You," Nick said. "I thought you were my friend. You're no one's friend but your own. I'll be back in the office on Wednesday and not a day before, and I damned well don't want you as my partner. I'd take a rookie or work alone before I'd work with you again."

"Nick, come on," Howard said. "You would have done the same thing, and you know it."

"No, Howard, I wouldn't have," Nick replied. "If I had been in your position, I wouldn't have saved up what I thought was evidence against you and taken it to management. I would have pulled you aside and asked you if there was anything going on, and if you had told me no, I would have taken you at your word. Now get the hell off of my porch."

Nick didn't give Howard a chance to reply before slamming the door in his face. Nick's shoulders sagged with relief; they were safe for the moment, but he had to be more careful. He ran up the stairs, taking two at a time, to tell Hana the news. He was shocked to see her packing.

"Hana, what are you doing?" he asked.

"They're here for me, are they not?" she asked softly.

"No, honey, they're not. They found you," Nick said.

"What do you mean, they found me?" Hana asked.

"I think Hiroshi helped you by having someone say they were you," Nick replied, taking the neatly folded kimono out of Hana's hands and putting it in the dresser.

"Why would he do that?" Hana asked, surprised.

"Whether he gets back to Japan or not depends on you being safe. He didn't do it for you; he did it because it suited his purpose, but be that as it may, he helped us out, and by extension, Kenji and Patricia."

"Do you know if they were arrested?" Hana asked.

"No, and I wasn't about to ask," Nick replied. "Later tonight I'll go over to Abby's, and if they're not there, I'll go to Ralph's to see if they're there. If they're not at either place, then they've been arrested, and I'll have to find out where they are."

Somehow, Nick didn't think they had been arrested; he didn't know why he was so sure about that, but he wasn't about to tell Hana and then find out they had been arrested.

"They took me off of suspension," Nick said later, when they were drinking tea.

"Will you return?" Hana asked.

"Yes, but I'm going to request a different partner," Nick said.

"Is that wise?" Hana asked.

"The man was selling me out to get a promotion; I can't trust him," Nick replied.

"That's true, but you know him now. You know what he's capable of, and if you don't work with him, how will you know what he does and whom he speaks to?" Hana asked.

She had a valid point, Nick realized. "You're right, but I won't pretend to be friends with him."

Later that evening, Nick looked outside and didn't see any signs that he was being watched. On the spur of the moment, he decided to take a walk. He had learned his lesson the hard way; he would take nothing at face value again. He was halfway back when he saw the car with two agents sitting in it.

"Son of a bitch," he muttered under his breath as he walked up to the car.

The man in the driver's seat jumped when Nick angrily banged on the window.

"What are you still doing here?" Nick asked.

The two men looked at each other and then at Nick.

"Well?" Nick demanded.

"We were told to keep watching you," the man in the driver's seat said.

"By who and why?" Nick asked, although he already knew the answer.

"Howard. Nick, he doesn't believe you," the man said.

"Believe me about what? Hana Takeda and her son are both at Manzanar," Nick replied.

"Yes, well, you know he was counting on that promotion and—"

"This has become personal," Nick finished.

The man's silence was Nick's answer. He liked the two agents in the car and decided to give them a warning. "Look, fellas, I'm going to give you a free piece of advice: stay away from Howard. I've been exonerated, and this is spending money that the government needs for the war. If this comes to light, Howard won't be the only one to lose his job."

A minute later, Nick watched the car as it turned the corner and went in the opposite direction of his house. Nick sat out on the porch for a half hour watching the street. When he was sure he wasn't being watched, he went into the house, kissed Hana goodbye, and headed over to Abby's house.

The first thing Nick saw was the car parked across the street; these men, he didn't know. Nick parked in front of the house, got out, and crossed the street. The driver saw him coming and rolled down the window.

"Help you?" he asked.

"I'm Agent Nick Alexander, and I want to know who told you to watch this house and why," Nick said, as he showed the man his identification.

The man squinted to see the identification and then said, "Howard Gibbs—said something about a woman named Hana Takeda who might be hiding here."

"I see; when did he tell you to do this?" Nick asked.

"A couple of hours ago, wasn't it, Chuck?" the man said, talking to his partner.

"Somewhere around there," Chuck replied. "But I have to tell ya, I thought the whole thing sounded funny."

"Why's that?" Nick asked.

"Can't really say; it just didn't feel right. So is the woman here or not?"

"She isn't here; they found her at the camp," Nick replied.

"Fuck!" Chuck swore. "I missed my kid's birthday party for some Jap broad that's where she belongs?"

Nick bit his tongue before he spoke. "You might catch the tail end of the party if you hurry."

"What about our orders?" the driver asked.

"I'll take care of it," Nick assured him.

When the car was gone, Nick went back to his car; it was obvious that Abby and the rest of them were gone.

"You looking for Abby?" a voice called out just as he was about to get into his car.

"I was; do you know where they went?" Nick asked.

"Nope, but it looked like they were going to be gone for a while. They even took that colored girl with them," the neighbor, an older man said.

"Thank God!" Nick whispered.

"What's that?" the man asked.

"I said 'thank you,'" Nick said as he got into the car.

He sat in the car for a few minutes before pulling away. This was way too close; he needed to get all of them out of the city. Howard had just proven that he wasn't about to give up, although his reasons had become personal instead of professional. After checking the rearview mirror, Nick drove over to Ralph's.

Patricia heard the car door first. She grabbed Niko and called for Kenji. "Somebody's coming!" she said and headed up the stairs, with Kenji close behind her.

A few minutes later Ralph called upstairs, "Come on down; it's Nick."

They ran down the stairs and hugged Nick, who assured them that Hana was all right.

"She's worried about all of you, but she's all right," Nick said. "I can't stay long, but I had to make sure you were all right. I'll be back in the next few days, and in the meantime, Ralph, I want you and Abby to think of a place where we can take everyone, and I want it to be out of the city. We'll work on the logistics once we've figured out where we're going. But we're all safe for the moment."

Nick stayed for a few more minutes and headed home. He did a mental calculation of how much money he had in cash and in the bank. By his calculations, he had somewhere in the neighborhood of fifteen thousand dollars; it was a hefty sum, but it wouldn't last long if he had to support seven people, including himself. He knew that Patricia and Kenji had some money, and so did Ralph and Abby. Between all of them, they'd be all right, but the problem was getting everyone to wherever they were going.

Hana was in the bedroom when she heard the noise from downstairs. At first she thought it was Nick, but he always called out to let her know it was him. She heard drawers opening and closing and books hitting the floor, and then footsteps approaching the stairs. Hana ran to the closet as silently as she could, got in, and squeezed into her hiding place. The bedroom door opened but didn't close. It wasn't Nick; he always closed the door. Hana held her breath as the intruder walked around the bedroom and past the closet where she was hiding.

It seemed like hours before the intruder left the bedroom, but Hana stayed where she was, not coming out until she heard Nick's voice in the bedroom.

Nick pulled into the garage, got out of the car, and went into the house. The first thing he noticed was the papers lying on the floor.

Hana.

He didn't dare call her name because the intruder might still be in the house; he could only hope Hana was somewhere in the house, hiding. Nick searched the bottom floor first. His office was totally destroyed, his papers all over the floor. Fortunately, he never took notes or kept records of any conversations he had with anyone regarding the Takedas, Ralph, Abby, and Mitch. It was for his safety, as well as theirs.

Satisfied that the downstairs was secure, Nick went upstairs and started in the spare bedroom and found it intact. The bathroom was empty, which left his and Hana's room.

"Hana? Honey, come out. It's me, Nick."

Hana flew out of the closet and into Nick's arms. "He came just after you left; I thought it was you coming back, but you didn't call to me, so I hid."

"Good," Nick said as he looked around the bedroom. Like the other bedroom, it was untouched. He wondered what it was Howard was looking for.

By the end of July 1943, General Henri Giraud was the commander of the Free French Forces in North Africa; the Japanese abandoned Kiska Island in the Aleutians.

Sicily and the Italian mainland were bombed by the Allied forces; the invasion began with the goal to liberate Europe.

The Red Army began a major offensive; exiled Polish leader Wladyslaw Sikorski died in an airplane crash; and the Battle of Kursk began when the German and Soviet forces met on the Eastern Front in Kursk, which was located approximately 280 miles south of Moscow. It would be the final strategic offensive that the Germans would be able to mount in the East.

Four-hundred-and ninety Poles were tortured and killed at Dominopol by the Ukrainian Insurgent Army. Rome was bombed for the first time by the Allies; Palermo fell during the Allied invasion of Sicily, inspiring the coup of Benito Mussolini's government; and the Allies bombed the city of Hamburg,

Germany. Hamburg was a major port and industrial center and the site of the world's oldest dynamite factory, which was constructed by Albert Nobel. The attack, which occurred during the last week of July 1943, created a firestorm that killed 42,600 civilians and wounded thirty-seven thousand, practically destroying the city.

Everyone was on pins and needles. The only bright spots were Niko, who was growing too quickly for Patricia's taste, and Patricia's twenty-second birthday. When she thought about it, it didn't seem like four years had passed since she and Kenji met, got married, were separated, and now had a baby. The war still raged on, and the Japanese as well as some other nationalities were still interred. She no longer listened to the war news; it frightened her too much, and if she didn't hear it, she could almost, but not quite, convince herself that there was no war.

Kenji, like Patricia, didn't want to hear anything about the war; to him, it was a senseless loss of life that he could and never would understand. All of them, with the exception of Nick and Hana, were still at Ralph's house, and no headway had been made on finding a place outside of the city.

"I just don't know of anyplace that would be secluded and big enough for all of us," Ralph told Nick one evening.

"I could ask around, but I don't think I should draw any more attention to myself; kicking Harold's ass gave me more attention than I needed," Nick said.

"You know for a fact that he was in your house that night?" Ralph asked.

"The bastard practically admitted it," Nick replied. "Anyway, keep looking and I'll keep my ear to the ground," he said as he stood up to go home.

"Is Abby's house still being watched?" Ralph asked.

"No, why?" Nick replied.

"They wouldn't expect us to go back there."

“You have a point, but they don’t know about this place,” Nick replied.

“And that’s why it should remain a safe house,” Ralph said. “I think we need to forget getting out of the city for a couple of reasons: the first and main one being getting everyone there, the second reason being we haven’t found anyplace big enough or secluded enough.”

“Talk to the others tonight and see what they think. I’ll be back tomorrow night, and I plan to bring Hana, so make sure the gate is open for me,” Nick said.

“Damned war!” Hiroshi grumbled. The air outside was hot, making the barracks almost unbearable. The woman who was his bedmate knew better than to say anything, as Hiroshi had started addressing her by the name of “whore” instead of her given name. Tonight she was moving back into her own space with her sister; she had taken enough of Hiroshi’s verbal abuse and his frequent comparisons of her to Hana.

The woman realized something that Hiroshi didn’t realize or acknowledge: he missed his wife and his son. The problem was that his wife was no longer his wife and he had burned his bridges with his son. She didn’t know the whole story, but she knew regret when she saw it. Hiroshi was now a bitter, lonely man who had made several costly mistakes, and it was much too late to rectify anything.

She knew she could get almost anything she wanted from Hiroshi because she had helped conceal the fact that his wife was no longer at the camp, but she wouldn’t. He had suffered enough in his life and would continue to do so without her help.

Hiroshi no longer talked about going to Japan; deep in his gut, he knew Japan was going to be defeated. He couldn’t explain how he knew that, any more than he could explain how he had known that Hitler was going to be trouble, and that he had to get Hana and Kenji out of Japan before anything happened.

He looked over at the woman whom he had been sharing a bed with and felt a measure of guilt. Not that he had taken her to his bed, but because of how he had treated her. He knew she was planning to leave him, and he couldn't blame her, but he didn't want to be alone.

Hiroshi took a good, hard look at her: she was rather plain, but not ugly. She was good in bed, doing whatever he asked of her, and she had good, wide hips; she was made for having babies. He wondered what she was planning to do when and if they were released from what he considered to be hell. He wondered if Nick would just give him the money instead of paying his way back to Japan, but maybe there would be no choice. He was a spy; he had actively conspired against the United States, and he refused to sign the loyalty oath. Most of the others who refused to sign were sent off to other places, but not him, and he wondered how much of that was Nick's doing. In the end, it really didn't matter, Hiroshi decided.

The woman rose to leave, but Hiroshi stopped her; he was going to do something he had never done with either Hana or Kenji. He was going to apologize.

Kenji kept watching Ralph. He wasn't well, but rebuffed any of Kenji's attempts to talk to him about it.

"For the last time, I'm fine!" Ralph exclaimed.

"No, Ralph, you are not fine," Kenji replied. "Your cough is worsening and it sounds wet, but yet you cough nothing up. When you walk even a short way, your breathing becomes labored. You must go to the hospital or call the doctor."

"No!" Ralph yelled.

Kenji was unfazed. "Why are you being so difficult about this?"

"We're going to need all the money we have," Ralph replied.

"Ralph, money will mean nothing if it costs your life. I am begging you on behalf of all of us. Please go to the hospital."

"He's right, you stubborn old coot," Abby said from the doorway.

"Not you, too," Ralph said.

"Yes, me too; now get your body to the car. I'm taking you to the hospital," Abby said.

"Who's going to the hospital?" Nick asked as he walked in with Hana.

Kenji briefly forgot about Ralph when he saw Hana. "Mother! You look well," Kenji said, hugging her.

"As do you; where are my daughter and grandson?" Hana asked, looking around.

"They're upstairs," Kenji replied, hugging her again.

Abby hugged Hana next, then Ralph.

"All we need now is Hattie and John," Abby said and then grabbed her purse. "I'll be back, and Ralph, tomorrow we go to the hospital, even if we have to tie you down."

"Ralph, are you ill?" Hana asked, concerned.

"Nah, I'm fine. It's just Dr. Kenji over there and the old woman think I'm sick," Ralph explained.

"If I may say so, Ralph, you do not look well," Hana said softly.

Nick started to say something, but Ralph stopped him, "Don't say it!"

"I won't; I think you've gotten the message. If you don't want to go to the hospital, then I'll have someone meet you at Abby's house. It's your choice," Nick said.

"Hana?" Patricia said when she came into the room.

Hana and Patricia hugged, and Patricia handed Niko over to Hana, who hadn't seen him for months.

"You are so handsome and strong, like your father!" Hana said as she hugged and kissed the squirming baby. "And you have your mother's eyes," she added as she sat down, holding the baby.

Patricia stood next to Kenji, who had his arm around her waist, and watched Hana hug and kiss Niko. Kenji was pleased that she looked well and noticed the wedding band on her finger. She was still wearing a kimono, and that had to change. If they were stopped, it would be a dead giveaway. Patricia's clothes would be too big, but they would have to do until they could get her some better-fitting clothes.

"*Kirei*, Mother cannot keep wearing a kimono; do you have anything she can use?"

Patricia looked at Hana and then down at herself. "Everything I have would be too big, but you're right about the kimono," she said. "Maybe we could fix something up."

"Mother, could you go with Patricia? She'll help you with clothing."

Hana handed Niko to Nick and followed Patricia upstairs.

"I know she needs different clothes, but it would look strange for me to buy women's clothes. Maybe Abby and Hattie could get her some," Nick said.

A few minutes later, Abby came in with Hattie, who immediately took Niko from Nick and John.

"Now we're all here," Abby said, kissing Niko on the head. "Where's Patricia?" she asked, looking around the room.

"Upstairs with Mother," Kenji replied. "She needs other clothing; it is too dangerous for her to keep wearing a kimono."

"I have some clothes that are too small for me," Abby said. "They'll be big on her and they're outdated, but she's welcome to them. The issue is how to get them to her."

"I'll swing by your house tomorrow on my way home from work," Nick said, turning when he heard Patricia and Hana come down the stairs.

Hana almost drowned in Patricia's dress, but it was an improvement. Patricia had taken the belts from the kimono and used them on the dress so it didn't hang so badly. At first glance, no one would realize Hana was Japanese, which was the goal.

Hattie and Hana hugged each other and exchanged pleasantries while John stood back and watched. Hana made her way to him and bowed slightly. "Hello, John."

John gave an awkward bow and said hello. He had gotten used to Kenji only because he spent more time with him and he was a man, whereas Hana he had met only once or twice, and he hadn't spoken to her.

Nick gave everyone a few more minutes to visit before bringing up the topic of discussion. "You all know what happened at our house a few weeks ago, and it's prompted me into thinking that we need to move to someplace outside of the city. The problem has been finding a place that's large enough for all of us, and getting us there. Ralph and Abby have been looking, and so far, nothing has turned up. Ralph brought up a solution, and I want to know what you think about it.

"Right now, no one knows about Ralph or this house, and Abby's house is no longer being watched. Ralph suggests that we go back to the way it was before you had to come here and that we keep this house as a safe house. I would still like to get out of the city—I don't trust Howard as far as I can throw him. Any suggestions?"

Patricia spoke first. "I would feel better if we were all together. Part of the stress comes from worrying about you and Hana."

"I understand that, Patty," Ralph said. "But it just isn't safe for all of us to be in one place. As it is, there's too many of us at Abby's, but people have gotten used to seeing me, and it would raise more questions if I disappeared. I agree with Nick that we need to leave the city, but logistically, it isn't possible."

They talked for almost two hours before deciding to go with Ralph's suggestion. Just as they were getting ready to go, John spoke up. "You can come to our place if you needs to; it ain't big, but nobody would look for ya there."

The room went silent; this was the first time John Middleton had volunteered to help in any way.

"Daddy, thank you," Patricia said, hugging him.

"Yes, thank you," Kenji said. "I feel better knowing that Patricia and Niko will have another place to go to if the need should arise."

Patricia gave Kenji a curious look, and then her eyes clouded over as she understood what Kenji was saying: he wouldn't come with them if something happened.

Kenji saw the look and felt a stab in his heart, but they had to accept the fact that they could be caught, and he would die before he let Patricia or Niko spend a day in one of the camps or prison. The events of a few weeks ago had brought that possibility back to him.

Thirty minutes later, Hana was back in the trunk of Nick's car, and Abby was taking John and Hattie back home.

Nick noticed the dark-colored car sitting on the corner, but pretended he didn't. He knew who it was: Howard Gibbs. He wasn't worried that Howard had seen Hana—he couldn't have—but he was angry that the man still wouldn't leave things alone. Apparently, the ass whipping hadn't done its job.

Nick drove home within the speed limit, pulled up to the garage, and got out to open it. Out of the corner of his eye, he saw the car slowly drive by and then speed up. He pulled into the garage and locked it before letting Hana out; she wasn't safe here. Nick knew that as long as Howard Gibbs was in the picture, none of them would be safe. The issue was how to eliminate the threat.

"Nick?" Hana asked anxiously.

"Hana, you're not safe here. I need to take you back to Abby's."

"No—"

"Sweetheart, listen to me; Howard Gibbs followed us home. I'm afraid he's going to come here one day when I'm not here and arrest you. Now go upstairs and pack a few things while I call over to Abby's."

"Nick—"

"Go on," Nick said as he kissed her.

As Hana climbed the stairs, she had an inkling of what Patricia must have felt when she watched Kenji leave for the camp. She swallowed the lump in her throat and packed her few belongings. She remembered Patricia's courage and pulled herself together. It wasn't as if Nick was going to a camp; this was only temporary until he talked to this Howard Gibbs.

Nick was looking out the window when she came downstairs. He had spotted Gibbs parked down the next block, and he had to deal with him before he could take Hana out of the house.

"Wait here," Nick said and slipped out of the door. He walked around the block and came at Howard's car from behind.

He crept up to the passenger side, opened the door, and jumped in before Howard knew what was happening.

"Nick!"

"Drive, you son of a bitch," Nick hissed.

After a brief hesitation, Howard pulled away from the curb.

"Go to the park; you and I still don't understand each other," Nick said.

Nick directed Howard to a remote section of the park and made him stop the car. "Why are you still following me?"

"Because I think you're hiding something or someone," Howard replied.

"And who or what would that be?"

"Hana Takeda or someone else."

Nick laughed. "Do you know how fucking crazy you sound? You said yourself that they found Hana Takeda at Manzanar, and you still haven't told me what you think it is I'm hiding."

"I don't know, but I know you're up to something. Why else would you be friends with a nigger?"

Nick almost punched Howard, but refrained.

"Are you listening to yourself? You've gone from accusing me of hiding a woman who is in a camp to accusing me of being up to something because I'm friends with a colored person. Tell me where the guilt lies," Nick challenged. "Is it illegal to talk to a colored person? And what am I? Am I a magician who can make people appear and reappear?"

"No, but you're one slick motherfucker," Howard replied.

"Let me ask you this," Nick said. "Does the director know you're using a government car for personal use?"

Howard paled.

"I didn't think so," Nick said. "I'm prepared to make you an offer."

"You don't have anything I want except for proof that you're a spy for Japan and God knows who else."

Nick laughed; he couldn't help it. "That is the most asinine thing I've ever heard you say. You have nothing to support your accusations. That's why you're still following me; you're trying to get back into the good graces of the director. You searched my house; did you find anything? No, and do you know why? There's nothing there to find. Here's my offer: you get the hell out of here and I won't turn you in."

Howard looked out the window and then turned back to Nick. "I have an offer of my own: you let me look through your house, and if I don't finds anything, I swear to God, I'll leave you in peace. And it has to be now."

"Now?" Nick asked.

"Now," Howard replied.

Nick weighed his options. If he said no, he would never be rid of the arrogant prick, but if he agreed. . . . The wild card was Hana. If they were caught, the others would be safe because as far as anyone knew, Kenji was still in the camp.

"All right; let's go," Nick said, to the surprise of Howard.

"I can go through your house?"

"You can do whatever the fuck you want."

"What about your wife?"

"She's away visiting her cousin; are we going or not?" Nick asked.

Howard started the car and headed toward Nick's house. Nick said several silent prayers that Hana would hear the car and hide.

Hana paced back and forth; she was worried for Nick. He had been gone for quite a while. She was about to go into the kitchen when she heard a car pull into the driveway. She knew it wasn't Nick's car; his car was still in the garage. Hana grabbed her bag and ran upstairs as fast as she could. She made it to the closet when she heard a voice she didn't recognize, followed by Nick's.

She opened the closet door and got in, taking her bag with her. Hana huddled in the corner of the closet and covered herself with the old clothes Nick had planned to get rid of, and she waited.

"Go ahead and look," Nick said, as he looked around for any signs of Hana. "And this time, you make a mess, you clean it up."

Nick stood in the doorway to his office as Howard opened drawers and riffled through papers.

"I would offer you a cup of coffee, but that's reserved for friends," Nick said as he followed Howard to the kitchen.

Howard didn't reply as he looked through drawers and the kitchen cabinets. From the kitchen, he went to the living room, where he looked in the coat closet.

Nick started to get nervous when Howard went upstairs. Howard started in the spare room, opening and closing drawers and checking the closet, becoming more frustrated that he wasn't finding anything.

He took a cursory look into the bathroom before heading to the master bedroom. Nick was glad he had told Hana to pack her things. but hoped that she hadn't left anything non-American behind. The last place to look was the closet.

Hana heard the bedroom door open and cringed. She tried to make herself into a smaller ball and held her breath as she heard Nick's voice and then the voice of the man searching the room. The closet door opened so suddenly that Hana almost yelped.

"You break it, the cost is yours," Nick said.

She could tell he was close to the man, and she suspected why. *Go away*, she willed the man. *Go away.*

"Satisfied?" Nick asked.

The closet door closed, and Hana sagged with relief.

"Now, you bastard, you've searched my home and found nothing. Not even the woman who is in Manzanar," Nick said. "I expect you to keep your word and stay the hell away from me, and that means you don't con some rookie into doing surveillance for you. The minute I think you've gone back on your word, your ass is mine. Now get the fuck out."

Howard didn't reply as he walked to the front door. That would be the last time Nick would ever see Howard. He would be gone by the time he arrived at the office the next day.

Nick waited until he saw the taillights of Howard's car disappear before running up the stairs, calling Hana's name. Hana came out of the closet and hugged Nick.

"It's all right; he won't be back," Nick told her.

"You're sure?" Hana asked.

"I'm sure," Nick assured her and held her tight. "It's late; let's go to bed."

Hana nodded, knowing that it wasn't sleep Nick had in mind. Nick let her go and went back downstairs to check the locks on the windows and doors. He put a chair under the doorknob of each door and what he called a security stick at the base of the patio door. The only way in now was to break a window. Satisfied, Nick went back upstairs and loaded his gun. Hana's eyes grew wide when she saw the gun. She hated guns; they had always frightened her, and she hated the fact that Nick thought he might need his.

Seeing Hana's fear, Nick put the gun in the top drawer of his bedside table, got undressed, and waited for Hana. As he waited, he thought about their options. The best plan was to take Hana to Abby's, but now that Howard wasn't a threat, she would refuse to go. Nick still wondered if there wasn't a place somewhere that would be big enough for all of them and decided that the next time he drove up to Manzanar, he would look around.

Hana came to bed wearing only the one of Nick's shirts, even though she had something of her own that she could wear. Nick wrapped both arms around her once she was settled and stroked her dark hair until she fell asleep. His intent had been to make love, but Hana was exhausted and needed to sleep—so did he, for that matter.

The next morning, Hana didn't get up as she usually did; instead, she held on to him.

"Hana, it's all right," Nick assured her.

Hana nodded, but she wasn't convinced. She didn't want Nick to leave, and she didn't want to be alone in the house. "Nick I . . . I'm afraid. I do not trust that he won't be back."

Nick weighed his options. Hana did have a point; what if Howard did come back, even though he gave his word?

"All right; get dressed. I'll take you over to Abby's for the day. No one will be there, but you'll be safe."

Hana breathed a sigh of relief; she had already decided that if she had to stay in the house alone, she was going to hide in the closet for the day. She understood why he chose Abby's house instead of Ralph's; if they had to leave, there would be one less person to worry about.

After Nick took Hana to Abby's, he went into work. He became curious when ten o'clock came and there was no Howard. He went to Howard's office, finding it cleaned out.

"He's gone," a voice behind him said.

"Where'd he go?" Nick asked, looking at the empty desk.

"Word has it he transferred to the Sacramento office."

"Kind of sudden, isn't it?" Nick asked.

"Yeah, well, he didn't have too many friends here, but when he started accusing you of being a spy and broke into your house, he lost the few friends he had."

Nick turned around to face the speaker. "Lou, isn't it?" Nick asked, recognizing the agent as one of those who had been watching Abby's house.

"Yeah, I just got transferred here," he replied. "Gibbs took my spot in Sacramento, but I have to say I was pissed at first, but man oh man, I like LA."

It occurred to Nick that Lou seemed to know a lot for someone who had just transferred in and was determined to keep an eye on him. It also occurred to him that Howard knew what was coming. That's why he was still following him; he was hoping to save his job here, but not finding anything sealed his fate.

"I hear you're newly married," Lou said after a minute.

Nick's guard went up; it could be just idle chatter, but he didn't think so. "Yes," he replied.

"That's nice. Me? I don't ever plan to get married—too many women to fuck."

Nick found the man slightly repulsive, but smiled at the comment. "Welcome aboard, Lou," he said, extending his hand.

"Thanks; hey, do you suppose they'd mind if I used this office instead of the one over in the corner?" Lou asked, shaking Nick's hand.

Warning flags went up. Lou was up to something, and Nick was determined to find out what. "I don't think so, but you better check with Maggie over there. She'll be able to tell you if that spot's spoken for," Nick advised. He watched as Lou made his way over to Maggie and started to flirt with her. He saw Maggie nod her head yes and knew that Lou was going to be moving into Howard's old office. Nick cursed under his breath, and headed to his office and closed the door.

Kenji and Hana watched Ralph with growing concern. Kenji searched through the medical journals that went wherever he did to see if he could figure out what was wrong with him. After searching for several hours, he finally narrowed it down to something in the respiratory system and not the heart, which was of some relief. After another two hours, Kenji decided it was likely that Ralph had pneumonia and he had to get to a doctor, but Ralph was adamant about not going. Kenji put the books away and went to look for Ralph.

He was sitting at the kitchen table drinking a cup of coffee when Kenji found him. Ralph looked up when he heard Kenji come into the room.

"Morning," Ralph said.

"Good morning, Ralph," Kenji replied, as he sat at the table across from Ralph.

"Want a cup of coffee?"

"No thank you," Kenji replied. "Ralph, I believe I know what is wrong with you—"

"Don't start that again!" Ralph exclaimed. "I'm fine!"

"I believe you have pneumonia and you must see a doctor."

"I'm not going to spend money on a doctor—" Ralph started to say.

"Yes you are, old man," Abby said from behind him. "And we're going now."

"Abby—"

"Don't you 'Abby' me! You're sick and you know it. Why you refuse to go to the doctor I don't know or understand, but you are going."

"I can't," Ralph said softly.

Kenji and Abby looked at each other, but it was Kenji who spoke. "Tell us why."

With halting words and tears, Ralph told them about Ada and his refusal to spend money on a doctor.

"That's why I can't go. I can't do something for myself when I refused to do it for my wife."

No one spoke for a few minutes.

"Ralph," Kenji said. "We're sorry for your loss, but that doesn't change the fact that you'll die if you don't go to a doctor."

Ralph looked away. "No."

"You selfish son of a bitch!" Abby snarled.

Both Kenji and Ralph stared at her; they had never heard her use a curse word stronger than "damn," and they had never heard her call anyone names.

"You came into our lives, got us to love you, and you don't care enough about us to live?"

"Abby—"

"No, you listen to me! I'm sorry that your wife died. Whether she would have lived had you called the doctor, I don't know, but I do know this: we wouldn't want you to die if there was a way for you to live. We all love and need you. You're part of this totally unorthodox family, so get your coat. I'm taking you to the doctor."

Abby grabbed her purse and waited by the door. When Ralph didn't move, Abby grabbed his hand and gave it a hard squeeze. "Ralph, please."

Slowly Ralph got up and headed for the door, with Abby following him.

Patricia came downstairs with Niko just after Ralph and Abby left. Kenji reached for the baby and kissed him when he had him in his arms. He told her that Abby had taken Ralph to the doctor, even though he protested.

"Thank God! I was worried about him," Patricia said, as she made breakfast for them.

"I was, too," Kenji replied as he readjusted Niko in his arms. "*Kirei*."

"No."

"*Kirei*, we have to talk," Kenji insisted.

"I know what you want to talk about, and I don't want to hear it," Patricia said, already crying. She hated these talks; it meant Kenji was thinking they were going to be found. He had wanted to talk soon after they moved back to Ralph's, but she wouldn't allow it. Now he was demanding that they talk.

Kenji gave her a minute to calm down before continuing. "If anything happens, I want you and Niko to go to your parents' home. This war cannot last forever, and when I'm released, I'll look for you there. Don't forget to take the money; your parents will need help keeping you and Niko fed."

Patricia took a deep breath. The thought of them being apart again was too much; this war was too much. All she wanted was to live in peace with Kenji and Niko. Patricia stood at the sink shaking. He was right; they needed to have a plan, but. . . .

"*Kirei*," Kenji whispered in her ear; she hadn't heard him move. "It is just a precaution and nothing more. I have to know that you and Niko will be cared for."

Patricia turned around in his arms. "I know; I'm just so tired of it all, and I know you are too, but—"

Niko began to cry, interrupting her thought. Patricia went to go comfort him, but Kenji stopped her. "He will be fine for a moment; finish your thought."

Patricia hesitated. "I'm scared so much of the time. When you were in the camp, I was scared something was going to happen to you; now I'm scared they're going to find you and take you away from us, and now there's Ralph."

Niko's cries became more insistent; Kenji let Patricia go and went to pick the baby off of the floor, picking up the blanket he had been lying on at the same time.

"Come with me, *Kirei*," Kenji said as he headed toward the living room. He sat on the couch, laid the baby across his lap, and began to lightly stroke his back; in minutes he was asleep.

"I love how you are with him," Patricia said.

"He's a good, strong boy," Kenji said, still stroking Niko's back. Then he turned his attention to Patricia. "*Kirei*, you are one of the strongest people I know. Many women would have run by now because of the difficulties, but you're still here. I sense your fear; it is evident when you sleep, and between that and Niko, you're not resting. Tonight, Abby will take care of Niko and it will be just you and me, talking and making love."

Patricia nodded; it had been quite a while since they spent any real time alone and even longer since she'd had a good night's sleep.

Kenji put his arm around her and encouraged her to rest her head on his shoulder. "Sleep now," he said, kissing her head.

Patricia snuggled closer and closed her eyes; the next thing she knew, Abby and Ralph were coming into the living room.

"Isn't that a sight?" Ralph said.

Patricia had slept for over an hour and felt better. Niko was still sleeping across Kenji's lap, with Kenji's free hand resting lightly on his back.

"What did the doctor say?" Patricia asked.

"That the old coot will probably live until he's as old as Methuselah; he's got pneumonia, just like Kenji said," Abby said. "But if he hadn't come in, he would have died."

"Did he give you any medication?" Kenji asked.

"Something called penicillin," Ralph replied.

"And you'd better take all of it!" Abby said firmly as she went to the kitchen to get Ralph a glass of water.

Ralph took the first dose of the antibiotic and handed the glass back to Abby; he looked at them with tear-filled eyes and cleared his throat. "Thank you all for everything."

"Ralph," Patricia said softly. "You're family, and we all love you."

Ralph nodded and said, "I love you all, too, even that bossy old woman back there, but I have some things I haven't told any of you, and I would like to do that now, if I could."

All of them listened, spellbound, as Ralph talked about his life in South Carolina, Ada's death, his two sons leaving him alone, and the death of the black man in the woods.

"I was a coward; I did nothing to help that man, and I will always carry the guilt for letting Ada die and for not helping that man. That's part of the reason why I helped Kenji when he first came here, looking for a place for him and Patty. I didn't expect to come to think of you as family, and then came the old woman, Hana, and John and Hattie, all of whom have treated me with such warmth and respect."

No one spoke for several minutes, but Patricia broke the silence. "They would have killed you, too, and then you wouldn't be here with us."

"And you went back," Abby added. "You could have left that poor man hanging there, but you didn't. But not only that—you cried for him. In my book, that doesn't make you a coward. I don't know what to tell you about Ada other than what I told you earlier, but Ralph, we still love you and need you so stop being a damned martyr."

"Patricia and Abby are both right," Kenji said quietly. "Those men would have killed you, and we would have been denied the honor of knowing you as a friend and as family. I think you will always feel some guilt, but as Abby said, you cried for another human being who died in a horrific way. I am honored to call you my friend."

Ralph was speechless; he had expected to receive anger instead of the love and acceptance he was receiving.

"Have you tried to reach your sons?" Patricia asked.

"One of them is dead; he died at Pearl Harbor—and Kenji, don't you start feeling guilty; you weren't there. The other one is in South Carolina and has a least one child. He lost an arm over in Europe. Nick found out for me and got his number."

"Did you call?" Abby asked.

"I did and he . . . he wouldn't talk to me. He hung up," Ralph replied.

"I am so sorry," Patricia whispered as she got up from the couch and hugged Ralph.

"It's all right," Ralph said, returning the hug. "I have you all."

By the end of September 1943, John F. Kennedy's *PT-109* was sunk in the Solomon Islands; General George S. Patton was relieved of duty for ten months following an incident where he slapped Private Charles H. Kuhl with his gloves as he, Patton, was visiting wounded soldiers from the Sicilian campaign; the Battle of New Georgia in the Solomon Islands was won by the Allies; the Battle of Kursk was the first successful Soviet summer offensive of the war; and martial law replaced the Danish government while the Nazis occupied Denmark.

Allied forces, under the command of Bernard L. Montgomery, invaded Italy; an armistice was signed; and Italy dropped out of the war.

Germany began evacuating civilians from Berlin. Iran declared war on Germany after the surrender of Italy; the Allies landed at Salerno, Italy; the Germans commenced the Holocaust of Viannos, which lasted for three days; the Cephalonia Massacre, in which over 4,500 Italians were executed and another three thousand were lost at sea, began.

The people of Naples staged an uprising, believing the Allied forces were near. Many civilian lives were lost, and the Allies didn't appear.

The Danes sent many of their Jewish countrymen to Sweden via boat and saved the lives of many.

SEPTEMBER 1943

The move back to Abby's house had been made, and much to everyone's relief, Ralph was much better. Niko was crawling and getting into everything, but no one minded; it gave them something to do and provided some much-needed laughter.

Kenji and Patricia were glad that Niko had started sleeping through the night, although he was an early riser. More often than not, Kenji got up with him and let Patricia sleep; during his time alone with Niko, Kenji began to speak to him in Japanese.

"It is important that you know the native tongue of your father so you can teach it to your children, and they to theirs."

One morning, Patricia heard Kenji telling Niko this and realized they had never resumed her lessons. She tried to remember the phrases he had taught her and they came back to her rather easily. She waited by the doorway to give Kenji time to finish his time alone with Niko.

As she waited, she realized that as frightened as she was and was going to be, she loved her husband and her baby. The only things she would change if she could would be the hardships they had been through, but then maybe not—if anything, it made them stronger. She amended her thought: the only thing she would change was the fear, but then maybe even the fear had its place.

"I know you're there, *Kirei*," Kenji said.

"How do you do that?" Patricia asked for the thousandth time.

"I just have very good hearing," Kenji replied, chuckling.

"Did you have breakfast yet?" she asked.

"No, but Niko did, and he ate everything," Kenji said. He turned around to look at Patricia; something was different about her.

"*Kirei*, are you well?" he asked.

"I'm all right; what do you want with your tea?" Patricia asked, changing the subject.

"*Kirei*, you're lying to me," Kenji said softly.

"No, I'm not." Patricia said.

In her mind she really wasn't lying. She really was all right—just pregnant, and she didn't know how to tell Kenji. She even knew when it happened. It was the night at Ralph's house when Abby took Niko for the night; they had made love several times, with Kenji not pulling out in time once. They went through the usual agonizing over a possible pregnancy, but relaxed when Patricia bled just a little bit the following week; but it was nowhere near her usual menses. That had been a few weeks ago. Now she had the nausea but no vomiting and she was tired, just as she had been with Niko.

Just when she thought Kenji had let the subject drop, he brought it up again. "*Kirei*, you may not be lying, but you are keeping something from me. Now what is it?"

Patricia didn't say anything, but started to cry, which alarmed Kenji. She only cried when she was afraid or very happy, and he sensed that these weren't happy tears.

Ralph happened into the kitchen; he looked at Patricia and then at Kenji. He was about to leave when Kenji handed Niko to him. "Please, will you look after him for a few minutes? Patricia and I need to talk."

Ralph took the baby and left the kitchen, muttering about reading the paper together.

Kenji took Patricia's hand and led her to the small room Ralph had built in the back. When they were sitting, he hugged her close. "*Kirei*, tell me why you're crying," he urged.

"I . . . I'm sorry."

"What is it that you're sorry about?" Kenji asked calmly.

"I'm pregnant," she whispered and started crying again.

"*Kirei*, why are you sorry?"

"Because it's hard enough hiding with one baby, but two? And the house is already crowded and—"

"*Kirei*," Kenji interrupted. "I'm not angry, if that's what concerns you. I would be less than honest if I said the timing is good, but we'll manage as we always have, and who knows? Maybe this war will be over by the time the baby comes."

"You're not mad?"

"Why should I be angry?" Kenji asked. "I could never be angry with you, and I was there, too."

They talked together for a few more minutes; they would have to tell the others sooner rather than later. Any plans would have to be amended.

Hana was in the kitchen when she first heard the front door open; she stopped what she was doing and waited for Nick to call out. When she didn't hear him, her heart began to race. Whoever was in the living room was headed toward Nick's office.

She weighed her options. She wouldn't be able to make it upstairs without being seen or heard, and there was no real place to hide in the kitchen. That left the outside, but there was no place to hide out there either, other than the small storage shed in the back yard. Not knowing what else to do, Hana slipped out the back door, closed it behind her, ran to the small shed, and found it locked.

Hana hid behind the shed, trying to calm down enough so she could think. There were only two places she could go: Ralph's or Abby's. But everyone was at Abby's. She knew the general direction of where Abby lived, but had never actually seen the street address or the house, for that matter. She looked up at the sun, trying to figure out how long it would be till dark. *Not soon enough*, she thought to herself as she looked around. She couldn't just start walking; it would only be a matter of time before someone realized she wasn't American.

Hana took another look around, lay on her stomach, and crawled under the shed. It was barely high enough for her to squeeze under, but she managed. Just as she made it under the shed, she looked toward the house and saw a man looking out the kitchen window.

Lou knew Nick wouldn't be home for at least another hour. He, like Howard, believed that Nick was hiding something.

There was something about the way Nick had acted on the night they had been watching the house that triggered his suspicions.

After he had gone home that night, he called Howard.

"Nick showed up at the old woman's house."

"What did he want?" Howard asked.

"He wanted to know why he was still being followed, because the woman had been found. But here's the thing: when Chuck made a comment about a Jap broad being where she was supposed to be, I thought he was going to punch him."

"We all know he had a thing for the Jap, but she's at the camp. He's hiding something else."

As Lou went through Nick's house, he noticed that the house was masculine; there was nothing to indicate that a woman lived there, with the only exception being a slip on the bed.

"What are you up to?" Lou mumbled as he went from one room to another. "And where is your wife?"

Lou went back downstairs to the kitchen and stopped. Someone had just been here; the potato on the counter hadn't started to blacken yet, and the sink was still wet. He checked the cabinets and the pantry before deciding to make a more thorough search of the house, although his time was growing short. It was now clear that Nick was hiding someone, but whom?

Lou went back upstairs to Nick and Hana's room and began to look through the dressers. He grinned when he found some of Hana's underthings.

"Little one, aren't ya?" he murmured as he touched the underwear.

He looked under the bed and finally went to the closet. He was so intent on what he was doing, he never heard Nick come in until the barrel of his gun was against the back of his head.

"What the fuck are you doing in my house?"

Lou didn't say anything but moved suddenly, hoping to startle Nick into either dropping the gun or falling backward so he could escape, but it didn't work.

"Do that again and I swear to God, I'll shoot," Nick said calmly. "Now turn around."

Lou turned to face Nick.

"Did you really think I didn't know what you were up to?" Nick asked.

"Who else is here?" Lou asked, ignoring Nick's question.

"Do you see anyone else?" Nick asked.

"No, but the evidence is here."

"You really are a stupid son of a bitch, aren't you? Taking Howard's office so that you're close to me, asking about my private life, and then you come into my house uninvited—I believe that's called breaking and entering—and then you wonder why someone would hide? Downstairs. Now."

Even though Nick was outwardly calm, his heart was pounding. Where was Hana? She wasn't in the closet—Lou had it half emptied; he would have seen her. Maybe she was in the spare bedroom, but she had already started making dinner, so she had to be downstairs somewhere.

"Sit down," Nick said as he picked up the phone.

"Who are you calling?" Lou asked.

"The police; I found you in my house going through my personal things," Nick replied.

"You really are a slick bastard," Lou said.

A police car came a few minutes later and took Lou away. He wouldn't be out until sometime in the morning, and then he would have to explain what he was doing in Nick's house. Nick had had enough; he was resigning and that was the end of it.

He walked through the house calling her name, becoming panicked when he reached the last room where she could possibly be.

Hana was cramped, hungry, and thirsty, but she didn't budge from her spot. It was almost dark, and Nick should be home by now, unless he stayed late. She froze when she saw the silhouette of a man in the yard. It looked like Nick, but she couldn't be sure; she couldn't really see his face.

Her heart pounded as the man came closer to the shed; he was almost to the shed when she heard her name.

"Hana, baby, it's me."

Hana slid from under the shed and ran into Nick's arms, sobbing.

"Shhh, it's all right," Nick whispered as he picked Hana up and carried her into the house.

He set the tea kettle on, wet a washcloth, and washed Hana's dirty face and hands. He had to get her out of here; this was the second close call they'd had, and the next time they might not be so lucky.

He made her a cup of strong tea and went to his office. Lou hadn't ransacked it like Howard had, but it had been gone through. He went to the small closet, removed a small tackle box, and carried it to the kitchen. Hana had finished her tea and waited silently for Nick to say something.

"We're leaving," he told her as he opened the tackle box. It contained several official documents, including his passport and four thousand dollars in cash. He had been slowly withdrawing money from his bank account over the past several weeks in anticipation of having to leave. In the morning, he would go to the bank to withdraw the rest of his money and get the cash from his safety deposit box. After that, he would go to the office and resign, but for now, they would go to Abby's house.

"All right, baby, go take a quick shower and I'll pack for us. We're going to Abby's."

"I'm so sorry to have been so much trouble to you," Hana said, looking down at her hands.

"Hana, you aren't the problem, and if I had to do it all again, I would—except I wouldn't have taken so long to tell you how I felt. Now go on and get cleaned up," Nick said, giving her a kiss.

When she was out of earshot, Nick called Abby. "Make room because we're coming over. I'll tell you when we get there."

The nights were already getting colder at Manzanar. People were going to bed wearing their hats, gloves, and whatever else they could to keep warm. Hiroshi had convinced the woman to stay with him and stopped calling her a whore but her name, Ani.

The longer the war continued, the more disillusioned Hiroshi became with Japan. The stories about the torture of prisoners grew worse; the stories about the extermination of the Jews continued to the point where he had to admit there had to be some truth to them.

Being in the camp had given him a lot of time to think about his choices and where they had led him. He never would have accepted the black girl into his family, but maybe there could have been some compromise. He definitely shouldn't have conspired with Joben Saito to have the girl hurt and, from his point of view, that's where things went to hell.

He should have listened to Hana. If he had, he might still have his wife—but then, maybe not. He regretted working with Joben; it had led to nothing but trouble. They still would have ended up here, but. . . . He wondered if Hana would talk to him when this was over. He wanted and needed to apologize to her for everything. He wanted to apologize to Kenji, too, not because of his views—he still didn't want the black girl in his family—but for the fact that he had been in on the plan to hurt her.

Hiroshi snuggled closer to Ani, closed his eyes, and tried to block out the howling wind.

SEPTEMBER 30, 1943

Nick kissed Hana awake. "I've got to go, but I'll be back by this afternoon."

"Nick, please stay here," Hana said softly. "Don't go."

"I'll be all right; you just stay here and do what Ralph and Kenji say."

Hana hung on to Nick; she had a heavy feeling in the pit of her stomach. "Nick—"

"I'll be back, I promise," Nick said as he kissed her again. "I love you."

Hana watched Nick leave with a heavy heart and started to cry.

Nick went to the bank and withdrew his money, saying that he was buying a summer place for him and his wife. He then emptied the contents of the safety deposit box and headed to the office.

He walked into a decidedly cool reception, but he shook it off. He no longer cared; this was his last day at this place. He went to his office and found the director and the assistant director sitting in his office.

"Nick, have a seat," the assistant director said grimly.

An hour later, Nick was under arrest for the suspicion of being a spy.

Chapter 17

DECEMBER 8, 1943

Ani looked around as she followed Nick to the back of the dress shop; seeing no one, she relaxed slightly and looked up at Nick.

"Who are you, and why did you agree to pose as Hana Takeda?" he asked.

Ani blinked; she was unprepared for Nick's bluntness. "I am Ani," she said softly. "I have agreed to become Hana to compensate for an error on my part."

"Error? What error?" Nick asked.

"It was I who told them about your meeting with Hiroshi and about the papers."

"Wait, told who? And do they know you're posing as Hana Takeda?"

"The man at the office," Ani replied. "I was put with Hiroshi to report what he did and whom he talked to. I told them that Hiroshi wasn't spying, but then I mentioned the papers and they told me I had to keep watching him. They are not aware that I am pretending to be Hana."

"The man who told you to spy on Hiroshi; what's his name?" Nick asked.

"Mr. Mitch; I know because I heard someone say his name once," Ani replied.

"Describe him to me."

"He's tall, but not as tall as you, and he is thin with brown hair."

That's Mitch, all right, Nick thought. "Did you describe me to him?"

"Yes, because I did not know your name, but I have seen you here before, visiting with Hana and her son."

"How many times have you seen me?" Nick asked.

"Two times, and both times you were talking with Hiroshi."

The more Nick heard, the more it was becoming clear that Mitch was involved in this spy thing somehow and that he and Hiroshi were collateral damage.

"Have you seen me more than twice?" Nick asked.

"No, only those times. I'm sorry I said something about the papers; I didn't know what they were."

"Ani, did this man promise you something in return for helping him?"

Ani looked down and then back up. "He promised me a job and a place to live when the war was over. Is this not true?"

Nick didn't lie to her. "I don't know, but don't count on it. And don't give him any more information about Hiroshi. If he asks if I talked to you, don't lie—tell him yes and tell him this: Nick knows."

"Damn it! Answer the phone!" Mitch hissed. Everything had hinged on Nick being in prison; there was supposed to have been evidence linking Nick to the informant at the White House, so what in the hell happened to it? When Nick called to tell him he had been arrested, Mitch thought that meant everything was good, and now he was here.

"Fuck! Fuck! Fuck!" Mitch screamed and slammed the phone down.

He paced as he tried to figure out his next move. If he stayed, he was as good as caught, and so was his Japanese contact to whom he had been feeding information. He had to reach him and tell him to destroy the radio, but wait a minute. . . . They wouldn't come after him, at least not right away. He had time to think. First they would go after the jabbermouth at the White House who talked too much. It would cut off any flow of information, but he wouldn't be caught, and he still would have a chance to somehow plant the evidence on Nick. *If* his fucking contact would pick up the phone!

He hated using Nick the way he had, but this was war, and the emperor needed all the help he could get. It was a stroke of sheer luck when he was approached about joining the agency, and it was only because he had been living and working in Japan for years and spoke several of the dialects fluently that he had been asked. His Japanese wife and son still lived in Hiroshima and were waiting for his return, and he did plan to return, as soon as he could. He had seen them last in 1940, just before he came to the States to take care of some business matters, but he called and spoke with them whenever he could.

After he had accepted the position, it was relatively easy to set up his network, especially in the Japanese section of town. That idiot Joben Saito was instrumental in helping him do that; Mitch had a brief moment of anxiety when he heard that Saito was at Manzanar. . . .

For all of Saito's bravado, he was a coward and would have talked to save his own ass, but Takeda took care of that for him, or at least Mitch assumed it had been Takeda. Like everyone else who suspected him, Mitch had no proof, but it didn't matter. Saito was dead and no longer posed a threat.

Somehow, he had to put the attention on the jabbermouth and then take himself out of the equation and put Nick back in. They still needed to get rid of the shortwave radio, and that shouldn't be too difficult, but maybe. . . . He could call in an anonymous tip and somehow connect the man at the White House to Nick and then to his contact here. It could work—it had to work—and then he would start his escape plan and make his way back to Hiroshima, where his wife and son were waiting for him.

Nick stopped at the hospital before he left the camp; there was no way he was staying after what Ani had just told him. He would be dead by morning. Mitch was the spy, but he couldn't prove it. Any evidence he had against Mitch would be circumstantial, and he needed definitive proof. He didn't know who Mitch's contact here was, and there was no easy way to find out—there were over ten thousand Japanese at the camp. The questions were: whom was Mitch getting his information from, whom was he giving it to, and why in the hell would he spy for Japan?

He found Dr. Mynt in his office, packing.

"Where are you going?" Nick asked, surprised.

"Back to private practice, I guess. What brings you here?" Dr. Mynt asked as he threw some books into a box.

"Business; why are you leaving?" Nick asked.

"I spent too much money—they found some young hotshot who claims he can run this place on a lot less money," Dr. Mynt replied.

"They can do that?" Nick asked.

"Appears so; how are my friends?" he asked, meaning Kenji and Ralph.

"Fine, but worried about his wife and baby. . . . When were you going to leave?" Nick asked.

"As soon as I can get a ride to Independence; why?"

"How would you like to see your friends again?" Nick asked.

"I would like that, but where would I stay? I'm sure their house is full."

"Yes, but mine isn't," Nick replied.

"Well, damn, I guess I'm going to visit friends! Let me grab a few things and we'll be on our way."

"A few things" consisted of pain medications, sedatives, antibiotics, IV tubing and fluids, and surgical equipment and garb.

"Always be prepared!" Dr. Mynt quipped as he filled a box with the supplies and then grabbed several syringes. A few minutes later they were on the road, headed down the mountain.

Ani waited for two hours before she went to Mitch's office and timidly knocked on the door.

"What?" Mitch asked impatiently; he still hadn't been able to reach his contact in the office.

"Mr. Alexander, he came to talk to me," Ani said, just as she had rehearsed.

Mitch stopped what he was doing and looked at her. "Well, what did he want?"

"He told me to give you a message."

"Just spit it out! I'm busy!" Mitch snapped.

"He said to tell you that Nick knows."

"What? What does he know?" Mitch demanded.

"He did not say; he only said to tell you that Nick knows."

"Get out!" Mitch said as he stood up.

Ani didn't need to be told twice; she practically ran out of the office and to the space she shared with Hiroshi, and packed her few belongings. She was gone before Hiroshi returned from his evening walk.

Patricia was actually feeling better, but Kenji wouldn't let her out of bed.

"Can I at least go downstairs and sit on the couch?" she begged.

"No, *Kirei*, I don't know what's causing these episodes, and I want you in bed if it happens again."

She was tired of being in bed and missed being around people, even though people came and went all day to keep her company. Kenji brought Niko up several times a day and allowed him to sit or lie on the bed beside Patricia, moving him when he became too rambunctious. Kenji split his time between Niko and her and was rapidly approaching the exhaustion point again and, like everyone else, he was worried for Nick.

Patricia watched Kenji as he read through his books again, trying to prepare for every eventuality, including a cesarean section. He already had Abby sharpen and sterilize her sharpest knives and had her seal the sharpest ones in canning jars. The bedroom was beginning to look like a hospital ward; everything was moved up from the basement and arranged in the room.

Patricia was petrified and tried not to show it by talking about whatever came to mind. She looked over at Kenji and saw his eyes closing, and noticed for the first time the lines of worry around his eyes. He needed sleep; he needed to feel like the man he was, and the only way that was going to happen was for the war to end.

Hana peeked into the room and saw Kenji sleeping in the chair; she nodded at Patricia and closed the door.

"Kenji?" Patricia called softly.

He was instantly awake. "*Kirei*? Are you all right?"

"I'm all right; I just need you here beside me for awhile. Your mom is watching Niko," she added.

Kenji kicked off his shoes and slid into the bed beside her. He lay on his back and put an arm around her. It was the "I want to say something" position. Patricia didn't say anything but waited.

"I heard you talking to our baby this morning," he said. "You told her that she would be all right, that she is strong, and that she is a Takeda. So are you, *Kirei*. You may not be a Takeda by blood, but you are a Takeda in that you have the courage and strength for which our family is known. I am proud that you are my wife."

Patricia kissed Kenji's cheek, reached up, and began to stroke his forehead until he was snoring softly. In his sleep, he turned on his side, pulled her tight against him, and rested a hand on her stomach. For the first time since this pregnancy began, Patricia felt hope that just maybe the baby would be all right.

"Paul, there's something I need to tell you," Nick said as he drove down the mountain.

"Go on."

"Hana Takeda is my wife."

"I figured as much when I saw that wedding band, but it isn't legal."

"No, not yet," Nick replied.

"Is she going to be all right with me at your place?'

"She might be a little nervous at first, but she'll be fine," Nick assured him.

"What do you know about the pregnancy?" Paul asked.

"Not much other than what Kenji told you; are they going to lose the baby?"

"I don't know—maybe. But I'll know better once I see her. You know, that boy is going to be one hell of a doctor."

"He already is," Nick said proudly and told Paul about the preparations Kenji had already made.

They talked all the way to Abby's house, not even stopping to eat, partly because Nick was in a hurry to get home and partly because he didn't trust Mitch not to have something planned. Nick kept watching the rearview mirror for signs that he was being followed. If Paul noticed, he didn't say anything as he continued to chat about this and that.

It took Hiroshi several hours before he realized Ani wasn't coming back, and he couldn't say he blamed her. He had absolutely nothing to offer, and at one time he was a conspirator against America. She had helped him by continuing to be Hana, and that was more than he could have asked for, but he wondered why she didn't at least say goodbye.

Hiroshi huddled under the blankets, missing the warmth of Ani's body, and actually considered finding one of the *shoufu*—whores—to come warm him. No one would think twice about it since he and "Hana" had been divorced. He did a mental count of the money he had left and the money he had saved from his meager earnings at the camp and decided to pass on the whore. Surely there would be someone who would be willing to sleep with him for warmth and companionship and cost nothing.

As he shivered under the covers, he thought about what Nick had said about Kenji and realized that he was right. He didn't have to agree with Kenji's decisions to be proud of him, and he had been the one to teach him honor and courage. And he, Hiroshi, had been the one to lose his honor, as well as everything else. He had to ask himself: If he had the chance to approach his son, would he? And what about the woman? Could he bring himself to acknowledge what he tried to have done to her? And what if there were children? What then? He was certain Hana would have accepted them if there were any. He compared himself to Hana and Kenji; they had each other and people who loved and cared for them while he had no one who would risk their freedom to help him. He closed his eyes and fell asleep, undecided about what he was going to do.

It was almost nine o'clock when Nick pulled into Abby's driveway and beeped the horn, announcing his arrival. Hana ran to the kitchen and waited by the door for Nick to come in. As soon as he was through the door, she threw herself into his arms and hugged him.

"Are you hurt?" she asked, as she ran her hands up and down his arms.

"I'm fine, sweetheart," Nick assured her and kissed her. "I brought an old friend with me," he said and motioned for Paul to come in.

"Paul? That you?" Ralph asked, coming into the kitchen when he heard voices.

"How are you?" Paul asked. "Nick told me you had a 'bout of pneumonia."

"I'm good; Dr. Kenji said that's what it was and made me go to the doctor. It sure is good to see you!" Ralph said, shaking Paul's hand.

"The same here; where's Kenji?" Paul asked.

"Upstairs with Patty," Ralph replied. "He's been beating his head against the wall trying to figure out what's wrong with her and the baby."

"Well, I hope we can figure it out; is it all right to go upstairs?"

"Yeah, but before you do, you should meet two people," Ralph said. "Wait here."

He came back later with Abby in tow and Niko in his arms. "Abby, this is Paul Mynt; he's the one that gave Kenji and Patty a place to spend the day up at the camp. And Paul, this is Abby; she owns this house and has been helping Patty and Kenji from the beginning."

Abby and Paul shook hands. "Are you hungry? We have some leftovers from dinner."

"That would be very nice. Thank you," Paul said with a smile. "And who is this young man?" he asked, smiling at Niko.

"This is Niko, Kenji and Patricia's boy; he's coming up on a year old in February and as smart as a whip!" Ralph bragged.

"Hello, young man!" Paul greeted Niko. None of his normally brusque manner was evident as he looked Niko over with a practiced eye. "You're a fine young man, and we're going to see what we can do about your mama," he said, patting Niko on the leg.

Patricia lay awake listening to Kenji snore and feeling his warm breath blow over her face. She didn't do much, but she felt like she did something besides just lying in bed and letting him take care of her. Eventually she fell asleep after repeating several times to the baby, "You will be all right; you have to be."

Kenji stirred and tried to move slowly so he wouldn't wake her.

"I'm awake and I really need the bathroom," she said.

Kenji got up first and then helped Patricia up.

"Kenji, I'm fine," she said, as he held on to her as they walked to the bathroom.

He waited outside the door for her, helped her back to bed, and then used the bathroom himself.

"Feel better?" Patricia asked.

"I do, thank you. Did you rest?" Kenji asked.

"I slept some. . . . Who's here?" Patricia asked, straining her ears.

"I don't know, but stay put," Kenji replied.

After helping Patricia back to bed, Kenji crept down the stairs, listening, and stopped. Dr. Mynt?

Ralph was on his way up to get him when he saw him on the stairs. "Nick's back, and guess who he brought back with him?'

"Dr. Mynt is here?" Kenji asked. "How is this possible?"

"Doesn't matter," Ralph replied. "He's here, and maybe the two of you can figure out what's happening with Patty and the baby."

Kenji shook Paul's hand several times. "How is it that you're here?"

"Let's just say it was a financial move on the part of the government. So tell me what's happening with Patty."

Ralph bristled; he was the only one who called her that.

Abby noticed and intervened. "Ralph gets a little territorial with his names; apparently he has the sole rights to calling Patricia 'Patty.'"

"What? Oh, I see," Paul said. "Kenji, may I go up to see Patricia?"

"Of course, but let me go tell her you're coming up."

When Kenji was gone, Paul looked around the kitchen. "You have one hell of a household here."

"Yes, we do," Nick replied as he helped Abby set the table for him and Paul.

"*Kirei*, are you awake?" Kenji asked softly.

"Yes, who's here?"

"Nick's back, and he brought Dr. Mynt with him."

"Nick's home? Is he all right?"

"Yes, *Kirei*, he's fine, but Dr. Mynt would like to see you. May he come in?"

"As long as you stay," she replied nervously, as she remembered the last time a doctor had seen her in the very same room.

An hour later, Patricia had been examined from head to toe with Kenji holding her hand. She answered every question, some of them rather embarrassing, as honestly as she could.

"What do you think?" she asked anxiously.

"I think we might be looking at a vitamin deficiency," Paul said. "Your baby isn't even a year old and you're pregnant again—add that to the fact that you aren't eating near enough fruits and vegetables. Maybe there wasn't enough time for your body to fully recover, but I want you to eat double helpings of fruits and vegetables, particularly fruits high in vitamin C and vegetables like spinach and beets."

"The baby is all right?" Patricia asked.

"I think so, but of course I can't swear to it. But I would like for you to stay in bed for a few more days, and then we'll see."

Paul reached into his bag, took out a small packet of pills, and handed them to Kenji. "This is a mild sedative; it won't hurt the baby, but will help Patricia get some rest. Only give her one if she's anxious and can't sleep. I'll be staying over at Nick's, so I'll be available."

Patricia reached for Paul's hand. "Thank you."

"You're welcome," he replied, giving her hand a squeeze.

He looked around the bedroom, taking in the instruments that had been sterilized and stored in canning jars.

"I check the seals several times a day," Kenji said.

"Amazing," Paul breathed as he took in the makeshift hospital room. "I brought some surgical instruments with me; I'll bring them up and you can put them where you want. Just a question: are you really ready to perform a cesarean on your wife?"

"If need be . . . yes," Kenji replied. "I have the procedure memorized and have studied the diagrams. I look at it several times a day, but I'm glad you're here."

A week later, Patricia was allowed out of bed. She felt better and ate her vegetables, even the ones she hated, reminding herself that it was for the baby.

Hattie and Ralph met Paul during their weekly visit.

"Say, Paul, you play chess, don't you?" Ralph asked.

"Sure I do; want a game?"

"Play, John; I'll watch."

Ralph laughed as John beat Paul not once but three times.

"It's good to watch someone else get their ass whipped," he said, laughing at the expression on Paul's face.

By the end of January 1944, the Battle of Monte Cassino, a.k.a. the Battle for Rome, began. It would consist of four battles fought between the Allied forces and the German and Italian forces, with the goal being to take Rome—the Americans were driven off during the first battle.

The 1st Ukrainian Front of the Red Army entered Poland; Filipino troops fought the Japanese in the Provence of Ilocos Sur in the Philippines; Count Ciano, Italy's foreign minister and the son-in-law to Mussolini, was executed by fascist government sympathizers; the Royal Air Force dropped 2,300 tons of bombs on Berlin; the US Army 36th Infantry Division attempted to cross the Rapido River with heavy losses; and Operation Shingle—the amphibious landing against the Axis powers in the area of Anzio and Nettuno, Italy—began.

The American 45th Infantry Division would hold their ground for four months against German artillery and troop attacks.

The Japanese killed forty-four Indians and civilians in the Andaman Islands, which was located between India to the west and Burma to the northeast. The Indians and civilians were suspected of spying; this would come to be considered the worst atrocity during the Japanese occupation of the Andaman Islands. The American forces landed on Kwajalein Atoll and other islands held by the Japanese.

Ralph read the paper from front to back, still looking for any news of the release of the Japanese from the interment camps. He remained the source of information about the war if anyone wanted to know anything.

The feeling that he wouldn't live to see the end of the war had long departed, but only because Abby and Kenji made him go to the doctor. If he hadn't, he would have been dead by now.

From time to time, he thought about his only living son, Lawrence, and thought about trying to call him again. What stopped him was remembering the cold tone in which Lawrence had said, "It's nobody." But still. . . . He thought and then turned his attention back to the paper.

"This can't last much longer," Ralph muttered as he took note of the latest death count. He felt as Kenji did: war was a terrible waste of human life. The man who started this wasn't out on the battlefield; he was hunkered down in a bunker or somewhere safe from the bullets and grenades.

He looked down at Niko, who was playing with the wooden blocks Nick had made and sanded down. "I hope to God there isn't another war in your lifetime," he said.

Patricia was back on bed rest; her time of feeling better was over, and the same complaints of not feeling well had returned, but with increasing intensity. Ralph could hear the anxiety in her voice as she talked with Kenji and Dr. Mynt, and then her quiet sobs. He closed his eyes and said a quick prayer for all of them.

Paul came down a few minutes later, looking grim.

"What's happening?" Ralph asked.

"I don't know, but the baby's heartbeat is erratic at times, and then it goes back to normal."

"What does that mean?" Ralph asked anxiously.

"It means we might have to take the baby by cesarean," Paul replied. "We need her to carry that baby for as long as she can, and this is too soon."

"She needs to be in a hospital, doesn't she?"

Paul sighed. "Yes, but you and I both know what'll happen if she has that baby in a hospital: they'll take it, and all of us will be tossed into prison. The only thing we can do is hope and pray for the best."

"How is she?"

"Scared; I made her take one of the sedatives so she'll sleep."

Ralph hesitated and then asked the question he didn't want to hear the answer to. "Paul, is the baby going to die?"

"I don't know," Paul replied.

"Do they know?" Ralph asked.

"They know, but they're hoping for the best."

Ralph went silent. *When are those two going to catch a break?* he thought to himself.

Kenji held Patricia in his arms and gently rocked her until she fell asleep. He was as scared as she was, but he wouldn't and couldn't show it. She needed him to be confident, even if he didn't feel that way; if he fell apart, then so would she.

It had taken considerable coaxing to get Patricia to take the sedative. Her fear was that it would somehow diminish the chances of the baby surviving.

"Patricia, honey, we need you to carry this baby for as long as you can, and in order to do that, you have to stay in bed, rest, and stay calm. The pill is a light sedative that will help you get some rest, and it won't hurt the baby."

The heartbreaking part for Paul was when Patricia asked him if the baby was going to die. He had to swallow hard and blink back tears as he answered her, "I don't know. It's possible, but we'll do the best we can so that it doesn't happen."

Kenji kissed Patricia, eased her onto the bed, and lay down beside her. As he watched her sleep, he thought about their time together. They had been through more hardships than a couple that had been together for twenty years, and while there were happy memories, there were far too many ones filled with pain.

Paul offered to explain the situation to everyone else, and Kenji accepted. He wasn't leaving Patricia alone if he could help it. He wasn't concerned that Niko wouldn't be cared for; he knew he would be, but he had to be careful that he himself didn't neglect him.

"*Kirei*," he murmured, "we will get through this."

Patricia opened her eyes and closed them, still feeling the effects of the sedative. Just as she drifted back to sleep, her eyes snapped open. The baby. Their baby might die.

Kenji woke as soon as he felt her stir and relaxed when she drifted back to sleep for a few minutes, only to tense when she woke again shaking.

"Th—this isn't fair," she cried as she clung to him. "This isn't . . . what did we do that was so wrong?" she sobbed.

"Nothing, *Kirei*, we did nothing wrong," Kenji assured her.

"Do you think if I had told you sooner that I was sick, it would be different?"

"No, *Kirei*, I don't. It's as I said before: the fault lies with no one," Kenji replied as he fought back tears. He hated that there was nothing he could do to ease her fears.

Dinner was quiet, with all of the women sniffling.

"Is there any chance the baby will be all right?" Abby asked.

"There's a chance that everything will be all right," Paul said, "but there is the possibility that the baby could die."

"What about Patty?" Ralph asked. "She won't die, will she?"

"I won't lie and say that it can't happen, but she's strong and healthy. She should be fine," Paul replied.

Hattie and John remained silent; they were each saying silent prayers for Patricia and the baby as Hattie held Niko in her lap.

Of all of the women, only Hana knew the pain of losing a child. She gave Nick's hand a squeeze and excused herself. She went upstairs and found Kenji and Patricia talking quietly; she paused and listened to Kenji's soft voice as he tried to soothe a very anxious Patricia.

She tapped on the door and waited for one of them to tell her to come in. Kenji responded to the knock and seemed glad to see her.

"May I have a moment with my daughter?" Hana asked.

Kenji kissed Patricia before getting up from the bed, and kissed Hana on the way out.

Hana sat on the bed beside Patricia and took her hand.

"What happened to your baby?" Patricia asked softly.

"Kenji told you about his brother?" Hana asked.

"Not much, only that he died."

"I do not know for certain," Hana replied. "Kenji was two years of age at the time, and Hiro was four. We knew he wasn't well but thought it was something he had eaten; he loved sweets as much as Kenji does and often overindulged. Over two days his condition worsened, and we called for the doctor. He died two days later."

"How do you deal with something like that?" Patricia asked.

Hana hesitated. "Patricia, there is no easy way to deal with something like that, but you have something that I didn't have at the time. You have a husband who is willing to grieve and stay with you. Hiroshi cried for a moment, became stoic, and then left me to grieve alone."

"He didn't help you?" Patricia asked, stunned. "He left you alone?"

"No, he didn't help or stay with me, but you have Kenji and all of us to help you if the baby should die. You will not have to go through this alone."

"Hana? I don't want her to die," Patricia said, crying again.

"None of us wants her to die," Hana soothed. "But maybe she won't. Maybe she will be born beautiful and strong. Maybe she will have a major contribution to make to the world. I told you what I did because I wanted you to know I understand that kind of pain."

Patricia hugged Hana and asked to speak Hattie.

A few minutes later, Hattie was sitting on the bed, holding Patricia as she cried.

"Mama?'

"Yes, baby?"

"If she dies, she'll go to heaven, won't she?"

"Yes, baby, I believe *if* she dies she will go to heaven."

Patricia nodded and prayed for the life of her baby.

Mitch still hadn't figured out how to connect the White House informant to Nick, and his time was getting short. Already people were sniffing around and asking him questions that were hitting a little too close to home, but that wasn't the worst of it—he still hadn't talked to his contact at the office where Nick worked.

His contact in the camp still had the radio, and it was probably time to have it destroyed. He still hadn't figured out what Nick knew or thought he knew—maybe it was a bluff, but then maybe not. It was time to leave and go home to his wife and son. He had done all he could do for Japan and the emperor without giving his own life.

He started to pack his papers into his briefcase without really looking at what they were. Afterward, he went to his room to grab his suitcase to leave; his Japanese contact was on his own.

When he got to his room, he found his office contact waiting.

"What in the hell are you doing here?" he asked. "I've been trying to reach you!"

His contact looked at him but didn't respond.

"What the fuck happened down there? Nick is supposed to be in prison and he showed up here! What happened?"

"I couldn't get the evidence."

"What do you mean, you couldn't get the evidence? All you had to do was put some papers in the damned desk! What was so hard about that?" Mitch asked.

"Mitch—"

"Don't 'Mitch' me! What the fuck happened?"

"Mitch, don't—"

"Mitchell Jackson, you are under arrest for the act of treason against the United States of America," a voice from behind him said.

"No! Nick Alexander is your spy!" Mitch yelled. "Lou! Tell them!"

"It's over," Lou said sadly.

Mitch had one hope left, and that was that they didn't know who his contact in the camp was. Without him and the radio, the evidence would be circumstantial; they couldn't prove anything, as he had never met the man at the White House face to face.

That hope was dashed when a military policeman came in carrying the shortwave radio, while another had his contact in handcuffs.

Elam stepped forward and looked at Mitch. "You almost destroyed the life of a man you called a friend and you conspired against your own country; why?"

"That's your fault!" Mitch replied. "You're the ones that approached me and asked me to help you! I simply took advantage of the opportunity to help Japan."

"But why? Why would you help the enemy of this country?" Elam asked.

"I haven't considered myself an American citizen for years," Mitch replied. "My home, my wife, and my child are in Japan. I never wanted to come back here, but I did for the emperor. As far as Nick is concerned, I never wanted to use him the way I did, but this is war and he was collateral damage. But let me ask you this: how did you know it was me?"

"A few things: First of all, Nick brought it to my attention that the only person who knew how often he came up here was you. He also told us you were a little too willing to help him with a few things of which he won't divulge the details, and then there's your office contact. He fucked up; he ran his big mouth and talked about things there was no way he should have known about—things that were at the White House level. It wasn't hard to see what happened, and then there was your contact here; we've known for a while that the radio was here, but we weren't sure where the information was coming from. And, as you know, we thought it was Nick and Hiroshi Takeda working together, but we couldn't pin anything on Nick without concrete evidence.

"You weren't the only one with people working for you. Takeda was cleared, and the same contact was gathering information for us. You, your buddy Lou here, and your contact here are going to prison for a good, long time," Elam said.

"Wait!" Mitch cried. "My wife, my son! They're in Japan!"

"Not my problem," Elam replied and walked away.

Hiroshi patted the behind of his new wife. Physically, she resembled Hana much more than Ani had, and personality-wise, she was similar to Hana as well. He liked her well enough, especially since she was young enough to give him children and would follow him no matter where he ended up.

He had already told her she was to be his wife and she hadn't objected when he picked a day and found someone to perform the ceremony. In a way, it simplified things since he and Hana were supposed to be divorced. There was no longer the chance that he would mistakenly call Ani by her real name since they weren't together.

In the time when he was alone—before he married Dai (the irony didn't escape him that his new wife's name was the same as Joben's daughter)—he thought long and hard about what he should do about Kenji, if anything. Nick's words about Kenji being a man of honor and courage kept coming back to him. Maybe it was time for him to start making his way back to being the man who taught his son what it meant to have honor and courage. If he had to apologize to the girl, then so be it, but he didn't think he would ever change his views about her. But at the very least, he would try to make his amends with his son.

He still had one worry—the loyalty oath. Could he still take it? Tomorrow he would go up to the office and find out. His hope was that he would be able to stay in America and start over. If that happened, he vowed he would never conspire against this country again.

JANUARY 30, 1944

Patricia and Kenji had their good days and their bad. On the good days, Patricia was hopeful that everything would still be all right.

Kenji and Dr. Mynt checked for the baby's heartbeat two or three times a day and were always relieved when they heard it. It was still in the normal range and on occasion erratic, and it was still much too soon for the baby to be born. By their calculations, Patricia needed to carry the baby at least until April, and then they would take the baby by cesarean.

"Do you understand that there are no guarantees?" Paul asked when he, Kenji, and Patricia talked about their options. "The baby could be stillborn."

"We understand," Kenji said, holding Patricia's hand. "We will deal with whatever happens."

"All right, then," Paul said. "Let's keep our fingers crossed.

That afternoon, Kenji and Niko were reading with Patricia. Kenji had started reading to Niko whenever he had the chance and began teaching him very simple Japanese words.

Patricia felt a twinge in her back and moved to get more comfortable; twenty minutes later there was another twinge. *Oh God*, she prayed silently, *not yet; it's too soon.*

The twinges stopped, only to return an hour later.

"K—Kenji?" she stammered. Tears were already forming as she realized she was in labor.

Kenji looked up from the book, took in her frightened expression, and knew he had to calm her. "All right, *Kirei*, I'll be right back. Breathe as we have practiced," he said as he calmly picked Niko up and carried him out of the room.

He spoke to the boy in soothing tones. "You must be a good boy; your mama needs me."

Kenji kissed Niko and handed him to Ralph.

"Please, have Abby call Dr. Mynt, and could you—"

"I'll take care of him, and we'll make sure Hattie and John get here."

As Patricia waited for Kenji to come back, she prayed for the life of their baby.

"Please, God, don't take her!" she repeated over and over like a mantra, completely forgetting about the breathing exercises.

It seemed like hours before Paul got there and took over.

"I've got it; she needs you," he said as he started an IV.

"*Kirei*, I'm here," Kenji said over and over as Patricia cried, begging for the life of the baby.

Three hours later, Patricia was resting quietly, the labor stopped. Paul checked the baby's heart rate, and for the moment it was regular. Ralph brought in an extra chair, and Paul and Kenji spent the night in the room with her, with Paul leaving only when Kenji helped Patricia use the bedpan.

By late morning, Paul felt confident enough to go to Nick's for a quick shower and change of clothes.

"Keep those fluids running and keep her calm. I'll be back in a little while."

Kenji nodded and walked Paul to the door. "I cannot tell you how grateful we are that you're here."

"You're welcome, but Kenji, we have a long way to go," Paul cautioned.

"I know, but still, we're grateful for your help."

By the end of February 1944, the battles at Monte Cassino and Anzio continued; the Narva front was formed between the German and Soviet forces near the eastern border of Estonia; the Marshall Islands were almost in the hands of the US; Operation Overlord—the planned invasion of France—was confirmed; SHAEF—Supreme Headquarters Allied Expeditionary Force—was established in Britain by General Dwight D. Eisenhower; there was an anti-Japanese revolt on Java; the Soviets initiated the Narva Offensive; a monastery located on top of Monte Cassino was destroyed by bombs dropped by the Allies; diplomats from the USSR and Finland met and signed an armistice; the light cruiser HMS Penelope was torpedoed—415 crew members died; Leipzig, Germany, was bombed for two nights straight; and the Marina Islands of Saipan, Guam, and Tinian were attacked by US Navy planes.

The house took on a festive mood as preparations were made for Niko's first birthday. The only hard part was that Patricia couldn't actively help get ready for it. Paul and Kenji talked about moving her downstairs for the party and decided against it, even though there had been no further episodes of premature labor.

"I want her where all the equipment is if we should need it," Paul said.

Kenji wholeheartedly agreed, so the party was going to be held in the bedroom so Patricia could attend.

Paul managed to catch Kenji alone for a few minutes when he was in the kitchen getting Patricia a glass of juice and everyone else was busy. "Son, you're one hell of a doctor, even without training. I can only imagine what you'll be like when you're trained. When this war is over, I'd like to help you get into medical school."

Kenji was stunned. "What? Why would you do this?"

"As you know, my wife died some years back, and we never had children. It would be a travesty if you didn't go to school because of finances. As a matter of fact, I've been in touch with a friend of mine. He knows all about you, and when this is over, he would like to meet you."

"I don't know what to say," Kenji said softly.

"I'll tell you what to say," Paul said. "Say your prayers that this damned war ends soon so we can get back to living normal lives."

Kenji nodded his head in agreement; that day couldn't come soon enough for any of them. He thanked Paul profusely, even though "thank you" just didn't seem adequate.

Kenji went up the stairs carrying the glass of juice, stopping at the door when he heard Patricia's soft melodic voice reading to Niko, who had fallen asleep. He waited until she finished before going into the room.

"*Kirei*, I have good news for us," he said as he took the book and handed her the glass of juice, reminding her to drink all of it.

Patricia listened, shocked and then thrilled at the news that Kenji would be going to medical school with Paul's help. It confirmed her belief that things would get better for them. Then she had a thought: what if they held the fact that she was black against him? Kenji, sensing her change of mood, asked her what was wrong.

"What if they won't let you in because of me?" she asked.

It took Kenji a moment to realize what she was asking. "*Kirei*, let us not look for trouble where there may be none. If that does happen, we'll deal with it then. For now, let's concentrate on the child we have and the one that's coming."

Patricia nodded. She wasn't going to spoil this for him; she could see already he was feeling better about himself simply because the opportunity to care for her and Niko the way he wanted to was now possible.

Paul smiled to himself. His original plan was to tell Kenji about financing his education after the war was over, but they had been through so much that he felt they needed something positive to look forward to, just in case the baby didn't survive. The smile on Kenji's face was all he needed to know he had made the right decision.

He had already written several letters to his friend and set things up with the school, just in case something happened, and also made sure his lawyer had a copy of the arrangements.

The birthday party was a happy affair, with everyone laughing as Niko opened his birthday presents and flung the paper up in the air. Nick and Hana gave him more blocks that were sanded down and painted with letters of the alphabet; some were even painted with Japanese symbols. Ralph and Abby ordered storybooks, and Ralph gave him one of his old stethoscopes; Hattie and John gave him a sweater Hattie knitted; and from Patricia and Kenji he got a new blanket for his bed that Patricia ordered for him, using her maiden name.

The chocolate cake made by Ralph was the highlight of the party. "This was my mama's recipe," he said when everyone took a bite and proclaimed it "delicious."

He turned to Hattie and said, "I haven't forgotten about us opening up a restaurant when this war is over."

"Now, Ralph—" Hattie said.

"It's a done deal," Ralph said, cutting her off.

After the party, Kenji took Niko away to give him a bath. He had chocolate cake all over his face, hands, and clothes, but looked as though he had enjoyed himself.

Patricia cornered Paul; she wanted to thank him for what he was doing for Kenji.

"Patricia, Kenji is a natural healer, and I'm happy I can help, but what about you? Have you thought about school?"

"We've talked about it, but that was before Niko came along," Patricia replied. "I want Kenji to go first; it's been hard on him not being able to care for us in the way he thinks we should be cared for."

"But this isn't his fault or his choice," Paul said.

"On an intellectual level he knows that, but on an emotional level he feels as though he failed us somehow. But what you did for him today was . . . unbelievable, and I wanted to thank you for both Niko and myself."

Patricia kissed Paul on the cheek and then looked at him. "Thank you for everything."

Hiroshi and Dai had settled into a routine of him going to work at the camp nursery while she worked at the dress shop.

They made love every night, and much to Hiroshi's frustration, there was still no pregnancy—but then, did he want his child to be born here? There was still no word of when they would be released from the camp, and for all he knew it could be another year, if not longer.

The only other thing that pleased him was that he was able to take the loyalty oath. While he was aware that he could go to prison here, he wouldn't be going back to Japan. After talking with Dai, he decided that if he managed to stay out of prison, he would try to find Kenji and apologize.

"But what of his wife?" Dai asked.

"What of her?" Hiroshi replied. He had decided he simply couldn't accept her.

"You cannot accept him and not her; she is a part of him and carries the Takeda name, and what if there are children?" Dai asked.

"I cannot accept this," Hiroshi said stubbornly.

"Hiroshi, how is it that you became involved with Joben Saito? It was because of the attitude you have now. You've talked about apologizing to her for your role in her attempted rape and murder; are you not going to even do that?"

Hiroshi hesitated; his shy, quiet Dai had backbone, just like Hana did. The thought occurred to him once again that he had married a woman very much like Hana. He also had to wonder if it was an unconscious decision and a way to rectify the mistakes he had made in their marriage.

"Then what?" he asked.

"That is for you to decide, but Hiroshi, you must try to make amends with your son. If you don't do this, you will regret it for the rest of your life."

Mitch sat in his cell. He hadn't been allowed to call his family to let them know what was happening to him. He hadn't even been given an agent to interrogate him, and he wondered why. He knew Lou had spoken to an agent several times and was being transferred to another facility, but he didn't know where, nor did he care.

His only concern was for himself and his family.

Nick sat in Elam's office wondering what he wanted. Hana didn't want him to come, but curiosity had gotten the better of him.

Elam leaned back in his chair, assessing Nick. He had been a damned good agent, and even though he was hiding something, he would give his right arm to have him back. It had been Nick who had figured out who the real spy was, and it had been right here in this office, under Elam's nose.

"Nick, I know we fucked you over and I can't apologize enough for that, but could you see your way clear to come back?"

"Why? So you can start trailing me again if I don't mention my wife or I don't hang around the office after work? No thanks," Nick replied.

"All right, let me ask you this," Elam said. "What would it take to get you back here?"

"Nothing," Nick replied. "Because I don't trust you or anyone else in this office."

"Fair enough, but what if I let you handpick your partner and let you interrogate Mitch?"

Nick's eyes widened. "I pick my own partner?"

"Yes, and you can't tell me you don't want to talk to Mitch," Elam replied.

Nick was going to say no, but gave it some thought. Since he'd been away, he hadn't been able to keep track of what was happening regarding the release of the Japanese from the camps. If he did this, he would be in a position to know in advance if trouble was headed their way. Hana was going to be upset, but this was for all of them.

"I want back-pay," Nick said.

"Done."

"If there are any questions about me professionally or personally, I want them brought to me."

"Done."

"I want Lou's office."

"Done."

"I want total control over who my partner is, meaning I don't want to have to clear it through you."

"Done."

"Put everything in writing, and then we'll talk," Nick said, as he stood up to leave.

Lou stared at the walls of his cell, wondering just what he had been thinking. How had he allowed himself to be put in this position? His life as he knew it was over; the one thing he had been proud of—being an agent for the United States—was now gone.

He had allowed Mitchell Jackson to convince him that Nick was a spy, even when his gut told him Nick was no more a spy than he was. He agreed with Elam that Nick was hiding something, but to frame him as a spy was more than he was prepared to do; that's why he hadn't left the evidence on Nick's desk and then pretended to find it.

He was looking at a long time in prison; by the time he got out, he would be older by twenty years, making him fifty when he was released. He asked himself if he could do twenty years in prison, and if he did, what would he do when he was released? This job was all he knew and all he had ever wanted to do.

Once it came out what he had done, his family refused to talk to him, and knowing his family as he did, that wasn't going to change. Ever. He had no wife, but a fiancée who also refused to talk to him, so what was left?

He looked at the pen and paper lying on the cot and sat down to write. The first letter was to his family, the second to his fiancée, and the last one to Nick.

An hour later, the agent in charge of him found him hanging from the ceiling of his cell. The letters were arranged neatly on the cot, with a note on top of them.

"Please make sure these are delivered."

Hana reacted as Nick thought she would. There was a mixture of fright, fear, and anxiety as she listened to his rationale. She had become accustomed to being relatively safe, especially when Nick was home, and she wasn't prepared to go back to hiding in the closet if someone came to the door unexpectedly. She cried as Nick held her in his lap and tried to make her understand that he wasn't going back because he wanted to; it was because he felt he could protect them better if he did.

Three hours later, Hana reluctantly agreed. "But we must do something different; I cannot go through the day not knowing if you are safe."

Nick saw her point; not knowing about his safety had been a big factor in her anxiety before. "Why don't we do this? I could take you over to Abby's before I go to the office, and I can call you there. It means you'll have to ride in the trunk twice a day—"

"I don't care about that!" Hana exclaimed, hugging him.

The next thing was telling everyone else.

The initial reaction was much the same as Hana's, with Ralph being the only one who agreed from the beginning.

"It only makes sense," he said. "We haven't been able to leave here for one reason or another, and let's face it, without Nick at that office, we're blind."

"What if they try to frame him again?" Patricia asked when Nick told her.

"I don't think that's an issue," Nick replied.

"Why not?" Patricia shot back. "It seems to me they're a little too anxious to get you back."

"I agree," Abby replied.

"As do I," Kenji added.

Nick took a deep breath before he spoke. "I understand your anxiety, but as before, everything will be in writing. My acceptance will depend on my demands being met, but you all have to admit that having me there gives us a safety net, and better that only one of us ends up in prison than all of us."

No one could argue with his reasoning. Nick noticed that neither Paul nor Patricia's parents offered their opinions, and asked why.

"Well," Paul said, "you've already made up your mind, and I can't find fault in your logic."

"I thinks the same," John said. "You gonna do what you gonna do."

"And?" Nick asked, knowing there was more.

"I—we want to thank you for what you did and what you doing, not just for Patricia but everybody here."

That wasn't what Nick was expecting to hear. "You're welcome," he said softly, not knowing what else to say.

On Monday morning, Nick met with five potential partners. After the general chitchat, he asked several questions, with the last being the one that would decide who his new partner would be.

"How do you feel about the Japanese and their interment?"

The first candidate was immediately disqualified.

"Are we talking off the record here?" he asked.

"Of course," Nick replied.

The man looked around to make sure no one was listening before he continued. "You know what's wrong with this country?" he asked. "We have too many foreigners! All of the Japs should have been given a one-way ticket back home."

"What about the ones born here?" Nick asked.

"They're Japs, aren't they? And let me tell you something else, the niggers and the . . ."

Nick let the man finish and then thanked him for coming in. "Thank you for your time, and I don't believe we'll be a good fit," he said, with no explanation of why he felt as he did.

The second candidate wasn't much better, spouting the same rhetoric as the one before him.

"Why do you feel that way?" Nick asked.

The man gave him a confused look. "The Jap is our enemy; they attacked this country and don't deserve to be here," he replied.

"And your attitude about black people?" Nick asked.

"They're here to stay; that doesn't mean I have to like it or like them. Why are you asking these questions?"

"Let's just say I believe in the live-and-let-live philosophy," Nick replied. "And . . . I don't appreciate racism, no matter the group. Thank you for your time."

The third man was better, but he had clear issues with dealing with people of other races, and Nick just had a bad feeling about him.

The fourth man he just didn't like; the man reminded him a little too much of his last partner, Howard.

He took a thirty-minute break, during which he called Hana to assure her that he was fine and not tossed into a cell somewhere.

The last man was younger than Mitch by maybe ten years. He was quiet, very soft-spoken, and extremely intelligent. Nick took him through the same questions as he had the others and then asked him the questions about the Japanese and the blacks.

"Is this off the record?" the man asked.

Nick sighed; he didn't know if he could sit through another spiel about the Japanese needing to be shipped back to Japan and the inferiority of black people.

"Speak your mind," he said and braced himself.

"You seem like a straightforward kind of guy and one that wouldn't give up another man's confidences. Am I right?"

"For the most part, that's correct," Nick replied, wondering what the man's point was.

"Mr. Alexander, I have no problem with people of different races or cultures; hell, it's what makes the world interesting. I am not happy with what happened to the Japanese and some of the other races—being locked up, I mean—especially when some of our own people were spies. I myself am not lily white; there's American Indian as well as some other races in me, so I'm hardly inclined to be racist."

Nick liked him and after talking with him for a few more minutes decided that Charles W. Hawthorne was his new partner.

"One request, please," Charles said as she shook Nick's hand.

"What's that?"

"Please call me Charles and not any of the usual nicknames that people use."

Later that afternoon, Nick went to the cell to see Mitch. When Mitch saw him, he stood up and waited for Nick to reach him.

"Sit down," Nick said, indicating the chair in the cell as he sat down.

Nick stared at Mitch for several minutes before speaking. "I thought we were friends," he said.

"We were," Mitch replied. "But this didn't have anything to do with friendship; this is war."

"Nothing to do with friendship?" Nick asked. "I trusted you and you almost succeeded in having me thrown into prison for being a spy! My question is why? Were you being threatened? What did they have on you?"

"Nick, there's a lot you don't know about me, and what you do know are all lies. I'm married, but my wife isn't staying in Texas with family. My wife is Japanese; she and my son live in Hiroshima. I haven't considered myself an American citizen in over twenty years. I consider myself Japanese and not American, and I will always consider myself Japanese."

"But you're not Japanese," Nick said.

"I am legally a citizen of Japan," Mitch said.

"You have dual citizenship," Nick said, understanding. "But why me?"

"You were the best choice; when you started pumping me for information about the camps and then you started coming up every couple of weeks, I wondered what was going on. I did some snooping and heard what you did for Hana Takeda and the other Japanese woman. I also heard through the grapevine that you were sweet on her, and I knew then that you were who I needed to cover myself. My Japanese contact was already at Manzanar; he was one of the several hundred that came here to build the camp before it opened."

"Who else worked with you?" Nick asked.

"I suppose it doesn't matter anymore," Mitch said to himself more to himself than to Nick. "Joben Saito helped me set up the network, but getting Hiroshi Takeda to join was the icing on the cake. Once word got out about him, others stepped forward to join."

"Are these others still active?" Nick asked.

"Yes, and I'll tell you who and where they are in exchange for something."

"What do you want?" Nick asked, already knowing the answer.

"I want to go home—to Japan," Mitch said.

"I can't authorize that, and you know it."

"But you can go to Elam Martin," Mitch countered.

"You have to give me something; he's not going to take your word for it."

Mitch thought a minute. "All right, I'll give you one name to check out; if it's true, then you go to Elam."

"Deal," Nick said, and waited as Mitch wrote a name down on a slip of paper.

Nick's new partner, Charles, was waiting for him in his office when he returned from seeing Mitch.

"So what's first?" he asked.

"Did you find an office?" Nick asked.

"Yes, I took the one in the corner over there; someone said it used to be yours."

"Just how much do you know about what happened to me?" Nick asked.

"All of it, once I sifted fact from rumor," Charles replied.

"And you're not concerned?"

"Should I be?" Charles asked.

"Not at all."

"Then I'm not concerned," he replied, shrugging.

Nick filled Charles in and asked for his opinion.

"I think we should take it to Elam and let him decide," Charles said.

Nick had already made that decision but wanted to find out what Charles was thinking. "Why?"

"I don't know Elam all that well, but what I do know is he's going to say no. He won't deal with Jackson, no matter what he's selling."

"Go on," Nick urged.

"Why should he? We've got the Japanese contact from the camp who, from what I hear, is singing like a bird."

"So why bother Elam with it?" Nick asked.

"That way you can tell Jackson you asked, and if Elam decides to talk to him and it comes up, he can back you."

"Good," Nick said, realizing he had made the right choice in picking Charles as a partner.

Charles called it right.

"No deals," Elam said. "He can't tell us anything that his Japanese contact can't tell us. Oh, and by the way, Lou hanged himself and left something for you."

Elam handed Nick the envelope. "I could be wrong, but I think it's a letter of apology."

Nick tucked the letter into his pocket without looking at it; he would read it later, after he talked to Mitch and when he got home.

Mitch paced the small cell, his mind on his wife and son. The bitch of it was that his wife didn't want him to work for the US; in fact, she had begged him to say no.

"I should have listened to her," he muttered.

He turned to see Nick standing in front of the cell with a younger man, who he presumed to be Nick's new partner.

"Did you talk to him?" Mitch asked anxiously.

"I did and I'm sorry, he said no," Nick replied.

"No?" Mitch asked, shocked. "Did you tell him I had names?"

"I told him that, and here's the problem," Nick said. "Your camp contact is giving up everything he knows."

Mitch sat down on the cot; he was never going to see his family again. He was going to die in this country alone, but the worst of it was that his family wouldn't know.

Nick felt sorry for him, but not enough to talk to Elam again. This man had been perfectly willing to let him rot in prison for a country that wasn't even his.

"One more thing," Nick said as he stood to leave. "Your partner Lou killed himself."

"He . . . he what?" Mitch asked.

"Your partner is dead," Nick repeated and walked out to the sounds of Mitch calling his name.

Chapter 18

By the end of April 1944, anti-fascist strikes occurred in northern Italy; the Soviet Air Force bombed and destroyed the city of Narva; the Australians prepared for an attack on western Australia by the Japanese that was based on faulty information; the Japanese attempted to invade India, initiating a four-month battle around Imphal; and the Japanese attacked American forces on Hill 700—the battle lasted five days, with the Japanese retreating.

The Soviets carried out an air raid on Tallinn, Estonia. Eight hundred civilians were killed and twenty thousand were left homeless, but the military objects were left almost untouched; the National of the French Resistance approved the resistance program; the third Battle of Anzio began—the small town of Cassino was destroyed; Vienna was bombed; Hungary was occupied by Germany. In response to a bombing that killed German soldiers, 355 Italians, including seventy-five Jews and over two hundred members of various groups in the Italian resistance, were killed during the Fosse Ardeatine massacre in Rome.

The Allied bombers hit Budapest, Hungary, and Bucharest, Romania, ahead of the advancing Red Army; General Charles de Gaulle took command of all free French forces; the Japanese surrounded British forces at Imphal and Kohima, India.

The German troops began to evacuate Crimea; the Japanese launched a major offensive in central China with some success; the Slapton Sands tragedy occurred, in which over five hundred American servicemen were killed in a training exercise in preparation for D-Day in Devon, England. Preparations for D-Day continued throughout southern England.

MARCH 1944

Everyone watched Patricia closely; she hadn't had an episode of early labor since the one in January. Even Kenji, who had never really prayed to the Christian God, added his prayers to the prayers of the others. Both he and Paul monitored the baby's heart rate, and on occasion the irregular heart rate showed up. As for Patricia herself, aside from the anxiety and being tired of being in bed, she was healthy, confirming Paul's belief that the problem was with the baby and not Patricia.

Kenji started rereading his medical journals in preparation for med school; seeing him so excited made Patricia happy and did more to help her than anything. Kenji would let her ask him random questions from the books, making her an active participant.

"You know, *Kirei*, you could be a doctor," he told her one day.

Patricia laughed at him. "Sure I could."

Kenji wasn't laughing. "Why do you find that funny?"

"You're serious?" Patricia asked.

"Very."

"I guess I never thought about it; I didn't think I would get to go to college until we talked about it," Patricia replied.

"I understand, but *Kirei*, think about it, and if not a doctor, then a nurse."

"Why do you think I would be good at being one of those? I thought we decided I would be a teacher."

"I think you would do well at whatever you decide to do, but Patricia—*Kirei*—your grasp of the material in these books tells me you would do well."

"Let's get you through school first, and then we'll talk about me," Patricia replied.

Kenji took the book from her and laid it on the floor. "Enough study for now; you need to rest. We have only a few weeks more and we'll bring our baby into the world," he said as he lay down beside her and took her into his arms, laying his hands on her large stomach.

"Do you think she'll be all right?" Patricia asked as she placed her hands on top of his.

"I hope so, *Kirei*. In a few weeks, we shall see."

"What if she . . . what if she's dead?" she whispered.

"We'll deal with it as we have dealt with everything that has come our way: together."

Patricia hesitated before speaking again. "Your mother told me about your brother, Hiro," she said softly.

"What did she tell you?"

"She told me how they thought he got sick because of something he ate and that he liked sweets as much as you do."

"What else?" Kenji asked.

"She told me how your father left her alone after Hiro died."

"Are you afraid I will leave you to mourn alone?" Kenji asked.

"I . . . I don't—"

"*Kirei*, we have been through so much pain and joy together—more pain than what is fair. The times I left you were because I had to and not because I wanted to, but when our baby is born, I will be here. If she's stillborn, then I'll be with you; if she's born handicapped in some way, I'll be with you and we will love and care for her together."

Patricia snuggled closer and closed her eyes. Even though she knew in her heart Kenji wouldn't leave her alone, she had to hear it, and now that she had, she could rest.

Paul made a point of becoming friends with a physician from the hospital with a goal in mind; he needed anesthesia for Patricia for when he and Kenji did the cesarean. He and Kenji discussed the options and decided to go with ether since it was the safest, but it took time for it to be absorbed.

"We could start early, around five, and by six we should be ready to go," Paul said.

He also needed an oxygen tank and a mask; he wondered if Nick could help in some way without compromising himself.

"I don't know, but . . . we could go back up to Manzanar. It would actually look good for me to do that," Nick said. "Do you have anyone up there you would trust?"

Paul gave it some thought. "There was a nurse I had a thing with, and she might help me."

"Can you call up there?" Nick asked.

"Sure," Paul replied, "but we need a back-up plan in case she can't or won't help us."

"That's reasonable, and in the meantime, I'll see what I can come up with," Nick replied.

Hiroshi had come to a decision: he had to talk to Hana and Kenji. He would try to find them after he and Dai were released from the camp. He was still undecided about Patricia, but conceded that Dai was right. He couldn't very well try to make amends with Kenji and not her. Maybe there could be some compromise; maybe he could apologize to her and then make some attempt to be civil to her, at least in public. If there were children, he would have to do the same thing, but he wasn't sure he would ever accept them or her.

As of yet, Dai still wasn't pregnant, and Hiroshi continued to tell himself that he really didn't want his child to be born here. He was grateful that the days were getting warmer, although the nights were still cold. At night, he and Dai huddled together for warmth and Hiroshi realized he had never held Hana like this. So many mistakes, but one of the biggest was the way he had acted when Hiro died.

He vividly remembered that Hiro had been sick, but they thought he had eaten too much of something. None of them were expecting him to die, but when he did, instead of staying and comforting Hana, he left her alone with a dead child and Kenji. Why he was thinking about that now he didn't know, but the intense feeling of guilt hit him so hard that he held Dai tighter against him.

"Hiroshi," she asked softly, "what troubles you?"

Hiroshi told her about Hiro's death and his actions. By the time he was done, he was weeping.

"Why did you leave her alone?"

"I have no answer for that other than to say I was in my own pain," Hiroshi replied.

"But husbands and wives are to share in all things, are they not?"

"Yes, that's true," Hiroshi conceded, realizing something: While he had been a good father to their children, he had never been a good husband to Hana. She had never said anything, and he had interpreted her silence as happiness and acceptance.

His thoughts went from Hiro's death to all the nights he spent with the *shoufu* once it became clear that Hana wouldn't give him another child to replace the one they had lost. Once again he had the thought that he was the one at fault. He had bedded Ani for months, and she never got with child, and here was Dai who he bedded nightly, even before their marriage, and she still was barren.

"Go to sleep, Dai," Hiroshi said. "I am done talking for the night."

MARCH 20, 1944

Patricia was sitting up in a chair when the first contraction hit; she fought the urge to panic and took a deep breath before calling Kenji's name. He helped her back into bed, called down for someone to call Paul, and started an IV to get fluids going.

"Breathe, *Kirei*," he encouraged as he started the IV.

When it was started, he sat beside her on the bed and rubbed her stomach with one hand and held her hand with the other. "Keep breathing, *Kirei*; Paul will be here soon."

Patricia tried not to panic; she tried to think of anything but losing the baby. Giving up, she began to pray, forgetting about breathing. She gripped Kenji's hands and cried through her prayers. "God, please don't do this to us; please don't take our baby!"

Kenji felt his own tears flow as he listened to Patricia beg for the life of their baby. He added his own prayers, knowing that everyone else was praying for them, too.

Paul arrived a few minutes later and examined Patricia. "Patricia?" he called gently. "If we can't stop the labor, we'll to have to take the baby and hope for the best. Do you understand?"

Patricia stopped praying long enough to listen to what Paul was saying and then looked at Kenji. "Kenji?" she asked, her fear obvious.

"We understand," Kenji replied for the both of them.

Paul got things ready while Kenji sat with Patricia to keep her calm. Ralph had already left to pick up Hattie and John while Abby watched Niko and set pans of water on to heat, and she called Nick and Hana while she waited.

It was touch and go for an hour or so before the contractions stopped. Everyone breathed a sigh of relief when there were no further contractions for the rest of the evening.

"I think we're all right for now," Paul said to Patricia. "But I want you back on bed rest."

Kenji brought Niko to the room so Patricia could kiss him goodnight. Paul suggested that she take a sedative so she could rest, and Patricia didn't argue with him. They were too close to their goal of April 15 for her to argue with Paul or Kenji about her care. If they wanted her in bed, then in bed she would stay, and she would do it gladly.

After Niko was in bed, Kenji gave Patricia the pill with a sip of water and stretched out beside her. He wanted her to rest, so he didn't talk; instead he rubbed her stomach, gratified to feel the baby move under his hands. It wasn't long before Patricia was sound asleep.

Ralph looked at his son Lawrence's phone number and debated calling him, but he couldn't quite make himself do it. He had no plans of dying anytime soon, but he still needed to make amends with his son if he could, and there was no time like the present, he decided. He did a quick calculation of the time difference and picked up the phone. He was going to call his son and hope he would at least get to talk to him.

He picked up the phone, dialed the number, and waited. It rang several times before someone answered—Lawrence.

"Hello?"

Ralph closed his eyes, said a silent prayer, and then responded, "Lawrence, this is your father. . . . Please don't hang up."

"What do you want?" Lawrence snapped.

"I just wanted to apologize," Ralph replied. "I'm sorry I waited so long to call the doctor for your mother. It's a mistake that—"

"I don't give a fuck about your sense of guilt! It doesn't change the fact that you were a selfish bastard who let her die because money was too hard to come by."

Ralph felt tears forming as he tried to come up with an answer to Lawrence's accusations, except they weren't accusations—they were the truth.

"I'm not going to try and justify my decision, because you're right. I was being selfish and I should have called the doctor a lot sooner than I did. It's something I will regret until the day I die."

"What do you want from me? Forgiveness?"

"No," Ralph replied, "I just wanted a chance to tell you how sorry I am."

"We went back," Lawrence said softly.

"Went back home?" Ralph asked.

"We went back to live with you because we didn't want you to be alone, and you were gone—you didn't leave a note or anything!"

"Oh God, Lawrence, I'm sorry. I didn't know; I didn't think you were coming back, so I left."

"You knew where we were; why didn't you call us or ask us to come home? When you didn't, we thought you didn't want us."

Ralph's throat tightened; it had never occurred to him that the boys just needed time; he thought they hated him as much as he hated himself. "It . . . I wanted you to come home, but I thought you hated me. . . . "

"Pop, we were angry, sad, and scared kids! We didn't know what to do or think! We only knew that Mama was dead and that you didn't call the doctor because you didn't want to spend the money—but we still loved you."

Ralph was openly weeping. "I am so sorry! Thank you for talking to me. I'll let you go now."

"Pop, wait," Lawrence said. "Baby boy died at Pearl harbor."

"I know," Ralph replied sadly.

"How?"

"I have a friend who found out where both of you were—that's how I got your number. I also know you lost a limb over in Europe."

"Why now, after all these years?" Lawrence asked.

"I'm not going to live forever," Ralph replied. "I have some friends who might lose their baby, and I started thinking more and more about you and your brother. You were never far from my thoughts, and I decided it was time for me to contact you again."

Lawrence was silent for several seconds; when he spoke, Ralph could tell that he was crying. "We missed you."

"I missed you too, and Lawrence, I can't say this enough, and I know it doesn't change anything, but son . . . I'm sorry."

"I am too. You have three grandkids," Lawrence said.

"Was that one of them that answered the phone the last time I called?"

"Yep, that was the oldest, Kenneth. He's the oldest of the three; he'll be fourteen in a few weeks. Dianne is next, and she's eleven, and then there's Eli—he'll be nine in the fall."

"Your wife?" Ralph asked.

"Sally. She's the one that told me if you ever called again I should talk to you. By the way, where did you go after you left here?"

"I moved to California; LA, to be exact."

"You've been there all this time?" Lawrence asked.

"Yep, I have good friends here."

He was going to tell Lawrence about everyone and stopped himself. Lawrence may have been his son, but he hadn't seen him in over twenty years. He changed the subject, "Where are you living?"

"In town. Sally's mother lives there, and she wants to be close by in case something happens."

"She sounds like a good woman; what are you into?" Ralph asked.

"I'm working in the office at the mill, and I'm part of a group that's out to protect our interest."

Ralph felt a drop in his stomach; there was only one group he could think of that would do what Lawrence was talking about. Visions of the dead black man he had cut down from a tree and buried flashed in his mind.

"What group would that be?" Ralph asked.

"I can't say over the phone, but let's just say that the white race is in danger," Lawrence replied.

"Oh my God, Lawrence, you're in the Klan?"

There was no response.

"Your kids and wife—"

"I have their full support," Lawrence said, the pride evident in his voice.

Ralph was glad he had stopped himself from saying anything about Abby and the rest of them.

"Look, Pop, I gotta run, but I'm glad you called back. Is there a number where I can call you?"

Ralph thought frantically for a response; giving him Abby's number wasn't a good idea.

"I'm at a friend's house, since I don't have a phone at my place. I'll call you, how's that?"

"Sounds good, and Pop? I'm really glad you called back."

Ralph had mixed feelings about the phone call. On one hand, he was glad that he called and that they were able to talk, but on the other hand, he wouldn't be able to tell his son about the people he had come to love and consider family. That wasn't exactly true, Ralph realized. He could tell him and take the chance of losing his blood family again.

"What are you so deep into thought about?" Abby asked as she walked into the kitchen carrying a very hungry Niko.

"I just talked to my son," Ralph replied.

"It's about time," Abby replied. "What did he say?"

Ralph told her the gist of the conversation. "Abby, he's in the Klan! He's a part of the group that whipped that man to death, and he thinks it's all right."

"What did you tell him?" Abby asked.

"I didn't say anything," Ralph replied. "I didn't want to lose him again, but not saying anything isn't right either. I wanted to tell him about all of you, but I can't."

"Ralph, when it's time, you will. None of us will be angry if you don't tell your son about us, so don't let that worry you."

Ralph didn't reply immediately. "You know," he said a few minutes later, "I know exactly how Patricia and Nick must feel, not being able to go out or talk about their wives and husbands."

"It has been difficult for them, but as you can see, they've managed. But the thing is this: If you tell your son about us, he won't take it well, and as you say, you could lose him again. Is that a price you're prepared to pay for telling him?"

It was a good question.

"I can't tell him now, anyway," Ralph replied. "It will have to be after the war's over, so I have some time to think about this."

Later, when he was alone, Ralph realized something: He was doing the same thing he had done when he saw the black man being whipped. He sat back and watched because he was afraid. Maybe he didn't have to tell Lawrence about Abby and the others, but he could tell him about the black man and hope it would start him thinking.

Ralph picked up the phone and called Lawrence back.

"Pop?"

"Yeah, son, how long have you been in that group?" Ralph asked.

"Three months or so, why?"

"I want to tell you why I really left. Your mother dying and you boys leaving was a part of it, but not all of it."

Ralph took a deep breath and told Lawrence the entire story without stopping, even when he was crying.

"Pop, look, I'm sorry you saw that, but the nigger must have done something to deserve that," Lawrence said.

"Son, no one—and I mean no one—deserves to die like that, and I don't care what color he is or what he did. That man—not nigger—that man died simply because he was black, and he probably did nothing more than not move fast enough when a white man told him to do something."

"Pop, you don't understand; they're taking our jobs and looking at our women and children—"

"I understand plenty," Ralph shot back. "I understand things are hard, but neither your mother nor I taught you to hate."

"I don't hate anyone!" Lawrence shot back.

"All right then, when they tell you to go with them to hang or whip someone to death, what are you going to do?"

"It's not like that!" Lawrence replied.

"Uh huh, they haven't asked you yet, have they?"

"No, because that's not what we do."

"But you just said that maybe the nigger deserved it; is that what you really believe, or are you saying what they want you to say?"

Ralph blinked back tears when he heard the dial tone in his ear.

APRIL 15, 1944

5:00 a.m.

"Are you ready, *Kirei*?" Kenji asked, kissing Patricia gently on her lips.

"I'm scared," she replied, holding his hands.

"I know; I am, too. But remember that no matter what happens, I'm here and so is everyone else."

There had been one more incident of premature labor since the last one, but it hadn't lasted as long. The baby's heart rate had remained normal except for the occasional irregularities. The last few days were the hardest, as the date and time for the cesarean approached. Kenji and Paul had even discussed not doing it at all, but letting Patricia deliver the baby naturally.

"That will increase the stress on the baby's heart," Kenji said.

"I agree, but I wanted to get your thoughts on it," Paul replied.

"My goal is to have both Patricia and the baby well and alive, and I don't think her having the baby naturally will do that. I know there are no guarantees with the cesarean, but I think we have a better chance, even with the risk of infection," Kenji replied.

"Are we ready?" Paul asked as he came into the room.

"We are ready," Kenji replied for the both of them.

6:00 a.m.

Patricia was finally in a deep sleep, with Kenji holding her hand. He kissed her forehead and went to wash up, taking care to wash under his fingernails and all the way up his arms to his elbows. He was shaking as he slipped on the surgical garb and gloves before joining Paul at the makeshift surgical table, which had been constructed by Nick and Ralph several weeks before and stored in Abby's room until it was needed. The night before, Hattie, Hana, and Abby had scrubbed it with boiling water with lye mixed in and covered it with one of the sheets that had been boiled just for this event.

Paul opened the sterile surgical supplies and gave Kenji a reassuring smile through his mask before making the cut into Patricia's abdomen. He stopped to look at Kenji. "You okay?" he asked.

"I . . . I'm all right," Kenji replied, once again grateful that Paul was with him.

"All right, here we go," Paul said as he completed the incision. "Got the suction ready?" he asked.

Kenji nodded and got ready to apply suction from the contraption he and Paul had put together after much trial and error.

6:10 a.m.

Kenji looked down at Patricia to be sure she wasn't in any distress and breathed a prayer of thanks that she didn't appear to be in any discomfort.

"I'm through the uterus," Paul said calmly as he reached in to retrieve the baby.

6:15 a.m.

Paul got a hold of the baby and began to lift her out as Kenji suctioned the excess fluid. A few seconds later, Paul lifted out a baby girl, who was breathing, but not crying. "Come, on kid! Cry!" Paul urged as he slapped the baby's bottom and was rewarded with a cry. Both he and Kenji let out a sigh of relief as Kenji clamped the cord and Paul cut it.

"Take the baby and check her out while I finish up here," Paul said.

Kenji cried as he listened to the baby's heartbeat; for the moment it was normal, but she would be checked frequently. The tears continued as he gave her the first bath of her life and wrapped her in a warm quilt made by Hattie.

"Welcome, little one," he said as he kissed her.

11:00 a.m.

Patricia slowly opened her eyes and looked around. She tried to move and felt a stab of pain in her abdomen. The baby; where was her baby? She was about to panic when she heard Kenji's soft voice talking to someone.

"Kenji?"

"I'm here, *Kirei*," he said as he came to the bed, holding the baby in his arms. "Look what we have."

"She's all right?" Patricia asked anxiously.

"She's beautiful, as is her mother," Kenji replied as he put the baby in her arms.

"Her heart?" Patricia asked as she examined the baby, checking her fingers and toes.

"Regular, but she still has the occasional irregularities; other than that, she appears to be healthy."

"She's beautiful," Patricia said. "Have the others seen her yet?"

"No, I wanted you to see her before anyone else. Do you still wish to wait before naming her?"

"I don't know; what do you think?" Patricia replied, wincing in pain as she tried to get into a more comfortable position to nurse the baby.

"I would like to name her, but I leave the choice up to you."

Patricia gave it some thought. "Can a baby have more than three names? I don't know if we'll have another girl or not, so I was thinking about giving her the names of our mothers plus Abby's."

"That's a nice thought, but so many names for such a little one," Kenji said, touching the baby's foot.

"I know, but. . . . "

"All right, *Kirei*, in what order would you like the names?"

"How about Hana Marie Abigail Takeda?" she asked. "Marie is my mother's middle name; she always told me if I ever had a daughter not to name her Harriet," she explained, seeing Kenji's puzzled expression.

"What will we call her?" Kenji asked as he thought about the name.

"Marie."

"Then Marie it is. Are you up to visitors? They're aware that they can't stay long, but they want to see you and the baby."

Thirty minutes later, everyone had gotten a peek at the baby. Hattie, Hana, and Abby all cried when they heard the baby's name.

"She's a beautiful baby," Hana said, touching her granddaughter.

Kenji shooed everyone out and got the baby and then Patricia ready for bed. As he worked, he had to wonder if the survival of the baby meant that things would continue to get better for them. He placed the baby in Patricia's arms and went to get Niko.

"Mama!" Niko called when he saw Patricia. The only thing that stopped him from taking a running start and jumping onto the bed was Kenji, who said, "No, *musuko-son*, your mama is in pain."

Niko stopped and looked up at Kenji, waiting for further instructions. Kenji took Niko's hand and walked with him to the bed. He sat down, picked Niko up, and sat him in his lap.

"Niko, this is your *imoto-san*, your little sister."

Niko gave the baby a curious look and then looked back at Kenji.

"Her name is Marie, and you must be a good big brother and help keep her safe."

Niko looked at Marie and then at Patricia.

"Give Mama a hug," Patricia said, holding out her hand to him.

With Kenji's help, Niko lay on the bed next to Patricia and kissed her cheek. He kept glancing at the baby, as if trying to decide if he liked her or not. When she cried, he jumped a little and then reached out to touch her face, smiling when she stopped crying.

Paul stayed for the next two days to make sure there weren't any complications.

"I think she's going to be fine, but she has to take it easy. I want her in bed for another few days; then she can get up in a chair, and no lifting anything heavier than the baby."

"Paul, we can't thank you enough."

"You're welcome, and I'm glad things turned out all right. Keep an eye on the baby's heart rate and call me if anything changes. I'll be back later this evening."

Patricia had fallen asleep with the baby in her arms and Niko curled up against her side, playing with one of the baby's feet.

"Come, Niko, we must let Mama sleep," Kenji said softly as he helped him from the bed.

"Baby," Niko said, looking at Patricia and Marie.

"Yes, she is our baby."

Kenji left the door open so he could hear Patricia if she called and helped Niko with his bath. For the first time since he had escaped from the camp, he felt a real glimmer of hope.

He laughed when Niko splashed him with soapy water. "You're right, Papa does need a bath."

He dried Niko off and oiled his skin before combing his thick curly hair. "And you are in need of a haircut," he commented as he ran the comb through the curls. That finished, he helped Niko use the toilet and wash his hands before tucking him in for a nap in his bed, which was in a corner in his and Patricia's room.

Kenji peeked at Patricia and the baby and decided to take a quick shower while they slept. He was exhausted but happy; all would be perfect if only the war would end.

By the end of May 1944, D-Day was set for June 6, 1944; Crimea was liberated and the Red Army moved in; Chinese troops invaded Burma; the Battle of Monte Cassino ended—the Allies were the victors; there was increased bombing over targets in France in preparation of D-Day; the Allies were moving toward Rome; the Germans were in retreat in Anzio; the invasion of India was over; and the Japanese retreated from Imphal, India with heavy losses.

Patricia and the baby were doing well, although Marie still had the irregular heartbeat every so often. Niko soon became the protective big brother, watching everyone who went anywhere near the baby, including Kenji and Patricia.

Patricia was up and out of bed, finding that the more she moved around, the better she felt. The incision to her stomach was healing, but Kenji still checked it no less than three times a day.

One day, when both children were sleeping, Kenji brought up the subject of school. "*Kirei*, I have decided on a course of study, and I would like your opinion."

"You'll be good no matter what you do," Patricia replied. "But what are you thinking about doing?"

"Obstetrics," Kenji replied. "I've been here for the births of both of our children, and it was the most amazing thing to participate in and witness. What do you think?"

"I think if that's what you want to do, then you should do it," Patricia replied. "Have you talked to Paul about it?"

"I have, and he agrees."

"Then you have your answer," Patricia replied. "Things are going to get better, aren't they?"

"I believe so," Kenji agreed as he glanced over at the sleeping babies.

Ralph looked at the phone; he hadn't spoken to his son since the day he told him about the black man. He picked up the phone, put it back, and then picked it up again, dialing the number before he could change his mind.

The phone rang three times before Lawrence picked it up.

"Lawrence?"

"Pop? I'm glad you called."

"Is everything all right?" Ralph asked.

Lawrence hesitated before he spoke again. "Pop . . . you were right about them. They asked me to go with them for a ride and . . . and they picked up some ni—black boy who was walking home and they strung him up! Right there in front of me! I tried to stop them, but then they started calling me a nigger lover and threatened to hang me alongside the boy."

Lawrence stopped talking for a second and then continued, "I didn't say anything else, but they told me if I opened my mouth, they would come after me."

"What are you going to do?" Ralph asked.

"I dropped out; I still believe that our jobs are in danger, but that boy wasn't doing anything! He was just walking home. I'm thinking about moving, but I don't know where to."

Ralph was silent; he wanted to help, but he wasn't sure of how unless. . . .

"Son, I have a house here that's got plenty of room if you want to move out here." After he made the offer, he wanted to take it back; he hadn't thought of the ramifications of it.

"I don't know, Pop; I'll have to talk to Sally and the kids about it. Are there jobs out there?"

"There are some, especially in the city, but Lawrence, does Sally know about what happened?"

"I told her, and she's scared. I think she would leave if it weren't for her mother being here. If we came, we would have to bring her with us. Can you call me in a week or so?"

Ralph hung up after telling Lawrence that he would call back. He could have kicked himself; in his eagerness to help his son, he may have put all of them in danger again.

Hiroshi, along with everyone else in the camp, was enjoying the warmer weather. He no longer actively sought out news of the war; he simply no longer cared. He ignored the rumors of the supposed pending release of the Japanese from the camps; he wouldn't believe it until he was walking out of the gate with Dai.

He took a little of the money he had saved and bought a notebook and wrote a note each to Hana and Kenji and waited for Nick to make a visit so he could give them to him. He wrote to Hana first but didn't put her name anywhere on the letter, just in case it was intercepted somehow.

I am still here and have had much time to think. I have made many foolish decisions over these past few years, and I would like to offer my apologies for any shame or pain that my actions may have caused.

Live well and be happy,

H.

The next one was to Kenji.

I offer my sincerest apologies for my lack of honor and courage. I also add to this my apologies to anyone I have caused harm to by my actions. I am told that you have acted with nothing but honor and courage and that I should be proud of you. I would like for you to know that I am proud of you, and that I concur with the person who told me he would also be proud to call you son.

H.

When he was finished, he tucked the notes away for safe-keeping until he saw Nick again. He looked over at Dai, who was busy tidying their space; she still wasn't pregnant, and even though he didn't want a child born here, she should have been pregnant by now. He was finally beginning to come to grips with the fact that the problem was him and not the women, and if that were the case, Kenji would be his only child. That meant he had to make amends with him, which meant he had to accept the woman and any children they had together. It appeared as though he really had no choice at all but to accept the woman as Kenji's wife.

The idea still made him ill.

By the end of June 1944, a provisional French government was established; Operation Overlord was postponed because of high seas, but began on June 5; American, British, and French troops entered Rome and fell into Allied hands, making it the first Axis capital to do so; Operation Overlord began with five thousand tons of bombs being dropped by one thousand British bombers on German gun batteries on the Normandy Coast in preparation for D-Day.

D-Day began on June 6 with 155,000 Allied troops landing on the beaches of Normandy.

Stalin launched an offensive against Finland, hoping to defeat it before going on to Berlin. Six hundred and forty-two men, women, and children were killed in a town near Limoges, France, in a German response to resistance activities; Germany launched a V-1 flying bomb against England—a secret weapon Hitler believed would allow the Germans to win the war; Saipan was invaded by US Marine and Army forces; Elba was freed; Assisi, Italy, was captured by the Americans; the British won in the Burma campaign; and the National Committee of the Republic of Estonia made a declaration to the "people of Estonia."

Each time Ralph talked to his son, he hoped he would decide not to move into his house. Not knowing what else to do, he talked to Nick.

"I don't know what to tell you, Ralph," he said. "You know what could happen if he comes, and the only way around it is if you move back to the house with them, which means you wouldn't see Kenji or the kids."

"I know, I know," Ralph grumbled. "Maybe they won't come, and if they do, maybe it'll be after the war."

"Maybe," Nick said. "But you're still going to have to tell him at some point."

"I know that, too, but if the war is over, then there's no danger to Kenji, Hana, and the kids."

"True," Nick conceded, as thoughts of his own family crossed his mind.

"What are you going to tell your folks?" Ralph asked.

"The truth," Nick replied. "I'm tired of hiding and lying about Hana, and before you ask, they're going to be very angry."

Ralph nodded in understanding; it was going to be a very interesting time.

JUNE 6, 1944

Hana was in the kitchen when someone knocked on the door and then tried the knob. Hana ran up the stairs to get Nick, who was in the shower.

As soon as he heard her come in, he stuck his head out and grinned at her. "Room for one more!" he teased.

"Someone is at the door!" Hana said, completely missing the invitation to shower with him.

"Go hide; I'll come and get you when it's clear," Nick said as he got out of the shower.

By the time he made it downstairs, the doorbell was ringing almost nonstop.

"All right!" he shouted when he reached the door and looked through the peephole.

"Nick!" Charles shouted.

Nick opened the door to a panic-stricken Charles.

"What's wrong?" Nick asked.

"Mitch, he told Elam about the things he did for you."

"And?"

"Elam's on his way over here," Charles replied.

"All right, what else?" Nick asked.

"That's all I know, but I thought I'd better tell you."

"Thanks, why don't you come in? I was just getting out of the shower when I heard you banging on the door."

Nick let Charles in and showed him a seat. "I'll be back in a moment," he said as he went into the kitchen.

Hana hadn't set the table yet, which was good, but even if she had, he could invite Charles for supper and that would explain the place settings. As far as Hana's absence went, he could say she was out of town again with relatives and that he had opted not to go.

Nick went upstairs and shut the bedroom door behind him.

Hana stayed in the closet and waited.

"Sweetheart, stay put until I come for you," he whispered as he took a shirt from a hanger.

Hana didn't reply but nodded; she was nervous, but she trusted Nick.

Charles hadn't moved from the spot where Nick left him and was looking more nervous by the minute.

"Charles, calm down; I've been through this a time or two."

"Maybe you have, but I haven't," Charles replied.

"I was about to make dinner; would you care to join me? My wife is out of town for a baby shower and I hate cooking for one."

"Ah, sure," Charles replied.

"Good, I hope you don't mind eggs," Nick said as he headed toward the kitchen.

"No, that's fine. Where's Mrs. Alexander again?" Charles asked.

Nick froze; Charles had been duped into coming here.

"Who sent you here?" Nick asked.

"Elam," Charles replied, not bothering to lie.

"Did Mitch really talk to Elam?"

"I can't really say. I only know what Elam told me."

"And he sent you here to see what I would say or do," Nick commented.

"Nick, I'm sorry; I didn't know."

"He really isn't coming, is he?" Nick asked.

"He said he was, but given what just happened, I don't know," Charles admitted. "What do you want me to do?"

"Have dinner. We'll talk about this, that, and the other, and that's exactly what you'll tell Elam when he asks you what we did," Nick replied calmly, but inwardly he was fuming.

Finally, Dai was pregnant and Hiroshi couldn't have been happier. It was another chance to fix old mistakes and another chance to raise a child who would bring honor to the Takeda name. He was having second thoughts about making amends with Kenji, and said as much to Dai.

"Why do you do this?" she asked. "Kenjiro is still your son, and you must make things right with him."

"But you are giving me a son," Hiroshi replied.

"What if it is a female? What if something happens that the child isn't born? Hiroshi, you mustn't change your mind on this or you will live to regret it."

In the end, Hiroshi conceded that at the very least he needed to talk to Kenji and make his apologies to the woman. He agreed because Dai had a point; something could happen during the pregnancy, and the child could be a female, which would leave Kenji as his heir, although he had nothing to leave him.

Ralph called his son Lawrence to see how things were going.

"Hey, Pop!" Lawrence greeted. "Things are all right, I guess. Sally's mother took a fall the other day, so she's been staying over there."

"Sorry to hear that," Ralph said.

"Yeah, well, she'll be all right."

Ralph sensed there was something more that Lawrence wanted to say. "Something else on your mind?" he asked.

"Me and Sally been talking about your offer every chance we get, and we talked to the kids about it, too."

Ralph's heart pounded.

"We've decided to take you up on your offer; the thing is that we can't leave until August. One of Sally's sisters and her husband are going to move in with Mom."

"Do you know when in August?" Ralph asked, his mouth dry.

"Nancy and her husband are supposed to get here sometime during the first week; we'll leave here the following week. I'm figuring on about a week to get there."

"That's fine."

They hung up a few minutes later, with Ralph promising to get the phone numbers of the schools close to the house.

The baby was growing by leaps and bounds. Kenji checked her heartbeat three times a day and was always pleased to hear that it was regular. Patricia was up and about and taking on more of the responsibility of the children, with Kenji's help.

They talked about his going back to school and finally decided he would go into obstetrics. When it came to talking about her schooling, Patricia would change the subject.

One day, Kenji refused to be distracted. "*Kirei*, why do you keep changing the subject when we talk about your schooling?"

"Because it's a long ways off," Patricia replied.

"We could have you go first," Kenji said.

"No, we can't," Patricia said. "We've been waiting for this for a long time, and besides, Paul said he would pay for your education, not mine."

"I can wait—"

"No, Kenji," Patricia said firmly. "You have been so happy ever since Paul told you he would help you with school, and I'm happy for you, so no more talk about you waiting and me going to school."

Kenji dropped the subject, but was determined that somehow Patricia was going to go to school.

"Papa?" Niko called.

"Yes, Niko?" Kenji asked.

"Read?"

Niko loved stories and loved to be read to; it was something Kenji and Patricia both encouraged, so when he asked to be read to, it was done with no complaints.

"Go get your book and bring it to me," Kenji said, as he tousled Niko's curly hair.

When he was gone, Kenji kissed Patricia; it had been a long time since they last made love, and he was eager for it.

"A few more days," he had replied when she asked about it; that had been almost a week ago. As anxious as he was, he wanted to be sure Patricia was healed from the cesarean. *Four more days*, he told himself as he waited for Niko to come back with his book.

Abby and Ralph had already agreed to watch Niko and Marie. Niko would stay with Ralph, and Marie would stay with Abby. As of yet, Kenji hadn't said anything to Patricia in case something happened that plans had to be changed. He had already been to the basement, changed the sheets on the bed, cleaned the little makeshift bathroom, and put clean towels and washcloths on the little bench that held the washbasin.

Just thinking about it made his loins tingle. Four more days.

Hana came out of the closet soon after Charles left.

"Stay up here," Nick told her. "Elam is up to something."

"I didn't trust that man no matter what you said," Hana said as she ate the eggs and toast Nick had cooked for her.

"I know, sweetheart, and I didn't trust him either; that's why I have everything in writing."

"Why does he not leave you alone?" Hana asked.

"I don't know, but I intend to find out," Nick replied, taking the dirty dishes away from her. "Get ready for bed," he said, kissing her.

Hana watched Nick leave the room. She was frightened for him, but she was more frightened of this Elam Martin, because he had the power to take Nick away from her. She didn't want Nick to confront him, but knew he would and nothing she could say would change his mind. She hoped that whatever Nick said to the man wouldn't get him thrown in jail.

Nick took the dishes downstairs and double-checked the locks on the doors and windows; as soon as he got into the office, he was going to confront Elam. For all practical purposes, Elam had reneged on their agreement, and Nick was going to call him on it and then quit.

Hana was in bed when Nick went back upstairs; she lay on top of the blankets with nothing on but one of his dress shirts. Every once in a while she wore one of them to bed instead of her slip; she never explained why, and Nick didn't really care. He loved unbuttoning the shirt one button at a time as he teased her skin with kisses and nips until she giggled.

When he looked at her, which was something he thought he would never tire of, he saw something in her face that he hadn't seen for a while—real fear. Not nervousness but cold fear, and he thought he knew why. He climbed into the bed next to her and took her into his arms.

"You're trembling," he commented.

"I . . . I'm frightened of this Elam Martin; he means to take you away."

"I know," Nick commented. "That's why I'm going to beat him at his own game."

"Don't confront him; he will use it as a reason to put you back in jail."

"He can try," Nick replied.

"Nick, please don't provoke this man," Hana begged.

"Hana, it'll be all right; I promise," he assured her, and then he kissed her. It seemed like it had been a long time since he had made love to her and felt her skin next to his. In all of their time together, he had never tasted her; she wouldn't let him. When he asked her why he couldn't taste her, she could never explain, although she took his cock into her mouth many times. Tonight Nick decided that was going to change.

"Hana, do you trust me?" he asked.

"Yes," she replied without hesitation.

"Will you trust me to do something that you've never let me do?"

"What do you want to do?" she asked, already knowing the answer.

"I want to taste you; I want to feel you come on my tongue," Nick replied. "Will you trust me enough to do that?"

Hana hesitated; part of her wanted to experience him in that way, but part of her was afraid.

"What are you so afraid of?" Nick asked as he rubbed her back.

"It . . . it's a new thing to me."

"My guess is that you're going to love it," Nick said as he kissed her, not giving her a chance to reply.

He started with the top button of the shirt and worked his way down, stopping to suck on Hana's hardened nipples as he unbuttoned the rest of the shirt. He could hear her murmuring encouragements to him in Japanese and felt her tense the lower down her body he went.

"You are so beautiful down here," he said as he kissed the top of her mound, eliciting a gasp from Hana. He found it hard to believe that her husband had never explored this part of her, but then again, Hiroshi Takeda had only looked for his own pleasure.

"Open your legs, baby," Nick urged.

Reluctantly, Hana opened her legs; her body was stiff with fear of what was to come. Nick kissed the top of her mound again, but slid his tongue between her outer lips. Hana gave an involuntary jerk and let out a soft, almost inaudible moan; it was enough to keep Nick going. Spreading her outer lips, Nick began to lick and nibble around her clit, not touching it with his tongue until Hana was moaning louder and trying to grind herself into his mouth.

When he thought she was ready, he touched her clit with the tip of his tongue and flicked it. He heard Hana call his name the way she did when she was going to come and stopped to give her a chance to calm before starting again. This time he took her clit into his mouth and sucked gently until Hana was coming; she screamed as she bucked under him, her hands entwine in his hair.

Nick moved up beside her and hugged her as she trembled from the orgasm.

"Did you like that?" he asked when she was calm and breathing normally.

"Y—yes," Hana replied shyly.

"I'm glad because I liked doing it," Nick replied as he pulled her up on top of him and eased her onto his cock.

It didn't take Hana long to come again, with Nick coming as her orgasm waned.

Nick covered them up with a blanket, and as Hana slept he began planning how he was going to deal with Elam Martin.

"They're coming," Ralph said to Abby later that night.

"When?"

"Mid-August."

"What are you going to do?" Abby asked.

"I don't know yet; I only know that I can't tell them about Kenji, Hana, and the kids. Patty, you, Nick, and Patty's parents aren't going to make a difference, or I hope not, anyway," Ralph replied. "Why did I open my big mouth?" His face was filled with anxiety, fear, and pain as the realization that he may have put his family in grave danger hit him.

"Because Lawrence is your son and you did what any parent would do: you wanted to help your child," Abby replied.

"I'll have to move back into the house," Ralph said. "I can't take the chance that they'll come here."

"Maybe they won't come," Abby said with a hopeful expression on her face.

"Maybe, but Lawrence wants me to get him a list of the schools close to the house."

"We have some time yet," Abby said. "We'll work it out."

The next morning, as he dressed for work, Nick replayed what he was going to say to Elam in his mind.

Hana was quiet as she watched Nick dress; she didn't want him to go to the office. "Please don't go; stay here with me, or we could go see the grandchildren."

Nick stopped what he was doing and went to her. "Hana, I have to go in. I promise to call over to Abby's as often as I can."

"But—"

"I'll be fine," Nick said, hugging her.

Hana didn't argue with him any more—she knew it would have been pointless—but she really wished he wouldn't leave. In a rare show of aggression, she walked up behind him, wrapped her arms around him, and then reached down and began to stroke his cock. Immediately he hardened, placed his hand on top of hers, and pressed down.

"I'm going to be late," he said, even as Hana's strokes became faster and harder and his breathing quickened. Nick turned around so he was facing Hana. "Baby, that feels good, but I still have to go."

Hana nodded as she undid Nick's belt and unzipped his slacks before reaching in and pulling his cock out, rapidly stroking it until he came with a loud moan, his semen landing on her stomach. Gently she tucked his now-flaccid cock back into his shorts, zipped him up, and redid the belt.

"Hana—"

"Don't say anything; just come home to me," Hana said as she stood on her tiptoes and pulled him down for a kiss.

"I love you, Hana. What I'm doing is for that reason."

"What are you going to do?" Hana asked, suddenly alarmed.

"Quit my job and come home to you," Nick replied, kissing her again.

An hour later, Hana was tucked into the trunk of the car and he was pulling out of the garage when he saw Mrs. Hallowell standing at the edge of the driveway. Nick groaned; he was already late, and he would be later still if he had to get Snowbird down from a tree.

He stopped the car when he reached the old woman. "Good morning, Mrs. Hallowell; is Snowbird up in the tree again?" Nick asked pleasantly.

"Good morning, Mr. Alexander! Snowbird is in the house, but I wanted to tell you something."

Nick got a nervous feeling in his stomach. "What is it?"

"A man came to my house the other night and was asking me all kinds of questions about you," she replied.

"What kind of questions?" Nick asked.

"Well, he wanted to know if I had ever met your wife, for one thing, and I told him that I had—when did you get married?" she asked.

"Not real long ago, but why did you tell him you met my wife when you haven't?" Nick asked.

"I didn't like him! Especially when he told me not to tell you that he had been here."

"What did this man look like?' Nick asked.

"Tall, good-looking man, dark hair that was getting a little thin."

Elam.

"Thank you, Mrs. Hallowell; was there anything else?"

"No, that's about it. When *will* I get to meet your wife?" she asked.

"Soon, I hope. She's away visiting family; her sister is having a baby, and she wants to be there," Nick said, lying smoothly. "I have to go now, but thank you again for the information."

"Son of a bitch!" Nick swore as he pulled out of the driveway and headed over to Abby's. He watched carefully, making sure he wasn't being followed. After leaving Hana at Abby's with promises to call frequently, Nick headed to the office.

The office was in an uproar when he got there.

"What's happening?" he asked Charles when he saw him.

"D-Day," Charles said excitedly. "The Allies have landed on Normandy."

As good news as that was, Nick had other things on his mind. "Is Elam here?"

"He's in his office," Charles replied, too excited to notice the ominous tone in Nick's voice.

Nick left the general office area and walked into Elam's office without knocking, slamming the door closed behind him. "You deceitful bastard!" Nick hissed, not caring that Elam was on the phone.

"Clyde? I'll call you back," Elam said and hung up the phone. He looked at Nick for a moment. "What's crawled up your ass?"

"You!" Nick shouted.

"Me? What did—"

"Mrs. Hallowell told me she had a visitor and described you to perfection."

"Nick—"

"Shut the fuck up!" Nick snarled. "You reneged on our deal when you went to my neighbor and asked about me; you reneged on our deal when you didn't come to me with any questions regarding my personal life; and yes, I would have told you it was none of your damned business, so here's what's going to happen. Effective now, I'm done, and if I see one car or agent watching me, my house, or my friend's house, I'm going to the top. I'm sick of this shit!"

"Nick, let me explain."

"I don't want or need an explanation for why you're spying on me again," Nick said, and then an idea hit him. "That's why you asked me back, isn't it? You wanted to be able to keep an eye on me, even though I proved I hadn't done anything wrong. What's really going on here, Elam?"

"Nothing," Elam said. "I just know you're hiding something, and it's bothering me like a bad rash."

Nick gave Elam an incredulous look. "You mean that this is all because of your curiosity about my private life?"

"Come on, Nick—"

"No, I'm done here, and do me a favor: put Charles with Avery as a partner. He's the best agent in the office."

Nick walked out without looking back. He really was done with this; he would sit out the rest of the war with Hana and the others.

Elam watched Nick leave and cursed under his breath. One of his best agents had just walked out the door, and when the director found out, there would be hell to pay. The problem was that he had no good excuse for it; going to see the old woman had been a spontaneous decision, and he really hadn't expected the old woman to say anything. He had seriously underestimated their relationship.

He decided to wait before letting the director know that Nick had quit; he would give him a few days to cool off and then approach him again about coming back. What he didn't understand is why he just couldn't leave Nick alone. He knew he was hiding something, but weren't they all? Elam made a promise to himself: if he could convince Nick to come back, he would leave him alone.

Hana nervously paced the living room; Nick hadn't called her yet, and she had visions of him sitting in a cell somewhere. She tried to occupy herself with caring for Niko and Marie so Kenji and Patricia could have some much-needed time alone, and had moderate success.

She heard a car horn beep three short times. Nick.

Hana picked the baby up and hurried to the kitchen, with Niko following close behind her, and waited by the door. As soon as Nick walked in, she hugged him, almost crushing the baby between them.

"Whoa, careful there!" Nick said. "I don't think Kenji and Patricia would appreciate a smashed baby."

"Are you all right? What happened?" Hana asked.

"I'm fine, and I quit," Nick replied, taking the baby from Hana.

"You're not going back?"

"I'm not going back," Nick confirmed as he kissed the baby on the head.

"Will they come for you?" Hana asked.

"No, sweetheart, they won't come after me," Nick assured her.

Hana nodded, although she wasn't completely convinced. She was just happy he was home.

"Where's Ralph? I've got news that I'm sure he doesn't have," Nick said.

Ralph was making some slight changes to the little room he had built off the back door for Kenji and Patricia. The weather was warming up, and he was trying to find a way to let more of the outside air in without making it easy to see someone sitting inside.

"Hey, Nick," he greeted, not looking up.

"Hey," Nick replied as he watched Ralph work. "I've got some news I bet you don't have."

"Yeah? What's that?"

"D-Day."

"What's that?" Ralph asked, finally looking at Nick.

"Yesterday the Allies landed in Normandy."

"You don't say?" Ralph asked. Nick now had his complete and undivided attention.

"That's what I heard when I went in this morning."

"What do you think it means?" Ralph asked.

"Hopefully an end to the war," Nick replied. "There's one more thing: I no longer work for the government. Elam reneged on his agreement, and I'm done as of this morning."

Ralph didn't reply at first. "Nick, I don't like it. What does this man want with you? You've been cleared of spying, he shows up and begs you to come back to work, and now he's fucking with you again."

"He wants to find out what I'm hiding," Nick replied. "I don't think it's because he has anything against me; I think it's because he can't stand not knowing something about me or anyone else, for that matter. Make no mistake—if he finds out about Hana, Kenji, and the kids, all of our asses are going to be sitting in prison somewhere, so we need to be careful."

Ralph nodded in understanding. "Actually, I'm glad you're here," Ralph said. "My son and his family have decided to take me up on my offer to move here."

"When are they coming?" Nick asked, already thinking of an alternative safe house for everyone.

"Mid-August," Ralph replied.

"What are you going to tell him?" Nick asked.

"I can tell him about everyone except for Hana, Kenji, and the kids," Ralph replied. "Although it galls me."

"We need to come up with another safe place," Nick said in response.

"I know; I've been thinking about that."

"Any ideas?"

"Not a one, but I'm working on it," Ralph said.

The day was finally here. Kenji made sure both children were bathed and dressed for the day while Patricia was in the library reading. She wanted to help with the baths, but Kenji wouldn't let her.

"You deserve time to yourself, and besides, once I'm in school, you'll be too busy for such pleasures, so go and relax."

Patricia agreed with him, but she still wanted to help. Finally she gave in and went to the library to read, admitting that it was nice to have some time to herself. As she picked out a book, she wondered what Kenji was up to, but whatever it was, she hoped it involved some alone time for them. She missed him, and it had been months since they made love—other than in the way they used to before they were married—and if she was ready, then he had to be, too.

Kenji bathed Niko first, helped him dress, and sent him to Ralph. When he bathed Marie, he took his time and examined her, listening to her heartbeat, satisfied that there were no irregularities.

"You are beautiful, just like your mother," Kenji murmured to the baby as he dressed her and then brushed her dark hair.

He carried her downstairs and handed her to Abby. "If you need anything, call down to us and we'll come up," he told her.

"Don't you worry," Abby replied, cuddling the baby. "We'll be just fine."

"Thank you for doing this," Kenji said softly.

"You're welcome," Abby replied. "Everything you wanted is already downstairs," she added.

"*Kirei*?" Kenji called when he went into the library.

"Back here!" Patricia yelled from the back of the library.

Kenji found her sitting on the floor with her back to the wall and sat down beside her.

"Where are Marie and Niko?" she asked.

"Niko is with Ralph, and Marie is with Abby. They will be caring for them while we spend the day and night together."

"All day and night?" Patricia asked, surprised.

"It's arranged," Kenji said, standing up and holding his hand out to her.

Patricia took his hand and suddenly became nervous. While Kenji had seen the scar and tended to it, he hadn't seen it in the context of them making love. While she knew it wouldn't matter, it still made her nervous. She absently touched the barely noticeable scar on her cheek and remembered that it hadn't mattered to him then.

Kenji looked down at her and touched her face. "You will always be my *Kirei,* no matter how many scars you have."

"How did you know I was thinking about that?" Patricia asked.

"I remember when you got the scar on your cheek," Kenji said, tracing the scar with a fingertip. "You were so afraid that I would find you ugly. I didn't then and I don't now. You're as beautiful as ever," he assured her.

Patricia felt tears burning her eyes; he always made her feel beautiful, no matter the fact that she didn't quite see herself in the same way. She let him lead her to the basement; he turned on the lights and led her down the stairs.

Patricia looked around the basement that had been their home on and off for the past couple of years and where Niko had been born. Fresh flowers were in vases all around the room; a plate of sandwiches sat wrapped on a small table alongside a pitcher of water and glasses of juice. The washbasin was filled with steaming water with a bar of soap and clean towels, and washcloths next to it on another small table. The bed was freshly made and already turned back.

"You did all of this?" she asked when Kenji came back down the stairs.

"With help from Abby and Ralph, yes," Kenji replied as he wrapped his arms around her.

Patricia leaned back into him, her insecurities about her scar forgotten as she felt Kenji's hardness pressing into her back. She turned around in his arms and looked up at him. "I have missed you so much."

"And I you," Kenji replied as he kissed her.

Patricia started to undress, but Kenji stopped her. "Let me; I love undressing you."

Patricia felt her nipples tighten and was glad that she had pumped her milk into bottles while Kenji gave the babies their baths. Her womb clenched and the fluids of arousal soaked her panties. She loved being undressed as much as Kenji loved doing it. Unable to be still, she began to unbutton his shirt, taking time to touch his chest and play with his nipples, leaning in to take one into her mouth.

Kenji moaned softly and sped up undressing her. Both of them knew that the first time would be quick, but the times afterward would be gentle and unhurried. Finally Patricia stood naked in front of him; he stepped back, looked her up and down, then dropped to his knees. He wrapped his arms around her hips, rested his cheek on her stomach, and then kissed a trail down the length of the incision.

Patricia wrapped her arms around his head and held him close; it was several minutes before either of them moved, and then it was Kenji who moved first. He took Patricia's hand and led her to the bed, easing her into it before lying next to her. For a few moments, they lay front to front before Kenji moved so he lay on top of her and eased into her. It only took a few thrusts before he felt his orgasm begin, and he quickly pulled out and rubbed against Patricia's thigh. As much as he loved their children, he couldn't allow himself to get so lost in the moment that he came inside of her; there couldn't be another pregnancy. For one, it was much too soon, and they simply couldn't afford it, especially if he was going to go to school.

Kenji rolled off Patricia and reached for a washcloth so he could clean her thigh. When he was finished, he got between her legs and, without teasing, took her clit into his mouth and nibbled on it until Patricia came with her face covered with a pillow to stifle her screams.

Someday, Kenji thought to himself as he listened to Patricia's screams of pleasure, they would be in their own home where how loud she screamed wouldn't matter.

He held a shaking Patricia in his arms and waited until she calmed.

"Are you all right?" he asked.

"I'm perfect," Patricia replied and then fell silent.

"You're thinking," Kenji said.

"Have you ever wished that we hadn't met?"

"No," Kenji replied without hesitation, "but there was a time that I wondered if I shouldn't have married you, and it wasn't because I doubted that I loved you—it was *because* I love you. Being with me has brought you so much pain and sadness."

"But it's also made me happy," Patricia interjected.

"What about you?" Kenji asked. "Have you ever regretted the decision we made?"

"As scared as I was and still am, I've never regretted being with you, and if I had to do it all again to be here with you, I would," Patricia replied. "I do have a question: do you ever think about your father?"

Kenji hesitated; he had been meaning to talk to her about his father, but something always came up. "I have been thinking about him lately," he admitted.

"And?"

"I don't know, *Kirei*. He's not the man who taught me honor and courage, and I'm not sure I can get past what he tried to have done to you."

Patricia touched his face and then kissed him. "What if I told you that I could and that if you wanted to make peace with him, even if he doesn't accept me, I'd be fine with that?"

"I would say that you have a good heart, but if he cannot accept you and our children, then he cannot accept me," Kenji replied.

Patricia chose her next words carefully. "Kenji, we can't teach our children forgiveness if we can't forgive others ourselves. What your father did was wrong—there are no two ways about it—but if you don't at least talk to him, what will you tell Niko and Marie when they're old enough to ask about him? If you talk to him and he turns you away, then you've done all you could do and it will be up to him to make the next move, and you can tell our children that."

Kenji thought about what she said. "I understand, but *Kirei*, you are my wife, and I will not deal with a man who cannot or will not accept you as such."

"How will you know that unless you talk to him?" Patricia countered.

She had a point, Kenji realized. Actually, several points. "I concede that you are right on several points," Kenji said. "If the opportunity presents itself, I will speak to my father, but if he can't respect and accept you and our children, I'll have nothing more to say to him."

"That's fair," Patricia said as she reached down and began to stroke his cock until it was fully erect.

The following week, Nick was at home with Hana and Paul when the doorbell rang. Hana ran up the stairs while Paul cleared away the extra place setting at the table. Nick peeked out and saw Elam at the door with Charles; he fought the temptation to ignore them and opened the door.

"What do you want, Elam?" Nick asked, after greeting Charles.

"To talk," Elam replied.

"There's nothing to talk about," Nick replied. "You went back on your word to stay out of my private life, and you interrogated a sweet old lady."

"That was a spur-of-the-moment decision," Elam replied. "It was a bad one, and I'm sorry."

Nick laughed. "Your apologies mean nothing to me, but why are you here?"

"Can we come inside?" Elam asked.

"No, have a seat on the porch and I'll be right out," Nick said and closed the door in their faces.

"Who's out there?" Paul asked.

"People from the office," Nick replied as he ran up the stairs.

"Sweetheart, you don't have to hide in the closet, but stay up here," Nick said as he helped Hana out of the closet.

"Who is it?" she asked.

"Elam Martin and Charles."

Hana's heart rate jumped. "Why are they here?"

"My guess is that Elam got his ass chewed about me quitting," Nick replied as he hugged her. "I'll be back in a few minutes."

While Elam waited for Nick to come out, he used the time to think about his proposal to Nick. If Nick refused, then Elam was in deep shit. It occurred to him that he made many of the same mistakes Howard Gibbs had, in that he just couldn't leave Nick alone. The difference was that Howard had his reasons and Elam didn't; he was just curious about a man who guarded his private life so intensely. The truth of it was he didn't believe Nick was married. He had always believed Nick to be a homosexual; it only made sense. He was never seen with a woman and rebuffed any advances made toward him by the women in the office. The wedding ring was a means to get the women to leave him alone.

Elam stood up when Nick came out.

"You have ten minutes to tell me what you want."

"Nick, I overstepped my bounds when I went to talk to your neighbor. She makes the best cookies, but at any rate, it won't happen again."

"What is it you think I'm hiding?" Nick asked.

"You want the truth?" Elam asked.

"Yes, let's lay our cards on the table. Just what in the hell do you think I'm hiding?"

"All right then, I have never seen a man guard his private life the way you do. I also think that the excuse about keeping work and your home life separate is a bunch of bullshit, and that doesn't explain why no one has ever seen your wife—not even a fucking picture! Which leads me to one conclusion: You're not married and you're wearing the ring to keep the women off of your back, which leads me to another point—no one has ever seen you with a woman. Every man in that office, married or not, has banged a woman working there—except for you."

Nick saw where this was going and struggled not to laugh. "Elam, first of all, my private life is just that: private. I don't care that the rest of you talk about your wives or girlfriends, and whether you believe it or not, I do try to keep my work life separate from my home life. As to why no one has ever seen my wife, I maintain that it's none of your fucking business as long as I'm doing my job. I know what goes on behind closed doors at the office, and I don't give a damn, but just because I don't partake in used goods doesn't mean anything. I just don't like leftovers. But that's not what you really think, is it? Go one and say it," Nick urged.

Elam had the sense to be embarrassed and tried to back out. "Look, let's just drop it and talk about what we need to do to get you back in the office."

"Let's not drop it," Nick said. "I'm sure that Charles is interested in hearing your theory about my private life; tell him what you were thinking."

"I . . . I thought you were a homosexual," Elam mumbled.

"Hmmm, based on what? The facts you just stated? It seems like you haven't learned anything about circumstantial evidence," Nick said. "Just to clear things up, I am married, and you can believe me or not. And I am not a homosexual, but what if I was? Does that place me back under suspicion of being a spy? And what were you going to do with the information? Blackmail me to keep me under your thumb? Publicize it?

"This is my last warning to you: Leave me the fuck alone. If I even see a car that looks agency drive by here or following me, or if I find out you've been asking questions about me or my wife, I'll make a phone call. So ask yourself, is finding out what you think I'm hiding worth losing your job at worst and being demoted at best?"

Elam was at a loss for words; he had given Nick enough ammunition to get him fired, and Charles was a witness who would stick by Nick. "All right," Elam said. "I get it, and I'm done snooping in your private life; will you come back to work?"

"There's not a chance in hell of that happening," Nick replied.

"But—"

"No, and there's nothing you can offer me to make me change my mind. After you leave, I don't expect to see you again, and by the way, good luck explaining to the field office director why I quit . . . again."

Nick stood up, nodded at Charles, went inside, and began to laugh. "Homosexual, of all things!" he said and laughed again.

He went upstairs still laughing and told Hana about the conversation with Elam. She didn't find it funny and told him so.

"Sweetheart, it's all right," Nick said, still chuckling. "You should have seen Elam's face when I made him say it."

"Nick, I still don't trust him, and you made him look bad in front of a subordinate. Just be careful, even though you no longer work there."

"You're right, but I'm tired of the games. I'm tired of hiding you and not being able to take you out to dinner or for a walk," Nick replied.

"I know this has been hard on you," Hana replied. "But surely, this can't last much longer, can it?"

"I hope not, but there's still the issue of our marriage. It isn't legal, and as far as I know, we won't be able to be legally married anytime soon," Nick replied. "But then at least you won't have to hide every time someone comes to the door and we can go out, even if we have to act like we're not married."

"Will your family hate you?"

Nick sighed. "They won't be happy," he replied and then realized they were talking as if this was going to end tomorrow, but then, who knew? *Maybe it could*, he thought to himself.

By the end of July 1944, fourteen-year-old diarist Tanya Savicheva died of starvation; her diary, which depicted her family's death, became famous.

Minsk in Belarus was liberated by the Soviets; the largest Banzai charge of the war took place on Saipan, and 4,300 Japanese lost their lives. Saipan was deemed secure with the Japanese having lost over thirty thousand troops; many civilians committed suicide at the encouragement of the Japanese military. Tokyo was bombed for the first time since April 1942; President Roosevelt announced that he was planning to run for a fourth term; Colonel Claus von Stauffenberg attempted to assassinate Hitler at headquarters in Rastenburg, East Prussia; US Marines landed on Guam; and the Majdanek concentration camp was liberated by the Soviets.

Kenji fingered the necklace he had given to Patricia for her birthday a few years before; she had given it back to him when he was getting ready to get on the bus going to the camp. He had promised to give it back to her when they were together again and wondered if this qualified and decided not. They could still be caught. He put the necklace back in his wallet; he would wait until the camps were closed before he gave it back to her.

Patricia's birthday and their anniversary—the second one—was on the same day, July 8. Patricia would be twenty-four and it would be their third anniversary; although they celebrated January 1 as their anniversary, July 8 was the legal date.

He wanted to get her something special and, with the help of Hattie and Abby, managed to buy her a new dress and a small bottle of perfume. The dress was hanging in Abby's closet, and Hattie would bring the perfume as well as the cake. Niko looked forward to John and Hattie's visits because they always brought him a treat of some kind; he had inherited his father's love of sweets.

Patricia's birthday was just a day away, and Kenji couldn't wait to see her in the dress. She would also wear her hair down the way he liked it, and she would put on just a dab of the perfume he had gotten her for another birthday.

"Papa, help me," Niko said, tugging at Kenji's pant leg.

"What do you need help with?" Kenji asked as he bent and picked Niko up.

"I want to read."

Kenji smiled at him. "Why am I not surprised?" he asked and kissed Niko on the cheek.

"Love you, Papa."

"I love you, too; now which book are we reading today?"

Patricia watched Kenji and Niko together and smiled. Niko was learning from the best, she decided. Her father was teaching him, too, but Kenji was teaching him gentleness, whereas her father taught him toughness. That wasn't to say that Kenji wasn't tough; he was, but in an entirely different way. He could defend himself and them if need be, but he hated violence of any kind and had been fortunate that they hadn't encountered much violence, other than what he saw at Manzanar.

She heard Marie crying and left Kenji and Niko to their reading to tend to her.

"What's wrong, baby?" she cooed as she picked the baby up. As soon as the baby was in her arms, she knew what the problem was. "Poor thing, I'd cry, too," she soothed as she laid the baby down and removed the source of her discomfort. She washed Marie's bottom and applied oil to it before putting on a clean diaper. "Better?" she asked as she kissed the baby's head. Marie gurgled her response.

Patricia took Marie to the kitchen, where Ralph sat sipping on a cup of coffee. He hadn't been himself lately, and Patricia wanted to know why.

"I haven't said anything yet except to Nick and Abby, but my son and his family are moving out here. They're going to live in my old house."

"That's wonderful!" Patricia exclaimed.

"No, it isn't," Ralph said glumly.

"I don't understand," Patricia said.

"Patty, by them coming here, there's one less safe place for you, Kenji, and the kids to go to. And they can't know about Kenji, Hana, and the kids; he'd turn all of us in."

"You can't know that," Patricia replied.

"I can and I do know that to be true; he was a member of the KKK, and even though he no longer participates, he believes in what they teach."

"When are they coming?" Patricia asked.

"The middle of next month," Ralph replied.

"Maybe it will be all right," Patricia offered.

"Maybe," Ralph conceded, not really believing it.

The next day, Hattie and John came over early to help get ready for Patricia's birthday, with Hana and Nick showing up soon afterward with their birthday gift for Patricia. Abby had Patricia in her room under the pretense of helping her pick out something to wear for the party.

"There's something in the closet for you," Abby said when Patricia came into her room. "It's from Kenji."

"In your closet?" Patricia asked.

"Yes, and he'd like you to wear it," Abby replied as she went to the closet and pulled out the dress.

Patricia stared at the dress; she hadn't had anything new since the wedding dress Abby had bought for her.

"It's beautiful!" Patricia looked at the lemon-colored summer dress and cried. "He shouldn't have; we'll need the money for school and—"

"Patricia, put the dress on, kiss him, and say thank you. It means a lot to him," Abby said.

Patricia nodded; Abby was right. She put the dress on with Abby's help. It was just a tad too big, but the yellow looked nice against her dark skin. She undid the French braid that she now wore her hair in and brushed it out until it lay neatly against her shoulders.

"You look lovely," Abby said when Patricia was dressed. "Wait here."

A few minutes later, there was a tap on the door and Kenji walked in.

"Happy birthday, *Kirei*!" he said, walking up to her.

"The dress, it's beautiful. Thank you!" Patricia said, hugging him and then pulling him down for a kiss.

"It looks beautiful on you," Kenji said, stroking her cheek gently. "I have something else for you." He held out the small box that contained the bottle of perfume.

"Kenji—"

"Open it," he urged.

Patricia took the box and opened it. She lifted out the small bottle of perfume; it was the same brand as the other and a floral scent as well.

"You always remind me of spring flowers," Kenji told her as he took the small bottle from her hands, opened it, and put a dab behind each ear and on her wrist. "I wish I could keep you to myself for just a little while longer."

Patricia stood on her tippy toes and kissed him on his chin. "Thank you for the dress and the perfume, but it would have been a good birthday without them because you're here."

"All right, you two!" Ralph called up. "Supper's waiting!"

Kenji kissed Patricia one last time before taking her hand and leading her downstairs. Everyone complimented her on her appearance, which she attributed to Kenji's good taste in clothes.

"No, *Kirei*, *you* are what makes it beautiful," Kenji said.

After dinner, Patricia opened her birthday gifts. From her parents she got another used copy of one of the classics; Abby got her another sweater; Ralph gave her some nice-smelling bubble bath; and Nick and Hana gave her an envelope containing $100.

"I can't take this!" she gasped. "It's too much money!"

"We want you to have it," Hana said. "When this is over, you can buy whatever you like with it."

Nothing Patricia said could persuade Nick and Hana to take the money back; she ended up thanking them profusely. The money would be added to their savings, most of which they still had only because Abby and Ralph refused to take any money from them.

"I haven't given my gift yet," Paul said.

"Yes, you have," Patricia said.

"No, I haven't; it's kind of a gift for the both of you," he said as he handed a thick folder to Patricia.

Patricia looked at Paul and then opened the envelope. Inside was the application to the UCLA School of Medicine and several tests.

"Don't sign your name just yet, but I figured we might as well get the ball rolling," Paul said. "The tests are aptitude tests to see if you need to repeat anything. You don't happen to have your transcripts from Nagasaki, do you?"

"I have them here with me," Kenji replied.

"Good, let me know when you plan to take the test. I have to sit with you; I know you won't cheat, but that was a stipulation for getting the tests for you."

"Of course!" Kenji replied, still in shock.

Patricia hugged Paul and kissed him on the cheek. "Thank you!"

"You're welcome," Paul said, hugging her back.

Kenji was speechless; he knew Paul was going to help, but. . . .

"Thank you many times over," Kenji said, his voice soft and choked with emotion. It was at that moment he really believed that all of them would make it through intact and together. Once again, he thought about the necklace in his wallet that was wrapped in the embroidered handkerchief Patricia had given him for his twenty-first birthday and decided to wait; he didn't want to tempt fate.

After the party and the kitchen were cleaned up, Ralph decided to call his son. He hadn't spoken to him in over a week and was hoping they had changed their minds about coming, at least until after the war.

"Hey, Pop!" Lawrence said cheerfully when he answered the phone.

"Hiya, son, how are things?"

"Good! I'm glad you called; I have some good news for you."

"What's that?" Ralph asked nervously.

"Sally's sister and her husband got here earlier than we thought, so we're pulling out of here next Saturday."

Ralph's stomach dropped. "So you're thinking it'll take you a week?"

"Maybe longer; Sally wants to do a little sightseeing since she's never been out of the state, but to be safe, let's say a week."

"All right then; we'll see you then."

"Wait, Pop, how do we get ahold of you?" Lawrence asked.

"Well, it's like I said, I use my friend's phone, but I suppose you can call here and leave a message." Ralph reluctantly gave Lawrence Abby's number and then hung up.

"What's wrong?" Patricia asked when she saw Ralph's face.

"They're coming; they're going to be here in two weeks tops."

"It'll work out; you'll see," Patricia said, patting his arm.

"I hope so," Ralph replied, but he didn't believe it would be all right. He had a very bad feeling about his son and his family coming to his house. He almost picked up the phone to tell him not to come, but he couldn't think of a good enough reason to renege on his offer.

"Please, let this just be a case of nerves," he prayed.

Lawrence leaned back in his chair after talking to his father; he didn't really want to move to California, where he knew there were plenty of niggers and spics living; he liked it just where he was. The plan to move had come up when he told the leader of the local Klan about his conversations with his father.

"This sounds like a good opportunity to start another group; of course you would be the leader since you would be starting it," Dr. Malcolm Rhodes said.

That was the deciding factor. When Lawrence spoke to his father, he led him to believe that while he didn't condone the lynching and whippings, he agreed with the belief that the white race needed to be protected. He left out the part that he was often the initiator of the lynchings, as he had been with the black boy he told his father about. If his father knew any of it, he would have taken back the offer to live in his house.

Sally was thrilled with the idea of him running his own group, as were the kids, but it was also the idea of moving to someplace different. He didn't know what was going to happen once his father figured out what he was really up to. It was clear by the way his father cried over the dead nigger and the way in which he corrected him by calling him a man that he had become a nigger lover.

Lawrence planned to look for their own place as soon as they arrived, to prevent any issues. The Klan had given him plenty of cash, and he got asking price for the house. He wished he could sell the land that his father owned, but since it was still in Ralph's name, he couldn't. He did, however, allow the Klan to use the house for meetings; it was perfect since it was out of the way, far from town, and the perfect place for lynching niggers and nigger lovers.

The thought that his father would be angry that his home and land were being used in such a way didn't bother Lawrence in the least; he simply didn't care. He looked around the kitchen, which had boxes stacked in every corner. They really were leaving here for another life.

He made one more call before going to bed.

"Doc? It's all set; we're leaving next week."

Lawrence hung up and smiled. He was proud to be a member of a group that was going to protect the white race.

Chapter 19

By the end of August 1944, the 442nd Combat Team was actively fighting in the war, although they were generally prohibited from fighting in the Pacific Arena. These restrictions weren't placed on Americans of Italian or German ancestry, who were allowed to fight in Europe, mainly because they outnumbered those of Japanese ancestry.

The second Warsaw uprising began, led by the Polish Home Army, the Polish people expecting help from the Soviets who were approaching; the rebellion would last for sixty-three days, and help didn't arrive.

Florence, Italy, was liberated by the Allies; the Germans destroyed some of the historic buildings and bridges as they retreated; the trials of the conspirators against Hitler began; Japanese POWs escaped from a prison near the town of Cowra, Australia, in which two guards died; the Germans, in anticipation of the Krakow Uprising, rounded up all of the young men in Krakow.

In Seattle, Washington, the Fort Lawton Riot occurred. The riot began with a conflict between US soldiers and Italian POWs in which a prisoner named Guglielmo Olivotto died. This led to a court-martial of forty-three soldiers, all of them black. (In 2005, the book *On American Soil* helped convince the US Board for Correction of Military Records that the prosecutor, Leon Jaworski, made a huge mistake and that all convictions should be reversed. President George W. Bush signed legislation that allowed the army to give back-pay to the defendants or their survivors.)

Guam was freed by American troops; Guam and the Marianas would be turned into major naval and air centers to be used against the Japanese homeland. The French Resistance, inspired by the approach of the Allies, began an uprising; Romania broke from the Axis powers and joined the Allies; 168 captured Allied airmen arrived at the Buchenwald concentration camp near Weimer, Germany, where they were fully shaved and starved; Paris was liberated; the Soviets entered Bucharest, Romania; and the French government was turned over to free French troops.

Ralph paid little attention to the news or the newspaper; he was too distracted by nerves over the arrival of his son and family. The last hope that they might not come was dashed when Ralph called just as Lawrence was signing the papers for the sale of his house and asked for the names and phone numbers of the schools near Ralph's house.

He and Abby had gone to the house several times to clean and make sure there was no evidence of Patricia, Kenji, and the baby being there, but Abby had a point. "So what if he finds anything? You could always say you had a family living here with you before the war, and if they stumble across anything Japanese, then say they had to go to the camps, which isn't a lie."

The big problem was that he would be living with strangers. Kenji and Patricia had been strangers, too, but he knew where they were coming from, whereas with Lawrence, he just didn't know. The feeling that there was more behind the move than Lawrence had let on niggled at him, even though the reasons Lawrence had given for the move were perfectly reasonable.

Ralph looked at the calendar; they would be here in less than a week. In less than a week, he would be separated from the people whom he loved and who loved him, as irritable as he could be. The issue of his house no longer being safe had finally been resolved; Nick found a house not too far from his that was for sale and bought it at well below asking price. There was nothing else they could do; his hope was that once the war was over, he would be able to sell it for what he paid for it. If not, then Kenji and Patricia could live in it.

Hattie, Abby, and Patricia had already been over to the house several times, cleaning and getting it ready while he and Nick made any repairs and stocked it with essentials. In order to make it look like a move-in was happening, Nick would spend the day there and on occasion sleep there. He and Ralph shopped around for cheap furniture and beds to complete the illusion.

Several times, Ralph tried to apologize for telling his son that he could live with him.

"Ralph! Give it a rest!" Nick said one day as they worked on the back yard. "No one is upset with you; you did what you thought you needed to do."

Up until now, Ralph hadn't shared his concerns about the reason for Lawrence's move. "I think there's more to it," he told Nick.

"Like what?"

"I don't know, but there's something else going on," Ralph replied.

"Do you want to know what I think?" Nick asked. "I think you're nervous because you haven't seen him in so long and you'll be meeting your grandchildren for the first time."

"Maybe you're right," Ralph said, but the niggling persisted.

Lawrence had never realized how beautiful the West Coast was; he thought that even the ocean looked and sounded different. He had hoped to be at his father's by now, but Sally wanted to stop at every historic site she saw and begged to spend the night at a hotel where the beach was just a stone's throw away.

He had always been unable to deny her anything, and agreed. He watched as she and the kids ran up and down the beach and put their feet into the water, only to take off running again. Their laughter and happiness warmed him, and he was beginning to be glad that they were moving when he saw that even Kenneth seemed happy.

He turned his attention to the reason for the move and what he needed to do once they got there; the first thing he had to do was find out if there were any groups already in existence, and if there were, he would have to seek them out. If there were just a few people here and there, then he would try to pull them into one group. He also had to find a place to meet if the group couldn't meet at the homes of the new members. Realistically, it could be weeks before he knew what had to be done, and he had to find a job to boot.

He was distracted from his planning when Sally sat down beside him, her eyes lit with happiness and a smile on her face.

"Thank you for this; I know you're eager to get to your dad's house."

Lawrence put his arm around her and kissed her temple. "You and the kids deserve this and so much more," he replied.

Sally hesitated before she spoke. "Do you really want to do this? Couldn't we just move here and keep to ourselves?"

"I thought you were behind me in this," Lawrence said.

"I am, but I was just thinking that we could just . . . you know."

Lawrence took his arm from around his wife. "I'm doing this for us and our kids and their kids," he said. "I can't very well expect others to do all the work while we reap the benefits of it. This is a war, and we need every man, woman, and child to join in if we're going to keep the niggers, the nigger lovers, and the rest of them under control."

Sally laid her head on Lawrence's shoulder; it would have been pointless to say anything more on the subject. His mind was made up. As for herself, she didn't have any bad feelings toward anyone and agreed that the races should be kept separate, but Lawrence was her husband, and she had to support him, no matter what she believed.

Like him, she found the West Coast beautiful, and she was glad to be away from her demanding mother and the town they had lived in. That Lawrence indulged her as much as he was doing surprised her a little, but then, he rarely told her no. He was so excited about leading his own group, and that was the reason for the surprise.

As she laid her head on Lawrence's shoulder, she closed her eyes and listened to the sound of the ocean as it hit the shore. The thought that she could stay where they were forever crossed her mind, but there was no way that was going to happen—Lawrence was on a mission, and there was the matter of the money the Klan had given them to get started out here to consider.

Kenji studied every day in preparation of taking the tests; he had given Paul a target date of September 30, which gave him six more weeks to learn all he could.

Patricia would watch him study to the point of exhaustion and put her foot down. "Kenjiro Takeda, put that book away right now!"

"Just a little longer, *Kirei*," he said, sounding like Niko when he didn't want to go to bed.

Patricia walked up to him, took the book out of his hands, sat in his lap, and kissed his face until he was laughing.

"All right, *Kirei*, you win," Kenji said, still laughing and kissing her back.

"You study too hard," Patricia said as she rested her head on his shoulder.

"It's with you and our children in mind that I study as hard as I do," Kenji replied. "*Kirei*, things are going to get better for us; I feel it. Marie surviving was my confirmation of this belief; things are already improving, and from what I hear, the war will soon be over."

"Not soon enough to suit me," Patricia replied, kissing his cheek. "I'm going to get ready for bed," she said, standing up. "You have ten more minutes, Dr. Takeda," she called as she walked away.

Kenji watched her walk away and closed the book. She was right; he had been studying hard, and he was tired. The thought of lying in bed with Patricia in his arms sounded like the perfect way to end the day. He realized that all the things they had talked about doing would be possible in a few years, but in the meantime, he would be thrilled to walk down the street with her and their children.

"Please, let this war end," he prayed to no god in particular as he made his way to their bedroom.

Both children were sound asleep when he reached the bedroom, and Patricia was already in bed waiting for him. He looked at her and smiled. The mischievous sparkle in her eyes that he had always loved was slowly making its way back, another indication to him at least that things really were going to be all right.

Kenji stripped, climbed into bed, and put his arm around her. As tired as he was, he wanted to talk. "I've been thinking about what you said about my father."

"And?"

"I can't see my way around what he wanted to have done to you, but if you can see your way to forgive him, then I will at least try."

"I think you'll be glad you did," Patricia said.

"I've also been thinking about what we will tell our children when they're old enough to ask about us, and *Kirei*, we will tell them the truth—all of it."

Patricia thought about it and decided he was right; she was going to tell him that she agreed when she heard his soft snores. She kissed his cheek and closed her eyes; a few minutes later, she was asleep.

Elam hadn't called or made an appearance since he and Nick last talked, but Charles came by frequently, always calling beforehand. According to Charles, things at the office were much the same with one major change: Elam Martin had been demoted to field agent.

"It turns out that you weren't the only person whose life he was prying into without cause," he told Nick over a cup of coffee.

"Who else?" Nick asked.

"Some of the higher-ups," Charles replied. "Including the director himself."

That shocked Nick; surely Elam wouldn't have been that stupid. "Why was he doing this? It had to be more than just curiosity."

"I don't know, and he's not talking. He's lucky he still has a job. From what I hear, he only has a job because he's been with the agency for so long and was instrumental in arresting Mitch and his partners."

Nick's head spun; it didn't make sense, but it didn't matter. He was out of the game, and it was going to stay that way. He had already started making preparations to reopen his law office; he wanted to leave the mystery and intrigue to those who liked that sort of thing.

"Who replaced Elam?" Nick asked.

"No one, as of yet."

It then struck him that this wasn't a strictly social visit. "Other than to say hello and to fill me in on the office scuttlebutt, why are you here?" Nick asked.

Charles looked a little uncomfortable and squirmed under Nick's gaze. "The director sent me, because he knows we were partners for a short time," Charles replied.

Nick knew what was coming, but waited for Charles to finish. "He wants you to replace Elam."

"Why didn't he ask me himself?" Nick replied.

"I think he's well aware of your feelings toward . . . shall we say, authority? He knows you've been fucked over too many times to count, and he thought you would at least listen to me," Charles replied.

"No."

"You're not even going to think about it?" Charles asked, surprised by Nick's quick response.

"There's nothing to think about," Nick replied. "I meant it when I told Elam that I was done."

"Nick—"

"Tell the director he has my thanks for the offer, but the answer is no," Nick said, cutting Charles off.

Charles smiled. "I told him you would say no."

"But you asked anyway."

"I had to try," Charles said.

"So what office is Elam working out of?"

"Ours for now, but he's looking to be transferred to another office. As you can imagine, he doesn't have many friends where we are. Everyone is wondering if he was snooping into their personal affairs, and if he was, what did he find out?"

Nick and Charles talked for a few more minutes before Charles excused himself. "I'm taking a nice young lady out for dinner."

"Good for you!" Nick said as he walked Charles to his car.

"I think she might be the one," Charles said as he got in.

"Then by all means, keep me posted," Nick replied.

Hana waited anxiously in Nick's office; she knew of Charles, and based on what Nick had told her about him, she liked him. She wondered what the discussion was about and hoped it wasn't about Nick going back to work at the office. She had gotten used to having him around; she breathed easier knowing he was safe, and she liked helping him get ready to open his law office again. That's what she was doing when Charles came to the door, and she continued sorting through his papers while she waited for Nick to come back.

Nick called her name to let her know it was safe to come out; as always, when he saw her, he was struck by how beautiful she was and how he was stupidly going to let her get away just because she was Japanese.

"What did Charles want?" Hana asked.

Nick told her the gist of the conversation, stopping to reassure her that he wasn't even thinking about taking the position when he saw the panicked look on her face. "Relax, baby; I told him no."

Hana relaxed breathing a sigh of relief. "Thank you," she said, hugging him.

Nick hugged her back, but his mind was working; something wasn't right about the whole Elam thing. What did he not know? He decided that he didn't care. He was where he wanted and needed to be.

Ralph paced the living room; Lawrence and his family were due at any time now. He had already made several searches through the house and was finally satisfied there was nothing that could invite questions he didn't want to answer.

"I don't want to be here," he murmured, already missing the laughter and noise of the children, and Niko begging him to read to him. He missed Abby and her calling him "old man." He didn't know how he knew it, but he knew that Lawrence being here was going to be trouble.

He checked the food in the oven and then the place settings. "Six," he mused, "and five of them strangers." Abby had offered to stay for moral support, but he turned her down; now he was wishing he hadn't. Just as he was considering calling her to ask her to come back, he heard a car horn out front.

They were here.

Sally looked at the house and then at Lawrence. "It's awfully big," she commented.

"He said he had plenty of room, and I guess he does," Lawrence said as he looked at the house and then the yard.

Sally looked, too, and was thrilled; she loved yard work, and this yard needed it. She looked back at the kids, who hadn't said anything since they arrived.

Lawrence turned around in his seat. "Listen up, mind your Ps and Qs, you hear me? Grampa doesn't know why we're here, and we need to keep it that way. You can't use the words nigger, kike, fag, spook—none of it, you got it?"

The two younger ones nodded their heads that they understood; Kenneth, the oldest one, looked out of the car window with a bored expression on his face.

"Good, now let's get out."

Ralph's heart hammered and his stomach twisted as he watched Lawrence and his family get out of the car. He took a deep breath and went outside to greet them.

"Lawrence?" he called as he approached the car.

"Pop?"

Father and son stood looking at each other for several minutes until Sally stepped forward. "Hello, I'm Sally, and these are our children: Kenneth, Dianne, and Eli."

After the introductions, Lawrence held out his remaining hand to Ralph, who took it without hesitating.

"Well, come on in; you must be tired and hungry," Ralph said as he walked away. He led them into the house, showed them where the bathrooms were, and took the food out of the oven.

"Two bathrooms!" Sally gushed as she washed her face and hands.

"How about that?" Lawrence replied quietly.

Lunch was quiet, and what little conversation occurred was stilted. The kids looked at Ralph, but beyond the initial hello hadn't spoken.

Sally once again stepped in. "I love your yard, do you mind if I work in it?"

"Sure, have at it," Ralph replied. "There's a yard out back if the kids want to go out to play. . . . " Ralph suddenly remembered Kenji's work area; there were poles out there that he had written on in Japanese.

Damn it! he thought to himself as he watched the faces of the younger kids light up. *Maybe they won't notice*, he thought. If they did, he would do as Abby suggested. He would tell them that he had rented a room to a Japanese man, but he had to go to one of the camps.

"Grampa?" Dianne called.

"Yes?"

"Do you have fruit trees?"

"I have a lemon and orange tree in the back," Ralph replied. "Help yourself."

After that, the atmosphere relaxed slightly, but not by much.

Lawrence and Ralph appraised each other before Lawrence finally spoke. “Thanks for letting us stay here; it’s a nice place.”

“You’re welcome,” Ralph replied. The niggling feeling was back.

“I hope we won’t be here too long; I sold the house back home and plan to buy one here.”

“Stay as long as you need to,” Ralph replied, secretly hoping that they would be gone sooner rather than later.

“Thanks, Pop; I plan to start looking for a job in the next few days. Any suggestions?”

“Well, you sold insurance at home. There are a few companies around like National Life—you might have some luck there,” Ralph said. “And it helps that you have a car.”

Perfect, Lawrence thought to himself. If he could land a job like that, it would be easier for him to meet people and make contacts.

Ralph showed the kids where their rooms were and then showed Lawrence and Sally where they would be sleeping, which happened to be the same room Kenji and Patricia had slept in.

“It’s like it’s a place all unto itself,” Sally said, looking around.

“The man who lived here set it up that way; he kept to himself.”

“You mean a Jap slept in this room?” Lawrence asked, forgetting himself.

“I mean that I rented this space out to a very nice young man who happened to be Japanese,” Ralph replied.

“Is that the bed he slept in?”

“No, it isn’t,” Ralph replied.

“Well, I guess that’s something,” Lawrence muttered under his breath.

Ralph bit his tongue and continued to show Sally around. He left Lawrence and Sally in their room and was walking by one of the kid’s rooms when he heard a disturbing conversation.

“Did you see how many niggers and spics were walking around?” Ralph recognized the voice of the oldest boy.

"Shhh, Daddy said we can't say those words here. Grampa might hear." The voice of the little girl, Dianne.

"So what if he does?" Kenneth replied, his tone curt.

"He doesn't know why we're here!" Dianne replied.

After that, the conversation changed to something mundane. Ralph moved on to the kitchen to clean up the lunch dishes. As he cleaned, he wondered what Lawrence was up to and how he was going to find out. *The oldest one*, he thought as he remembered the boastful way the boy had talked; he only had to wait until he could get him alone.

Everyone missed Ralph, especially Niko. He wandered around the house calling Ralph's name. "Unc Ralph!"

"Uncle Ralph isn't here," Patricia said, reminding him for the tenth time.

"Where he go?" Niko asked.

"Uncle Ralph has a son; he's with him," Patricia said, picking him up.

Abby looked at the phone, wishing that Ralph had one. She was worried about him; he had been so nervous when she left, but insisted that she leave.

"Stubborn old coot!" she grumbled as she made lunch for all of them. "I should have stayed."

Kenji heard her grumbling to herself when he went into the kitchen for a drink of water. "Is there anything wrong?" he asked.

"I don't know," Abby replied. "I'm worried about that stubborn old coot."

"He was very nervous," Kenji said.

"More than nervous," Abby replied. "Scared is more like it."

"He'll be fine," Kenji replied, finishing his water. "Let me help you with lunch."

"I'm almost done; why don't you go spend a few minutes with Patricia and the children?"

Kenji hesitated and then nodded. Abby, he realized, really was worried about Ralph. He also wondered if there weren't some romantic feelings between Abby and Ralph; he was fairly certain there were feelings on Ralph's end, but Abby was a little harder to read.

He had often wondered why Abby never remarried but didn't feel that it was his place to ask—but he did ask Patricia.

"I don't know why she never remarried; the only thing I know was that her husband wasn't a nice man," Patricia replied.

"She's quite worried about Ralph," Kenji said, taking Marie from Patricia.

"I know she is," Patricia replied as she helped Niko wash his hands. "But I don't know if her worry is groundless—even he was worried."

Kenji kissed Marie on her head and carried her to the bedroom to check her heart. "You're doing well, little one," he said with a smile as he finished her exam.

He met Patricia in the kitchen, where there was an intense conversation going on between Abby and Patricia.

"If you're that worried, you should go over there," Patricia said.

"He didn't want me to stay when I offered," Abby countered.

"Abby, we're talking about Ralph, who wouldn't go to the doctor until you and Kenji made him go," Patricia said. "This isn't any different; he would have said no even if he had wanted you to stay."

Abby sighed. "You're right. I'll go over after we eat lunch."

"Why do you suppose Ralph is so frightened?" Kenji asked as he lifted Niko up into a chair.

"I don't know, and I'm not sure he does either," Abby replied. "I do know that it has something to do with his son being here; he keeps saying there's more going on than just the need to move."

"What do you think?" Patricia asked.

"I don't know," Abby replied. "Maybe I'll know something after I go over."

They ate lunch in silence, each of them wondering about what had Ralph so frightened, and worrying about his safety.

Ralph listened to the way the kids talked, taking note of how the kids spoke very carefully around him. Part of that he attributed to them not knowing him, but the other part was because they had been told to watch what they said. The only one who seemed to be at ease around him was Lawrence's wife, Sally.

"Thank you again for letting us come here."

"You're welcome; it's nice to meet you and the kids," Ralph replied, meaning it. "So how are things back home?"

"Pretty much the same." Sally laughed. "Slow and boring. I'm glad we moved."

"Lawrence told me about that black boy that got hung; the Klan still giving you trouble?"

Sally tensed; Lawrence didn't want her discussing the Klan with anyone. Ralph saw her tense and at first attributed it to her being afraid, but then wasn't sure if it was fear or nerves that he was seeing.

"I . . . we . . . I mean, they've left us alone," she replied, which was sort of true.

She's lying, Ralph thought and let the subject drop.

Lawrence saw Ralph and Sally talking and got nervous; Sally couldn't lie if her life depended on it, and it was much too soon to let the cat out of the bag.

"Hey, Pop! This really is a nice place you have here," Lawrence said as he walked outside. "Is it paid for?"

Ralph wondered why Lawrence would ask such a question, but he answered it. "Yep; it's mine, free and clear."

"Are they any others like this around?" Lawrence asked.

"I'm sure there are; if you want and when you feel like it, we can go looking," Ralph said, as eager for Lawrence to be out of his house as Lawrence was to be gone.

In some ways, Ralph wished he hadn't contacted his son, but in some ways he was glad he had. One thing was clear to him: Lawrence lied to him. He was still very active in the Klan; the proof was in the way the kids talked, but he needed real confirmation of his suspicions. All he had right now was what Nick would call "circumstantial evidence." He had to talk to the oldest boy.

A car horn beeped, making them all look up.

"Who's that?" Lawrence asked.

"That's my friend Abby," Ralph replied, glad that she had showed up.

They watched as Abby climbed out of the car and then reached inside, coming out with a plate covered with a towel. "Hello!" she called as she walked toward them.

"Hello," Sally greeted.

"Lawrence and Sally, this is my friend Abby."

Abby and Lawrence looked at each other a few seconds before acknowledging each other.

Abby didn't like him, and judging by his reaction, Abby realized that he didn't care much for her either, although he tried to hide it. As for herself, she didn't know why she disliked Lawrence. There was something about him that didn't ring true, but she liked Sally. Abby looked up to see the kids watching her curiously; she smiled at them and only got a response from the two youngest ones. The oldest one gave her an insolent look that she wanted to slap off his face, but she continued to smile as the introductions were made.

"I made some sugar cookies for you," she said as she handed the plate to Sally.

"Thank you!" Sally exclaimed, a little surprised by the show of hospitality. "What do you say, kids?"

"Thank you, Miss Abby!" Dianne and Eli said.

"Kenneth!" Lawrence said sharply.

"Thanks," Kenneth grumbled and walked away.

"I'm sorry about that," Lawrence said, but offered no explanation for his son's rude behavior.

"Come on in!" Ralph said, his relief that Abby was there evident. "I'll make some coffee."

Lawrence was the last one in. He didn't like Abby; she was what he would call a free thinker and was probably a nigger lover, right along with his father.

He watched as Abby and his father acted like a couple that had been together for years instead of just friends and decided to question them. "How long you two been friends?"

Abby and Ralph looked at each other, but it was Ralph who spoke. "Since around 1940 or '41; why are you asking?"

"No reason; it just seems like you two are closer than friends. . . . Don't get me wrong, I think it's great," he said with what he hoped was a sincere smile.

Ralph was about to tell Lawrence that it was none of his business when Eli came running in. "Dad! There's Jap writing on some poles out there!"

Ralph didn't react; he was glad he had already covered himself by telling Lawrence that he had rented out space to a Japanese man.

"Is that so?" Lawrence replied.

"Yeah, you wanna see?"

"No, it's all right. Grampa had a Jap . . . I mean, Japanese man living here for a while."

Neither Abby nor Ralph missed the conscious effort it took for Lawrence not to use the derogatory term. Ralph, Abby realized, was right; there was something not quite right about Lawrence, other than the fact that he was a racist. Her gut told her the same thing that Ralph's gut told him: Lawrence was up to something. The other thing she noticed was that while Lawrence was polite to Ralph, he wasn't what she would call respectful; there was something in his tone of voice that was condescending and something else. . . . Disgust? But she couldn't be sure.

She stayed for an hour, and it seemed like a long hour to her; she felt sorry for Ralph and wished he could leave with her.

Ralph walked her to her car, not speaking until she was ready to get in. "Drive safely."

"Ralph, something isn't right with your son," Abby said with a smile just in case they were being watched.

"I know; do me a favor and call Nick. Ask him if that friend of his can do a check on my son."

"What are you thinking?" Abby asked.

"I think he's still involved with the Klan and my inviting him was the perfect opportunity for him to come and cause trouble," Ralph replied.

"Ralph, be careful; I don't trust him or that oldest boy."

Ralph didn't need to be warned; his guard had gone up as soon as he met Kenneth. There was something missing in the boy's eyes when he looked at Ralph; later, Ralph would realize that what he didn't see or sense from the boy was compassion.

Lawrence watched from a window as Ralph and Abby talked; they needed to find their own place as soon as possible. It was only a mater of time before one of them screwed up and exposed why they had really moved. Abby didn't trust him, and neither did his father.

The first thing tomorrow, he would find a phone and call the insurance company. With his experience and the fact that he had lost his arm in the service of his country—a fact that he played to the hilt—he'd be hired right away. Once that happened, they would start looking for a house. He was glad they hadn't unloaded the trailer; it was one less thing to slow them down from moving.

Lawrence moved away from the window when Ralph headed back toward the house; he didn't want him to know that he was being watched.

Abby made it home to find Nick's car in the garage. She was glad to see him; it would save her a phone call, and it would be easier to explain what she saw and felt in person.

Nick was lying on the floor on his back playing "airplane" with Niko, who was laughing hysterically.

"All right, Grampa Nick," Patricia said, "if you don't stop, he won't settle down enough to go bed."

"Okay, kiddo, time for the landing!" Nick said as he gave Niko one last swoop.

"More!" Niko exclaimed when Nick set him on the floor.

"Not tonight," Nick said gently, "your mama says it's almost bedtime."

Niko pouted and looked hopefully at Kenji, who was holding Marie in his lap.

"Do as Mama says," Kenji said softly, but there was a note of authority in his voice that Niko knew better than to question or resist.

"Yes, Papa," Niko said, went over to Patricia, and took her hand.

"Go say goodnight to Grampa Nick and Grandma Hana," Patricia urged.

Niko said his goodnights, kissing Abby last. He looked around and then remembered that Ralph was away. He climbed up the stairs with Patricia and Kenji behind him; he hated bedtime.

Hana rocked Marie as Nick helped Abby make tea.

"What's wrong?" he asked.

"I'll tell you all about it when Patricia and Kenji come back down. I wish that John and Hattie were here, too, because this might affect them, as well."

"Does this have something to do with Ralph's son?" Nick asked.

"Yes, but. . . . You know what, it's early yet, and I wonder if John and Hattie are still up. I don't want to do this twice."

"I can drive over there if you want," Nick offered.

"Do you mind?"

"Not at all," Nick replied. "Should I tell them to come prepared for a pajama party?"

"Yes, that way you or I won't have to go out again, and if they're going to stay, ask Hattie if she has any extra eggs for breakfast in the morning."

Kenji and Patricia read with Niko and said prayers in both Japanese and English; they kissed him good night and closed the door behind them.

Kenji stopped Patricia before she headed down the stairs. "I want to kiss you before we go back to the others," he told her as he pulled her into his arms.

Patricia wrapped her arms around his waist and for a moment felt a flash of insecurity; he was so nice and trim, and she had yet to lose the weight from Marie.

"I love you, *Kirei*," he murmured after he kissed her.

"I love you, too," Patricia replied.

It had been quite a while since they had any real alone time. Making love with Niko and the baby in the room was challenging at best, so it happened only on occasion.

"Maybe it's time to see if my mom and dad can stay over and watch Niko and Marie for a night," Patricia said, giving him a tight squeeze.

"I think you're right," Kenji agreed, returning the squeeze

"Are you planning to study tonight?" Patricia asked.

"I am, but why don't you study with me?"

"Because one of us needs to be awake to keep ahead of Niko and Marie," Patricia replied. "But I'll study with you for a little while anyway."

Nick hadn't returned yet when they went back downstairs.

"He went to go get your parents," Abby said when Patricia asked where Nick was.

"Why? What's happened?" Patricia asked.

"Nothing yet; I'll explain when they get here."

Patricia and Kenji looked at each other and then back at Abby; it wasn't her to be so cryptic. Marie was sleeping contentedly in Hana's arms, and neither Kenji nor Patricia made a move to take her away. Hana only saw the children once a week, and Marie was young enough that she still slept a good bit of the time. She was already sleeping through the night and was a sound sleeper, so taking her to bed was no problem.

Nick came in with John and Hattie in tow.

"I got some eggs and bacon here for the mornin'," Hattie said as they came in. "I got a chicken, too, in case we still here."

"Wonderful!" Abby said as she took the bag of food from Hattie and hugged her. She spoke to and hugged John. It was still a shock to him whenever Abby hugged him; white women just didn't hug black men.

"Where's Ralph?" Hattie asked. She knew that his son was coming, but she wasn't sure of where he would be staying.

"He's staying at his place with his son and family," Abby replied.

"Are the babies all right?" John asked anxiously.

"They're fine," Abby replied. "Niko is already in bed and Marie is in the living room with Hana, Kenji, and Patricia."

"They're all right? Patricia and Kenji?" he asked.

"John, relax, everyone is fine," Abby replied.

"Then why did Nick come get us?" Hattie asked.

"We have a problem—or what could be a problem," Abby said as she put tea cups on a tray and handed the tray to Nick.

A few minutes later, they were all sitting in the living room. Hattie sat in a rocker with Marie, who had stayed asleep during the transfer from one grandmother to the other.

"You sure is a pretty one," Hattie said, looking down at the sleeping baby.

"She's beautiful like her mother," Kenji said with a smile.

Whenever he said or did anything that made Patricia happy, Hattie's appreciation of Kenji grew, as did John's. It had taken him a while, but he no longer saw Kenji as an enemy. Kenji was a man who happened to be Japanese and who loved his daughter and their children, and although he had never said this, he had come to regard Kenji as a son.

Everyone listened as Abby talked about Ralph's nervousness and now fear as the time for Lawrence's arrival drew near. "He wasn't this nervous when he went up to Manzanar with Nick to get Hana and Kenji," she said.

"He tried to tell me that something wasn't right," Nick said. "I thought it was just nerves about seeing his blood family after so long. He was afraid he was bringing danger here, but is he right?"

"All I can tell you is this: Lawrence is as racist as they come, and that oldest child Kenneth gave me the chills," Abby said. "But there's something else. I didn't like the way Lawrence talked to Ralph. His tone was condescending, and there was an underlying tone of disgust or contempt—maybe both."

"Is he in danger?" Hana asked.

"I don't think so . . . at least not yet," Abby replied. "But Nick, he wants you to do something."

"What's that?"

"He believes that his son is still involved with the KKK, and he wants to know if you could call your friend Charles and see if he can find out what Lawrence has been up to."

Nick hesitated; he hadn't told them about the offer to take Elam's position and that he was trying to stay as far away from the office as possible. He looked over at Hana, who nodded her head so slightly that no one else noticed. He didn't want to do this, but the safety of his family might depend on it.

"I'll call him in the morning," Nick said. "But I can't promise that Charles will help me or that we'll find out anything. What we need to be thinking of in the meantime is a way to keep everyone safe. Abby, based on what you saw, do you believe Lawrence is capable of hurting Ralph?"

Abby thought for a moment. "Yes, and I think his grandson, Kenneth, could hurt him as well. The thing that concerns me is that Ralph doesn't have a phone or a car, and no way of getting help."

"So you thinks that this Lawrence is out to do what, exactly?" John asked.

"I don't know; maybe start a group here? And if that's the case, then it affects all of us," Abby said.

"The KKK has been looked at several times by the FBI over the years; they tend to grow in numbers, die down, and resurge again," Nick said. "But the really frightening thing is that some of the members are members of our government—I mean mayors, senators, and the like."

"How do you fight a group like that?" Patricia asked.

'I'll tell you how!" John said. "You get people together and you kick their asses!"

"Which will only lead to more violence," Kenji said softly; he was remembering the riot at Manzanar.

John was going to reply when Nick interrupted, "The question on the table is how to keep everyone safe."

"What are the chances that they'll show up here?" Patricia asked, thinking about the babies.

"Not likely," Abby replied. "Ralph didn't tell them where I lived, but they do know that Kenji stayed there. One of the kids found some writing in your workout area."

Kenji looked alarmed.

"It's all right; Ralph told them that he rented out space to a Japanese man who had to go to one of the camps, and they bought it."

"Why you thinks he here to cause trouble?" Hattie asked.

Abby related the difficulty that Lawrence and the children seemed to have in not using racial slurs. "And he wanted to tell me something, but his son was watching us through the window."

"We've got to get Ralph out of there," Patricia said.

Everyone agreed, but the consensus was on how. Then Nick had a flash of inspiration. "Abby, how would you like to get married?"

Abby sputtered on her tea and stared at Nick. "Wh—what?"

"Let's think about this. You said that Lawrence already thinks that you and Ralph are an item, right? So why not use that to our advantage?"

"You know, for someone who says that they don't like intrigue and mystery, you're damned good at it," Abby said dryly.

Nick chuckled. "So what do you think?"

"Let's say that we do this. They're going to want to visit, and it can't be here," Abby said.

"What about the other house?" Patricia asked. "We could move there and—"

"Too risky," Nick said. "But . . . Abby and Ralph could live there, at least during the day, and to cover things here, Paul could move in when he gets back from San Diego."

"That would get Ralph out of the house, for the majority of the time anyway," Abby said. "But I want a phone put in at the other house."

"I've already arranged for that, but what we have to do next is figure out a way to let Ralph know what's happening," Nick said.

"I could go back over there," Abby replied.

"No, I think I will," Nick replied. "I want to get my own read on Lawrence and his family. I'll find a way to get Ralph alone."

An hour later, the group broke up. Nick kissed Hana before helping her into the trunk of the car. It occurred to him that while the day was coming that he wouldn't have to hide her, there would still be hardships, but they would deal with those as they came; now the priority was keeping his family safe.

Dai's pregnancy was progressing well. Hiroshi found himself being attentive to her in a way that he had never been with Hana. He found himself being less and less concerned about the sex of the baby and more concerned about its welfare.

Now as he rubbed Dai's tired feet, he thought about Kenji and Hana, and all the mistakes he had made with them. One of the things Hana had told him during the whole Patricia fiasco was: "The world is changing, and we need to change with it." He had to wonder just how much the world really had changed;

the war was coming to an end, if the gossip was to be believed—possibly by next year.

It saddened him that their baby would be born here, and he had already begun to do what he could to minimize the amount of dust that gathered in their space. Tomorrow, while Dai rested, he would look for another place, one that wouldn't be as dusty. The chances of finding one was slim to none, as the camp was packed full, but still he would try.

Another thing he had to start thinking about was where they would live when they were released. They had a little money, but not enough to buy a house or even rent one, unless Nick still gave him the money he was going to use to get back to Japan. The immediate problem would be where they would go for the first few days after release and how he would support them.

"Hiroshi, do not trouble yourself over what cannot be controlled," Dai said softly.

Once again it struck him how much like Hana Dai was, but there was a difference: he had married Hana because he had to; he had married Dai because he wanted to and he loved her. He was beginning to understand Kenji a little more and felt a flash of shame that he hadn't tried earlier. But Dai was right: There was nothing he could do to change the past, and there was nothing he could do about their lives after their release for the time being except for one thing. He was going to make his peace with Hana and Kenji, and he would learn to accept the woman his son had chosen to spend his life with.

Hiroshi was surprised at the sense of relief he felt once he consciously decided to make amends. He felt better and lighter than he had in a long time. He slowly moved Dai's feet from his lap and got into the small bed with her. He closed his eyes and inhaled her scent, and said the words that he had never said to Hana, "*Watashi wa tsuma o aishite* (I love you, my wife)."

Dai turned over and looked at him with tears in her eyes. "*Watashi wa tsuma o dana* (I love you, my husband)."

The words were as awkward to hear as they were to say, but Hiroshi liked the sound and feel of saying them. He hugged Dai close and kissed her, something else he rarely did with Hana, and rubbed her back until she slept.

Hana was quiet as they got ready for bed; she was frightened for everyone, but she was very frightened for Ralph. She knew firsthand what hate could do to a family.

"What's on your mind?" Nick asked as he undressed.

"I'm worried for Ralph; what if he doesn't want to go along with this plan?"

"He will," Nick assured her.

"How do you know this?" Hana asked.

"Ralph isn't a stupid man; he'll understand that this is the only way we can keep him safe and with us."

"So much hatred," Hana murmured.

Nick waited for her to continue; he knew that there were major problems regarding Patricia and Kenji, which was why he had left home, but Hana had never told him the entire story. "Want to talk about it?" he asked as he sat next to her on the bed.

Hana looked down. "I'm so ashamed of the way we were and of the way we treated Patricia, and I allowed it to happen. I knew Hiroshi was planning something and I kept my silence; if I had spoken. . . . Patricia was almost raped and would have been killed if she hadn't fought back and injured the man that attacked her."

Nick put his arm around Hana and let her talk; it was a long time in coming.

"When we first came to this country, we were filled with such hope, even though it was obvious that we were not welcome here, but we worked hard and became successful with our business and were able to send for Kenjiro. Hiroshi had such high hopes for him and planned on Kenji bringing much honor to our family."

Three hours later, the tale was finished.

"Hana, listen to me," Nick said. "What happened was terrible, but thank God Patricia came out of it all right. I also know that she loves you and bears you no ill will. Should any of it have happened? No, but it did, and you've made your peace with Kenji and Patricia."

"But Hiroshi has not," Hana replied.

"That's for Hiroshi to worry about," Nick replied. "Come on, sweetheart; let's get some sleep."

Hana lay awake long after Nick was asleep; she had that sick feeling in her stomach again.

Nick called Charles first thing in the morning and asked to meet him for coffee.

"Sure, you want to come to the office?" Charles asked.

"I'd rather not," Nick replied. "How about the diner just a few blocks down from there?"

"Mackie's? Sure, what time?"

"It's seven now; what about nine?" Nick asked.

"Nine is fine," Charles replied and hung up.

Nick looked over at Hana; he knew she hadn't slept, but didn't know what to do for her except let her know that they all loved her.

"I know," she replied. "Thank you and please be careful."

Lawrence watched Ralph with a mixture of contempt and anger as he chatted with a black man as if they were best friends. The one thing he noticed was that the lines here were more blurred than at home; there seemed to be a blending of the races here that would be unacceptable at home. He had his work cut out for him.

When Ralph came in, Lawrence put on a fake smile. "Who was that?" he asked.

Ralph hesitated before replying. "That was Mr. Jackson from across the way; he takes his walks past here some mornings and we talk."

"So he's a friend?"

Ralph was going to say no, but then he remembered the man he had buried. "Yes, he's a friend, and on occasion we eat lunch together. Is that a problem?" he asked and then walked away, not giving Lawrence a chance to reply.

"So," Charles said, "you want information on Lawrence Goodman. Can I ask why?"

Nick didn't see any reason not to tell him, so he did.

"The KKK? Shit, Nick, just between you and me, we're investigating some of these guys. Where'd you say he was from?"

"South Carolina; Abbeville, I think," Nick replied.

"Why do you think he's here? Lawrence, I mean?"

"My guess is that he's here to recruit and start a chapter."

Charles blew out a breath and then smiled. "I might be able to help you without sneaking around. Can I come by later this afternoon?"

"Yes, just call first to make sure I'm there. I have some errands to run."

Ralph was sitting on the front steps when Nick pulled up. Sally and the kids were working in the back yard—even Kenneth was helping.

"Nick! You're a sight for sore eyes! How's everything?"

"Good, but we all miss you and are worried about you," Nick replied. "Where's your son?"

"At a job interview."

"His wife and kids?"

"They're in the back yard; what's going on?" Ralph asked.

"I'm going to talk fast, so just listen and nod your head and laugh," Nick said, looking behind Ralph.

"All right. . . . "

"We think that you're not safe here; your son is up to something, and we think we know what it is."

"You don't say?" Ralph asked and laughed.

"We have to get you out of here, so you're going to ask Abby to marry you."

Ralph stared at Nick, his mouth open.

"Laugh!" Nick said, laughing as if he was just told a very funny joke. "You and she are going to live in the house I just bought, and Paul will move into Abby's house.

"That's the funniest thing I've ever heard!" Ralph said, laughing, but his eyes were filled with disbelief.

Two weeks later, Ralph and Abby were married in a small ceremony in Ralph's back yard. Ralph had moved most of his personal belongings the week before. The wedding was held there because he didn't want Lawrence to know where he and Abby were living unless he absolutely had to. He had come to the conclusion that Nick and Abby were both right: his son and grandson were dangerous. That conclusion came after he finally got Kenneth alone.

"What do you think of California?"

Ralph suppressed a shudder when Kenneth looked at him with cold gray eyes. "Too many niggers and spics walkin' around like they own the place."

"Kenneth—"

"And too many fucking nigger lovers. If I had my way, all of you would be dead."

"Where did you learn so much hatred?" Ralph asked.

"My daddy says we're at war and we all need to step up. Do you know what that makes you if you don't help? A traitor, and traitors die by hangin'."

Ralph swallowed hard; he had brought these people here. They weren't family except by blood; his real family lived a few blocks away from here, and he wanted to go home.

"I suppose you won't mind telling me why you came here then," Ralph said.

"We're here to spread the word!" Kenneth said as though he were a minister here to spread the word of God.

"Sweet Jesus, boy, who taught you to hate like this?"

Kenneth wouldn't answer him but asked a question of his own. "Why do you love the niggers and Japs so much? They ain't your kind."

Ralph thought about his answer. "Son, let me tell you something. There's good and bad in every race. Hate has never done anyone any good, but it's caused a lot of harm. Hate is wasted energy; we have to live on this earth together, so we might as well learn to get along."

"Dad was right about you," Kenneth said as he looked at Ralph in disgust and then walked away. Ralph realized that this boy, his grandson, hated him and could and would kill him without remorse.

That conversation occurred three days before the wedding, and every night after that, Ralph slept with a knife under his pillow and a chair under his doorknob.

The night before the wedding, Lawrence asked Ralph about the house. "What are your plans for the house?"

"I hadn't thought too much about it; why do you ask?"

"I would like to buy it. Sally and the kids really like it, and if you and your new missus have another house, then you won't need this one," Lawrence replied.

"So you're planning to stay here permanently?" Ralph asked.

"Appears so; so what's your asking price?"

"I . . . I don't know," Ralph replied.

"I did some checking; it seems that the average asking price is around five to six grand."

"That sound's about right, but—"

"I can pay cash, and I'll even throw in extra for the furniture," Lawrence said.

"I'll have my lawyer friend draw up the papers," Ralph said.

If he were honest with himself, he would have admitted that the house felt tainted somehow, but what he told himself was six thousand dollars would go a long way toward contributing to the support of his real family.

The wedding was quiet, short, and to the point. When it was over, Ralph kissed Abby on the cheek. Abby went through the motions, hoping Ralph wasn't expecting them to have sex; even after all they had been through together, she had never told any of them about Lorena. If Ralph expected them to have sex, she would have to tell him. There was no way she could fake it.

Right after the wedding, Nick handed Lawrence the papers to sign for the purchase of the house, and Lawrence handed Ralph an envelope containing seven thousand dollars.

"This is too much!" Ralph protested and began to count out a thousand dollars.

"No, take it," Lawrence said. "You're leaving the house fully furnished."

As Ralph left his house for the last time, he looked around and felt a weight lift off his shoulders. He was glad to be leaving his son and his family behind.

It was another week before Charles got back to Nick.

"We need to talk; when can we meet?" he asked.

The urgency in Charles's voice alarmed Nick. "What did you find out?" he asked.

"Is your friend still living with his son?"

"No, but—"

"I'm on my way over."

Nick hung up the phone; whatever Charles was going to tell him, it wasn't good.

Hana was standing behind him, wringing her hands. "Nick?"

"Charles is on his way over; he found something out, and apparently it can't wait."

Lawrence enjoyed his new job as an insurance salesman; he played his handicap to the hilt, embellishing the story of how he lost his arm to get the maximum sympathy.

As he had suspected, there were people who felt as he did, but they were scattered. He did find out that there was a small group of Klansmen in the area, but they weren't organized. It became his goal to have a meeting by the end of September. Things were moving right along and much better than he could have planned.

Charles knocked on the front door fifteen minutes later; Nick looked behind him to make sure Hana was out of sight.

"Nick, your guy is not a nice man."

"All right, tell me something I don't know," Nick said as they walked to the living room.

"You're sure your friend is out of that house?"

"Yes, now will you tell me what you found out?" Nick said impatiently.

"First of all, you were right. He's here to start a new group, but that's not the only reason he left South Carolina. The FBI is investigating a rash of hangings that happened about a month before he left."

"What are you saying?" Nick asked.

"Your friend and his son were the instigators in over half of them."

"Just how many hangings are you talking about?" Nick asked, his stomach rolling.

"Twelve that we know of, and Lawrence and Kenneth Goodman led at least eight of them."

"They're murderers," Nick stated.

Kenji had two more weeks in which to get ready for his tests; it helped that Paul had moved in, because he could ask questions that weren't in the book.

"You're going to do fine," Paul encouraged.

"I hope so; so much depends on it," Kenji replied.

"By the way, I picked something up for you when I was in San Diego," Paul said. "I'll be right back."

Kenji sat in the library; it was much too quiet. He missed Ralph and Abby's bickering about what spice to put in the soup, and he missed the dinnertime conversation. It occurred to him that when he and Patricia finally had their own home, it would be quiet as well.

"Here it is," Paul said as he handed Kenji a sack.

"What is this?" Kenji asked.

"Look inside," Paul urged.

Inside of the bag were a physician's reference book, a stethoscope, a penlight, and a lab coat. "Paul, I can't accept these things; you've already done so much for us."

"Kenji, I'm doing nothing more than helping a promising young man reach his dream of becoming a fine physician, and all physicians need the things in that bag."

"I don't know what to say."

"You don't have to say anything," Paul replied. "Just help someone else when you're able."

Later that night, with Niko and Marie asleep in the bedroom across from theirs, Kenji told Patricia about Paul's gifts.

"*Kirei*, I don't know how to thank him."

"He told you how he wanted to be thanked; when we can, we help someone else," Patricia replied.

"How is it that our paths keep crossing with such good people?" Kenji asked.

"I don't know; I guess I would like to think that God or gods are watching out for us," Patricia said as she snuggled closer.

It took them a couple of nights to get used to not having Niko and Marie in the room with them, but they adapted quickly, taking advantage of the privacy to make love and talk.

"What do you suppose Charles found out about Lawrence?" Patricia asked, changing the subject.

"I don't know, but I think it will be bad," he replied quietly.

Patricia didn't reply; she had the same feeling, but she was glad that Ralph was no longer in the house.

Abby and Ralph settled down in the new house; fortunately, Ralph wasn't expecting them to consummate the marriage.

"I know the wedding was just for show to get me out of that house," Ralph told her.

Abby breathed a sigh of relief that she didn't have to explain why she wouldn't have sex with him. She looked around her small bedroom and wondered how Patricia, Kenji, and the babies were doing; she missed them horribly and decided that in the morning she and Ralph would go over to visit. They had stayed out of sight for a week, long enough to have been on a short honeymoon and back.

Both she and Ralph were anxious to hear what Nick found out about Lawrence.

"Maybe it won't be bad," she told Ralph when they talked about it earlier in the week, but she knew it would be and braced herself to be able to help Ralph when they found out just how bad it was.

"You didn't see the way that boy looked at me," Ralph replied. "He could have slit my throat and not given it a second thought. Abby, I brought these people into our midst and jeopardized everyone in the process."

"You wanted to help your family—"

"They're not my family anymore," Ralph said sadly, "and that's my fault. If I had stayed or even left a note, maybe they wouldn't be this way. Lawrence told me that he and the youngest one went back to the house, but I was gone. I should have left a note!"

"How do you know he's not lying?" Abby asked.

"Why would he lie about something like that?" Ralph asked, not thinking.

"He lied to get here, didn't he? He told you he was out of the Klan, but yet your own grandson confirms that they aren't; they came here to start another chapter, and he used you to do it."

"Abby, I'm sorry."

"Ralph, you have nothing to be sorry for; you couldn't have known."

"But I knew something wasn't right—I should have told them not to come."

After Charles left, Nick looked at the clock. It was just past nine, and Ralph would still be up. He decided to drive over; this wasn't the kind of thing he wanted to say over the phone. Nick ran up the stairs to find Hana sitting on the bed; the closet door was open in case she had to get in quickly.

"What did he say?" she asked.

"Honey, it's bad," Nick said. "I have to go tell Ralph that his son and grandson are murderers."

"They killed people?"

"Yes, at least eight, but probably more. It's part of the reason they came here."

"Poor Ralph."

"Yes, it's going to be hard for him," Nick replied.

Ralph and Abby waited nervously for Nick to come over. Ralph was so nervous that he vomited dinner; he knew it was going to be bad, especially when Nick wouldn't tell him anything over the phone. Abby felt helpless as she heard Ralph throwing up and then water running as he washed his face and hands.

A few minutes later, Nick was at the door. Abby answered it, her own stomach now churning.

"Ralph, sit down," Nick said gently.

During the drive over, he had debated the best way to tell Ralph about his son and decided to be straightforward.

Abby sat next to Ralph and took his hand in hers, and then nodded at Nick.

"Lawrence and Kenneth . . . Ralph, they've killed at least eight people along with the Klan. There are many more murders, but they've been linked to at least the eight I mentioned."

Ralph was stunned; he wanted to say, "Not my boy! He wouldn't do something like that!" But he couldn't. He didn't know his boy anymore, and his grandson, too? He was just a child!

"What else?" he whispered.

"The FBI now knows that he's here, and they're going to arrest him and your grandson."

"They're going to take them back to South Carolina, aren't they?" Ralph asked.

"Yes."

Killers—his son and grandson were cold-blooded killers.

"I have a favor to ask," Ralph said.

"All right."

"When they're arrested, I want to talk to them before they leave."

"I'll see what I can do," Nick replied. "Ralph, I'm so sorry."

"Not your fault, and I never should have let them come here. I endangered everyone for murderers, and don't tell me that I couldn't have known! I should have listened to my gut and told them not to come."

"Ralph, any of us would have done the same thing; they're your family—"

"No, they aren't," Ralph said quietly. "You, Kenji, Patty, and the rest of you are my family. When are they going to arrest them?"

"By the end of the week," Nick replied.

Ralph nodded and blinked back tears.

Nick left a short while later with a heavy heart. He knew that once Lawrence was gone, there would be someone else to take his place. He began to rethink his decision to stay out of the agency.

Lawrence was on the phone when Sally came into the kitchen; she already knew whom he was talking to.

Doc.

She hated the beady-eyed little man; she hated what he taught and hated herself for allowing him to teach her children that hate, but Lawrence was away fighting in Europe and Doc had helped her with the boys, telling her that Lawrence asked him to look after all of them while he was gone. At the time she hadn't realized what he meant, or she convinced herself she hadn't.

While she agreed that the races shouldn't mingle, she didn't agree with the name-calling and discrimination that was so rampant. In her mind, separation wasn't the same as discrimination; the blacks would just have their own things. She never voiced her views to Lawrence because as his wife, she had to support him, but of the three children, it was Kenneth that swallowed everything the Klan taught hook, line, and sinker, and he was the one that worried her the most. It had gotten to the point that if she asked him not to use racial slurs, he would accuse her of being a nigger lover and threatened to go to Doc. It became easier to let it go than to argue with him. The one thing she did insist on was that he didn't use that language in front of the younger children; she knew she had failed when she heard Eli calling Markie, a little black boy he had played with since they were both babies, a nigger.

When Lawrence came back from the war minus an arm, it got worse. He wasn't only angry about the blacks; it was now the Jews, because in his mind that's why he had lost his arm. He went so far as to say that they should have let Hitler go until he killed all of the "Jew bastards" and then gone after him.

She didn't contradict him.

Sally had really hoped that once they got here, Lawrence would love it so much that he would let go of the Klan, but he didn't. And Kenneth . . . he frightened her with the way his eyes blazed whenever Lawrence talked about taking control and killing every nonwhite person in sight, whether they be man, woman, or child.

Kenneth, she realized, was lost to her, but she still had two other children she could save. The question was how, and whom she could go to for help.

Ralph.

She really liked the gruff old man, and so did Eli and Dianne, and she was sure that he liked them. When she heard Lawrence laughing about watching someone swinging from a tree, she knew it was long past the time when she needed to get her and her two younger babies out of the house.

By the end of September 1944, the Allied troops entered Belgium; Finland agreed to an armistice with the Soviets; Brussels was liberated by French and American troops; the Warsaw uprising was still in progress; the first Allied troops entered Germany; the Battle of San Marino began and ended; there were signs of civil war in Greece; and the Germans surrendered to Canadian troops in Calais, located in northern France.

SEPTEMBER 4, 1944

Sally was in the kitchen trying to figure out a way to get her and the younger children out of the house. Kenneth seemed to know that something was happening and followed her throughout the house.

"Why don't you go out and use the workout area?" Sally asked.

"Why are you tryin' to get rid of me?" he asked.

"I'm not; it's just that it's so nice out, and all I'm doing is housework."

Kenneth gave her a suspicious look but went outside, leaving Sally alone. She looked out the back window and saw Kenneth doing chin lifts. She poured herself a cup of coffee and sat down to think; she knew she couldn't go back home, which meant she either had to stay here or go somewhere else. Of the two options, here was the most reasonable, and Lawrence would hunt her down if she went somewhere else. She thought about leaving the two younger ones with him and then coming back for them, but they were already talking like Kenneth and Lawrence, and he would never let her take them.

A tap on the front door broke her concentration; puzzled as to who it could be since they didn't know anyone other than Ralph, Sally went to the door.

"Ralph! I was just thinking about you!" she exclaimed when she saw him and Abby on the steps.

"I left something in what was my bedroom, and I came to get it, if that's all right," Ralph replied, surprised at the warm reception.

"Sure it is! It's so nice to see the both of you. I was just having a cup of coffee; would you like some?"

"Uh . . . no—"

"We would love some, wouldn't we, Ralph?" Abby interrupted.

"Sure," Ralph said, looking around. "Where are the kids?"

"In the back; they just love the fruit trees!" Sally said, fully aware she was babbling. "Dianne ate so many oranges the other day that she made herself sick."

Ralph and Abby looked at each other and then back at Sally.

"Mama!" Kenneth called out as he came into the living room.

He stopped when he saw Ralph and Abby; his eyes narrowed as he stared at them.

"Kenneth, you remember Abby, your grandfather's new wife—"

"I know who they are," Kenneth said in a tone that made it clear that their presence wasn't wanted or appreciated. "What do you want?"

"Kenneth!" Sally exclaimed.

"I just came to get something I left, and then we'll be on our way," Ralph replied.

"We were going to have a cup of coffee first," Sally said.

Kenneth was going to say something, but thought better of it and walked away. Abby watched the entire scene without saying anything; what she noticed was that Sally was afraid of her son.

As soon as Kenneth left the room, Sally's shoulders slumped in relief, a fact that neither Ralph nor Abby missed.

"Ralph, why don't you go get your watch and I'll help Sally make the coffee," Abby said, taking Sally by the hand.

Abby looked around for Kenneth and spotted him in the back yard playing with the younger two children. "Sally, what's happening here?" she asked. "And don't say 'nothing'; you're scared half to death of your own child."

Sally hesitated and then spoke quickly, "I want to leave and take Dianne and Eli with me; I don't agree or believe in everything that Lawrence and Kenneth do. I want to leave before it's too late for Dianne and Eli, but I have nowhere to go, and I don't have any money."

The back door banged just as Ralph came into the kitchen. Kenneth looked at each of them before speaking. "Why are you still here?"

Ralph took Abby's hand and led her to the living room, not speaking until they were outside. "That boy is dangerous," he said.

Abby told Ralph what Sally told her.

"I don't know, Abby; Lawrence lied to me, too."

"She's scared," Abby insisted. "Take my word for it. I know a frightened woman when I see one. The question is, what are we going to do?"

"What do you propose we do? If we help her, Lawrence and Kenneth will come looking for her, and not only that, we'll have undone everything we fixed by getting married."

"True, but if Lawrence and Kenneth are arrested, she could stay here. The house is paid for, and we could give her some of the money back."

After discussing it again, that was what they decided to do.

Charles called Nick to keep him in the loop. "We're arresting Lawrence and Kenneth Goodman in the morning; bring your friend down to the office if he still wants to see them."

"What about the wife and the other two kids?" Nick asked.

"They can stay or go; there are no warrants out on the wife," Charles replied.

"What time?" Nick asked.

"We're going to grab the husband when he leaves the house to go to work. The kid, we'll grab at home."

"Charles, be careful; the kid's gonna fight you."

Nick hung up a few minutes later and called Ralph. "Ralph, they're going to pick up Lawrence and Kenneth tomorrow around nine; are you sure you want to see them?"

Ralph hesitated. "Yes."

"I'll pick you up at eight-thirty."

After they hung up, Nick wondered about the wisdom of Ralph going to see his son and grandson, but it was Ralph's call to make.

Kenji and Patricia were studying together while Marie slept and Paul kept Niko entertained. As far as Paul was concerned, Kenji was ready to take the test now, but understood why he wanted to wait. He had waited this long, and he wanted to be sure he was ready. In a few weeks, they would know if he was accepted; Paul was certain Kenji would be a shoo-in and wished that he and the dean of the school could meet in person.

He wondered about Patricia and her plans; she was every bit as intelligent as Kenji and would do well in school. Having two children would make things difficult, but it could be done if she really wanted to go to school. He decided to talk to her about it when he could catch her alone.

When Kenji answered the final question correctly, Patricia looked up at him. Like Paul, she believed Kenji would pass all of the tests with no problem.

When she asked him why he wanted to wait, he had a good answer for her. "*Kirei*, taking the test early isn't going to get me into school any faster. The studying gives me something to focus on, and I want to be sure that I'm ready."

She couldn't find fault with his logic and went back to drilling him. When he didn't answer the question, she looked up to see him watching her intently.

"What?" she asked.

"I was just thinking that you are so beautiful, so intelligent, and that I'm a very lucky man."

"All right, sweet talker, what else?"

"Nothing else; I'm blessed to have you and our children, and I love all of you."

"Kenji, what aren't you telling me?" Patricia asked.

"I promise you there's nothing else. It's just that I think about Ralph and his family and I realize I'm fortunate to have all of you, and that includes your parents, Abby . . . everyone."

"We're lucky to have you, too," Patricia replied softly.

SEPTEMBER 5, 1944

Lawrence hummed a happy tune as he got ready for work; he was selling insurance policies so fast that he had quickly become the number-one seller, which hadn't made him any friends. There was another reason for his excitement: he had finally rounded up enough like-minded people that he was going to have his first meeting tonight. One of the potential members had a room with a pool table and other amenities that made it conducive to meetings. The other reason why he was having it there as opposed to at home was that he wasn't ready for anyone to know where he lived just yet. When he told Sally that the meeting would be elsewhere, he wondered about the relief that she had tried to hide, but wrote it off as nerves; after all, she was the wife of the leader of a new chapter of the Klan.

Sally had breakfast ready for him when he came downstairs; he kissed her and then the two younger kids, and gave Kenneth a curt nod of greeting.

"Daddy, can you bring us some candy when you come home?" Eli asked.

Lawrence tousled Eli's hair. "I'll call later and see if you've been good or not, and if you are, I just might have a treat for the both of you."

He finished his breakfast, picked up his briefcase, and headed for the door. "Don't forget that I won't be home for supper!" he called back to the kitchen before stepping out.

He got into his car and drove to the office; as always, he was early. He was so lost in his thoughts that he didn't notice the two men following him from his car to the office. He had just unlocked the door when he heard his name called.

"Lawrence Goodman?"

Lawrence turned around to see who had spoken to him, assuming it was a perspective client. "Yes, what can I do for you on this fine day?" he asked cheerfully.

"Lawrence Goodman, you are under arrest for the—"

Lawrence stopped listening after he heard the word "arrest" and tried to rush the two men. Where he would have gone had he succeeded, he didn't know, but he had to try. Both men anticipated the move and trapped him between them, but still Lawrence struggled. He looked around, hoping that someone was on the street so he could yell for help, but there was no one.

One of the agents continued informing Lawrence as to why he was being arrested. Finally, he gave up the struggle and went with the men; he would call Doc when he was allowed his phone call.

Kenneth was in his room when the agents came for him. They told Sally who they were, and for just a brief moment, Sally thought about warning Kenneth, but then she saw this as her chance. If they were here for Kenneth, they must already have Lawrence.

"Where is your son, ma'am?" a tall, skinny agent asked her.

"Who are you?"

"We're with the FBI, and we have a warrant for the arrest of one Kenneth Monroe Goodman. Where is he?" he replied, showing her his identification.

Sally's mouth was dry and her heart pounded as she considered what she was about to do. "He's in his room, but could you try not to hurt him?"

"We'll do our best," the tall agent said.

The other agent looked like a thick tree stump with arms and legs; if either of them would hurt Kenneth, it would be this one.

"Please, he's just a boy," Sally said, looking at the man.

The thickset agent looked at her, nodded, and then followed his partner up the stairs. A few minutes later, Sally heard Kenneth's angry cries and curses as the men restrained him.

"Hold still, son, and you won't hurt yourself," one of the agents said.

"Sons of bitches! Let me go, damn it!"

"Kenneth Monroe Goodman—"

"Motherfucking nigger lovers!" Kenneth screamed at the top of his lungs.

They finally got him down the stairs, still kicking and screaming. He only stopped when he saw Sally; he looked at her with a coldness that shook her to the core. "I told Daddy that you wasn't to be trusted."

"Kenny—"

"Shut up!"

Sally watched as the men took Kenneth away. Thankfully, the other two children were still out back playing in the yard. The next thing was: what was she going to tell them?

Ralph sat nervously in what had been Nick's office; the agents that had arrested Lawrence and Kenneth would be returning any time now. He didn't know what he was going to say to either Lawrence or Kenneth, but he knew that after this, he would never see either of them again unless it was in the newspapers or on the news. Once again, he cursed himself for bringing them here, but what was done was done.

An hour later, Nick came to get him to take him to see Lawrence and Kenneth.

"Are you sure about this?" Nick asked for what had to be the tenth time.

"No," Ralph confessed, "but I have to."

Nick nodded; he wanted to advise Ralph to go home and not to torment himself, but he kept his peace.

Lawrence sat on the cot of his cell; he still hadn't made his phone call—they wouldn't allow him to. Kenneth was also allowed a phone call, but like him wasn't able to make it. They had talked about the possibility of being caught and each of them was to call a different person; that way, their chances of reaching someone was doubled.

Lawrence could see Kenneth across the way, madder than hell; he was proud that Kenneth wasn't crying like some sissy-assed schoolgirl. He was taking his capture like a man.

He froze when he saw Ralph and a man he recognized as Ralph's lawyer friend go to Kenneth's cell. He strained to hear what was being said.

"What do you want, nigger lover?" Kenneth snarled.

"Nothing, I guess," Ralph said sadly and walked away.

Lawrence was confused; Ralph hadn't been at Kenneth's cell for more than a few seconds and now he was coming over to his.

The two men looked at each other, neither understanding the other.

"Lawrence, what happened to you?" Ralph asked. "We never taught you such hatred."

"What happened to me?" Lawrence asked. "Look at my arm, old man! I lost it fighting for this country and I come home to no job because it's gone to one of your friends! Baby boy died at Pearl Harbor; the Japs killed him—"

"I understand that you're angry, but Lawrence, you killed innocent people! Those people did nothing to you! Maybe this is my fault; maybe if I had stayed at the cabin or came to get you, this wouldn't have happened."

Lawrence laughed. "You really are a stupid old man! Remember all those trips we took with Grampa? He told you that he was taking us fishing or hunting, but that isn't where we went. . . . "

"You're lying," Ralph said softly.

"No, I'm not, and you know it, but here's the thing: you can arrest me and send me back for trial, but there isn't a jury in the South that will find me guilty. And Kenny? All he has to do is make tears well up in those pretty gray eyes of his and he's free. *And* on the off chance that we are convicted, there will be someone to replace me, and you know what? You and all of your darkie-loving friends will die right alongside of them."

Ralph didn't know what to say, so he said nothing; he looked at Lawrence sadly and walked away.

As soon as Lawrence could, he made his phone call to Doc. "Kenny and I are under arrest."

"Yeah? That's too bad," Doc replied.

"You're sending someone, right?"

"Ah, can't do that; the FBI is down here hot and heavy. You're on your own until you get back home, and then we'll see what we can do for ya."

"But—"

The line had gone dead.

Kenneth got the same reaction, only he was too young and inexperienced with life to understand the ramifications—they were being left to fend for themselves.

Sally walked around the house, wondering what she was going to do. She was waiting for the call from Doc, telling her not to worry about anything, that he had it taken care of. When the phone call didn't come by five, she knew what had happened: the Klan had all but abandoned Lawrence and Kenny. If they helped them, it would be after they were taken back to South Carolina.

Dianne and Eli had asked her repeatedly where Kenneth was, until she finally told them the truth. "Kenny and your father are in jail."

"Why?" Eli asked.

"He and your daddy did some really bad things," Sally replied.

"You mean hangin' them ni—"

"Stop it!" Sally yelled. "That's enough of the name-calling. I don't ever want to hear that word again!"

"But Mama—" Eli started.

"No, it's too late for Kenny, but I won't let you hate like that, so no more name-calling."

"Are we going back home?" Dianne asked.

"No, I don't think so," Sally replied. "I'm hoping that Grandpa Ralph will let us stay here."

"But what if he doesn't? " Dianne asked, as a tear ran down her face. "I don't want to go back home; we like it here."

"I know, honey, I do, too. We'll just have to wait and see what happens," Sally replied, giving the girl a hug.

Sally couldn't help but notice how the house seemed more settled without Kenneth's constant glaring and Lawrence's constant talk about his group. She decided to enjoy the peace while she could; for all she knew, Lawrence and Kenneth could be back home tonight. She also knew that the prosecutor would have a hard time convincing a jury to find either Lawrence or Kenneth guilty—they were white men and they would be believed over any black person who testified against them. If they were freed, they'd come back here, and she wasn't sure she wanted that. It wasn't a question of whether she loved Lawrence—she did, and Kenny too for that matter, but the hate. . . .

She reexamined her own feelings and had to admit that she was a racist as well. Maybe not to the extreme that Lawrence and Kenny were, but a racist nonetheless. Sally sighed; she would think about the racism issue later; she had dinner to make for her two remaining children.

Ralph was silent on the drive back home. To hear the anger and hatred in Lawrence's voice and to see the eyes of his grandson had hurt more than he thought, but he was relieved that Lawrence and Kenneth were leaving the state, even if temporarily. It would give Sally time to make up her mind about what she wanted to do.

She was a racist even if she didn't consider herself one, and Ralph wanted nothing to do with her, which was unfortunate because he did like her and the kids. But they were a threat to what he considered his real family. Ralph knew what Abby would say when he told her his thoughts; she would want to try to help her somehow. The woman was a soft touch.

Abby anxiously waited for Ralph to come back. Like Nick, she wondered if his going to see his son was a good idea. She was so worried about it that she had mentioned it.

"I have to," was all that Ralph had said.

She had the morning to think about Sally and the two children. Lawrence had bought the house, so they should be able to stay there if they wanted to; the other question was about their financial status. They could give back some of the money from the sale of the house, but what would happen after that ran out?

"Damn," Abby swore softly; she liked Sally but didn't quite trust her, and she definitely didn't trust the kids, simply because they were kids. If Sally stayed, everyone else would still be in danger, whereas if she left. . . . But Abby's gut told her that Sally didn't want to leave.

She jumped up when she heard the front door open; as soon as she saw Ralph's face, she knew it had been bad. She walked over to him, hugged him, and then kissed his cheek before taking his hand and leading him to the sofa.

"Jesus, Abby, they have so much hate in them," was all he said.

SEPTEMBER 30, 1944

Kenji kissed Niko, Marie, and finally Patricia in the doorway of the library. Today was the day that would determine their future.

"You're going to do great!" Patricia said, giving him a hug.

"I hope so; so much depends on my doing well," Kenji replied.

A few minutes later, Kenji was sitting at the table. His mouth was dry and his heart pounded; he simply could not fail—he couldn't.

"Ready?" Paul asked.

Paul put the first test down in front of Kenji. "This portion of the test is the shortest part," Paul said. "You should be able to complete it in less than an hour."

Kenji nodded, closed his eyes, and opened them again.

Paul sat across the room, sat down, picked up the paper, and then quietly said, "Go."

Kenji looked down at the test and almost panicked; he was wasting time, but he couldn't think. He closed his eyes and took a deep, cleansing breath and then another until his heart rate slowed and his head was clear, and then he started the test, finishing a full twenty minutes before the hour was up.

"Do you want to take a break?" Paul asked.

Kenji nodded and rushed out of the library to look for Patricia. "*Kirei*? Where are you?" he called.

"In the kitchen!" she called back, wondering what the problem was.

Kenji quickly went to the kitchen and hugged her. "It's going to be fine!" he told her. "It's really going to be fine."

"I already knew that," Patricia replied, hugging him back.

Seven hours later, the tests were done. Kenji was tired but confident that he had passed each test with high marks. The hardest part of the test had been the essay on why he thought he should be considered for a place in the program. He was tempted to write a flowery essay about all that he had done without the benefit of training, but didn't. His essay consisted of one short paragraph:

> *I believe I should be considered because I believe I was brought into this world to somehow ease the suffering of my fellow human beings, regardless of their race, nationality, or station in life. I believe that being in the medical profession will allow me to do this.*
>
> *Thank you for your consideration,*
>
> *Kenjiro Takeda*

Paul looked over the essay and smiled; this was no less than he expected. The fact that it was short and to the point would be what caught the eye of the person making the final decision.

"Take the rest of the evening off; I'll watch the kids," Paul said with a smile.

He had looked over Kenji's answers to the tests and wouldn't be surprised if his scores were among the highest, if not the highest, in the history of the school.

Kenji found Patricia giving Niko a bath while Marie lay on the floor next to her. "It's done, *Kirei*," he said, sitting beside her and picking up Marie.

"I'm sure you did fine," Patricia replied as she leaned over and kissed his cheek.

Now would come the hard part . . . waiting for the results.

Lawrence wondered why he and Kenneth hadn't been extradited to South Carolina yet. When he asked, his question went unanswered; Kenneth, he knew, had been moved to another part of the building. He hadn't seen him since their arrest and wondered what, if anything, he was telling them.

It had been almost three weeks since their arrest, and not a word from South Carolina; he wondered what was happening there and how long they would be kept here. He talked to Sally once and she seemed to be doing all right, but he detected a change in her. He had always known that she didn't like the violence that came with being in the Klan, but he thought she had come to accept it as part of the package.

When he asked her about going back home, he didn't like the way she had hedged.

"We like it here and the kids are in school, making new friends and all." What she hadn't mentioned was that some of those friends were nonwhite.

"You need to start making preparations to go back home," Lawrence said firmly and then hung up.

Doc sat in the FBI's field office, looking around in shock. There was a traitor in their midst; there had to be in order for the feds to have so much information. The question was, who? He had been so sure that the feds would leave after a few days of no one talking and that he would be able to send some help to Lawrence and his boy, but the feds were showing no signs of leaving. He trusted no one, not even those he thought trustworthy, but the longer this went on, the more he was coming to realize that like in any war, there was acceptable loss of life. He would have to give up Lawrence and Kenneth.

They were soldiers, he rationalized, and would understand that in order to continue the work, he would have to sacrifice them.

As he sat there, he began to formulate what he would tell the FBI. He would tell them about the eight deaths that they were asking about and then lead them to believe that Lawrence acted on his own. Whether they would buy it remained to be seen, but it would take the pressure off, and if all went well, they would try to put all the hangings on Lawrence and his boy.

As far as Sally went, he couldn't have cared less. Lawrence had always been careful about not telling her any secrets and what she knew the feds already knew, so she wasn't a threat, but Lawrence would want her home. Doc had to concede that it wouldn't look right if Lawrence was here and she stayed in California, but he saw no easy way of getting her to come back. According to Lawrence, Sally and the kids really liked the West Coast. In the end, he decided to let's Sally's conscience dictate whether she came back or not.

By the end of November 1944, the Soviets had entered Yugoslavia; the Warsaw Uprising was over; the Polish Home Army was defeated by the Germans; Field Marshal Erwin Rommel was under suspicion for being one of the bomb plotters in the assassination of Hitler—he committed suicide after telling his wife that he was innocent; Red Army forces were in East Prussia; Hitler ordered that all men ages sixteen to sixty sign up for Home Guard duties; Aachen was the first major German city to be captured; Charles de Gaulle was recognized as the head of the provisional French Government; Japan was being systemically bombed by B-29s using Tinian Island in the Marianas as a base; and Romanian troops and the Red Army liberated Romania.

General John Dill died in Washington, DC, and was the only foreigner buried in Arlington Cemetery; Belgium was liberated; President Roosevelt was elected for a fourth term; San Marino, a small state on the Italian peninsula, declared war on Germany; Hitler left his wartime headquarters at Rastenburg, East Prussia, and never returned; and soon afterward, he would move into the bunker where he would ultimately commit suicide.

Everyone hoped that Kenji would have the results of his tests before his birthday rolled around. When it became obvious that it wasn't going to happen, they tried to relax. Hattie, Hana,

Abby, and Patricia were all in the kitchen making Kenji's birthday dinner while the men watched Niko and Marie play in the middle of the living room floor.

All of the men noticed that Ralph was quieter than usual and that he hadn't really been himself since his son and grandson had been arrested by the FBI, but he wouldn't talk about it, not even to Abby. The truth of it was that he was trying to forget the entire thing.

Lawrence and Kenneth were both still in custody in the LA Field Office, and no one knew when they were going to be sent back to South Carolina. Ralph had agreed with Abby that the house belonged to Sally, but balked at giving her any money. It turned out to be a moot point because Lawrence had left plenty of money at the house the morning he was arrested.

"It ain't your fault," John said out of the blue.

"Yes, it—"

"Shut up and listen!" John said crossly. "It ain't your fault! Your son made his choice, and you ain't responsible for that. He knows right from wrong, and he chose to teach his son the wrong, so stop your mopin' and get the hell over it!"

All of the men looked at John; they had all been thinking the same thing, even Kenji, although he wouldn't have said it in that way.

"Well, damn," Ralph muttered in surprise.

"He's right, you know," Nick said. "No one is holding you responsible for Lawrence's actions, so you should stop taking the blame."

"I . . . thank you," Ralph said quietly. He was still quiet, but beginning to come out of his fog. John and the others were right; his only error, and it had been a big one, was to bring Lawrence into their midst. He wasn't responsible for the choices Lawrence made or for what he decided to teach his family.

By the end of the dinner, Ralph felt more like himself, much to Abby's relief. She wondered which of the men had finally gotten through to him; whoever it was, she wanted to give him a big hug and kiss.

After the dishes were cleared, it was time to open gifts.

"Niko and Marie helped make your gift," Patricia said as she set down a box wrapped in paper that Niko had colored.

Kenji smiled at his children and opened the package; inside were dozens of small sugar cookies.

"Niko, come to Papa," he said softly. When Niko reached him, Kenji picked him up and hugged him. "Thank you for the birthday cookies; every time I eat one, I will think of you." He repeated the same thing to Marie when he held her.

"This is from me," Patricia said, handing him a small box.

Kenji opened it and gasped. It was a pen he had been eying in one of the catalogs that Abby got in the mail. "*Kirei*, you shouldn't have!" he exclaimed as he looked at the pen.

"Of course I should have! A doctor needs a good pen, doesn't he?" Patricia said as she kissed his cheek. "Happy birthday."

Kenji, to Patricia's surprise, kissed her on her lips in front of everyone. He was always openly affectionate to her, but he rarely kissed her on her lips in public. Afterward, he blushed, making her blush with him.

The rest of the gifts included updated medical journals, books, and pencils, but there was one more gift: Nick and Hana were going to take care of Niko and Marie for the night and the next day and night.

"Two nights?" Kenji asked.

"Two nights, and no arguments," Nick said. "Everything we thought you might want or need is downstairs."

"Patricia—"

"Helped plan it," Nick said. "And you both deserve it. Happy Birthday, Kenji."

Suddenly Kenji couldn't wait for the party to be over with. The last time he and Patricia had more than one night alone was before Niko was born. Hattie and John were the first to leave, after wishing Kenji a happy birthday and kissing both babies goodnight; Ralph and Abby followed them out to give them a ride home.

Paul went back to Nick's to wait for news of Kenji's test results. He had spoken to his friend at the college the week before, and they were still going over the tests.

"What's taking so long?" he demanded.

"Paul, are you sure you were in the room with him at all times?"

"Yes, why?"

"These test scores are the second highest in the history of the school. When can we meet this young man?"

Paul had to think fast. "If you'll recall, he's the young man I mentioned when I was working at Manzanar."

"Oh, yes, the young Japanese man."

"Yes, him; when can I expect a letter of acceptance?"

"As you know, we like to meet our candidates first, but because of the circumstances, that isn't possible. You can expect a letter of conditional acceptance in a few days, the condition being that we meet with the young man before we formally accept him."

Paul hung up the phone and breathed a sigh of relief. He had really wanted to tell Kenji at the birthday party, but wanted to see his and Patricia's faces when they opened the letter.

As soon as Niko and Marie were in bed, Kenji and Patricia said goodnight to Nick and Hana. Kenji went downstairs first, turning on the light as he went. The room was set up with everything Patricia could think of; Kenji looked around and then ran back up the stairs, coming back with the box of cookies.

He set them on the table by the bed and took Patricia into his arms. "This, *Kirei*, is one of the best days of my life. Thank you."

"I'm glad," Patricia said.

"Did Marie really help with the cookies?" Kenji asked.

"She really did; she's a really good sugar sprinkler."

Kenji laughed and wished he had a picture of the cookie baking; he wished he had a picture of a lot of things, beginning with their wedding—both of them. When he had a chance, he would ask Nick about buying them a camera. Years later, when he and Patricia were old, he wanted to be able to take the pictures out and show them to their children and grandchildren.

"What are you thinking about?" Patricia asked.

"That I wish we had pictures of our weddings. The only picture I have of you is the one Nick took when you were carrying Niko."

"I remember everything," Patricia said. "From the first time I saw you get off of that boat until now, and I don't think I'll forget any of it, either."

Kenji kissed her. He wouldn't forget any of it either, and he often thought about the first time he had seen her, never dreaming that their paths would be joined together. He moved his lips from hers, kissing her cheek as he pulled her tight against him.

"I will never tire of the way you feel," he murmured against her cheek. "I love you, *Kirei*, and that will never ever change."

It was then that he decided to return the necklace to her. He pulled back and took out his wallet. "*Kirei*, when I left you that first time, you gave me your necklace. I have carried it in my wallet wrapped in the handkerchief you embroidered for my twenty-first birthday."

Patricia remembered. It seemed like a lifetime ago that she watched Kenji get on that bus; even now it hurt to remember it.

"I told you that I would return it to you when I knew I would never leave you again, and while the war isn't over and the camps are in operation, I believe I am able to keep my word and never leave you again."

Patricia started to cry; she hadn't forgotten about the necklace but hadn't asked about it. She thought maybe it had been lost or stolen. "You still have it?"

"It has never left my person; I've been waiting for the right time to return it to you."

Kenji took the necklace from the handkerchief and put it around Patricia's neck. "I am never leaving you again."

Patricia touched the pendant, which was in the shape of a circle. "I love you, too," she said through her tears. "You came back just like the soldier in the song, you—"

As Kenji kissed her, he began to hurriedly undress her, anxious to feel her skin next to his. Patricia fumbled with the buttons on his shirt, became impatient and ripped his shirt open, and then struggled to unfasten his pants while he unzipped her dress and pulled the bodice over her shoulders.

He pulled back and helped Patricia with his pants, then finished undressing her. Patricia lay back on the bed and waited while Kenji looked at her for a few seconds before lying on top of her and sliding in and then going still; he wanted to be inside of her for as long as he could before he had to pull out.

"No, *Kirei*, don't move. Just lie still," he breathed.

They lay like that for several minutes before Kenji began to slowly thrust in and out of Patricia, pushing himself in as deeply as he could go and then pausing before pulling back. Patricia clung to him, crying out as she came; Kenji pulled out just as her orgasm waned, ground himself hard against her, and came with his face buried in her neck.

Afterward, they lay wrapped in each other's arms, not speaking. The pendant of the necklace rested on Kenji's chest.

"It really is going to be all right, isn't it?" Patricia asked.

"Yes, *Kirei*, it is," Kenji replied. "We're going to go to the places we talked about. I'll take you, Niko, and Marie to Japan and show you where I lived, where I went to school, and I want to show you off to my family."

"I'm not so sure about that," Patricia replied, remembering the reaction of Hana and Hiroshi.

"It will be a few years before we can go; maybe things will have changed by then," Kenji replied.

"Maybe, but you know what I want more than anything?" Patricia asked. "I want to sit on that park bench with you."

"The one across from the grocer's?" Kenji asked.

"That one, and I don't care what anyone says or thinks," Patricia said.

During the rest of the night of talking, making love, and planning, they left the basement long enough to see Niko and Marie and to eat and shower. It felt like a second honeymoon.

The letter from UCLA came the following week. Paul told Nick and Hana and then called Ralph and Abby.

"Do you know what it says?" Abby asked.

"Of course I know what it says!" Paul retorted. "Get your asses over there or I'll give it to him without you."

Niko was playing with Marie when the phone rang, and Patricia was in the kitchen making dinner. She turned the stove off and hurried to the phone. "Hello? Sure, we'll be here," she said.

"Who was that, *Kirei*?"

"Paul; he said he'd be over after dinner."

Kenji's stomach dropped. "He must have received word about school."

Dinner seemed to take forever. The time until Paul, Hana, and Nick showed up seemed even longer still. Ralph and Abby rang the doorbell ten minutes later with John and Hattie in tow.

"What happened?" Patricia asked.

"Nothing bad," Paul replied. "But you might want to sit down."

Kenji sat on the couch next to Patricia, holding her hand. Nick held Marie, and John held Niko in his lap.

"The letter from UCLA came today," Paul said.

Kenji's grip on Patricia's hand tightened.

"I thought you might want your family around when you opened it."

"Do you know what it says?" Kenji asked.

"Yes, I know, and I'm not going to tell you, so open the letter," Paul said as he handed the letter to Kenji.

Kenji held the letter in his hand, looked at it, and handed it to Patricia. "I want you to open it."

"No, you should open it; you did all of the studying," Patricia replied.

"But you were at my side and you helped me prepare. Please, *Kirei*, open it."

"Damn it! Somebody open the letter!" Ralph said, sounding like his old impatient self.

Patricia took the letter, whispered a silent prayer, and opened it. She read silently, her eyes growing wide and then wet with tears. "You did it! You're in, pending a face-to-face meeting with you whenever you're released from the camp! Kenji, you're going to be a doctor!" Patricia cried, throwing her arms around him.

"I passed all of the tests?" Kenji asked.

"Every single one! Your scores are the second highest in the history of the school—congratulations!" Paul said.

"This is possible only because of you," Kenji said, his eyes glistening with tears.

"It's possible because you're a bright young man; it would have happened with or without my help," Paul replied.

"We can only say thank you," Kenji said, standing up and giving Paul a deep bow of respect.

"You're welcome," Paul replied.

Suddenly the living room erupted into applause and cheers; Hana, Abby, and Hattie each hugged Kenji, and each man shook his hand.

John was probably the proudest of the men. "Hot damn! We got ourselves a doctor in the family!"

Abby and Hattie made coffee and tea, while Patricia and Kenji read and reread the letter together.

"It's really happening!" Kenji said, hugging Patricia.

Sally looked out of the front window; there was still no word from South Carolina, and she hadn't heard from Lawrence since that last call telling her to be ready to move. She hadn't even begun to pack and decided that she wasn't going to; she was staying put. There was enough money to last for quite a while if she was careful, and she planned to find a job of some kind, even if it was babysitting.

She hadn't seen Ralph since the arrests, but Abby stopped by frequently, always bringing a treat for the children and staying to have a cup of coffee with her. She found Abby to be a good friend, even though it was obvious that Abby didn't trust her. In any case, she was grateful for the friendship and told Abby so.

"Sally, I won't lie to you and pretend to understand what it is you and your Klan believes. I'm here because you're all alone, and everyone needs a friendly face."

"But you don't trust me."

"No, I don't, and that's because you, your husband, and your children came here under false pretenses. You took advantage of Ralph's guilt to come here to spread your hate."

"I tried to talk him out of starting the group—"

"Do you agree with what he teaches?" Abby interrupted.

"Some of it, but not the part about the hangings or whippings. I just think we weren't meant to mix with other races is all."

"Does that make you any less racist?" Abby asked.

"Yes, it does! I'm teaching my kids not to use the ugly words that Lawrence and Kenny used, I—"

"Still living with the same attitude," Abby broke in. "Are you also teaching them respect for those who are different, or are you teaching them that everyone needs to be kept in their own little compartment? When they finally put Lawrence and Kenneth on trial, what are you going to do?"

"I . . . I have to at least stand with him," Sally said weakly.

Abby sighed. "Sally, I can't tell you what or what not to do, but your husband and your son killed innocent people. Ralph slept here with a knife under his pillow and a chair under the doorknob because Kenneth told him that traitors like Ralph were supposed to die. Do you understand what I'm saying? They weren't going to stop with the blacks; they were and are going after people who disagreed with their teaching of hatred and who aren't white."

Abby left a few minutes later; she had made her point, or hoped she had.

"Abby?" Sally called. "Tell Ralph that I really am sorry."

Charles sat across from Lawrence in the interview room; he disliked the man from the first time he saw him and disliked him a little more with each subsequent meeting. He had some news for Lawrence, news that might make him want to give up some information about his fellow Klansmen.

"Your friend down there, the one you call once a week or so? Doc, is it? Well, he's been giving the agents in your hometown quite an earful."

Lawrence snorted. “Yeah? What’s that? The dates for the county fair?”

“Interesting that you should mention dates,” Charles said calmly. “He gave us the dates of the hangings that took place over a four-month period, and guess what? You and sonny boy over in the other cell have been placed at each one.’

“You’re lying!”

“Not only that; he says the Klan didn’t order those hangings, and he called you a loose cannon.”

“Liar!”

“He also had several photographs with you and that crazy kid of yours posing next to the bodies of your victims.”

Lawrence couldn’t say anything; was it possible that Doc had given him and Kenneth up?

“There’s this one picture that was so bad the agents looking at it threw up; it was the one with the black man tied to the back of a pickup truck. There was a before and after picture, and you and Kenneth were the only ones in both of them,” Charles continued.

“Son of a bitch!” Lawrence swore.

“So you know what that means, right? It means that your racist ass is going to prison; it means that your proclamation about no white jury convicting you is bullshit! And do you know why? Because if they don’t, in the face of all of that evidence, it’s going to call a whole lot of attention to every known chapter of the Klan, no matter where they are. You and your son are acceptable losses,” Charles said and then wondered what would happen if he told Lawrence that he had black blood as well as the blood of some other nonwhite races.

“Oh, and there’s one more thing: Sonny boy over there is spilling his guts, too. He’s one fucked-up kid, you know? Did you know he was going to kill your father, his grandfather, and . . . your wife?”

Lawrence’s head snapped up. “That isn’t true.”

“It is; he said that your father was a traitor and should be treated as such. It’s what you taught him, isn’t it? And your wife? He didn’t think she was a true believer and thought she was planning on calling the police or something—again, the whole traitor thing."

Lawrence was deathly white; it was true that Kenny had taken to the teaching of the Klan like a fish to water, but he was going to kill Sally? Ralph he could understand, but his own mother?

Charles watched Lawrence process the information and stood up to leave.

"Wait, can I see Kenneth?"

Charles kept walking, pretending not to hear the request; he had no intention of honoring it.

The evening after Kenji received his acceptance letter, Nick and Hana were getting dressed to go over to Abby's for a celebration dinner.

"I wish we could go to a nice restaurant to celebrate," Nick said as he straightened his tie.

"Maybe we can do that when Kenji graduates," Hana replied as she tapped Nick on the shoulder and turned around so Nick could zip up her dress.

"I'm planning on it," Nick said as he zipped up Hana's dress and wished they had another hour before they had to leave. "Baby, just think about it; our kid a doctor!"

"You've never said that before," Hana said quietly.

"What? 'Our kid'? Of course he's our kid, just like Niko and Marie are our grandkids," Nick replied, surprised at her surprise.

"It's just nice to hear you say it," Hana replied.

They were on their way out to the garage when the phone rang; Nick almost didn't answer it but thought better of it.

"Hello? Charles? What? Slow down! Oh fuck!"

Chapter 20

Nick looked around to see if Hana was within earshot. "What the fuck happened?" he hissed.

"We're not sure," Charles replied. "We were getting ready to put them in the car and then the kid was free."

"Someone in the office helped them; it's the only explanation," Nick said. "Did you send a car to the mother's house?"

"As soon as the kid made a break for it."

"He's on foot?" Nick asked.

"I think someone picked him up. Look, I gotta run; I'll keep you posted."

"Take this number and call me there," Nick said and gave Charles Abby's number.

"Nick, is something wrong?" Hana asked.

"No, baby, nothing for you to worry about," Nick replied. "Let's go or we'll be late."

Hana knew Nick wasn't telling her the truth but let it go, understanding that he didn't want anything to ruin tonight's celebration.

As Nick tucked Hana into the trunk of the car, he wondered if he should say anything to Ralph, and decided against it. Hopefully they would catch Kenneth before he had gone too far or at his mother's house.

Kenneth lay in the back seat of the car that had been waiting for him when he escaped. He didn't know who his benefactor was, and he didn't much care. All he knew was that as soon as they were outside, his cuffs were unlocked and he saw the waiting car on the corner and took off at a run. Even now, he didn't know who the driver was, and it was for the best. If he was caught again, he wouldn't know a name or a face.

He didn't speak to the driver as they headed to what he assumed was his mother's house, although he was sure that would be the first place the police would look for him. The fact that he didn't know where he was didn't bother Kenneth; this place was no different than home, except that the woods were missing. He had an excellent sense of direction, thanks to his father and Doc, who would take him into the woods and leave him with nothing except the shirt on his back.

At first he thought they were just being cruel, but he had learned to enjoy the outings and the challenges they presented. Now he was glad for the training; he would survive here, as he did at home, and his father would be proud.

Lawrence was as surprised as anyone when Kenneth got away, and like the rest, he knew that the help had come from the inside. The only question was, who? He hoped that Kenneth had the sense not to go home, where they were probably already waiting for him.

Charles walked into the interrogation room and sat down; he hated the smug son of a bitch sitting across from him, but hid it.

"Seems you lost someone," Lawrence said with a smile.

"For the time being," Charles replied, smiling back at him. "You know what, though? Your kid just made the most-wanted list, and when we find him. . . . "

That took the smile off Lawrence's face; Charles noticed, pleased, that the lie had worked.

"He's just a kid—"

"Who helped you murder at least eight people, and I'm betting there's more than that," Charles interrupted. "You could help him and you both if you tell us who helped you."

"I don't know; I was as surprised as you were—and a hell of a lot happier," Lawrence replied, smiling again.

Charles tapped his fingers on the table. "No matter, your ass is still out of here."

"What? What about Kenny?" Lawrence asked.

"What about him? We'll find him, and if he has a weapon and shoots, we shoot back," Charles replied coolly.

Sally finished folding the laundry from the day and was going to make fresh lemonade for the next day when she heard the tap on the door. She glanced at the clock and got to the door just as Eli opened it; she recognized the agent as one of the men who had arrested Kenneth several weeks before.

"What's happened?" she asked anxiously.

"I'm here to let you know that Kenneth escaped and may be headed here."

"Escaped? How? Aren't they on their way back to South Carolina?"

"It happened when we were getting ready to leave. Ma'am, does Kenneth know anyone who would have helped him?" the agent asked.

"No . . . he never left home, and they hadn't started the meetings yet. The first one was supposed to be on the evening of the day you arrested them," Sally replied.

"Do you know where the meeting was to be held?"

"No, I'm sorry, I don't."

"All right, if you remember anything, stick your head out of the door. A car will be there and in the back all night."

"And then what?" Sally asked.

"We hope to have him back in custody by the morning," the agent replied as he walked away.

Sally closed the door and whispered a prayer that Kenneth was found; he considered her one of the enemy and would have no problem killing her.

Nick pulled into the garage and beeped the horn, announcing their arrival. He got out, closed the garage door, and helped

Hana out of the trunk. He forced himself to smile, but knew he hadn't fooled her.

"Nick—"

"I'll tell you later," he said, as Ralph came out to greet them.

The odor of frying chicken and fresh biscuits filled the garage, making Nick's stomach grumble, even with the news he had just received.

"Well, come on in!" Ralph exclaimed.

Nick followed Hana in and watched as she was warmly greeted by everyone, John included. He made his way to the living room, where Kenji was on the floor with Niko and Marie.

"Hiya, kids!" he greeted.

"*Ojiisan* Nick! Grandpa Nick!" Niko exclaimed happily, getting up and running to him.

Nick picked Niko up and kissed him on the cheek before setting him down and picking up Marie, who just giggled.

"How's Dr. Takeda?" Nick asked.

"I'm not a doctor yet," Kenji replied.

"The hell you're not!" Nick replied. "You just don't have the credentials yet."

"That's a few years away," Kenji said, "but I'm glad to have a few moments alone with you."

"Something wrong?"

"No, all is as well as can be expected, but I have a request."

"What do you need?" Nick asked.

"I have only one picture of Patricia and none of the children. I would like for you to purchase a camera for me. Is this possible?"

"Sure it is, but developing the pictures might be a problem," Nick replied.

"Do you know this process?"

"Well, yes, but it's complicated and. . . . Who am I talking to?" Nick asked, laughing. "Yes, I can get you a camera, and we can set the basement up as a darkroom; just give me a couple of days."

"Thank you, but please don't tell Patricia. I want to surprise her."

"*Obaasan* Hana!" Niko said, jumping up again.

"*Ohayo ichiban no mago* (hello, number one grandson)," Hana said in Japanese and English. She took Marie from Nick and kissed her.

"She's doing well," she commented as she kissed the baby again.

"She is, and we're grateful for that," Kenji said, standing and stretching.

"I only came to see you and the children; I must get back to the kitchen. Dinner is almost ready," she said, handing Marie back to Nick.

Nick and Kenji watched as Hana went back to the kitchen.

"I've never properly thanked you for caring for my mother," Kenji said.

"No thanks are needed," Nick replied. "I love her."

"I know this, but thank you. I am proud to call you Father."

"Wh—what?" Nick stammered.

"I know I have a father with whom I will attempt to make amends, and even though I call you Nick, I look up to you as a father."

"I—oh God, Kenji; I'm proud to call you my son," Nick replied, his throat tight.

He had to wonder what it felt like to have a son of his flesh, but if it felt anything like this, it had to be beyond description. Nick put the baby on the floor and hugged Kenji. "You really are my kid!" he exclaimed and meant it.

Kenji returned the hug, his throat as tight as Nick's had been.

"It's ready!" Patricia called as she walked into the living room. "Everything all right?" she asked as she looked at Kenji and Nick.

"Everything is perfect," Nick replied, looking at Kenji.

He had a son; it didn't matter that he was in his twenties. He had a family that he never could have dreamt of in his wildest dreams, and he would die to protect all of them.

Kenneth closed his eyes, not worried about where he was going; he had figured out a while back that he wasn't going to his mother's house and that it was probably for the best. He would have killed the traitorous bitch and ended right back in jail. He hated the fact that Dianne and Eli were still with her, but there was nothing he could do about that. If they adopted her views, he would take the fact that he had to leave them into consideration.

The car finally stopped, and the driver got out without speaking. Kenneth waited a few minutes and then got out, stretched, looked around, and followed the man into a small house. The smell of cooking food made his mouth water as he followed the voices coming from the kitchen.

"Take a load off," a gruff voice said from the stove.

Kenneth didn't move; instead, he looked around. "Who the fuck are you?" he demanded.

"Friends; now sit down and eat before it get's cold," the man said, ignoring Kenneth's tone.

"I said, who the fuck are you?"

"Sit your ass down and eat!" someone said from behind him.

Kenneth spun around to see who had spoken. He recognized the man as one of the agents from the office. "Why did you help me?"

"Let's just say that our politics are the same."

"You got a name?" Kenneth asked.

"Just call me Frank," the man said. "Sit down and eat; Angie will show you to your room when you're done."

Kenneth sat down and began to eat; he kept his eyes on the people around him and looked for possible escape routes. He had already decided that he wasn't staying here; somehow, he was going back to South Carolina. The hell with his mother; he needed to be home so he could help his father escape.

Everyone ate their fill of chicken, mashed potatoes, gravy, corn, and biscuits.

"Mama and Ralph made the cake," Patricia said, cutting a big piece for Kenji and setting it in front of him.

"Thank you for the delicious dinner," Kenji said with a smile. "Perhaps Mother and I could make a traditional Japanese meal for you sometime."

"That would be wonderful!" Abby said.

The talk was animated, with no one except Hana noticing that Nick seemed a little distracted. At eight, the phone rang.

"I'll get it!" Nick called, standing before anyone had a chance to move.

"Tell me you got him," Nick said.

"No, but we know who helped him, and we know where he is," Charles replied.

"Who?" Nick asked.

"One of the junior agents . . . Lincoln Phillips."

"I don't know him," Nick replied.

"That's because he came after you left."

"How'd you find out?"

"You know that old black janitor, Harvey?"

"Sure, he's a deaf as a doornail; what about him?" Nick asked.

"Well, old Harvey isn't as deaf as he lets on. As a matter of fact, I think his hearing is better than mine."

"He heard someone talking," Nick commented.

"He heard a lot of someones talking," Charles replied. "They didn't care because they assumed, like all of us, that Harvey was deaf."

"Is someone on the way to pick up the homicidal brat?" Nick asked.

"They should be arriving about now."

"Good, call me when they've got them. If I don't answer here, hang up and try my home number."

"Who was that?" Abby asked from behind him.

"Charles, just giving me some information," Nick replied.

"Nick, what are you up to?" Abby asked.

"Nothing! I promise."

Abby didn't believe him, but he had walked away before she could say anything.

Since it was a special night, Niko was allowed to stay up fifteen minutes longer, and the grandmothers got to tuck him and Marie into bed.

"*Oyasuminasai*, Papa and Mama (goodnight, Papa and Mama)," Niko said with a bow.

"Well done," Kenji said with an encouraging smile. "That is a big word for one so young."

"Thank you, Papa," Niko said, beaming at the compliment. He kissed everyone, including Marie, good night and followed Hana and Hattie up the stairs.

"That's one sharp little boy!" Paul commented as he watched Niko climb the stairs.

The phone rang one more time, and Nick raced to answer it.

"What's going on?" Abby asked no one in particular.

"You got him?" Nick asked.

"Sure did, and a few others as well; they'll be charged with aiding and abetting, but are you ready for the big news? Guess who was with them?"

"I don't know, who?"

"Elam Martin."

"What the fuck was he doing there?" Nick asked.

"When he was checking up on people, it was for a recruiting mission. His goal was to plant some of his people in offices around the country—Lincoln was one of his."

"He was looking at me as a possible recruit?" Nick asked.

"No, he really was looking for something on you," Charles replied, "and on the director, but whatever it was, he didn't find it."

"So where is the son of a bitch?"

"Sharing a cell with his little buddy, Kenneth," Charles replied.

"Are you going to be there for a while?"

"I can be, why?"

"I want to come down and see Elam," Nick said. "I'll be there in an hour."

Nick hung up the phone and went back to the living room.

"What happened?" Abby asked.

"I'll tell you when Hana and Abby come down," Nick replied. "Patricia, is it all right for Hana to stay here tonight?"

"You don't even have to ask," Patricia replied. "Both of you are always welcome here."

Hana and Abby came down a few minutes later. Nick filled everyone in on what happened.

"But they got him, right?" Ralph asked.

"They got him, as well as Elam Martin."

"Your boss?" Abby asked.

"Yes, apparently he was trying to get like-minded people placed in field offices in order to help advance the cause of the Klan."

"But he works for the government!" John said.

"True, but remember that I said they come from all walks of life. Look at where Lawrence came from—one of the leaders is a physician."

The room went silent as everyone realized that while one war might be ending, another one was starting.

Elam looked at Lawrence and turned away; he wanted to say something, but didn't know who might be listening, not that it mattered. At the very least, he would lose is job; at worst, he would serve time for aiding and abetting. He wondered who had talked; he looked around the cell and saw Harvey sweeping the floor and disregarded him. Elam, like everyone else, believed him to be deaf.

Seeing no one else, he spoke to Lawrence. "We tried; you're on your own now."

"Shut up!" Lawrence hissed, looking at Harvey.

"He can't hear; he's deaf, and even if he did hear, he'd be too stupid to understand," Elam said.

Neither man saw the flash of anger in Harvey's eyes as he continued to sweep the floors and gather the trash.

"Thank you for at least trying to get my boy out of here," Lawrence said, looking across the room at Kenny.

"Your friend Doc called me at home, which was a very stupid thing to do, by the way."

"Doc called? How do you know him?" Lawrence asked, surprised.

"He's a friend of an acquaintance of mine who foolishly gave this friend of yours my number."

"So now what?" Lawrence asked.

"You and your son are being extradited to South Carolina, and from what I hear, there will be a trial. What in the hell were you thinking, posing for pictures like that?"

"We didn't know we had a turncoat!"

"Which is why you shouldn't have posed in those pictures!" Elam shot back.

"You're a fine one to talk; you've got a turncoat, too! Why else would you be sitting in here with me, unless this is a setup. Is that it? Is that why they put you in here with me—to get information?"

Elam looked at Lawrence and started to laugh. "I'm in here because of you and that crazy-assed kid of yours! I was doing just fine until your sorry asses blew into town."

No one noticed that Harvey had left the cells.

Charles waited on the other side of the door for Harvey to come out. "What'd you hear?" Charles asked.

"Sumthin' 'bout a man named Doc who called a friend of Mr. Elam's, who gave Mr. Elam's name to Doc."

"Did they mention the friend's name?'

"No sir, but Mr. Elam was none to happy 'bout the call."

Charles slapped Harvey on the back. "Thank you for your help; you just helped put away some pretty bad men."

"You welcome, but you ain't gonna tell nobody that I can hear, are ya?"

"No sir! Your secret is safe with me," Charles assured him.

Nick nodded at the old janitor as he passed by, not indicating that he knew he could hear.

"What else did you find out?" Nick asked.

"Elam has knowledge of Doc; as a matter of fact, he's spoken to him. It was at his request that Elam got involved, but there's someone else."

"Who?"

"We don't know, but whoever it is has ties here and in South Carolina."

"Have you started checking the backgrounds of. . . . Sorry," Nick said.

"No problem; are you sure you don't want to come back?" Charles asked.

Nick didn't answer him, but went down into the cells.

Elam stood up when he heard footsteps approaching; he raised his eyebrows when he saw Nick and Charles.

"Well, look who it is: the agent who doesn't want to be an agent."

"Getting acquainted with your new roommate?" Nick asked as he pulled up a chair.

"What do you want, Nick?"

"Nothing, really; I just wanted to see what two real Klansmen look like, and I have to say I'm not impressed.

"And Lawrence, I hope you enjoyed your stay with us; your father—"

"He isn't my father."

"Glad to hear it, because he doesn't consider you a son, but I want to give you a warning: If by some miracle you don't get convicted, stay the fuck away from California and keep your crazy-ass son with you. If I see or even get wind that you're here, you're a dead man."

Lawrence laughed. "You can't tell me where I can and can't go."

"Come back to this state and I will kill you."

"Hey! Everybody! Did you just hear that? This agent just threatened me!" Lawrence called out.

"I didn't threaten you," Charles said.

"Not you! Him."

"I'm not an agent," Nick said as he stood and walked away.

As he drove back to Abby's, he thought about Charles' question. Did he want to go back? Then there was Elam's comment about the "agent who didn't want to be an agent."

"I could do so much good," he muttered and then thought about Hana and the rest of them. "But I wouldn't be a field agent," he mumbled and wondered if that would make a difference to her; somehow, he didn't think so.

Hana lay on the bed in the basement with her eyes closed. No matter what Nick said and how angry he got at the people at his office, he missed it. She saw his excitement when a new problem or danger came up and they had to figure a way out of it. He loved what he did and had probably never really realized it. Part of her, the selfish and frightened part of her, liked where he was—safe with her and the others. The other part of her, the wife who wanted her husband happy, wanted him to go back to what he loved doing, and she would have to learn to deal with the fear.

She tossed and turned for an hour before she finally made up her mind: she wanted Nick to be happy, and opening his law office wasn't going to do it, at least not now. When he came back, she would encourage him to go back to work, if that's what he wanted to do.

Hana drifted off to sleep while she waited for Nick to come back.

"What were you and Nick talking about?" Patricia asked as she got ready for bed.

"I told him that although I have a father, I also look up to him as a father," Kenji replied as he hung up her and then his clothes.

"What about your father?"

"I will try to make amends," Kenji replied. "I will give him the opportunity to know his grandchildren."

"I'm glad to hear that," Patricia replied. She knew it hadn't been an easy decision for him to make because of what his father had planned to do to her, but he and his father needed to talk. After all, if her father came around, maybe Hiroshi had as well.

"Kenji, I don't care whether he likes me or accepts me; it's you and the babies that I want this for."

"I understand that, but I will not accept anything less than respect for you as my wife and the mother of my children. If he cannot give us that, then I will have nothing more to say to him."

"So, Dr. Takeda—"

"*Kirei*, I'm not a doctor yet," Kenji interrupted.

"But you will be."

"Yes, but I'm not one yet," Kenji insisted.

"We're all proud of you, Dr. Takeda," Patricia said, walking toward him. "And we all love you."

Kenji put his hands on Patricia's hips and pulled her into him. "I love you, too," he said. "I'm finally making steps toward being able to care for you and our children."

Patricia wanted to tell him that he had always cared for them, but didn't; no matter what she said, he didn't and wouldn't see it the same way she did. Instead of replying, she stepped in closer, wrapped her arms around him, and pressed tightly against him.

"I feel bad for Ralph," Patricia said, laying her head on Kenji's chest.

"As do I, but he is not alone; he has us," Kenji replied, walking backward to the bed and sitting when he felt the back of his knees touch the sides.

Patricia remained standing in front of him, looking down at him as he looked up. She smoothed his hair back and ran her fingers through it. He really needed a cut, but she liked the length and didn't mention cutting it; when he went to school, it would have to be cut, but until then. . . .

She bent down and kissed his forehead, his eyes, and then his nose before finally reaching his lips. Kenji scooted back on the bed, pulling Patricia with him, and lay back. Patricia moaned softly as Kenji's hands stroked her back before reaching down to her ass and pulling her tight against him. Patricia straddled Kenji's hips, crying out as his naked hardness touched her.

Kenji flipped her to onto her back and slid in with a sigh, and stilled for several minutes. Patricia didn't move; she loved the feeling of being filled with him as much as he loved filling her, and as much as she didn't want him to, he would have to pull out. Ever since Marie had been born, Kenji had been religious about pulling out; it was too soon for another baby, and the last pregnancy had scared him, even though he had never told Patricia that.

He began moving slowly and deliberately, maximizing the pleasure he knew Patricia would feel. He stopped just long enough to look down at her and tell her that he loved her before he sent her over the edge.

Abby and Ralph sat in the living room in silence. Abby didn't know what to say or do for him, other than sit with him. That there were people in the government who were sworn to protect involved in this was disturbing and frightening. It meant that her neighbors could be in this group, and how would she know? It meant that even when Kenji, Patricia, Hana, and Nick could go out in public, they would still face hardships. She pushed the thoughts aside and thought about the good things that had happened during the worst of times: Kenji and Patricia were together with two beautiful babies, and Kenji was going to medical school, with the help of Paul. Nick and Hana were together; John had finally accepted Kenji and often called him son, and they all considered one other family.

She remembered the letter she had written when Kenji and Patricia had become her family and reminded herself that she needed to say something to Nick about it. When she died, everything she had was going to Kenji and Patricia; she had no one else to leave it to, and even if she did, she would have made the same decision. She knew that Ralph was leaving everything to them as well; they were going to be all right if they could just get past this war.

"You don't have to sit with me," Ralph said. "I'm all right."

"I know you are," Abby replied. "But I'll sit with you anyway."

"How can a parent teach their child to hate like that?" Ralph asked, more to himself than Abby. "They killed eight people! Eight people who had done nothing wrong! God help me, but Abby, I hope they hang the both of them and every Klansman along with them."

"Ralph, I know you're angry, but they're still your family."

"The hell they are! You, Kenji, Patty, and the rest are my family! I forgot that fact when I brought Lawrence and his family here."

"What about Sally and the two remaining children?" Abby asked.

"What about them?"

"I don't think it's too late for them," she replied.

"Maybe," Ralph conceded, "but I don't trust her."

"Understandable, but she and those children are alone."

"What is it that you want me to do, Abby? She's a racist just like—"

"Yes, she's a racist, but she never wanted anyone hurt," Abby said. "She believes that the races should be kept separate but that everything should be equal. Those children had no choice in the matter, and we have a chance to change their minds."

"And I get to know my grandchildren; is that it?"

"That's it," Abby said.

"I'll think on it," Ralph replied.

The agent tapped on the door again, making Sally jump.

"Ma'am, it's safe now; your son is back in custody."

"Is he all right? Did he hurt anyone?" Sally asked anxiously.

"Not that I'm aware of," the agent replied.

"Did he get hurt?"

"Again, not that I'm aware of. Good night, ma'am."

Sally sat down, relieved and feeling guilty because of it. Kenneth was her child, and she was supposed to want him and Lawrence home with them. "I love them, but I don't want them here," she whispered to herself. "I don't want them here."

Paul looked through his financial statements; there was enough money to send Kenji through school several times over. He still hadn't talked to Patricia, because it seemed like things were always in the way or something was happening with them—the children or regarding the safety of the family that he now considered his. He had spoken to Kenji about Patricia's interest and found out she was thinking about teaching, and while teaching was a noble profession, Paul thought she would be wasted in that field; it wouldn't be enough of a challenge for her.

She could be as fine a doctor as Kenji, but there were several issues. She had no college background, and there were the children to consider. What he wondered was if there was a way for Patricia to test out of some of the prerequisites and if there was some way she could take the other classes while Kenji himself was at school.

He took out a piece of paper and wrote a letter to his friend at UCLA, to be mailed in the morning. When the letter was written, Paul took a minute to think about the first time he had met Kenji and smiled. It didn't take him long to recognize the inherent talent Kenji possessed and for him to decide to help however he could. What he hadn't expected was to find someone with the same capability and a family to boot. He planned to talk to Patricia as soon as possible.

Nick pulled into the garage at Abby's house and quietly went down to the basement. He had made the decision not to go back to the office; he couldn't and wouldn't put Hana through the anxieties of the past. He loved her too much for that.

The bedside lamp snapped on as soon as the door to the basement opened; Hana was awake and waiting for him.

"Why aren't you sleeping?" Nick asked as he kicked off his shoes and undressed.

"I did for a short time," Hana replied. "Is everything all right?"

"It's fine; how are you?"

"I'm fine, and I have been thinking."

"What about?" Nick asked as he settled on the bed next to her.

"You and your job. . . . I think you should consider going back."

"Hana—"

"Please listen to me before you say no," Hana said, touching his lips with her fingertips. "You miss it, even though you don't say it; I see how your eyes light up when there's a problem to be solved or when something like tonight happens. These are emotions that sitting in a law office will not elicit. Am I frightened? Yes, but I want you to be happy."

Nick didn't know what to say; it was so unexpected, and he didn't realize he was that transparent. "Hana, I don't how to respond; how long have you been thinking about this?"

"For a little while, but it was while you were gone tonight that I really took the time to think through it," she replied. "Nick, have you been thinking about this, too?"

Nick pulled Hana closer and kissed her head. "I'd be lying if I said I hadn't, but you and this family come first."

"If you're concerned about how I'll deal with the anxiety, I'll learn to cope as I've learned to cope with so much since my arrival to this country."

Nick told Hana about the position of director that had been offered to him.

"I wouldn't be a field agent, but . . . I would make it my priority to deal with the likes of Lawrence Goodman and Elam Martin. That alone would make me a target—"

"Do you want to do this thing?" Hana asked, interrupting him.

"Hana, it's not that simple," Nick replied. "If it were just me, I'd say yes, but it isn't. I have to consider all of you and what could happen if I do. I could become a target, and if the time comes that we can go public, the rest of you could become targets, too, and if anything happened to any of you—"

"I think the decision is ours to make," Hana said softly. "You should talk to the others."

Nick fell silent. If he did this, he would have to take every precaution to keep everyone safe. There wouldn't be a problem at the moment, but later there could be, and he just wasn't going to risk it. The fact that Hana loved him enough to even tell him to go back to work spoke volumes.

"No, I'm not going to do it."

"Nick—"

"You have no idea of what you just did means to me, and I love you for it, but Hana, my place is with you and this family, and there are other ways I can help deal with these jerks besides putting you all in the line of fire. When this war is over, I'm going back to practicing law, and I'll work from behind the scenes."

"And what will you do in the meantime?" she asked.

"What I'm doing now—doing what I can to keep all of us safe and together," he replied.

"Are you at peace with this choice?" Hana asked.

Nick thought for a minute before replying. "I am completely at peace with this; now go to sleep."

Hana snuggled closer and closed her eyes; a few minutes later, she was asleep.

On December 18,1944, the legality of Executive Order 9066 was clarified; Korematsu vs. the United States voted six to three that in general, EO 9066 was constitutional; Justice Hugo Black held the opinion that the need to protect against espionage outweighed the rights of the plaintiff Fred Korematsu and anyone of Japanese descent (Korematsu's conviction for evading internment was overturned in 1983).

By the end of December 1944, Heinrich Himmler ordered that the crematoriums and gas chambers at Auschwitz concentration camp be torn down and destroyed; the bombing of Iwo Jima began; the Battle of the Bulge began; the third fleet of Admiral Halsey was hit by a typhoon, capsizing three destroyers; and eighty-six American prisoners were executed by SS troops in the Malmedy massacre.

The Battle of Bastogne was at its height—the Americans were running low on ammunition when the Germans demanded surrender; the message of "Nuts" was sent back by General McAuliff; the American counter-attack of the "Bulge" began.

The Belgian transport ship SS *Leopoldville* was sunk off the coast of France; more than eight hundred lives were lost—most of those were American servicemen; racial tensions within the US military boiled over in the Argana race riot on Guam—the racial tensions between the 3rd Marine Division and the all-black 25th Depot Company of the US Navy began in August 1944 when the 25th Depot Company began loading operations at the newly created naval supply depot. The Soviets launched the Battle of Budapest; and Hungary, now led by a Soviet-controlled government, declared war on Germany.

Hiroshi looked over at Dai; she was due soon, and he wished they were somewhere better than this. There were increasing rumors about release, and everyone was still talking about the Korematsu decision and how that meant they would be released, but Hiroshi wasn't going to believe it until he saw it.

The notes he had written for Hana and Kenji remained hidden; Nick hadn't been up for him to give them to. He looked at Dai again and covered her with another blanket, to which she murmured, "Thank you." He had been making her speak English on the chance that release was imminent.

The pregnancy had gone well and the doctor at the hospital assured both of them that the baby was healthy. Hiroshi hoped so; this child and Dai were a second chance for him.

The problem of where they would go had been solved two weeks before. One of the higher-ups saw Hiroshi working in one of the greenhouses and liked his work.

"Very nice," he said as he looked at the healthy plants. "What did you do before the war?"

Hiroshi bowed and murmured his thanks before replying, "I owned a nursery much like this one."

To his surprise, the man handed him a card. "You do good work; if this mess is ever over, come see me. I'm in need of a good gardener."

Hiroshi bowed again and then spoke, "Please, may I bring my wife? "

The man hesitated. "Can she clean?"

"Yes, sir, but she is with child—"

"There's a small gatehouse in the back that you can use; we can talk about wages when this is over."

Hiroshi couldn't believe their luck; he couldn't wait to tell Dai. All they had to do was wait for the war to be over and make their way back to LA. When he told her, she was as excited as he was.

"Good things are happening already!" she said and hugged him.

One thing clouded the moment; he didn't know if he would go to prison or not. After thinking about it for several minutes, he decided not to dwell on it.

Ralph read about the Korematsu decision with interest and told Abby about it.

"What do you think?" she asked.

"I don't know, but let's keep our fingers crossed," he replied.

Paul finally had a few minutes alone with Patricia; Kenji was in the basement playing with the children so she could have a few minutes of peace.

"Patricia, have you given serious thought to college?"

"Sure, I think I would like to be a teacher," she replied.

"Why a teacher, as opposed to something like a doctor?" Paul asked.

"I don't know. . . . I don't think I have enough brains to be a doctor."

Paul looked at her and chose his next words carefully. "Patricia, teaching is a wonderful profession and I agree that you would be an excellent teacher, but I think you need to do something more challenging."

"Like what?" Patricia asked.

"Med school. . . . "

"Have you been talking to Kenji?"

"A little. . . . "

"Did he tell you to talk to me about this?"

"No, but—"

"Why do you think I'd be any good at being a doctor?"

"Patricia, I heard you studying with him. You did more than just ask the questions; you asked him to explain what the answers meant, and you understood!"

"Yes, but—"

"Now you listen here, young lady!" Paul said gruffly. "You and that husband of yours have two of the finest minds I've ever seen, and it would be a shame to waste yours, so I took the liberty of writing to my friend at UCLA, and he wants to meet you."

"What? UCLA? Paul, what for?"

"If he likes you—and he will—we're going to work out a curriculum for you so you can go to college and test out of some of the basic courses."

"But . . . but. . . . The money and the babies and—"

"The only thing we have to work out is the childcare, and you have plenty of willing babysitters."

"College? Me? Does Kenji know?"

"Do I know what?" Kenji asked from behind her.

Patricia was crying so hard that she couldn't talk.

"*Kirei*? What's wrong?" Kenji asked, handing Marie to Paul and taking her into his arms.

"I believe those are what are called tears of joy," Paul said and then explained his plan to Kenji.

Kenji was speechless; his *Kirei* was going to get what she had always wanted and they would do it together. "How can we thank you?" Kenji whispered, his own eyes wet with tears.

"You just did," Paul replied, his own throat tight. He left them alone, taking Marie and Niko with him.

"*Kirei*, you are going to be an excellent doctor! Did I not tell you? Paul sees what I did. We'll open our own practice and. . . . "

Patricia listened in a daze; she was really going to college! She wanted to run to her parents to tell them but she wouldn't—not until Kenji could tell them with her.

"We have to call Abby and everybody so they can come over. . . . Kenji?"

"Yes, *Kirei*?" Kenji replied, looking down at her. His eyes misted over again when he saw the one thing he had missed so much: the sparkle in her dark eyes.

Paul heard them talking and smiled; they were finally catching some much-needed breaks.

After much discussion with everyone, Nick reopened his law office. Surprisingly, it felt good to be back; he really had missed it. After much more discussion with Hana and the rest, he changed his specialty from corporate law to criminal law—prosecution, to be exact. He was hired by the city with the understanding that he kept his own office, and if any Klan cases came up, he would get to prosecute. The only thing he really wished was that he could prosecute Lawrence and Kenneth Goodman.

He kept up with what was going on with the case by talking to the prosecutor in South Carolina. He really had expected the man to be one of the "good ol' boys" and was pleasantly surprised when the man was otherwise.

"Mr. Alexander," William H. Mahoney said, "not all of us down here agree with what the Klan stands for and is teaching. I plan to do everything in my power to see that the Goodmans get what's coming to them."

"I'm glad to hear it," Nick replied. "Would you object if I called periodically for updates?"

"Not at all! As a matter of fact, I would like to bend your ear from time to time."

The last bit of news Nick received was promising: the Klan wasn't touching Lawrence and Kenneth Goodman with a ten-foot pole.

Nick looked around his office; the only thing missing were pictures of his family. He carried some in his wallet. Kenji had turned out to be quite the shutterbug. There were albums of pictures at Abby's house; each album was stuffed full of pictures of everyone and everything.

He packed his briefcase and got ready to leave; there was a gathering at Abby's, and he wondered what it was all about. When he asked Paul, he became secretive and told him that he would find out when he and everyone else got there.

When he pulled into the driveway, Mrs. Hallowell waved him down. "I'm sorry, Mr. Alexander, but Snowbird is in the tree again. Could you?"

"Of course," Nick replied and went to Snowbird's favorite tree and lifted the cat down. "There you are," he said, handing the cat to the old woman.

"Thank you so much!" she said, rubbing the cat behind its ears.

Nick smiled and walked away; he was very anxious to see Hana.

"Hana! Where are you?" he called.

"I'm here!" she called from his office.

"What are you doing?" he asked when he went into the office.

"Organizing your files," she replied as she stood up. "How can you know where everything is?"

"I just do—or, should I say, did," he replied, looking around the office. He had to admit that it did look better—more functional, although it always had been neat.

"Get dressed; there's a meeting over at Abby's tonight," he said as he kissed her and looked around the office again.

Patricia hugged Paul so many times that he laughed every time he saw her coming. It was good to see her and Kenji happy; they still had a long road ahead of them, but at the end of it was a bright and happy future.

Kenji bathed Niko and Marie while Patricia made sandwiches and punch, refusing help from Paul.

"You've done more than enough."

"Why don't you let me help you with the sandwiches?" Paul asked and was shooed away.

"She is right; you've done more than enough for us," Kenji said.

"I've done nothing but—"

"Helped give us and our children a future," Kenji said.

An hour later, everyone was there and wondering what was going on. Kenji wanted Patricia to share the news, but she didn't think she could pull it off without crying, and made Kenji do it.

"I know all of you are wondering why we asked you here," Kenji said. "You are already aware that I'll be going to medical school when the war ends or the internment camps are closed. Today we've received more good news. Paul. . . . " Kenji stopped talking; his throat had tightened. "Paul has offered to pay for Patricia's college education; she will be a physician and. . . . " Kenji was openly crying. "And . . . we don't know how it is that our lives have crossed paths with people such as yourselves. People who risked their lives and freedom for the two of us and our children. We are honored to know you, to call you friends and to call you family.

"My baby gonna be a doctor?" Hattie whispered.

"Yes, Hattie, your little girl is going to be a doctor," Paul said, touching her hand.

Hattie hugged Paul so tightly he had to pat her back so she would let him go. John stood silent with tears running down his face; his Patty Cakes was going to college. His Patty Cakes was going to be the first of his family to go to college.

Suddenly the room erupted into excited chatter, and hugs and kisses. Abby pulled Patricia aside and hugged her. "I told you change was coming! I am so happy for you!"

"If you hadn't taught me, this wouldn't be happening," Patricia said.

"I think it would have—maybe not like this, but it would have happened," Abby said, hugging her. "Patricia, I love all of you. Always remember that."

Patricia frowned and pulled away. "Abby?"

Ralph interrupted the question she was going to ask by asking one of his own. "When does school start?"

Patricia looked at Abby, who had already walked away, and turned her attention to Ralph. Abby sat in a corner watching quietly; she loved these people who had been a family to her in ways that she never could have imagined. She made a mental note to call Nick at his office sometime in the next few days.

By the end of January 1945, American troops crossed the Siegfried Line into Germany; the Soviet Union began the Vistula-Oder Offensive against the Nazis in Eastern Europe; Raoul Wallenberg, a Swedish architect and businessman who rescued thousands of Jews in Nazi-occupied Hungary, was arrested by a Soviet patrol in Hungary; the Battle of Holtzwihr occurred (Lieutenant Audie Murphy, who later became an actor, would earn the medal of honor); concentration camps Auschwitz and Birkenau were liberated; the *Wilhelm Gustloff* was sunk by three torpedoes from the Soviet submarine *S-13* in the Baltic Sea. There were ten thousand people aboard, most of whom were civilians; up to 9,400 people were thought to have died—the greatest loss of life in a single ship sinking in war history; 813 American POWs were freed from the Japanese-held camp at Cabanatuan City, Philippines, by 121 American soldiers and 800 Filipino guerilla fighters; and Private Eddie Slovik was executed for desertion. He was the first American soldier to be executed for this offense since the American Civil War, and also the last.

JANUARY 2, 1945

Ralph was back to religiously reading the paper, looking for any news that the war was over. As always, he skimmed through the paper and then started at the beginning and read it front to back. During the initial skimming, his eye caught the number 9066.

"What now?" he asked as he went to the article.

His heart began to pound after the first paragraph; then he began to shout for Abby. "Abby! Come quick!" he called several times.

Abby ran into the room, wondering what the excitement was all about. "Ralph, wh—"

"They're free! They're turning them loose!"

"What are you talking about?" Abby asked.

"We have to go to your house and tell them! Come on!" he said, jumping up and grabbing Abby's hand.

"*Ralph*!" Abby yelled. "What on earth are you talking about?"

Ralph shoved the paper at her. "Look!"

It took Abby a minute to see what Ralph was talking about. "Oh my God! Ralph! Oh my God!" Abby screamed and hugged him. "Call Nick and . . . and Ralph, they're free!"

Nick hadn't looked at the paper yet and was about to when Ralph called.

"Nick! They're free!"

"Ralph, calm down and tell me what you're talking about."

"Do you have the paper?" Ralph asked excitedly.

"Yes, and—"

"Look on page two!"

Nick looked and then blinked.

"Nick? Do you see it?"

"I see it! I'll meet you at Abby's!"

Nick grabbed his briefcase and ran out of the office.

"Mr. Alexander!" his secretary called after him.

"I'm out for the rest of the day! Take the day off!" he yelled back.

Nadine didn't have to be told twice; she packed up her belongings and was gone ten minutes later.

Nick drove home as fast as he could, parked the car in the garage, and ran into the house calling for Hana.

"Nick? What—"

Nick picked Hana up and kissed her. "Baby, it's over! Not the war, but you don't have to hide anymore!"

"I don't understand—"

"Get into the trunk and I'll tell you when we get to Abby's," Nick said as he laid her in the trunk.

Kenji was studying with Patricia, helping her get ready for her interview. He could tell she was nervous, but he had every confidence in her and told her so frequently. He wanted her to set up the interview, but she refused.

"I'm not starting school without you, so stop asking."

"At least do the interview," he insisted.

"No, not until you can start school."

She was so adamant about it that he stopped asking.

They heard the beeping of car horns and jumped. Paul stuck his head in the library and told them to stay put until he found out what was happening.

A few minutes later he stuck his head in the door; tears were running down his face as he told them to come out.

Kenji and Patricia went into the living room to see everyone, including her parents, waiting.

"Kenji," Ralph said, his voice choked with emotion, "they've rescinded the order—you don't have to hide anymore."

Patricia was the first of them to fully understand. "Kenji, you're free! You can go outside and play with the babies!"

Kenji stood still, not fully comprehending what he was being told.

"Kenji," Nick said, "it's over."

"I . . . we're free?" he asked softly. "We can go outdoors?"

When he fully understood, he grabbed Patricia and hugged her so tight that he almost hurt her. When he released her, his face was wet, and he headed toward the door.

"Wait!" Nick called. "We have to drive you out of the city and come back with you in the car or else people will know you've been here."

Kenji stopped at the door, his shoulders slumped.

Patricia went over to him. "One more night, sweetheart," she said, rubbing his back.

Kenji turned to look at her; she had never called him anything other than his name. He nodded and took her back into his arms; it was only one more night.

"We'll stay here tonight," Nick said. "We'll plan to leave here at six, drive out of the city, wait a couple hours, and drive back. Abby, do you think you ladies can whip up something for us to eat in the morning?"

Patricia held Kenji tight; they didn't have to worry about him being taken away anymore. In a few hours, he would be free.

Hiroshi heard the rumblings, but he didn't believe it until the head of the camp announced it.

"You are free to leave! You will be given twenty-five dollars and a bus ticket! The first bus to Los Angeles leaves in two hours!"

"Dai! Our child will not be born here! Did you hear? We're free!" Hiroshi said as he began to pack their belongings. He planned to be on the first bus out; he didn't want them to spend one more night in this Godforsaken place. He didn't know where they would stay when they got there, but then he wondered if the greenhouse was still there and if anyone was using it.

Dai started to get up to help him pack.

"No, stay put; I'll do it," Hiroshi said as he checked for their money and the card from the man who would become his employer. He crossed his fingers and hoped that no one remembered his status as a spy until they were long gone.

An hour later, he and Dai stood in line waiting for the buses to come; he held their bus tickets in his hand, and their money was tucked away safely in his pocket. He held his breath every time a guard walked by, and didn't breathe easy until they were sitting on the bus.

Hiroshi put his arm around Dai and kissed her temple. They had survived; the nightmare was behind them.

Three hours later, they were in LA and warm for the first time in weeks. Hiroshi helped Dai from the bus and took stock of his surroundings.

"We have to walk, but we'll go slowly," he told her as he picked up their bags. Two hours later, they were at the greenhouse. Hiroshi closed his eyes in shame as he remembered what had almost happened there; he almost couldn't bring himself to see if it was open, but there was Dai to think about.

"Wait here," he said as he walked around the back and found the key that he had kept hidden in a tree.

He walked around the front, unlocked the door, and went inside. It looked just as it had when he last saw it, down to the bloodstains on the floor. Hiroshi went back out to get an exhausted Dai and their belongings, brought her in, and locked the door behind them.

He took her to the room Kenji had used when he used to stay there and eased her onto the cot; she was asleep in minutes.

Hiroshi walked around using only a match as a light, wondering if any of the supplies were still there and edible. If not, then they would be hungry until the morning, when he would go find them something to eat.

It occurred to him that the greenhouse was as it was when he and Hana had first arrived and, like he and Dai, had spent their first night here. He heard Dai mutter and went to check on her; she had gotten too warm and threw his coat off her and had gone back to sleep. He found the supplies, but none of it was good. At first light, he would go find them something to eat.

Kenji paced like a caged animal; the morning seemed so far away. "Just a few more hours and I can sit on that park bench with *Kirei*," he murmured.

Patricia put Marie and Niko down early because they would be going with them in the morning. She also wanted to tend to Kenji; he made her nervous with the way he kept looking at the front door.

She walked up behind him and put her arms around him. "We made it; you promised that you would never leave again, and you kept your promise."

Kenji turned around in her arms, hugged her, and began to softly sing the song about the soldier who returned home to his beloved. They gave up their bed to her parents while Abby slept in the room with the babies; Ralph and Paul bunked downstairs, leaving Nick, Hana, Kenji, and Patricia alone to wait out the night.

"Baby, we made it," Nick whispered in Hana's ear. He still wouldn't be able to publicly acknowledge her as his wife, but she could answer the phone without fear, and she wouldn't have to hide.

"Tomorrow, when we return, I want to go to the park bench and sit with you," Kenji said when he finished the song.

Patricia could only nod her head; she was crying again.

Everyone was up by five; by five forty-five, Kenji was in the trunk of Abby's car with a wide-awake Niko, who was always looking for an adventure. Hana was in the trunk of Nick's car with a very fidgety Marie, who would soon be lulled back to sleep by the motion of the car. Patricia and her parents rode with Ralph, and Abby rode with Nick, which turned out to be a good thing; it gave her time to tell him about the letters.

She waited until they were well on their way before she spoke. "Nick, I want you to do something for me."

"All right."

"I have several letters—they all say the same thing, but one is at my attorney's office, one is in my jewelry box at the house where Kenji and Patricia are, and one is at the house where Ralph and I are staying."

"What's in the letter?" Nick asked.

"If anything happens to me—something really unexpected, like dying—I want you to make sure my wishes are carried out."

"Abby, you'll probably outlive all of us—"

"I don't think so, but at any rate, as you know, I have no family to speak of other than you and out little group. I'm leaving everything to Kenji and Patricia. The letter instructs my executor, which is you, by the way, to keep the house and any assets in my name so the government can't take them, and once this madness is over, everything is to be put in Patricia and Kenji's name. I believe Ralph wants the same thing done with his assets as well—all of it goes to Kenji and Patricia."

"Abby, are you ill?" Nick asked.

"No, but I want and need to know that I have everything in order, just in case. Will you do as I ask?"

"Of course, but Abby—"

"Thank you, Nick," Abby said, ending the conversation.

Patricia held Hattie's hand as the car headed away from the city. The last time she had come this way was when Kenji was at the camp and they came to see him. That day seemed like a whole lifetime ago, but today, when they drove back into the city, Kenji and Hana would be free. Actually, they were free yesterday, but Nick had a point—they couldn't be seen outside before today; people would notice and ask questions.

"It sure pretty out here," Hattie commented. This was Hattie's first time outside of LA, and she was as awed as Patricia had been on her first trip outside of the city.

Patricia looked out the window and saw several buses approaching. She knew what they were and she cringed; a bus like those had taken Kenji away from her. She wondered what the people on those buses were going to do since their homes, businesses, and money had been taken from them. She wondered about Kenji's father and what had happened to him.

Kenji taught Niko simple Japanese sentences to keep him occupied; he had grown tired of this particular adventure and wanted to see Patricia.

"Mama is sitting right where my feet are," Kenji said gently.

"Where is my sister?"

"She's in the car with Grandma Hana; we'll see them soon," Kenji replied. "Recite the alphabet to me."

Hana held Marie in her arms to cushion her from the rough ride. She needn't have worried; Marie seemed to like the sometimes-bumpy ride, laughing when Nick hit a particularly bumpy patch. She couldn't believe it; she would soon be free to walk around without fear of being discovered.

Like Patricia, she wondered about Hiroshi and then decided that whatever happened to him, it wasn't her concern.

Nick pulled over and stopped the car, with Ralph following close behind him. He jumped out, opened the trunk, and took Marie, who was none the worse for wear, from Hana, and then helped her out. Kenji was already out of the trunk of Abby's car and was hugging Patricia while Niko ran over to check on Marie, or "Rie Rie," as he called her.

Hearing Niko's voice, Marie giggled and reached for him. Niko smiled and took his sister's hand, laughing when she did. Hattie and John walked around the car, looking at the mountains that surrounded the camp. It was chilly, and both of them could only imagine how cold it was in the mountains.

Abby and Hattie got out the snacks and passed them out. Everyone nibbled, but all of them were anxious to get back. Instead of waiting two hours, they waited an hour and headed back, following one of the buses. Kenji, Patricia, Hana, and the children all rode back with Nick, while Abby, John, and Hattie rode back with Ralph.

Kenji held Niko on his lap with one arm around him and his free arm around Patricia, who was holding Marie. When they got to Abby's house, Paul was there, waiting to greet them.

Patricia handed Marie to him and got out, but Kenji stayed put. "Kenji?"

Kenji looked at her and swallowed hard before getting out, still holding Niko. He sat Niko down and walked down the driveway and to the street. A breeze ruffled his hair as he closed his eyes and let the sun warm his face; he turned to look at Patricia and held his arms out to her. Patricia took off running, not stopping until she was in Kenji's arms. People were watching, but they didn't care. There were a few rude comments, but they fell on deaf ears.

"*Kirei*, walk with me," Kenji said.

By now, anyone who was home was out on their porch watching Patricia and Kenji as they started their first walk together since Kenji's interment. They walked around the block and headed back to the house to find everyone waiting for them.

"How'd it feel?" Ralph asked.

"It was . . . amazing," Kenji replied. "I know we've just come back from a long drive, but Ralph, could you drive us to the grocer's?"

"Whatever for?" Ralph asked.

"There's something we promised each other we would do."

"All right then, come on. Abby, do you need anything, since we're headed to the store?" Ralph asked.

"How about a nice roast to celebrate?" she asked. "I think I have enough potatoes, but let me check."

She came back a few minutes later with a grocery list. "And don't forget the onions!" she called after Ralph.

Fifteen minutes later, Kenji and Patricia were sitting on the bench across from the grocer's. Several people looked at them in disgust, but most ignored them. They only left the bench when they saw Ralph coming out of the store with several sacks of groceries.

"I think she bought out the store!" Ralph said as he put the bags in the trunk.

The house was abuzz with activity when they got back. "What's going on?" Ralph asked.

"Nothing, we're just celebrating!" Abby said, hugging him. "Where's the roast? We need to get it in the oven before it gets too late."

Nick slipped away to make a quick phone call to South Carolina.

"Anything new?" he asked.

"No, but these sons of bitches are going to prison, so don't worry about that," William said.

"Good. Was there any mention made of the person who put Elam and Doc in touch with each other?"

"No, but I'm going to tell you something: this whole Klan thing is going to get a lost worse before it gets better."

"I'm afraid you're right," Nick agreed and then hung up. He would think about that another day. For now, his family was safe.

Hiroshi left Dai sleeping while he went to get them something to eat. Several places refused to serve him before he found one that would. He bought enough food to last them the day and headed back to the greenhouse to find Dai awake and nervously waiting for him.

"I have food for us," he said as he set the bags down.

"What is this place?" she asked.

"This used to be my nursery, before it was taken," Hiroshi replied.

"Is this where it happened?"

"Yes," Hiroshi replied. "I had nowhere else to take you. I'm sorry."

"Hiroshi, it's all right. You're no longer that man, and your son, when you find him, will see that."

Hiroshi nodded in gratitude and offered Dai a cup of hot tea and a roll. "Later we'll need to find a phone to call our employer. By tonight, I hope we'll be someplace more comfortable."

Nick wondered about Hiroshi and where he would have gone. He knew he had left the camp; his name was crossed off the list. When he saw Kenji alone, he asked him.

"The only place I can think of would be the greenhouse," Kenji said.

"Where is it?" Nick asked.

Kenji gave directions and asked to go with him.

"Don't you want to stay here and celebrate?" Nick asked.

"If he's there, then I must talk to him," Kenji replied.

Nick shrugged. "I'll meet you in ten minutes by the car."

Kenji pulled Patricia aside. "*Kirei*, Nick and I are going to the greenhouse to see if Father is there. It's the only place I know that he would go to."

"How do you know he's left the camp?" Patricia asked.

"Nick called. *Kirei*, don't be frightened; we'll be back soon," Kenji said as he kissed her.

Patricia gave him a weak smile. "Be careful."

Hiroshi sat on the floor while Dai took a nap. As she slept, he wondered how he was going to find Kenji and where he could use a phone to call his employer. He leaned his head back against the wall and closed his eyes; he was almost asleep when he heard someone at the front door. He looked over at Dai, who was still sound asleep, and crept out to the front of the building.

He could see the silhouettes of two men standing in front of the window. He looked around for something to use as a weapon and ironically picked up the same garden tool Patricia had used to defend herself against Vernon. He heard Dai stir and hurried back to shush her, but she had gone back to sleep.

"I don't think anyone's here," Nick said, looking around.

Kenji looked at the door and then down. "He's here; see how the soil is disturbed?" He knocked on the door. "Father! Are you here?"

Hiroshi froze. Kenjiro? Here? But he didn't answer.

"Father, it is me, Kenjiro, and Nick! If you're here, open the door!"

Dai was now awake. "Hiroshi, who's here?"

"My son."

"Are you not going to talk to him?" she asked.

Hiroshi got up slowly and walked to the door. "Kenjiro?"

"Yes, Father."

Hiroshi opened the door and stepped back to let Kenji and Nick in. Kenji and Hiroshi looked at each other, not speaking.

"When did you get here?" Nick asked.

"We arrived last evening," Hiroshi replied, not taking his eyes off Kenji.

"We? Who's with you?"

"My wife, Dai; she's with child."

That galvanized Kenji. "Is she all right?"

Hiroshi blinked at Kenji's concern. "She's tired, but otherwise all right."

"When is the baby due?" Kenji asked.

"Soon, we're not exactly sure. Kenjiro, why are you here?" Hiroshi asked.

"May I see her?" he asked, ignoring the question.

"She's in there, but—"

Kenji was already walking into the room.

Dai looked up at him and then at Nick, and tried to sit up.

"No, don't get up," Kenji said gently as he looked at Dai's face. "I'm going to look at your feet; do I have your permission?"

Dai looked at Hiroshi and then nodded her consent.

Kenji felt her ankles and then her feet before asking how she felt.

"I am tired, but well."

Kenji nodded and stood up. "You cannot stay here; she needs a good night's rest and a good meal."

"There's no other place for us to go," Hiroshi replied.

"You will come with us," Kenji said.

Hiroshi, Dai, and Nick all stared at him.

"Father, you and I have had our differences, and I'm sure we still do, but your wife and child have nothing to do with what has occurred between us. Now please, gather your things so we can leave."

"Kenjiro, we cannot—"

"You can and you will; now come. This will give us an opportunity to talk."

"Kenji, are you sure about this?" Nick asked as they waited outside for Dai and Hiroshi.

"I cannot leave them here," Kenji replied. "He and I will talk, and if we cannot reach an agreement, then he can go his way. But his wife is carrying my brother or sister; we must give them shelter, if only for tonight."

Patricia kept watching the front door and listening for the beep of a car horn. She kept herself busy with Niko and Marie, but prayed that Kenji would be back soon. She understood what was happening; she would be afraid every time he left and wouldn't breathe easy until he was back. After what felt like an eternity, she heard the car horn and ran out to the garage. She hugged and kissed Kenji, as if he had just come back from a long trip.

"I'm fine, *Kirei*," he assured her, touching her face. "I've brought others back with us."

"Who—"

Patricia gasped when she saw Hiroshi Takeda standing by the car with a very pregnant woman. Patricia and Hiroshi looked at each other without speaking.

Dai looked at Patricia, then at Kenji before looking at Hiroshi. She looked back at Patricia and smiled at her. "I am Dai Takeda; I am pleased to meet you."

"I . . . I'm Patricia Takeda. It's nice to meet you, too; would you like to come in?"

Dai smiled and bowed, and followed Patricia into the house.

All activity stopped when Patricia came into the house followed by Dai, then Kenji, Nick, and Hiroshi. Hana looked as if she had seen a ghost; Ralph cursed under his breath; John's hands were balled into tight fists, and he was glaring at Hiroshi.

"Kenjiro, maybe we should leave," Hiroshi said softly.

"No, please stay," Patricia said. "Everyone, this is Hiroshi and Dai Takeda; please make them as welcome as you made Kenji and me."

"He the one that—"

"Yes, Daddy, but it's past history." She took Dai by the hand and led her to the living room. "Would you like to use the bathroom or anything?"

"No, I am fine. Thank you for your kindness."

"You're welcome," Patricia said. "Why don't you sit down and rest? It's going to be a while until we eat."

Kenji watched Patricia with a pride that words couldn't begin to describe; her capacity to forgive amazed him, and he would be certain to mention that fact to his father when they talked.

Hiroshi watched Patricia as well and was struck by the way she stood up for him and Dai, even after the way he had treated her.

"Father, dinner is at least two hours away. I would like to take this time and talk with you."

Hiroshi nodded and followed Kenji down to the basement.

"Are you hungry or thirsty?" Kenji asked.

"No thank you, and thank you for your kindnesses to us," Hiroshi said. "Kenjiro, I was going to seek you out to ask your forgiveness. I have been wrong in so many things, including the treatment of you, your mother, and the one you chose to spend your life with. I endangered you and your mother by my association with Joben Saito and . . . I am truly sorry for the harm that almost came to your wife. On many occasions, I accused you of having no honor or courage and of disgracing this family. The disgrace is mine; I'm the one who lost all honor and courage. You were right to disown me as you did. I beg your forgiveness."

"Why now?" Kenji asked.

"When I was at that place, I had much time to think. At first, I was so angry and filled with hate toward you, your mother, your wife, and this country. I refused to see that I made many wrong choices out of arrogance, fear, and anger. Among the worst of those choices was the plan to hurt Patricia. If I could undo any of it, I would; I would have made an effort to understand why you fell in love with her. I would have listened to your mother; she tried to warn me about Joben Saito. She tried to tell me to leave you be, but I made her choose between us."

"Did you kill Joben Saito?"

"Yes, because I blamed him for what happened. I was angry with him because he betrayed me by leading the Americans to believe I was the leader of the spy ring. Kenji, I know you don't understand why I did the things I did—"

"I understand perfectly," Kenji said softly. "It was about control and prejudice; it was about you not wanting to learn how to live with others different from us. But you still haven't explained to me why, other than forgiveness, you seek me out."

"This child is my second chance to do things differently. Part of that is coming to you and asking forgiveness, but not just from you—from your mother and your wife. Kenjiro, I am sorry for my betrayal of you, your mother, and of everything I have taught you." Hiroshi bowed his head and waited for Kenji to speak.

"You are here because *Kirei*—Patricia—has forgiven you. I was filled with such anger toward you that I didn't care whether you lived or died, but my *Kirei*—she cared. When we went to register that first time, she included you and Mother in her prayers for safety. Even as you were planning her rape and death, she prayed for you. It is she that talked to me about forgiveness and how I couldn't teach our children the concept if I myself didn't practice it. I came to realize that she was and is right, but I will tell you this: our children will hear the story of how hate almost took their mother away. I also must tell you this: I love Patricia, and you must accept that as well as accept her as my wife, and treat her with the respect she is due."

Hiroshi looked at Kenji and nodded. "Please, may I speak with her?"

Kenji hesitated and then nodded; a few minutes later, he was back with Patricia.

"Patricia, I humbly ask your forgiveness. I made many wrong and foolish choices in my disillusionment. I offer you my apologies."

"I forgave you a long time ago," Patricia said softly. "But I think you need to say something to Hana."

"That was it?" Hiroshi asked.

"What is it you were expecting?" Kenji asked

"I don't know," Hiroshi said.

A few minutes later, Hana came downstairs with Nick. Kenji nodded and went upstairs; whatever his father said to his mother and Nick was between them.

He found Patricia in the library, staring out of the window. "It's over," he said, putting his arms around her.

"Does he know about Niko and Marie?"

"He does, and he'll show them respect even if he doesn't accept them," Kenji replied.

"When is the baby due?"

"Soon; they aren't exactly sure when. *Kirei*, I cannot even begin to tell you the pride I felt when you stood up for Dai and my father."

"Dinner!" Abby called through the door and walked away.

Kenji turned Patricia around in his arms and kissed her. "You are and always will be my *Kirei*."

They walked out in time to see Niko staring at Hiroshi.

"Who are you?" he asked suspiciously.

Everyone waited to hear what Hiroshi's response would be. Hiroshi knelt down and looked Niko in the eye. "You are as precocious as your father was as this age. I'm your grandfather. Your papa is my son."

"I have two grampas—Grampa Nick and Grampa John!" Niko said.

"Now you have a third," Hiroshi replied.

Niko looked at Hiroshi for just a few seconds longer before looking back at Kenji and Patricia. The expression on his face seemed to be asking, "Is this true?"

Kenji gave a slight nod of his head and Niko looked back at Hiroshi, still not sure about this stranger.

"*Youkoso*—welcome," Niko said with a bow and walked away to stand by his parents.

Kenji touched his head gently while Patricia held Niko's hand.

"He's a handsome boy," Hiroshi said softly. "Is he the only child?"

"We also have a daughter," Kenji said.

"May I see her?"

Hana stepped forward with Nick close by, holding a squirming Marie, but stopped out of touching distance. Hiroshi looked at Marie and smiled.

"She is very beautiful," he said, but made no move to touch her.

Ralph watched the scene with mixed emotions. On one hand, he was glad that Kenji and his father were making amends and wished that the reunion with Lawrence had ended this way, but he was still angry with Hiroshi. He didn't know all the details about what happened between Kenji, Patricia, and Kenji's parents, but he knew enough to know that Patricia had been in danger.

"It's ready!" Abby called out.

Dinner soon regained a festive atmosphere, although no one other then Kenji, Patricia, Hana, and Nick spoke to Hiroshi. Nick pulled Hiroshi aside and asked him his plans.

"I have employment if I'm able to use a phone to call him; he says he has a place for Dai and me to live," Hiroshi replied.

"I see," Nick said. "I'm sure you can use the phone here, and I owe you some money. That should help."

Hiroshi nodded. "I wouldn't accept if it were not for Dai and the child."

"Understood. I'll bring it by tomorrow; let me show you where the phone is."

They were intercepted by John. His anger was obvious, and both Nick and Hiroshi felt the heat of it. "You only live right now cos my girl tell me not to kill you."

"I am in her debt—"

"You do anything to hurt her or them babies, there ain't nothin' she can say to stop me from killin' you," John hissed and walked away.

"You got off easy; the last man that hurt Patty—the man you hired—is dead," Nick said. "And let me add a warning of my own: Everyone in this house loves Patricia, Kenji, and those babies. You make one false move toward any of them, you've signed your death warrant."

Nick left Hiroshi standing by the phone and went to find Hana. Hiroshi was very much aware of just how fortunate he had been and knew that Patricia's father and Nick would carry out their threats. He made the phone call and was told to come to the house in two days' time, which meant he needed to find someplace for him and Dai to stay for the next two days.

Abby was talking to Dai when he went back to the living room. Whatever they were talking about was pleasant, because of the smile on Dai's face. Dai looked up when she heard Hiroshi come into the room.

"It is settled; we'll report to the place of our employment in two days' time," Hiroshi said.

"You'll stay with me and Ralph until then," Abby said.

Hiroshi was speechless. These people were willing to help him, even though they knew what he had done. He also knew it was because of Dai and Patricia that he was being helped.

"You have our thanks," he said.

"The men are in the backyard if you want to go out there," Abby said.

Kenji watched his father come into the backyard. There was a part of him that was still very angry with him, and he supposed it would be for a while, but there was a part of him that was glad he had made the effort.

"Come join us, Father!" Kenji called out when Hiroshi hesitated.

The group of men went silent as Hiroshi made his way toward them. Ralph and John tensed; it wouldn't have taken much for them to beat Hiroshi to within an inch of his life.

When he reached the group, he looked at John. "When I came here, I thought that it was only Patricia, Kenji, and Hana I needed to make my apologies to. I was mistaken; I also owe an apology to you and your wife. Mr. Middleton, I offer to you my apologies for the wrongs I have committed against your daughter, Patricia. I have no excuse except for arrogance and ignorance for my actions; please accept my apologies."

Hiroshi finished the apology with a bow, to which John gave no response. Instead, he changed the subject and asked Ralph if there was time for a game of chess.

"You didn't expect him to just shake your hand, did you?" Nick asked.

"No, but—"

"Hiroshi, you're lucky you're still standing," Nick said and walked away.

"He's right," Kenji said. "You're very fortunate you're still standing."

"Your friend Abby has offered us a place to stay until we go to our new place of employment."

"This doesn't surprise me," Kenji replied. "Father, these people, all of them have become my family. They took me and Patricia in even though they could have gone to prison for it. These people have loved and supported us through everything, so you will pardon me if I tell you that I am glad we've talked, but at this point in time, I don't completely trust you."

The words hurt, but it was no less than he deserved. "I understand that I have lost your respect and trust; I only ask that you give me a chance to regain those things."

"We shall see," Kenji replied.

Patricia watched from the kitchen window and breathed a sigh of relief; her father had managed to curtail his anger, and Kenji and Hiroshi were talking. She could tell from Kenji's stance that he was tense and still angry, but at least they were talking.

In all honesty, she wondered how long the new-and-improved Hiroshi would last.

Chapter 21

By the end of March 1945, Ecuador, Syria, Paraguay, Turkey, Egypt, Finland, Peru, and Argentina declared war on Germany. Syria declared war on Germany and Japan; the Battle of Budapest was over. Tokyo and Yokohama were bombed by American Naval Vessels; Iwo Jima was invaded by the US Marines (the American flag was raised on Mount Suribachi on February 23); Germany was bombed by nine thousand bomb; there were US incendiary raids on Japan; the Philippines was liberated; a number of Japanese cities were firebombed by the US—Tokyo was one of the cities; Patton's troops took Mainz, Germany; and General Eisenhower broadcasted a demand for the surrender of Germany.

Mitch sat in his cell thinking about his family. He knew that Japan was being bombed and that Tokyo was one of the cities involved, but he didn't know about Nagasaki. His stomach was in knots because he still hadn't spoken to his family since before his arrest, even though he begged for a phone call.

"Please! I just need to know they're safe!"

The agent in charge looked at him in anger. "You betrayed this country; you don't get to ask for favors." And he walked away.

It was at that point that Mitch came to believe he would never see his wife and son again. The thought of suicide briefly crossed his mind and was gone. He would take whatever they dished out, and as soon as he was free—if it ever happened—he was going back to Japan, and he was never stepping another foot into the United States.

Hiroshi looked at his infant son and smiled. Dai had survived childbirth and was working in the main house of their employer while he tended the grounds. He found it hard to believe that they were free. He spoke to Kenji, Patricia, and the grandchildren at least once a week; the conversations were still tense, but becoming easier. He finally accepted the fact that he and Kenji would never again share a close father and son relationship and that Kenji would never entirely trust him or take him at his word, but there was no one to blame for this except himself.

He also realized that a few short years ago he would have scoffed at working for someone, but now he was thankful for the job. The money Nick had paid him went a long way toward making their lives more comfortable. He was able to buy all of them American clothes and furnishings for the house. It had been very dusty from months of being vacant, but between him and Dai, and with some help from Kenji and Patricia, the little house quickly became a home.

Every so often, the old anger would rise, especially when he heard about Japan being bombed, but Dai would bring him back to reality. "Did our home country not attack this country?" she asked.

"Yes," he replied and then realized it was this anger that had gotten him in trouble to begin with. At that point, he would begin to count his blessings and remember the promise he had made to himself and Dai. She was good for him; she in her own quiet way kept him grounded without making him feel emasculated.

The baby cried out for attention, drawing Hiroshi from his thoughts.

"What is it?" he cooed at the baby, as he checked his diaper. This was something he had never done with Hiro or Kenji, deeming it woman's work. He changed the diaper, picked the baby up, and went outside to enjoy the mild air until dinner was ready.

"I am a very lucky man," he said as he rocked the baby.

Patricia was on pins and needles. Today she was going for her interview with Dr. Brown at UCLA. Kenji was staying behind, but Paul was going with her.

"*Kirei,* you will be fine," Kenji assured her. He had already met with Dr. Brown, but said nothing about his relationship to Patricia, not wanting to diminish her chances in any way. He kissed her at the door and wished her luck after she kissed both Niko and Marie.

"Good luck, Mama!" Niko called after her.

Patricia didn't think she had ever been so nervous. Her hands were cold and clammy, and her heart pounded so hard she thought she could hear the beats.

"Kenji is right," Paul assured her. "You're going to be fine."

Patricia nodded, not trusting herself to speak.

By nine forty-five, Paul and Patricia were sitting in the reception area. She didn't miss the curious and sometimes hostile stares she got as she and Paul walked down the hall. She didn't allow herself to be intimidated, often meeting the stares with one of her own. The people had two choices: they could speak to her or ignore her. When spoken to, she returned the greeting; the others, she ignored.

"Dr. Mynt, Dr. Brown would like to speak to you privately," the receptionist said right at the stroke of ten o'clock.

Paul gave Patricia a reassuring smile before standing and going into the office. Patricia looked around the reception area and felt eyes on her. It was the receptionist giving her a curious look and looking like she wanted to ask Patricia a question. When she spoke, it wasn't a question, but a statement. "You must be something special."

"No, I'm not," Patricia replied.

"Yes, well you're here, aren't you?"

"Yes, but—"

"Patricia, come on in," Paul said from the door of Dr. Brown's office.

Patricia looked at the receptionist before she stood up, but the woman had already gone back to her work.

Dr. Brown was a bear of a man who dwarfed Paul, but his face was pleasant, his eyes friendly. “Please sit down, Miss Middleton,” Dr. Brown said.

Patricia frowned. *Middleton?* she thought and corrected what she perceived to be a mistake. “Excuse me, but my last name is Takeda,” she said politely. “Middleton is my maiden name.”

Out of the corner of her eye, she saw Paul smiling.

“I see,” Dr. Brown said. “I assumed you would want to go by your American name to make things easier for you.”

Patricia looked at Paul and then at Dr. Brown. “My name is Patricia Ann Takeda,” she said firmly.

“All right then; just how is it you have a Japanese last name?” he asked.

“I wasn’t aware that my last name mattered,” Patricia replied, not answering the question that had an obvious answer.

“It doesn’t; it’s just that things are going to be difficult enough for you, and people are going to ask.”

“Let me tell you something,” Patricia said heatedly. “I’m not interested in making things easier! You have no idea of what my husband and I have been through since we met, so if you think that people glaring at me and calling me names is going to bother me, forget it! And one more thing: I’m proud of my last name, and if using it means that I can’t come to school here, then I guess I won’t be coming here for college.”

Dr. Brown blinked rapidly in surprise. “You wouldn’t come here if we told you that you couldn’t use your Japanese last name?”

“No, I wouldn’t,” Patricia replied without hesitation. “So tell me now: is my using my married name going to be a problem?”

“I guess not,” Dr. Brown replied, taken aback by Patricia’s bluntness.

The rest of the interview went smoothly; Patricia answered the questions clearly and succinctly, not offering any more information than what was asked.

“All right, Mrs. Takeda. Have a seat in the reception area while I speak with Dr. Mynt.”

Patricia stood and thanked Dr. Brown for his time. When she got back out to the reception area, the receptionist looked up.

"How'd it go?" she asked.

"I don't know," Patricia said honestly.

"I bet you did just fine; my name is Cynthia."

"I'm Patricia Takeda; it's nice to meet you."

"Takeda?" Cynthia asked.

"Yes, why?"

"There was a Takeda in here a couple of weeks ago to interview for a spot in the med program; he was a real looker for a—"

"My husband," Patricia said tersely.

"What? Oh my God, I'm sorry!"

"It's fine," Patricia said. Patricia didn't believe the woman; she knew exactly who she was when she brought it up, probably even before that.

"Really, I'm sorry," Cynthia said. "Sometimes my mouth just runs and I don't think about what I'm saying."

Patricia didn't reply. The woman was a snake.

Paul came out a few minutes later with a big smile on his face. "Well, Patricia Ann Takeda, you have a few tests to pass, and when you pass those, we'll start figuring out your schedule for classes."

"I did it?" Patricia asked.

"You sure did!" Paul replied, laughing.

Completely forgetting where she was, Patricia jumped up and hugged Paul, earning a disapproving glare from Cynthia.

Kenji was grateful that both children were active; it took his mind off Patricia and her interview. He had every confidence in her; it was Dr. Brown he was concerned about. Kenji didn't like the way in which the man fished for information instead of being straightforward.

He also didn't know which last name Patricia was going to use; he told her that if she had to use her maiden name to get in, she should do it.

"Would you deny knowing me to get into med school?" she had asked.

"Of course not!"

"The same goes for me," she replied. "If I use my maiden name, in effect I'm denying you, and I won't do it."

"*Kirei,* just think about it," he urged. After that, the discussion didn't come up again.

"Drs. Kenjiro and Patricia Takeda," he murmured, liking the sound of it. He would be finished a few years before Patricia, but then he would be able to support them while she attended school.

"Papa, when is Mama coming back?" Niko asked.

"Soon; I miss her, too," Kenji said, hugging Niko. "Go choose a book so we can read to your sister."

Niko ran into the library and chose a book he thought Marie would like while Kenji checked her diaper. Kenji changed her diaper and then listened to her heart, smiling at the strong and regular beat. "All right, pretty one; let us see what book your brother has chosen for us."

Marie smiled at Kenji and touched his face, making him smile in return. "Papa loves you." The words "I love you" were rarely spoken to him by his father; it was assumed that he was loved, but with his own children, Kenji wanted and needed for them to hear him say it.

He had rarely heard his father tell his mother that he loved her, and now he knew why. They hadn't really loved each other, but those words had become three of his favorite words of the English language, and he used them often.

They were partly through the third story when Kenji heard Nick's car pull into the garage. He put Marie on the floor and told Niko to play with her.

"Kenji!" Patricia called as soon as she was in the kitchen.

"What happened?" Kenji asked anxiously.

"I did it! All I have to do is pass the tests and I'm in!"

Kenji hugged Patricia. "I had no doubts!" he said, kissing her.

"You should have heard her," Paul said. "She held her own."

"I can believe that," Kenji said. "*Kirei*, which last name did you use?"

"Takeda; what else would I have used?" she asked.

"There was no difficulty?"

"I simply told him that my last name was Takeda and if I couldn't use it, then I wouldn't go to school there," Patricia said stubbornly. She knew what he was thinking: he was thinking that she should have used her maiden name as a means to an end.

"When he called me Miss Middleton, I had to make a choice and I chose you. My last name is Takeda, and when I'm finished it will be Dr. Takeda, so no more talk about which name I should have used."

Kenji hugged her again and kissed her. "Now we have to get you ready for your tests. Do you know which ones?"

"Math, science, and English," Patricia replied, "but no studying today. Today I want to enjoy being a student and enjoy being with my husband and children."

"I agree, and maybe we could bake cookies," Kenji replied, remembering that he and Niko had eaten the last one.

"How about we invite everyone over for dinner?" Paul asked. "And I want to help."

While Paul went to the store, Kenji called everyone. When he was finished, he stopped Patricia from what she was doing and kissed her. "I am proud of you," he said. "All of us are."

"We really made it, didn't we?" she asked softly.

"Yes, *Kirei*, we made it. We have a long ways to go, but I believe the worst is over."

Patricia agreed. They still got funny looks and heard rude comments, but they were free to be together, and for her, that was all that mattered. Her next wish was for Hana and Nick to be legally married, but she didn't look for it to happen any time soon. Nick and Hana were getting around being seen together by Hana acting as his housekeeper and cook. Nick hated it, but as Abby reminded him, it was better than her having to hide.

Patricia worried about Abby, although she couldn't say why. She looked the same and sounded the same, but something was different. Several times, Patricia caught Abby looking at them as if she would never see them again, and it scared her. She hadn't said anything to Kenji, mostly because he was so observant and he didn't seem to notice anything different. Maybe Abby had always been that way and she was just noticing because things had calmed down considerably since Lawrence Goodman and his son were gone, but she didn't think so.

Sally had stopped calling her mother; she was tired of hearing about the trial and about how she wasn't a good wife because she wasn't at Lawrence's side. And she was tired of hearing that she wasn't a good mother because she refused to come home for Kenny's funeral.

"Mama, he was going to kill me!"

"No he wasn't; he was a good boy," her mother insisted.

"No, Mama, he wasn't. He and Lawrence were both killers, and I won't pretend otherwise."

The final straw was when her mother called her a traitor to the Klan and the white race.

"I'm sorry, Mama," Sally said and hung up.

That conversation had been a month ago, and she hadn't spoken to anyone from home since. She only knew what was happening with the trial because of Ralph and Abby, who got their information from Nick.

Now that she was away from home and Lawrence, she was beginning to rethink everything she had been taught about the separation of the races. She had managed to get the younger two children to stop using racial slurs, although they slipped on occasion.

They still had plenty of money, and it helped that the house was paid for. The kids were finally enrolled in school and were making friends, but Sally was lonely. Abby and Ralph showed up for lunch once a week, and that was the extent of her social life. She admitted that she did miss Lawrence and she had friends because of his contacts, but even after all this time, she still didn't know anyone and wasn't sure about how to go about meeting people.

When Kenji called Ralph and Abby about dinner, Ralph offered to make a dessert and then asked a question.

He told Kenji about Sally and the children, and wanted to know how he and Patricia would feel if they came to dinner with them. Kenji was hesitant and wanted to talk to Patricia first.

"I understand," Ralph replied.

"Do you trust her not to bring these Klan people here?" Kenji asked, knowing that Patricia would ask the same question.

"I won't lie to you," Ralph said. "I don't totally trust her, so why don't we do this? We'll have dinner here; that way, she won't know where you are."

"Can you wait while I speak to Patricia?"

Kenji was back a few minutes later. "Patricia wants to have dinner here; she is tired of hiding, but she says that you must warn Sally before you bring her and the children here."

"Kenji, are you sure you want to do this?" Ralph asked. "I won't be offended in any way if you don't."

"*Kirei* is right; the time to stop hiding has come. Invite her and her children."

Sally was finishing the laundry when Ralph and Abby showed up at her door unexpectedly.

"Is something wrong?" she asked.

"No," Abby said. "We just want to talk to you for a few minutes; can we come in?"

Sally blushed at her bad manners and invited them in, offering them something to drink after they were sitting. While Sally got the drinks, Ralph told Abby that he wanted her to tell Sally about the others.

"You're better at explaining things like that," he whispered.

Sally came back with a tray of iced tea and cookies. "I just made these this morning," she said as she set the tray down.

"They look delicious," Abby said, taking one.

"So, what brings you by?" Sally asked, glad for the company.

"Well, we wanted to invite you and the children to a celebration tonight," Abby said, setting her glass of tea down.

"A party? We would like that! What are we celebrating?"

Abby told Sally about their family, leaving out that Kenji had been hiding at her house and Hana at Nick's. She mentioned that Hana and Nick considered themselves married even though it wasn't recognized as a legal marriage. She ended by telling her about Kenji, Patricia, the babies, and Hattie and John.

Sally was quiet for several minutes before she spoke. "Why haven't you told me before?"

"Because I wouldn't let her," Ralph said. "When I brought Lawrence and the rest of you here, I brought danger to these people, whom I consider to be my family. I don't trust you, and I'm going to be honest—I wish I hadn't asked you to come."

"So why did you?"

"I really don't know," he replied.

"If you don't trust me, why are you telling me about these people?"

"Because if anything happens to any of them, I'll know you had something to do with it," Ralph replied.

"I would never do anything to hurt anyone!" Sally protested.

"So you say," Ralph replied. "But here's the other reason you're invited: Kenji and Patty think it's time for people to come out of hiding and show these Klan bastards that we're not afraid of them."

Abby watched the conversation between Ralph and Sally with interest.

"Are all of these people going to be there?" Sally asked.

"Yes, as we said, they're family," Abby replied.

Sally debated long and hard before answering. "I thank you for the invitation, but I'm not quite ready for that just yet. It doesn't mean that I won't ever be, but . . . but please tell Patricia and Kenji that I said congratulations."

"Thank you for being honest with us," Abby said. "And we'd better get going; we have to get a few things at the store."

Abby and Ralph left a few minutes later to go to the store. After they were gone, Sally wondered if she had made the right decision by declining the dinner invitation. What good did it do to teach the children not to call names and to tell them to respect others if she kept them separated from those different from themselves? She told Abby she wasn't ready to mingle with other races, but would she ever be ready? Maybe it was one of those things that had to be done and they would learn as they went.

She would give them an hour to get home, and then she would call and ask if she could change her mind.

Nick and Hana were thrilled for Patricia.

"So many good things are happening!" Hana said as she fixed Nick's lunch and sat it in front of him.

"It's about damned time!" Nick exclaimed as he stood up. "Baby, you sit; I'll fix my plate."

Even after all their time together, Nick wanted to be sure that Hana knew she wasn't his servant and that he liked caring for her in the same way she cared for him.

"I'm not hungry," Hana said. "I'm too excited for Kenji and Patricia to eat. Both of them going to be doctors! I'm so proud!"

"I can tell, and so am I," Nick said. "But you still need to eat something; dinner is a long ways off."

Hana sat down and nibbled at the sandwich she had made for Nick; she really was excited for their children, and then she wondered if they had invited Hiroshi. Like everyone else, she remained skeptical about Hiroshi's apparent turnaround. Even Niko was very wary of Hiroshi, and he was normally a very friendly child; he was to Dai and the baby, but Hiroshi. . . .

"What are we taking to dinner?" Nick asked as he ate the rest of the sandwich.

"I would like to make a Japanese dish; are you able to take me to the oriental market?"

Nick glanced at the clock. "Sure, if we leave now."

Hana went to grab her purse and met Nick by the car; the novelty of not having to hide hadn't worn off yet, and she doubted that it would.

Hiroshi had started work early that morning so he would be done in time to get them to Kenji and Patricia's house for the celebration. He had been both pleased and surprised by the invitation and suspected that Patricia had been behind it. She would actually go out of her way to make him, Dai, and the baby welcome, whereas Kenji's greeting to Dai and the baby would be warm, but the greeting to him would be civil and cool.

"I was so stupid," Hiroshi said as he trimmed the plants growing around the house. He was also aware that he was being watched, not only by Kenji but by every male in the family, especially Patricia's father. He was the only one who didn't acknowledge him when spoken to, and tonight would be no different.

His employer turned out to be a good friend as well as employer, making a car available for his and Dai's use whenever they needed it. All in all it was a much better life than he had imagined; he had a wife, a healthy child, and a home, but something was missing . . . his own business. He liked Mr. Somers and his family and he truly did appreciate the job, but he wanted more.

He knew that Mr. Somers was always looking for another business to dabble in and wondered if he would be interested in the nursery business. The old nursery just sat there, and as far as he knew, no one had bought it and it was still empty. On his next day off, he would work up a business proposal and present it; he wouldn't really own the business, but the illusion would be there. If he could make this happen, he would be content with his life and completely let go of the old hatreds, which were almost gone.

Sally answered the phone on the first ring. “Hello?”

“Sally? This is Doc.”

Her mouth went dry; she hadn’t spoken to Doc since before they left South Carolina. Her first thought was that something had happened to Lawrence. “Is something wrong?” she asked.

“No, just calling on Lawrence’s behalf,” Doc replied. “Are you and the young ones all right?”

“We’re fine.” She didn’t believe him; he wanted something.

“Good, glad to hear it. Lawrence says you have a big house.”

Sally didn’t respond.

“I have a friend heading out your way and was hoping you could put him up for awhile.”

No response.

“He won’t be there for long and—”

“I’m sorry, but no,” Sally said, hardly believing she had said it.

“Lawrence—”

“I don’t care what Lawrence said; I don’t want your friend here.”

There was a tense silence, as each of them thought about what they were going to say next.

“You’re not going to help further our cause?” Doc asked.

“Further your cause?” Sally asked. “It was your cause that turned my son into a killer! It was your cause that has my husband in jail and standing trial for murder! And where are you? I don’t hear anything about your Klan helping him . . . if anything, you handed Lawrence and Kenny over to the authorities on a silver platter, and you’re asking me for help? Go to hell, Doc, and take your precious Klan with you!”

Sally slammed the phone down; she was literally shaking with anger. That phone call was the first time she had admitted out loud that she blamed the Klan for what happened to Lawrence and Kenny. It was also then that she realized she needed and had to go to this party and that Abby was right—racism was racism. She also knew that changing her thinking was going to take conscious thought and effort. She waited until her breathing calmed before she picked up the phone and called Abby.

The phone rang several times, and just as she was about to hang up, Ralph answered the phone. She noticed his hesitation when she told him she had changed her mind about the party.

"Why'd you change your mind?" he asked suspiciously.

"Abby was right about a lot of things," Sally replied. "Including racism. The Klan just called and asked me to house one of them."

"What'd you say?"

"I told him no and that I blamed them for Kenny's death and Lawrence's being in jail."

Ralph was silent for a few seconds. "Sally, Lawrence was a grown man and responsible for his own actions. He didn't do anything he didn't want to do, but Kenny was a different story," he said. "Kenny had problems to begin with, and the Klan—and that includes Lawrence—exploited that. What I'm saying is that I agree with you about Kenny, but not Lawrence."

Sally listened without interrupting, realizing that Ralph was right; Lawrence had already changed by the time he got back from the war. The change had actually started before the war, but Kenny. . . . There had always been something different about him, a cruel streak that got worse as he spent more and more time with Doc and then Lawrence.

"You need to ask yourself this: why do you really want to come? Is it to prove to yourself that you're no racist?"

Sally felt his anger and knew where it was coming from; he was still angry that he allowed them to come, and angry that he had been used by Lawrence.

"Ralph, I understand what you're saying," she said, "and I will even concede that part of my reasoning is to prove to myself that I'm not as bad as Lawrence and Kenny were, but let's face it: you're mad at me for what Lawrence did."

"No—"

"Yes, you are," she interrupted. "Just so you know, I tried to talk him out of starting this new group, and he wouldn't listen. I'm sorry that things between you were so bad, and I'm sorry that he used you to get here, but that isn't my fault, and it isn't Dianne's and Eli's fault either."

Ralph was silent. She was right; he was angry with her.

"One more thing," Sally said. "You couldn't have known what Lawrence was up to; he took advantage of your guilt, and you did what I would have done. . . . You offered him a home for his family."

"Sally, look, you're right and I'm sorry," Ralph said. "You have no idea how much these people mean to me; they became my family when I had none, but listen, if you want to come, we'll come and get you."

"I would like that, and I'll make sure the kids are ready and understand what's happening."

Ralph picked Sally and the children up at five o'clock; the children looked at Ralph as if they wanted to say something, but weren't sure if they should.

"You got a question?" Ralph asked.

Dianne and Eli looked at each other and then at Ralph, but it was Dianne who spoke. "Is it true that you have a family that isn't white?"

"Yes, it's true," Ralph confirmed. "What else?"

"Some of them are Ja—Japanese?"

"That's also true, and yes, they speak English."

"Mama says that there are n—black people, too, and that one of them is married to a Japanese."

"That's also true, and I expect all of you to treat them with respect because if you can't, then you should stay home," Ralph said firmly.

"We can do that," Dianne said.

The ride to the house was quiet, with Dianne and Eli holding hands.

"Relax!" Ralph snipped. "You aren't going to be eaten."

Sally looked over at Ralph and murmured, "They're just nervous."

What Ralph wasn't saying was that he was just as nervous as they were; this would be the first time that he allowed people who had been a part of the enemy camp this close to his family.

"Sorry, I'm a little nervous, too," he finally admitted.

He pulled into the garage and beeped his horn to announce their arrival. Sally got out and looked around, not sure what to expect. Abby came out and welcomed them with a hug.

"Come on in! And you brought sugar cookies? Kenji will be your friend for life," she said as she led Sally and the children into the house.

Like before, when Hiroshi and Dai first came, the kitchen went silent.

"Everyone, this is Sally Goodman, Ralph's daughter-in-law, and her children, Dianne and Eli," Abby announced and then introduced everyone in the kitchen.

"Hello and welcome!" Patricia said.

"Hello, and thank you for having us," Sally replied as she nudged Dianne.

"Th—thank you," Dianne said shyly, but as soon as she heard Marie's giggle, she forgot her shyness and smiled.

"She loves babies," Sally said by way of explanation.

Eli still hadn't spoken; it wasn't that he wasn't used to seeing black people, it was that he had never seen blacks and whites in the same house, having a good time. His eyes widened when he saw Kenji walk into the kitchen carrying Marie, with Niko following behind.

His and Dianne's mouths dropped open when Kenji walked up to Patricia, said something that made her smile, and kissed her.

"Sally and children, that's Kenji, and the little one's name is Marie—and the young man behind him is Niko."

Kenji smiled at them and said hello, while Niko just looked at them.

"Niko, please greet our guests," Kenji said gently.

Niko looked up at Kenji and then back at what he considered to be intruders. He gave a slight bow and mumbled a welcome.

The last introductions were made when Hiroshi and Dai arrived with the baby. Both Dianne and Eli remained glued to Sally's side as the dinner preparations continued.

They were shocked again when Nick kissed Hana and then Patricia on the cheek; this never would have happened at home, at least not openly.

Sally got up her nerve and walked over to where Patricia was standing washing dishes.

"I know it's not much, but I brought cookies; I made them just this morning."

Patricia smiled her thanks and began chatting with Sally. By the time the dishes were done, Sally was more relaxed and drying the dishes as Patricia washed them.

Dianne and Eli stood in a corner watching the activity, not quite sure what to make of it.

"Hey, Eli!" Ralph called. "Why don't you help me and John pull the table out?" Happy for something to do, Eli ran off to help, leaving Dianne alone.

"Dianne, would you like to help in the kitchen?" Patricia asked.

By the time dinner was served, the awkwardness had decreased markedly. Dianne was holding the babies, even offering to help change dirty diapers.

Everyone, though, was watching not only the Goodmans, but Hiroshi as well. During a lull in the activity, Kenji pulled Hiroshi aside. "How are things with you?" he asked.

"We are well," Hiroshi replied. "I'm glad for this private moment."

Kenji waited for him to continue.

"I just wanted to tell you that I'm proud of you and what you have accomplished under very difficult conditions."

"Thank you, Father."

"And that pride extends to Patricia and my grandchildren."

Kenji's face remained impassive as he thanked his father. "I thank you, but you must understand that while I have forgiven you, our relationship can never be as it was."

"I know, and I understand," Hiroshi said. "I know I have never told you this, but Kenjiro, you are a good son, a good father, and a good husband."

Kenji didn't reply, but gave his father a bow of respect, which was returned.

As he walked away, Kenji had to wonder if the change he was seeing was in fact real. For his father to say he was proud of Patricia and the children was a big step.

After checking on Niko and Marie, he went back to the kitchen and stopped short. Hiroshi was talking to Patricia, holding both of her hands in his. He watched as Patricia pulled away and gave Hiroshi a hug, which was returned. Even so, he wasn't fully convinced of Hiroshi's apparent change of attitude toward Patricia, the children, or things in general.

By the end of the evening, the children were playing, together with Dianne, the self-proclaimed babysitter. The adults were in the living room, chatting but keeping a close eye on the children. Sally kept looking at Patricia and wanted to talk to her alone. The opportunity didn't present itself until it was almost time to go.

"Patricia, thank you again for allowing us to come; it couldn't have been easy knowing what you do about us."

"You're welcome, and I'm glad you came," Patricia replied with a smile.

"Can I ask you a personal question?" Sally asked.

Patricia hesitated and then gave her the go-ahead.

"H—how do you handle the racism? And what about your children?"

"I don't really know how to answer that except to say that you know black people have always been discriminated against. Will that change? I hope so, but as far as me and Kenji are concerned, the only thing that matters is what we think and feel for each other."

"I understand that, but you're adults; what about your children? What's going to happen when they're called names and teased because they're mixed?"

"First of all, even if they were all black or all Japanese, they would still be teased just because they aren't white. Secondly, they're being raised with a sense of self-worth and to respect everyone no matter their color, nationality, or beliefs, and yes, that respect extends to your Klan. Why? Because they're still human beings, and hate is such a wasted emotion. If you don't believe me, talk to Kenji's father or my father, for that matter; they can tell you the price they paid because of hate."

Sally felt her respect for Patricia grow and realized she could learn a lot from her. "Thank you for answering my questions, and I hope I didn't offend you in any way."

"No, you didn't. The only way to learn is to ask, and if I feel it's too personal, I'll say so."

"You ready?" Ralph called out.

"Thank you again," Sally said, hugging Patricia.

Lawrence looked out of his jail cell; he had lost weight and wasn't sleeping at night. He still mourned for Kenny and was angry that he hadn't even been allowed to attend his services so he could say goodbye. The authorities were afraid that the Klan would try to help him escape. His only consolation was that Kenny had died fighting the good fight.

He was angry about something else. The Klan, the ones Kenny had died for, hadn't come to see him and weren't even helping with his defense expenses, choosing to distance itself from him. He still believed in what the Klan believed, but if he escaped a prison sentence, he wouldn't rejoin them. They couldn't be trusted. He would strike out on his own and start a new group whose members would be handpicked by him, and no one who was caught would ever be left behind. There were several people he had to deal with if he ever got out: one was Doc, for handing over the evidence; and then there was that agent, Charles, who had so glibly told him about Kenny's death; and then the one who wasn't an agent . . . Nick. Added to that list was the prosecutor and anyone else that was part of this, including the judge, if he was found guilty.

He spent his days in the courtroom memorizing names and faces and the roles they played, but the first one to go was going to be Doc. At some point during the trial, he realized that if he was going to survive, he needed to take care of himself, and that meant he had to start eating, sleeping, and getting back into shape. He also decided that if he was sent to prison, he might be able to start his group there; maybe prison wouldn't be such a bad thing after all.

By the end of May 1945, the Battle of Okinawa began; several concentration camps, including Buchenwald, were liberated; Spain broke off diplomatic relations with Japan; Ernie Pyle, a war correspondent, was killed by a sniper on le Shima, a small island off Okinawa; Hitler celebrated his fifty-sixth birthday; Hermann Goering sent a radiogram to Hitler's bunker asking to be declared Hitler's successor; and Albert Speer made a last visit to Hitler to inform him that he ignored the Nero Decree for scorched earth (the Nero Decree was issued on March 19, 1945, ordering the destruction of the German infrastructure). Himmler also made a secret surrender offer to the Allies, which was rejected; when Hitler heard about the offer, Himmler was shot.

Benito Mussolini and his mistress, Clara Petacci, were caught in northern Italy and shot and hung; Hitler married Eva Braun on April 29, and they committed suicide on April 30. Joseph Goebbels was appointed Reich Chancellor, and Karl Donitz was appointed Reich President.

Hans Krebs was sent to negotiate the surrender of Berlin, but was not given permission to grant an unconditional surrender, so the negotiations ended without an agreement. On May 1, 1945, Goebbels and his wife killed their six children and then themselves; the war in Italy was over; the Battle of Berlin ended, and German troops throughout Europe were surrendering; the Prague uprising began; German soldiers in Amsterdam opened fire on a crowd celebrating liberation; Kamikazes had success off Okinawa; Nagoya, Japan, was heavily bombed; the Georgian Uprising on Texel ended, concluding the hostilities in Europe; the head of the SS, Heinrich Himmler, committed suicide.

May 6, 1945—the last day of fighting for American troops in Europe.

May 7, 1945—Germany surrendered unconditionally to the Allies in Rheims, France. The surrender was signed by Alfred Jodl on the behalf of Germany.

May 8, 1945—The ceasefire took effect one minute past midnight.

Nick picked up the phone as soon as he heard it ring; he already knew who it was.

William.

"I'm sorry, Nick, but if he gets any prison time, it won't reflect the severity of the crimes he committed."

"How much time are you talking about?" Nick asked.

"Four years . . . maybe."

"Four years for more than eight murders? Are you serious?"

"I know, but it's better than nothing," William replied.

"Why so little time?"

"Nick, you have to understand the mentality of the people here. Many of them think Lawrence Goodman is a martyr in the cause of the white folk. The only reason he's getting any time at all is because of those pictures."

William was right and Nick knew it, but it stuck in his crawl. If Lawrence had been a black man, his punishment would have been much more severe. As a matter of fact, it wouldn't have even gone to trial; he would have been hanged before that happened.

"This is one fucked-up world," Nick told William.

"Yes, my friend, it is," William conceded.

"Keep me posted, will you?" Nick asked. "I want to know what happens to the son of a bitch."

Nick hung up with a sense of disquiet; deep down, he knew he hadn't seen the last of Lawrence Goodman.

Patricia was ready for her tests—or as ready as she was ever going to be. The afternoon before the test, Hana and Nick took Niko and Marie to their house. Paul went over to Ralph's and Abby's to spend the night there, with plans to be back to begin the test at ten the next morning.

"Make sure you get a good night's sleep and try not to worry; you're going to be just fine," he said.

By one o'clock, the house was empty, and neither Kenji nor Patricia knew what to do at first. They hadn't been alone in so long that it felt strange.

"Let's walk," Kenji said, holding out his hand.

He had started walking again soon after the interment camps closed. He never tired of feeling the sun and breeze on his face as he walked, and he took Patricia with him as much as he could. They were now known in the neighborhood and rarely bothered anymore. There were a few neighbors who spoke to them and even fewer who carried on conversations with them, but that bothered neither of them just as long as they were left alone.

Patricia put on her shoes and met him by the door; Kenji took her hand and led her outside. It was a beautiful day, the sky a clear blue and a soft breeze blowing. Kenji put his arm around Patricia's waist and led her off the porch.

"We're on our way," he said softly as he pulled her tight against his side.

When Patricia didn't reply, Kenji looked down at her. "What worries you?" he asked.

"What if I don't pass?" she asked worriedly.

"You will, and if by some slight chance you don't, we'll try again," Kenji said. "But I have every confidence in you."

They continued their walk, arriving back at the house an hour later. Kenji made Patricia sit while he got them something to drink; as he poured the lemonade, it occurred to him that they were totally alone, that Patricia could scream her pleasure and no one would hear or disturb them. It would be the first time since their marriage that they had such an opportunity. He felt his manhood stir in his pants at the thought of hearing Patricia scream in pleasure. He carried the drinks to the living room to find Patricia gone.

"*Kirei*?" he called.

"Up here!" Patricia called from upstairs.

Kenji went upstairs, taking the drinks with him. He went to their room to find Patricia completely nude and on the bed; she had the same idea. Kenji set the glasses of lemonade on the dresser and walked toward the bed. He was now fully erect; the front of his slacks tented far out.

Patricia watched as he undressed and felt a spurt of wetness between her legs in anticipation of feeling his hardness in her, but Kenji had other ideas. He knew that one of her favorite things was when he made her come with his mouth; it was when she screamed the loudest and had to almost smother herself to contain the screams.

He lay beside her on the bed and began by kissing her, taking his time to run the tip of his tongue around her lips before slipping it inside her warm mouth. As he kissed her, his hands played with her breasts, focusing on her nipples, which were fully erect and begging to be suckled.

Kenji broke the kiss and began to work on her neck, earning moans of pleasure. He stopped when he noticed that she was trying to quiet.

"*Kirei*, it's just us," he reminded her and then went back to work on her neck. He moaned himself when he felt her hands running through his hair and pulling gently when he hit a spot that was particularly sensitive. He kissed her chest before taking a nipple into his mouth and sucking gently.

"Oh, God, that feels good!" Patricia said as she wrapped her arms around him. Kenji had to agree; he loved the feel of her hardened nipple against his tongue and lips. She no longer produced milk, which saddened him a little because he had enjoyed the taste of the fluid that had sustained their children. He had fond memories of gently drinking from her when her breasts were so full of mother's milk that they were painful.

He suckled on the other breast, taking as much time with it as he had the other, biting gently and then sucking as she liked him to do. Slowly, he left a wet trail of kissed down her body, completely bypassing the part of her that he craved to taste.

Kenji kissed the inside of her plump thighs as he ran his hands down and then up her legs. Patricia, he knew, wanted him to hurry. He could tell by the impatient movements she made and by her moans of pleasure that were mixed with sounds of impatience. He ignored the throbbing of his cock and its demand that it be buried deep inside of his *Kirei,* but it had to wait until he made her scream his name. Finally, he was where they both wanted him to be. He took a minute to just look at her, to smell her scent, before he spread her lips wide open with his thumbs.

Patricia felt as if she was on fire; making love with Kenji had always been nothing short of wonderful, but today it seemed different. Maybe it was because she didn't have to muffle her screams or because they didn't have to hurry in case one of the children needed them, but whatever it was, she enjoyed it.

She wanted to hurry him along and even tried to give him a little nudge, with no success. She realized that his thinking was the same as hers, and he was simply in no hurry. She closed her eyes and enjoyed the sensations of his touch against her skin, gasping when he took a nipple into his mouth, crying out when he bit and then sucked on it.

Now he was at the place where she wanted him to be; she lay shaking with anticipation of feeling his lips wrapped around her throbbing nub. She knew he would tease her to maximize her pleasure, and when she finally released, it would be sudden and all-consuming, and he wouldn't stop until she released again after that first time.

Kenji touched her clit with the tip of his tongue and moved it back and forth as he slid one long finger as deep inside of

Patricia as he could go and then slowly withdrew it. He could hear her calling his name as her hips rose to meet the thrust of his finger and to press herself harder against his tongue.

Several times he brought her to the edge and pulled back, leaving her throbbing clit to kiss the inside of her thighs or to talk to her softly. “I will love you forever, *Kirei*. No matter what comes our way, I will always love you.”

And then he would go back to nibbling at her gently. When he felt that she would scream the loudest, Kenji took her clit between his lips, rolled it, and then began to suck. Patricia’s scream began as a low moan that gained in volume, as well as intensity.

“Kenji!!” she screamed at the top of her lungs as the orgasm swept her away, and still he didn’t stop.

Scream for me again, he thought as he continued to suck and nibble at her clit. He was rewarded for his efforts a few minutes later.

Kenji held Patricia tightly against him and thanked her.

“For what?” Patricia asked when she could speak. “You did all the work.”

“I am thanking you for everything—for staying with me when things were hard and for the two beautiful children you have given me.”

“I should be thanking you, too,” Patricia replied. “You could have left just as easily as I could have, and I do believe that you had a part in making those two babies.”

“Just think, *Kirei,* both of us will be doctors,” Kenji mused. “It will be a long road, but after what we’ve been through, I know we’ll make it.”

Patricia didn’t reply. She wanted to return the favor. She started at the top, just as Kenji had done with her, and worked her way down to his feet and then back up. When she got to his cock, she stopped and looked up at him. She knew what she would see: his eyes would be mostly closed, but she would still see the light brown of his eyes through a slit, and there would be a slight smile on his face. She loved that look; even though he looked young for his age, that look took away a few more years

. . . the worry wasn't there. She kept her eyes on him as she took the head of his cock into mouth and held it there, moving nothing but her tongue along the underside. She watched as his eyes closed completely in pleasure and he bit his lower lip. Closing her eyes, she slid her lips down his cock and stopped just at the point where her gag reflex would kick in, and slid back up.

"*Kirei*," Kenji said softly and began to thrust into her mouth, slowly crying out as Patricia played with his balls. "I like that," he whispered. "Pull a little harder."

Patricia didn't immediately comply; he wasn't the only one who could tease. Instead, she released him from her mouth and began slow, leisurely strokes with her hand wrapped snugly around his shaft. When she felt him grow, she stopped and started again when he calmed.

"You tease me," Kenji said, his voice strained.

She was teasing him, but it was about to end; she took the head of his cock into her mouth and pulled on his balls as she sucked hard. She heard her name being called as spurt after spurt of his essence coated her tongue and slid down her throat. She suckled from him until he begged her to stop, the head of his cock being so sensitive now that it was almost painful.

Kenji opened his arms to her without speaking; when she was settled, they fell into a deep, relaxed sleep.

Paul was at the house thirty minutes early. Patricia was already up and very nervous.

"Patricia, honey, you're going to be fine," Paul assured her. "Don't look at the big picture; just deal with what's in front of you."

Patricia took a deep breath and nodded; Kenji had told her the same thing several times during the night when she woke up nervous. Each time, he would talk with her in low, soothing tones until she fell back to sleep; she now found herself wishing he could be in the room with her. It was unrealistic, but a wish all the same.

At ten o'clock sharp, she was sitting in the library, waiting to begin the first test. For one of the few times in her life, Patricia felt insecure about herself. She could feel the tears welling up in her eyes and felt the first one as it rolled down her cheek. She was so scared and nervous . . . she couldn't do this.

"*Kirei*," Kenji said from beside her and put his arms around her.

"I don't think I can do this," she said softly as she laid her head on his shoulder.

"Is this my *Kirei* who went through so much with me? Is this the same *Kirei* who would not use her maiden name to get into school?" Kenji asked, kissing her cheek.

"That's different," Patricia said.

"How so?" Kenji asked. "This is just another challenge that we face together." Kenji sat with her for a few more minutes, talking softly. When she was calm, he kissed her and wished her luck.

Paul came in right after Kenji left. "Ready?" he asked.

Patricia took a deep breath and let it out. "I'm ready."

Paul set the first test in front of her. "You have two hours, starting now."

Patricia looked at the test and then at Paul, who gave her a reassuring smile. She read through the test, as Kenji suggested, and then started at the beginning. The farther into the test she got, the more she relaxed and realized that she had worried about the English part of the test for nothing. She actually finished it with ten minutes to spare.

"Take a break," Paul said as he stood up to stretch.

Patricia found Kenji sitting on the floor with his back against the wall outside of the library. He jumped up when she came out and hugged her. "I'm sure you did well," he said, leading her to the kitchen for a drink and a snack.

"I think so, too, but I'm worried about the math and science part," she replied.

"Remember to take your time, and if you don't know an answer, skip the question and go back to it," Kenji said as he walked with her back to the library. “I’ll be waiting here,” he said, pointing to the spot where he had been sitting earlier.

“You don’t have to sit on the floor; why don’t you take a walk or something?” Patricia asked.

“I’ll wait for you, and we can take a walk together before Niko and Marie come back.”

He kissed her again for luck, sat on the floor, and started reading his medical journals. Unable to concentrate, he closed his eyes to rest. Once school started, rest would be in short supply for the both of them. One of the things they needed to be careful of was that the children weren’t neglected and that they continued to take care of each other. They had to be sure there wasn’t another pregnancy, which led him to wonder about birth control of some type. It wasn’t that he didn’t want more children with Patricia, but he still hadn’t quite gotten over the fact that the last pregnancy had been a difficult one for them, and a baby would interfere with school. When the test was over, he would find a time to talk with Paul.

Patricia finished the last test right when the time limit came. She was tired, shaky, and her head hurt to the point of nausea. Paul took the test from her and led her out of the library.

“She’s whipped,” he commented, handing her off to Kenji, who took her to the living room and laid her on the couch. She was asleep in minutes.

Two weeks passed before Paul called to tell them that he had the results.

“Did I pass?” Patricia asked.

“Don’t you want to tell everyone at once?” Paul asked.

“I passed?” Patricia asked, almost too afraid that she had misunderstood him.

“Yes, sweetheart, you passed!” Paul exclaimed and then laughed when Patricia screamed in excitement.

"I'm going to college!" Patricia screamed at the top of her lungs. "Thank you! Thank you a thousand times over!" she exclaimed.

"Don't thank me; you did all the work," Paul replied.

"But you made this possible! I think we need to have a party!"

Paul laughed; for Patricia, any good news was a reason to have a party, and he understood; until recently, there hadn't been much to be happy about.

"Fine, but this time I'll provide the food," Paul said. "And I'll call everyone; you and Kenji enjoy some time alone celebrating."

Kenji hugged her. "I knew it; I knew you would do well!"

The food for the party consisted of sandwiches, fruit, cake that Paul bought, and lemonade. "This way no one has to cook, and everyone can concentrate on having a good time."

Sally and her children were now fixtures at any get-together and had long gotten used to seeing Kenji kiss or hug Patricia. While Sally was growing to care for these people, she still wasn't convinced of the wisdom of interracial marriages and the effects it could have on the children. She had to admit that Niko seemed well adjusted, but then, he hadn't started school yet. There would be no way for him to pass as anything but what he was: a child with parents of two different races. She could only hope that it wouldn't go too badly for him and Marie, when she was old enough to go to school.

She wondered how Patricia and Kenji were going to handle it when the children came home from school in tears because of the names they had been called or when they came home bruised and bloody from being beaten up. It would be something she would talk with Patricia about later, but not now—this was a celebration.

Ralph noticed that Sally seemed to be bothered by something. "Are you all right?" he asked.

"I'm fine; I was just thinking about Patricia's babies. They aren't going to have an easy time of it."

"No, they aren't, but they'll be all right," he replied. "With parents like those two, they'll be fine."

"I hope you're right," Sally said quietly.

Hiroshi was happy for Patricia and made a point of telling her so, but he was happy for another reason. He had approached Mr. Somers about reopening the nursery, and he had agreed.

"I'll buy it, you run it, and when it starts making money, we'll figure out a way for you to buy it from me."

The Hiroshi of old would have shared the news, not caring what else was going on, but today was Patricia's day. While he had apologized to her and told her that he was proud of her, he hadn't taken the final step. He hadn't accepted her as a daughter. It was something he was going to do, even if the relationship between he and Kenji remained as it was. He kept an eye out for an opportune time to speak with Patricia privately.

Patricia wasn't the only one noticing a difference in Abby. Hattie and Hana both noticed and decided to corner her to find out what the problem was.

"I'm fine!" Abby said with a smile.

"Excuse me," Hana said. "But I, for one, don't believe you. Are you ill?"

"No, I'm not ill," Abby replied.

"I'm with Hana," Hattie said. "You ain't actin' right, so either you tell us what's goin' on or we get Kenji and Paul over here."

"Hana and Hattie, I promise you that I'm fine," Abby said. "But if you must know, I found out a few months ago that a dear friend of mine died, and I didn't get to say goodbye to her."

"When was this?' Hana asked.

"January, soon after the interment camps began to close."

"Why didn't you say somethin'?" Hattie asked.

"Because for the first time in months, there was something to celebrate, and I didn't want to bring sadness into it."

Abby had started looking for Lorena in the spring of 1944, but hadn't told anyone. She hired a private investigator, who had finally located Lorena's family toward the end of December, just a week or two before the interment camps began to close. She had found out that Lorena died just before it was official that the camps were closing.

Since she had never shared that part of her life with anyone, she suffered the loss alone. In the back of her mind, she had always held the hope that somehow she and Lorena would find each other. That hope had died with Lorena. Part of her sadness was due to the fact that she didn't look for Lorena sooner, and she didn't know why. She could have looked for her after Lionel died, but she didn't.

"Abby, you keeps sayin' that we a family, but you suffer alone," Hattie said. "I understands your reasons, but we been through too much together for you to go through this by yourself."

"You're right, and I should have said something, but Hattie, I just couldn't do it! There has been too much sadness, and believe it or not, I feel better now that I've shared my loss."

Neither Hana nor Hattie looked convinced, but had no choice but to take Abby's word for it. Abby knew they didn't believe her, but it was mostly the truth. Her only goal now was to live long enough to see Kenji graduate from med school and Patricia graduate from college. She would have to be more careful about how she acted; if Hana and Hattie picked up that something wasn't right, then it was possible someone else had, too. The women returned to the party with Abby really feeling better; she listened to the laughter that filled the house and felt even better.

Sally had come a long way; she was still a little uncomfortable, but that was to be expected. Dianne and Eli had become fiercely protective of Niko and the babies. When the neighborhood children said unkind things as they passed by and Dianne was there, she made her displeasure known. It made Abby glad that they had taken the family in and showed them that it was possible for races to get along without racism. Their very unorthodox family was growing; she just might have to live long enough to see how things turned out.

Patricia stepped outside for a breath of fresh air; the house had become stuffy with so many people in it, and she wanted a moment to herself. She closed her eyes and whispered a prayer of thanks that she had passed her tests, but more importantly, that she was surrounded by family. She also whispered a prayer for Kenji; he hadn't truly forgiven his father, even though he thought he had. While she didn't expect them to have the relationship they had before the war, she had hoped he would have warmed toward his father by now.

She was now convinced that Hiroshi was sincere in his change and meant his apologies. She didn't know what it would take for Kenji to believe it, but decided it was out of her hands.

"Patricia, may I speak with you?" Hiroshi asked.

"Oh, sure," Patricia replied.

"Patricia, I have already told you that I am very proud of you and Kenjiro; both of you have shown remarkable courage and honor in a very trying time. I have also apologized to you for my part in making that time even more difficult, but there is one thing that I haven't done, and I would like to do that now."

Patricia didn't know what to expect, but gave her consent.

"I once told Kenji that you would be a taint to our bloodline, and at that time, I believed that to be true, but that belief was based on stereotype and hatred. Kenji has since told me that you are an added strength to an already strong bloodline. I am in agreement with him; your family is strong in honor and courage. Your capacity to forgive still amazes me, and I am honored to call you daughter."

Patricia was speechless; Hiroshi Takeda had really done a complete turnaround. Neither of them noticed Kenji standing in the doorway, listening. Tears ran down his face as he heard the truth in Hiroshi's words; he stepped outside, into Patricia's line of sight and saw that she was crying, too. She hugged Hiroshi and held a hand out to Kenji; in a few long strides, he reached them and put his arms around both of them.

"This is all I wanted," he whispered in Hiroshi's ear. "I wanted nothing more from you than this."

Dai watched from the kitchen window and smiled; her prayers had been answered. Now she and Hiroshi could truly be happy.

By the end of July 1945, aircrafts from the *USS Ticonderoga* bombed airfields on Kyushu, Japan, in an attempt to prevent special-attack aircraft from taking off; the Allies decided to split Germany into four areas of control; Osaka, Japan was heavily bombed; the Japanese on Okinawa were defeated; and the United Nations Charter was signed in San Francisco.

General MacArthur announced that the Philippines had been liberated; Norway and Italy declared war on Japan; US Navy aircrafts took part in the bombing of Tokyo for the first time; the Trinity test—the first test of a nuclear weapon—took place at Alamogordo, New Mexico; at the Potsdam Conference, the Allies agreed to insist on an unconditional surrender from Japan; and it was also at this conference that President Harry Truman hinted that the United States had nuclear weapons. The Potsdam Declaration was issued to Japan; the Japanese battleship *Haruna* was sunk by a US aircraft; the USS *Indianapolis* was sunk by a Japanese submarine; and the United Sates commenced air attacks on the cities of Kobe and Nagoya in Japan.

Everyone, including Hiroshi, was asking the same question: "Why doesn't Japan give up?" It was the topic of many discussions whenever the men were together; even John and Hiroshi agreed and were beginning to talk, if even about the war. Of everyone, John was the only one who actively mistrusted Hiroshi, and it didn't matter what Patricia said.

There was one point John wanted clarified. "It ain't got nothin' to do with him being Japanese; that man tried to hurt you, and I ain't about to forget that."

After a while, Patricia stopped trying; as long as John was at least civil to Hiroshi, she would leave it alone. Excitement was mounting; Kenji and Patricia would be starting classes in the fall, and Abby, much to Patricia's relief, seemed to be better.

There was a double celebration planned—her birthday and her and Kenji's anniversary, which was July 8. The party was going to be that evening, and both she and Kenji were shooed away from the kitchen. Dianne and Eli took care of Niko, while Abby took care of Marie.

"What are we supposed to do all day?" Patricia asked.

"Our house is empty; go there," Abby said.

"Come, *Kirei*, I have a gift for you that we both are going to like," Kenji said, taking the car keys from Ralph.

"But Niko and Marie—"

"Are going to be fine," Abby interrupted. "Now scoot! And we'll see you at five."

Kenji grabbed Patricia's hand and led her out to the garage, where Paul was waiting. He handed Kenji a small box, kissed Patricia on the cheek, and wished her a happy birthday before heading into the house.

"What's in the box?" Patricia asked.

"Our anniversary gift," Kenji replied with a secretive smile.

"Well, what is it?"

"You'll soon see," he replied with the same secretive smile.

He had talked with Paul about what was available for birth control. "Is there anything reliable?" he asked.

"There's something called a diaphragm that's supposed to be reliable if used correctly," Paul replied. "I'll see what I can find out."

And that's what was in the little box that Patricia held in her hands and was shaking to see if it rattled. Kenji had known in advance that they weren't going to be allowed to participate in the preparations for the party and had arranged to use one of the bedrooms at Ralph and Abby's for the day.

Patricia asked questions about the box all the way to the house, becoming exasperated when Kenji wouldn't tell her anything. He parked in the garage and helped Patricia out of the car by taking her hand. Instead of leading her into the house, Kenji pulled her into him by her hips. "You are every bit as beautiful as you were the first time I saw you."

"Yes, well, a little heavier—"

"Beautiful," Kenji interrupted, moving his hands from her hips to her face. He traced the scar that Vernon Monroe had given her with a fingertip. "Come, I want to give you our gift."

He unlocked the door and led her to the bedroom that Abby had fixed up for them.

"We get to spend the day in bed?" she asked.

"The entire day is ours," Kenji said as he sat her on the bed. "Open the box, *Kirei*."

"Are you sure there's something in here?" she asked, shaking the box.

"I am positive; now open it," Kenji urged.

Patricia opened the box and looked inside, frowned, and looked up at Kenji. "What is that?"

"That, *Kirei*, is our anniversary gift," Kenji replied. "It is a form of birth control."

Patricia gave Kenji a dubious look.

He explained how it worked and how he wouldn't have to pull out when it was time for him to release.

"So, you see, you cannot get pregnant—or that is the theory—and I can release inside of you."

"And I suppose you know how to put this thing in?" she asked, still not sure about the diaphragm.

"Yes, I know how to put it in, and I can teach you to, as well."

"So what happens if we use this thing and I still get pregnant?"

"Then we'll deal with it," Kenji replied. "*Kirei*, I have read all the literature available on this form of birth control, and it is actually more reliable than me pulling out."

"Well, I'm willing if you are," Patricia replied as she reached over and began to unbutton Kenji's shirt.

A few minutes later, she was lying on the bed, waiting for Kenji to insert the diaphragm.

"It is in place," he announced after checking it again. He lay next to her and kissed her. "Happy anniversary and birthday, *Kirei*."

There was no teasing as Kenji nipped and sucked at Patricia's nipples until she was whimpering. Kenji moved to between her legs and in one movement slid deep inside of her and sighed; it was a feeling he never tired of and was sure that he never would.

Patricia began to move first, prompting Kenji to move. They moved together slowly, allowing their orgasms to build. Patricia reached up and pinched Kenji's nipples; she pinched again when she felt Kenji swell within her.

"I'm going to—" he didn't get the rest of the sentence out; instead, he moaned as he released inside of her for the first time since before her pregnancy with Marie. He pressed his pelvis tight against Patricia's mound and ground against her, triggering her release.

He laid sprawled half on top of her, only moving when his cock softened and slipped out. After they napped for an hour or so, he helped Patricia remove the device, wash it in warm water, and put it back inside the box.

"I'll have to come up with a better way of cleaning it before we use it again," he said as he got back into bed.

"I think I like that little device," Patricia said sleepily.

"Nick! Phone!" Ralph called from the kitchen.

Nick's heart pounded; Lawrence had been found guilty of murder, and the sentencing was today. He hoped that he would go away for years, but it wasn't going to happen. Whatever the sentence was, he would keep it to himself for the day; he didn't want the likes of Lawrence Goodman ruining a good day.

"William?"

"Yeah, it's me," William replied, sounding tired.

"What happened?" Nick asked.

"Well, the son of a bitch got off with just four years, like I said."

"Damn it, William! That's not right!"

"I know and I agree, but as I mentioned before, it's better than nothing."

"But eight people died!" Nick replied.

"I know, but there's another reason why I called," William said. "I have it on good authority that once he's out, he's going to want to settle the score."

"What are you saying?" Nick asked.

"He's going to go after everyone who had anything to do with this, including their families."

"Did he say that?" Nick asked.

"To anyone who matters? No, but the person who told me has nothing to gain by lying."

"Who's your source?" Nick asked.

"It's better if you don't know, but Nick, don't ignore this. From what I hear, he's planning to break away from the Klan and start his own group. He's going to start his group while he's in prison, so warn anyone who had anything to do with apprehending him."

"What are the chances that he'll be out before the four years are up?"

"Honestly? Good," William replied.

"What are you planning to do?" Nick asked.

"I don't know yet. . . . I was thinking about moving out your way."

"Really?" Nick asked surprised.

"Yeah, I've already gotten a few death threats and a couple of broken windows on my car and house."

"When were you thinking about coming?" Nick asked, trying to think of where he could stay.

"It won't be for a week or two."

"Let me know, so we can have a place for you to stay."

"Will do, and you all be careful."

Nick hung up the phone and cursed under his breath. He had been right when he thought he hadn't seen the end of Lawrence Goodman. He would have to tell the others in a few days, but he could tell Charles sooner than that. Once again, he found himself in the position of having to protect his family, and once again, he wondered if he shouldn't have taken Elam's position just so he could have his ear to the ground. But then again, he had Charles, and he would have the protection of the police, which meant he had to start figuring out who he could trust.

Lawrence knew where he was going to spend the next few years: the South Carolina Penitentiary. His sentence was for four years, but it would be shorter; at least that was what his lawyer said.

"Keep your nose clean and you might be out in two," he said.

Two years, four years—it really didn't matter that much to Lawrence. He really had no one other than the two men he had struck up a friendship with. He hadn't told them his agenda; they had yet to prove themselves. They talked a good talk, but did they really believe what they said? He had learned his lesson the hard way when he was still mourning Kenny and needed a friend. He had spouted off to his cellmate that people were going to die; he spouted off about the blacks and the Jews and about how the white men had to stick together.

Too late, he realized that the man he had spouted off to was a snitch. He figured it out when the man was moved from their cell the next morning, under the premise of seeing his lawyer. Lawrence bought it at first, but then the man—Joe Waters—didn't come back. Later, he found out that he had actually been talking to the prosecutor and had been moved to another cell.

It was time to test the loyalty of his new friends; he wanted Joe Waters dead before they were transferred to the state pen. How and where they did it was up to them, and he didn't want to know about it. His goal was to protect himself. He didn't order the men to kill Waters; if they interpreted it that way, then that was their problem.

By later that evening, Joe Waters would be found dead in his cell.

The phone rang again just before Patricia and Kenji got back to the house; this time, Nick answered it and was surprised to hear William on the other end.

"I hate to bother you again, but I wanted to let you know that my informant was found dead in his cell."

"What? What happened?"

"His neck was broken. . . . I think Lawrence is responsible somehow, but I can't prove it."

"Are you still planning to come out here?" Nick asked.

"I believe so," William replied. "I can do more alive than dead, don't you think?"

"Give me a heads up when you leave," Nick reminded him before hanging up.

He called Charles next and told him about the sentence Lawrence had received and issued a warning.

"He's out for revenge, so just watch your back and we'll keep in touch."

Nick hung up the phone just as Patricia and Kenji walked in. He pushed Lawrence Goodman out of his mind for the time being; tomorrow would be soon enough to think about how to deal with him.

As Lawrence waited in his cell to be transferred to the state pen, he mentally crossed one person, the snitch, off his list and began to plan how he could get to the next person on his list.

Review Requested:

If you loved this book, would you please provide a review at Amazon.com?

CPSIA information can be obtained
at www.ICGtesting.com
Printed in the USA
FSOW01n1230210515
7275FS